M of the
Fool 5

J.M. CLARKE

MARK OF THE FOOL 5
©2023 J.M. CLARKE

Aethon Books
www.aethonbooks.com

Print and eBook formatting by Josh Hayes. Artwork provided by Shen Fei.

Published by Aethon Books LLC.

Aethon Books is not responsible for websites (or their content) that are not owned by the publisher.

ALSO BY J.M. CLARKE

Mark of the Fool

Book One

Book Two

Book Three

Book Four

Book Five

Book Six

Check out the series here:

(tap or scan)

CHAPTER 1

A "TRIUMPHANT" RETURN

Alex Roth and the guard had been making their way to the encampment for some time. The forest was close to disappearing behind the rolling hills. A handful of surveyors who'd accompanied Ripp to investigate the fire and explosion were headed back to camp with them, but the majority had gone to the burned-out windmill. There'd be lots of monster remains waiting for them.

"A horde of monsters right under our noses?" Ripp gaped. "Just hiding in that old windmill?"

"Yeah, I think they were using tunnels to hide from our patrols. And they were just outside our territory too."

"They were clever alright, hiding right outside our borders like they did. It seems they knew our land stops right before the forest."

"They probably did. They had birds watching us all times of the day and night."

"Birds? What kind of birds?"

"Regular birds, like crows and owls and such. Just local birds that one wouldn't really notice."

"So, they had spies hiding in plain sight, the tricky bastards."

"Yeah, well they won't be watching anyone anymore," Alex said.

The swiftling threw a glance over his shoulder at the imposing forest receding in the distance.

It would be a long, late night.

Alex had the clawed monster all trussed up and was dragging it behind him on a makeshift sled. There was no way he would have left it near the windmill to become scavenger food; that corpse might have a valuable story to tell.

"You know, I think I've passed near that windmill close to half a dozen times." Ripp stopped and pulled out a map of Greymoor, tapping the diagram. "Never saw nothing... Then again, I don't think I've ever gotten closer than half a mile. Not close enough to see this thing."

He inclined his chin to the aeld tree comfortably nestled in Claygon's arms. The golem stepped softly in the midst of the party—or as softly as a giant clay construct that weighed thousands could—swaying his arms to ease the impact on the sapling.

Surveyors were throwing uncertain looks at the tree. One apprehensively passed her hand back and forth through the green-golden light, and little sparkles danced off the aeld, like it was amused, adding to its well of emotions.

Nerves. Anxiety. Giddiness. Excitement. Curiosity. Fear. Amusement.

All bubbled from the sapling as it bobbed along in Claygon's hands, reminding Alex of Brutus when he was a pup. He remembered those countryside excursions the Lus would take them on to the mill, or to see the sights in the next town over. He, Selina, Brutus, Theresa, and two of her brothers would ride in the back of the wagon. The cerberus pup would bound around the back of the cart, barking at birds, sniffing the air, and excitedly following every sight with all six eyes. His tail would be wagging so enthusiastically, he'd almost topple over. Yet, he'd always return to his master's side—pressing against her for reassurance—whenever a flock of birds burst from a thicket, or a farmer's bellow echoed through the hills.

He was curious and young. New to the world and its sights and sounds.

And youth brought both excitement and apprehension.

So it was with the tree, Alex supposed.

He hoped it would be comfortable in its new home.

"The aeld tree only came to be there recently," Alex said. "It's... it's a long story. Maybe it can wait until morning?"

"Wouldn't be so sure about that," Ripp said. "There were a few awake in the encampment when we left. Not everyone heard the blast, but it was loud enough it got a few people up and moving."

"Right..." Alex said. "Well, hopefully, there won't be too many questions tonight. I'd love to see my bed."

"We'll hope that happens for ya," Ripp said.

At first, it looked like he'd get away clean.

The front gates opened quietly, and though the sentries crowded atop the walls, they weren't shouting questions, only talking softly to each other as they watched the procession come through. Two stone golems closed the gates, and Ripp went to report to the ranking Watcher of Roal on duty.

A few guards patrolling the interior of the wall peppered the young wizard with questions, but he held up his hands.

"Friends, everything's been resolved. I'll tell you more in the morning," he said wearily. "It feels like it's been a night and a half, and I just want to—"

"Mr. Roth!"

Professor Jules' voice shattered the peace along with all Alex's hopes of crawling into bed. The straightforward and mighty alchemy professor marched out of the sea of tents, her robes in disarray, her hair wild and eyes wilder.

"What is *that*!" She pointed to the aeld, which gave off a short burst of fear.

"Professor, Professor!" the young wizard hissed. "Not so loud, you'll scare it."

"Scare *what* exac—" Her voice dropped to a whisper as she strode up to him, his golem, and the glowing tree. She squinted, peering up at the sapling in Claygon's hands. "Is that an aeld tree?"

"Uh, yeah..." Alex said.

"Why do you have an aeld tree, Mr. Roth?"

"Well, do you remember that report my survey team made at the end of summer... right after we got to Greymoor?"

"Oh by every lord that ever wore a crown! Could you be *any* vaguer? I have a lot to think about!" Professor Jules crossed her arms. "Refresh my memory."

Alex reminded her of their encounter with the Crich-Tulaghs, blue annis hag, Gwyllain, and the promise the asrai had made.

"I see... and how does that translate to you getting such a tree in the middle of the night?"

"Well..." Alex explained the events of the evening, and with every word, Jules' eyebrows rose higher.

"You did *what*?" she whispered.

"Uh... well, I uh..." Alex stuttered. "I uh..."

"Uh-huh," she said impatiently. "Say it again. Slowly. Like you're explaining something to a child. A *dull* child. And listen to yourself when you do, *very carefully*."

"I uh… well, I went for a walk."

"Yes?"

"Then, I… I met Gwyllain."

"And Gwyllain is who?"

"The asrai fae… that my team saved."

"Right, so you met an asrai fae when you were out for a walk in the middle of the night."

"Yeeeeah…" he said slowly.

"And then?"

"I went with Gwyllain and Claygon to the forest just outside Greymoor."

"Right."

"And then I summoned a bunch of monsters."

"Right…"

"And uh… we fought… a small army of monsters."

"You, your summoned creatures, and the asrai you'd met? …Only once."

"Y… yeah. Wait, no. Claygon was there too."

"Right, and you fought an army of monsters, a Hive-queen, a pair of hags… by yourselves. In the middle of the night. Miles away from help."

"Well, you know… that's not," Alex coughed. "I mean, that's one way of putting i—"

"And then you started an immense fire," she continued. "In the middle of the forest… by yourself. And you put it out with a *bigger* fire?"

"Yeah, that uh… you summed it all up pretty well."

"Are you *out* of your *mind*?" she hissed, stepping forward so she was less than a foot away from him. "You could've gotten yourself murdered in the fields like someone's prey!"

"I had my training, Professor," Alex defended himself.

"And you also had plenty of people to help *here*. That is why the university organises *expeditions*, not *solo quests*. Leave such things for knights-errant and other fools!"

Alex's lip twitched. One day, she'd understand the irony in that statement. "I assessed the situation, Professor, just like Baelin taught me. And just like you taught me. I had plenty of resources: I was fresh, and my mana was fully charged. I had Claygon with me. Meanwhile, my friends were exhausted from the day's battle and my cabal's mana had run completely dry. Completely."

"There are others in our camp."

"Yes, Professor," Alex said. "But most of them were exhausted or were recharging their mana. And... this wasn't really part of the expedition's mandate. How would it look to the university's board if they found out I convinced expedition members—who have no other connection to me—to go out on a potentially dangerous side-mission for my purposes? Plus, I could've been on a time limit and... this might be out of line, but I've been trained for combat. I did what I thought was best."

"Oh dear, you're starting to sound like Baelin." Professor Jules gave him an unhappy look. "I suppose you do raise some valid points, though, and I can see that you did give this some thought, at least. But... in future, could you avoid doing such things alone, especially in the dark of night?"

"Yeah, if I can avoid it," Alex said.

She peered at him for a long moment. "What's done is done, but remember, Mr. Roth, safety first, always."

He considered what she'd said.

"I know, Professor, but with all respect, the world isn't always a safe place. I'm never reckless and I think that's a way of keeping myself safe."

She muttered something about Baelin and corrupting influences before her eyes lit up.

"By the way, what *is* that you're dragging behind you?"

Alex thought fast. 'Keep the details limited.'

"It's this really interesting-looking monster that I don't remember seeing in the Thameish bestiary. Look at its claws, just those alone would be worth studying, I think. It might be rare, so I brought it back so scavengers wouldn't get it."

She looked it over, all smiles.

"I'll have it taken to the research tent." She rubbed her hands together, turning back to the aeld tree. "Hello there, little fellow. Welcome to Generasi territory. I hope Mr. Roth takes the very best care of you."

"Actually, I wanted to talk to you about that, and some other things I left out. But for now, would it be alright if I plant the tree here, right in the middle of camp? I think it'd be a boon for everyone."

"Of course you can, that'll be a good thing. I suppose it would be wrong to badger you for more details right this second. You look like wild bulls trampled you. We can talk tomorrow, Mr. Roth. You can just leave the specimen right there."

"Right, thanks, Professor." Alex left the clawed cadaver, and he and Claygon made their way toward his tent.

Behind him, muffled muttering came from Professor Jules: "The reports about this are going to be... wait, are they even necessary? He did act on his own after all, and—"

She quickly strode through the tents, heading in a different direction.

Alex stealthily picked his way through camp, trying not to awaken anyone. His pace was slow and steady, with Claygon trying his best to be stealthy, and failing with every step. Alex was thinking about the morning, certain it'd be filled with questions from his friends and others, so the longer he could delay them, the better. Ahead, his tent waited, calling to him like heavenly bells.

He quickened his step.

He was almost there.

Then a menacing shape loomed out from the dark, blotting out the moon.

Alex whirled toward the shape, but its moves were swift, blocking any route for escape.

Grimloch. The menacing shape was Grimloch's.

The shark man grunted, his black eyes focusing on the wizard.

"Huh, was sleeping. The light woke me up. Thought we were under attack."

"Jeez, what is with everything trying to scare me to death tonight?" Alex asked, his heart pounding.

"Dunno. Maybe don't make scaring you so much fun," Grimloch growled. "We being attacked?"

"No...?"

"Good enough for me." He paused. "Why do I still *feel* so much fear then?" His black, doll-like eyes turned to the sapling. It was shedding waves of panic. "Why is this tree scared? It's a tree. Not meat."

Alex's mind whirled. He was too mentally exhausted for this. "Yeah, Grimloch... not meat. Can I go to bed now?"

"Sure you can," the shark man said, making no effort to move.

"Okay, then... and uh... please don't wake anyone else up."

"I won't."

"Especially Theresa."

"I don't have to."

"Okay, the—Wait. What do you mean you don't have to?"

"She does life enforcement, Alex," Grimloch growled. "Even longer than me. Her senses are sharper than mine. So if you woke me up, you really think *she'd* still be asleep?"

Alex gulped. "You're telling me she's standing right behind me or something, aren't you?"

"No."

The young wizard glanced backward. No one was there. He sighed in relief. "Okay, then. Then I'll—"

"She's standing right behind *me*." Grimloch grinned.

A familiar form slid out from behind the towering shark man, one that moved as quietly as a silence-spider. Eyes flashed in the dark. The look of a death stalker marked her face.

"Evening, Alex. Nice night for a walk," Theresa said, her voice dangerously calm.

Chapter 2

Just Communication

"Y-yeah." Cold sweat dotted Alex's brow. "N-nice night for a walk, eh?"

Theresa in no way looked as though she believed it was a nice night for a walk. The exact opposite was true. Her death stalker face was more grim reaper than peacefully strolling hiker. As she nodded to the sapling—its fear spiked.

'I'm right here with you, little guy,' Alex thought.

"Well, uh—" He put on his brightest, grandest smile. "It's an aeld tree! Surprise! Only took a great big fire, and fighting some Ravener-spawn... and, uhm, some other monsters to get it. Simple."

The silence fell on him, crushing down like a pair of hands choking the breath from him.

"No, no, stop thinking like that," Alex thought. "Why is my mouth going rogue *right now*?"

"Alex..." Theresa took a soft, careful step toward him. "You're thinking out loud."

Alexander Roth, a Hero of Uldar and favourite of the ancient wizard, Baelin, barely resisted the urge to scream.

"So..." Theresa said. "You went out... all by yourself... Remember when you said that anything could happen, and if the worst did, you wanted me to look after Selina?"

She let the words hang.

"I mean, sure," Alex said. "If you wanna put it *that* way, but language is such a varied and... imprecise... *subjective* tool of communication—jeez, is it getting hot out here or is it just me?" He chuckled nervously, looking to Grimloch. "Am I right?"

"It's always warm on the surface compared to the deepest trenches of the sea," Grimloch rumbled.

Silence.

"Grimloch?" Theresa asked, her voice uncharacteristically sweet. "Would you mind giving my boyfriend and me a bit of privacy? Just for a little while."

"Or... *or!*" Alex said. "Y-you could chaperone young people who're alone on a dark night. Haha, protect them from danger."

"That sounds boring," Grimloch said. "I already got my fun out of this. I'm getting a snack and going back to bed." He looked at Theresa. "Kill him quietly."

"H-hey!" Alex protested.

"What? You deserve it. You knew about a good fight and didn't share. That's cold." Grimloch shook his head like Alex had spit on his ancestors, then he strode off in search of some sort of meat.

Like his neck was a rusted gate hinge, Alex slowly turned to face Theresa—who was advancing on him menacingly.

'It must be *menacing night* in Thameland,' he thought, backing away, straight into Claygon's immovable form.

Thmp.

"H-hold on now."

With a single step, Theresa was right in front of him, so close he could feel her breath on his neck.

"Tell me. Everything," she said quietly.

Alex Roth might have been branded a Fool by the god of his land.

But Alex Roth was not fool enough to lie to the woman who knew him like she knew her own hand.

Taking a deep breath, he told the story, leaving no details out, and even adding things he couldn't tell Professor Jules. In low tones, he described to the huntress that the clawed monster in the windmill was kin to the pair they'd fought at Patrizia DePaolo's ball. She was shocked to hear that it was working with a Hive-queen. He told her about the conclusions he'd come to, and all the questions and suspicions he still harbored.

Theresa did not interrupt.

She didn't snap at him.

Didn't blame him.

And, in a way, that was even more unnerving.

It was the silence, the death stalker face, and those eyes boring deeper into him with his every word. By the end, he would've preferred going another round with the Hive-queen.

"And then I met Ripp, and we came back home," he whispered. "And that's pretty much it."

For a moment, an apology was making its way to his lips... but he bit it back. He firmly believed he'd done nothing wrong. Any apology he gave would simply be false words to avoid conflict.

And he owed Theresa many things...

False words weren't among them.

After what felt like a lifetime that even Baelin might call 'long,' Theresa let out a heavy sigh.

"Okay," she said, gathering her thoughts.

Alex knew better than to say anything: he just gave her time.

She crossed her arms over her chest. "Alright... I'm not mad at you." She paused. "Okay, I lied. I'm a *little* mad at you."

He nodded, leaning in to show that he was fully listening to her.

"Look, I'm not stupid: I know you can handle yourself. I've seen it, over and over again. You're tough, you're smart, and we haven't been training with Baelin for nothing. And... well, maybe I'm the last person who should criticise you for going off into the wilderness on your own. You know... since I basically half-lived in the Coille. And you're a lot better equipped for dangerous situations than I was back then. I won't tear you down for going out there, and besides, you had Claygon with you."

"Okay, to be fair," he interrupted her. "When you went into the forest, the worst thing you could've met back then was a wild boar or a bear. Or maybe a cerberus? But, like, they're a lot less dangerous than entire dungeons of Ravener-spawn."

"Alex. Are you really trying to tell me that what I did was better than what you did? Right now? When I'm trying to *help you*?"

"Uh..." he murmured.

What the hell *was* he saying?

"Yeeeeeees?" he offered.

"Oh, by the Traveller, *Alex*," she said, a pained note in her voice. She wound her fingers around the cuff of his shirt. "I... Don't change, okay? Look, I mean it. I'm not mad about you going out there... but why didn't you wake me up?"

"You were tired from dealing with those Cold Belchers. Everyone was. But I have my sleep spell to use, y'know? So, I was fresh in no time. I figured it wouldn't be fair to any of you if I woke you up to possibly end up in some dangerous situation when you weren't 100%."

"While that does makes sense, you could've just *told* me. Then I could have said if I was fresh enough or not."

"You would've forced yourself to come with me, or you might've... trust me, you *really* didn't want to face those bastards when you were tired. They were fast, there were a lot of them, and they were *motivated*."

"And I still would've wanted to at least know. You're a big boy, Alex, but... if something happened, then I would never know where to look for you. Never would've known what happened. You just would've been gone. My mother said that to me, and she was right. Never knowing what happened to you would be... unbearable... for life."

"Yeah... but..." He winced; a dark image rose in his thoughts, and he had to push it aside. "If you'd forced yourself to come with me and then something happened to you because of a situation *I* dragged you into... I know I couldn't live with myself."

She sighed. "Alex. Alex. Alex. This is me. I'm not stupid. I wouldn't get into something I couldn't handle. I've been in Baelin's classes too. I know how to measure a fight I can't win, or a hunt I can't complete. Even if I'd just hang back to back you up if you got in over your head, or even if I stayed behind, but *knew* where you were, that'd be a lot better than nothing. Besides, remember that night I walked into your room back in Alric?"

She looked at his shoulder. "I walked with you. Just like you walk with me. Let me *keep* walking with you. Just tell me. That's all."

Alex chewed his lip, imagining if the worst had happened: his body would lie beneath the windmill among the crumbled remains of Claygon. Gwyllain would have disappeared into a hag's belly, and his body would've followed. By the time surveyors tracked him to the woods, there might've been nothing to find but crumbled bits of clay, and maybe some bloodstains.

And then, Theresa, Selina, and Mr. and Mrs. Lu would've been left with a cruel hope that he might be alive somewhere. The kind of false hope that shattered people with futile quests and fruitless dreams.

"Okay, yeah... that part wasn't cool. You deserved to know." He sighed. "I'm sorry."

"You don't have to be sorry, just... If you've got to do something like that again, tell me where you're going. I'm not your shepherd or your grandmother: I don't need to know everywhere you go. But if you're going up against a horde of monsters, please tell me. I know you said Gwyllain thought the monsters were probably gone, but he wasn't sure."

"Yeah, okay." Alex wrapped her in a hug.

She stiffened, then hugged him so fiercely, he had to exhale. "Welcome back," she said. "I'm glad you're in one piece."

"Thanks... me too," Alex smiled. "Next time, I *will* tell you. As a matter of fact, if you can come, I want you right beside me next time."

"Next time?" She looked up at him.

"Yeah, I mean... If the aeld tree grants me a nice big branch, then I'll have the body for my staff. But I'll still need to power it. And that means breaking a dungeon to get its core."

Theresa paused. "I hope it's a silence-spider dungeon."

"Oh? Why?"

She gave a little growl. "Because you got another go at a Hive-queen. I want one too."

"I'll see what I can do."

He and Theresa talked for a while before exhaustion caught up with them, replacing their words with yawns. Claygon stood patiently in the moonlight, cradling the sapling as Alex and Theresa shared a goodnight kiss, then hand in hand, walked toward Alex's tent. The golem followed, being as quiet as he could.

No one poked their heads out from any of the sea of tents they walked by. Most were likely still deep in sleep.

"Night, Claygon. Night, little tree," Alex and Theresa said, crawling into his tent and closing the flap behind them. With Claygon holding the aeld, it wasn't long before the soft drone of snoring drifted from within. And so, the golem stood beneath the stars, nestling the magical sapling, bathed in its green-golden light. Clouds drifted above. Guards patrolled the walls.

And—under the joined light of moon and aeld—Claygon's head moved slightly to face the little tree. If Alex had been awake to stand in that light, he might have noticed a wave of surprise rising in the sapling's aura. Surprise, followed by inquisitiveness. And inquisitiveness followed by a sense of... focus.

If he had been awake and present...

He might have thought that the golem and sapling were communicating.

The next morning found a great commotion among the Generasians.

In the centre of the encampment was the familiar sight of Claygon, holding the decidedly *un*familiar aeld tree. Burlap wrapped its roots in place of Alex's cloak, and summoned water elementals misted its roots and soil. Mixed with another dose of leasú-todhar dust, the water sank into the wrapped soil, feeding the aeld while the wizards discussed when, if, and how to plant it... as they waited on some expert help with their decision.

"I'm walking here! I'm walking here!" Professor Salinger's familiar voice drifted through camp, rising above the crowd. The dark-haired magical botany professor pushed his way through those assembled to witness whatever was going to happen.

When he reached the tree, he brushed himself off as though he'd just rolled through a field of dust.

"Well, look at what we've got. This is a treasure! I've been briefed. We've got to get this lovely in the ground as quickly as we can!"

"Indeed," Baelin's deep voice rumbled, and Alex could see his horned head rising above the other professors'. "I've had the wonder of having an aeld tree grow on some property of mine, and I must say, we are most fortunate, because it was quite the boon. I agree with Professor Salinger, it should be planted with all haste in a spot where it has plenty of room to grow. We must also give it proper care and attention. Now, where is the scoundrel who wrenched such a prize from the hands of our enemies?"

The professors—as one—looked to where Alex was still eating breakfast, and Baelin—his eyes twinkling with delight—made his way over to the young wizard.

"Well done, Alex! You left, you saw, and you conquered, just as a Proper Wizard should," the chancellor said. "And now you feast on the breakfast of champions. Well done."

"See? You did nothing wrong," Grimloch grunted at Alex.

"I would not go so far," Prince Khalik said, buttering a chunk of bread. "You did not *share*."

"Oh, come on, not you too," Alex said.

"Now, now," Baelin cut in. "There are more than enough monsters in this land for everyone. There shall be plenty of opportunities in the future."

He looked at Alex. "Now, Professor Jules told me a little of what occurred last night. And... showed me a most interesting sight."

He glanced toward the research tent where specimens from the windmill had been taken. One was the clawed monster. Alex's hunter.

Baelin gave him a pointed look. "I do believe you may have more to share with me. And it seems we just might have some planning to do."

CHAPTER 3

CONFOUNDING THE CONFOUNDING VARIABLES

"So... it may have been targeting you and spying on both you and the rest of our team for a good while," Baelin said, annoyance marking his tone. "*And* it also had the wherewithal to set a trap for you by observing your asrai friend's movements and using the aeld tree to bait *you*. *That* is most interesting. And let us not forget the alliance between it and these two blue annis hags... That level of cooperation speaks to more intellect than I originally prescribed to these creatures."

His gaze shifted, settling on a shelf near the tent's entrance. Najyah preened herself, happily oblivious to the ancient wizard's stern gaze. Alex had to admire her courage; he didn't think he could have been quite as nonchalant under Baelin's scrutiny.

Shifting his position on the carpet, he took in his companions.

Prince Khalik's arms were folded across his chest and his jaw clenched under his beard. Isolde's index finger rapidly tapped on her right knee, while Thundar scowled with his powerful arms also crossed. Theresa thumbed the hilt of one of her swords. Brutus panted beside her.

Confidants and close friends—everyone who knew Alex was the Fool —had been invited to meet with the chancellor in a tent he occupied when he was on site. He'd cast the same spell that masked conversation that he'd used when he and Alex strolled across campus the morning after Alex, Thundar, and Khalik's night spent knocking back plum brandy in the name of science. Sitting cross-legged on the tent floor to examine last night's events in detail made privacy from passersby vital.

Baelin's nostrils flared. "One also has to consider the avian spies. That also speaks of a much deeper measure of intelligence. Not only did these monsters have the patience to observe us for months before acting, they chose mundane creatures that reside naturally and abundantly in the area as spies."

His expression turned darker. "Blast it, I never once suspected the feathered snoops!"

Now Najyah *did* look at the chancellor, her feathers puffing up in offence.

Prince Khalik swore in Tekish. "I do not understand how I could have been so careless not to have noticed. An eagle is my familiar. Who better to note suspicious birds than me? This... ambush happened, in part, because of my failure."

"Blame will not bring us forward, Khalik," Isolde said.

Tap. Tap. Tap. Tap.

Her finger drummed even faster. "We must focus on the potential repercussions and possible sources of this danger. What shall we do about these birds? Do we watch each one that flies above the encampment or perches nearby?"

"No." Baelin shook his head. His bronze beard-clasps clinked. "I'd rather leave safeguarding the camp to Watcher Shaw, Professor Jules, myself, and others tasked with security. Our meeting should focus on weighing theories that Alex has presented: looking at whether or not these creatures follow the Ravener, or the demon, Ezaliel."

"Well, we know from dissecting them that they certainly are not demons," Isolde said. "Though demons do attract cults made up of many sorts of mortal worshippers."

"Indeed, some cults even use demonic chaos to craft their own mutants by warping flesh," the chancellor said. "Though such experiments mostly lead to warped abominations that die within moments of their creation, and even those that survive tend to be only useful as mindless fodder in battle; little better than beasts of burden. Albeit beasts of burden with extra claws, limbs, and fearsome teeth. Still, such experiments do produce a creature of high value on the rare occasion. Perhaps it was one of those."

He looked at Alex. "Then again, your unique status lends some credence to the idea that these creatures have spawned from your Ravener. After all, some Ravener-spawn are rarer than others, and it could be that this is some unknown creation that has not yet appeared in the bestiaries."

"Yeah, we don't really know what the Ravener can and can't do," Thundar grunted.

"There's *some* information in the history books. Most previous generations of Heroes had their final battle against the Ravener recounted in songs, poems, and recorded in epic tales," Alex said. "Although... we wouldn't be here studying dungeon cores if the books had everything about Thameland's oldest enemy in them."

"Indeed. Ezaliel has proven to be quite the confounding variable. For every hypothesis, there is enough evidence to give the impression that it could be true, but not enough to confirm one while denying the other. So, we must act as though both could be true."

Baelin scanned the group. "I do believe this question will be a waste of breath, but do you still feel comfortable remaining with the expedition? Keep in mind that *one* fact can be confirmed: for whatever reason, you've been targeted. Actions were tailored to hunt and trap you, or indeed, those of you who were involved in saving this asrai...

"You are all capable young people. Full of life. Full of vigour. Full of trained judgement and mounting power. However, an important aspect along the path of the Proper Wizard is assessing what—among life's many complications—are challenges to be confronted, and death sentences to be avoided. Know that whatever the situation might have been last night, there is a chance that Alex, or *all* of you, might still be targets. Or all of us, for that matter. So, with that in mind, considering Alex's personal involvement with last night's clash, do any of you feel the need to excuse yourself from further involvement with the expedition?"

A chorus of *no's* filled the tent.

The chancellor then looked to Khalik. "And that goes for you as well? Are you sure?"

"Without doubt," the prince said. "I would not be worthy to be called wizard or any title if I were to back away now. *I* was not the one in danger last night."

The ancient wizard nodded. "Magnificent. You all may make your own decisions, but I am glad you've chosen to stay the course. Now then. Plans. I have no doubt you will be out in Greymoor and in the land beyond for expedition purposes, *and* your own personal goals, so be vigilant. Find more of these creatures if you can. Capture them if you can, unless you would be risking all to do so. I shall send surveyors to search out cells of Ezaliel's cultists. They must be captured and interrogated about this matter and other foul dealings pertaining to their master." He said that with distaste. "As for this... creature... the next time the Heroes or a Thameish delegation comes to Greymoor, I will make inquiries about them. Perhaps someone has encountered such a creature before. And with that, does anyone have any further thoughts or questions?"

"You want us to group up?" Thundar asked. "Not travel alone and stuff like that?"

Baelin looked at the minotaur like he'd suddenly sprouted two pairs of horns. "Of course not! I give you—as always—the autonomy to move as a large group or as a smaller one as needed. Indeed, perhaps at times, it would be better to break your team up for infiltration or other tasks of that nature. You are all capable. I shall not throw objections in your way. Though the same cannot be said for Professor Jules."

Baelin focused on Alex. "I suspect that when she learns the monsters were specifically targeting you, she will strongly argue that you be removed from the expedition for your safety. Naturally, I will go against this. At times such as these, we cannot run from the enemy. After all, turning your back to a wild beast is an excellent invitation for it to chase you, and if you forever run from every beast... then you will live in fear of the cave lion for your entire life. That is not the proper way."

"Indeed," Khalik said.

"Right," Alex agreed.

"Now then, I will go and speak to Professor Jules. You all have duties to perform, and Alex, you have a tree to plant. Noon is approaching, and I do not want you to miss your opportunity."

"Yeah," Alex said, standing.

Baelin started for the tent flap, the carpet muffling the sound of his hooves. "Hmmmm... hmmm... hmmm... missed opportunity..."

"What was that, Baelin?" Alex asked.

"Hm... a thought occurs. The confounding variables involved with these clawed monsters will make it more difficult to get answers. We will show the Thameish the creature's remains, but if they have no knowledge to share, then we must rely on cultists. And, of course, cultists tend to be fanatics. If we cannot get them to talk, or if what they say is useless, we would be back to square one. I'd much prefer to increase our options."

The ancient wizard looked at Alex, nodding as if confirming something to himself.

"I think, my boy, you and I should go on a little hunt."

"What do you mean?" Alex asked. "You mean we go looking for more clawed monsters?"

"Oh my, no." Baelin absently ran his fingers through his beard-braids. "If these beasts *do* come from the Ravener, then that *should* mean they are made by dungeon cores. A thorough examination of one could help unlock the secrets of these mysterious creatures."

"But we've examined them thoroughly," Isolde pointed out. "We have not found anything about how they create monsters."

"Indeed, and that is why I will rearrange my schedule to pursue one *personally*. It is true that we have examined the remains of dungeon cores." Baelin drew himself up to his full height. "But perhaps it's time to capture and study a *live* one."

"You've gotta time it right," Professor Salinger was saying, standing within the circle of wizards. As Alex approached the magical botany teacher, he could see him craning his neck, squinting up at the sun. "Ah, yes, we're lucky. Sunny day. Not a cloud in the sky. Perfect aeld-planting weather. Caufield!"

He pointed at one of his assistants who clutched a portable timepiece inches from his face. The young man's bloodshot eyes blinked slowly, never straying from the device. "Professor?"

"Now remember, you must tell me the *exact* instant it becomes noon. Not one second after or two before. The more precise we are, the better and—Aha! Roth!"

He pointed at the gathered wizards. "Come on, people, let him through, let him through."

Everyone cleared a path for the broad-shouldered wizard making his way to the centre of the crowd. There, Salinger, his assistants, Claygon, and the aeld tree stood under the near-noon sun, waiting beside a great hole in the earth, and a large mound of soil.

Waves of curiosity alternated with acknowledgement as Alex approached the tree. It was starting to recognise him.

"Hello." He nodded to the aeld. "I hope everyone's taking good care of you!"

A wave of contentment drifted from it.

"Feel that? That should be answer enough," Salinger said. "You have to be part of the digging, Mr. Roth. It's becoming more comfortable around me, but there's been a lot of noise and new sights it's still adjusting to. You saved it, so you should be here to calm it."

"Got it." Alex rubbed his hands together.

"Perfect," Professor Salinger said. "Someone get this man a shovel!"

"A shovel?" the young wizard asked, spotting a group of students nearby. Some were stretching like they were warming up for a competition, some held sturdy-looking shovels, while a pair were placing incense into censers.

A young man stepped forward, pushing a shovel into Alex's hands.

"We're not using magic?" the Thameish wizard asked Salinger.

"No, it's better if we do this by hand." The professor picked up his own shovel. "When it comes to spirit trees, it's important to give respect, make something of a ceremony out of the planting process, and even present a sacrifice. It's all part of the ritual."

"Ceremony?" Alex asked. "Gwyllain—uh, the asrai that brought me to the aeld—didn't say anything about a ceremony."

"Ah, well, not everyone or every culture believes in the same things, but there's been a lot of correlated data that speaks to increased spiritual plant health when the spirits within are appeased," Salinger said. "Which means, having a ceremony for major events like planting, having sacrifices, and all that good stuff."

"Sounds almost religious." Alex held the shovel in one hand, stretching his fingers and wrists.

"That's because it comes from religion," Professor Salinger said. "From the early, early mortal days, certain cave paintings and oral traditions speak of the worship of spiritual plants as predating the common worship of deities. There was even a theory that our world hung in the branches of a *world tree*. Another tradition says the first seeds of all spirit trees fell off the back of an Earthborne."

"What's an earthborne?" Alex asked.

Salinger shrugged. "No one's been able to find out. Could've been an earth elemental, some sort of extinct race of people or monster, or even a title from ancient tribal times. Nobody knows. The point is, ceremony and spiritual plants are woven all throughout mortal history. And, aha!"

"Sorry we're late!" Khalik's voice boomed.

The prince pushed through the crowd, flanked by Thundar, Theresa, and Brutus. Grimloch brought up the rear.

"We had other duties to attend to," the prince said. "But we are here now and ready to help."

"Perfect, the more the merrier," Salinger said. "Get 'em some shovels."

His assistants handed each newcomer—except Brutus, naturally—a shovel. Grimloch's looked more like a child's garden spade in his giant hands—drawing looks of amusement.

"Are we not using magic?" Khalik asked.

Salinger just sighed. "Blah, blah, blah—spirit likes ceremony. Better to do it by hand. I don't have time to go over it agai—"

"Professor!" Caufield cried. "Two minutes to noon!"

"—Yes, yes, definitely no time! Alright, I want all of you to follow my instructions *precisely*." He quickly counted everyone holding a shovel, then uttered an incantation. The earth trembled, and X's appeared around the hole at equidistant points. "Everybody pick an X and claim that spot as your own. Then, when you hear me start singing and shovelling, follow my rhythm as closely as you can. You won't know the words to the song, but the tune's simple and easy to pick up, so just hum along. It'll help you keep rhythm and serve the ritual. Now hurry, get in place!"

The diggers glanced at each other then scrambled into position.

Casting another spell, Salinger caused the mound of soil to shudder and separate, dividing into smaller piles. They glided around the hole like earthworms, each taking a position behind a digger.

"You've got your soil." Salinger unwrapped the burlap from the aeld tree's roots, then raised his shovel and took a position by an X. "I'll start the song precisely at noon. Alex, when I point down, have your golem lower the sapling into the hole."

"Got it."

The two wizards holding the incense burners positioned themselves directly north and south of the circle, lighting the incense with a quick incantation. Smoke drifted from within, floating from the censers and falling to the earth, where it hung like a low cloud of mist on a cold spring day. The scent was soothing as all waited in silence.

And then…

"Noon, Professor!" Caufield cried.

Salinger took a deep breath.

Then he fell into song.

CHAPTER 4

ANCIENT RITUALS AND NEW APPLICATIONS

T he words sounded ancient.
 Primal almost.
 The melody was simple yet rang with power.
Professor Holden Salinger's voice filled the centre of camp, carrying with it ancient syllables and a tone which held respect, reverence, and esteem. In a moment of deja vu, Alex felt like he was back in the church of Alric, listening to the choir sing hymns in Uldar's name. His and Theresa's eyes met, exchanging a look of reminiscence.

As Salinger placed his palms together, it struck Alex how similar the poses of prayer were among deities' faithful, no matter the deity, and no matter the culture. He wondered if there was something to that, or if it was just one of life's endless quirks.

The professor's voice fell, finishing a verse, and though he wasn't the best singer, he carried the tune well enough for the others to follow. As his melody repeated, those in the circle joined in, humming along, their voices blending with his words.

Once a single voice became many, the little aeld seemed to suddenly flourish, brimming over with life.

Its aura brightened, pulsing in time with the ceremonial song, pouring out pure glee to all in the circle. The wind rose—blowing the sapling's leaves in harmony with the pulsating light. They waved to the song's melody, keeping a steady rhythm, like a heartbeat.

'It's singing,' Alex thought. 'In its own way, it's joining the song.'

Smiling, he used the Mark to learn Salinger's words, and though he didn't know the meaning, he joined in.

Their voices carried into the air, rising with the wind.

Then Salinger caught Alex's eye and pointed to the hole before him.

'Alright, Claygon,' the young wizard thought. 'Lower the aeld. Gently now.'

Claygon carefully lowered the tree, stabilising its root ball in the waiting hole. Professor Salinger nodded his approval, providing a signal to the participants in the ritual to be ready. He then positioned his shovel over his mound of soil and filled the blade. Everyone followed his lead, then moving as one, they sprinkled fresh earth over the young tree's roots.

With each blade of soil, Professor Salinger's assistants swung their censers back and forth, shedding white smoke, dispersing it over the earth and into the hole, mixing it with the growing mound of soil.

Shovel by shovel, verse by verse, and swing by swing, the hole filled with smoke and fresh earth as the sapling's light grew ever brighter. Its incandescence spiked to near blinding when Alex spread the last of the soil over the young tree's roots, protecting them from the elements. With the planting complete and the earth tamped down around the little tree, allowing it to settle in the middle of the encampment, the magical botany professor raised his shovel before him like a knight making an oath of fealty.

"And so, we honour this spirit in its new home," he proclaimed. "May it grow and prosper, and may it share that prosperity with us. Would you like the honour of watering it now that it's safely in its new home, Alex?"

"Of course." Alex summoned Bubbles and brought out another pinch of leasú-todhar. He sprinkled Gwyllain's gift over the soil around the roots—a light dusting which left a cerulean glow across the soil—and sent a happy little wave through the tree's aura.

As Bubbles watered it, Alex patted its trunk. "Welcome to your new home. I hope our care for you matches the good fortune you'll bring us."

"And then what happened?" Selina demanded, leaning over her textbook.

"Well, not much after that." Alex took a sip of water, putting it on the ground beside him, well away from their books.

Another sunny noontime, but this one found the Roth siblings on campus a couple of days after the planting ceremony, with Alex going over blood magic notes and tutoring Selina in magical theory. They were taking a short break, and he was regaling his sister with tales of the windmill, Gwyllain, blue annis hags who had a taste for fae, the aeld tree, and the clawed monster.

Leaving out parts of the story that weren't for random ears to overhear.

"I fed and watered the tree for a few days, took care of my duties, and before we knew it, it was time to come back home. And here we are." He shrugged. "So that's basically it. Now we just keep feeding and nurturing the tree, and do our best to help it grow."

"Awesome!" Selina's green eyes sparkled. "Can I see it?"

"Well, I'm not sure about that, actually," Alex said. "We can't really bring visitors into the encampment whenever we want. And the land's still not safe... Y'know, like I *just* said. Plus, I'm pretty sure Professor Jules would tear me in half if I brought my sister there. I don't know... Maybe when the research castle's finished? It'll probably be safer then. There's still lots of monsters back home."

"Hrm... Well, I hope I get to see it one day..." She paused. "What's home like now? With all those monsters there?"

Alex blew out a breath. "I haven't actually been back *home*, home, not to Alric at least. Let's just say I get why everyone has to leave until the Ravener's defeated."

She swallowed. "I hope the tavern's okay. And the rest of town... If a big battle happened there like it did at the windmill, it doesn't sound like there'd be much of our hometown left."

Alex sighed. "Well, the army tries to defend towns and cities, especially important ones. So maybe Alric will be okay. It's important to Thameland because the Cave of the Traveller's nearby."

Selina frowned. "But... it's our home. We live there. Lots of people do. It has the summer festival, and the church, and the magistrate's office... Wouldn't that make it important enough?"

Alex considered that. There were many ways he could answer her; many sweet lies he could tell to paint the picture of a kinder world for her. But, when it was all said and done, a half-truth would still be a lie. And Selina had grown beyond sweet lies that were meant to shield children.

"Well, *we* think it's important." Alex leaned back against Claygon's leg, his hands resting on the grass. "You know how the world just seemed to move on in the Rhinean Empire and here in Generasi, even while all of Thameland was running from the Ravener? It's kinda like that. We think our town's important, but there's a lot of people out there who think *their* town's more important than ours. And the officials who decide where the army goes make those decisions. Since the Cave of the Traveller's important to *everyone* in Thameland, it means they'll likely protect our town more than other towns."

Selina's frown deepened. "Hm. Kinda like how the flour in that windmill was probably important to somebody? But you needed to blow those monsters up, so using it to burn them was the better choice."

"Exactly. It's... kinda grim when you think about it... but maybe healthy in its own way. The world's a great, big, wide place, with good things and bad things happening to people we've never even met. They don't know about the things that happen to us, and we don't know about the things that happen to them. So basically, we just have to decide how much of our lives and spirits we use for others... and who we use them on."

"Hmm, you sound like Baelin," she said.

"Yeah, I think he's rubbing off."

She giggled. "You're not scary like he is."

"Hey!" he said, pretending to be offended. "I'm sure those monsters were plenty scared of your mighty brother."

"More like mighty, *lame* brother." She rolled her eyes.

"Well, the sister takes after the brother."

"No she doesn't."

"Yes she does."

"No she doesn't!"

"Yes she does!"

They glared at each other. "Well, the tree wasn't scared of you. If you were so big and scary, it'd be scared of you, wouldn't it?"

"Of course not. I just saved it like it was a damsel and I was a brave knight from a fairy tale! It could *feel* my aura of mighty goodne—Wait, what are you doing?"

Selina had leaned over the grass, pressing her palm to her lips and puffing her cheeks out. "Trying... not... to... throw up."

"Ugh." He looked up at the branches of the large tree they were sitting under. "I should have Claygon pick you up and put you on one of those branches up there."

"He wouldn't do that." She patted Claygon's foot, smiling sweetly at the golem. "Would you?"

For a brief, horrifying moment, Alex imagined his golem's first true display of sentience would be to side with his sister. He studied Claygon's face with his breath held, looking for signs of imminent betrayal... There weren't any.

His golem was his usual stoic self.

Smiling smugly, he turned his attention back to Selina.

The smile dropped.

A deep frown had creased her brow, she looked like something unseen was pressing on her shoulders, like she carried the weight of the world on them.

Before he could say anything, she spoke up.

"Alex... do you think the tree would be afraid of *me*? Do you think it'd sense my... fire affinity? You said it was afraid of the fire you started."

"Oh no, I don't think so," he said. "I *did* start the fire, yet it doesn't fear me. I don't think there's any reason for it to be afraid of you."

"Yeah, but you only used fire. Fire's... *part of me*..." she said, sucking her lip between her teeth. "And... it's a tree."

"Well, I don't think it'd sense your fire affinity. As far as I know, aeld trees can't sense elemental affinities. Besides, if you treat it kindly, I'm sure it'll have no problem with you. You're *not* just a walking ball of fire. I mean, fire has its own place in the wild. It clears the way for new growth, and burnt things feed the soil. Professor Salinger says fire means renewal. And listen, I used fire to put out the fire in the windmill. It can be used for a lot of different things, just like Shiani said. Point is, though... I used fire and it wasn't afraid of me, so I don't think it would be afraid of you. I think it reacts more to how folks treat it."

He raised an eyebrow. "Did something happen? You don't usually talk about this stuff."

She looked away, her hand falling on her textbook. "In our next class... we'll be learning more about affinities. So... I've been thinking."

"Oh. What're you thinking about?"

"I don't know..." she said. "Lots of things, I guess."

He thought about what to do. A part of him considered talking to her teacher about maybe letting her go to the library during that course... What would that accomplish? It would just make her more afraid and teach her that she should run from knowledge she might not want.

And if he supported that sort of thinking, he would be telling her that Alric was just as special to everyone else in Thameland as it was to them.

And what good would that lie do in the long run?

Alric was only special to the kingdom because the Cave of the Traveller was so close to it, and the transportation potential it had was enormous. If they came to understand how to control the magic, then the Kingdom of Thameland could be a far different place after the war. A network of teleportation gates could transform Thameland from a remote kingdom to a trade mecca in under a decade.

That was what gave Alric value, not the fact that people lived in it and loved it.

And Selina had a fire affinity. Nothing would change that. She wasn't going to grow out of it. It couldn't be removed. She couldn't will it away. As far as anyone knew, elemental affinities were as inherent to people as their soul, mana, or flesh and blood. Even more inherent, in the case of flesh and blood: shapeshifting magic could *change* the flesh.

No known magic could change an affinity.

Would he really leave his sister with the idea that she should run away and hide from the knowledge of something that was inherent to her?

No. That wouldn't help her. He'd have to let her decide for herself, just like he'd done before.

"Well, what do you want to do?" Alex asked. "It sounds like your teacher's just going to go over what the affinities are like, right?"

She nodded.

"She won't force you to do anything with them?"

"No." Selina shook her head. "She even said that we weren't allowed to do any magic for a long time."

"Right... so it sounds like you'll just be finding out how some of this stuff works."

"Yeah, I know," she said. "I'm a little scared... but..." Her hand fell on the knife belted at her waist. "But I want to find out more."

He smiled, leaning over to squeeze her shoulder. "You're brave. Good for you."

She looked up at him. "But... could you tell me about that fire you made one more time, and how it fought the other fire?"

"Sure," Alex said. "I'll tell it as many times as you want."

CHAPTER 5

THE ORIGIN OF AFFINITIES

Selina's class was all abuzz with excitement. They were hovering in front of her classroom door like eager bees over a flower field—chattering to one another, giggling, and periodically adjusting hefty bookbags on their shoulders.

Seven of the eight students kept watching the door as if willing it to open, and if staring at it long enough would make it fly open.

Selina—the eighth student—wasn't so excited.

She felt like sprites were flying around inside her belly, some excited and others panicking. She was nervous, not knowing quite what to expect, so a part of just wanted to go back home.

And what good would that do?

'You want to be a wizard, right?' she thought. 'Alex and Baelin keep talking about how dangerous it is and...' She remembered the Games of Roal and demons. Demons who mindlessly attacked them, turning what was a fun day into a terrible scary one, full of sharp teeth and wild magic and red. 'How can I handle stuff like that if I'm too scared to even go to class.'

Her hand dropped to her belt instinctually. Of course, there was nothing there; she wasn't allowed to carry her birthday gift from the Lus in school, which bothered her. Having the knife was comforting, in the same way holding figurines she'd made when she was small used to be.

'I wish Abela was here,' she thought for the hundredth time since she'd started learning magic theory with her other classmates who were rich in mana. Abela was her closest friend, except she didn't have enough mana to become a wizard.

Her friend didn't seem bothered by that fact in the slightest, but Selina still wished that she and her best friend were in all the same classes, especially ones that made her nervous.

She'd made friends with other kids in her magic classes, but it wasn't quite the same.

"I'm so excited," Mariama said from nearby, her dark plaits bouncing as she bobbed on the balls of her feet. "I've been trying to find out more about wind affinity, but my big sister hardly tells me anything. Ugh, you're so lucky, Selina."

"Huh?" Selina was dragged from her thoughts, turning to Mariama and two other students who were watching her with a mix of curiosity and awe.

She fought the urge to make a face. Most of the kids in her classes looked at her that way since her affinity was revealed. It wasn't their fault she didn't like thinking about that day. They didn't know about what happened to her mother and father.

"How am I lucky?" she asked.

"Your brother teaches you all kinds of extra stuff." Mariama pouted. "My sister says that I can't learn *anything* unless our teachers teach it to us. It's *so* annoying."

"Alex doesn't teach me all *that* much," Selina said. "Just a little bit more about spell arrays. He tells me what they do and stuff."

"But that's what I mean!" Mariama said. "I'd love to learn that stuff now. Instead, it's all this boring history stuff. I want to know *magic*, not history!"

"Well, a lot of the spell array stuff is... well, I'm not sure you'd like it," Selina said. "It's a lot of detail. There's a lot of things I had to learn just to start understanding it."

"But you're *starting*. It's so unfair. You get a head start over the rest of us." The other girl rolled her eyes.

"I think Selina's right," Chelios said.

The younger Roth sibling looked at the tall, tanned boy making his way over to them. A broad smile brightened his face. "All the nuts and bolts of it isn't for everyone. My father started teaching me a little bit about magic arrays and—I like it loads—but I think most people would find it boring. Not me, though."

"Oh yeah, it's very cool!" Selina said excitedly. "Did he tell you how a Bohr Array Section works? How it controls how much a spell can spread? When you see a radius listed in a spell-guide, you can change that radius if you change the Bohr Array's configuration. It's tricky, but it's a lot like changing the specs for a building. It's okay to do it as long as you know what each part of the structure's for, and what changes could happen if you rearrange stuff."

Chelios stood frozen like a deer in the path of a charging dragon.

"Uh... well, I mean yeah," he said, withering under her earnest gaze. "I mean sure... yeah. The Bohr Array... yeah, I always thought that most people—not me—would think it's the bor*ing* array!"

Some of the other kids burst out laughing.

A shudder went through Selina.

'Ugh, that was an Alex joke,' she thought.

"But seriously, you must be really excited," Chelios said. "What with all those fire sprites and how they gathered around you on testing day. Mr. Powell said your fire affinity is super strong, right? You must be so excited!"

"Uh..." Selina said, a wave of discomfort going through her. "Well—"

Click.

The door opened, revealing the smiling face of Miss Sutton. "Well, well, it's so good to see all of you so diligent this early in the morning. Hello, everyone, come in! Come in!"

Selina sighed with relief as the other students rushed into the room.

Their wizardry classroom was a hall of wonders. Glass terrariums and tanks held earth and water where small magical creatures lived. They were cared for by the students. Longoean ash spiders, scotiatic coffee lizards, and cobic shine-fish crawled or swam behind the glass. Some paused what they were doing to watch the children as they ran into the classroom.

On the other side of the room, a raised bed of rich brown soil was filled with dozens of plants. There was a butterfly bush that—when it was hungry—would periodically uproot itself to drink nectar from nearby flowers, then settle back into the soil when it was full. There were flowers that bloomed every day at noon in shades of gold, like the sun. Others grew tiny berries that shed entire rainbows of colourful light. One plant —Selina's favourite—had leaves that looked like salt crystals, each pulsing with inner electric lines.

They reminded her of Isolde's lightning bolts.

Miss Sutton took her place at the front of the class as the eight students found their seats. A minute of chattering passed—then a loud *hem, hem* brought everyone's attention to the front of the room.

"Very good, class," Miss Sutton said. "I'm glad to see so much excitement today. If only you'd had such enthusiasm for our lesson on the

History of Spell Arrays." She watched them from behind thick, red-framed bifocals.

A bit of grumbling went through the class, and Chelios raised his hand.

"Yes, Chelios?" Miss Sutton asked.

"*I* liked spell arrays, Miss Sutton," he said, his voice filled with pride and his chest puffed up.

The teacher smiled sweetly. "I'm very glad you did. But today, as you all know, we won't be talking about spell arrays. We'll be talking about affinities and their history. Just a bit of it, at least. This information will be on the final test, so I suggest you take notes, pay attention to my hand-outs, and—as always...?"

"Do your homework," the class droned, with all the enthusiasm of children who'd repeated those words dozens of times.

"Exactly!" Miss Sutton said in cheery tones.

She snapped her fingers.

Poof!

There was a burst of light and smoke—as though she'd set off a small firework—and chalk appeared in her hand. On the board, she drew symbols, four of them in four directions: up, down, left and right.

Raging flame to represent the element of fire.

Flowing waves to represent the element of water.

Craggy stone to represent the element of earth.

Rushing wind to represent the element of air.

And in the centre of it all, she drew the symbol for mana.

"Can any of you tell me what the primary elements are?" she asked, facing the class. "Yes, Milintica."

A boy with a long dark braid wrapped in leather ties had raised his hand. "Earth, Fire, Water, and Air. But some say there's different elements: wood, fire, earth, metal, and water."

"That's correct. Those are the elements that people in Tarim-Lung teach in their systems of magic. They are also correct," Miss Sutton said, drawing a symbol of a tree and a symbol of a steel bar. "In those lands, their mana vents are inhabited by powerful spirits of wood, fire, earth, metal, and water. They drink in wild mana from the vents and release it as energy tied to their elements. So, for them, their system is more appropriate. However."

She tapped the four elements she'd drawn. "When it comes to elemental planes, the primary elements are the four you named first. All others, such as Ice and Magma, are called Paraelemental planes, which form gateways between the four primary elemental planes. Now, when it comes to affinities, mortals are only born with—if they have any affinity at all—an affinity for one of the four primary elements. Do you have any idea why that is?"

The children looked at each other, but no one raised their hand.

"Well, that was actually a bit of a trick question." Miss Sutton smiled. "There really is no fully right answer."

"There isn't?" Chelios asked.

"No, I'm afraid. We learn more about magic every day. Knowledge is not a dead thing to look at once and never think about again. Knowledge lives. Knowledge grows. Knowledge changes. People agree and disagree about things we think we know. And until one is proven right beyond doubt, we must be open to the idea that the things we believe can change."

Selina thought about fire.

Before fire had shattered her family, she used to think it was beautiful. One of her very first memories was of fire. The way it danced. The warmth and scent. Its light. But ever since the night her parents died, fire was shame. How could she love something that could do something so awful?

Then when they'd left Alric...

Fire nearly killed them in the Cave of the Traveller... And it had also saved their lives from the swarm of spiders. It'd burnt the Hive-queen and let them escape. She'd seen fire magic used to fight those demons that tried to kill everyone.

And Shiani had told her about how her people viewed fire so differently.

Selina had peeked at Vesuvius' glowing flames in a mix of wonder and shame. Changes. Changes. Changes.

She tuned back into the lesson to find Miss Sutton moving on.

"—the most accepted theory as to why mortals are born with affinities for the elements is because way, way, *way* back in history, many mortals *worshipped* elements." The teacher drew a pair of hands pressed together in prayer. "Some of your families might worship deities and some might not, but a long time ago, people worshipped spirits, mighty monsters, and even the elements themselves. Can you think of why that would be?"

Selina remembered what Shiani had told her about how fire helped her people. Then she thought about the farmers around Alric and how they would pray for rain. Or how the fishermen would pray that the river would have lots of fish in the spring.

She raised her hand.

"Yes, Selina?"

"Um, is it because the elements are so important in our lives?"

"Exactly!" Miss Sutton praised her. "And the further back in time we go, the *more* they affected mortals' lives. Before we figured out how to build shelter, we had to hide in caves or be at the mercy of the weather and hostile tribes. Before magic and divinities came into the hands of mortals, fires were unstoppable in villages. So people worshipped and sought the good blessings of the elements."

She drew a line from the clasped hands to the symbols for mana. "As we know, the elemental planes are powerful planes of magic, with elements being strong and powerful beings. Being around them can leave a mark on someone's mana, one that can even reach out through time to touch their children's-children's children. So if you have an affinity for an element, it might mean that your family had something to do with that element way back in time."

Miss Sutton pointed to a world map on the wall next to the obsidian stone she was drawing on. "This is supported by the fact that there are far more people born with elemental affinities in the Rhinean Empire, where people *still* worship the elements to this day. And..."

She tapped an area on the board. "Most people in the Rhinean Empire born with elemental affinities are born near the Peaks of the Elements."

Selina recalled the four peaks. Each mountain had been within sight of the portal they'd taken out of the Cave of the Traveller. Alex had blocked her from seeing the mountain of fire. Maybe there was a connection there? Mr. Lu once told her that her last name—Roth—used to mean "red" in the old Rhinean tongues. Fire was orange, but it could also be red. Was there a connection?

She swallowed.

Changes.

"Other theories say that exposure to an element or elemental in childhood can give someone an affinity, but that's questionable since everyone's exposed to wind, earth, and water every day, yet affinities are still quite rare, all things considered," Miss Sutton explained. "The theory about the worship of elementals in the past is the most accepted one we have today. It's called the Ancient Elementals theory."

She chuckled. "There was also a theory that Mana and Elemental affinities were given to us by powerful beings from the stars. That's called the 'Ancient Aliens' theory, which is *not* accepted. So, please don't confuse the two if you read about it or hear it discussed. At a later date, we'll talk about which areas of the world have the greatest population of folks with elemental affinities. For now, let's talk about what an affinity actually does, and how it affects your mana. You might be surprised at how you can use it."

'At how you can use it...'

Selina remembered how Alex had used fire to fight fire.

The young girl leaned forward in her seat, paying close attention, opening her mind to the lesson.

And changes.

CHAPTER 6

THE CHANGING FLAME

"How many of you have been to the rainbow tower?" Miss Sutton asked.

Selina, Chelios, and two other students raised their hands.

"Good, so some of you have seen how glass prisms break light into colours." The teacher drew a triangular prism on the board. "Those of you who haven't been to Noarc's tower, have you seen coloured glass or a coloured gem, like a ruby or a sapphire?"

The other four students raised their hands.

"Excellent! That will make this easier to explain. Now, I have a simple question for everyone. At least I hope it's simple." She drew four tall rectangles on the board: one red, one green, one yellow, and one blue. The chalk shimmered, changing colour each time it touched the board, and returning to its natural colour after the blue rectangle was completed.

She then drew four straight lines, one ending against the left side of each coloured rectangle, creating an image of a light beam striking the rectangle.

"Now, let's say the straight lines are light, and the rectangles are coloured glass. Each beam of light strikes the coloured glass on the left side, then comes out on the right side. What colour will each light beam be when it emerges on the right?"

Someone snorted.

Selina and some of her classmates looked at each other, waiting for someone else to answer.

The question did appear to be *too* easy; there must have been a trick to it. Unsure, Selina didn't raise her hand, but neither did anyone else. *No one* wanted to be the one taking a chance at being wrong when the answer seemed so obvious.

Miss Sutton mimed looking at a timekeeper. "Come on, we're not moving on until one of you answers."

Reluctantly, Mariama's hand went up. "Uh... well, if it went through the red rectangle, the light would turn red. If it went through the blue one, it would turn blue. If it went through the yellow one, it would be yellow, and the green rectangle would turn it green."

Miss Sutton watched the young girl squirm for a few moments. Selina had the feeling her teacher was enjoying herself, then she finally broke the tension with a big smile. "You are... absolutely correct, Mariama!" She drew the appropriately coloured lines exiting the right side of the rectangles.

"And now you know the basics of what we call the Filter Theory, which is the most accepted theory for how affinities work." She tapped her belly. "Like we've talked about before, inside all of us there's a mana pool, and around that mana pool are our mana fibres. We haven't been able to examine them visually, but people with affinities have described how their own fibres *feel*. And what they say *seems* to indicate that mana fibres in people with affinities are shaped slightly differently than in those without."

She tapped the coloured rectangles. "Imagine that each fibre also acts as a kind of filter, filtering the mana you make in such a way that it's "touched" by a particular element. So what does this mean in practice? It means that the mana you produce is much more efficient at powering spells of your own element. Spells you cast of that element will require less mana and be far more powerful than average."

She looked at Mariama and Selina. "Which means that your mana will be much less efficient at powering spells of the *opposite* element. The stronger the affinity, the less efficient it will be, and the more likely the mana will be to 'act up' while you're building a spell array. For those with a very strong affinity, casting spells of the opposite element might even be dangerous."

Selina nodded. She'd expected that would happen.

Miss Sutton continued the lesson, explaining how affinities were used throughout history. She talked about the ancient kingdom of Windemere where those with a wind magic affinity were seen as blessed people, and how they used their spells to power windmills so each harvesting season the grain was efficiently turned into flour. The kingdom always had flour to trade for other goods with their neighbours. She explained how people with water affinities used spells that changed currents to push ships through the ocean even when there was no wind.

Then she spoke of fire.

"In the lost Kingdom of Ozuko, there were many people with fire affinities. And they had two jobs: to make clean water and to help make it rain," she explained.

Selina's hand immediately shot up.

"Ah yes, Selina?" Miss Sutton asked.

"I thought you said that people with fire affinity couldn't use water magic very well, or at all?"

"Aaaaah, but here's the thing, Selina. If you apply magic and science *together*, then you can do all sorts of things that might surprise you." She picked up a cup of water from her desk. "Watch closely."

With a short incantation, Selina felt a wave of heat pass through the room and a gathering of mana near the cup in her teacher's hand. Something about the mana felt... comforting.

Then came a hiss and a bubble as the water boiled, sending a line of steam into the air.

"Take note of the steam. When water boils, it *evaporates*, meaning it turns into vapour. However, if it gets cold enough, then it will turn into water again. That's a process called *condensation*, which is what we call the moisture that one sees on a window in colder climates during the cold season. Now, here's the interesting thing about evaporation and condensation."

She muttered another incantation, and the mana Selina sensed felt... awful. Strange. Unfriendly. As Miss Sutton finished the spell, a thin wall of ice rose from the floor beside her. It was no thicker than a pinky, and no wider than Selina's arm-span, but it would've been even taller than Alex.

The teacher brought the steaming cup close to the wall of ice and—as the steam touched the frozen surface—it began turning into water droplets that quickly froze into icy protrusions on the wall.

"Each of those droplets are pure water," their teacher said. "When water evaporates, it leaves many impurities behind. Contaminants like sand, grit, and even salt. So, for example, if you were to boil seawater, you would make pure steam. Then when it condenses, you have pure water that you can drink. We call this *distilled water*. You understand? If you have or ever develop an interest in alchemy, you'll be using distilled water a lot."

"So... wizards with fire affinity could boil sea water to make pure steam?" Selina asked.

"Exactly, and if you evaporate a *lot* of water at once, then it will travel up into the clouds where it is *much* colder. Then, if that much water condenses all at once, and under the right conditions, it can trigger or increase rain. See? With science and magic together, there's many amazing things you can do, if you learn about electrical currents, how heat travels, the minerals in earth, and the way water flows. And—Selina?"

"How does heat work?" she asked.

Silence spread through the class.

"Oh my, well, that's an advanced question," Miss Sutton said. "Well... um... how can I put this? This is *very* much oversimplifying it, and you'll learn much more about heat during magical theory and alchemy courses in later years. For now, heat is a bit like 'energy on the move.' When something burns, energy is being released as heat and flame. The fire feeds itself on air and fuel, and heat results. Heat conducting along metal is energy travelling along it."

Selina's mind was working quickly.

A tiny hope bloomed in her chest.

She thought back to what Alex told her about using more flame to fight the fire in the windmill:

"*The thing is, the fire needed the wood, air, and monsters inside the mill to keep burning. So if I made a bigger fire, it would eat all the fuel and air inside the mill. Then the first fire wouldn't be able to burn anymore,*" he'd said.

Fire to eat the fuel of another fire.

Fire to stop fire.

Fire to end fire.

Fire would burn up all the fuel, and then there would be no more heat after that.

And now this stuff about heat... Fire was transforming energy. Changes. Changing.

Heat was something moving from one place to the other... so wherever the heat was going would get hotter, wouldn't it? So then...

She put her hand up again.

"Yes, Selina?"

"What is cold?"

Miss Sutton chuckled. "You are just *full* of difficult questions today, aren't you? Cold is hard to describe, but the easiest way I can explain it is that cold is where heat and energy *isn't*. The less heat and energy in the air…" She made a little shivering motion. "The lower the temperature will be."

"So…" Selina said, her hope growing. "If you can move heat and fire, can you create cold?"

Miss Sutton paused, thinking about the question. "In theory… you might be able to, but it would be very difficult, I would think. I imagine it would be a lot easier to have a wizard just cast a spell of elemental water, or a spell of paraelemental ice. There's no real necessity for such a thing, but who knows? Does that answer all your questions?"

Selina Roth's mind was on fire. She barely managed to squeak out a: "Y-yes, those are all my questions. Thank you, Miss Sutton."

"You're most welcome. Okay, then," her teacher said. "Now, let's talk about how air magic works. With air, we—"

Selina wasn't listening.

Her imagination was aflame. What if fire didn't have to come with shame? What if she could use it—just like her brother used the Mark—to do something different? Something *good*? Fire and ice.

Snow from fire.

Good fire that ate destructive fire.

An Eater of Flame.

Silently, she sat, trying to pay attention to the lesson while her mind danced with images of flame. For the first time in years, those images didn't completely fill her with shame and fear.

A sense of wonder returned, and though some shame remained, for the first time, she felt like she could do something about it. Hope. Selina's mind drifted back to Miss Sutton's voice when she heard "assignment for next class" and realised her classmates were all standing.

Immediately, she was out of her chair, shoving books into her book bag, and heading to the line forming by the teacher's desk. She waited patiently for her turn, knowing her question wasn't going to be a short one. It seemed like everyone had long questions that needed long answers today. Mariama's was about the elemental plane of air, and how that intertwined with lightning magic. She was second to last in line just before Selina; whose patience had been erased by the time Mariama's turn came.

When the young girl had gotten her answer, she noticed Selina standing there. "You want me to wait for you?"

"No. You go ahead. I'll catch up to you in a minute."

Mariama shrugged. "Okay, see you in a bit."

Chelios—flanked by two friends—paused at the doorway, giving Selina and Miss Sutton a wave goodbye.

Selina was almost vibrating with excitement.

"Umm... I was wondering if I could ask you kind of a hard question, Miss Sutton?"

"Oh my, well, you've been asking me hard questions all morning, Selina. You certainly had me earning my wages, that's for sure." Miss Sutton smiled, placing a book in her bag. "I'm glad today's lesson sparked so many questions in you. It shows how engaged you are and that you're making some sound connections from the material. That's the definition of learning. So, tell me what you're curious about?"

"Ummm... Making a spell that could... move heat and fire and then make things cold where the heat was... Could someone make a spell like that?"

"You seem really interested in that." Miss Sutton frowned, then cleared her throat. "Your brother has told me... something of your past. Are you doing okay?"

"...Yeah, I'm okay," Selina said.

"I didn't want to be indiscreet in front of the other children, but... I'm glad I have the chance to check in with you. Just so you know, if you ever find parts of our lessons involving fire affinities too difficult, don't hesitate to excuse yourself for a bit." She smiled and patted Selina's shoulder.

"Now, to answer your question... If someone could make a spell like that. People don't usually make spells unless it's out of necessity, and most people use cold magic to make cold, or water magic to make water. It might technically be possible, though. I think you'd need to ask a wizard far more experienced than myself."

The words *technically be possible* were enough for Selina.

"Miss Sutton, when you have help hours after school, I wonder... if you could teach me a little more about how heat and fire magic works?"

Miss Sutton's smile was soft. "Whatever I can. And whatever you're comfortable with."

And so, a door had opened for change to come to Selina Roth.

Just as a wildfire brought change to the land.

What would grow after that change?

Selina was hopeful for something good.

CHAPTER 7

REDUNDANCIES

For the first time, Alex Roth walked toward the portal to Thameland with only Claygon at his side. He drew quizzical looks from the portal staff, since the expeditionary force was accustomed to seeing him with his teammates. This change of routine was something the attentive staff paid close attention to. Some waved and wished him a 'good morning,' and he replied in kind, but never slowed his stride.

Today's event was too important for him to be late.

It had been nearly a week since the windmill blaze, and normally, he and his teammates wouldn't be returning to Greymoor so soon.

But today was a special day.

Alex had received a message the night before that was written in a familiar hand. It had read:

Alex, my boy, I have managed to clear my schedule but just for tomorrow. Apologies about the short notice. I have taken leave to inform your professors of a one-time possible absence on your part. Professor Hak was very complimentary of your work, and actually said that—if you did not choose to attempt it this semester—that she would propose you Challenge the Exam for credit for next semester's first-year Blood Magic course.

I chose not to tell her of the little book you are penning. I thought that should be your 'little' surprise. In any case, should you accept, your professors are forewarned.

I hope to see you on the morrow, say at, seven o'clock, for a nice little safari.

If you choose to accompany me, please press your charm pendant to the bottom of the note, and I'll be alerted.

Do make sure to come equipped for battle tomorrow and bring both a lunch and supper; I shall meet you at camp beside your lovely aeld tree. I've heard it's growing well.

Oh, and do bring headwear. Reading the weather indicates that it will be a sunny autumn day in the area where we will be trekking. Yet, it will also be bitterly cold. I did not train you for battle only to have you felled by frostbite or sickness!

Yours faithfully,
Chancellor Baelin

Of course, angry dragons couldn't keep Alex away from Baelin's orb hunt, so he'd eagerly taken the charm pendant from around his neck and pressed it to the message.

There was a flash of light, a hiss of flame, and—when the young wizard lifted the pendant—symbols were inscribed as though they'd been branded into the paper.

He hadn't wasted a second after that.

He'd prepared his gear for the morning, had a quick Restful Slumber, gave a hurried explanation to Theresa and Selina, then ran out the door at sunrise with his golem by his side. Selina and Theresa stood on the balcony waving goodbye, with Selina excitedly bouncing on the balls of her feet.

His little sister seemed about ready to burst recently, but—if Alex asked her what was going on—she'd only say:

"I'll tell you later, okay? It's a secret for now."

He didn't push. After all, who was he to begrudge anyone their secrets.

'Maybe she has a surprise for us,' he thought as he stepped onto the portal. 'Maybe something's happening at school, or maybe... wait? Could there be a boy that she likes in one of her classes? Should I be expecting that? Is she old enough for that? Oh, by the Traveller, what am I supposed to do? Be protective? Be cool with it! She's only eleven; she can't be—'

Whooom.

Alex and Claygon sank into the portal with his body peacefully still, but his mind panicking.

By the time they emerged in Thameland, he was a bit calmer.

'Get your mind right,' he said to himself, stepping off the portal and greeting the Watchers on duty. 'You can't go into this with your mind in some chaotic, half-crazed mess. Calm down and only start panicking when Selina tells you she's getting married... Stop it!'

Alex shook his head while stepping out of the teleportation tent. He watched the sky for signs of snow.

The early morning was bright and crystal clear, nothing but sun and feathery white clouds, yet a deep chill hung heavy in the air. The rains had been frigid lately, coating yellowing grass between each tent in light frost.

Winter was coming, and the first snowfall wouldn't be too far off, making Alex wonder how expedition members who'd never experienced cold and snow would find the bitter cold. Pulling his cloak around himself, he and Claygon moved through the encampment toward his and Baelin's meeting place—the aeld tree.

Looking around, Alex whistled in amazement.

Construction on the research castle had continued, making it nearly impossible to refer to the site as an 'encampment' anymore. With the inner wall complete, the builders had moved on to the next phase and were now at the stage of replacing tents with outbuildings.

The research tent was already gone, and in its place stood a large stone building that was a smaller version of the Cells. He could only imagine how thrilled Professor Jules must be with the finished research building since he was just itching to get inside himself.

Other structures—including a bathhouse, tool storage, and a sleeping barracks—were still under construction but near completion. They ought to be finished by week's end.

But to Alex, the most remarkable sight before him was near the centre of camp.

There, what looked like a half-finished mass of stone had been erected. The keep of the castle was surrounded by scaffolding and a mountain of building stones. In front, most of the grass had been removed, replaced by paving stones: a courtyard in the making.

In the courtyard's centre, a field had been cleared for an expansive garden bed filled with enriched soil where newly sprouted earth-enriching magical plants were growing. They'd been generously provided by everyone's favourite magical botany professor, Professor Salinger. And, in the centre of it all?

"Hello there," Alex said as he approached the aeld tree.

Stepping into its green-golden glow, a wave of peace and contentment came over him.

"Ah, I see you're in a good mood today." He placed his hand on its trunk in greeting, then took a pinch of leasú-todhar from his bag. "Nice sunny day for you, eh? I bet you're looking forward to that."

A wave of warmth came off the aeld, tinged by a touch of nerves as Alex sprinkled the cerulean dust over its roots. With each passing day, the tree had settled in, growing more comfortable in its new surroundings.

Though it still gave off the occasional wave of nervousness.

He couldn't blame it. Had he been trapped—for the Traveller only knew how long—and at the mercy of nasty monsters, he'd be pretty nervous too.

"I see you've still got a bit of nerves," he said, pausing to summon Bubbles. The elemental appeared and released a little burbling noise, then sprayed the soil with light, nourishing mists. "And I get that. I'm just happy to see that you're growing so well."

He wasn't sure if it was the leasú-todhar, the planting at noon ceremony, the magical seedlings growing alongside its roots, or all of those things, but the aeld tree looked *great*. Its green-golden glow shed a richer light than when he'd rescued it from the clearing by the windmill, its leaves were broader and looked like they'd been polished, and its trunk actually felt *warm*.

And...

In that short time, the trunk became a little thicker, the tree taller, and its branches fuller. Whatever the reason for its growth spurt, he'd keep giving it the best care. Maybe—

Teleportation magic. Coming from behind him.

The young wizard turned as the power spiked and a familiar horned figure appeared.

"Morning," Baelin said. "I see that you're early. Glorious."

"Whoa." Alex took a step back.

In all of his time around Baelin, he'd only seen the chancellor dressed in his magnificent robes, even while battling Leopold's summoned demons. Of course, those had been times when the ancient wizard hadn't had any forewarning.

Today, he was ready, the fight was of his choosing, and so he was dressed for it, as only the instructor for the Art of the Wizard in Combat could be.

The goat beastman had abandoned robes in favour of armour of brilliant bronze. A shirt of bronze chainmail, belted at the waist, clad his broad shoulders and torso, falling to his knees. His lower legs were protected by bronze greaves, and his forearms sheathed in polished gauntlets. A helm with guards that protected the front of his horns and shielded his head fit like a custom forged glove. In one hand, he gripped a staff that towered over him, crafted of a deep, black material that drew in the surrounding light. It was crowned by a jewel shaped in the image of a goat's eye that burned with an inner flame. At his waist, a brutal-looking spiked warhammer hung, backed by a curved pick. Glowing runes encrusted its head, and the mana it emitted made Alex's senses tingle.

"You're really not playing around today, are you?" Alex said in awe. "Have to admit, I wasn't expecting you to be someone who wore armour."

"And why not?" Baelin asked. "When one knows one is going into battle, is it not appropriate to dress for the occasion? One wouldn't till their fields wearing a silk dress, and one should not go into war wearing robes, if one can help it."

"Yeah, that makes sense, but... armour?" Alex asked. "I figured with the kind of protective spells you'd have, any kind of armour—even magical armour—would be... unnecessary?"

Baelin gave him an unamused look. He let out a sigh as though the world's weight had pressed the breath from his body. "Alex, I am not sure who should be more disappointed. Myself, or Professor Jules. What did I teach you in the Art of the Wizard in Combat? What have you been learning and applying during this expedition? Think about the reports you've been submitting for your COMB-2000 credit."

"Uh..." Alex paused. "A Proper Wizard doesn't ignore any source of power?"

"*Exactly.*" The chancellor tapped his hammer. "And why do we not pare down all safety procedures and equipment to their bare minimum, even when doing so would save both time and coin?"

"Redundancies are important in safety," Alex said, repeating some of the safety part of his first-year alchemy textbook word for word. "Safety procedures and equipment aren't meant to protect you in *ideal* conditions; they're meant to protect you under stress."

"Precisely," the chancellor said. "And so I have sheathed myself in protective force armour, but what would happen if that spell were to be pierced? What would happen if I encountered an enemy where such a spell would do little good? Why entrust my bodily health to a single layer of protection, when I can gird myself in protective spells, magical armour, and my own iron will?"

"Yeah, that makes total sense." Alex scratched the back of his head. "Didn't really think about that. I always thought that armour would be restrictive. And you'd be better off just relying on protective magic and increased mobility to be a shield for you."

"In some cases, your thinking would be quite apt," Baelin said. "But this armour has enough enchantments laid upon it to make it as light and cool as cloth, while at the same time, harder than castle-forged steel. Remember: as your resources expand, then normal limitations become... guidelines. Keep that in mind as you grow in strength and experience. I have known too many archwizards who thought themselves indestructible due to their magic, only to fall in a situation where their magic was denied to them. Keep that in mind."

Alex nodded, conjuring an image of some barren, terrible place where he couldn't channel his mana. "Maybe... maybe I'll start looking into some light armour for myself."

"Good man. In any case, let us depart. We have all day, but no sense in wasting time here when the wilds, adventure, and fabulous prizes call to us," his voice boomed, tinged in excitement. "Come, let us begin our sojourn. Do you have anything else to do or gather?"

"No, this is it," Alex said, turning to Bubbles. "Why don't you keep misting our friend here until you're pulled back to your home plane? How does that sound?"

With a burble, the water elemental continued spraying the contented aeld tree's roots.

Alex looked up at the sapling. "Alrighty, I'll see you when I get back."

Another wave of peace and calm came from the little tree as Alex and Claygon stepped up beside Baelin. Alex cast layer upon layer of magic on himself, preparing his full suite of defences. The chancellor cast a pair of defensive spells on himself, then cast greater force armour over Alex.

"And now for the finishing touch," the ancient wizard said, casting a flight spell on himself, Alex, and Claygon.

"Thanks. I'm ready and so is Claygon," the young wizard said.

Baelin nodded, a glint in his eye. "For blood and thunder, then. Into the hunt we go. Though... I suspect it will be less a grand hunt and more... nipping down to the shops for a biscuit sort of hunt." His laugh boomed across the encampment.

Raising his arms, he chanted an incantation.

Alex's senses tingled as teleportation magic enveloped the golem and pair of wizards.

Whoosh!

And then they were gone.

CHAPTER 8

CONVENIENCE

Alex appeared first, dropping into a fighting stance while surveying the area. Baelin's spell catapulted him across the land, and—wherever he was—it was markedly chillier than Greymoor. The sun was lower on the horizon than it had been earlier, casting the light of dawn in a deeper shade.

"West, then," Alex said. "We must have travelled west."

The wind rustled through a stand of pines, needles whispering as the evergreen branches rustled. The aroma of conifers hung in the air, mingling with bird calls and... something else.

His enhanced hearing detected something in the distance.

Something *wet*.

A heartbeat later, the air shimmered, signalling Claygon and Baelin's arrival.

"Ah yes, there's your peculiar quirk at work," the chancellor said. "Hmmm." He scanned the trees. "Well, it appears we are roughly on target."

When he banged his staff on the ground, the jewel shuddered, rippling like a pond, and a swarm of glowing, magical eyes surfaced. One pair. A trio. A dozen. Two dozen.

More than a score of Wizard's Eyes circled the ancient wizard like a mass of loyal bees. With a gesture, he sent them off and—as they flew away—they began to fade, gradually turning translucent, then vanishing.

"My Wizard's Eyes will have the area scouted in no time," Baelin said. "In the meantime, we can prepare and proceed toward our target dungeon, it lies northeast of here. We'll fly, of course, and I'll cast a spell to disguise our voices, so they blend with the sound of the wind, and another to mask our scent. Oh! And I should also cast the one spell that every wizard going on a hunt should never leave home without. Might I cast it over you and Claygon?"

"Of course," Alex said, keeping his voice low.

With a quick incantation, the chancellor waved his hand and a massive pulse of power flowed, pouring mana over Alex, making his form shimmer like waves of heat on a scorching day in Generasi.

"Whoa," the young wizard whispered as his hands faded before his eyes.

A few breaths later, Baelin and Claygon were also as invisible as the wind blowing around them. But, seconds later, Alex came back into view, but only to his own eyes; to all other sighted creatures, he was invisible.

Making a quick guess at the spell Baelin had conjured, he suspected Greater Invisibility... or perhaps something more powerful. The strength of the mana had nearly brought him to his knees.

"Hold on now, I'm not quite done," the chancellor's voice said.

Another wave of mana washed through the air. Alex felt it concentrating around his eyes, and then, Baelin and Claygon's slightly translucent forms shimmered back into being.

"I trust you can see us now?" Baelin asked.

"Uh, yeah. What spells were those?" Alex marvelled.

"The second one was True Seeing." The ancient wizard waved a gauntlet before Alex's eyes. "A very handy sixth-tier spell. It cuts through most invisibility magic, illusions, and even shapeshifting to reveal the world as it actually is. It *can* be defeated by mundane disguises and more powerful magics, but nonetheless, it is a spell I would recommend that no wizard of sufficient power be without. Keep in mind, it isn't infallible, but it will save your life time and time again."

Baelin chuckled. "About a millennium ago, there was this trend for assassins who were inclined toward magic to learn just enough wizardry to pick up Greater Invisibility, then use it to wreak havoc upon any head of state who someone had a grievance against. They charged a king's ransom for their services, eventually gaining enough wealth to establish their own dynasties."

Alex frowned. "Wait... Was an assassin known as the Crimson Mantis a member of one of these dynasties?"

The ancient wizard raised an eyebrow. "Indeed! I must say, I am surprised you know of him."

"Well, Khalik mentioned him. He was making this pretty unsettling joke about him a while back. So... what happened?"

"Hm?"

"With the assassins?"

"Ah, well, let us just say that court wizards and high priests—anyone with magic powerful enough to pierce invisibility—became highly valued in realms that, up until then, did not bother with them," Baelin said. "I found myself working as a hunter of these assassins for a time. Of course, by the time monarchs had seen the wisdom in hiring wizards and priests to guard them against such magical threats, any assassin with foresight had concluded which way the wind was blowing, and either retired or moved on to different methods. Still, some of the younger, less experienced ones tried to keep the trend alive."

Baelin burst out laughing. "I swear, Alex, you do not know comedy until you see a young man—dressed all in black leather in the summertime—confidently saunter across a crowded ballroom with a smug expression and a knife in his hand, convinced that no one can see him. Ooooh the look on his face when my first disintegration spell hit him."

Alex's eyebrows rose. "So, one moment he's walking across the ballroom, and the next he's dust?"

"Hah! Well, at least a *part* of him was! You see, if you become very adept, you can gain a certain *finesse* with a disintegration spell: you can actually choose which parts of something you want to turn to dust, and which parts you want to remain intact. With enough practice, you can use it with the precision of a sculptor."

Alex swallowed. He wasn't sure he liked where this was going. "Then this young assassin... what did you do to him?"

"Hah, I disintegrated his skeleton and left the rest! You've never seen a human body lose all of its skeletal integrity just like that, have you? *Ploop!*" Baelin snapped his fingers for emphasis then made a motion with his hand like paste splattering on the ground. "It becomes no more than a mewling pile of meat! Let me tell you, the other three assassins hiding in the rafters got the message rather... *quickly*. Fled immediately, even left their associate to his own limited devices! *And* they led me riiiight to their base. Aaaaah, what a delightful evening that was!"

Alex stared at Baelin in abject horror.

"Ah well, I suppose you had to be there." The ancient wizard wiped tears from his eyes. "Or perhaps you'll see the humour when you are older and more... experienced."

Alex chuckled nervously. "Y-yeah, maybe. So what was that other spell then? Greater Invisibility?"

"Ah that? Not quite. It's something of a homebrew, so to speak... Which I shall not reveal the details of. A wizard—even a teacher—cannot give away *all* their secrets, after all!" Baelin smiled, tapping a bronze beard-clasp with a gauntleted finger. "Now then, come, we have a hunt to engage in!"

He floated about a foot above ground. "You and Claygon follow me."

The goatman glided northeast and—after a moment of Alex trying to right his whirling mind—he and Claygon rose a foot in the air and floated after him.

The trio melted into the trees.

Deeper and deeper into the forest they flew, with the wind rising and rustling the pines. The canopy grew thick and the light dim. Alex cursed internally. The wind muffled his hearing while the dim light turned the forest into a blend of shadows. His eyes scanned their surroundings; he was with Baelin and Claygon, which was comforting, but he'd rather that his senses weren't muted while they were in these woods. Anything could be prowling through the shadows.

He imagined silence-spiders and Hive-queens creeping through the canopy. Maybe another clawed creature poised to swoop down on them, or even a pack of them.

Monsters were fond of amb—

"Oh! Would you look at that!" Baelin stopped, bending down suddenly.

Alex held his breath.

What was it? Tracks? A burrow? Had they reached the dungeo—

"A four-leafed clover!" The chancellor straightened up, happily pinching a tiny clover—roots and all—between two gauntleted fingers. There was a rush of teleportation magic and the clover disappeared. "Hah, an auspicious sign for our hunt, wouldn't you say?"

Alex sighed in relief. "You scared me. I thought you'd found the dungeon or something."

"I have."

"Like we'd just stumbled across i—wait, what now?"

"I have, my boy!" Baelin chuckled. "I was given quite detailed directions by our Thameish friends, so the Wizard's Eyes had no problem locating it. It is roughly two miles to the north, and we should reach it right in time for the best morning light."

"O-oh," Alex said, relaxing.

"But please continue monitoring our surroundings as you were. I wouldn't want your habits dulled just because we possess precise knowledge of where our destination is."

"Right..." Alex said.

"Oh, and feel free to chat. Keep in mind that any sounds we make are being disguised. Our discussion is merely mixing in with the sounds of these trees groaning around us from the wind. Nothing to worry about."

The more Baelin talked, the more dispensable Alex felt. "O-okay."

Floating ahead, the chancellor glided silently in between evergreens while Alex and Claygon followed. The golem's upper arms were crossed and his lower ones were folded behind his back. Baelin chatted away like he was a village elder out for a leisurely nature walk with his grandchildren.

Alex enjoyed the conversation as the light grew. But he also kept his ears and eyes sharp, knowing slacking off wasn't an option. Baelin might appear relaxed, but Alex didn't miss his head turning to either side, his goat-like eyes examining their surroundings with precision. The eye in his staff shifted, watching the canopy above, while he took in the constant stream of information from his Wizard's Eyes.

So, when he floated past monstrous sets of tracks pressed into the forest floor, Alex could only assume he'd 'missed' them on purpose. It must be the teacher in him testing his student.

"Baelin." Alex floated down, hovering over the footprints. "There's some tracks down here."

"Ah, excellent. I was hoping you were paying full attention. And what can you tell me about these tracks?"

The young man's eyes narrowed.

Whatever left them was huge. The ground was wet, and the footprints were at least a couple of inches deep. There had been a lot of weight behind them. The creatures that made them were broad, as the tracks were nearly as wide as they were long. An imprint of four bulbous toes extended from the front of a foot.

Images of those tracks were in one of the Thameish bestiaries they'd all had to study. He remembered Isolde cringing at the drawing of the foot, and remarking on how it looked like it was in desperate need of a proper pedicure.

"They're Skinless One tracks." Alex examined the forest floor and the tree canopy, noticing branches and other debris scattered around. The creatures were tall enough to knock some fairly high branches off the trees. "Big, stupid, nasty, and strong enough to crack stone with a good blow from one fist. They're the siege engines of the Ravener."

"Very good. Our Thameish sources informed me that it was indeed a dungeon occupied by these Skinless brutes. The signs of their destructive natures will increase the closer we get to the dungeon itself."

"Yeah," Alex said, a plan forming in his mind. "They're a nasty a bunch. But at least they're not exactly the sharpest or most cunning of the Ravener's spawn. We should be able to ambush them pretty easily. Even without magic."

"Indeed," Baelin said. "Now let's move on and survey our enemy and see how we might do that."

With purpose, the chancellor led Alex and Claygon through the woods. Farther ahead, a loud commotion drowned out the sound of the wind, announcing the dungeon and its monsters were near. The cracking of branches. The heavy thump of giant feet hitting the ground. The wet squelch of naked muscle.

The monster's presence had taken a toll on the surrounding trees. Branches were torn away, bark shredded, and pines uprooted; no tree had been spared.

Trees thinned—more roots were unearthed—until at last, they spotted Skinless Ones moving between the pine trees.

They towered over Claygon—each perhaps seventeen feet tall and over ten feet at the shoulder. They were a gruesome sight, and their name was undeniably fitting: humanoids bloated to an impossible size, with physiques utterly devoid of a single shred of skin. Copper-coloured muscle with fibres thicker than ropes corded their massive forms, writhing with their every movement. Wide, lipless mouths exposed thick, flat teeth meant for crushing. A broad forehead protruded from their faces like a step. A hole where a nose should have been, and enormous bloodshot eyes that constantly teared from the cold wind, completed their faces.

"Horrible things," Alex shuddered, whispering to Baelin and Claygon as they floated between packs of the creatures, unseen and unnoticed.

"They are not the most pleasant-looking creatures, are they?" Baelin agreed, emerging through the trees and floating above a cliff. "And they are as common as ants. Pfeh. Vile things."

Alex and Claygon came through the tree line and looked down. A vast ravine dotted with a honeycomb of gaping cave mouths reaching deep into the earth lay below. The Skinless monsters, as abundant as ground wasps guarding their nest, milled about.

"Jeez," Alex murmured. "It looks like they're pretty established down there. With that many, they could easily overrun a small city."

"Indeed, which is why we will stop them here," Baelin said. "Suggest a plan of attack."

"Well..." Alex scratched his chin in thought. The beginnings of a beard were forming, and it was starting to itch. "My thought is, we have Claygon distract most of the creatures. He can stage an attack from outside: lots of fire and lots of explosions. That'll draw most of the monsters' attention to him while we slip into the dungeon. Your Wizard's Eyes can scout out where the core is, and then we fly in and take it. I'm thinking that the dungeon might sense our mana through your spells—we don't know everything these cores are capable of—but even if it can, you can fight off its defences while I grab the core."

Alex pointed to the tunnels below. "Then we use your and Claygon's power to bury the dungeon. What do you think?"

Baelin thought for a moment, nodding. "Hmmm, a fine plan that makes use of the resources at our disposal. Quick and efficient. Good job. You have taken your lessons to heart," Baelin said with pride.

"Thanks. So I guess we can fly above, you can remove the invisibility from Claygon, and—"

"Oh now, just because I approve doesn't mean we're going to *do* all of that." Baelin smiled, his eyes tracing the lines of the ravine.

"What do you mean?"

"Do you know what one of the advantages of overwhelming power is, Alex?" The ancient wizard raised his staff.

"What?" Alex asked.

"*Convenience*," Baelin said, his voice taking on a dark note.

Then a tidal wave of mana rose around them.

CHAPTER 9

ONE PERSON'S ENTRANCE...

Power gathered around the chancellor like light blazing from the sun.

The air shook.

Alex's mana senses screamed.

His mouth went dry.

He'd seen the ancient wizard exert his power before, but he was never quite prepared for the magnitude of raw power he commanded. The eye on Baelin's staff blazed like a falling star, while the incantation pouring from the goatman's lips throbbed in his ears.

The Skinless monsters stopped what they were doing, sensing that *something* wasn't right.

Then the skies began to darken at ferocious speed.

And their world shook.

As Baelin's spell completed, the ravine shuddered.

Crack!

Monsters bellowed, towering cliffs melted into cascades of broken earth and stone. Trees wavered and collapsed. The earth roared and rock heaved from the soil.

And then, the bottom of the ravine split apart.

A quake rumbled through the dungeon, tearing it in two, sending Ravener-spawn tumbling into crevices that opened beneath them like hungry mouths. As frantic cries rose above the roar of earth and stone, Skinless Ones scattered throughout the forest thundered back to the ravine to find cliff faces heaving and buckling, sending them plummeting to their deaths.

"First the egg is cracked," Baelin shouted as the dungeon split apart, revealing scores of collapsing chambers underground. "And then it is *scrambled*."

His staff's eye flashed.

A wave of power soared and struck the air.

The wind screamed.

"Stay close, Alex. Even I might be unable to guarantee your safety if you stray," the ancient wizard warned.

It took all of the young wizard's will not to wrap himself around the chancellor's leg like a terrified cat. He'd become much braver from his adventures... but this? This was what he imagined the end of the world could look like.

The unnatural clouds shifted and boiled like rushing water, turning on themselves. And they turned. And turned. The air spun faster and faster.

Alex was witnessing the phenomenon Baelin was creating, but his mind couldn't believe it.

He remembered the tour guide at Noarc's tower telling them about violent events in the atmosphere of the Barrens when too much wild mana seeped into the air. Whirling winds that levelled everything they touched were created.

If he remembered correctly, the phenomenon was called...

Whoosh!

A tornado.

The air whipped and swirled into a funnel that reached down from the sky, shrieking as it touched the ground. Chaos filled the ravine. The tornado hungrily tore through widening crevices, grabbing earth, stone, and Skinless Ones like they were weightless. Boulders the size of wagons spun in dizzying patterns, upheaving trees or terrified Ravener-spawn; it didn't matter.

In the space of heartbeats, what was once a fearsome dungeon capable of destroying a good-sized army was merely dust in the wind. Yet, in all of the destruction, Alex, Claygon, and Baelin remained safe in a bubble of air so still, it was like being in a quiet meadow. Within the bubble of peace, the Thameish wizard witnessed ruined monsters and debris spiraling past them like he was watching a storm from the safety of a cozy hall with a fire blazing in its mantel. Then a thundering bellow reached him.

Horror was being dragged from deep underground.

A Rampart-crusher—an enormous tentacled creature resembling a skinned squid—fought against the wind. Its body was bulbous, as wide around as a Skinless One was tall, and from its frame, a dozen tentacles flailed, each ending in a grasping, six-fingered hand. It drilled its fingers into the earth, clinging to what little solid ground remained.

Naked muscles flexed, straining to hold on.

Bulbous eyes rolled in distress.

And—in the grip of one oversized hand—Alex saw their prize.

"Baelin!" He pointed. "I see the core!"

"I've had a Wizard's Eye on it this whole time. Look at that!"

There was a pulse of mana, and stone walls rose around the Rampart-crusher, trying to shield it from the brutal winds.

Baelin waved a hand like he was shooing a fruit fly.

The wind changed.

Boulders, felled pines, and Skinless Ones launched at the walls, striking them with the force of trebuchet stones. Mana flowed, more walls rose, and abruptly fell in a barrage of Baelin's making. The Rampart-crusher shuddered as jagged stones raked its flank.

Several raw-looking tentacles split from its torso.

The bellow that followed was lost in the howling wind as it was dragged from its handholds and cast into the gale.

End over end it spun, flailing, still desperate to keep its grip on the dungeon core. But for all of its stone-shattering might, it was powerless in Baelin's whirlwind. The ancient wizard watched it whip through the air, then extended his hand, muttering an incantation.

Mana shuddered.

And a black orb shot from the Rampart-breaker's fingers, tumbling through the violence around it, straight for Baelin's outstretched hand.

Shcwoop!

The core slipped into the bubble of calm and dropped into the chancellor's waiting palm.

"Excellent, we have our prize," he said in a cheery tone. "Now, let us finish this. I'll show you a favourite trick of mine."

With a word of power, Baelin waved his hand.

Shards of obsidian glass materialised in the tornado, whirling counter to the wind. Countless slivers raced through the air like hunting birds, shredding wood, earth, and flesh where they struck. In heartbeats, Ravener-spawn shriveled into masses of pulp. Near death, the mangled Rampart-breaker raised a tentacle and reached for the orb it was meant to serve and protect, then plunged from the sky.

When the work of the shards was done, only howling wind and the groaning of trembling earth remained.

"And that is that." Baelin waved his staff once.

The wind died.

The earth stilled.

And the obsidian shards vanished.

A noise deeper than thunder erupted from below as mounds of dirt, timber, rocks, and flesh struck the ground as one. Menacing clouds cleared as though they were never there, revealing the gentle light of the early morning sky.

"Bloody hell," Alex swore.

Where a powerful dungeon once stood, a wasteland of shredded monsters and overturned earth replaced it. It looked like titans had run through the land with the abandon of uncontrollable toddlers smashing sandcastles. Or massive bears digging up anthills.

Massive *rabid* bears.

"Holy shit," Alex swore again, stunned by the display of pure power.

He definitely wanted to be Baelin when he grew up.

He hovered in the air shaking his head, feeling even more redundant than earlier, but by the Traveller, did he ever have a story for Theresa and the cabal!

"As I said," Baelin said cheerily. "Convenience! Well, now let us find a place to settle for a time. We'll see if anything comes to investigate the commotion I made. I suspect we might be visited by stragglers, but we could also be lucky enough to have one of those creatures who are so taken with hunting you show up. However, in the meantime..."

The chancellor held the dungeon core out to Alex.

The orb gave off a wave of frantic energy, and its attention fell on him. Its mana recoiled. There was a recognition from the core like there had been in the chitterer dungeon.

Alex could also feel its fear.

"Care to give it a go?" Baelin asked.

When the dust had literally settled, Alex and Baelin were more or less camped roughly fifty yards south of the ravine. Baelin had conjured a pleasant little campfire while his Wizard's Eyes patrolled the area. Claygon watched the ravine. Alex had tasked him with clean up, and at the first sign of stragglers, his beams were primed and ready to start blasting.

The chancellor was watching Alex.

And Alex... watched the dungeon core.

Over a year ago, he'd been in a similar situation, holding a living dungeon core in his very hands. He could *feel* its displeasure. Its mana stung the air, vibrating like a nest of angry bees. Yet, for all its anger, it could do little without a Ravener-spawn, like a ship without a helmsman.

And it would fight him with everything it had.

He swallowed.

Cold sweat slicked his palms as he called on the Mark, focusing it on the task ahead: controlling a dungeon core. Memories from his struggle in the Cave of the Traveller came back with full force. That battle had tested him to his limits even though that core had been weakened. The mana it held was depleted, yet it still put up enough resistance for him to struggle. How much of a fight would this fresh, enraged one give him?

He reminded himself he was more skilled at mana manipulation now, unlike back in the Cave of the Traveller when he'd been escaping priests and Heroes.

"Are you ready?" Baelin asked. "If you are at all hesitant, perhaps you would rather I give it a go first? My original idea was—since in this—you are more experienced than I, you should try to control it first."

"No, no." Alex rotated the orb, examining its smooth, black surface. "That's alright, I... I want to do this. I need to do this."

"Well, then do away, whenever you are ready."

Alex nodded. "Are you sure you want to try this here instead of back at camp?"

"I would rather we attempt the process here in the wilderness where —we have less constraints—considering your situation. Should anything be revealed, it will be revealed to no one but us. If we successfully engage with this orb and gain a better idea of what we're dealing with, as well as determine that your secret will not be exposed, we can bring our prize safely back to camp."

"Yeah, that makes sense," Alex said, fighting nerves.

He'd been wanting this confrontation, even imagining it, yet now that it was right in front of him, his mind kept conjuring reasons to wait.

But no.

Time and opportunity were here, he should use them.

The most powerful wizard in all of Generasi was at his side. He was away from anyone that could be at risk, and the orb was at his mercy. Delaying was only feeding his nerves.

"Alright, nothing for it," Alex said.

Taking a deep breath, he threw his mana into the dungeon core.

And met a resistance he was not prepared for.

He'd been wrong: the dungeon core didn't come at him like a swarm of angry bees. It came at him with the full fury of a servant of the Ravener. Just like in the chitterer cave, but with an intensity and desperation he couldn't have imagined. Its mana pushed the young wizard back with a hostility that felt personal, promptly expelling him.

Alex frowned, considering what he'd just confirmed.

This thing's power was as beyond the orb's in the Cave of the Traveller as the sun's was to candlelight. This orb wasn't drained, and it was also fueled by resentment. If he'd met this much resistance in the Traveller's Cave, his mind might be mush now.

'Explains why people controlling dungeon cores isn't *exactly* common knowledge,' he thought. 'Well, Mr. Mark, we overcame Ito's Spiral. Let's see if we can out-wrestle this thing.'

Calling on the Mark, Alex threw himself into the core again and again, pitting his skill and power against its desperation. And at first, desperation won out. Easily.

Baelin watched—as still as a statue—for an hour while Alex struggled to even enter the core's mana pathways. Yet the ancient wizard never complained or asked a single question. He was merely patient.

And so was Alex.

With each failure, he learned a little more about *how* the dungeon core resisted him. He learned its pathways: how many mana entrances there were, how quickly its mana could fight him, and the way its power moved through the orb.

As the Mark pointed out what he did *right*, he began forming a strategy. The dungeon core resisted his mana with pure overwhelming force. Like a predator. It didn't seem to do *finesse*. It was all about brute force.

And so, he split his mana into thousands of strands—as with Hsekiu's technique—and attacked the dungeon core from every entrance.

Its power sought to block him, but his strands moved with the agility of vipers. Panic rose within it as it tried to fight him off, but too many of his strands moved in too many directions. The core split its attention, throwing power at him over and over again.

And forced him out.

He started again.

With each attempt, the young wizard went a little farther.

Alexander Roth bent all of his will and skill to the task, learning more of its pathways as he did. Its mana trembled.

Now it was easier, like learning the steps of a dance.

He persisted through the early morning, feeling closer to something important. The core's centre. The dungeon core seemed delirious, frenzied.

Alex was determined.

And he'd done this before.

Calling upon a familiar memory from the Mark, he shifted his mana.

Whoom.

A connection.

For an instant, the world disappeared. A thousand images poured into his mind as they had in the Cave of the Traveller when he controlled the core. Dark caves. Battles in places he'd never seen before. A dark la—

The images abruptly vanished, like they'd been halted.

When Alex's senses returned to the world around him, Baelin was standing.

Mana flowed from the core, reaching out toward the ravine.

The sound of grating stone echoed through the air.

"Alex!" the chancellor shouted in triumph. "My Wizard's Eye witnessed a wall rising from the dungeon's remains! You did that?"

"Yeah," the young wizard panted, sweat pouring from his brow. "Yeah, I did. I *actually* did that!"

"Well done, my boy!" Baelin patted him on the back. "This is an excellent step forward. Did you... learn anything? Anything that might help us track these clawed creatures?"

"No," Alex said. "I saw some images..." He told the chancellor what he'd seen. "But I have no idea what they were. And they were cut off too quickly. I think something didn't want me poking around."

"Hm, well, it will not have a say in the matter," Baelin said.

"Right... but, by the Traveller, I can't believe it." Alex stared at the dungeon core. It had forced his mana out again, but with less force than before. The more of its power he used, the less it was able to resist. "After a year... sometimes I'd get this notion that I'd imagined what I'd done. But here it is... solid proof. Baelin, this is big. History-changing big. It brings up so many questions—I-I've got to go back in."

"Hold now." The ancient wizard placed a hand on his shoulder. "Why not let me have a go? You are exhausted. No sense trying again when you are worn down."

"Yeah, I suppose you're right." Alex panted, offering Baelin the orb. "It's all yours. I could use the break, and if *I* could do it, you'll do it in no time."

"Oh, pfah, what's a few thousand years of experience?" Baelin chuckled, holding the orb between his palms. "Now, let us see what *I* can see."

Alex felt the ancient wizard's mana spark with overwhelming power.

It was profound, like the tornado he'd commanded.

Very little would be able to stand before it, including the dungeon core...

Which was why Alex was stunned when Baelin frowned.

Without a sound, the chancellor turned the orb over, fixing it with a piercing gaze. He seemed to be looking deep within it. Heartbeats passed while he turned the core, his mana boiling around him.

Alex waited for the rush of the dungeon core's power doing the chancellor's bidding.

But it never came.

Heartbeats turned to minutes.

Minutes became an hour.

Yet there was no rush of force. There was only the chancellor's deepening frown.

"Alex..." he finally said. "I... cannot do this."

The Thameish wizard thought he misheard. "Pardon?"

"I cannot do this." Baelin's voice held a note of astonishment. "It is impossible for me."

CHAPTER 10

...IS ANOTHER'S WALL

"Impossible!" Alex shot to his feet. "For *you*? That... *that's* impossible!"

"Nothing is impossible," Baelin said, turning the orb over again. His goat-like eyes scanned every detail. "But for the life of me, Alex, I cannot even begin to challenge this... *infernal* thing."

The young wizard's eyebrows arched toward his hairline. "No way, I mean... I can feel its mana. And I can *definitely* feel yours. There's no way you can't beat this."

"It is not a matter of power," the goatman said. "It is a matter of... Wait, perhaps I am being hasty." He handed the orb back to Alex. "Have you had enough rest?"

"Yeah." Alex moved closer to Baelin. "What do you need me to do?"

"Try and activate the dungeon core again," Baelin said. "Let's see if anything has changed. Perhaps it metamorphosed a defence against further tampering."

"Sure. I'll give it another try." Alex took the dungeon core and dove into it, finding the pathways, using the Mark as he went. The defences were much easier to break through this time. In minutes, he reached the core and—

Rumble.

Another rock wall rose through the debris that used to be the dungeon. Alex frowned.

'So even though the dungeon's destroyed, it still has control over terrain. I wonder just how far this thing's range is, and if it can establish a *new* dungeon.'

63

But, more importantly, at least for now…

"I'm in," Alex said.

"I see that. This is absolutely fascinating." The chancellor's focus was on the orb, his face tensed in concentration. "Let's try something. We'll both hold it while you use your mana to activate it. Go slowly and I'll follow what you're doing *precisely*."

"Got it." Alex held the orb toward the ancient wizard.

As his gauntleted hands pressed against the core's surface, Baelin's ocean of mana unfolded, nearly dropping Alex to his knees. Together, they reached into the core, the young wizard feeling like a tiny minnow swimming beside a massive whale.

Impossibly tiny.

And the *finesse*.

His mana was agile, but Baelin's was quicksilver. No effort in movement; it simply *was*. The chancellor shouldn't have a problem overwhelming and controlling the core, yet here it was. He just couldn't do it.

"Alright, so follow my mana," Alex said, letting his power gather by the dungeon core's entranceways. "Do you sense where I am?"

"Indeed, I feel where your mana gathers." Baelin frowned. "What am I looking for there?"

Alex's brow creased. "The entry points. They're right where my mana is."

The ancient wizard's frown deepened. His mana searched for entryways. "I sense nothing."

"Really?" Alex asked, confused. What was going on? "Okay, I'll take you to them, right to where they are. Just follow my lead."

The chancellor closed his eyes, moving his mana toward the entranceways while Alex guided him.

"Closer," the young wizard said. "Closer. You're getting there. Closer… closer… there! Right there! Stop!"

Baelin's mana paused squarely above the entrances. "Here?" the goatman asked, obviously baffled. "I sense no entrances, none at all."

"Okay, maybe… maybe it's done something so they're invisible? Or… maybe it's hiding them?" Alex tried to puzzle it out. "It could be using some sort of mana-sense-based illusion."

"Hm," the goatman mused. "Perhaps."

"Either way, go ahead, push your mana down into the dungeon core," Alex said. "Like I'm doing."

He demonstrated, which was even easier now. Each time he activated the orb, it used mana, so it had much less strength to fight him.

"Hmmmm." The goatman cocked his head as though listening for something in the distance. "What in the... your mana just felt like it disappeared. As though it went off into nothingness. Let me try."

Baelin's mana pushed down... except nothing changed.

It was like there *were* no entrances, so his mana was futilely pressing against a solid wall.

"What is going on...?" Alex murmured, his nerves stretching. "You're sure you can't do what I'm doing?"

"No... I cannot." Baelin sounded quite bewildered. "It is... it feels like there *is* no mana apparatus there to interact with. Honestly, I can feel the mana within the thing, but—for all intents and purposes—I may as well be trying to find pathways to magically interact with the average rock."

He pulled his mana back and stroked his beard-braids, lost in thought. When he opened his eyes, they were alight with intrigue. "Well, this is *absolutely* fascinating. It would seem that dungeon cores have apparatuses that can only be interacted with when held by certain individuals. Whatever the qualifications... it appears that I do not possess them."

The chancellor's voice was as calm as Alex's spirit was frantic.

What was this? Did this really mean that not everyone could take over dungeon cores? Why? Was that done by design, or was it accidental?

The young wizard tried reasoning things through, thinking about both dungeon cores and golem cores and how similar they were in mana. If dungeon cores were *made* to be controlled... then...

"*Who's* supposed to control them?" Alex wondered. "This... oh jeez, this is big!"

"Indeed." Baelin eyed the ink-black orb. "If dungeon cores have apparatuses that are only accessible to those having certain qualities, that speaks more to a purposeful design choice, rather than a random accident or natural development, or even an evolution. It lends credence to the theory that dungeon cores—and perhaps even this Ravener creature—are constructed."

He stroked his beard. "But we cannot know much more until we understand what criteria allows one individual to interact with these dungeon cores, and what *prevents* another from doing so. Hmmm... So what are the differences between you and me?"

"Well," Alex said. "You're miles more powerful than I am. You're older. I'm human and you're not. I'm Thameish and you're not. Hmmm... I worship Uldar, and you don't."

Alex's faith in Uldar had waned considerably compared to before he was Marked—these days, he prayed to the Traveller more than to Uldar—but he hadn't stopped believing in Thameland's god entirely.

"Indeed," Baelin said. "I *think* we might rule out the idea that you can control it because you are human. After all, Ravener-spawn control dungeon cores are a daily fact of life, and no autopsy has found that they share the least bit in common with humanity. They're not even mammals."

"True..." Alex murmured. "And me being younger would be a strange criteria. Not impossible, but pretty arbitrary. All things considered, I'm thinking it has something to do with me being Thameish. After all, I'm from Thameland, just like the dungeon cores."

"Indeed," Baelin said. "And the Ravener's mana does infest nearly every inch of this realm, however slight it might be. The thought occurred to me that those born here perhaps absorb a bit of that mana, while those born elsewhere would have no such exposure to it. Which would be a strong hypothesis... except for one simple fact: you were born during a time when there was no Ravener present, and—according to our Thameish allies—its mana is completely absent from the land between cycles."

"Right, and if the ability was triggered by being immersed in the Ravener's mana, then you should be able to activate a core, just like I did last year when we were in the Cave of the Traveller. At that point, the Ravener had only been back for a short while. So, I wouldn't have had much time to absorb its mana, yet I was able to control that core."

"Exactly... Ah, we did overlook one more difference between us." Baelin's eyes dropped to Alex's right shoulder. "Your Mark; what if that is the key to all of this?"

Alex blinked. "You mean... Heroes are supposed to control dungeon cores? Or maybe just Fools?"

"It is possible. We cannot rule it out. Either way, we have discovered something of prime importance," Baelin said. "You should experiment with it, see what can be done with it, and if you can work out how it creates monsters. That should run its energies down and weaken its mana, then it should be easier for you and others on site to handle it over the next few days."

Alex looked at him sharply. "Uhm... I kind of agree that we should let others try to access it to see if that helps us understand who's able to interact with this thing. But, what about those clawed things, what if they were after me because I took over that dungeon core? Suppose someone else controls one and ends up with a big target sign on their back?"

"Hmmmm, indeed... though... hmmm..." Baelin gave Alex's concerns some thought. "We will discuss what to do with it and how to experiment with a living core when we return to camp. In the meanwhile, go ahead. Run it as dry as you can."

"Got it," Alex said, trying to calm his spirit as he flew toward the ravine.

Hypotheses of all kinds raced through his mind while he looked at the dark orb.

Dread seeped into the pit of his stomach.

Just what in all of Uldar's mercy had they stumbled onto?

———

The Ravener felt it.

Another core had fallen to the Usurper.

Deep within its underground chamber—floating above the dark lake and surrounded by a grim army of guardians—its ancient mind thought on what should be done.

The Usurper still lived.

And it had received no word from any of its trusted Hunters.

They had likely failed. Probably dead.

And the Usurper still tainted the lands, taking things further and further out of balance. But what should be done now?

The Hunters had failed to this point... should it make more?

Would that make sense?

Or should it...

It reached deep within, searching far below the place where 'forms' of its typical servants were *kept*.

There, in the deepest recesses of its being, the shrouded terrain where unique servants were concealed waited. Servants it could spawn only if certain criteria were met...

And the situation had not fractured enough to justify bringing these to bear. Not yet.

Still, it began careful preparations to spawn at least one should things further deteriorate.

If the Usurper was not stopped soon, then that dangerous set of criteria could be met sooner, rather than later.

And all must be ready.

"And I think it's almost out of mana," Alex said. "There's a bit left, but not enough to really do anything with it right now."

He examined the ravine floor, where odd shapes rose from the debris. For the past hour, he'd been experimenting with the core, raising walls from the ruined earth, pressing holes in the ground, and shaping stone.

Rock formations were scattered far and wide, marking the ground with what could be best described as efforts ranging from rudimentary to more complex. He'd even created a small stone building using the core's power, and apart from missing some of the roof, it almost looked liveable.

"This... this could become addictive," he said. "I mean it's one thing to create things out of magic and alchemy, but this? Once you get the hang of it, you're basically shaping the land by sheer will alone. I wonder if this is what deities feel like?"

"The ones I have spoken to have not admitted to such a thing, but I do agree that there would be a certain... addictive quality to shaping things by will and purpose alone." Baelin thumbed his chin. "This is most fascinating. From what I've been told, dungeon cores gain power from mortal fear. There are always a dozen little anxieties during any given day at the encampment, especially for the young. So, it should be interesting to see if by having it in camp, it will regenerate mana from the 'little fears' of those around it. I must say, it is looking a little pale right now."

As Alex used its mana throughout the morning, the deep darkness it'd started the day with had faded until it was now the lightest shade of grey.

"Yeah, I noticed that too. Do we have anything else to do here?"

"Not for the present. The dungeon is destroyed, and we have gained our prize. All that's left to do is to bring it back to camp and inform the others of what we have been up to. Tonight, I will stay to aid in securing it, then brief Professor Jules when she arrives in the morning. We must set up containment procedures as well."

His goat-like eyes twinkled. "I'm very eager to experiment with our new sample. Who knows what other discoveries it might hold? I suspect learning how it works will be an involved undertaking. So come, today has been a most productive day for us. Perhaps having this living specimen in hand will soon bring us another one."

CHAPTER 11

ULDAR'S GUIDANCE

"You did *what*?" Professor Jules cried, not believing what she was hearing. On her desk was a light grey orb with a small ward surrounding it in a half-sphere, shimmering like water.

"I uh... I controlled a dungeon core," Alex repeated, looking up at Baelin for backup.

"Indeed, he controlled a dungeon core." Baelin shrugged.

Jules' eyes bulged, looking about ready to roll from her skull. Muttering, and with an air of desperation about her, the alchemy professor staggered from her chair, eyes fixed on a cabinet in her new office.

It was an impressive stone chamber lit by forceballs, and overflowing with polished alchemical apparatuses, endless shelves of texts, manuals, and constructs—mostly butterflies. A slew of protective equipment hung from ornate hooks, each pristine from meticulous care.

Beside these stood her objective, an elaborate cabinet with carved doors that flew open when her muttering turned to spell casting. Inside, a few bottles of amber-coloured liquid—maybe whiskey—were revealed. She reached for one with a shaking hand, then paused, seeming to think better of it, and went for a tin of tea and a silver tea set instead.

On one side of her desk was a pitcher of distilled water, which she poured into her teapot, then dropped in six scoops of loose tea leaves while saying something to herself that sounded like, "...strong today." The teapot was placed on a round, grey stone occupying one corner of the desk, then she pressed a glyph—one of fire magic—to the side of the stone, and turned back to Baelin and Alex. They were seated before her desk in sturdy maple wood armchairs with seat cushions filled with goose down, a gift from the Thameish court.

Professor Jules leaned forward, watching the orb. Then she took a deep breath, as if steeling herself.

"Excuse me, but *what*? How?" Her eyes travelled between the professor of the Art of the Wizard in Combat and his eager student. "How did you even *discover* such a thing?"

"Well," the chancellor jumped in. "We set out to obtain a live dungeon core for a bit of experimentation. And after subduing it, we thought we should give it a close examination. So Alex volunteered, since he's most keen to aid his homeland."

Professor Jules' look was piercing. "You examined a living dungeon core in the field, *alone*, Mr. Roth?"

Alex winced.

"Alone? Come now, Vernia, I am *old*, but I am no corpse. He was under my supervision and encouragement the entire time. I assure you, he was in no danger." Baelin smiled.

"I guess..." Professor Jules frowned. "Your protection should ensure safety... but even under your supervision in the Barrens, there have been mishaps..."

"As there have been in the Cells, unfortunately," Baelin said pleasantly. "That is the nature of what we do. It has its dangers, but we strive for safety and survival. And being prepared to act when danger comes. Yet, as I said, Alex was in no danger."

Professor Jules' jaw clenched and released. Alex imagined the word 'reckless' sped through her mind. "Everything you say is true, but also moot, considering the deed's already done." She looked directly at Alex. "Baelin's way might be considered bold, Mr. Roth. Do try to remember, safety trumps all, because without it, wizards would be as extinct as the tyranodopolus. Now, as I said, the deed is done, so let's not waste this opportunity. We can call it... setting up proper 'field examination safety procedures,' but I stress, don't make this type of thing a habit, Alex."

"Oh, do not stifle our students, Professor Jules. Think of the results." Baelin pointed to the orb. "This changes everything, does it not?"

"Yeah, it really does," Alex jumped in, caught up in what they'd learned about the core. "I didn't find out *how* it makes monsters like I was hoping to, but I did figure out how to make it alter terrain in a dungeon... or at least what was left of its dungeon."

"Truly?" Professor Jules' demeanour changed. Her eyes went wide. "That... that changes so much. We now have new and confirmable knowledge that mortals are capable of controlling dungeon cores. Which means Thameish understanding of their enemy will radically change! And then there's the fact that it could still alter terrain even after its dungeon was physically destroyed."

Her enthusiasm built as she turned to the map of Thameland hanging behind her. "Where did you say this occurred again?"

Baelin stepped around the desk and pointed to an area in northern Thameland. "Here. In this forest in particular. There *was* a ravine there where the core had made its dungeon."

"Was?" Professor Jules raised an eyebrow.

"It is still—by all technical definition—a ravine."

"...I take it you exercised your *usual* restraint when it comes to problem solving." Professor Jules shook her head and tapped the map.

"Ah, I see. And, Alex, you mentioned you were able to modify the dungeon core's territory even after the dungeon was demolished. A dungeon core frequently alters the shape and structure of its dungeon, so it's likely that its control over its 'home' is based on area, and not 'structural integrity.' Which would mean you could cave in an entire dungeon complex and—as long as the dungeon core is whole and has a Ravener-spawn to wield it—it could just reshape and rebuild. Hmmmm."

She made her way to a bookshelf, removing a leather-bound book and flipping to a passage near the beginning. "Yes, just as I thought. It seems there have been early Thameish accounts of dungeons being collapsed without destroying the cores... but the dungeons would always regenerate. Now we have a better idea as to why. Except... mortals controlling dungeon cores..."

She eyed the pale orb on her desk. "How did they never discover this after so many cycles? It's true that their magical technology is—from what I've gathered—centuries behind Generasi's. No offence, Alex."

"None taken," he said. "You're thinking the way I am: we know the church and previous court wizards researched the Ravener as much as they were able to. They enhance the Heroes' equipment with core remains, so you'd think *someone* would have discovered this."

"Yes... something just doesn't feel right," Professor Jules said. "Of course, we'll have to share this knowledge with our Thameish allies, but we should be careful when we do so."

"Agreed," Baelin said. "When we reveal all, we'll have to watch their reaction... carefully. Especially when one considers this next revelation. I cannot control the dungeon core."

Professor Jules squinted at Baelin. "You're teasing me."

"I wish I were," the goatman said. "Things went as such."

Baelin explained how he'd struggled in vain with the dungeon core. Not able to even sense its entryways. Jules' face grew ever more shocked.

"This further complicates things..." She looked at the core, curiosity and caution warring across her face.

Curiosity won out.

"Alright, so you've had no ill-effects from interacting with its mana?"

"No, none at all. Either for me or Baelin," Alex said.

"If that's the case, then I think I'm going to try it."

"What about safety, Vernia? After all, it's only been tested by Alex and me. Two testers isn't what one would really call rigorous testing, wouldn't you agree?" Baelin smiled, his face a mask of serenity.

Alex looked away, stifling laughter.

Jules glanced at Baelin, her focus still on the core. "You're clearly enjoying yourself a little too much, Chancellor, but we have to understand why Alex can control this thing but you can't, and the only way to get any answers is to experiment. Besides, you're here, as you assured me you were for Alex's safety." She returned his serene smile.

"Alright, then." Professor Jules cracked her knuckles. "Time to give it a go. Please drop the ward, Baelin."

Over the next few minutes, Alex watched Professor Jules examine, measure, and attempt to connect with the orb. Her puzzled expression grew deeper.

"Curious. Curious, curious, curious," she said. "If it weren't for the fact that you had a witness for your... core take-over or challenge, as it were, I'd ask if you'd gotten into some bad mushrooms. There's... nothing. No way for me to interact with it."

Baelin and Alex looked at each other.

"Let me try and guide you," Alex said. "We'll see if it's any different for you than it was for Baelin."

He touched the core with Professor Jules and felt her mana. She was powerful—one didn't become a professor at the greatest university of wizardry in the world by having poor skills and being weak—but he hadn't known just how powerful she actually was.

Baelin wore his power like a robe, while Professor Jules didn't. Within her, a *deep* pool of mana moved with *mathematical* precision. She would have made a frightening battlemage had she gone that route.

Yet, for all her precision and power... he couldn't guide her.

Like Baelin, she may as well have been trying to push her mana into a rock.

"This is... alarming," she said. "It implies that there is a design, a purpose to these dungeon cores that we don't yet understand. Gentlemen, I'm glad you discovered this sooner rather than later."

"What do you want to do?" Alex asked. "Let some of the other expedition members try to control it?"

She shook her head, taking the orb back. "No. Not yet. I want to run a few tests first. Then we'll figure out what to do from there. I'll pause everything we have scheduled for the next few days so we can learn what we can about this core. I have a feeling it will take time.

"Alex, we don't know what this means... The fact that *you* can connect to it while Baelin and I can't? That's very, *very* troubling to me. It is a living thing after all, so I think that you should err on the side of caution and take some time off from the expedition while we figure this all out. We don't know what any of it means yet, but until we get some answers and begin to understand what there is about *you* that lets you interact with it, then there could be some danger."

Alex looked at her straight on. "Is that a recommendation?"

"...Yes. I *recommend* you go home for a while. Don't worry about your alchemy credit; you have more than enough to miss a few days of lab work. I'm sure you already have plenty of material for your final report. But no, I am not *forcing* you to go home if that's what you're asking."

"In that case, if it's all the same to you, I want to see this through, at least as much of it as I can."

Professor Jules sighed. "Why doesn't that surprise me? Alright, then go and get your gear. We should get started on this right away. I suspect this might be a mystery that eludes us for a long time."

"You never know, Vernia, we might just get lucky," Baelin said.

"We'll see."

"Yeah," Alex said. "We'll see."

"I can't believe it," Carey whispered. "A living dungeon core. Right in front of us."

Fear rose in her chest. Here it was, a great enemy of Thameland.

An object more feared than devils and monstrous hags.

The subject of most of the scary stories told to her at bedtime, and the subject of many childhood nightmares. It was a vile servant of the enemy she'd sworn to use all of her knowledge and research against for as long as it plagued Thameland, or as long as she had breath in her body.

And now? Now she had her chance.

The core was pale. Samples of dungeon core remains they'd experimented on were always as black as midnight, so why was this so pale? She spotted Professor Jules in Analysis Room 1.

Now that the research building was completed, the teams had access to a suite of rooms for their research work, as opposed to the giant tent they'd been using. The equipment was organised and placed in the appropriate room according to its function, giving the researchers more space to do their work. Each chamber was sealed and reinforced as securely as one of the Cells back on campus, which was especially necessary today.

There was no telling what experimenting on a live dungeon core might bring.

"Well, here it is, everyone," Professor Jules said. "A living dungeon core. I want all of you to take extra caution with today's experiments: while the core doesn't seem to be 'living' from an organic perspective, it does have intelligence. There's no information available on what to expect once we begin our study since, as far as we know, a living core has never been studied. That said, I want to learn as much as we can, as quickly as we can. This is a very exciting moment, but do keep safety foremost in mind."

She gestured to the equipment. "Today, you'll be examining its mana traits: its signature, conductivity, and so on. I want to know if there are any variances in those properties compared to cores that have been crushed. While this project has come up suddenly, it must take priority. Any questions?"

"What about the rest of the team?" someone asked, looking around the room.

Roughly about a third of the regular team was assembled for Professor Jules' briefing. Carey noted Alex Roth and Isolde Von Anmut were missing.

"They're split between Analysis Rooms 2 and 3, and are prepping the equipment there. As soon as you're finished with your preliminary studies, I want the core's other properties tested immediately. Any other questions?"

Silence.

Carey watched the dungeon core and exhaled.

It was time to work.

"My lord Uldar." Her head bowed as she whispered a prayer. "Guide me. Guide my mind. Steady my hand. Keep me sharp. Let me find the way. Let me seek our enemy's weaknesses so that your Holy Heroes may destroy it forever."

As she finished the prayer, she swallowed her fear, then looked at the dungeon core in surprise.

Was she imagining things... or was it a little darker than it had been mere heartbeats before? She pushed the thought away and got to work.

Under Professor Jules' guidance, the team began running a series of tests on the dungeon core, passing it from one researcher to the next and placing it in various machines. An air of tension hung in Analysis Room 1, but the researchers kept pushing on.

"Alright, Carey." A third year student handed her the core. "Attach the mana conductor, then we'll start the tests."

"Right, I'll have it done in a tick," she said, carefully taking the core in her gloved hands.

Shock ran through her. She could sense the orb's mana—as faint as it was—and... something else. Agitation maybe? *Was* she imagining things?

Carey focused her full attention on the dungeon core, trying to see if the agitation she'd sensed was real or imagined. Maybe it was because she was so nervous. She passed her mana over the orb, searching for the best place to attach the mana—

Wait, what was that? What were *those*?

She ran her mana over the core again.

Were those... entrances?

Excitement rose in her chest.

Uldar had guided her.

Chapter 12

Usurpers

'Oh, come now, Carey, don't be so silly!' Carey admonished herself. 'This was examined by Professor Jules quite thoroughly, no doubt with upmost care and caution as per usual. What are the chances that you—a student—would notice something she did not?'

She chuckled at her own silliness.

"Uldar brings low those with too much pride," she muttered to herself.

She looked at the other students, still gripped by the giggles. All of her highly qualified colleagues—many of whom were upper years and far more skilled than her—had handled the dungeon core.

Of course they would've noticed such a thing.

It was a mana rich, cross between a creature and a device, and it would be only natural that it would have mana pathways.

Her laughter drew the eye of the closest student, a thin young man named Nadir. "Well, what has you giggling?" he asked.

"Oh, pshah, it's nothing. Absolutely nothing of relevance," she said. "One has to laugh at oneself sometimes."

"Once you're done with your private joke, we've nearly got the machine prepped. You'll want to hook up the core any second."

"On it, on it, sorry for the delay!" she said, her having a little bit of a singsong note in her amusement.

'By holy Uldar, I do so hope they don't think I've lost it,' she thought, returning her attention to the core. 'You know what, I should try and map out these pathways as best I can so I can know best where to attach the apparati. Uldar guide me... I'm sure the others would be able to do the same. It would be no good to embarrass myself.'

Humming a little tune, Carey separated her mana out into agile little portions—as she'd learned to do through her alchemy class—and slipped her mana into the dungeon core.

She gasped.

Oh, it did *not* like that.

The little mana left inside the core rushed at her, trying to push her out. Jumping back in surprise, she nearly dropped the core.

"You alright over there?" Nadir asked, his eyes narrowing through the lenses of *'you've been acting a bit funny...'* He glanced down at the core. "This is a new experimental subject. If you're feeling off—"

"Oh, I'm fine, just dandy," she said. "Just felt something from the mana within the core."

"Right, its mana was moving around a little bit when I was handling it too," he said. "You're sure you're alright with it? If it's too much—"

"I'm fine," Carey insisted, flushing with embarrassment beneath her mask.

Her fear of monsters invading the encampment was not exactly a secret among the other members of the expedition, to her humiliation. The last thing she wanted was to be treated like she was some unhelpful coward.

She turned back toward the core, anger burning in her chest.

'The Heroes might battle your kind in their own way with their own power, but I am also a child of Uldar. Of Thameland. I'm a member of the London family. You shan't scare me again!' she thought.

Squeezing her mana back through the entrances, she sought to map out its inner pathways. The core fought her with everything it had, which wasn't much. Its inner mana was nearly spent, and its attempts to drive her away were so feeble that she could've overrun it while asleep.

Reaching deeper into the core along its inner pathways, she felt like she'd hit the centre. The core had grown more and more frantic, but there was little it could do.

'Oh, pipe down, you!' she thought. 'It's been ever so trying, dealing with you. Now how do I reach the other side of you—'

She froze.

A connection was forged.

Mana flared.

Images pushed themselves into Carey's mind, causing her to shriek and drop the core. A heartbeat later, the images disappeared, leaving her shocked and breathing hard.

The dungeon core lay on the stones at her feet, unharmed, but paler than it had been a moment before. All the other researchers stared at her, their eyes wide through their lenses. Professor Jules rushed across the room and seized Carey by the shoulders.

"What... what did you do?" the professor whispered. "I felt a surge of mana..." She looked down at the core. "Did you... did you do something with the core?"

"I..." Carey murmured. "I don't know. I was experimenting with the pathways, trying to find the best entrance to attach the mana—"

"Wait, back up," Professor Jules said. "You *felt* the pathways?"

"Er, yes?"

Professor Jules looked at the rest of the research task. "You're all done for the day. Pack up and clean up the laboratory. Nadir. Go get Alex Roth, then find Watcher Shaw and tell him to contact Chancellor Baelin. It's an emergency. *Go. Now!*"

"Uh, yes!" Nadir rushed for the door.

"Professor?" Carey murmured. "What's happening? What... what's going on? What did I do?"

"Carey..." Professor Jules turned back to her, her eyes growing gentle and her voice soft. "It would appear that... you momentarily took control of a dungeon core."

Carey's thoughts froze.

Wait... *controlled* a dungeon core? That didn't make any sense. Why would a mortal be able to control a dungeon core? They were the enemy. That didn't make any sense. Only Ravener-spawn could use dungeon cores, right?

"...*What?*" Her mind whirled. "What does this mean, Professor?"

"I don't know yet, Carey, I don't know," Professor Jules said.

It struck the Ravener like a bolt of lightning.

All seemed to shake around it and its thoughts fell into chaos. Many of its guardian monsters looked toward it, sensing the distress. Some looked for hidden opponents in the caverns—there was nothing they could do.

This enemy was too far for them to strike.

Much too far.

No... that was not right.

The term *enemy* had become *enemies*.

Now there was not one Usurper.

There were two.

The situation had degraded. Two Usurpers meant that either another mortal had accidentally taken over a dungeon core or—even worse—it meant the first Usurper was communicating with others.

Telling other mortals *how* to take more dungeon cores.

Things needed cutting off before they degraded even further.

And now, certain criteria had been satisfied.

First, it would make more Hunters. It did not matter if the first pack were still hunting or if they were dead. The Ravener had refrained from making *too* many Hunters at once to avoid them being discovered.

Its assassins' greatest strength lay in mortals not knowing of their existence.

But such secrecy mattered less now.

And so did subtlety in general.

As another batch of Hunters shimmered into being, sliding from the Ravener's deep black surface, it reached deep into itself.

Down toward the monstrous forms held within the deepest part of it.

There. One was available to it now, triggered by this emergency. It would cost an immense amount of mana to craft, and it had not produced such a creature in several cycles.

But it did not hesitate, pouring its power into the form. It would take time to craft such a fearsome beast, and once completed, the Usurpers would know the meaning of terror.

For few Ravener-spawn were as terrible as the creature it now forged.

A Petrifier.

Carey looked petrified sitting in her chair in Jules' office.

"Do you... need a drink?" Alex asked, gripping his knees to steady himself.

"Hm? Oh, yes, I would like that ever so much," she said, looking toward the door. "Will Professor Jules be back soon?"

"I think so," Alex said, rising from his seat. Before she'd departed, Jules had given Alex permission to fix Carey anything from her cabinet. "She said she'd be back with Baelin, and apparently, he's already on his way."

"Good... good." She nodded, shifting uncomfortably in her chair.

Bottles and cups rattled as Alex prepared tea.

"I... Professor Jules said you'd also controlled the core?" She looked up at him.

"Yeah," Alex said, putting the pot on the heating plate. "When I was experimenting with it in the field. We didn't exactly want to make that public until we found out more. I guess we found out more pretty damn fast."

She gave a laugh tinged with hysteria. "By holy Uldar... So the two of us then. Wait, the two of *us*? What about Professor Jules and Chancellor Baelin?"

Alex paused, about to place the tea leaves into the infuser. "She didn't tell you that part? I guess she didn't have time... Carey, they couldn't do it."

She looked at him sharply, her eyes very wide. "Alex, you're not making any sense at all. I did it, so it should be *terribly* easy for wizards of their caliber."

"They can't even attempt it."

Alex explained the professor's and chancellor's experiences.

"What... then... why you and I?" she asked.

"I... I'm not sure," Alex said.

"Right..." she murmured.

The only sound in the room was the bubble of water coming to a boil. As that bubble rose into a sharp, hissing whine, Alex poured the water and placed the infuser into the cup, covering it with a saucer to let it steep.

He waited, eyes fixed on the cup.

His mind, however, was anything but quiet. The young wizard was frantically noting similarities between him and Carey, and contrasting them with their teachers.

They were leading him in some fairly... disturbing directions.

'This completely destroys the theory that only Heroes or even Fools can do it. Completely destroys it. So think, what do you and Carey have in common? She and I are both wizards,' he thought. 'And *that's* important. Hijacking a core requires mana manipulation. That means mana. That usually means wizard. Okay. Okay, what else do we have in common? Well, there's the obvious...'

He picked up the saucer and stirred the tea. "Cream? Sugar?"

"Sugar," Carey said. "A lot of it."

He spooned a couple of scoops into the tea and his mind kept working.

'Right, there's the obvious similarities,' Alex thought. 'We're both young, we're both Thameish, and we're both followers of Uldar. By the Traveller, why in all the hells would a belief in Uldar be the criteria to activate a dungeon core? Or even being Thameish? What in all bloody hells does that even mea—'

"You're not being sensible!" Professor Jules' voice boomed from the hallway.

Alex and Carey looked at each other and then toward the door.

There was a deep voice that said something in the hall, but even Alex's sharp ears couldn't quite pick it out.

"You have to think of—" Professor Jules' voice boomed before falling low. Perhaps she'd started speaking quieter.

What certainly wasn't quiet was the sound of boots and hooves coming closer. They sounded like they were in a hurry and—

Thoom.

Alex and Carey jumped as the door banged open and both Professor Jules and Chancellor Baelin swept into the room, shutting it behind them.

The ancient wizard looked serious, while Professor Jules was agitated.

Alex slowly handed Carey her tea, and she took it with a trembling hand, sinking into her seat.

"Alex, Carey," Professor Jules said. "I want you off the expedition until further notice."

Alex gasped.

Carey yelped, nearly dropping her tea.

"Hold on, don't panic." Baelin held up a hand. "You are not being removed from the expedition."

"Baelin," Professor Jules said. "This is *too strange*. Too many unknowns. Too many possible dangers. Think about it: about a dozen students handled the living dungeon core today, and the only ones that... found its mana pathways are our *Thameish* students? Baelin, this quite frankly stinks, and until we find out more, I think our students should be *out* of Thameland."

"And *I* disagree. Carey and Alex are two valuable members of the research team, and they are *grown* adults, not children to be hidden."

"And we are dealing with forces we're just starting to understand here," Professor Jules said. "Listen to me. First, we find out that the dungeon cores have a nearly *apocalyptic* reaction with chaos essence, then

Alex gets attacked while just outside of Greymoor in an event that looks suspiciously like a trap, then we find out that the dungeon cores can seemingly only be controlled by Thameish students?"

"Or followers of Uldar," Baelin noted calmly.

"Followers of Uldar?" Carey cut in. "Wh-why would that be the reason we could control dungeon cores? They're our... they're our god's eternal enemies."

Baelin looked like he was about to say something, then thought better of it. "Before we get too hasty, Vernia, why do we not ask the students in question what their choice would be, considering everything?"

"I'm staying," Alex said without hesitation. "With this discovery, I want to dive deeper into this as much as I can."

A moment of silence hung in the air.

Then all three other wizards looked at Carey.

CHAPTER 13

THE CHALLENGES OF FAITH

"I ... no, no, I don't want to go," Carey said with a hint of iron in her voice. "Every day, the Heroes and our army fight monsters across the land. They stay in the fight. They persevere. What right do I have to scurry off like a scared little mouse? I could never face my family ever again." She looked directly at the alchemy professor.

Jules looked back at her for a long, silent moment. Then she closed her eyes and drew a breath so deep, her body shook.

"Miss London," she measured her words. "I strongly recommend that both you and Mr. Roth return to campus. It won't be for long, but until we determine if you'll be safe here, I think you should step back. You can still work with the expedition on the Generasi side of things. In time, we'll be bringing samples back to the Cells for processing, further experimentation, and prototyping. You could both make your contribution there. Any thoughts, Mr. Roth?"

"No thanks," Alex said. "I get what you're saying, Professor Jules, and I know you're trying to keep us safe. But I think I'd be more useful here on site, and one reason, ironically enough, *is* because I'm Thameish. I've also got Claygon, and I can handle myself. Baelin won't always be here to break dungeons across his knee, which means we'll need all hands on deck."

"We have plenty of Watchers," Professor Jules countered. "Your help is appreciated, Mr. Roth, but..." She turned to Baelin. "Tell them what you told me."

The chancellor's nostrils flared. "There might be a chance that you two could be hunted for this discovery. Those images that were revealed when you took control of the core—"

"—I saw something too!" Carey cried, turning to Alex. "What did you see?"

"Uh..." He looked at Baelin, who nodded and remained silent. "Well, it was strange. These images of monsters and places I'd never seen before suddenly flashed into my head. They were only there briefly, though."

"By Uldar, I think we saw the same thing, and what I saw only lasted for a few seconds too! What does it all mean?"

"Well, it could mean there's a degree of communication between dungeon cores," Baelin said. "Perhaps you saw images of other dungeons, considering there were monsters in what you both experienced. That could indicate the presence of some hivemind or communication apparatus existing between dungeon cores."

He looked at Carey solemnly. "In full disclosure, if I were this Ravener and I knew someone had discovered how to control my dungeon cores—the means of producing my soldiers... my armies—I would stop at nothing to ensure that individual was eliminated. I am not saying this to scare you, but before you make a decision... I feel you should know what you could be up against."

Carey sat up a little taller in her chair. "Thank you ever so much for that, Chancellor Baelin, but... I still want to see this through. There's... I have so many questions now. How can I leave when they're yet to be answered?"

"Exactly," Alex agreed. "I'm staying too. And hell, we've got a castle here with some of the best trained combat wizards in the world. This might be *the* safest place in all of Thameland."

"I... I think so too," she said, her lower lip trembling ever so slightly. The determination in her voice matched her fear.

"Excellent," Baelin said. "Spoken like Proper Wizards."

"I..." Professor Jules frowned. "I don't like this, Baelin. It's our duty as instructors and leaders in this school to see that our students use caution and not assume unnecessary risks."

"The path of wizardry is a dangerous one, Vernia. You yourself know this," he said. "If one wanted to live a completely safe life, one would be better served becoming a tailor, perhaps. Or opening a shop to peddle fruits and vegetables. Magic is a deadly art, and wizards must know how to make their own decisions in the face of those dangers. We cannot shield them from all risk, we just cannot, nor should we even try. We'll simply be doing them a disservice when they're no longer hidden beneath our wings. We also shouldn't be the ones to decide what risks they choose to face."

"The path of wizardry was a lot more dangerous *before* we came up with safety regulations, proper mentorships, and the like." Jules shook her head, her eyes growing distant. "No more using apprentices to provide blood for sacrifices, or tricking them into diving into ancient, dangerous ruins to fetch dubious artefacts. Young wizards are no longer turned into mulch by an angry demon they accidentally summoned... most of the time. We don't want to go back to the dark old days. Remember, they were put aside for very good reasons. It's up to us—those with wisdom and experience—to guide and protect our young wizards."

"What you are suggesting is beyond that," Baelin said firmly. "I understand the need for caution, but if we start stepping too far into that realm, we risk taking away a student's agency. You remember that idiotic meeting we attended a few years back, don't you? Where it was suggested that our curriculum be altered so nearly ninety percent of courses are pre-selected for students in an effort to promote—" he made air quotes, and his look grew disgusted "—'optimization and universal skill building in the modern wizard'? You fought against that as hard as I did, arguing that such a thing would defeat the choice afforded every wizard."

"That's different, Baelin," she said. "What you're arguing is the equivalent to saying that every student should be given the choice to *not* wear safety equipment in the lab, because enforcing such rules would take away from a student's experience. I am not proposing we kick students off the expedition, only that they serve from a *safer place*."

"And these students are in their second year. They undertook this expedition knowing that there would be dangers, monsters, and an entire warzone to be wary of. They knew there would be unknown substances to experiment on. I do not think we would serve them well by drawing a line for them. When they are out in the world and the unexpected happens, we won't be there to whisk them away. I believe exposure to the unknown now will give them skills to deal with it later."

'Grandma, Grandpa, please stop fighting!' Alex screamed internally, carefully returning to his seat.

Carey's eyes darted back and forth between the two wizards.

Neither Baelin nor Professor Jules had raised their voices during their discussion—there was a deadly calm in their tones—but it was clear that hooves and heels were dug in.

They even seemed to have forgotten that Alex and Carey were still in the room, growing increasingly wide-eyed.

"This is an unknown among unknowns," Professor Jules said. "How many expeditions were destroyed by an expedition leader saying 'oh, just a little farther'? Remember the Silt Cave Disaster? We lost Professor Collins and five promising graduate students because of foolhardy decisions."

"A false equivalency, Vernia. And you know it. You love your students, and you should, but if you coddle them—"

"Coddle them?" Professor Jules' eyebrows shot up. "I want to keep them *alive*. Baelin, with all due respect, this is not some barbarian age where folk have to fight and die every day for their meat. We're in a time of science and magic—"

"And faith," Carey whispered, but if Jules heard her, she didn't look her way.

"—and these two young wizards have an excellent future ahead. Simply having them pause the headlong rush into dangerous mysteries, I believe is more about being 'reasonable,' and less about 'coddling.'"

"And I think you are underestimating our students' capabilities," Baelin said, pride filling his voice. "I accepted the position as chancellor of the university because I also love wizardry and seeing new wizards entering the world prepared for its trials. But those trials are often dangerous, and if we train our students to run and hide from shadows *even when* they are in a safe location backed by some of our best security forces, then what are we teaching them? We're teaching them to cower, to run."

He gestured to the pair of young wizards. "Neither student has requested anything unreasonable. Alex has proven combat capabilities. He's taking my course and is also performing so excellently in the expedition, that—quite frankly—he would have to literally spit on his written final exam not to gain credit for year two of the Art of the Wizard in Combat. Allowing autonomy to challenge and assess the world is important for his growth, or he'll be unprepared for the dangers of the wider world."

He looked at Alex. "Do you not agree?"

Alex swallowed nervously, not wanting to get caught between the two wizards and their opposing points of view. He saw reason in both arguments, and he'd come to care dearly about both professors. It almost felt like he was being pulled into one of Mr. and Mrs. Lu's arguments.

"Uh..." he said carefully. "I agree with both of you, but... I dunno... I've gained power. If I don't use it, then what's the point? I want to do things as safely as I can, but I think I can handle whatever's coming. And if there is something nasty coming, why should I hide back in Generasi while my colleagues are here facing it?"

Professor Jules looked like she was about to say something then bit it back. Worry had taken over her expression.

"Well spoken, Alex." Next, Baelin gestured to Carey. "Carey, on the other hand, has no combat experience. Do you?"

Carey flinched. "Not really."

"But you are an excellent alchemist, and you have not said that you have any desire to suddenly rush into battle and risk yourself even though you're not experienced or equipped for such rigours, have you?"

"No," Carey said. "I do want to continue working on the frontline ever so much... but here in the encamp—er, castle. If I went out there, I know I'd just be a danger to myself and anyone else with me. So, I'll stay where I can best help... especially because... there's only the two of us who've engaged with a dungeon core so far, yes?"

She looked at Professor Jules, whose nod came reluctantly.

"Then I must stay, I simply must! We have to learn everything we can about all of this. And, my countrymen... I am terribly frightened, to be sure, but I won't let my fear send me retreating like a coward."

Silence hung in the air.

"And there you have it. Reason. If we deny them now, Vernia... we would not turn them into Proper Wizards... we would turn them into cowards."

Professor Jules' jaw flexed rhythmically.

"I..." she said. "I... seem to have been outvoted. Well, I can't stand in your way if the three of you want this so much. But know that I disapprove. I very much disapprove."

She sighed, shaking her head. "Well, what do we do—"

"Professor, why are Alex and I the only ones who managed to do this?" Carey asked. "Why us? What is going on, and why would mortals even be able to control a dungeon core?"

Professor Jules cleared her throat. "Well, Miss London, it might be too early for a hypothesis, but there are two obvious commonalities between you and Mr. Roth. First, you are both Thameish, and secondly, you are both followers of Uldar."

Carey paused, working through Jules' answer.

And the colour began to drain from her face.

"But... why in Uldar's name would that allow us to control these... these... devil-orbs?" she cried. "They are our enemy, so, why? Why would we... maybe Uldar's grace is simply so mighty, that it lets us seize control of dungeon cores against their will?" Her eyes darted. "M-much as a mouse would bow to a lion in the southlands!"

Baelin and Professor Jules looked at each other.

The ancient wizard cleared his throat. "Perhaps that might be a fair hypothesis. Power can be a tipping factor in many situations. But... I was unable to even attempt this myself, and the same is true for Professor Jules."

"Oh, that's alright, Chancellor Baelin," Carey said. "There's no shame in not being as powerful as a god—"

'Carey, no!' Alex screamed internally, feeling like he was watching a rudderless ship steaming toward a reef.

"—especially one as great as Uldar," the young woman finished, her tone filled with the innocence of a child reporting the colour of the sky on a given day.

Professor Jules gasped.

Alex considered having Claygon break down the walls and yank him from the room.

Baelin stared at Carey, a look of shock on his face for the very first time since Alex had known him. Then he threw his head back and a booming laugh filled the room. "Oh my, Carey, there was a time... there was a time..." he said, wiping a tear from his eye.

He had an edge to his voice right below the surface that Alex caught, leaving him feeling like the spectre of death had just flown by.

"Well... let us say for a moment that you are correct, and that your deity, Uldar, is my better," he said. "It could be possible. Not all deities are made from the same stern stuff, after all."

He stroked his beard. "But there are two issues with your hypothesis: the first being—*you* and Alex are not Uldar. You are not priests either and so do not wield his divine power for yourselves. The second issue is that it's not about power, it's that the dungeon core's entrances do not even *appear* for others aside from you and Alex, so far. It's as though they're *designed* only to be accessible by certain individuals. Which indicates something... less than accidental."

"Wait, you're suggesting that there's some... purpose to allowing children of Uldar... of Thameland, to control dungeon cores? Whose purpose?" Carey asked.

Baelin shrugged. "That I do not know, my child. Your guess is as good as mine."

"The thing is," Alex cut in. "The historical records cover how Uldar fought the Ravener the first time, right? They also cover how Heroes rose up to fight him in subsequent times… Except information about those first battles are vague. We don't even know where the Ravener came from."

"But why… why Uldar's children?" Carey muttered, her eyes growing distant. "Why… why would Uldar's own be able to control… and why does no one know of this? We must tell the church right away!"

"I don't know about that, Carey," Alex said. "Our kingdom's been fighting the Ravener for… at least a millennium, maybe longer. This should be common knowledge among our people. It couldn't have stayed hidden for this long, unless…"

"Unless someone or something wanted it to remain hidden," Professor Jules finished. "Which is why details must be revealed cautiously."

"But…" Carey had begun to shake. "Someone *must* know!"

"Yeah, I agree," Alex said, watching Carey as his mind worked. "That's why I think we should start by only telling a few people. People that are already close to the expedition."

Carey looked at him sharply. "Who?"

"The Heroes."

CHAPTER 14

CHALLENGED BELIEFS AND ALTERNATE PLANS

"Hmmm. That's not a half-bad idea," Baelin said. "It should also increase trust between us and them... though, I doubt they would be likely to believe us by our word alone."

"I know I wouldn't," Carey said, appearing more shaken as the realisation that mortals could control dungeon cores played in her mind. "I never would have believed it."

"Which is why we need at least one of them to try it. We should invite them back here," Alex pushed on. "Listen, if this is half as big as it looks, they should know. Imagine if they could turn the Ravener's own weapons against it?"

He crossed his arms over his chest, considering possibilities. "We know you need mana and mana manipulation for it to work, and of course being Thameish goes without being said. I bet Drestra could do it, probably Cedric too. That way, we let them know what's happening, and they get a heads-up about enemies... from the Ravener or... elsewhere."

"You mean cultists?" Carey asked.

Baelin, Alex, and Jules exchanged a quick glance.

Professor Jules cleared her throat. "Carey, the likelihood that this was *completely* unnoticed by everyone in Thameland for all of history is... well, it's possible, but highly unlikely."

"Indeed," Baelin agreed. "In a situation like this, if such a fact is unknown by everyone who has any reason to know it, even after the passage of so much time, I would have to say it's most likely that some... entity or entities do *not* wish it to be known."

"What?" Carey blinked her large eyes. "Are you saying you think... you think there's some kind of conspiracy? I don't mean to be disrespectful, but that just sounds like absolute madness! Right round the bend! It... I'm sure it can all be explained. Look at all that our teams have discovered so quickly about the dungeon cores. Secrets that eluded our kingdom and the church for centuries! I mean... I mean..." Her words stopped, and a pained look crossed her face. "I mean... of course we have Generasi's advanced magics and technologies to work with..." Her voice dropped. "Yet, I was able to interact with the core without magics or technology; I simply picked it up." She was almost whispering now, a catch in her voice. "Someone surely should have figured this out by now..."

She looked paler. "By Uldar... what is going on?"

"I don't know, and that's why I'm thinking we tell the Heroes. That way, they'll be warned since this information would matter most to them, and the way I see it, they'd be least likely to be in on... whatever's going on, if there is something going on," Alex said.

"And if they are, we can watch their reactions firsthand, and—should they prove to be treacherous—dispense with them before they can even consider striking us," Baelin said.

Alex looked at him somberly, knowing he was right. If the Heroes did turn out to be enemies, better to catch them alone and off guard than with the full backing of...

He really would like to know who the hell they were fighting.

He waited for Carey to raise a protest, but she remained silent.

Alex watched as her body language seemed to wilt. There was a slump to her shoulders, like a terrible weight had been placed on them. Everything about the way she looked spoke of turmoil, despair.

He remembered what he'd felt like in the Cave of the Traveller. All the sudden questions. All the doubts. The fears. Hijacking that core had shaken him. After all, who wouldn't be shaken if they learned that what they'd been taught from childhood, what they'd believed without question, should actually be questioned. That their god's and their homeland's eternal enemy could be controlled by mortals, and no one had ever told them that?

Except, it was even worse for her.

After his experience in the Traveller's Cave, he'd assumed that all mortals could control dungeon cores. Now, he'd come to understand that not all mortals could, and if dungeon cores could only be controlled by people of Thameland or specifically followers of Uldar, it meant that something was *terribly* wrong with their understanding of the Ravener, their struggle, and...

Alex gripped the armrests on his chair.

...Maybe even Uldar himself.

Uldar's gift to the people was to destroy the Ravener's first incarnation, and—then—to create the Heroes. But if his children could control dungeon cores, then why... why would he not tell them that?

Why bother with Heroes at all, why not encourage followers—who were most powerful in magic—to take command of the cores and use their own monsters against them?

Alex remembered Baelin's distaste for deities, and indeed, many were selfish, petty, fickle, and arrogant. Others were kind, though, and wanted the best for their followers. He'd been *raised* on stories that Uldar was kind and caring.

The evening of his eighteenth birthday had changed his thinking and taken away some of his reverence for his god, but it hadn't entirely died. Now? Here he was wondering exactly what the great and 'holy' Uldar intended.

What *was* his plan?

The more he thought, the more disturbing possibilities came to mind. And that was troubling for him, someone whose faith in Uldar had become casual at best.

What about someone as devout as Carey?

She could either fall into denial and hold on to her faith, make excuses and look for other possibilities, become angry and treat what was before her as lies...

Carey shifted in her chair, clutching her knees and chewing her lower lip. Her feet were planted squarely on the stones: all signs of someone trying to ground themselves. Her mannerisms spoke of...

...Doubt.

Alex felt a stab of sympathy in his heart. Carey had never been his favourite person in Generasi, annoying at times, though fairly harmless. She'd always been a good lab partner and wasn't malicious. Did she deserve to have her world shattered?

As someone who'd lived that several times in his life, he didn't think so.

"You know, perhaps we should let this issue lie for now." Baelin broke through Alex's thoughts, also watching Carey carefully. "It is... trying in many ways, as some revelations can be. I agree with Alex's idea of reaching out to the Heroes, and you, Vernia?"

The alchemy professor frowned, seeming to mentally calculate things. "Ugh... if I wanted this sort of intrigue and danger, I would've become a court wizard. I... yes, I think it's a good idea. Sitting on this for too long might reflect negatively on us if it were to come out... accidentally."

"Speaking of that," the chancellor said. "Until we are ready to reveal this, I will be calling all members of the expedition to a meeting. And I strongly recommend the use of pact magic to ensure this does not leak outside the team before we are ready."

Jules looked at him sharply. "*Really*? Are you sure that's necessary?"

"I believe so," Baelin said gravely. "I am sure that, at the very least, the researchers who were in your lab today will already be asking what has happened, and with information as sensitive as this, I would prefer it didn't find a winding road into some demon summoner's hands this time. It might sound distrustful... but I won't risk betrayal again. It has already cost us too much, and we're still dealing with fallout in the form of cultists to this day, right here in Thameland. Is there any opposition?"

Alex didn't even have to think about it. "No. I think it's best. And I also get why."

"Fair enough," Professor Jules agreed.

Her words were followed by a drawn out silence.

"Hm? Sorry?" Carey blinked, pulling herself from her thoughts. "Er, yes, yes. I'll swear not to tell a soul by way of pact magic."

"Good," the ancient wizard said. "Then we will do so. And I'll make sure the Heroes of Thameland are contacted as soon as possible. If nothing else, if one of them chooses to attempt controlling a dungeon core, then we'll have another data point to go by."

"Pacts... pacts..." Drestra whispered, drawing symbols in the dirt with a stick. "Can I trick him? Is there some loophole I can exploit in Lord Aenflynn's words? Maybe I can... no, no, no."

She scratched out the idea, thinking back to the old stories.

Games of wordplay often came up in stories of the fae. There were too many disturbing tales of mortals who'd made deals with fae, only to have the otherworldly creatures trap them with some hidden meaning in their own words. Which was the problem: *most* of those stories were about fae tricking *people* with words, not the other way around.

And Aenflynn was a fae lord. She doubted he'd be obliging enough to leave her some easy-to-find loophole to capitalise on. After weeks of mulling over the problem, she still hadn't come up with anything that the ancient, clever fae wouldn't immediately see through.

Worse, even if she were to trick him, it wasn't as if he'd be doing them a one-time service and then she'd never see him again. His armies would be fighting by their side, and mortal children would be held in the fae realm. Even if Aenflynn miraculously honoured a deal he was tricked into, suppose he instructed his troops not to fight as hard as they could? Or what if he took vengeance out on the children given over to the fae realm?

At the end of the day, the best thing to do was to honour the spirit of the deal and make sure the fae lord walked away satisfied.

If they—

Crack.

She caught the sound of a dry leaf crunching beneath a light footstep and whirled around. A familiar white-robed figure was making his way through the trees.

"Merzhin?" she called out.

"Holy Sage. There you are, by Uldar's holy will." His high-tenor voice sounded relieved as he broke through the trees. "The Holy Champion sent me to find you. We have made ready to travel to the fae wilds again. Are you prepared to go?"

'No,' Drestra thought.

"Yes." She stepped away from the patch of ground she'd been writing on, rubbing the symbols away with her foot. "Let's get this done."

Together, they made their way back to camp as Merzhin glanced back at her.

"Did you have a pleasant time communing with the wilderness?" he asked, an awkward friendliness in his voice. "I've always found it so delightful how the Witches of the Crymlyn weave the reverence of nature into your worship of Uldar. It's an admirable denomination, I think. For—"

He cleared his throat. "*—lo, did Uldar make all the fields fertile and the forests lush, and his benediction made the rivers and seas forevermore hold plenty so that his children might feast of his land for all their days. For this land is his greatest domain and his greatest gift to all who follow the sign of the hand.*"

He made the sign of the hand before his chest. "*Always,*" he finished the recitation of the holy scripture. "I find that some focus too little on the agrarian sides of Uldar's great domain."

Drestra gave him a long look. "We worshipped the spirits, fae, and land long before Uldar. It only made sense that he join them, not be worshipped instead of them."

"Mmm, yes, *fae*." Merzhin almost seemed to spit the word. "I have no idea why we're even still entertaining this nonsense. Surely even *you* must be tired of it by now. This fae lord increases his price each time we are undecided. And how can we decide? What he wants from us is too monstrous to even consider. We're wasting time, don't you agree?"

"No," Drestra said flatly. "I don't think we are. I think we'd be foolish not to look at everything if we're going to win this war."

"Faith in Uldar and his gifts shall win us the war," Merzhin said. "Unshakeable faith. Your faith is light, Holy Sage. It is thin, like dried wheat. Have faith. Trust in Uldar and us. Look at how many cycles we have overcome the enemy and understand that we will succeed."

"I'm not having this argument again, Merzhin," Drestra said.

"All of this desperation weighs heavily on the spirit. You give yourself to a higher power—"

"Enough," Drestra warned him.

He sighed. "Very well. I will drop it for now."

"Not just 'for now'" she grunted, turning her thoughts back to the problem at hand.

As much as she hated to admit it, Merzhin was right. The way things were going, these moon-timed meetings with Aenflynn were a waste of time. The fae lord, of course, had all the time in the world to spare.

He was an immortal or near-immortal creature, and his people weren't the ones being harmed by the Ravener. The fae even called the Ravener's attacks the Times of Plenty. The Heroes had far less time to spare, and less hope as he simply raised his price each time they delayed their decision.

Now the number of children he was requesting had risen to a level that even made her uncomfortable. She just couldn't let go of the thought of gaining those powerful forces for the war effort.

'Think about the *spirit* of what he wishes,' Destra thought. 'Taking fae changelings and making them comfortable here is no problem... it's the children going over to the fae that's the unbearable part. Does it *have* to be children? He wants something to replace the forces he's giving us. That means power. Mortal children would grow up in the fae world and live longer than adult mortal soldiers. Which means he wants power that will last. Military support for us now... military growth for him later. We can't hand him just any sort of power. What if he turns it on us? Meaning it needs to be something that we can give him that won't turn on us... and something that will last—'

"Drestra! Merzhin!" Hart's voice boomed, echoing through the trees. "New information's come in! There's a cult to the east that needs paying a not so friendly visit to, and the priests have called for you, Merzhin. Drestra, the Generasians have called for us... and they made it sound urgent!"

CHAPTER 15

SUPPOSITIONS AND STORIES

"Oh, by Uldar, the Traveller, and all my ancestors," Theresa shook her head, holding it between both hands. "I can't believe this. Only you and Carey?" she said, looking up at Alex. "I just can't... I can't believe this."

"I think there would be few who could," Prince Khalik said, leaning against the wall and crossing his muscular arms. "This would be like the people of the four Kingdoms of the Blue Delta learning that the machine gods that plague them every dry season were actually the servants of their kings. It is... shattering, potentially."

"I'm wondering if it's just people who're Thameish that can control it, or if it's those who follow Uldar," Theresa said, watching the activity around them. "And it doesn't look like we're the only ones with questions."

Jules' and Baelin's briefing had been more than an hour ago, and its ripple effects were being felt everywhere in the encampment. Researchers, guards, and builders had paused their work—freed from their tasks for the rest of the day—and many huddled in their own little groups, discussing the news. A noise like thunder announced Vesuvius tromping through the half-finished courtyard with Tyris perched high on his back.

Her eyes lingered on Alex as they passed him and his friends, but she didn't stop. Sitting under the branches of the aeld tree, Meikara and her medical colleagues talked among themselves, often stealing glances Alex's way with expressions ranging from curiosity to fear. And the blood mages weren't the only ones watching the Thameish wizard. Some were outright staring, whispering like insects droning in the courtyard. Others watched the tents and partly finished outbuildings, probably looking for Carey, but they were out of luck. The young woman had returned to Generasi as soon as the team finished binding themselves to a pact of shared secrecy.

It was Baelin's magic, and it would curse anyone who broke the pact with a growing agony that led to paralysis.

Between what Carey had described to Professor Jules as a sour stomach, a chalk-like complexion, and a deep need to return to campus to think, Jules had offered her a potion to settle her stomach, which she was sipping on when Alex had last seen her heading to the teleportation circle.

Baelin had also left the encampment, teleporting away to pick up the Heroes, while Jules was locked in her office, tackling a mountain of paperwork from the unexpected direction their research had taken.

That only left Alex, and while some folk would have cast politeness to the wind and come rushing over to pepper him with questions, it was clear that he and his friends wanted privacy. They were wedged in a corner of the inner wall, away from everyone.

There were some who still might've been bold enough to casually saunter over anyway—acting nonchalant—but Grimloch, Brutus, and Claygon made for a fine deterrent. A large hunk of meat disappeared into the shark man's mouth, and gnashing teeth made short work of it as he stared at passersby with his dead eyes. If the briefing had bothered him in any way, you'd never know it by looking at him. He was enthusiastically tossing his food in the air and snatching it with his teeth like he was playing his own game of catch. If Baelin and Jules had announced that a meal would be late, Alex had no doubt he would've looked more concerned.

Brutus had two heads tucked into a bowl of dried meat, while his third whined softly, watching his master and licking her hand.

Claygon was silent, of course, but his head was turned toward the aeld tree, like they were communicating as it gave off its soothing light in the middle of the courtyard.

Leaning against the golem, Thundar was chewing on a carrot, his furry brow was creased in thought. Isolde paced back and forth, muttering to herself with her hands clasped behind her back.

"It is most curious," she said. "And it calls into question so many historical and ideological events. Even spiritual ones, depending on what the answer to this puzzle turns out to be."

"Yeah," Thundar said. "I guess to get some answers, we'd need to find a Thameish person who's got mana and doesn't worship Uldar to get them to try and hijack a core."

"Or an Uldarite who isn't Thameish," Alex said. "But finding them is going to be like hunting for a tick in a field. Just about everyone in Thameland worships Uldar, or at least pays some measure of respect to him."

"Best bet would be someone who emigrated here," Theresa said. "It'd have to be someone who moved to Thameland and became a subject of the kingdom but didn't join the church. Someone we can trust."

"That'd be easier to do, but... well, I think any pool of people who lived in Thameland and didn't believe in Uldar would be small to begin with. Even smaller now because they might've started believing in him when the Ravener came back," Alex said. "Or maybe it'd drive them away... I dunno. One thing we know for sure, they would've been hard to find in the first place, but nearly impossible since almost everyone's left Thameland."

"One thing we must understand is *when* someone is considered Thameish," Isolde pointed out. "Is it when they have moved here? Is it if they were born here?"

"That part's easy at least," Theresa said. "Heroes only come from Thameish folk, but we know that some past Heroes came from other lands originally. The Traveller was supposed to be from somewhere else, and there was a Chosen a few cycles before who was born in Rhinea and came to Thameland when she was five. She and her family swore an oath to the king when they came here, so that made her Thameish enough to be marked as the leader of the Heroes in her time."

"Ah, well that does help narrow things down," Isolde said, shaking her head. "But either situation proves grim. We Rhineans take pride in historically offering our Thameish cousins shelter while your Heroes battle the Ravener, but there are those who do not approve of this arrangement.

"Some of our nobles complain about having to house and feed the Thameish when they arrive because taxes on all Rhineans are raised by the emperor. The collected funds are then used to support those who fled your kingdom. It is our duty, but some chafe at it. Were they to learn that some of your people could *control* the dungeon cores of your enemies..."

"Oof, I didn't even think of that," Alex said. "Support would probably dry up hard, wouldn't it?"

"Do not think so little of the majority of us. Most would gladly continue to aid our allies. Though certainly some would, no doubt, begin to petition the emperor for a... *change* in policy. It could create some unfortunate discord."

"Ah, the wonders of politics and the greedy, shortsighted desires of petty nobles," Khalik grunted. "It does not bode well. I wonder. Has there been any change in the orb, Alex? I wish I'd had the opportunity to see it."

"Oh no, Jules has it locked down tight." Alex looked over at the research building. "At least a dozen Watchers and some golems were brought over from campus to guard it. Baelin even placed more than one ward on the door of the Analysis Room it's in. You'd have an easier time breaking into a merchant's vault than getting in there. As for how it's doing. Well, it's getting darker last I saw of it, which means its mana's building. No surprise there: dungeon cores feed off fear, and there's been enough fear and anxiety floating around here for it to feed off of."

"Can they communicate with each other?" Isolde asked, throwing a nervous look toward the research building. "The idea that we could have brought a spy into our midst concerns me."

"Nobody knows yet," Alex said. "That's something we were going to look into... before all this happened. It's one of the reasons it's been locked down under all those wards."

"Hm." Khalik smoothed his beard. "A core that creates monsters. A core that feeds on the fear of mortal kind to power itself. A core that strikes only at those from a certain kingdom... and yet, that same core can only be controlled by those it victimises... Such would be poetic if it were not so grim. And suspicious. It gives us a lot to speculate about."

"Hey, you're all looking like someone spit on your ancestors' graves, but ain't this a good thing?" Thundar asked. "Think about it. All the sinister shit aside, we just got ourselves a powerful new tool."

He began listing the benefits on his thick fingers. "For one, we've got something that could make *us* monsters. That means unlimited specimens and guards. No more fearing Ravener-spawn if we just throw their own creatures at them. Two, we can use it to change terrain in any way we want. Isn't that badass? We'd raise the castle even faster. Those mining operations the leadership's been talking about—the ones our fae friend found. Think about it, Alex—we wouldn't even have to use earth mages for that. One dungeon core and, *voom!*"

The minotaur spread his arms. "We can just open up the earth like we're cracking a walnut. Third, we can learn *exactly* how a whole living dungeon core works. Do you know what my tribe calls an animal whose behaviour we know *all* about? Prey, my friends, prey!"

"Mmmmm, quite true, Thundar," Khalik said. "If we can use the dungeon cores to change terrain, we could have roads throughout Greymoor before the season ends. But! While we know they can be made to alter terrain, we do not know if they can be made to make monsters. And even if they can, will those monsters also be under our control, or will they simply turn on us as soon as they appear? Then there is another issue: Alex, does anyone know how a dungeon core... makes a dungeon? How does it bring an area of land under its control?"

"Once we get through the initial tasks and make some data sheets, that's probably the next thing we'll be working on," Alex said. "But there's been no time for any of that. Folks are reeling, and with the Heroes on their way, we probably won't have time to run full experiments for a while."

Theresa gave Alex a long, meaningful look, then looked away. "Experiments... I feel like I'm in the middle of a giant experiment right now."

"What do you mean?" Alex asked softly.

"It would've been *one* thing if it turned out that *any* mortal could use the dungeon cores," she said carefully. Grimloch still didn't know about their experience in the Cave of the Traveller and what they'd learned there. Very few people outside of the cabal did. "But it's like it's *tailor made* so only its *victims* can control it. Imagine? If a deer found out that the only living creatures that could control wolves were other deer. It's like a joke."

She looked up at the clear sky, her eyes focusing on a dark cloud moving from the east. It was still distant, but it was threatening. The wind had a crisp bite to it. First snow would come any day now. "Does Uldar *know* his people can control dungeon cores? He'd have to, wouldn't he? So then why bother with Heroes? Why send five young folks to fight and die if any one of us, if we have mana, can just take control of our enemies? Why?"

"Hmmm, I have a couple of theories," Khalik said. "There was once a story I heard as a boy. Two lions were attacking a mine in the north of Tekezash, killing miners and making them into their meals. Now, you must understand, mortals are not the usual prey of lions: they have learned to fear us, our weapons, and our magics over the millennia. So this was strange. The other thing that was strange was that these were *male* lions, and not young ones either. Mature male lions would normally be leading prides and letting most of the lionesses do the hunting. And finally, the lions were beyond cunning. It was uncanny. They seemed to know the ways of humanity. How we hunted. What our weapons were.

So, for ten months, the lions killed at will. They seemed unstoppable. And then something odd happened."

He tapped the shortsword at his waist. "A slew of mercenaries were hired to kill the beasts... many died. There was one, a young man from the kingdom of Tsava, who joined the hunt with four others. His companions were hunted and killed, but when the lions stalked him, he called out in Tsa—his mother tongue—for them to stop. And wouldn't you know it? They did."

"Why?" Isolde asked.

"Well, as it turned out, they understood commands in Tsa. The young mercenary took the lions with him while an investigation was done, and it so happened that a rich merchant and hunter from Tsava had a pair of trained hunting-lions escape his pens. That is why they were so clever. They were trained to hunt at his side, so they used the skills they'd been trained to."

"Jeez, what happened to the merchant?" Alex asked.

"He happily took his prized lions back and rewarded the young mercenary... Only for the lions to run away again. As it happened, the young man had been a kinder master than their former one. And so, they went back to him. Together, they hunted monsters all over the region. But the point is, these dungeon cores might be some mortal's creation. Maybe some ancient wizard made them—one of your countrymen from the past perhaps. And then the cores went out of control. Maybe this Ravener took them then, and now *you* must take them back."

"Not the craziest theory I've ever heard," Alex said.

"I got a theory too," Grimloch jumped in. "But if this one's right, you've got a *big* problem."

CHAPTER 16

HEROIC TRICKS AND DIVINE GIFTS

"What do you mean, a big problem?" Khalik asked.

"You'll understand when I finish. Mmmm... any of you landbound people ever heard the story of Bowar-Og?" Grimloch rumbled, picking his teeth with a bone.

"No, I cannot say I have," Khalik said.

"Naw," Thundar said.

"No," Theresa and Alex echoed.

Isolde shook her head.

"Right." Grimloch licked the last of the meat juices from his fingers. "Bowar-Og was a folk hero. Both above and below the waters. There *were* a lot of songs about him."

"Were?" Khalik asked.

"*Were.* They're not sung anymore. He used to go around with his harpoon fighting sharks, sea serpents, and even some of my people, because back then, some of us were at war with some of the selachar. He made his living with his trident, spearing all kinds of monsters. What he really specialised in was bandit hunting. It'd always be the same: bandits would come to an area, people would send out a call for help, and the bandits would kill a bunch of knights and wandering warriors. Bowar-Og would always defeat them. Some would die by his spear and the rest would run. Then, a rival of his started asking questions. She'd noticed that he fought a lot of bandit bands, and they'd always have their faces covered, they'd have different names, different weapons, different armour... but they'd always be the same races with the same stocky shapes. So she followed him one tide and..."

He growled. "She saw him *meeting up* with the bandits."

"Oh..." Khalik's eyes grew. "Oh *no.*"

"What? Were they bribing him?" Isolde suggested.

"No. He was their leader," Grimloch snarled. "Got an idea in his head that they'd make more money if they faked bandit attacks then had him stop them instead of robbing travellers and raiding villages. It was always the same setup. Bandits would swim into some remote village, attack some sea cows, crush coral houses, and maybe kill a guard or two. The village would send out a cry for help, and Bowar-Og would answer. He'd fight them singlehandedly, he'd kill any new recruits his band had picked up, and let his crooked buddies run away. Then the villagers would heap all kinds of wealth on him, which he'd take and share with the other crooks."

"Oh shit," Alex said. "They wouldn't get as much wealth in the short-term as if they raided villages, but in the long-term, they're hunted by less people, and they get rewards from 'bandit subjugation' over and over again. They'd make a lot more over time if they were smart about it."

"How'd it resolve?" Theresa asked. "I doubt anyone would've believed their Hero was a bad guy... especially if it was one of his rivals who was pointing it out."

"That's exactly right. People didn't believe her at first," Grimloch growled. "So she kept quiet and got a group of people together from villages Bowar-Og had saved and took them into the deep. They went to a bandit camp in an ocean trench, and who'd they find? Bowar-Og, sitting with them, laughing and drinking. They didn't like that too much, so they set a trap. Next time those bandits swam into a town and Bowar-Og appeared promising he'd stop them, a bunch of mercenaries—paid for by all the towns he'd 'saved'—surrounded and captured every last bandit. Didn't take them long to start squealing on their silent partner. The townsfolk took Mr. Hero, gave him twenty shallow cuts, and left him in megalodon waters with the rest of his bandit band. They told him that he'd have no problem fighting his way out if he was half the monster hunter he said he was."

Grimloch grinned. "He wasn't."

"Oh dear," Isolde said.

"Yeah, that's the fun part of the story. So anyway, maybe it's like that here. These dungeon cores are supposed to be like golems, from what I hear, right?" He jerked his thumb toward Claygon. "Maybe some old wizard made 'em so they could 'solve problems for money' and now here they are, still causing trouble."

'Some old wizard...or someone else...' Alex thought, considering a very grim possibility.

From the look Theresa threw him, she'd thought the same thing.

"Reminds me of a story from my tribe," Thundar said. "They say that in our early days, one of the gods we used to worship sent down a bunch of golden bulls to protect us. Well, he didn't bother telling *us* about it, so we just saw a bunch of great, big mammoth-sized monsters on our lands, grazing on grass, and before the bulls could do anything, our warriors attacked 'em. Well, the bulls got pretty testy that those they were trying to protect attacked 'em, so they swore revenge on us. It finally came out that they were there to help us, but not until long after we'd killed every last one of 'em."

He shrugged. "Maybe Uldar, or some ancient wizard or something, made dungeon cores to help the people and, I dunno, there was some kinda misunderstanding, and now everyone's attacking them."

"Right..." Alex said. "Well, it's hard to tell either way. I'm starting to think our history's so incomplete that anything could be right. But ya have to wonder if it's incomplete on purpose."

"Yeah, I'd love to get into the church archives in the capital," Theresa said. "Maybe there's hidden stuff there we could dig out."

"Yeah, me too," Alex said. "And I—"

He paused.

Teleportation magic was coming from near the aeld tree.

"Let's leave this for later. We have company. Baelin's back with the Heroes."

The air shimmered and four forms materialised beside the aeld: Baelin, Cedric, Hart, and Drestra.

"Welcome back," Baelin said to the Heroes, who were looking a little wild-eyed.

"If this were a regular day, I would offer you a place to sit and have a proper meal before we proceed, but I fear this is too important to let lie for long. Perhaps a quick beverage will suffice for now?"

Cedric chuckled nervously. "Heh, you're talkin' like all o' you've just stumbled on the end o' the world or somethi—"

He paused, spying Alex's group by the wall. "Well, hello to you, Isolde an' the rest o' yous! Pleasure to see you all again..." He frowned as the cabal and their companions strode over. "Is normally what I'd say if all o' yous didn't look like y'were walkin' to your own funerals. What's happened? Y'get attacked?"

The three Heroes looked around, and Drestra gasped when she saw the aeld tree. Her slit-like pupils grew as she took in the beautiful sapling.

"An aeld tree!" Her voice filled with warmth. "We had one protecting the main square of our village. I can't believe you have one. How did you manage to get it?"

"That's a long story," Alex and Baelin said at the same time, then looked at each other.

The chancellor cleared his throat. "And one that will need to be explained at a later date. I have already informed Professor Jules of our arrival, and Alex will take you down to see her in our new research building. She'll be waiting for you, and I'll see you all there shortly."

Without another word, the ancient wizard vanished in another pulse of teleportation magic.

Hart shifted his helmet and scratched his head. "The atmosphere around here's pretty tense. Reminds me of when my band found out we were on the losing side of a war we were hired for in Rhinea."

"It's not that bad... probably," Alex said.

None of the Heroes looked reassured.

"That was fast. I'm glad you're here," Professor Jules said, meeting Alex and the three Heroes just outside the research building. "Baelin's not with you?"

"He's getting Carey," Alex said. "He told us to come see you and wait for him."

"I see. It appears that Carey won't have much time to herself after all," she said, as the Chosen, Sage, and Champion exchanged puzzled glances. "Well, welcome back to the three of you, if only these were more relaxed circumstances."

"Okay, *now* all o' yous are startin' to scare me, and that's not an easy thing ta' do, so what's this all about?" Cedric said. "First, we gotta get here fast, so fast that Baelin's gotta meet us at the closest place he could teleport to. Now we're here and no one's tellin' us anythin'—" He looked at Alex. "Your friends all slink off with hardly a word. S'been bloody spooky is what it's been."

"Forgive us. We're not trying to be clandestine for effect, Cedric," Professor Jules said. "It's just that the quicker and smoother this all goes, the better. Now, walk with me."

With a billow of her cloak, she turned and led the group into the research building and down a steep flight of stairs.

They reached the vault, and Hart whistled when he saw how many Watchers were standing before the doors, guarding them.

"What've you got in there, the Ravener?" He laughed.

Jules and Alex didn't say anything.

"Look, I was just making a joke. What in the hells have you got in there?" he asked.

"You'll see," Professor Jules said, approaching the vault doors.

She whispered something Alex couldn't hear, and abruptly, a pulse of magic flashed. With a creak, one of the doors to the chamber swung open, revealing a pedestal with a familiar orb on it.

"S'that a dungeon core?" Hart cried, his hand falling on the hilt of his sword. "A living one?"

"Why do you have a *living* dungeon core?" Drestra demanded.

"All locked up in here like s'the king's jewels, why in Uldar's name?" Cedric asked. His morphic weapon slid off his arm, turning into a spear in his hand.

The Watchers tensed.

"We were experimenting on it," Professor Jules said calmly. "And we found something that you need to see."

"See? Can't you just tell us?" Drestra asked.

"No," Professor Jules said. "It's better if you see it firsthand."

"You can relax," Alex jumped in. "There's no Ravener-spawn around to control it, and even if there were, the dungeon core's really low on mana right now..."

He took a close look at it.

The orb was still a shade of grey, but definitely darker than the last time he'd seen it. Anxiety. Fear. Power for the enemy. All intertwined.

'I wonder how they'll react?' he thought.

Luckily, he didn't have long to wait.

There was a rise of teleportation magic.

Then Baelin and Carey appeared from thin air.

"Gah, y'took a few years off me lifetime," Cedric said to Baelin before talking to Carey. "Good t'see ya again, y'been holdin' up alright?"

Carey definitely did not look like she'd been holding up alright. Not at all.

"Oh dear," Jules whispered, watching her.

Her face was pale and puffy, her nose and eyelids were red and swollen, like she'd been crying.

She probably had been.

Clearing her throat, she lowered her head to the Heroes. "I... I'm alive."

Silence hung in the air.

"Alright, no sense in wasting any more time," Baelin said, heading to the pedestal and picking up the grey orb. "We have one more teleport to make, but before that—anyone object to a flight spell being cast on them?"

Only Hart had concerns.

"You're not going to teleport us into the middle of the sky, are you?" he asked the wizard.

"Of course not. I would warn you if I were. It is just that... the ground is not exactly stable where we are going. But you shall see soon enough."

———

With a surge of teleportation magic, they appeared above the ravine. Below them, the land still looked like it had been ravaged by titans, and a cold wind swept the air.

No Ravener-spawn walked below, but hordes of animals did. Birds and insects crawled and flew through the valley, feasting on the mangled corpses of Skinless Ones.

Drestra gasped. "What happened to this dungeon?"

"I did," Baelin said simply. "One does not need a god's power to wreak terrible wrath."

"Ugh, well, that's a rank smell," Cedric waved his hand in front of his nose.

Carey took a mouthful of her stomach potion.

"What is this place?" the Chosen asked.

"A dungeon reported to us by your military," Baelin said. "And one that's still active."

"Still?" Hart asked, scanning the ruins below them. "With it all gutted? Oh yeah, because the dungeon core's still intact, I guess."

"But why bring us back ta the dungeon?" Cedric asked. "If we're here ta pick through them ruins, that's goin' t'be a bit of a nasty affair."

"No, that will not be required," Baelin said, holding the orb out to Alex and Carey. "Now, let's proceed."

Carey looked at Alex. "You go first. I... I don't think I can, yet."

"Okay," the young man said softly, taking the core.

He took a deep breath and turned to his fellow Heroes.

The last couple of visits, they'd spent time together, and he felt he'd gotten a good feel for them, at least to some extent. These three weren't fanatics. They were young, thinking folk who wanted to help others and destroy the Ravener.

Depending on how they reacted... everything could change.

CHAPTER 17

CONVICTIONS

"When ya called us up here, I never thought I'd be watchin' one o' yous carryin' around a livin' dungeon core." Cedric eyed the orb like it was a coiled snake. "Never seen anyone do that before... Almost expect it t'bite ya or somethin'."

"Yeah, if I think about it, it's the first time I've ever seen a live one up close like this." Hart inspected the core. "It's got kind of a sheen to it. Almost looks like a giant pearl."

"But more dangerous than any jewel," Drestra said, her voice crackling like flame. She looked from the orb to the Generasians. "Are we... supposed to see an image in it? Like in a crystal ball?"

"No," Alex said. "Nothing like that. As a matter of fact, you'll want to watch the wrecked dungeon down there. Oh, and Cedric, Drestra? Pay attention to your mana senses. You'll know why in a sec."

The two Heroes frowned, and Hart already had his large eyes trained on the ravine, scanning the debris and dark crevices below.

"Right... I'm watching," Cedric looked down.

"What am I looking for?" Drestra asked.

"You'll know it when you see it," Alex said, directing his mind to the core then shattering his mana into hundreds of streams and pouring it into the dungeon core. He called on the Mark and attacked the core from all sides, expecting resistance... but he needn't have bothered. The orb was stronger, but not strong enough to stop his mana. It rushed through the entrances, bypassing the core's weak attempts to eject him, and then he was in, right where he wanted to be, in the centre of the dungeon core where its magic originated.

Alex's mana had entered a control centre of sorts, like a windowless room filled with levers, dials, and buttons that drove the core, deploying its power in countless ways.

Eventually, the research team would have to explore and map it, but not today. Today was for controlling the dungeon core for the Heroes to see. So he moved his mana, sending it flowing into the centre of the core, then 'pulled a lever.'

A sudden rush of dark mana poured out.

"What?" Drestra cried. "Beware, everyone! The core, it's—"

Thoom!

From the bottom of the ravine, a five-foot wall erupted, shedding soil as it rose. Carey made a choking sound as the colour drained from her face, then she began to whisper, making the sign of Uldar over her heart.

"I can hardly believe it, even though I'm seeing it for myself," Professor Jules murmured, taking a notepad from her robes. She conjured a pair of Wizard's Hands and a pen. One held the notepad steady, while the other began to record her observations.

Baelin simply said. "And there we have it."

As for the Heroes?

They were stunned.

"Wha—?" Hart grunted, drawing his blade. His head pivoted between the orb and the wall. "What just? Cedric, Drestra! What happened? What in all the Ravener-spawning hells did I just *see*? Since I can't do any of that fancy stuff like sensing mana, *what just happened*?"

"No..." Cedric's jaw dropped. "Noooo bloody way. No. No, I must've been bewitched 'cause I'm bloody-well seein' things! Feelin' things that don't make any bloody sense! I thought I felt mana come outta the core and flow inta the gorge down there, then that bloody wall popped up!" He was wild-eyed.

Cedric ground his teeth, his gold tooth glinting in the sunlight. "No, no, no. *No*. Can't be. Did the dungeon core do that on its own? They can't do that! They need a monster to control 'em! Everybody knows that. I learned that shite from the priests a day after I got marked!" He touched the golden scales glowing on his bare chest.

"Drestra!" The Chosen turned to the Sage. "Drestra, your mana sens-es're better than mine! Drestra? *Drestra?*"

But the Sage wasn't moving.

It was like she'd become a statue in midair. Her cloak and veil blew listlessly in the brisk autumn wind. She was shivering, though Alex suspected it wasn't from the cold. Her golden reptilian eyes slowly slid from the wall below, up to the dungeon core in Alex's hand.

"Impossible," she murmured. "I felt your mana... I felt it flare and go into the core... and then that wall came out of the ground. It felt like when a dungeon commander's controlling a core... it's... oh by the spirits! Did *you* do that?"

Alex slowly nodded. "Yeah. It takes a lot of practice with mana manipulation, and when the core's fully powered, it'll fight you like a demon, but yeah. You saw what you saw, and you felt what you felt. I truly controlled it."

His eyes drifted from Hero to Hero, noting their body language.

Cedric oozed disbelief. He'd crossed his arms defensively, and his openness wavered before Alex's eyes. He was trembling. Drestra was stiff, and though her veil hid most of her face, her emotions came off her in waves, just like the aeld tree.

Disbelief. Fear.

...Anger.

As for Hart?

Alex couldn't really read him. The Champion's body language was a jumble, too alien for him to distinguish one past Champion from the next. But his face?

Shock had faded.

His jaw was set.

His eyes were measuring. Calculating. Like the experienced soldier he was.

All of a sudden, a deep sound boomed off the ravine and soared above the trees as Cedric burst out laughing. His head was thrown back, his eyes were closed. But the laughter had no trace of humour. It was harsh and cynical, and he kept it up until he was coughing, breathless, and his voice was hoarse.

When he finally opened his eyes, they were hard, ringed with anger, and something else. Mixed emotions? Maybe uncertainty? Maybe fear?

"Look, if'n this is some kinda bloody joke that you people are puttin' on, then s'not bloody funny." The Chosen's voice was like flint, and his eyes raked over all four Generasian wizards before returning to Alex. "What's this, some sort o' illusion? Some trick?" They flicked back and forth between Carey and Alex. "The two o' you should know better, bein' fellow Thameish an' all! Draggin' us all the way out here for some cruel trick. I'd expect that from the fae, but you lot?"

An eyebrow rose, his eyes filled with suspicion, and Alex watched him closely. There was something fighting within him. Confusion? Recognition and denial? Desperation? Horror? Either way, Cedric's outrage was shaky. Anger was leaving his voice. "An' you, Alex, back in the—"

"Stop," a deep voice cut in.

Hart was looking at Cedric with an expression that could've been carved from stone. "Stop. You're not making any sense and you know it. Why would this be a joke? You sound like you've lost your mind."

Cedric whirled on Hart, going red in the face, then bit back his words. His attention turned to the orb. "Bloody hell... just... bloody hell," was all he said.

"And now you can see why we wanted to show you this," Baelin said. "And why we kept quiet about the details until you could see it for yourselves. You didn't believe your eyes when the evidence was right in front of you. You certainly wouldn't have believed anything we simply told you, and I cannot blame you. As we've been discussing, this has been an unforeseen development that calls many things into question."

"Many, many things," Drestra agreed. "How... how did you learn about it?"

Alex glanced at Baelin. "We were here investigating a dungeon and looking to get our hands on a living dungeon core to see if we could figure out how it made its monsters. But... while I was messing with it... well, you just saw what happened."

"By Uldar," the Sage said. "This is... this could change the war. But how did you make it work? Did you use some special mana technique from Generasi?"

"No," he said. "As a matter of fact, you and Cedric could probably do it with a few minutes of practice. The core doesn't have much mana left, so it won't be strong enough to stop you."

"What... *what*? By wildfire," the Sage swore. "Well, if you could do it... and Cedric and I could—"

"Ugh, bloody hell, can't bloody believe it." Cedric ran both hands through his hair. "Can't bloody believe what I'm listenin' to. Mortals controllin' dungeon cores? Not even the most crazed doomsayer could think up such bloody nonsense."

Drestra looked at him, then at Baelin. "So when you did it, Chancellor Baelin, you must have—"

Now it was Baelin's turn to laugh. Cedric and Drestra startled, but Hart was still focused on the ravine, calculating.

"Oh, no, I cannot do it," the chancellor said frankly. "Unfortunately, I could not even begin to try."

He explained how he couldn't interact with the dungeon core.

Now Hart's focus shifted back to the wizards. "It kinda sounds like a gate that only opens for some folk, but not others." He looked at Alex. "And if it only opened for you, why do you think Drestra and Cedric'd be able to do it?"

"Because I, to my dismay, did it too."

The Heroes' heads abruptly turned toward Carey.

"I'm afraid it's true," she said. The young Thameish woman set her jaw and held out her hands to Alex. "Would you be ever so kind as to hand me the dungeon core?"

A determined look had taken her features, and Alex did as she asked. "You need... any guidance?"

"No, it'd be better if I did it myself," she didn't try to hide her bitterness, "and show off this... *gift*—" disgust had joined the bitterness of her words "—that's been given to us."

"What d'you mea—" Cedric started but trailed off.

Carey's eyes were closed. She gripped the orb tightly between both hands, and her knuckles paled. Alex felt her mana pierce the dungeon core.

She was slower than he was; minutes passed as they floated in silence, with Drestra, Cedric, and Hart watching the core, Alex and Baelin watching Carey, and Professor Jules' Wizard's Hands taking notes.

Time dragged by, Carey stayed focused, until finally, she found her way into the centre and took a deep breath.

Alex felt her mana twisting, trying to catch on to... anything inside the core.

Then a rush of dark mana exploded.

Thoom!

In the valley below, earth shuddered, and a patch of soil became a spewing mound of mud. It reminded Alex of Vesuvius' shell.

"Damn my eyes," Cedric muttered. "Damn my bloody eyes!"

Carey handed the dungeon core back to Alex without a word. Her fingers clenched and released, her face quivered as though she were fighting tears, but beneath that, her anger was unmistakable.

"There you have it. So far, I'm the only one—aside from Alex—who can control this thing." She bit her lip, her tone resentful. "Do you want to take a guess as to what Alex and I have in common that no other member of the research team does?"

"You're both Thameish," Hart said. "I remember that there's nobody else from Thameland who's part of your expedition."

"There's another thing, holy Champion: we're both *followers* of Uldar," she said, and her words were solemn, like she was pronouncing a death sentence.

The air seemed to grow colder.

"...Oh. *Oh*," Drestra said, her voice very quiet. "*Oh*."

"It just keeps gettin' better n' better," the Chosen said, looking up at the sky, his eyes searching through the blue. "What're you thinkin' up there, Uldar? What's the plan in all this?"

"Why... would only our people be able to use it?" Drestra asked.

"That's not the question you need to be asking," Hart growled.

All eyes turned to him.

"This tells me something. Either we've been lied to, or every scholar, priest, and Hero who came before us have been the biggest idiots ever born." He shook his head, clearly irritated. "And you can't tell me *nobody* ever picked up a dungeon core in the last how many thousand years and thought to fiddle with it. C'mon, I've seen enough wizards to know they're all the same—no offence meant to you four—poking around in all kinds of different magic stuff. I can't believe that not even one of them ever tinkered with a core. It'd be like expecting a fish not to bite at a worm. Way too tempting to ignore."

"You're thinkin' folk're lyin' to us?" Cedric asked.

"Yeah, I kinda do," Hart said. "It wouldn't be the first time I've been hired by someone to do a dirty job, only to find out the job's a hell of a lot dirtier than they said. Mercenaries get lied to all the time. You know why?"

He bared his teeth. "Because a lot of lords think we're fodder. And I sure as hell don't like being treated like *fodder*."

Alex saw doubt go through the other Heroes.

This... this was going better than he could have hoped.

Drestra looked at Hart. "You're right, something is wrong. This is too big to *never* have been noticed. And the fact that we've only seen followers of Uldar control this core, well... it makes me wonder. You said Cedric or I could do this, Alex?"

"Yeah," he said.

"Good." She held her hand out. "I want to try it and see for myself. Then... we have a *lot* to talk about."

CHAPTER 18

THE NEXT STAGE

The Hero took the dungeon core between her hands.

It wasn't the first time she'd seen one, of course, but it was the first time she'd had any interest in examining a living one. Representatives of the church and the Thameish army had shown her and the other Heroes drawings of dungeon cores in the capital the first time they'd ever met, which was soon after they'd been marked for Uldar's work.

The priests had filled their heads with as much knowledge of the Ravener as they had time for. In other words, a lot of information in very little time since dungeons and Ravener-spawn had been springing up and running wild all over the kingdom. Those days seemed so long ago, yet it'd been only a little over a year since she'd been marked at eighteen.

It was hard to believe that she'd been away from her home in the Crymlyn for only over a year now. It felt like a lifetime at times, but in fact, she'd just turned nineteen not too many months ago.

Undeniably very, very young for her kind.

Since they'd left the capital, she'd seen dozens of living cores over the course of their battles. Some had been so powerful—so fueled on the fear of mortals—that their darkness would have eclipsed the deepest, moonless night. Those battles were fierce and prolonged. They'd also fought dungeons with cores so starved of mana, that they'd been nearly colourless, and thankfully, were destroyed with ease.

In all of those encounters, neither she, Cedric, nor any priest had ever thought to stop, pick up a dungeon core, and examine it. Destroying them as quickly and as decisively as possible then moving on was always the end goal of every battle. In the war against the Ravener, there was no time to stop and wonder about the nature of dungeon cores. Today, they'd have to make time, so she took a good hard look at the core she held.

Visually, there was nothing unique, interesting, or unusual about it. Nothing to hint at the world-changing revelation that this thing—no bigger than the average mortal head—had revealed. Rubbing her hands over it only told her one thing: that it was even smoother than ice.

No more delaying, then.

Time to see if she could get inside.

Taking a deep breath, Drestra reached deep into her mana. The Mark of the Sage flared, and it was like the light of the sun flowing through her body. Power sparked at her fingertips as she found the mana entrances and wasted no time in going forward.

"Wait!" Alex called suddenly.

Drestra paused. "What's wrong?"

"Before you keep going, I just want to warn you that we have no idea if there'll be consequences from doing this," he said. "It may be possible that taking over a core could make you a target of the Ravener."

"That's absolutely true," Professor Jules said, her face a mask of concern. "These are uncharted waters, as it were, and we don't have nearly enough data to say for certain what taking control of one of these cores could mean for you. To be fair, as long as you can feel the entrances to its mana pathways, that proves you can do it, so there's no need to go any further."

Drestra looked down at the orb. "I need to see this for myself. Besides, I'm a Hero of Uldar. I'm already one of the Ravener's targets, wouldn't you say?"

Her power flowed, and she felt the dark mana rising, desperate to eject her.

'How strange...' she thought. 'I never thought that one of these things could feel fear.'

But there was no mistaking how its mana frantically thrashed.

It was *actually* afraid.

'What a curious thing, and how very satisfying,' she thought before pushing deep into its mana pathways and quashing all resistance. Drestra was no expert in mana manipulation. It was a complex art and most witches in the Crymlyn relied very little on it. But considering its weak resistance—alongside the overwhelming power of her mana and the Mark

—she didn't need it. Before long, she'd made her way to the centre of the core.

...and there was something curious in there.

Something that she could interact with if she just moved her mana in the right way. She felt around like she was in a dark cave, moving her mana in different ways until... she connected.

Whoom.

Drestra gasped in astonishment.

It was true!

Images of darkness flowed through her mind, but before she could catch and make sense of them, they abruptly vanished, like they'd been cut off. Mana flowed from the dungeon core into the ravine, then her mind shifted, and for a moment, she felt it connect to something below.

Unfamiliar thoughts filtered to her through the orb; suddenly, she knew what she could do. If she could just reach them—

"Oh, *bleeding hells!*" Cedric cried.

There was a shimmer along the wall Alex had made.

And from it?

A monster was being born.

The Ravener was incensed.

Things were escaping its grasp!

There were *three* now!

Three!

In its dark chamber, mana was still constructing the spawn that would put an end to these Usurpers. Its Hunters sensed their master's distress. The guardians filling the cavern roared as one, the noise echoing through the tunnels.

Its thoughts were not on them.

They were churning, assessing the situation and its protocols. It examined records deep within, reaching back through all the cycles all the way to memories of the first battles against the first Heroes, long dead.

Five glowing golden symbols ran through its memories, but it was not Heroes that were its focus: cycle by cycle, it measured the number of times that Usurpers were more than two.

Aside from very specific circumstances in the earliest cycles, more than two Usurpers existing at the same time had occurred but twice since those early days. It examined its options.

Time to block the Usurpers.

First, it severed the usurped dungeon core from its link.

Then, it released some of the restraint placed on the other dungeon cores. They would still be limited in the kinds of spawn they could create, but now, they could birth servants faster. More efficiently.

This would create more fear and more fuel, hopefully leaving the enemy too distracted to organise.

After that? It could do nothing more.

It retreated into itself, waiting for the Petrifier to be ready.

Alex stared at a half-formed Skinless One emerging from the wall. Only a misshapen torso had come through, only to then collapse in a writhing heap of flesh. The dungeon core was almost completely clear now. Drestra using it to produce the partly formed Ravener-spawn had taken all it had left.

Cedric swore.

Carey gaped, while Professor Jules' Wizard's Hand scribbled even faster.

Baelin simply watched, while Drestra was transfixed by the creature.

Hart's reaction was different. He acted.

In one smooth motion, he drew his thick longbow from his back, nocked an arrow and—

Twang!

—sent it rocketing downward with all his immense strength.

It slammed into the half-creature's forehead, ending its writhing.

Drestra swore. "*Hart*, why did you do that?"

Hart gave her a look. "Because a monster appeared, and I didn't feel like asking it over here for an ale. Why? Were you planning on doing something with it?"

"I wanted to *control it*," she said.

Alex's interest spiked. "What? Hold on now, you could've controlled it?"

"Yessss, do go on, my child." Baelin leaned in, his goat-like eyes gleaming with interest.

"There... there was a connection between me and the creature, coming from the dungeon core," she said. "And at the same time, I sensed something. I think if I'd moved my mana the right way, I might've been able to take control of it."

119

"Then you did not have control immediately?" Baelin asked. "Fascinating. The cores can create monsters, yet controlling them is a different operation. Incredibly fascinating. This information will certainly serve as quite the roadmap for future investigation."

"Absolutely," Professor Jules said. "I'm dying to know how it ticks. How it does *everything* it does. When you think about it, these dungeon cores not only produce matter out of pure mana, but they're able to create life. *Complex life*. If we could reverse engineer that... forget a revolution of magical technology; we could bring the entire *world's* technology and quality of life forward by millennia. Gah, you three are lucky. I'd love to be able to poke around in it myself."

"Yeah, that's the thing I *really* want to find out next," Alex said. "What's the exact criteria for accessing the core? Drestra, are you a follower of Uldar?"

Drestra was staring at the dungeon core, and Alex could almost see the gears turning in her mind. "Hm? I'm sorry?"

"It's okay. It's... I know, it's a lot to digest. But, are you a follower of Uldar?"

"Yes... though not as devout as many," she said.

"Damn. That means we still don't have an answer. It'd be really helpful if we could figure out what the *exact* trigger for being able to control a core is. Is it being Thameish? Is it following Uldar? Is it both? Is it some other variable that we haven't even considered?"

"Hmmm." Drestra's brow furrowed. "An interesting question. I—"

"Why are none o' yous not losin' your collective shite over this?" Cedric asked, his voice thin and strained. "You all seem so bloody calm while it's takin' everythin' fer me not t'start bloody screamin'. Look, if'n folk of Thameland can control these things then why're we botherin' fightin' all these cores? Why're they attackin' us? And why don't them church priests *talk about this*? You'd think it'd be a *wee* bit important! An' shite, if they've been lyin'..."

"I kinda want to bust down the doors of the cathedral, grab High Priest Tobias, and shake him until he squeals, maybe even dangle him from a parapet," Hart said. "But maybe I'll settle for Merzhin instead... Though I suppose we shouldn't spread this yet."

"Right," Cedric said. "We talk about this too loud an' too soon an' it'd be like kickin' a nest o' wasps an' fire ants barefoot. Who knows what's gonna come pourin' outta the ground, but whatever it is, y'know it's gonna be angry an' dangerous."

"And the Ravener is still trying to kill all of us," Drestra said. "If this spreads too quickly and in the wrong way... there'll be panic and more fuel for the enemy. If it really is our enemy. I don't even know anymore."

Cedric looked at the four wizards intently, eyes lingering on Carey. Despite the potion, she still looked like she was about to be sick. "Look, if'n you all want ta leave this land, I won't blame yous. This here's... s'pretty shit. We don't know where it's gonna go, an' this ain't your fight. Whatever the hell's goin' on, an' whatever the truth is, we were marked for this fight. Not yous. If'n you want to leave, I'd understand."

Jules and Baelin burst out laughing, and a heartbeat later, so did Alex. Even Carey gave a weak smile.

"Oh, you don't know us, Cedric," Alex said. "We're on the trail of maybe the greatest magical discovery of like ten lifetimes. I don't think wild dragons could pull us away now."

A wave of amusement showed in Drestra's body language.

"Well said, Alex," Baelin said. "We are here to aid *and* investigate. Of course we are going to stay, but you are right about one thing. This revelation should remain as known to as few as possible. Do not forget that the Cult of Ezaliel still wanders these shores. They must not hear of this. It would not be below them to use Thameish citizens to capture dungeon cores and enslave them to do their demonic master's bidding."

"Yeah, and... I hate to say it, but doesn't this revelation really look bad for the church... maybe even the king?" Alex scratched his head awkwardly. Speaking high treason and blasphemy in one sentence made him kind of nervous. "If there's enemies within our own ranks, and I feel that there are, we don't want to tip our hand."

"Aye... an' it is *our* hand, innit?" Cedric said. "I swear you bloody lot of foreigners—an' you too, Alex an' Carey—are the only ones in this damn war who've been tellin' us the whole truth."

The *whole* truth.

Alex winced internally, thinking about the Mark on his shoulder, hidden beneath his clothes and the spell he and Thundar had created. He hadn't told the Heroes the whole truth. He and Baelin hadn't told them who he really was or how exactly he'd *first* learned that dungeon cores could be controlled.

At least things were starting to move in a direction where it wouldn't be a disaster if they found out. They had growing doubts about the church now, as far as he could tell, and they might not be so eager to drag him off in chains if he came clean with them.

But not yet.

Let this information filter through their minds. Let it steep, then he'd see what he'd see. For now, they'd probably nurse it, discuss things, while the expedition focused on narrowing down the catalyst—

"Do you have time for another teleport today, Baelin?" Drestra asked.

The ancient wizard paused, looking like he'd been caught off guard.

"I do. I assumed this development would require time and attention. Why do you ask? Do you wish to return to your duties?"

"No, not yet. You said you weren't sure if the trigger was being Thameish or worshipping Uldar, right? So that means we need to test it on someone who's Thameish but does not worship him," the Sage continued. "If you have the time and can teleport all of us close to my home, then we might be able to get that question resolved."

She paused, in thought.

"Maybe even today, if we're lucky."

CHAPTER 19

THE WITCH'S SUGGESTION

"What?" Alex asked, excitement surging through him. "How? How're we resolving this today?"

Drestra's reptilian eyes were focused on the wizards and her fellow Heroes. "This is somewhat of an open secret, but I still don't want anyone going to the priests with what I'm about to say."

She looked directly at Cedric. "That means you too, Cedric."

His face turned red. "Wait... why're you lookin' at *me* like that?"

"Because you get along with those priests, and I know Hart, and from what these folks just said, I doubt any of them are going to be talking about this or what I'm about to say to priests or anyone else for that matter."

"After this shite, Drestra, I don't know what I'm thinkin' about priests." He crossed his powerful arms. "I ain't goin' t'go so far n' say that I hate all o' 'em, but... bloody hell, I trust 'em a helluva lot less."

Carey visibly winced. "I... I'm sure there's honourable members of..." was all she managed to say. "But we've made a pact not to speak of anything to do with the dungeon core, and of course, I won't say a word to anyone about what you're about to tell us, Drestra."

"Good, now that that's out of the way," the Sage said. "Deep in the Crymlyn, not every witch worships Uldar. Some practise only the old ways. Generations might well have passed, but to this day, they still despise the church and priests of Uldar. They've never forgiven or forgotten what they did. These are witches who're Thameish by birth and blood, but they reject him and his church."

"I could understand why," Baelin said. "So you're saying that one of those witches could be the perfect case study to test the core with. Hmm... And would you personally know one of these hold-outs? Someone you know *and* trust?"

"Yes," she said. "Someone I know well. The witches of the old ways don't have *much* to do with those of us who worship both Uldar and the old ways, but we still meet to take care of the swamp, and we unite in difficult times. One of my closest friends is one who still follows the old ways, and I'd trust her with my life."

"Excellent. Would she be open to testing the dungeon core? Perhaps not going as far as to attempt to control it, however. If they are able to access it with their mana, then we'll know without a doubt that they would be able to probe it. If they find no entrances for their mana? Then we can rule them and the question of being Thameish and a follower of Uldar out."

"That's what I was thinking," Drestra agreed. "Then we'll have an answer to one of our questions."

"How close can you teleport to the Crymlyn, Baelin?" Alex asked.

The chancellor's eyes seemed to lose focus, viewing something only he saw hovering before his eyes. "I took something of a tour of Thameland when we were negotiating with King Athelstan, and I did pay a visit to Wrexiff, which is Carey's hometown and quite near the Crymlyn."

Alex's blood ran cold. Going to a town would mean people, specifically, soldiers and priests.

"However," Baelin continued. "I think it would be wiser to teleport to somewhere in a nearby forest instead. There's less likelihood that priests will be in the wilderness to ask us our business and perhaps rather awkward questions, particularly when they see three Heroes in our party, which could lead to a tipping of our hand before we are ready to tip it."

Alex fought the sigh of relief he was suppressing. Things were shifting. With the Heroes being brought into the expedition's secrets, and him becoming more important to the city and the university, priests having the power to just drag him away was lessening. His own personal power was also a factor in how much had changed for him since he'd left Thameland.

When he was first marked, there was nothing he could physically do if a few priests caught him and dragged him off to war. Now, especially with Claygon beside him, any priests who considered grabbing him had better be prepared for one hell of a fight. Still, there was also Selina, Theresa, and her family to keep in mind. For now, keeping his secret until he was ready to reveal it was what needed to be done.

"That's reasonable," Hart said. "Honestly, the less people that find out about this the better. In war, you don't go sharing intelligence with anyone unless you're sure they're your ally, and right now, we don't know *who* our allies are."

"Hm. I like the way you think," Baelin said. "My proposal is that we teleport to a remote location I visited when we first arrived in Thameland. Just an out-of-the-way little spot in the wilderness. From there, I can teleport us to locations within my line of sight until we reach the edge of the swamp. Then, we can fly under the cover of trees until we reach our final destination. We will need to move quickly as I can't keep my more important meetings and tasks waiting indefinitely."

"Fine by me," Cedric grunted. "When y'find out the battle y'been fightin' for over a year might be tied up in some kinda great, big, dirty secret, you make that a priority."

"Would it be okay if I came with you?" Alex said. "I can bring Claygon for extra protection, and I really would like to be there for the test."

"Hah!" Baelin laughed. "It is adorable that you think extra protection might be needed."

"Hey, what if it takes longer than today and you have to go back to Generasi?" Alex pointed out. "It could happen."

"Well, let's hope it doesn't." He and Alex exchanged a subtle glance. "But you have a fair point. In that case, I think we should return to the encampment for supplies in case our stay has to be extended." He looked at Professor Jules and Carey. "Will you be joining us?"

"Hrm," Jules frowned. "As much as I want to see the experiment with my own eyes... I am not good in the wilderness, and even less so in a fight. And I have heard the Crymlyn Swamp is somewhat dangerous."

"You heard right," Drestra said. "We learn magic in part to defend ourselves."

"Mmm, then how about—when you've located Drestra's friend, and if she agrees to do the test, you teleport back to the encampment and fetch me? Then I can be there to observe the outcome without holding the rest of you back."

"I-if it's quite alright, I would be ever so grateful if that could extend to me as well," Carey said. "I would like to be there too. Please. If I'm not there, I think the suspense will drive me mad. But I also know I'd just be dead weight in a fight, and if folk who've manipulated these cores are actually targeted by monsters... or others, I don't want to be out there too long to get myself or any of you in trouble."

"A mature decision," Baelin said. "And the answer, of course, is yes. After all, it takes just a few droplets more mana and a scant few heartbeats' worth of time to do so. Now, if we're done here, let's return to camp and collect our supplies. Then, it's away to visit Drestra's community. The sooner we start, the more likely I can see our rather important journey through to the end."

"Absolutely," Professor Jules said. "And the sooner we'll have an answer one way or the other."

'But whichever way it turns out,' Alex thought, 'I get the feeling it's trouble. Big trouble.'

"You're heading back out so soon?" Theresa asked from the tent's entrance.

She watched as Alex shoved clothing into a rucksack and organised his supply of potions.

"Yeah," her partner said, checking the colour of a potion. "We should be back in a day... maybe three or four tops if things end up taking longer than we expect them to."

Theresa crossed her arms. "And it's just you, Baelin, and the Heroes?"

"And Claygon." He buckled the rucksack. "Don't forget Claygon. Oh, and I wouldn't say that I'm *just* travelling with Baelin and the Heroes: Baelin alone is probably the nastiest fighting force in all of Thameland. We'll be fine."

"And... no one else can come with you?" Her hands dropped to her swords, and she adjusted her chain shirt and bow slung on her back. As soon as he'd returned and the announcement was made that they were heading back out, she'd prepped for battle.

But disappointment soon replaced her excitement when the chancellor said they would be travelling alone.

"Yeah, I want you to come with me too." Alex's expression was both disappointed and apologetic. "But Baelin said he wants to keep the group as small as possible in case there's priests or soldiers around.

"It took some convincing for him to even let me bring Claygon along... Priests shouldn't be in the swamp, according to Drestra, but in these times, there's no guarantee where they might be. So moving in a small group means we'll be more agile."

"I know," she said, disappointment in her voice. "That... that makes sense. You just be careful out there, okay?"

"I will." He stood up, went to her, and wrapped her in his arms before kissing her. They stood near the tent flap, connected to each other for too short of a time. Then Alex spoke, trying to reassure her. "And with Baelin along, we'll definitely be okay."

"Yeah, true. And if you find something out there that can take *him*, you'll have bigger problems. I'm just worried that if you're out there long enough and he's needed back in Generasi... what then? Maybe you could suggest that—if he has to come back—he teleports me to your group. I'm no Baelin, but my swords should help, and the group would still be small."

"Actually, that's not a bad idea," Alex said. "I'll suggest that to him if he has to go back to Generasi."

"Good," she said. "I can have everyone's ba—wait, what are you giggling at?"

Alex had broken into unsuppressed giggles. Glancing behind and finding no one around, she stepped into the tent and closed the flap behind her. "What's suddenly got you so giddy?"

"Well, think about it," he snorted. "If you replace Baelin, that means it'll be a group of five. The Sage, the Chosen, the Saint—" His voice dropped to the lowest of whispers. "Then there's me, the Fool... and think about it."

"Think about what?"

"You practise life enforcement." He grinned, his eyes dancing with amusement and triumph. "It's like you're our alternate Saint. We've got the whole Hero roster down!"

"Pfffft, I'm no Saint, Alex. And you know it."

"You're a saint to me," he whispered, his voice taking on a cheesy tone. "You're the only saint in my li—Mh!"

She pressed her hand to his mouth. "Alex, even if you were trying to be serious, I would never fall for that."

His mouth opened and her hand suddenly felt wet.

"Agh!" she cried, pulling her hand away. "Did... did you just lick my palm?"

"You don't seem to mind when Brutus does it." He laughed.

She stared at her hand, then frowned at him.

"Before you say anything," he warned, "I want you to remember that you chose me. You chose me above everyone else. You picked me —Agh!"

Theresa wiped her palm on his forehead. "There. Now we're both gross. We should—"

"We are nearly ready!" Baelin's voice boomed through the camp. "Hart, Alex! If you would be so kind as to join us, then we can begin!"

"Well, that's me," Alex said, kissing her three more times then shouldering his pack. "I'll talk to Baelin, and... if he has to come back, I'll see you in the Crymlyn."

"See you," she whispered. "Keep safe."

"I will."

Claygon was standing beside the tent and the three of them made their way to the glowing aeld where Baelin, Cedric, and Drestra were waiting, talking with their friends who'd come to see Alex off.

Hart strode from somewhere in the camp, having helped himself—with Baelin's permission—to supplies he'd loaded into an immense pack he carried on his back. He looked like a turtle... and giggling, Theresa whispered that she was wondering if Tyris might enjoy having *two* turtles around. Drestra obviously heard her; she'd started giggling.

Professor Jules and Carey were amongst the gathered expedition members.

"I'll make note of what we've observed so far," she said. "And then return to Generasi to let the other expedition leads know what's happened. What we've uncovered is obviously something they should know about without delay. If you come back today and I'm gone, just talk to Watcher Shaw, Baelin."

"I hope you'll all be safe," Carey said.

"Of course. Well, no time like the present. We're off! When we return, we will be one step closer to solving this mystery. Farewell to all for now," Baelin said.

Alex gave Theresa a little wave as the ancient wizard spoke words of power.

And then he, Alex, Claygon, and the Heroes vanished.

Theresa bit her lip. "Left behind again."

She looked at her swords.

Her fists clenched.

It was time to practice. Hard.

CHAPTER 20

THE TELEPORTATION SHUFFLE

I t was snowing.

Alex Roth appeared in a meadow, standing on a low rise overlooking a crossroads twenty paces to the south. A damp chill filled the air, and with it came wet, white flakes drifting from a sky of steel grey clouds. The wind was low, yet moist and brisk, and he wrapped his cloak tighter around his broad shoulders.

It wasn't cold enough for the snow to stay, but there was little doubt about one thing:

"Winter's almost here," Alex whispered as the air around him began to shimmer.

As one, the rest of the party appeared: the chancellor, the Heroes, and Claygon. Cedric and Hart immediately checked their surroundings—their hands on their weapons—searching for signs of danger, but Drestra was looking at Alex.

"Did you get here... before us?" she asked.

Alex shrugged. "I guess so? Quirks of magic can be weird."

"Aye?" Cedric raised an eyebrow, looking at the young Thameish wizard closely. "Have t'take yer word for it. Don't know much about teleportation magic."

"Magic in general is variable." Baelin surveyed the land with his hands on his hips. "For example, if one had need to codify the damage dealt by attack spells using pen and paper, I would imagine it would require some sort of complicated dice system to simulate."

"I'll take yer word for it." Cedric shrugged and his shining spear melded into a gauntlet over his arm. "For the most part, all I need t'know about spells is how fast they make Ravener-spawn go boom."

Baelin looked sharply at Cedric, his expression slightly hurt. "Oh, you will miss so much of the wonders of wizardry that way, Cedric. You cannot have such a plebian understanding of magic!" He stroked his beard-braids. "As a matter of fact, this is an excellent opportunity for a lesson in some higher forms of wizardry. Congratulations, almighty Chosen, wise Sage, and mighty Champion: today, you will be honorary members of Generasi University. I shall teach you a lesson usually only offered in Tele-4500—a fourth year course dedicated entirely to the study of teleportation magic."

"Ooooo!" Alex clapped excitedly, looking at his fellow Heroes. "You're all in for a *treat*!"

"Uh... I'll take your word for it," Hart said, his large eyes darting back and forth. He looked out of his element. "Won't be much good to me, unless I've got to explain to a wizard their own business. Then again, if I ever end up on a wizard-hunt after the war, I guess it'd do me some good to know more of their tricks."

Cedric and Drestra shot him horrified looks. The Chosen subtly inclined his head toward Baelin, who was—of course—standing right there.

The Champion shrugged. "What? It's a living. And a good one, at that."

"He's right! It *is* a living. And if I was offended by wizard-killers, I would be offended at myself! Young Hart, I hope you can use this knowledge for your economic gain in the future. As for Alex, Cedric, and Drestra..." Baelin turned north. "I am going to show you a lovely little trick *you* can perform when you learn long-range teleportation magic. It will make travelling far quicker and pleasanter."

"Uhhh, what tier's this fancy teleportation stuff?" Cedric leaned toward Alex.

"Teleport's fifth-tier," Alex said, rubbing his hands together. "Only three tiers away for me."

'And maybe only *two* tiers away soon enough, if Operation Grand Summoning Ascension keeps going well,' he thought.

"*Fifth*, y'say? Well, I don't think I'll be learnin' any o' that fancy high level magic any time soon, then," Cedric said. "An'...d'we got time for this, y'think?" He looked at the dungeon core which was stuffed into a satchel slung over Baelin's mail-covered shoulder. "Solvin' a mystery o' these cores seems a bit on the pressin' side."

Baelin looked at the Sage. "Drestra, regarding your friend whom we are about to visit, would you say she will likely disappear within the next ten minutes or so?"

Drestra raised an eyebrow. "No?"

"Excellent! Then I do believe we have ten minutes to spare for this little lesson." The chancellor smiled at Cedric. "Remember, young man, the opportunity to gain knowledge does not come often, and once you have knowledge, you have it forever."

"Right... Bloody hell, you sound like my nan," Cedric said. "I still don't think I'll be learnin' such magics any time soon."

"So do it later, then! It will be a good lesson for you, whether you learn it in two days, two years, or twenty years. Now, pay attention. Folk are usually willing to pay a lord's ransom to learn such tricks." The ancient wizard indicated a high hill far to the north with a nod of his head.

By Alex's estimate, it might be a fifteen-minute walk to its summit.

"When one is teleporting," Baelin explained, "one can only transport themselves and their passengers to one of two sorts of locations. The first is what most wizards use Teleport to reach: a place they have already personally visited. This has very obvious uses. For instance, I can do this!"

With a few words of power, the chancellor disappeared.

Heartbeats later, he was back and holding a porcelain cup of a steaming hot beverage. "See this?" He took a sip. "I retrieved it from my office in the university. And now—"

He vanished.

Cedric looked at Drestra. "Why can't you do that?"

She glared at him. "Why can't *you*?"

Baelin reappeared, empty handed. "—and now I have placed the cup in my office in the research building right here in Thameland. Learning Teleport essentially means you can wake up in the morning in your residence, go off to adventure somewhere in the wide world, and then be back home for supper! You can also use it to escape danger and accomplish a host of other tasks."

Drestra's eyes were very wide now, and she was hanging on to the chancellor's every word. Alex, of course, was enraptured too. He imagined himself visiting Theresa's parents for lunch and then teleporting back to Generasi in time for class.

"But of course," Baelin continued. "The restriction of needing to visit a location before teleporting to it is somewhat limiting. It means travelling to an area the old-fashioned way first. That is why I took some time to travel through Thameland some months ago, so that I could tele-port within reasonably close distances to just about any location on this grand isle you call home."

Alex raised his hand, and the ancient wizard gave him an amused look. "Yes, Alex?"

"Is there a way to get around that limitation?" he asked. "Some, I don't know, ninth-tier spell that lets you teleport to anywhere you can think of?"

"Possibly," Baelin said. "The Plane Shift spell, for example, lets one travel to another plane despite never having visited it before. Unfortu-nately, that spell simply transports you to *anywhere* on that plane. Most inconvenient. There *is* a graduate research team hard at work trying to develop a sort of 'Greater Teleport' spell of perhaps sixth or even seventh tier. In theory, it would be able to transport you to any location in the world—regardless of distance—so long as you could visualise it, even if you only had a mere passing description, or even a painting of the loca-tion to go by. But such a spell does not yet exist."

He spread his arms over the landscape. "Teleport is not always used to reach places that you have already visited. There is a second type of desti-nation that it is not *often* used to reach."

He pointed at his eye. "Teleport can also take you anywhere that you can see at present, provided you can see the *exact* location where you will be arriving. So, no teleporting deep into a thick forest, where you cannot see where you will appear. Now, most do not use Teleport for such purposes. There are lower-tier spells more often used for short-range travel. But—if you have enough mana—you can chain these teleports together in a nifty little method of travel that we archwizards like to call 'The Teleportation Shuffle'."

"Cute name," Drestra said.

"Kinda like a dance," Alex added.

"A dance of the cosmic power, perhaps." The ancient wizard chuck-led. "So let us say that you wish to go somewhere, but! Gasp! You have *not* been there before! Whatever shall you do? Well, for most wizards, they would be forced to use flight spells, mounts, or their own feet to journey there first. But what if I told you there was a faster way? A way that has the advantage of utter expediency! To demonstrate... I will cast a spell on you, so keep all limbs inside the wagon, so to speak."

Baelin spoke an incantation.

"Wait, wha—" Hart started.

The world vanished in a flash and—a heartbeat later—Alex was standing on the high hill to the north. The others materialised around him.

Cedric looked around. "Well, y'saved us a little bit of a walk. About five or ten minutes by my reckonin'."

"Indeed! But this is where the lesson truly begins." Baelin gazed over the landscape below. From the hill, they could see for miles and miles. Forests and wild meadows blended together across the land, and in the far distance, farmers' fallow fields and cottages lay empty.

Seeing them touched Alex. In happier times, cottage chimneys would be puffing smoke, and folk would be out gathering wood and other bounties of the land for winter. He spotted a far-off windmill, bringing back his last adventure in Greymoor.

'Hopefully, this trip to the Crymlyn'll be a *bit* less eventful,' he thought, patting Claygon's arm.

"So, we have a good vantage point from here," Baelin said. "And this is where the Teleportation Shuffle truly shows its worth. We can see far more of the countryside from this hill, which allows us to teleport much farther than we could from the crossroads."

"That makes sense," Drestra said. "You can see farther into the horizon."

"Yeah." Alex frowned, deep in thought.

Memories returned to him. Of seeing Mt. Tai through a portal in the Cave of the Traveller and of the four elemental peaks in the Rhinean Empire.

"If I were doing this," he said, "the first place I'd teleport to is the top of a tall mountain. Then I could see dozens of miles—maybe even farther —and be able to teleport a much greater distance."

"Indeed, now you are getting it, but hold on to that thought of your mountain," Baelin said. "There are additional complications to consider. For instance, let us say we wanted to teleport, oooooh... over there." He pointed to a copse of trees to the north; it looked to be at least two miles away. "What complications could occur when we got there?"

"Why do I feel like I'm bein' lectured by a clan elder?" Cedric muttered.

"Well," Alex jumped in eagerly. "First of all, just because we can see it, doesn't mean we know it's safe to teleport there. We could teleport in front of those trees and find an army of angry bears waiting. Or that the ground's unstable, and as soon as we get there, we fall into a sink-hole. Or find that there's gas leaking from the ground somewhere. Basically, the farther you're teleporting to without knowing the place, the less information you'll have about what you'll find when you get there."

"*Exactly,*" Baelin said. "Just because one can see it from a distance, does not mean we have the full picture of all threats that might be there. And that is why I told you to keep your mountain idea in mind, Alex."

He cleared his throat. "Let me tell you a story. There was once a very arrogant archwizard by the name of Yem the Invincible. He lived in the early days of wizardry, so there is an argument to be made that he was *the* most powerful mortal wizard of his day. So powerful, in fact, that he went wherever he pleased and whenever he pleased using the Teleportation Shuffle; he felt that his defensive magics could handle any threat. One day, he decided to teleport to the top of an extraordinarily tall mountain, tens of thousands of feet up to the peak. But there was an issue."

Baelin chuckled. "He was diving at the time in a pool of utterly clear water, and he'd spied the mountain from about one hundred feet below the surface. He teleported from deep within this body of water to abruptly ascend to a high summit. The shock of the sudden pressure changes combined with altitude sickness *destroyed* him in an instant. So, one could say that he wasn't so Invincible, was he?"

He roared with laughter at that.

"I... don't find that too funny," Cedric looked uncomfortable.

Alex gave him a knowing look and shrugged, while the chancellor laughed. "You get used to it, though it can take most people some time before—"

He paused, realising that two people were laughing.

Alex glanced over to find Hart Redfletcher doubled at the waist, slapping his knee. He and Baelin pointed at each other, then laughed harder.

"That's amazing!" the Champion said. "I got a story just like that!"

Alex looked at Cedric again. "Some people get used to it really fast."

CHAPTER 21

RANSOM AND DESCENT

After what seemed like forever, Hart and Baelin got their composure back, though tears of laughter still swam in their eyes and the occasional chuckle escaped them.

"So," Baelin said, a huge smile on his face. "You said you have a similar story to share? Mine was the appetiser, so let yours be the main course!"

The Champion wiped his eyes. "You want the story, well here you go. When I was about... maybe fifteen, the Ash Ravens—that's my mercenary band—had gone down to the Rhinean Empire for work. Word had travelled up to Thameland because of these two lords who were having themselves a little religious dispute."

He made a pair of fists. "The two of 'em prayed to the four elements, but one thought fire was the greatest and the other thought earth was. I can't even remember their names now, but let's just call them Fire Lord and Earth Lord for the sake of the story. Anyway, I didn't really get all the philosophical crap, but from what I understood, the entire business had been on the civil side... Until everything changed when Mr. Firelord attacked. You see, *bandits* sacked one of the temples in Mr. Earthlord's territory. Only problem was that when some of these *bandits* got caught, they started screaming that they should be ransomed to their families."

"What's that mean?" Alex asked.

"Oh, it's a funny practice," Hart said. "Say when someone like you or me or, y'know, bandits get captured, we'd have our heads lopped off or get thrown in a dungeon. Or both. But, when *knights* and rich nobles get captured, their families pay good gold to get them back. So they get to sit tight, made all comfortable, while their families get gold together. Not fair, no, but good business if you can catch one."

"Huh... so when they said they wanted to be ransomed back, it came out that they were knights," Alex reasoned.

"Right on the mark. As it turns out, they were all Mr. Firelord's knights. Not a good look, so you know, of course that meant war."

He made a walking motion with two of his fingers. "We go down there, hired by Mr. Earthlord, but one of his sons is put in charge, and Mr. Earthlord Junior's a right ass. Arrogant as an eagle but not nearly as bright, though he thought he was. But that's alright, we were gettin' paid so we let him believe what he wanted, and we just did what we're good at. We won battles for the little shit he should've lost."

Hart chuckled. "Now this is where he reminds me of your Mr. Yem. See, he had this set of full plate armour from his daddy. Tackiest thing you'd ever want to see. All gold inlaid and studded with gems like he was trying to outshine the sun. He even had servants polishing it every minute he wasn't wearing it. Would you believe he *actually* brought these four valets into battle just to start the polishing the minute they took him out of it?" Hart shook his head.

"Yes, I actually would," Baelin said with an amused smile.

"Anyway, in spite of how gaudy this plate looked, the damn suit was tough as hell. Cutting edge stuff. He could've taken a sledgehammer to the chest with that thing on and laughed it off. On top of that, daddy had wizards enchant every plate with all kinds of magic."

He put his hand over his chest like he was swearing an oath. "On *Uldar*, I once saw a knight lance him in the chest. Snapped the bloody lance in half and the little bastard didn't even move. The *other* knight got dismounted like he'd charged into a stone wall full force. Broke his neck when he hit the ground."

"Ah, *yes*." Baelin stroked his beard with interest. "I do recall a set of armour like the one you described being crafted in Generasi some half a decade ago. It was the talk of the warrior community, though mockingly at times. A king's ransom was poured into it for some of the best armourers in the city to put it together. I can see how it could give one the impression they were invincible."

"Oh yeah, he thought he was invincible, alright." Hart grinned. "And, like your Mr. Yem, he went wherever he wanted and did whatever he wanted. Every battle, he'd always lead from the back, sitting on his big, old charger and watching the battlefield from a nearby hill. He wanted to see every detail so much, that he always insisted on keeping his vision completely clear. No obstructions for him. Which meant... he'd always have his visor *up*."

"*Ooooh no*," Baelin, Cedric, Alex, and Drestra all said at the same time.

"Oh *yeeeeah*." The Champion smiled. "So there he was, sitting on his horse one day, far enough from the battlefield to be out of arrow range—so he thought—and even if one got lucky and hit him, he figured it'd bounce off his armour. I mean, his face'd be too small a target to hit, right? Well. *Bang!* Crossbow bolt *right* to the mouth! The hit took most of his teeth. Infection got the rest, and a good part of his jaw. Last I heard, his daddy said he'd be sipping gruel for the rest of his life!"

Baelin burst out laughing, sending Hart into more fits of laughter.

Drestra shook her head. Cedric grimaced. Alex shrugged.

'Don't... don't get influenced by them, Claygon,' he thought.

"Oh, what a delight! And it helps illustrate the point!" the chancellor said. "When you are teleporting anywhere, ensure that you account for multiple forms of risk that could be lying in wait! Then mitigate them. Get ready now. I'll be casting some spells on you."

With words of power, he cast a flight spell on each of them, followed by a spell of invisibility, Orbs of Air, and a spell of true seeing. Soon, the Heroes were looking at each other's translucent forms.

"This is incredible," Drestra said, marvelling at her companions. "We could go anywhere we want like this. Unseen, flying, and yet be able to see each other."

"Yeah." Hart stroked his stubble. "Imagine having entire strike teams cloaked like this. They could just slip into enemy ranks as a group, slaughter their generals in the morning, and then be off for beer and biscuits before lunch."

"Somethin' to work on for us. We'd have a helluva lot easier time with a whole lotta dungeons if we had this set up," Cedric agreed.

"Glad you are enjoying the experience!" Baelin said. "And with that, we have mitigated two risks: we no longer have to worry about the ground's integrity, *and* we're largely safe from attack in our invisible state. Let's be off to the next location!"

In a flash of teleportation magic, they were transported to the copse of trees Baelin had pointed out earlier, floating just above the ground.

"You see? This way, we do not have to worry about the ground's integrity. Now, to really show the technique's worth, please join me in flying higher into the sky." Baelin's translucent form smiled, then shot into the air.

Alex exchanged grins with the other Heroes and hurtled after the chancellor with Claygon at his side. He had to admit, despite the seriousness of their situation, he was actually having fun. All the teleporting and flying they were doing had also set his imagination on fire. Getting deeper into teleportation spells couldn't come soon enough.

They floated up beside the ancient wizard, who waited a few hundred feet in the air. "Now, take a look around."

Alex turned, scanning the landscape. From their height, miles of wilderness spread before them in every direction, and he took it all in as flakes of snow sifted over the ground. He shivered. They were only a few hundred feet up, but the chill ran deep. A woolen cloak suddenly appeared around Cedric's bare torso, and a trembling Chosen nodded at Baelin in gratitude, pulling it tight around him.

"And now, from this vantage point, we can make the jump for several miles at a time," Baelin said. "With uninterrupted views of the vista, we can travel long distances. This is why flight magic is the perfect complement to the Teleportation Shuffle. However, to avoid Yem's fate, you must always pay attention to your altitude, the cold, wind speed, and direction, and the weather and air pressure. Do not make the mistake of thinking, 'if I fly higher, I will just see farther!'"

He took on a grim look and watched the sky. "It might not look like it from here... but if you fly high enough, you shall find only death up there. Now, let us go!"

With a few words of power, Baelin catapulted them through space in a stream of teleportation. The world flashed around Alex. In one heartbeat, he was floating in the sky above a forest, the next, soaring through waves of sights and sounds.

A broad smile took his face.

Being immersed in so much teleportation magic was exhilarating, exciting, yet comforting, like coming home to a warm fire after a long day in the cold wilderness. There was almost a voice calling to him across time and space, welcoming him.

He wished it could go on forever, when Baelin suddenly stopped near a vast, expansive swamp.

"Let's do that again!" Alex said, whirling on the amused chancellor with the enthusiasm of a child.

"Now, Alex, we should at least *pretend* that we are adults at times," he said, smiling at all four Heroes. "And here we are. According to map coordinates and my calculations, this should be the southern end of Crymlyn

Swamp. When you recover, Drestra, would you please tell me if we are in the right place?"

'When you recover?' Alex thought, taking a look at the other Heroes.

Cedric, Hart, and Drestra were bent at the waist, looking more than a little grey. Their hands were pressed to their mouths. The Champion was shaking and gagging beneath the heavy pack on his back.

"Are you guys okay?" Alex asked them in alarm.

"They are fine... well, 'fine' might be a strong word," the ancient wizard admitted.

"Damn right it's a strong word. Flying through the air has its uses, but it just ain't natural," Hart managed to choke out.

"What they are experiencing is teleportation sickness. Which is less problematic than you might imagine. As a child, did you ever take to spinning around in a circle until you were so dizzy that you fell over?"

"Uh, yeah, more times than I care to remember," Alex admitted. He wasn't always the smartest of children.

"Teleportation sickness is essentially a disorientation-caused nausea akin to motion sickness," Baelin explained. "When one appears in multiple locations rapidly, the body can become a little... confused. Hence, the nausea."

"You didn't warn us about that?" Alex asked.

"It will not kill," the ancient wizard said. "And, through experiencing, one gains a valuable... well, experience."

"Feels like my insides're gonna pour out," Cedric moaned.

"I nearly threw up in my veil," Drestra said.

"It's like ten hangovers at once," Hart groaned.

"Oh, do not be so dramatic!" Baelin chuckled. "It will pass in mere heartbeats."

After more than *mere* heartbeats, the Heroes' translucent forms looked decidedly less grey.

"Hoh," Drestra sighed. "It will be a long time before I have enough mana to do that. Hopefully, I'll have the stomach for it by then."

"I am sure you will," Baelin said. "Now, are we in the right spot?"

"We are. And—what's better—I can point you to exactly where my home is," she said, adjusting her veil in the wind. "The witches I spoke of live more of a wandering type of life in the swamp. We'll have to go to my village to ask where they might be this time of year. Do you have the mana to continue teleporting us?"

Baelin chuckled. "Do I *have the mana*, she asks. How adorable. Lead the way and I will get us there."

With Drestra directing Baelin, they travelled through the sky above the Crymlyn, deeper and deeper into the immense swamp. The deeper they went, the more the young wizard realised just how immense it was. If Drestra and Baelin hadn't been there, he had no doubt they would have gotten lost, because the marsh was soon all he could see in every direction. He knew the swamp was said to be big—it appeared as a massive swath of land on maps of Thameland—but seeing something on a map and seeing it in-person, especially from the air, were two entirely different matters.

Most trees had dropped their leaves, giving the swamp a ghostly appearance. Skeletal tree trunks and branches reached up over misting frost-covered water, seeming to strain toward them as they passed by. Mudholes, shriveled bog plants, and peat dotted swaths of moss-covered ground.

Vulture-like birds—far larger than any bird that flew above Greymoor—screamed to each other. Alex mentally thanked the Traveller they hadn't been servants of two blue annis hags hiding in a windmill on a fiery night not so long ago.

A wave of excitement went through him. Not many in Thameland could say they'd visited the Crymlyn Swamp's borders, let alone flying over it and meeting the witches who lived there. He was about to live out some of the childhood ghost stories his father used to tell him.

…Without the gruesome endings, he hoped.

"There." Drestra pointed at a series of lines of white smoke to the north. "My village lies there. We should descend and come in over the water. And maybe drop the invisibility. Things were… tense when I was last here, and it wouldn't do to surprise everyone by appearing out of thin air in the middle of our village square."

"Spoken with true wisdom, young Drestra," Baelin said. "Then we will do just that, and I will conjure a boat for us to sail to your community's borders. Discovery awaits."

CHAPTER 22

THE DANGERS OF CRYMLYN SWAMP

The party floated from the sky, sinking beneath naked tree branches to stop above the frigid swamp water.

Baelin looked at Drestra. "There are no toxic gases here?"

"Not in this part of the swamp," the Sage said.

"Excellent. I shall cancel your Orbs of Air. We should know what the area smells like before continuing: swamps often have built up gases that can be quite explosive. So, it's always best to have a quick whiff of the air, see if we have anything to be concerned about."

With a wave of his hand, he cancelled the spell, and a foul smell of rotting vegetables and drying fish reached Alex's nostrils. Nearby, he spied a silver form breaching the water, quickly followed by a quiet splash. A small fish snapped a bug off the water's surface.

'Not many insects around,' Alex thought. 'Good thing we're so late in the year, or we'd be a feast for mosque—'

Splash!

Alex, the Heroes, and Baelin whirled.

Deep in the trees to the east—a splash much louder than a small fish hitting the water startled them. A bird's panicked cry was abruptly cut off.

Another splash, then... silence followed.

"What'n blazes was that?" Cedric asked.

"Could be any number of things. Some of the swamp's predators are very active this time of year," Drestra said calmly. "They fatten themselves in the fall then swim down to their caves for the winter. It's almost time for them to go into hibernation."

"Charmin'," Cedric said, his morphic weapon flowing off his arm and transforming into a spear. Now he was ready for whatever came, whether fish or predator.

'Watch out for anything swimming near us,' Alex directed Claygon. He drew a sleeping potion and a booby-trapped mana soothing potion from his bag. 'If anything jumps at us, squash it.'

The golem's head began to turn, watching the landscape in all directions.

Hart drew his bow and nocked an arrow. "What're the odds of these predators attacking an armed party?"

"Low," Drestra said. "They rarely attack my people when we're out on the water. Unless they're very, very hungry."

"Right," Alex said. "Of course this'll be the day they'll be starving."

"Unfortunately for them, any attack they attempt will only result in their *own* deaths," Baelin said, conjuring a swarm of Wizard's Eyes. He sent them out in all directions, his gaze unfocusing for an instant. "Hm, no immediate threats in the area. Excellent."

He turned to Alex and the other Heroes. "Stay here for a moment, will you? Remember that you are still invisible, but endeavour not to make too much noise. I shall return momentarily. Alex, will you hold this for a moment?"

Just as he had when he teleported away earlier, he gave the dungeon core over to Alex, then disappeared.

Four Heroes and Claygon floated, watching the swamp around them.

"So, this is your home, eh, Drestra?" Alex whispered.

"I was born here," the Sage said quietly. "I'd only left the swamp a handful of times before I was marked. This was my world for more than seventeen years."

"How did you deal with the smell?" Hart's face soured.

She shot him an annoyed look "I don't want to hear anything about how my home smells from *you*."

"What?" Hart asked.

Drestra looked at Alex. "This Champion here... It took Cedric and me weeks to convince him to bathe regularly. For a while, he reeked worse than a dungeon full of dead Ravener-spawn."

"Hey, we're out on a war campaign. A bit of a half-wash chases the bugs away, and doesn't waste time like some luxurious bath would," Hart said defensively.

"Your stink nearly chased *me* away," Cedric grunted.

Alex chuckled quietly, not particularly interested in commenting.

Calling on the Mark, he read the Heroes' body language; tension lay in all three of them. They seemed more relaxed around each other than before, though their tension spiked each time their eyes fell on the dungeon core slung over Alex's shoulder.

It looked like the gap was closing between the three Heroes. Maybe sharing the secret of the dungeon core had brought them closer, at least subconsciously.

'Hopefully, it keeps closing,' Alex thought. 'No matter what we find out.'

Minutes later, Baelin was back with a large, gracefully-shaped boat with a figurehead carved in the image of a hydra's nine snarling heads. The vessel was long—long enough to carry a party three times their size—and broad enough for Claygon to fit in with ease.

With a whispered word, the chancellor lowered the boat into the water and gestured for everyone to get in. "This comes from my personal collection, and it is indeed a favourite." He smiled fondly at the water-craft. "Hop in. Alex, I will take the core back. Oh, and do not worry about Claygon: the boat's enchantments ensure that it can carry *more* than our combined weight."

Alex handed him the dungeon core, then floated into the boat, watching Claygon. He had nothing to worry about. Even when Claygon settled in the middle of the vessel, it never sank below the waterline.

The enchantments Baelin had on it were powerful ones.

Hart and Cedric sat down next, rocking back and forth, testing its stability; they were soon nodding in satisfaction. Drestra was looking about, taking in every inch of it.

"Where are the oars?" she asked.

"Our manner of travel will not require oars," Baelin said, pointing ahead. "That way to your village, I take it?"

"Yes," she said. "There's curving paths and forks in the waterways, but I can guide you through them."

"Excellent."

The ancient wizard snapped his fingers.

"Holy sh—" Alex swore as the boat lurched forward under its own power.

Picking up speed, it glided through the marsh, kicking up mud and slushy water in its wake. And considering how fast it moved, it travelled with an eerie silence.

Alex wanted one, and no doubt so did the other Heroes.

"Prepare for the cancellation of your invisibility spells," Baelin said.

"As Drestra said earlier, it's better not to alarm her compatriots by suddenly appearing out of nowhere. We want to have a pleasant chat with them, not give them the impression we are thieves or spies."

"Great," Hart said. "Now any of these nasty predators will see us coming."

"Trust me, as long as Baelin's here, we have nothing to worry about," Alex said.

"You flatter me, but I shan't be raising your grades over mere words, Alex!" The chancellor waved a hand and their bodies shimmered, translucence fading to reveal them.

Everyone tensed, more cautious.

"Keep watching for anything nasty," Alex told his golem.

Claygon's head swivelled in all directions as he balanced in the middle of the boat.

"You're all too nervous," Drestra said. "At the speed we're going, we'll reach my village in minutes. And as I said, creatures in the swamp rarely attack people. We're fine."

And, indeed, her words were true…

…for approximately sixty seconds.

A minute of gliding through the swamp—with the Sage guiding the chancellor through the waterways' branching paths—saw Baelin suddenly sit bolt upright and snap a hand out to their right.

With a single word of power, he shot out a crackling sky-blue beam, sending it racing above the water, striking what seemed to be empty air about a hundred and fifty feet away.

Crack!

A monstrous scream ripped through the swamp, then was replaced by the sound of crackling. Rapidly freezing ice spread, coating an invisible creature swimming toward them, flash freezing it like an ice sculpture floating in the murky water.

"By the Traveller!" Alex swore. "What in all the hells is *that*?"

The creature's shape was mostly humanoid and probably ten feet tall, with a thick tail equally as long as the rest of its body. Hooked talons extended from fingers on massive hands, and its arms were so long, they must have scraped the ground when it walked.

"What in the—" Drestra leaned over the side of the boat, her reptilian eyes squinting at the creature. "I think that's an invisible marauder."

"A *what* now?" Alex asked.

He didn't remember mention of any such creature in the Thameish bestiaries.

"They're predators from deep within the swamp," she said. "Nasty things, and with a sadistic streak. They're smart enough to use tools, and cruel enough to hunt not only for meat, but for sport. They can also turn invisible, naturally."

"Well, it is now an invisible corpse," Baelin said matter-of-factly. "Against my Wizard's Eyes, that level of invisibility—no matter how natural—would not serve it."

The boat turned, gliding toward the frozen form.

The nearer they went, the more the monster's invisibility shimmered away, until only a slight translucence remained. When Baelin shot it, they must have been close enough for him to catch enough of its body with his true seeing spell, cancelling most of its ability to remain hidden.

It wasn't what anyone but another invisible marauder would call attractive. Green scales covered most of its body except for its back and tail. They were sheathed in a bone-like carapace. Its face had a human-like quality for the better part, but its mouth was that of a giant crab.

He whistled at its claws: they looked sharp enough to tear through petrified wood like paper.

"This... something's wrong," Drestra said as they pulled alongside the frozen body. "Invisible marauders stay much deeper in the swamp. They have a fear of mortals, and my kin—the ones we're looking for—cull their population as much as they need to."

She gave Baelin a worried look.

"We need to get to the village."

"Of course," he said, conjuring a rope which tied itself around the monster. "I think we should bring this creature with us to show to your people. If they aren't already aware of this... abnormality, then we can show them."

"I'm glad you saw it," Drestra said.

The boat took off again at speed, with everyone watching the trees and water. Baelin recast Orbs of Air over their heads in case something managed to get close enough to drag one or all of them beneath the murky surface.

Near Drestra's village, the trees grew thinner and signs of civilisation abundant. Ropes had been attached to tree trunks as mooring posts; curious, arcane glyphs were scratched into tree bark, and effigies hung from leafless branches high above. Alex stared at the effigies. They were figures of people made of sticks and straw woven together, then painted red.

They reminded him of diagrams he'd seen in blood magic books.

"Those weren't there when I was here last," Drestra said softly, pointing at the effigies. "They warn of dangerous areas that should be avoided or, at the very least, passed through cautiously. I wonder why they're so close to the village?"

"I guess we'll be finding out soon enough," Alex said to the Sage, his grip tightening on his potions while his eyes scanned for more attackers.

But the next sign of life they encountered wasn't a monster.

About a hundred and twenty feet ahead, five people shimmered into being, their forms having the same translucence as a spell of true seeing. They were crouched in what must have been a sentry post.

Each was pale, clad in rough, homespun clothing, and were decorated in arcane symbols drawn in red pigment. They held bows nocked with arrows that glowed with power.

"Ah, the sentries!" Drestra cried, jumping to her feet.

She called to them in a language Alex had never heard before—one with complex syllables and tones that ran from guttural, to musical—and caught the sentries' attention. They looked down at her in surprise.

"I come with the Champion and Chosen," Drestra said in the common tongue. "And with other friends too. Well met, Angharad!"

"Well met, Drestra," a sentry called back in a deep voice. He was young and not particularly tall, but he was broad of both shoulder and belly. "It's been too long!"

The sentries spoke quick incantations and shimmered out of invisibility while Angharad stepped forward. "Your timing's either good or terrible. You've come in dark days."

"What's happened?" she asked as the boat glided beneath the sentry post. She pointed to the invisible marauder tied to the back of the boat. "That thing was within a horn's blow's distance from the village. What is going on? Are our kin having trouble containing them?"

Angharad grimaced. "A lot has happened since you left, Drestra. And as for our kin? We lost contact with them about two months ago. You'd better come into the village. We have a lot to tell you."

CHAPTER 23

THE DEAD AELD

The Heroes and the Chancellor of Generasi glided through the swamp in his enchanted boat, following a vessel Angharad had unmoored from the mouth of a small cave formed by the roots of the same tree the sentries' post was in.

The witches' boat was small—more of a dugout really—just big enough to hold two sentries and Drestra. It was powered when a sentry spoke a short incantation and passed her hands over the oars, bringing them to life. The paddles responded, shuddering, groaning, then slithering over the portside and starboard of the dugout to dip themselves in the water, rowing as though ghosts were pulling them.

Drestra was eager to catch up on recent events in the Crymlyn and had joined the sentries on the trip to her home. Now they talked quietly in the dugout, leading Baelin, Alex, and the other two Heroes to the Sage's village.

"Well, this is unexpected," Baelin said. "I thought we would have our work done within hours, but the situation appears to be more complicated than I anticipated. Hmmm. Perhaps I will have to depart for a time and leave the task at hand to the four of you and Claygon."

The chancellor looked up at the sky, a frown taking his face.

Clouds were darkening and the snow was falling harder, not settling on the ground yet, but visibility was lower.

"The weather looks to be turning against us. Hm, listen well. Alex, this is something you must pay attention to in future when you attempt the Teleportation Shuffle," he cautioned. "It becomes far less useful when one's sight is compromised."

"Right..." Alex said, thinking about what might come next. It looked like they were on the verge of an adventure, and...

He glanced back at the ice-caked monster they were towing.

It could be a dangerous one.

So then why did he feel so... exhilarated?

There was a part of him that was looking forward to Baelin leaving them on their own. Something was brewing in the swamp, and uncovering it with Claygon, the three Heroes, and Theresa would be an adventure. The dungeon core's secrets, looking for answers in this strange place, being unsure of what was coming next, all of that was exciting, even thrilling. Having Baelin with them would probably mean they'd get answers faster, answers he was eager for.

But, when he really thought about it, the thought of having to work for those answers using his own skills, got him real excited.

'Baelin's definitely rubbing off on me,' he thought. 'But that's alright. He's someone I don't mind being influenced by.'

"Do you mind leaving us the boat?" Alex asked. "And the core?"

"Not at all," the chancellor said. "What would be the point of training and watching you grow into a Proper Wizard if I would not even trust you with such a meagre amount of responsibility."

"Right." Alex blushed and was about to say something else...

...when something enormous up ahead of them caught his attention.

"There's somethin' I didn't expect to see," Cedric murmured as he and Hart leaned over the side of the boat.

Ahead was what looked to be a living *wall* of trees. Not logs, but breathing trees that had grown so closely together, their trunks were fused in a continuous rampart of living wood. Their canopies wrapped each other in a permanent embrace. It was one of the most majestic things Alex had ever seen, easily competing with some of the wonders in Generasi.

"Wow, they must be even more incredible before the leaves fall," Alex shouted to those in the dugout, the wall looming higher the closer they came. Each tree was perhaps fifty to sixty feet tall.

"It is!" Drestra called back, pausing her conversation with the sentries. "I only wish you were seeing it in happier times."

"Yeah," Alex murmured, his eyes widening at what lay ahead.

The tree trunks curved, forming a gracious tunnel into a... tree dome? Tree house? He had no idea what to call it.

"This place is easy to defend." Alex could plainly hear the admiration in Hart's voice as they passed into the tunnel, sailing deeper into the structure of living wood. Inside, a dense forest of trees that thrived in swampland reached toward the clouds, their canopy forming a network of pathways on every side, including above. Some branches were thicker around than even Baelin's boat and had become a truly living structure birthed from a single organism.

Alex found he felt relaxed, their surroundings had a soothing quality that took the tension from both his and Cedric's bearing from the moment they'd slipped beneath the tree branches.

Hart was a different story. It wasn't that he was tense, it was that his focus was now in full military mode. He pointed to a host of places where archers and wizards could hide in the canopy and make use of those massive branches for cover, while peppering intruders with spells and arrows from atop other branches.

The Champion sniffed the air. "And it's humid in here too."

"Yeah." Alex turned his attention to the canopy. "Some of these trees have roots that go all the way down to the earth deep below the water so they're always slowly taking water up. They get completely *saturated*. Anyone coming in here with a plan that involves burning the Witches out would have a hell of a time burning anything, especially with Witches raining all sorts of nasty spells down on their heads."

"Yeah, that's what I was thinking," Hart said, squinting at the trees. "Good thing we're being escorted in. Look up there; they're already watching us."

"Indeed," Baelin said, his eyes looking ahead. "They have been monitoring us well before we entered the treeline."

Alex casually looked up, catching quick movements in the shadows of the branches. There were animals up there, steadily watching: squirrels, birds, and other creatures with sharp intellect shining in their eyes, which marked them as familiars. And they weren't alone. Sentries wrapped in cloaks the colour of tree bark lay on hunting blinds, concealed and peering at the newcomers with bows in hand. They appeared tense.

And ready for a fight.

Alex wondered what they'd been dealing with lately.

The boats sailed from the mouth of the tunnel to a large island within the fortress of trees. Before them, the main village of the Witches of Crymlyn Swamp rose. Nearby, a line of docks jutted into the water with a small flotilla of dugouts moored to them, and from there, a stone pathway led into a village... Though, that really wasn't the right term.

Luthering was a village.

What lay before them was a town nearly the size of Alric, except magical. The houses were a mix of wooden cottages, giant mushroom-houses, and magnificent trees with entire cabins growing in their branches. The Witches of Crymlyn were hard at work as Alex's group reached the docks.

Wood was being split for the long winter coming.

Hauls of fish, logs, and swamp vegetables were being carted toward storage houses by teams of otters the size of horses. A walking tree nearing twenty feet tall strode through the centre of the village, carrying a load of barrels in its many arms like they weighed no more than a bushel of sweet peas.

"How charming." Baelin smiled, watching as some of the witches pointed at the newcomers. Folk had begun to gather while the boats were tied off, but their numbers grew into a crowd when the sentries guided the group through the village.

Nearing the village square, Alex saw a large tree in its centre, one with a very familiar shape. It was an aeld tree. "Why is the aeld white, Drestra?"

"Sadly, it died."

He thought of his aeld tree in the courtyard of the encampment, so bright, so warm. He remembered the planting ceremony Professor Salinger performed for the little tree and how vibrant with life it had been. In death, this aeld had turned completely white, like freshly fallen snow, and while no glow emanated from it, it still held a muted light that caught one's attention.

It was sad that its spirit was gone.

Fittingly, in the centre of the village adjacent to the tree, a circular shrine of menhir stones stood, each at least as tall as Claygon. Witches knelt there—hands clasped tightly in prayer—within a circle. An arcane glyph marked each stone, though one was emblazoned with the white hand that was Uldar's holy symbol.

Alex's displeasure surfaced, but he pushed down the urge to scowl. Uldar's symbol was noticeably smaller than the other glyphs, visibly worn by weather and time, and spattered here and there with bird droppings. It looked like its maintenance wasn't top priority for the Witches of the Crymlyn.

'Well, depending on what we find out, maybe they'll be taking it down anyway.'

He looked back down as Angharad spoke to Drestra, then moved toward a large wood and stone hall the size of one of Uldar's churches, without symbols to honour him etched in its walls. Moss and ivy crawled over stone, and the thatched roof was bright green, as though it was still growing from the earth.

Two rows—with six pines in each—flanked the hall, releasing a pleasant woodsy scent, and a significant amount of mana. Alex watched the evergreens, wondering what magic lay in them as Angharad made his way up to a set of doors.

Drestra turned. "We'll see the village elder in a moment. Angharad is just letting her know we're here."

"What's been happening?" Alex asked. "Did the sentries say what happened to the other witches?"

"Yeah, are they okay?" Cedric joined in. "What about that friend you mentioned? Anyone hear from 'em?"

The Sage frowned. "Apparently, they've not been seen in any of their campgrounds or hunting areas. Search parties are out looking, but none of them have come back with any news. Everyone's concerned."

Cedric's eyebrows rose. "An' your people are *all* magic users?"

"Many, not all. But yes, magic users were among those who disappeared," she admitted.

"Sounds serious," Hart said.

"Indeed. Well, if fortune smiles on us, then we might find your friends quickly." Baelin looked up at the sky. "Though it appears fortune might *not* be on our side."

Above, the clouds were deep grey and threatening. Snow continued falling and the temperature with it. Flakes of white were settling on the ground now, more reluctant to melt than before.

"The weather has indeed turned against us," Baelin said. "And without knowing as much as I would wish to about the weather and climate systems around this area, I am reluctant to alter it. Hm, if only *you* were still alive."

The chancellor looked up at the aeld tree. "Would it be safe to assume that it lived for at least half a millennium? When did it die?"

"Yes, it was very old and well tended. It lived for about 700 years, but died when I was eight," Drestra said sadly. "Ah, if only you could've seen like I did when I was young. It lit up half the village when it was happy. Some of our people are looking for a sapling to replace it but haven't had any luck finding one. So when I saw yours—"

She paused, looking toward the hall.

Angharad had emerged and was waving them to the doors.

"Later, I guess," the Sage said. "We had better go in. The faster we learn what's happened, the faster we know what can be done."

The interior of the hall was dark, cozy, and within its four walls, the *oldest-looking* person Alex had ever seen awaited. A tiny woman—her face a mask of lines—sat on a blanket by a fire pit. Flames licked the sides of a cauldron large enough to hold a good-sized pig.

'...Or a person,' Alex thought, trying to dismiss the grimmer fairy tales he'd been told about witches.

Which was no easy feat when the spitting image of witches from those very fairy tales was sitting a few feet away. Reminding him, uncomfortably, of the pair of blue annis hags.

"Welcome to Crymlyn Village," the elder's voice croaked to her guests, now seated on thick blankets in front of her. "Or I should say, welcome *back*, Drestra-child. It is good to see you again. The other children have missed you."

"I missed them and you too, Elder Blodeuwedd. Mother." Drestra bowed her head, and her crackling voice held more sincerity than Alex had ever heard in it. Cedric looked at her with an eyebrow raised, but she didn't catch his gaze.

"But what's happened to our sister people?" the Sage continued. "Angharad couldn't tell me much."

"It was on purpose that not much was shared until you were brought before me," Elder Blodeuwedd said. She looked at Baelin and then Alex.

Her eyes seemed to glitter like diamonds in firelight.

"Welcome, strangers from the far lands to the south. Angharad told me where you are from. Or... perhaps not so welcome."

Alex watched her closely as she dug into a pouch at her side.

He looked at Baelin and Claygon, but the chancellor was focused on the elder witch as she pulled out a small, clay tablet.

"Do you outsiders recognise this?"

She held the tablet out to them, displaying a symbol carved into it.

"Oh *shit*," Alex swore.

A growl escaped his throat.

The symbol belonged to the Cult of Ezaliel.

CHAPTER 24

THE ELDER WITCH

"And just where did you come upon this?" Baelin asked, tension tingeing his voice.

Not anger. Not accusation. Not offence.

Just a hint of tension, like a hand beginning to curl its fingers into a fist. No threat yet, but a preparation.

"Here, in the swamp." Elder Blodeuwedd watched him calmly, those glittering eyes meeting Baelin's piercing gaze. Alex took in her body language: relaxed, utterly calm, even serene... yet tension was there. Her shoulders slouched, and her hands shook with a barely perceptible tremor.

But there was no sign of fear.

Alex wondered if the tremor was part of an illness. He was truly impressed that she could hold the ancient wizard's gaze so evenly.

He cleared his throat, hoping to coax a response from her. She was so focused on Baelin—likely feeling his powerful energies—that she was paying little attention to anyone else.

Her eyes briefly flicked away, and Alex spoke up, his words low and calm.

"Whoever came here with that... they were a problem for you, weren't they?"

As he spoke, some of the tension left the air. Drestra jumped in. "We know that symbol! It's the symbol of a cult of demon worshippers who've made their way to Thameland for reasons that bear no resemblance to anything good."

She looked at Baelin and Alex. "These two aren't cultists... they're friends. They've been nothing but helpful, honest, and forthcoming, Mother."

Elder Blodeuwedd held Drestra's eyes, then looked at Baelin.

She shrugged. "Strangers from outside the swamp came to the village one day, bearing this symbol. They asked for our alliance, military protection against Uldar *and* the Ravener, in return for shelter and serving as their guides in Thameland."

A frown creased her brow. "But we were wary of them. They smiled too easily and offered much we did not see proof of. And there was a presence to them. Like one sees in those who have sold themselves to foul magic. When I told them we would consider it, they left easily enough.

"Then, a few weeks later, our brothers and sisters disappeared... I must add that I hope Drestra's trust in you both is well placed." Her eyes drifted to the front door before she continued. "So, what brings you to Crymlyn Swamp? Angharad has told me you seek our kin, but not *why* you seek them. In truth, your timing is... curious. Strangers come from afar, then our people vanish without a trace. Then other strangers come looking for those same people. Why?"

"Drestra's friend is to help us with a question that we need answered, a private question for now," Baelin said smoothly. "What I can say is that we have a need to find your kin. And by we, I mean myself, my friend here, and our expedition."

"Don't forget us," Cedric said. "Bloody bastard cultists are addin' t'our troubles too."

"Mother," Drestra said. "I'd like my companions to join me in searching for our people. Please, give us your blessing."

"Hmmmm," the elder said. "These strangers seek our kin for their own business, and offer no false smiles and fantastical promises of gifts. And one of our greatest calls them friend. That gives me comfort that they do not have malice in their minds. Very well, daughter."

She dug a pinch of bright green powder from her pouch and tossed it in the fire. A whoosh preceded emerald flame that roared up the sides of the cauldron, peaking high above the rim before ebbing and calming to a flickering orange.

"There, now you have my blessing. Search for our kin in the Crymlyn. I will tell you where they were last seen... and if you find them—" her eyes drifted to Cedric, Alex, Baelin, and Hart "—I'll be sure a reward is prepared for you, for the Witches of Crymlyn Swamp believe that no help should go unrewarded."

Alex lowered his head. "Thank you," he said, taking on some of the notes in the elder's voice. "We'll do our best to find them, and those you sent after them as well."

The elder nodded. "Good. I will have a cottage prepared for your needs while you are here with us. And in the meanwhile, we can talk about where our kin were last seen as well as disturbing events that have come to our lands lately. You'll soon see that you'll need good luck and the spirits with you more than ever. I know you will guide your companions well, Drestra-child."

"Yes, Mother," the young witch said.

"Oh my, how lovely and nostalgic," Baelin said as their boat glided through the swamp.

The snow had picked up, but the wind was low, and the cold not *too* biting. Though that didn't mean the weather wasn't worsening. The atmosphere in the swamp felt ominous to Alex, especially with visibility now reduced to mere yards ahead, and the conversation with the elder replaying in his mind.

She had told them of *things* their scouts had seen deep in the marsh: monsters they'd never—in remembered time—seen before. Monsters whose descriptions were unnervingly similar to demons described in some of the university's summoning textbooks.

"What's nostalgic?" he asked Baelin, his eyes searching the trees before glancing at the clouds and noting the change in light, darkness would soon fall.

"This adventure," Baelin said, looking at Drestra sitting pressed to the vessel's bow, watching the swamp ahead. "It has been some time since I went exploring the wilderness to find something or someone. It used to be something I did as regularly as breathing."

"You miss it?" Alex asked, smiling.

"At times, but—overall—I have moved on to other things."

"Oi, how can y'be so calm?" Cedric glanced at Baelin. "I understand not bein' a'feared o' the wild, bein' that y'got so much power t'throw around an' y'got three of Thameland's Heroes an' yer student an' his golem wit' ya... S'not like we can't win a fight; s'just I'm worried for what's happened, an' if we're gonna find Drestra's kin in this deep swamp. The witches 'ave already searched fer weeks now."

"Indeed, but they do not have the mobility we do. Even if the weather has reduced the range that I can safely teleport us, we are still able to travel far more quickly than they can. Further, we have the strength of spell and arms to take more... direct routes."

"Yeah," Alex said. "I can understand why they'd need to be cautious too. If there really are demons lurking somewhere in here, that's not something just anyone can handle."

"And not when winter's so near," Drestra said. "It's a terrible time. We need almost every hand out hunting, harvesting, and making ready for the cold season."

She looked back at her companions, including Hart and Claygon, who were watching their flanks as they glided through the marsh. The Champion had his bow clutched tight, an arrow nocked.

"Thank you," she said in her crackling voice. "Thank you for helping with this. I owe you all."

"Think nothing of it," Baelin said. "As was said earlier, we are doing this for our own purposes as well. It's not a case of pure altruism, but rather it meets the needs of two groups aligning in a fortuitous or, rather, an unfortunate time. And we are—in many ways—fighting a war alongside each other, albeit with differing capacities. I am sure you will have a chance to return the favour one day. Especially as danger arises all around us... And speaking of that..." He looked past Drestra. "Do you see anything resembling the forked tree yet?"

"Actually, we should be close," the Sage said. "It should be ri—ah, there it is!"

She pointed ahead. Rising from the centre of the waterway was the tree they sought—and it was so straight and even, it looked like it had been whittled by mortal hands. The waterway ran past it, flowing deeper into the swamp, and the tree represented an unofficial boundary line that the witches used.

Everything past the forked tree seemed... darker. Trees were more twisted. Grasses withered. The water murkier.

Although those things weren't what caught Alex's attention... it was what was missing.

"Hey, didn't the elder say there was an effigy here? To mark the area ahead as some place to stay out of, or at the very least, be real cautious in? You know, a place where a whole damn search party disappeared? So, where's this effigy?"

"Aye, that's a bloody good question. I remember 'er sayin' it was right here." Cedric craned his neck, looking through the swamp. But the trees were thicker here, and his vision lower.

"How much you willing to bet it didn't just fall off by itself?" Alex asked, getting potions ready.

"I'm not taking that bet," Hart growled. "'Cos I'm no fan of losing coin."

"Indeed," Baelin said. "Those invisible marauders have sufficient intellect to plan, and it would be in *their* best interest if hapless wanderers stumbled into their territory. If Elder Blodeuwedd's theory proves correct, then demons deep within the swamp would drive invisible marauders out of their normal hunting grounds. Which means they would have to attract prey however and wherever they could, so removing the warning would be a good way to achieve that."

"That makes sense." Drestra's eyes hardened. "Well, we'll go to them, give them what they *think* they want. I'll go right *through* them to find out what happened to my kin if I have to. Thinking about them meeting the same fate as the one you froze is rather appealing."

"Yeah," Hart said. "Guess we'll be doing your people *another* service too: culling overpopulated pests!"

"Hah!" Baelin laughed. "I *knew* I liked the two of you."

As Hart and the chancellor grinned at each other, Alex felt a twinge deep in his chest that surprised him. An emotion he rarely felt.

'Is that jealousy?' he thought as he began conjuring Wizard's Hands, forceballs, and layering defensive spells over himself. 'Am I actually *jealous*? Of *Hart*? Come on, Alex, stop being crazy. At least pull the crazy back *a little*.

'It makes sense that they'd get along. Baelin, above all else, is a warrior like Hart. They've lived lives of war. And, they have the same dark sense of humour. So, why not?'

Once his defensive spells were up, he summoned Bubbles and five other small water elementals, sending them into the water.

"Hey, Bubbles." He patted the little water elemental on its... head? Its body, he supposed. Then he patted the others. "Hey, everyone. Welcome back. I need you to dive into the water and just follow us. If I tell you to attack something, that means you just suck all the moisture out of them, okay?"

Bubbles and the others made bubbling sounds, then slipped into the murky waters.

Cedric raised an eyebrow. "Really? Bubbles?"

Alex's face flushed hot. "I-it's appropriate."

The Chosen opened his mouth to reply, but then smirked. "Cute little things, either way. Don't look like they'd hurt a fly."

"You'd be surprised," Alex smiled. "They have some nasty tricks up their... sleeves, and so do *these* guys." He conjured a couple of swarms of water elemental beetles.

"Welcome back," he said to the swarms. "Thanks for your help last time, guys. This time, I want you to spread out, fly around and scout the area. If you land on anything you can't see, I want you to make a racket that'll bring the rest of the swarm, then start biting every invisible thing you've landed on. Buzz as loudly as you can, okay?"

The swarms scattered into the marsh in search of prey.

"Hm, I remember you used that strategy during the Grand Battle," Baelin said. "Though it will not be necessary now since we have the true seeing spell on ourselves."

"Yeah." Alex shrugged. "I figured what we have to do could take longer than you have time for, and you could be gone by nightfall."

"Indeed," Baelin said. "That is a distinct possibility."

"So yeah," Alex said. "Better to get in the habit of scouting out enemies before you leave, rather than being complacent."

"Ah, spoken like a Proper Wizard. Very well, keep your habits," Baelin said. "Now, has everyone else had time to prepare?"

The Heroes nodded.

"Good." He cast an invisibility spell over everyone. Even the boat vanished. "Let us see if we cannot find ourselves one good battle before I must head back. It would be a shame to leave you all to clean up this *entire* mess on your own."

With that, he gave the boat a quick command, and it glided past the forked tree and deeper into the gloom.

CHAPTER 25

A RUNNING BATTLE

It didn't take long before Baelin found the fight he was after.

They'd pressed deeper into the swamp where their surroundings turned rougher, and grisly remains of slaughtered birds, giant swamp otters, and enormous turtles that were eaten right out of their shells lay everywhere.

Alex imagined Vesuvius not being amused at the sight.

Then he cleared his thoughts.

The others were on alert, though Baelin *appeared* quite relaxed. Those goat-like eyes, however, scanned the marsh with that piercing gaze of his. Hart kept an arrow nocked on his bow string. Drestra held her hands out, ready to direct spells, while Alex had several booby-trapped sleeping and mana soothing potions in floating Wizard's Hands.

Claygon stood in the centre of the boat, his hands spread, ready to fire beams at anything coming too close.

Cedric had gone an extra step.

His morphic weapon shimmered, transforming from a spear into a magnificent recurve bow of gleaming silver with a silver string taut between its tips. The Chosen muttered a quick prayer to Uldar and conjured glowing arrows, much like those the centaur priests used at the Games of Roal.

Alex eyed the bow. 'I really gotta ask what the hell that weapon is once we get through this,' he thought. 'I wouldn't mind getting one for myse—' His thoughts paused and his face turned sour. '—oh, that's right. What am I thinking? The Mark and Uldar would never let that happen—'

"Shhhhhh!" Baelin hissed a warning.

Alex's bitter thoughts vanished.

The chancellor whispered a command that swept through the watercraft, slowing it. "Do not give any indication that you've noticed anything amiss, but something approaches."

Everyone went silent, their eyes searching the gloom. They remained still. Even their breathing was soundless while the boat drifted like an eel slipping through the murk.

Hart subtly looked left, indicating a spot through the evening light and falling snow, deep within the trees.

Alex's gaze shifted left.

A hundred plus feet away, Baelin's true seeing spell revealed translucent creatures moving noiselessly through the turbid swamp water, hunting for food.

More than two dozen invisible marauders inched closer, confident in their innate invisibility to keep them hidden. 'If those things weren't so deadly, the situation would be pretty funny,' Alex thought, fighting the urge to laugh. 'They're so sure we can't see them, that they're not even trying to hide. Guess what monsters, we can see you.'

Their actions might have been funny, but there was nothing funny about their appearance.

Some were scrawny, most bore long, jagged scars—like they'd fought for their very lives—on parts of their bodies not submerged in swamp water. Several had fresh wounds, open and raw. They'd been in a brawl recently.

Well, they were about to be in another one.

"Let 'em get closer," Hart said. "Maybe around sixty feet. Then we hit 'em hard and keep 'em from escaping back into the marsh."

Stock-still, they waited, watching their hunters swim closer, foot by foot, until...

"Now!" Hart shouted, and hell was unleashed.

The Chosen's and Champion's hands blurred on their bowstrings, launching a dozen arrows in heartbeats. Glowing bolts flashed from Cedric's bow like bursting fireworks, striking scaly skin, and holy power rampaged through convulsing bodies.

Hart's thick arrows had the speed and force of a small battering ram, sinking invisible marauders or flinging them through the air like limp dolls.

Drestra roared an incantation and aimed a spell at their attackers.

Orange light flashed beneath the line of marauders, illuminating the murky water. Steam exploded, scaly skin blistered red. Some died, but some survived and persisted, driven by one basic need: food. Prey had grown scarce.

They charged Baelin's boat, where some stopped mid-lunge, shrieking and clawing at their own flesh—Alex's water elementals were latched onto them, sucking their moisture, absorbing it like a sea sponge. The marauders clutched their throats, gasping for breath like caught fish until their struggles weakened and they mummified, sinking beneath the muddy waters.

Alex didn't bother using his Wizard's Hands, it wasn't necessary. Baelin had watched while his young companions fought the marauders, then when he was ready, he nodded and spoke a single word.

An enormous surge of power preceded the tell-tale signature of summoning magic.

The remaining marauders began to scream.

Below the monsters, the water churned in a spiral, red froth spun violently as scores of squat, foot-long fish materialised beneath the water's surface, tearing at the creatures like packs of starving Grimlochs.

In seconds, invisible marauders swirled in the water, dragged to the bottom of the swamp, or floating on the water's surface as no more than bones.

"Well, that's one way t'get things done," Cedric said.

"I don't think I'll be jumping overboard to get my arrows back," Hart grunted. "Good little fight, though."

"And less marauders to attack the village or anyone out foraging," Drestra said. "That was a *big* pack, I have to say. They only gather in larger groups for protection, so there's definitely a threat somewhere deeper in the swamp. I hope whatever they're afraid of doesn't have my kin."

"This ain't much consolation, but they'll regret it if'n they do," Cedric said.

"Thanks for summoning those vuncali fighting fish, Baelin. It was a good idea for now and for later. I think I get why you called them," Alex said. "They drew blood, now they'll look for more blood in the water and follow the smell, which should take them to wherever the wounded marauders came from. If we follow the fish, we should find what wounded them. That could give us some information about what's going on deeper in the Crymlyn."

Alex looked around. "If you have to go back to Generasi this evening, we'll have a great start for tomorrow."

"Ah! You catch on quickly," the chancellor said.

"Hey, you taught us to let today's advantages be the beginning of tomorrow's advantages," Alex said. "And I didn't exactly sleep through your class."

"No, you got top marks and for good reason! Well done, Alex," the ancient wizard praised him.

It took all of the young wizard's will to resist the irrational, childish urge to throw a smug grin at Hart.

They tracked Baelin's fish through the swamp, following the marauders' blood trails.

All of a sudden, it seemed the swamp had come alive.

Invisible marauder attacks were frequent. No sooner had they put a lone creature down, a pair, or trio would attack. Sometimes the attacks came from large groups. Though the Heroes, Alex, and Baelin eliminated them quickly, the spreading scent of blood attracted more.

They were starving and—as Drestra explained—weren't above cannibalism. Marauders emerged to feast on their own kind, dragging them away from the prying eyes of those who'd killed them.

But the Sage kept them from escaping, blasting them before they could grab their meal and leave.

"There's far too many of these," she said. "Each one we eliminate will make the winter and spring safer for my people." She looked at Baelin and Alex's summoned monsters. "I have to say, those spells are quite handy. We witches don't practise that kind of summoning. Our summoning spells require a lot of ritual and preparation to bind the spirits we ask for aid, and we always give something in return."

"Yeah, that's called subjugation-type summoning," Alex said, watching Bubbles and the other water elementals drink the moisture from a marauder's dead body. "It's not the friendliest way to summon monsters, but if your only goal is summoning a lot of creatures that'll get stuff done for you quickly? It's the best kind."

"Indeed," Baelin said. "At a quieter time, I can give you a crash course on the types of summoning that are possible, when it's convenient for us both."

"Thanks," Drestra said. "I learned some summoning spells in the capital like the ones you both used, but they weren't efficient for destroying Ravener-spawn. I find it easier to just hit them with fire, lightning, or ice..."

She watched the fish. "But having a small army that I can control... Subjugation-type summoning, you called it? Interesting. Anyway, this talk is just distracting us. We should leave it for another time."

Deeper into the swamp they went, fighting more marauders along the way. Soon the tang of blood was so strong, that rather than attracting starving marauders, it was driving them away in fear.

Things grew quiet and the Heroes, wizards, and golem moved through the water undisturbed.

"Pfeh, seems somewhat pointless for us to have been invisible when facing creatures that can turn invisible themselves. Blast it." Baelin frowned. "No doubt there are other foes waiting... Though I suspect the element of surprise has been lost. Loud, running battles tend to attract attention, whether you want them to or not. Hmmm. But it seems we aren't the only ones to have had such battles in this area."

"Yeah," Alex said. "I see what you mean."

Signs of terrible violence marked the foliage. Entire islands of grass had been burned away. Trees were downed. Skeletal remains of invisible marauders floated in murky water or poked through the roots of towering trees.

Their bones had been crushed, battered, burnt, or split. Probably by large weapons.

"Something's claiming this territory as its own," Drestra said. "Something new. I've never seen anything like this in our lands before."

"Probably them damn demons," Cedric said. "An' their cultists. Bloody hell, I didn' think they'd gotten this deep into Thamela—"

"Hold on," Hart said, pointing through the gloom. By now, between the deepening shadows of evening and the worsening snow, it was hard to see clearly.

It looked like there were masses rising from an island ahead, like giant tortoise shells, or piles of something. But what? A wave of dread went through Alex. The Orb of Air he wore cut all smells, and short of removing it, all he could do was wonder if the stench of rot was in the air.

Were they going to reach that island and find Drestra's kinfolks' bodies piled high, left to rot in the swamp? Demon worshippers weren't known for their kindness. From the Sage's manner, it was clear she also feared the worst. Her shoulders tensed the closer they came to the island, and her knuckles had turned white from gripping the boat.

It was Baelin who chased away their fear.

"Wizard's Eyes have checked what lies before us," he announced. "It appears those shadowy mounds are tents: we have found an abandoned campsite."

Sighs of relief came from each Hero while Drestra whispered a prayer of thanks to the spirits. Baelin's boat reached the island, and they disembarked, each scanning a different area with weapons, potions, and firegems ready.

All was quiet.

The campsite held half a dozen empty tents, scattered tools, and a rumpled bed roll left on the cold ground. Nearby, several sturdy mooring posts for good-sized boats stood, all empty.

Two objects in the centre of camp drew their attention.

The first was a dead campfire, which Drestra touched. Her frown deepened. "It's still warm. This camp was used very recently."

"And abandoned in a hurry," Alex noted, approaching the second object of interest.

It was a large, circular stone disk, large enough for a good-sized animal to be laid on. A summoning circle had been carved in it, and within the circle, a partly eaten corpse of an invisible marauder lay.

Cedric leaned down, touching it. "Hm, this body's still warm too."

Alex checked the snowy ground, noting footprints. He called on the Mark, and it showed him images of his time in the countryside of Generasi, tracking the vespara with Theresa. Noting the shapes of the tracks, their depth, and their stride length, he started to put a picture together.

The Fool crouched, peering at the mud.

"There were about ten... maybe twelve people here," he said. "All humans or races of similar height and weight. That looks like the imprint of a weapon rack over there." He pointed at a deep impression in the light layer of snow beside a tent. "And a few areas where people, maybe guards, sat. The edges of the island have impressions of piled logs. Probably for people to sit on and watch the swamp."

He went to the water's edge. "They posted sentries mostly on the side of the swamp we came from. They were probably watching to see if anyone made it this far while searching for the missing witches, in case an invisible marauder or other beast didn't get them first."

Alex pointed to the other side of the island. "All the mooring posts are on that side, which means they probably came from somewhere deeper in the swamp. I wouldn't be surprised if that blood trail your fish were tracking came from somewhere near here, Baelin."

The chancellor's eyes unfocused for a moment. "Indeed. There looks to be a battle sight not one hundred yards from here where my vuncali fish have tracked the trail."

"Right..." Alex said, tapping his chin. "That fits. It might be a bit early to come to conclusions, but I think this is an outpost. We may've found the cult's territory."

CHAPTER 26

THE DEMONS AND WITCHES

"The *cult's* territory?" Drestra's voice rose. "This is territory my kindred claimed too long ago to remember. While it's not someplace that is visited regularly, it belongs to witches, *not* foreign cultists."

"Yeah," Alex said. "It looks like they plan on settling here."

"The hell they do!" the Sage growled.

"What're ya thinkin'?" Cedric asked Alex. "An' how can y'tell all that from a few tracks? Y'must got good eyes."

Hart was silent, examining the ground, looking for his own evidence of Alex's theory.

"It's just a guess," the young wizard said. "But look at the campsite. It's well established. Look over there."

He pointed to a hill of trash on the side of the island. Garbage was piled high, and a deep pit had been dug beside it with burnt refuse at the bottom. A short distance away, what looked like a privy had been erected —a small shack that Alex had no intention of looking in.

"This camp's been here for a while. Mooring posts, weapon racks, the trash pile, a latrine... that all tells me these people are settled here. It doesn't look like they just dropped in for a few hours and then left. I think they've been using this place for some time, making it more of a semi-permanent camp, and judging by the way the guards were positioned... it feels like an outpost."

He tapped the Orb of Air around his head, his mind working. "You know... this is getting into speculation territory, but isn't the Crymlyn kind of the perfect place for a cult to permanently set up? The swamp's deep, it's big and it's hard to navigate. Uldar's followers rarely come here, which makes it easy to hide in and keep people away from coming in here. It's a good staging ground, all things considered."

"They need to get out of *my* swamp," Drestra growled. "I take it this camp was abandoned in a hurry?" She looked in the direction they'd come from. "They probably heard us fighting the marauders and left before we could get our hands on them."

"Aye, didn' wanna face us, bloody cowards," Cedric said. "This could be good news since it narrows our search."

"Indeed, that is what happens when you are able to swiftly repel whatever threatens you," Baelin said. "Hrm, but now time is turning against us."

He examined the sky.

The snow fell steadily, and as night advanced, the temperature was dropping. Thick flakes clung to everything they touched: mud, trees, rocks and the six allies exploring the island. Visibility was even poorer now.

"It does not look like the weather will turn stormy," the chancellor said. "But it will hinder our search. I believe this will be a good time for me to return to my other duties back home."

Alex wanted to keep searching.

They were so close to finding the cultists, and here they were about to lose the most powerful member of their team. It wasn't as if they were weak. Baelin was an unstoppable force, but he, Claygon, and the Heroes could also handle themselves. The cultists had a lot to worry about from them, but stopping the search at this point could mean losing an advantage they'd just gained.

The upside was that with Baelin leaving, Theresa would be joining them.

She wasn't Baelin—no one was—but she could handle her share of monsters.

"Well, if'n you'll be leavin', s'alright." Cedric laughed. "S'a bit unnatural for us Heroes t'be the ones bein' escorted everywhere we need t'go. But, vacation's over, s'time for us to do our work an' get rid o' nasty pests."

"Indeed," Baelin said. "And so I leave this operation in all of your capable hands. Here you go, Alex."

He handed the young wizard the satchel containing the living dungeon core. "I know you'll keep it well hidden, and well guarded safely in your hands."

"Right," Alex said, hanging the satchel across his torso. "When do you think you'll be back? You're kind of our ride back to the encampment."

"Once my duties are completed," the chancellor said. "You can expect me in a few days, briefly, at least. Hopefully, that will be enough time to clean up any troublesome leftover problems that might persist. Now, even though you are all competent young folks, I strongly recommend that you retire back to Crymlyn Village for the evening. Powerful you are, but the enemy knows the terrain—"

"So do I," Drestra cut in. "I've been living here my whole life. I know the land better than they could ever hope to."

"Indeed, if you do regularly venture this deep into your own swamp, there is still the issue of these cultists having a presence here for quite some time. Who knows what changes they've made, traps they've set, and hidden dangers they've left as deterrents for your people. During the day, I have no doubt you could overcome these limits. But in the dark?"

"I can see in the dark," the Sage said, her reptilian eyes flashing.

"But your companions cannot," Baelin pointed out. "In the daylight, you increase your advantages while decreasing those of your enemy."

"He's gotta point, Drestra," Cedric said. "Remember when we got attacked that night by the army o' Ravener-spawn at those standin' stones. Right terrible, that was, as y'said. We can break 'em come mornin'."

"Indeed, and I can make your quest easier before I go." Baelin turned, studying the landscape, soon spotting a thick copse of trees. "I shall conjure a teleportation circle and conceal it in that stand of trees, then link it with Crymlyn Village. Come morning, you can take my boat through the teleportation circle—which I trust will not be reduced to kindling in your battles—and be back here to resume your hunt. Who knows? If you're lucky, you might return to find those who abandoned this post, which will give you prisoners to interrogate."

"That'd be handy," Alex said, turning to the other Heroes with his attention more focused on Drestra. "I agree with Baelin. I think we should wait until morning, then strike hard and fast if they're here when we come back. I know you're worried about your kindred, Drestra, and so you want to get out there right away. But, if we get ambushed, our chances of finding cult members, your friend, and the rest of your kindred really narrows. Then, everyone loses."

The Sage's frown deepened at Alex's words. At last, her crackling voice sighed through her veil. "You... you're right. And if we're tired, that will make things even harder."

"Yeah," Hart agreed. "We'll leave for now, and break 'em good in the morning."

"Then it is unanimous. I am glad you all have chosen the more reasonable path," Baelin said. "Come, then let's be on our way."

The party boarded the boat, floating the short distance to the copse of trees Baelin had pointed out. It was the perfect spot: hard to access and dense with trees, yet wide enough for a teleportation circle that could accommodate the boat. Drestra cast a spell, animating the tree roots and bringing them to lifelike spider legs. They groaned, pulling themselves from the soil and scurried away, making enough room for even Claygon.

Then Baelin cast the teleportation circle and placed an illusion on it, hiding it from hostile eyes.

"This version of the spell has a command word keyed to it which I will share with you once we are back in the village," he said, watching the circle vanish beneath the illusion. "You will have to speak it before entering the circle or it will not transport you at all; keep that in mind. If everyone's ready, it seems our preparations are complete, so, let's be on our way."

With that, the party stepped into the magical circle and vanished from the swamp.

Zonon-In levelled a cold gaze down on the cowering mortal before her.

"And these trespassers differed from the ones you captured before?" she growled, her voice rumbling like both the roar of a wildcat and the chilling noise of blade sliding on blade. Her pincers clicked at her sides.

"Yes, mighty demon spirit." The cultist's forehead pressed so low, it scraped the mud beneath it. "They came through the swamp like they were on a vendetta, not quietly like past ones. But as you instructed, we conjured the wind demon to blow our boats away swiftly, and we escaped."

Zonon-In's growl rumbled through her tent. "So greater forces in this kingdom have found us."

There was a thrill in her voice that she didn't try to hide. A hunger for battle that this out-of-the-way post in the material world denied her. She fought the need to spring from her bone-throne, hoist her war-spear, and lead a warband of cultists and demons to find these enemies and slaughter them for a bit of fun.

But Ezaliel's orders were very clear: avoid all conflict until they had secured at least *one* of the curious prizes his unfortunately now dead wizard-servant had revealed to him—a bauble called a *dungeon core*.

His order was still unfulfilled. Countless search parties had ranged out of the swamp, seeking just one of these things, but were met by either the military forces of this realm, or some of the innumerable monsters that haunted the wilderness.

So she'd decided to wait until winter.

When the snows fell deep, their enemies' armies would be slowed while her ice demons cut across any mortal winter landscape like birds through the sky, then easily claim her master's prize. Ezaliel would reward her handsomely if the object proved as valuable as some said it was. She was in no hurry.

Their captives provided plenty of sacrifices and... entertainment. The cult's access to the larders of their 'guests' ensured there was plenty of sustenance and water to sustain all of their mortal servants for most of the cold season.

It was far more practical to avoid confrontation and simply move deeper into the swamp to conceal themselves from the hostility of mortals.

...Except she was becoming *dreadfully* bored.

Though not bored enough to disregard her master's orders. And besides, there were still *some* things she could do to keep herself entertained, like—

"Demon! Demon, are you there?" an arrogant voice called from outside her grand tent.

A wide grin split her face, revealing rows of dagger-like teeth leading to a small forest of mouth-tentacles. The cultist who'd reported to her shuddered before the undisguised malice of her gaze.

"You may go," she said to the man, resisting the urge to laugh as relief clearly washed through him. Humans were so amusingly small. Both in size *and* courage. "Tell the others that we will move shortly. You may also go and get yourself a reward from the quartermaster."

"Yes, mighty demon!" the cultist cried, facing her while bowing with each step as he retreated from her gaze.

How amusing! For a moment, the image of her claws reaching out to flay the man—just as he felt most relieved—came to her, but unfortunately, her pleasure would have to wait. The look of surprise that would have taken his face was something to savour.

She was patient and these were her master Ezaliel's followers, not her own.

Besides, there were other, more amusing targets that she was letting... ripen.

As if called by that thought, one of those very targets burst into the tent, his face a mask of adorably futile mortal anger. It was like watching an ant bluster about—highly amusing.

She imagined that this mortal saw himself very differently.

"I have heard that outsiders were seen close to our borders!" the man cried. "What will you do about this?"

"As my master commands," Zonon-In replied, massaging the note of amusement in her voice to be its most irritating. "And you are not my master, witch."

He growled. "This is not the deal we bargained for, demon. You said we would unite and throw down the Uldarite slavers who hold dominion in this realm, and bring the lands bordering the swamp into the hands of us witches! Instead, I see you lounging here while your followers use *my* people for your filthy rituals!"

"If you do not like it, you may... cast us out," Zonon-In said, her voice growing cold. "How many of your kindred joined you in betraying your people? Twenty?"

"*Thirty* brave souls who had grown tired of living in fear."

"Thirty magic users of *your* power won't get you very far against my master's many cultists, and my demon servants." She grinned. "I will make good on the bargain... um..."

"*Osian*!" he yelled in such an amusingly self-important way. "This is the tenth time—"

"Right, right, Rosian," she said, waving a pincer. "I'll remember this time. Remain calm. The deal will be made good, but my master's purpose must be satisfied first. I am a mere servant while you are the mighty leader of *thirty*—" she made her tone as condescending as possible "—brave traitors!"

"Not traitors! The others who did not follow are the traitors!"

"Oh, do you mean your more than one hundred kindred who decided not to deal with our followers?" Zonon-In asked. "Seems to me that you betrayed them when you went against the decision of your *former* group, but maybe my addition is off, and you have the majority behind you!"

"Just... never mind!" Osian snapped, and the demon grinned at her victory.

Frustrating this fool was too easy.

"What about the ones poking about our territory? We should capture and interrogate them, just like we did the traitorous Uldar-worshipping cowards from my village!"

"And we will... if they persist, as per my master's orders. Then you can have your little satisfaction, Assian."

"*Osian*!"

"Yes, that is what I said! Now, go. You humans need sleep, am I correct? You seem a little tired and grumpy. Perhaps some sleep will make you feel better."

Howling in frustration, the treacherous-witch stomped from the tent while the demon's rolling laughter chased him.

"By Ezaliel, that was fun... Still, I could use some variety in my sport." Her mouth-tentacles licked her lips. "Hopefully, those trespassers return and put up a fight. I would love to see to them personally."

CHAPTER 27

THE BABY ON THE MUSHROOM

"And look who I found!" Baelin said breezily as he reappeared in Crymlyn Village.

Beside him was the familiar figure of Theresa Lu, looking ready for war. She carried an immense pack over one shoulder, and both of her great-grandfather's blades were sheathed at her hips. In one gloved hand was her birthday gift from Alex, a powerful bow strung with the golden string she'd won at the Games of Roal. At her side, her ferocious cerberus, Brutus, stood—fierce, immense—and as hungry as ever... right until he bounded at the Thameish wizard, barking excitedly, and knocked him over.

"Aagh! Brutus! Stop! Why?" the young man protested as three large, wet tongues slobbered over his face while he floundered on the ground.

"Vengeance is mine," Theresa said quietly, helping him up from Brutus' ongoing tongue bath.

"Vengeance? *Really*?" The cerberus' assault persisted. "Brutus, you're drowning me! And I can't believe you'd hold a grudge like that, Ther—"

He watched her carefully.

She looked tired. In the moonlight, a sheen of sweat shone on her face, reflecting off the gathering snow, and her breaths came faster than usual. She looked like she'd been running.

"Aaaaahhhh, youth." Baelin shook his head and turned to Claygon. "You see how cruel life can be, my giant friend. I am literally one of the most capable archwizards in all this world, but as soon as a young man, a young woman, and might I add, an enthusiastic pup see each other, I am as forgotten as last week's weather forecast." He looked up at the sky mournfully. "To think I would live so long to see my days of glory pass away like this."

"No, wait, Baelin, I—" Alex started.

"Oh, *now* you pay attention to me!" Baelin began laughing. "Calm yourself. I merely jest. And on that note, I will take my leave of you young people and wish you the best of luck and good hunting. My goodbyes have already been said to the others, so do work well together, and most of all, simply take good care of my boat, your other package—" He looked meaningfully at the satchel strapped across Alex's torso. "—and yourselves. Farewell for now. I shall see you all in a few short days."

Theresa and Alex said their goodbyes to the chancellor, and in a flash of teleportation magic, he was gone.

The huntress looked around the fantastical village, letting out a breath that misted white in the cold. They were on the outskirts near the cottage Elder Blodeuwedd had ordered prepared for them.

"So this is the home of the Witches... It actually looks just as I imagined," she said.

"Yeah." Alex patted Brutus' head and mentally told Claygon they were leaving. "But where we're going tomorrow is a hell of a lot less fairy-tale-like. Come on, I'll explain once we meet up with the Heroes. They're in the cottage finishing up supper. You already ate? You want a hand with your gear?"

"Yeah, I ate, and I'm fine with my stuff, thanks," she said.

Their cottage was one of the houses set among branches of a great tree, making the sight of firelight from a cook-fire—flickering between wooden shutters—a very strange sight indeed. 'The tree probably has its own magical defences against runaway flames; otherwise, the practice of cottages in trees would be long dead. Either that, or all the trees would be,' Alex thought.

The village was still as the snow drifted down, leaving Alex and Theresa in a comfortable silence as they climbed up the carved staircase to the cottage door. Brutus' heads were turning every which way—his noses constantly sniffed the air—while he whined, longing to bound through the snow and explore the village.

"Hey," Alex said quietly. "You okay? You look like you've been running from demons or something."

"Yeah," she said, wiping her brow. "I was practising when Baelin came for me, that's all. I'm okay."

At the top of the steps, the Heroes' voices could be heard through the cottage door.

"So what's the deal wit' the elder; y'said she's your ma?" Cedric was asking.

"Yeah," Hart's deep voice spoke up. "She looks a little oldish for that. More like your grandmother, or maybe your great-grandmother. And she doesn't have your eyes?"

"Oi, Hart, y'can't jus' go askin' stuff about why someone's eyes look different. It's kinda rude," Cedric said.

"Cedric, it's alright," Drestra sighed, though weariness had entered her voice. "I'm used to those questions—"

The door creaked open before she could finish, and Alex, Theresa, Brutus, and Claygon stepped in, shaking off snow before Alex shut the door behind them.

"Welcome back!" Cedric lifted an earthenware cup of herbal brew. The witches had brought them a small keg of it with a supper of stew and skewered fish. It was good, filling food with an herbal flavour that Alex promised he'd ask about for his own cooking. Hart was enjoying the meal like it was his last one, making another trip to the stewpot.

"It's good to see you, Theresa. Welcome to Crymlyn Village," Drestra greeted Theresa, and squeezed the young woman's gloved hand, obviously happy to see her.

"Thanks, it's beautiful here, Drestra." The huntress gave her a hug.

Brutus went straight to the fire and curled up, warming himself while Alex took his partner's pack and placed it in a corner beside his own gear. Claygon sat beside it. The cottage was one large room, and each party member had claimed a corner of the space as their own.

"You two are just in time," the Sage said as Theresa and Alex came to warm themselves around a stone firepit in the centre. "Cedric and Hart just asked me about my mother."

"We heard," Alex shrugged. "I didn't really question your relationship, I mean, if she's your mum, she's your mum."

"True, but I've had such questions too many times to count, so I may as well answer now and get everyone's curiosity satisfied," she said, and the fire's reflection danced in her golden eyes. "Elder Blodeuwedd adopted me eighteen years ago. According to her, she found me bawling my eyes out on the cap of a giant mushroom in the swamp. There was no one around, just me. She told me it was a good thing she found me when she did because a giant swamp serpent was about two heartbeats away from swallowing me whole before she killed it. She took me home with her and raised me. She's the mother I've known my whole life. And that's the reason my eyes are different."

Silence followed as the others waited for her to continue her story... but she didn't.

Cedric gave a great yawn. "Aye, well, that's simple enough, isn't it? Kinda feel a bit dull-witted for not putting that together m'self."

"Yeah, that was a lot less epic than I thought it'd be," Hart said, turning his attention back to the remains of his supper.

Theresa simply nodded and said, "Thanks for sharing that with us. It must be annoying feeling you have to explain something so personal about yourself to whoever asks." She pointedly looked at the Champion and the Chosen, then went to unpack some of her things.

Alex subtly watched Drestra for a time, noting certain things about her body language: a closing off of her shoulders, a crossing of her ankles and hands, and her eyes not holding anyone's gaze, merely staring into the fire pit.

They were all signs of someone hiding something.

He took notice, though in the end, it was none of his business. Instead, he cleared his throat.

"Okay, guys, so... for tomorrow, I wanna make a couple of suggestions on how we do things."

The Heroes looked at him.

"Aye?" Cedric took a bite of fish. "Y'sound like some o' the knights that follow us into battle. What's it yer thinkin'?"

"Well, we're tough," Alex said. "Especially you three, but we don't know exactly what we're walking into in the morning. I think we should focus on recon. Drestra, how well do you know that area of the swamp?"

"Not very well," she said. "I've only been there a few times."

"Right..." he said. "I say when we go back, we head further into the swamp, but try to keep things quiet. We stay low and avoid fights with invisible marauders when we can. I'll be having my elemental beetles and water elementals scout for invisible threats. Baelin taught me a spell to summon a vuncali fighting fish, but I can only call one, not a whole school like he did, but at least we'll have one to track scents underwater."

"So scouting and skirmishing, instead of a full assault." Hart nodded. "Okay, there's some sense to that. I think we need to get our hands on someone who can answer some questions, though."

"Yeah, that was my next suggestion. Now, if they're cultists... it'll be hard to get them to say much, but there are ways. In the meantime—" Alex took out a notepad "—I'll be mapping our path through the swamp so we can get out of there fast if we need to. I'm thinking if we do manage to capture a cultist, we bring them back to the village and interrogate them here. If we try to do it out there, we're just asking to get ambushed while we're occupied."

"What?" Cedric raised an eyebrow. "No offence, but ain't that a little cowardly? Drestra's people've been stuck with them bastards for maybe a month or more now, an' we're jus' gonna go in there all sneaky-like an' then scurry back out? We're the bloody Heroes o' Thameland, we've fought armies! I think we can take care of a few bloody cultists. Hell, Hart handled an encampment of them devils all on his own, and I'm surprised you're not talkin' about rushin' in there and just takin' 'em out, Hart."

"I also don't want my people waiting any longer. Anything could be happening to them," Drestra said.

"Yeah," the young wizard said. "I get that. But the way I see it, one major problem we have is that we don't know what's *really* going on in that part of the swamp. We need information. Like, are your kin actually *in* those cultists' hands, and if they are, *where* they are. If we don't know those things, the situation could get even worse for them if we run in blind and start blundering about with no information. That's the thing about Ravener-spawn. They don't take hostages. At least not in my experience."

"No," Cedric said, calmer. "That's a fact, I've never seen 'em do that since we been fightin' 'em... an' aye, that makes things different."

"Yeah, no use in going in there, spells blazing, if we don't know *what* we're looking for or *where* it is," Hart agreed. "Still, I vote we kill as many of them as we can."

"Oh yeah," Alex agreed. "Once we get a prisoner, any cultist patrols we see? We turn them to dust. As a matter of fact, instead of going deeper into what they've got staked out as their territory..."

Drestra scowled.

"...it might be better to loop *around* it and see if we find another outpost."

"Yeah," Theresa agreed. "Baelin briefed me on what you all were up to, and this sounds like a good way to scout out the layout and size of their territory, kill some of them, *and* get ourselves a prisoner nice and early."

"Yes, that all makes sense," Drestra said. "But I don't want to move in too slowly. They've already run from us once. We should make sure more of them don't get the same chance."

"Oh yeah, trust me," Alex said. "They won't be getting away from us."

Alex and two swarms of elemental beetles materialised in the teleportation circle just after sunrise. Around him, six dimly glowing Wizard's Hands floated, each holding sleeping potions.

He dropped into a crouch, listening for sounds both near and far.

Only the natural noises of swamp life and muted whispering of the wind reached him.

A heartbeat later, the rest of the party appeared: Claygon, Drestra, Cedric, Hart, Brutus, and Theresa.

The huntress, Chosen, and Champion had bows in hand with arrows nocked on their strings. Claygon's head swivelled as he scanned the surroundings, while Brutus sniffed the air, his heads turning in different directions.

"Things look quiet so far," Alex whispered. "I haven't seen anything."

Then came Brutus's low growl.

The cerberus pointed his heads toward what appeared to be empty space about ten yards away. Alex's elemental beetles flew straight to it, hovering there.

He wasted no time. With a mental command, he called back the beetles and sent a Wizard's Hand to the empty space, crushing a sleeping potion above it. Mist sprayed, followed shortly by a harsh groan, then a splash. An invisible marauder dropped into the murky depths. A heart-beat later, three arrows slammed into it with terrific force. It was dead instantly.

"Good boy." Theresa stroked Brutus' ears.

"Right, let's get the boat in the water," Alex whispered.

Silently, the Heroes and Theresa carried the boat down a small bank, placing it at the water's edge. Using flight spells on Brutus and Claygon, Drestra let them float above the ground and into the vessel while Alex climbed aboard after a final look around.

He directed Claygon to crouch in the centre, then he cast Orbs of Air around everyone—except Brutus, whose heads would keep scenting the swamp air. And—with a quiet word—Baelin's vessel sailed into the water as silently as a waterbird.

They took a slow, winding route deep into the swamp, using Alex's beetles to scout for invisible marauders. There were none to be seen. Perhaps after yesterday, they might've decided to give this part of the swamp a wide berth. The boat drifted along soundlessly, progressing through the marsh, heading deeper into the swamp.

Around ninety minutes in, Brutus turned one of his heads starboard, growling at something to the right.

"What is it? What is it, boy?" Theresa whispered.

"Is it one o' them invisible things?" Cedric's voice was low.

Then he went quiet... the party looked at each other.

From the swamp, voices reached them.

CHAPTER 28

THE PATROL

The seven companions hid beneath a mud-covered tarp in the belly of Baelin's boat, moving stealthily toward unknown voices.

The cloth was draped over the sides, blending with their surroundings, and if they maintained a snail's pace, they shouldn't draw any more attention than the low, bumpy hills they were drifting past.

"Can anyone make out what they're sayin'?" Cedric asked, his voice barely audible.

"Something about a patrol," Theresa whispered, cocking her ear toward the voices.

Alex frowned, focusing on separating ambient swamp noise from people talking.

'There's... three of them,' he thought. 'They sound... stressed. No, not just stressed... scared. Like they're afraid of... maybe of being spotted? Could be the cultists we're looking for.'

He held his breath, listening intently, but while he could hear talking, the words weren't clear at their distance.

"Let's get closer," Drestra hissed. The Sage raised the tarp slightly, peering ahead, but all she could see were clumps of dense plants between them and the owners of the voices.

"We should just fly over there and ambush them. This is taking too long."

Alex started trying to reason with her, when Hart spoke up.

"That's probably not the best idea, Drestra." His voice was low. "While stomping them to paste would be fun, we gotta make sure things

180

don't get outta hand if we want a live prisoner. Any spellcaster worth their salt isn't just gonna sit there and let us jump them so easy. They probably have familiars, summoned monsters, and who knows what else on watch, so the minute they see us coming, I guarantee there'll be a fight... and that means a bunch of dead prisoners... and they can't talk."

"Yeah, they're demon worshippers; why wouldn't they have summoned demons watching for threats? That's what I'd do," Alex agreed.

Looking down, he considered the water, noting its murkiness. Even a demon swimming under the surface would have trouble seeing anything alive in all that murk. Especially if it just looked like more water.

"Hold on, I'm going to try something."

Alex concentrated, casting Summon Water Elemental through all of the Mark's interference, and conjured Bubbles beneath the tarp. The little water elemental bubbled happily, no doubt excited for his usual reward of a potion or two, or three.

"Hey, Bubbles," Alex whispered. "I need your help." He switched to a tongue of elemental water and pointed to where the voices were coming from. "I want you to go underwater and swim to the sound of talking. Have a good look around, pay attention to everything you see above the surface of the water: everything talking or moving around. Okay?"

The water elemental bubbled again, then rolled over the side of the boat and slipped into the water.

Not long after, the voices ahead rose in pitch. The party sat in silence, listening... but the talking began to fade.

"It seems like they're moving out of earshot," Theresa said. "I can hardly hear them now."

"Let's hope your elemental comes back soon," Drestra murmured.

As if summoned, Bubbles appeared a few heartbeats later, rising from the water so Alex could lift him into the boat. "Welcome back. What'd you find over there?"

He listened as the water elemental—unable to differentiate between humans and other humanoids—gave him a vague report that Alex was able to piece together to get a picture of what he'd seen.

"Hmmmm, no demons by the sound of it," he spoke in low tones. "My little friend says there's five things that look like us... I'm thinking human or close. He also said that there's something with wings circling above them, staying close, so I think it's a familiar."

"Demon?" Drestra asked.

"I don't think so," Alex said. What Bubbles had told him was that 'the flying, winged thing looked like that swarm of winged things that attacked us,' referring to the blue annis hags' giant flock of birds. "I think it's a bird familiar, to be specific."

"Well, if they're watching from above, it'll be hard to get to them," Hart said.

"We can still do it if we move in from where the trees are thickest. We can use them as cover." Destra pointed ahead to a swath of trees rising from the swamp. "A flying familiar could miss us if we keep our distance and keep the canopy above us."

"That's true," Theresa said. "Okay, so we'll keep the tarp covering us and the boat so we blend in like we're part of the swamp. All we have to do is make sure we keep moving cautiously." She watched the trees. "Let's go. I can pick out a path for us."

With the huntress and Drestra guiding, the boat glided on, closing the distance between the party and their prey. All the while, Alex, Cedric, and Hart peered at the sky from beneath the tarp, keeping the bird familiar in sight.

Soon, the voices grew louder.

Alex could pick out the odd snippet of conversation now.

'Jeez, they're loud,' he thought. 'It's like they want to be found.'

The closer they sailed, the clearer the voices, until Drestra gasped.

"I know that voice!" she hissed. "That's Llyworn!"

"Who?" Cedric asked.

"She's one my kindred from deep in the swamp!" Her voice was filled with relief. "We found them! But... I don't understand why they're going in the opposite direction to Crymlyn Village instead of rowing there as fast as they can?"

"Hmmm. That's what I'm wondering too," Alex said. "Maybe it's not really your people. Theresa and I've come across these monsters that mimic voices perfectly, and there's also demons that do the same thing. Hells, some of them can even change shape. What I'm saying is this could be a trap."

"Aye," Cedric said. "I could see that. We rushed 'em yesterday and gave 'em a scare. Now they send out a bunch o' nasty, dirty ol' demons to throw us off."

"Yeah," Alex said. "Could very well be."

"Mmm, let's get closer," the Sage suggested. "We need to hear exactly what they're talking about. Maybe see them if we can. I don't want some demon tricking me with shapeshifting or illusions. So, let's make sure this isn't a trap."

"Right..." Theresa said quietly. "Let's go around that island then. The trees are thicker up there, and we can hide under them when we get closer."

They moved in, and the voices grew louder and the words distinct.

"—is going to kill us if she finds us out here," a woman's voice said.

"That's Llyworn," Drestra whispered.

"And don't you think *Osian* will kill us if we don't act like we own our own territory!" a man's voice snapped back. "Now, stop arguing with me; you're going to alert half the damn swamp."

"A little late for that," Theresa whispered. "Who's that?"

"I don't know that one."

"Will you two quiet down and keep your eyes open?" a third voice hissed. "If those trespassers are still around, they're either going to be running from us or sneaking up on us, and I don't know about you, but I don't need my back decorated with fletching *or* acid arrows!"

"You're louder than the two of them put together!" a fourth voice snapped, and though he was quieter, his tone was even more stressed than the other three.

Alex frowned. Each of them sounded... agitated, even fearful, but that wasn't too surprising. It was the high level of frustration in each voice that was so striking.

"What're they talking about?" Drestra also sounded agitated. "What they're saying makes no sense if they're my kindred, but if they're not and this *is* a trap—and they're really demons or cultists—shouldn't they be acting... like they're on top of the world and not like frightened lambs?"

"It does seem strange, doesn't it? All that noise they're making will just put anyone looking for them on their trail," Hart whispered, peering out from the tarp. His large eyes focused through a gap in the thick tree cover. "I count five of them in the boat."

"Yeah, same here. They're maybe... two hundred yards away," Theresa said, then looked up. "Look. There's the bird."

"Where?" Hart's eyes searched the canopy. "I can't see—oh wait, there it is. Good, if it's hard for us to see it, then it'll be hard for it to see us."

Alex squinted at the sky, but couldn't find the bird, nor the five people in the boat below it. No... there was movement between the trees; no way he would ever have seen them before using blood magic to cleanse his body.

"Can you see what they're armed with?" he asked Theresa.

"Two of them have bows and they're standing; one's watching the bow and portside, the other's watching the stern and starboard," she said. "The others don't have weapons drawn, but... actually, one of them has an axe."

"Spellcasters," Drestra said. "That's a classic formation for our patrols. Two standing archers, one spellcaster on the oars, and two others ready to strike with their spells. If they *are* demons in disguise, then what terrible things did they do to my people to pry that information from them?"

"And is the familiar flying above also a tactic the witches use?" Alex asked.

"Yes," she said. "Whoever they are, they know our strategies."

A grim thought hit them, and everyone went quiet. It wouldn't be the first time traitors were found where friends were supposed to be.

"We have to catch them." Drestra's voice was hard.

"Agreed," Cedric said. "But with 'em havin' their eyes peeled and that bird up there, s'not like we're gonna be able to jus' creep up on 'em with nothin' but a tarp. It'd be simpler to rush 'em and just beat 'em down."

"Yeah, but if spells start flying, that'll alert everything in the swamp," Alex said. "And let's face it, some in that boat will end up dead, if not all of them."

"Right, takin' 'em alive means quiet-like, which means no blastin'." Cedric frowned. "How're we gonna get 'em, then? We three ain't exactly... used to tryin' t'nab enemies alive, that's not our rule for fightin' Ravener-spawn. We go all in."

Alex asked Drestra, "Do your people use Orb of Air spells?"

"Yes, of course," she said. "It's important for living in the Crymlyn, so it's one of the first spells we're taught."

"Damn," Alex swore. "I was thinking I could send Wizard's Hands at them, crunch some sleeping potions in their faces, and send them off to dreamland."

His mind was working on another plan when Theresa chuckled. "I have an idea. We have Orbs of Air around our heads. Now, the question is, can everyone here swim?"

The answers were all positive.

"Hmmmm. Drestra," she said. "Do you know a spell to keep us warm or dry us off if we get wet?"

The Sage nodded. "There were some environmental spells that I learned growing up. They'll keep you warm, won't beat a blizzard, but in temperatures that aren't extreme, they work quite well."

"That includes if we get *really* wet?"

"Yes, we'd still stay warm... why?"

"Good. I have an idea, but it means we're going to have to go for a little dip."

Brutus began to shake.

"Not you, boy, you'll stay here. And, Drestra, if you're okay with it, I need someone to stay here and protect my dog."

The Sage raised an eyebrow. "Really? Dog sitting?"

"Yeah, trust me, it's important," the huntress said. "Here's my plan."

"Hold it!" Llyworn squinted up at her familiar circling their boat.

The duck's squawking travelled through the swamp, drawing the attention of everyone in the boat.

"What is it, Darkwing?" she asked. "What do you see?"

She listened, confused. "What? What're you talking about?"

"What's he saying?" one of her compatriots asked.

"I'm wondering if he's taken to seeing things," she said. "He's telling me there's a boat about two hundred yards east... with a big statue lying in it."

"Well, *that's* a trap if there ever was one," an archer said. "Who puts a statue in a boat?"

"Still, we should at least get close enough to take a look," another witch said. "Report it to Osian, 'cos if we don't and it turns out to be something, we're all demon food."

"Right," Llyworn said, turning to the witch navigating the boat. "Take us east. Around fifty yards away from this supposed boat."

The navigator gave a short command to the animated oars.

They took them through the murky waters, weaving between trees and rough brush until the boat rounded a corner and was greeted by another boat drifting along the water's surface. A tarp obscured the stern, but lying in the vessel's bottom was what Darkwing had described: an enormous, ferocious-looking clay statue.

A large ruby-coloured gemstone shone in its forehead in the morning light.

Llyworn immediately knew *something* was not right. The statue was far too big to fit in the boat without sinking it. And why would anyone abandon such a valuable jewel in the swamp, and how did the statue get there in the first place?

Her eyes narrowed, watching the tarp. "Fire some arrows in there and into that statue. I want—"

Her eyes caught a flicker of movement in the water.

"Shite! Everyone, w—"

Something burst from the water beside them.

CHAPTER 29

THEY WHICH COME FROM BENEATH

The biggest man Llyworn had ever seen surged from the murky depths, seized the edge of their dugout, and pulled hard before she could even react.

The boat shifted violently to the left, groaned, then capsized like a toy boat in a storm. With a strangled cry, the witches hurtled over the sides.

Llyworn plunged deep beneath the surface and into the murky depths, gasping when she hit the frigid water. What saved her from aspirating was the Orb of Air around her head, and she thanked the spirits even as she frantically prayed for their help. Swamp water rose, and she sank lower, fighting rising panic. The last thing she saw above the water was Darkwing desperately shooting from the sky toward her.

Then, frigid, murky water enveloped her. Waving plant life reached for her, tangling her cloak as it spread like a sail. She flailed, terror gripping her, her father's diving lessons fleeing her mind. Llyworn kicked and grabbed for the surface, kicking up mud, silt, and weeds. Swamp water grew murkier from each frantic movement.

'Spirits, help me, I can't see!' Panic took her mind.

'Calm down or you'll die! Calm down and find the others. Call Darkwing!' she snapped at herself.

Fighting fear, Llyworn began chanting...

...as a pair of gloved hands reached from behind and clamped her mouth shut. A pair of legs wrapped around hers.

Terror surged. She struggled against them, trembling from panic and cold, but her captor held tight. She couldn't escape. A breath later, rope and murky water slid between her teeth, and she gagged as gloved hands tied the rope tight.

There'd be no spells for her now.

That iron strength spun her around, bringing her face to face with a young woman she could barely make out in the turbid water.

A young woman who snarled like a starving wolf.

———

Nearby, Alex swam up to the man with the axe while Cedric, Hart, and Theresa were restraining the others floundering in the frigid water. The axe wielder was panicking, swinging his axe in every direction and screaming into his Orb of Air. Alex moved behind him, grabbed his wrist mid-swing and yanked the axe from his hand.

The man's agitation grew. He kicked the water, trying to stay afloat while clawing at the Fool, who dropped the axe. He could just imagine the Mark deciding it was more 'weapon' than 'tool' right when he was underwater with a volatile, struggling man who'd probably like nothing better than to drown him. So, he grabbed the man's face and took his rope out to bind him.

His opponent lunged. Alex spun and dove, surfaced behind him, then looped the rope around his torso, pulling it taut. His adversary fought his capture but couldn't match Alex's strength. In heartbeats, he was subdued and being dragged up to the water's surface.

Alex's Orb of Air split the muddy surface, and he inhaled... only to be greeted with a face full of angry duck.

"Argh! Sic that thing, Bubbles!"

The water elemental emerged from below, blasting the bird with a cascade of water, driving it toward the bottom of the swamp. The duck righted itself and shot for the surface, but just as it took flight, Alex plucked the flapping waterbird from the air and bound it like he was trussing it for Sigmus dinner.

Soon, Theresa, Cedric, and Hart surfaced with captives in tow. The Chosen had actually grabbed two, his morphic weapon ringed one, squeezing tighter the more they squirmed.

He laughed, his golden tooth shining in the morning light. "Bloody hell, it was worth the cool dip, wouldn't cha say? We caught all of 'em."

"Great plan, Theresa." Alex smiled. "They were so busy watching what was happening above, they didn't think about what could be happening below."

Sitting on the tarp in the bottom of Baelin's boat a few yards away, Drestra, Brutus, and Claygon watched. The Sage had already dismissed a force shield spell she'd positioned over herself and the cerberus, protecting them against any attack on the boat... but an attack never came since the enemy abruptly found themselves over their heads in swamp water. Her eyes took in her companions and the prisoners, then she sighed, a long tired sound. "Good. You *did* catch them. Are any of you hurt?"

"Just cold," Theresa said, swimming toward the boat. "Let's get these people on board so we can get out of this water. Your spell makes it bearable, but not exactly pleasant. I'm not complaining. Look at the prisoners!"

"Yes, hurry back. They're turning blue!" the Sage said. "You have some protection from the cold water, but *they* don't."

She pointed at the captives; all were trembling, some were still fighting their gags and struggling against their bonds, but others were shaking so hard their movements were jerky and their complexions greying.

The duck, of course, was perfectly fine, still pecking at Alex with its bound bill.

"Right, don' want 'em freezin' before we get a chance ta have a little chat with 'em," Cedric said, swimming for the boat

"Yeah," Alex followed close behind, his mind already working on a new problem.

'We have prisoners, and there are ways to get them to talk, but we'd probably rather not use them,' he thought. 'How're we going to get them to talk, then? If I was them, I'd just keep my mouth shut as soon as the gag came off. Actually, their spellcasters'll probably try casting a quick spell as soon as their gags are off, but that's okay, a booby-trapped mana soothing potion will put a stop to that. Still, what's to stop them from just shutting up? And if they don't talk, what can we do to make them?'

He knew what Baelin and Grimloch would suggest. He'd cross that bridge only if there's no other way to find out what happened to Drestra's kin.

The questioning problem turned over in his mind as he watched the others swim to the boat.

'Claygon,' he thought. 'Thanks for being a diversion, buddy. Would you mind helping people back into the boat?'

Drestra startled as the golem stood and flew away, hovering above the water using Drestra's flight spell. Their backup plan—if they were spotted—was for Claygon to fly at the dugout, grab the archers and flip their boat over. But that was more of a contingent plan. It would have been messy and there was no way the people in the boat wouldn't have seen him coming then started spellcasting and making a lot of racket, alerting every cultist in earshot. Which would have meant a fight and nobody left alive to interrogate.

Fortunately, it hadn't come to that.

'Everything's going as smooth as—' Alex began a thought as he watched his golem hoist Theresa, Hart—and their prisoners—into Baelin's boat.

Drestra began casting spells of warming on the prisoners, raising their body temperatures. Hypothermia wasn't part of the plan if they wanted them to live, but as she warmed them, the look on her face could have frozen them.

"It really is you... What in all hells is going on, Llyworn?" The Sage scowled at the other witch. "What're you doing out here? Why aren't you trying to get back to the village?"

Cedric and Alex swam for the boat as Claygon flew toward them.

'Huh, that was kinda dumb,' he thought. 'We should've had Drestra cast flying spells on all of us too. Then we could've just flown the prisoners to the boat after we grabbed them. Ugh, tension really makes you miss things—'

Theresa had gone stock-still. Only her head moved, her eyes scanning the area like an owl.

Brutus jumped up barking, frantically sniffing the air, his hackles raised.

Hart's attention left his prisoner, turning to the swamp around them. His large eyes examined the trees.

A crawling feeling snaked up Alex's spine. Like someone's gaze was on him, watching him with eyes free of humanity.

Theresa's head stopped tracking. Her eyes went wide, and her bow seemed to leap into her hand as quickly as a single word left her lips.

"Demon!"

Alex whirled, spinning the prisoner and catching a shimmer of movement just above the trees. A small, angry imp glared down from the sky.

Its shriek pierced the silence when Theresa's arrow slammed into its chest.

More movement came from the trees below. Alex's senses tingled as mana built. A sudden flash of light illuminated the trunks.

"Oh shi—" He dove, dragging his prisoner beneath the water.

Rays of orange coloured the air and water.

Impact.

There was little left of his prisoner. Two beams had struck him, one in the head and one in the chest, and the water stained red.

The young wizard untied the mangled corpse while sending mental directions to Claygon.

'Attack!' he thought. 'Find whoever's shooting at us and stop them!'

A shadow passed overhead as Claygon flew toward their assailants. Alex cursed. His pack was in the boat, and he only had two potions on him.

'These'll do nicely, though.' He took the flight and haste potions from his belt, pushed one vial at a time into his Orb of Air, pulled the corks with his front teeth and drained the liquid.

The world slowed around him, and he sped away, splitting the murky surface, where flight took over. Alex soared, dodging a barrage of beams from up ahead.

He took stock of the area.

Claygon was racing for the trees. Hart's and Theresa's prisoners and Brutus were lying prostrate in the boat. The Champion and huntress kept low, firing arrows like a steady rain. Cedric had reached the boat and was transforming his weapon into a bow, while Drestra was beside him, covering their side of the vessel, deflecting beams with her force shield spell. Her eyes blazed and she fired bolts of acid in the attackers' direction.

Alex searched the water for Cedric's prisoners. He found them, floating face down with holes the size of their heads blown into their bodies.

'Shit! They're shooting at the prisoners!' He cast force shield, reaching the boat and grabbing his bag, then raced after Claygon. The nearer to his golem he went, the clearer what they were up against became.

A war party of cultists and demons, with few mortals among them, but a score of demonic warriors towered above boats made of what looked like the spines and attached ribs of titanic beasts covered with a demon's transparent hide.

The demons were all bulk, their skin covered in iron pikes. Their left arms terminated in club-like hands bearing claws as long as short swords, while their right arms ended in peculiar metal tubes. As Alex came closer, a demon tracked his flight with those tubes. Light and mana built up in each one, then exploded. Bloodred beams of force tore after him.

He dodged, but more rays chased him and Claygon from the boats below. The golem flew through the beams, as arrows and acid spells flew past him, striking cultists and demons. Their bodies tumbled overboard into murky water, foaming from acid.

A cultist pointed at Alex, and demons turned, firing a barrage of rays through the sky. A ray hit his shoulder as he spiraled through the cluster of red beams.

Grunting with pain, the Thameish wizard reached for mana soothing potions and dropped them on the assailants.

Vials burst, clouds of mana soothing potion blanketed the enemy. Rays of light and force began to sputter and die.

The demons staggered, calling to each other in their demonic tongue, but Claygon flew into their midst, ending all conversation. Massive fists went to work, and with each swing, someone—whether demon or cultist —became paste.

'Catch some, Claygon!' Alex thought. 'We need them for questioning!'

The golem switched tactics, reaching for their opponents rather than turning them to pulp.

And at that moment, things turned into a waking nightmare before the young wizard's eyes.

It was clear that the battle wasn't going in the cultists and demons' favour and they'd soon be taken alive, which led to something that Alex would remember, even if he reached twice Baelin's age. The cultists drew their blades and invoked a single name—Ezaliel—then died by their own hands, driving the blades into their throats. The demons bellowed at each other, then sprang, firing their beams and ripping one another to shreds.

Alex gaped in disbelief. Even the pair of demons Claygon had caught killed each other before anyone could begin to understand what they were seeing.

Demonic boats groaned as though they were alive, then shriveled like mummifying bodies in the Barrens of Kravernus. Skin withered. Bone crumbled.

In heartbeats, all that was left of the war band floated atop the water, pieces occasionally drifting to the bottom of the swamp.

"Holy hell," Alex swore. "What just happened?"

Silence returned to the swamp.

CHAPTER 30

PAINTING WITH THE COLOURS OF HORROR

Images of the carnage he'd just seen filled Alex's mind as he and Claygon flew back to the boat. He'd seen violent deaths before; he'd even helped cause some—Hive-queens, Mana vampires, monsters in the Barrens, even demons—but this was different. Mortals and monsters dying with such violence by their *own* blades, and at their own claws. It was unsettling, even for someone who'd seen more than his share of violence.

'That took... a terrifying amount of fanaticism,' he thought. 'It took a lot of will to do something like that.'

He glanced back at the ruins of the cultists' bodies.

'No way they would *ever* have talked,' he thought. 'Holy shit.'

Baelin's boat was gliding toward him, and he flew down to meet it.

"Everyone alright?" he asked.

"Yeah!" Theresa called back. "But what about your shoulder?"

He glanced at a red stain spreading across his shirt.

"I'm okay," he assured her, floating into the boat. "After what just happened, a wound to my shoulder isn't top of mind right now."

"Aye, c'mon then, let's get ya patched up," Cedric said.

The Chosen reached out, his power touching Alex's wound. Theresa casually caught his eye. Her eyes flicked to his Marked shoulder as relief passed through them. Thankfully, the beam hadn't hit his right side. Trying to come up with a reasonable explanation for why he didn't need to be healed when blood was staining his shirt would have brought Cedric's attention and questions. The Fool never thought he'd be thanking the Traveller for a wound, but here he was, thanking her for being shot on the left side.

"Did any live?" Drestra asked.

Alex shook his head while Cedric's divinity numbed the pain and healed him. "No... they either killed themselves or each other. It was pretty gruesome."

"Well, that's some scary shit," Hart said. "You see warriors do that sometimes; they're the ones you either have to worry about the least... or the most."

"What do you mean?" Theresa asked.

"I mean they don't care about preserving their own lives if their mission fails. They take a lot more risks than someone who wants to come out of a battle breathing. They also won't stop fighting, even when it's obvious you got them beat."

"Shite, s'like fightin' Ravener-spawn; they ain't got sense enough to stop fightin'." Cedric peered at Alex's wound and clapped him on the shoulder. "There we go, all mended as easy as ma's knitted cloak."

"Thanks," Alex said, looking toward the demons' boats. Brutus' necks were stretched in that direction, his snouts sniffing and growling at the dead.

"Wonder what the hell they were doing. Maybe following this lot." He nodded to the two prisoners shivering in the bottom of the boat.

"We won't know until we get some proper answers," Drestra said, dragging a corpse toward the vessel. "And... no matter what they were up to, their bodies have to be taken to Mother."

The teleportation circle in Crymlyn Village shimmered, drawing the eyes of witches passing by as Alex Roth appeared in the circle. Heartbeats later, his companions materialised around him.

Claygon carried three bodies—wrapped in the tarp—tucked beneath his arms, while Hart and Cedric had hold of the prisoners. The pair looked bone-tired and dejected, like their lives had ended back in the swamp water. The familiar was the only one still resisting, pecking at Alex and anyone else with the gall to come near it. Its eyes glowed bloodred. "You're staying tied up for now, duck," Alex said, keeping out of pecking range.

"Welcome back home... *kindred*." Drestra's tone was dangerous.

The prisoners couldn't say a word, but Alex didn't think they had any interest in conversation, even if their mouths weren't bound. The Heroes, Alex, Theresa, Brutus, and Claygon made their way toward Elder Blodeuwedd's hall, deep in the village. Witches dropped what they were doing and followed as they headed toward the standing circle and dead aeld tree; they were attracting a growing crowd.

Along the way, a bewildered young man pushed through the gathering and came up to Drestra. A frown creased his brow.

"What's all this?" he cried. "Llyworn? Is that you? You're alive?"

Every pair of witches' eyes were on the bound prisoners, their faces awash with confusion.

Llyworn glanced up, then quickly looked back down.

"What in the spirits' true names?" Angharad looked at Drestra in alarm. "Why do you have our kin tied up like common bandits?"

"Because, something is very wrong," was all she said, her voice cold enough to chill Alex's blood.

"Oh..." Angharad didn't push further. "You're taking them to the elder, I take it?"

"Yes, Mother will be able to figure this out."

"Right," the puzzled sentry agreed. "That's the best thing to do." His eyes drifted to the bodies under Claygon's arms. "And... them?"

The Sage's eyes hardened. "Those are more of our people, Angharad. We were attacked and things turned against them."

The sentry was silently eyeing the bodies.

The crowd whispered to each other all the way to the centre of the village and the elder's hall. To Alex's surprise, Elder Blodeuwedd was waiting outside, her face grim.

"Mother, I'm glad you're here," Drestra called as they dragged the prisoners toward the hall.

"The trees told me you were back, daughter," she said. "And that you were holding... captives?"

"Things... have grown complicated," Drestra said.

The Sage told of what they had seen, and the elder's face turned grimmer, watching the shapes wrapped in the tarp. "What about them?"

"Complicated," Drestra said again.

"Bring them within," the old woman said, her voice terrible. Her attention turned to the crowd. "Back to your chores! All of this gawking won't keep winter's bite away, and if our stores aren't fattened, we'll be burying some of you soon enough!"

The villagers were reluctant to leave, but slowly began dispersing throughout the village.

'She kinda reminds me of a storybook witch right now,' Alex thought —and of course kept that thought to himself.

Alex and Theresa's eyes met, then flicked to Cedric and Hart.

Their faces were blank, except for a slight smile playing at the edge of Hart's lips.

"Bring them," the elder said, her eyes fixed on the prisoners. As soon as Claygon—who was last to enter the hall—stepped through the doorway, Elder Blodeuwedd waved a hand.

The door slammed, the noise echoing in the soaring space.

"Follow me." The old woman led them to the rear of the hall and a staircase that ran deep below ground. She clapped her hands twice, and a host of paper lanterns filled with green glowing fireflies sprang to life, bathing the dark stairwell with an eerie light.

As the group descended—Claygon floated, his feet too massive for the steep, earthen staircase—Alex turned his mind back to the problem of getting the two prisoners to talk. He remembered Gustavo and Ferrero questioning him in Generasi. The pair of investigators had isolated him, trying to play on discomfort and anxieties to get to him.

The tactics hadn't worked on him, but they might work on prisoners who were involved in some way with demon worshippers. Alex was deep in thought when they reached the doorway of a large chamber beneath the hall. He let out a low whistle.

A ceiling at least twenty feet high, and perhaps twice that in length and width, rose above them.

The walls were lined with potion bottles, scrolls, jars with strange, withered things floating in them, and stone tablets covered in ancient sigils that were stacked high. In a corner of the chamber a firepit crackled, and above the flame, a black cauldron with dragons, and monsters of all shapes and sizes forged into its sides and lip, hung from a braided handle. The pot was large enough to fit Grimloch with room to spare. And in the centre of the room, a summoning circle carved upon a slab of dark stone waited, emanating an eerie quality that filled the space.

More green fireflies flitted about in hazy glass orbs, making the room feel even more... sinister, especially when Theresa whispered, "Is... is that blood?" She held on to Brutus.

Alex followed her gaze, finding dark, rust coloured patches staining the stone.

"This uh... y'got a nice place here, probably gets lots'a lips flapping," Cedric said awkwardly.

"This is *not* a nice place, child." Elder Blodeuwedd stared at him, then muttered a flight spell and rose high above the floor. She drifted past scores of over-packed shelves, pausing only when she reached one with bottles of potions stored in casket-shaped boxes.

The elder floated toward the prisoners, uncorking two bottles.

As an acrid scent wafted into the air, Brutus whined, backing away from the potions.

"Hold them steady, big man." The elder witch floated to Hart, who was eyeing the bottles like they were coiled vipers.

"Uhm, what's in those?" he asked.

"Ancient recipes known to few, using ingredients found only here in the swamp." She conjured glowing green Wizard's Hands to hold the potions, then took a tiny brush from the pouch at her waist.

The prisoners had been subdued, but they now found strength to struggle the moment the brush appeared. Hart's grip doubled.

'I bet Professor Jules and Generasi law would have a lot to say about whatever's about to happen,' Alex thought, looking at Drestra.

If she had a problem with what was happening, she didn't say. Hopefully, that meant the potions wouldn't melt flesh, or start turning anyone to stone, or anything gruesome like that. He remembered how Drestra had insisted her dead kin be returned to the village, so it was likely a safe bet she wouldn't approve of her living kin being melted.

The elder witch dipped the brush into the first potion bottle and spoke an incantation while swirling the liquid around. As words of power poured from her lips, the potion in the tiny bottle turned a sickly green and glowed like fireflies.

Every word she spoke repeated, filling the air, sounding like scores of voices echoing in the vast chamber. Blodeuwedd took the brush from the liquid and slowly painted the potion across the captives' foreheads. The witches' eyes rolled back, their bodies stiffened, and Alex startled when the angry duck tensed in his hands. She dipped the brush into the potion again and again, painting different sigils on their foreheads.

The prisoners alternated between stiffening like statues and shaking violently as Blodeuwedd went about her work. When their foreheads were covered, their throats were next. Llyworn began to gag.

"Oi!" Cedric cried. "Get the gag off 'er mouth b'fore she chokes!"

"It is alright," the elder said, painting symbols on the other witch's cheeks. "She will not choke, nor will she vomit."

Alex was puzzled.

He could feel mana pouring from the familiar and the prisoners in

Hart's grip. It ran out in torrents. Cedric was noticing it too and looked horrified.

"What's happening to them?" Alex asked.

"The purgative is taking effect." The witch dipped her brush in the other bottle. "It's like any tonic you would give someone to induce vomiting, only this makes a spellcaster 'vomit' up their mana, so to speak."

Alex shuddered, exchanging a horrified look with Cedric. Drestra, however, appeared as calm as if she was having a soothing cup of tea.

"They will recover their mana in a week's time, with no lasting damage," she said. "But in the meanwhile, there will be no spellcasting for them. And things will be easier for us."

Alex's stomach churned at the thought of that happening to him.

He told himself to remember not to make an enemy of the Witches of Crymlyn Swamp. Although, if that ever happened, to never, ever let them capture him alive. Maybe those cultists had taken the smart way out...

"W-what's that one now?" Alex asked, looking at the other potion.

The liquid glowed with a deep amber light.

"This relaxes the will," the elder said, painting golden-brown symbols on the wild-eyed witches. "It makes one tractable, unable to lie or deceive, so they become completely cooperative."

'Holy hell,' Alex swore internally. 'This is like fifteen kinds of illegal in Generasi.'

Still, there was a part of him—a part that worried him a little—that would have given a lot of coin to learn the recipes for those two potions.

"Are there any lasting effects to this one?" Alex asked.

"It can permanently damage one's will if the sigils are poorly applied, my curious child... Like in situations such as this, where I'm being distracted," she said pointedly.

Alex shut up. He didn't need the Mark's guidance to know when he was being politely told to be quiet.

"Keep a tight grip on them, young man," the elder said, dipping her brush again. "The second potion has a tendency to weaken the legs. Captives often collapse after it's applied."

"Oh uh... okay," Hart said, his voice shaky.

Alex, Theresa, Cedric, and Drestra looked at him sharply. The towering man had gone pale, and as hard as it was to believe, he actually looked scared. If Alex had eaten recently, he would be wondering if magical mushrooms had been in his food. The words 'Champion' and 'afraid' were as opposite as the words 'Baelin' and 'newborn.' The four of them tried to catch his eye, but they were fixed on the ceiling, pointedly avoiding sigils or potions used to paint them.

"Jus' when ya thought ya'd seen everything," Cedric muttered.

The elder shot him a stern look and finished drawing her symbols. Llyworn and the other witch abruptly relaxed. Hart kept them upright as light left their eyes. They stared blankly into empty space.

The elder rested her brush in a bucket on a nearby table, then floated to the potion wall and returned them to their storage boxes. She sealed them with a wave of her hand then faced her kindred, looking into their vacant eyes.

"Are you ready to talk?" she asked.

They nodded in unison, their movements sluggish, like they were moving through thick mud.

She looked at the five companions. "They're ready."

CHAPTER 31

AN INTERROGATION PROFESSOR JULES WOULDN'T LIKE VERY MUCH

"What are your names?" the elder asked.

"Llyworn," the young woman said, her tone distant.

"Rhodri," the male witch spoke without emotion.

Both were now freed from their gags—but their hands and feet were still bound. They were sitting in the middle of the chamber, near the cauldron. Elder Blodeuwedd and Drestra stood before them, while Alex and the others had positioned themselves behind the Sage and the old witch.

Looking into the prisoners' eyes and seeing no light, no spark of free will, was chilling. Even fear had been replaced by nothingness. Alex finally understood why such magics were forbidden in Generasi. Unconsciously, he reached for Theresa's hand and squeezed it.

Hart's eyes were everywhere but on Rhodri and Llyworn, while Cedric's jaw was tense, his arms crossed over his chest.

"What were you doing out in the swamp, Llyworn?" Drestra began the questioning.

"We... were hunting for those who made us leave our outpost," the young woman said.

She went silent. The Sage waited for her to continue, but no words came.

"You have to keep pushing for answers, Drestra," the elder witch said softly. "With the will unravelled, free thought is absent. You have to lead them through your questioning."

The Sage gathered her thoughts. "Was this outpost held by cultists?"

"Yes."

"Are you working with them?"

"Yes."

Silence followed a deep breath from Drestra.

"When did this happen, Rhodri?" A hard edge had come to her voice.

"Six weeks gone."

"How did it happen?"

"People came, offering an alliance," the man said, then fell into silence.

"Was this offer of alliance accepted?"

"Elder Gethin made them leave, but Osian met with them secretly and accepted their offer."

"Go on, what happened next?"

"Osian killed Gethin, then we helped the cult capture the others."

Drestra paused, her jaw clenching.

"The others, Llyworn?"

Alex focused on that part, wondering if every witch from deep in the swamp had allied with the cultists, or if there were some in need of rescue.

"Many didn't join," Llyworn said. "They were taken. Some joined us later, but some are used in demon rituals."

"What rituals?"

Llyworn recounted the demons' baser habits with a flat tone, like she was telling a tale of eating gruel for breakfast.

Theresa gasped, her gloved hand covered her mouth. Alex's jaw tightened. Cedric grimaced. Hart gave a low growl that rumbled from the bottom of his chest, and Drestra's breath caught. She stepped toward the prisoner, her eyes like stone, but Elder Blodeuwedd reached for her daughter's arm, hissing something beneath her breath.

'We've got demons to kill,' Alex thought.

"Stop!" Drestra cut the witch off. "Osian allows this?"

"Yes."

"Why?"

"The cultists promised to help us drive Uldar and his followers away from here," she said.

Alex snorted. Even if those demons did make good on their promise in some way, they wouldn't leave these traitors very happy about it. Demons were pure chaos, and their whims were nasty.

"What did they want in return?" the elder asked Rhodri.

"They wanted us to shelter them," he said.

"Is that all?"

"No, we have to guide them through the countryside so they can capture dungeon cores."

"What? Why would they want dungeon cores?"

"They believe there's hidden power or treasure in them."

The Heroes, Alex, and Theresa looked at each other.

Drestra leaned in closely. "Where are they camped, Llyworn? Describe it to me."

"Hold on," Alex glanced at a desk nearby and took a folded sheet of parchment and three pens from his bag. "Mind if I use that?"

Elder Blodeuwedd nodded, and Alex set the paper down, then concentrated, conjuring a pair of Wizard's Hands and handing them each a pen.

"Go ahead, Drestra, I'm ready for that description of the camp," Alex said. "I'll draw us a map and write down everything she says."

"Alright, Llyworn," Drestra said. "I'm going to ask you to describe your camp in detail. Let's start from the beginning. How would I get there from the village?"

The questioning continued, Drestra was thorough, making Llyworn break down every twist and turn to get to the cultists' camp. She asked about landmarks, where outposts lay, and the specifics of the cultists' defences.

Alex wrote down everything, then put the details together in his mind so Wizard's Hands could sketch out a rough map. Drestra and Blodeuwedd focused their questions well, and—once they had finished—Alex had questions of his own.

With the answers he was given, he mapped out the route to the enemy camp, and the details of how it was set up, but there was one important question still to be answered.

"Where are they keeping the prisoners?" Drestra asked.

"In the centre of camp, behind a palisade," Rhodri said.

"Are their mouths gagged to stop spellcasting?"

"Yes."

"Who's guarding them?"

"Demons."

"What kind of demons?"

"I don't know that."

"Describe them," Alex said.

He listened to the witch, carefully noting his description of the demons guarding the prisoners, as well as the other ones in the camp. As he wrote, he called on the Mark, focusing it on the task of identifying demons. It brought back memories of all the demonology and summoning books he'd read, and the illustrations in them.

Unfortunately, there were some—like the beam-shooting bastards and the demon leader—he'd never seen before.

"Describe the leader in detail, Llyworn," Drestra told her.

"It's an enormous, frightening creature, around three times the height of a tall man. Her eyes shine like fire and her skin's a similar colour. She has four arms, the lower ones have claws like crayfish pincers at the ends, and when she opens her mouth, it's full of teeth and tentacles. It's said that spells and spear tips don't seem to damage her."

Alex grimaced. "Oh, she'll be *loads* of fun."

"What is it?" Cedric asked him.

"She sounds like one of the higher demons. Some of them can resist mana and divinity. Nasty bastards. She'll be a tough one."

He tapped the page with his pen, circling a couple of numbers.

"Looks like we'll be up against maybe a few hundred cultists and half that number in demons, and many of them aren't exactly weak like the ones first-tier spells can summon, and that doesn't take into account those I can't name."

"Hundreds ain't too bad," Hart said. "We fight hundreds of Ravener-spawn all the time."

"Aye, but that's without havin' hostages ta worry about," Cedric said. "Can't exactly have Drestra drop a tornado o' fire on the camp an' call it a day."

"Yeah," Theresa said. "And if we attack in the open, they could kill the prisoners. Remember, they killed *themselves* rather than being captured, and they killed our prisoners first. It's like Hart said, they'll slaughter everyone if it looks like they're gonna lose."

Drestra let out an inhuman growl. "Did you see Ffion, Llyworn? You talked about sacrifices. Is she still alive?"

Alex could hear the tension in her voice, and realised she must've been holding back from asking that question.

"I saw her yesterday when I took food to the prisoners," the witch said.

Relief went through the Sage in such a wave, she looked like she was going to collapse.

"I'm happy for you, child," the elder said, patting her daughter's arm.

"Is that your friend?" Theresa asked.

"It is... We need to get her out of their clutches, and we need to kill those invading, filthy creatures." The Sage's hands balled into fists.

"No argument here," Cedric said. "We could strike hard an' fast, get the prisoners out before they can hurt 'em."

"Not with those beam-demons," Alex said. "They're so many of them that there's no way we could get the prisoners without a lot of casualties."

"Yeah," Hart agreed. "They could just spread out into the swamp and shoot us as we're leaving. We have a lot of folks to rescue, so we won't be moving fast either—Ah shit, the water. We'd need boats to get everyone out. Lots of places for a lot of people to die." He scratched the back of his head in thought. "I'm wondering if maybe we should wait for Baelin to come back. We know right where these cultists and demons are, so we wait for him, he turns us invisible and *then* we cut the heads off the snake before they know what hit 'em."

"There's too many," Drestra argued. "All it would take would be for just one demon to go after the prisoners. Who knows how many lives would be lost? And..." She looked at Rhodri. "How often do these sacrifices take place?"

"Every day," Rhodri said. "In the dawn ritual, a beast from the swamp is sacrificed on their altar, and in the dusk one, a beast and a witch are bled together, mixing the blood."

A heavy silence filled the room.

"And you let this happen? Why?" the elder witch asked.

"They wouldn't join us," Rhodri said flatly. "And their sacrifice is for our people's greater good."

"You mad bastard," Alex swore at the witch. Anger surged through him.

'Now I understand why Baelin hates fanatics so much,' he thought.

"We can't wait for Baelin; we have to get them out of there," Drestra said, her eyes on Llyworn. "And what about this camp? Is it permanent?"

"No, it moves every few weeks," the other witch said.

"Has it moved recently?"

"They were preparing for their next move when we left."

"Shit," Drestra swore. "We can't lose them again. When Llyworn and her ilk and those demons don't come back, everyone will run, and they might kill our kin when they're breaking camp. We can't let that happen."

"You're right," Cedric said. "Demons or not, we've beaten worse odds. Takin' the fight to 'em'll be easier than tryin' to track 'em while they're spreadin' out and hidin'."

"We should thin their numbers if we're going to try a rescue, though," Alex said.

"That's probably the best way to do things. Normally, I'd say we pick them off over time." Theresa frowned, organising her thoughts. "Like wolves picking off a herd of deer, but while we're doing that, they'll be killing prisoners."

Alex's mind was working.

Think. Adapt.

"Okay, we know the layout of their camp, right? What we need are ways to get in and ways to get out. You Heroes could probably break them by force, but that big demon worries me."

"Think we can't take it? Come on, man, you've seen us fight!" Cedric said, sounding hurt.

"You're all powerful," Alex said. "But... higher order demons and devils are on a level all their own. I'm *not* exaggerating when I tell you they're terrifying."

He thought about Hobb. The carnage one devil—alone—had unleashed on those demons in the arena was the stuff of repeating nightmares. The aftermath and the stories spectators told were cautionary tales Alex remembered well.

"I just don't like unknowns," he said. "And besides, it'd be one thing if we had her alone and surrounded, but she's going to have a ton of reinforcements with her. Demons, spellcasters, and the Traveller knows what else. And *we* have to worry about rescuing prisoners, while all she has to worry about is, y'know, gutting us."

"Aye, I still think we could take 'er. We fought some nasty shite, an' even wit'out Merzhin wit'us, there's few things in the land we've got t'fear." The Chosen grinned and there was a light in his eyes that reminded Alex of their first meeting outside Coille forest, when Cedric slaughtered an entire horde of silence-spiders all by himself.

"But, truth is, I don't think we're gonna be able to do that wit'out losin' a bunch of people we need to be rescuin'. We gotta break 'em up. Lure 'em out."

"Right..." Alex said. "If there were less of them in that camp, we'd be fine, but what could lure them out... Wait—" Inspiration struck. "Hey, you said the cultists are going after dungeon cores, right?"

"Yes," Rhodri said.

Alex stepped closer, an idea brewing. He remembered how Burn-Saw had recognised him. "How are they supposed to find them?"

"By tracking Ravener-spawn," he said. "And they have demons that can sniff out a dungeon core's mana, like bloodhounds."

"Oooooh, that's *great*." Alex grinned, his eyes twinkling.

Drestra's eyebrow rose. "What're you thinki—Oh." She began laughing.

"And let's say they find a dungeon core fairly close to their camp," Alex pushed, watching the captives closely. "What would they do?"

"They would send a war party," Llyworn said. "It was our job to guide them."

"How many in a war party?" Alex asked.

"At least half their numbers," she said.

"What does that mean?" the elder said. "What're you talking about?"

The companions were all smiles.

"Divide and conquer." Hart grinned. "I like it."

"Yeah, this is the perfect opportunity to split their numbers in half," Alex said. "And maybe lure out that big boss of theirs. If it works, we can save as many people as we can, and tear the cultists and their demons apart. But we'll have to act fast. They're getting ready to move, so they won't be as organised, and if we divide them, they'll be vulnerable."

"Is there anywhere in the swamp that would make a good ambush spot?"

Elder Blodeuwedd gave it some thought. "There are the Skull Pits."

"Skull Pits?" he asked.

"It's someplace we rarely go, and with good reason."

Alex raised an eyebrow. "Why?"

"There's quicksand there."

"Well," Cedric said. "Don't that just sound bloody perfect. Right, so let's get done wit' these prisoners an' get to work. We got a trap to set."

CHAPTER 32

THE BAIT IN THE SKULL PITS

"Now?" Zonon-In demanded. "You are sure?"

"Yes, leader," one of her higher-ranked demons growled from two crocodilian snouts. Its voice was like gravel. "Sniffers find mana scent: dungeon core near."

"Where?" The leader leaned forward, her eyes blazing.

The smaller demon cringed beneath her glare like a frightened imp. "South. One plus half mortal mile is what sniffers say."

"That's close." She turned to Osian who had entered her tent for some unrelated business of his own.

"What lies a mile and half south of here?" she asked the man, failing to keep disdain from her voice.

He startled amusingly, like he had pins placed in his boots. "I suppose that would be the Skull Pits. Terrible place full of quicksand. But, I was talking about my people. It appears they've disappeared."

"Ah yes," she said irritably. "The ones who left camp against my orders? And, what of the twenty I sent to get them back?"

"That has nothing to do with me. I want my people back." Osian's tone was testy.

"Then your ambitions are low. Why have small wishes when you could be wishing to be a king. Wouldn't that be nice for you? A human king? With your little jewelled crown and your sceptre?"

Osian ground his teeth, which was an excellent passing moment of amusement before she got down to real business.

"Osian, tell me, how would a dungeon core end up close to this camp?"

The witch frowned. "Well... dungeon cores appear without warning all across the land. There's no one rhyme or reason to it, and few, if any, can say how. The Ravener just sends them out, and they show up in caves or other places below ground."

"So it is possible." One of her pincers clicked with anticipation. "Hmmmm, this might explain certain things. This Ravener of yours started chaos in the swamp, then your people—who seem not to know what following orders means—vanish at the same time my patrol is destroyed." Her pincer clicked faster. "It seems a dungeon formed to the south and now its monsters are laying claim to our territory."

She looked at her demon. "Did the sniffers sense *much* mana?"

"Little mana," it snarled.

"Perhaps the core formed in the last day or so, which explains the low mana," Osian said. "They say it takes time for one to establish itself."

Zonon-In growled, her mouth-tentacles scraping her teeth.

This was an opportunity she'd be a fool to let pass. A dungeon core appearing so close while it was still weak. If she could take a punishing force and eliminate its guardian monsters and claim it, she would have a prize for her lord well before the time she anticipated.

Ezaliel might even grant her greater rewards than what was promised. Yes.

Yes, she would act, claim the prize, and if it was indeed the dungeon's monsters that had interfered with her forces over the past day, with them destroyed, her camp wouldn't be forced to move until a time of *her* choosing.

She rose from her bone-throne, towering above it.

"Gather a sizable force," she commanded her servant. "I want mortal followers assembled and waiting alongside my demons within the hour. Only the best fighters. Only those who can follow orders. From those, I will choose who will accompany me in an attack on this dungeon."

"Yes, leader." The demon snapped its jaws and backed out of the tent.

"Osian." Zonon-In's attention turned to the traitorous witch. "You will remain here since I cannot be sure you will follow my orders properly."

"What?" he cried. "We must expel these invaders from our home!"

"And if you didn't behave like an infant, I would bring you along. You could watch or fight, whichever you choose. But you can't even keep your own followers in line, and this situation is much too delicate for me to risk you going off on some mad plan for honour, or some other silly word you mortals make up."

She grinned. "Congratulations. You've acted so chaotically, you've managed to bring a *demon* up short. Not many can say that. You will stay here guarding the camp and make sure your people are ready to travel when the time comes."

Osian grumbled and swept from the tent. Her laughter followed him.

"Well, this is going to be a good day." She reached out and grasped air.

There was a shimmer, then a hiss of brimstone, and in a flash of red light, a war-spear appeared in her claw—nearly as tall as she—and made of burning brass. The end bore the skull of its former bearer and its barbed tip shed swirling, necromantic vapours.

"Time for some exercise," she snarled. "Oh, how I've missed these times."

***

"Well, it's done." Alex hurriedly placed the dungeon core back in his bag.

He'd sensed the orb's unique mana rise after he'd reached into its centre.

"Aye, now we wait for the signal." Cedric bit into a piece of jerky, tearing off a chunk of smoky venison. Brutus stared at him.

"Here's hopin' they come pourin' outta that camp like a whole nest o' angry wasps."

"Yeah," Theresa said, checking her arrows. "I hope Drestra, Hart, and the others will be okay."

"Don't worry about them; worry about *us*!" Alex laughed, checking his potions. He was taking stock of how many bottles were left since giving some to Hart, Drestra, and the witches accompanying them.

The plan was a simple one.

He, Theresa, Claygon, Brutus, Cedric, and a small mobile force of spellcasting witches from Crymlyn Village were deep in the Skull Pits. He'd just activated the dungeon core, letting it shed mana for the demons' mana sniffers to notice.

The idea was to trick them into sending out a force to find the core.

Meanwhile, Drestra, Hart, and another group of spellcasters were waiting out of range of the mana sniffers, close enough to the camp. If the demons took the bait, half of the army would be gone; the Sage and Champion could then infiltrate the camp and rescue the hostages.

When the fighters left, a witch would send a message by way of their familiar to Alex's team, letting them know how many enemies were coming for the core. Once the cult was deep in the Skull Pits, they'd find an ambush—not a dungeon—waiting for them. The witches knew the swamp, Alex had Baelin's boat, and between the entire group, they had enough flight spells, potions, traps, and skills to bury the enemy in swamp water and quicksand.

When the hostages were safe, Drestra was to shoot a blast of fire into the sky as a signal to Alex's team that the prisoners were on their way to the village with the witches, and the enemy camp was destroyed. The Champion and Sage would then come to reinforce the Skull Pits.

With everyone assembled inside the perilous terrain, they could break the army's back.

It was a good plan, Alex thought, one he and his companions had worked out together.

"Just hope they don't surprise us," he muttered beneath his breath.

"What was that?" Cedric asked.

"If they do, we'll be ready for them," Theresa said, giving Alex a small smile.

Brutus stood up, padded across the boat, and licked his face.

"Thanks, guys," he said.

"Y'got bloody good hearin', Theresa." Cedric was relaxing against the stern, toying with the glowing string on his bow. "Well, ain't this a bit strange?"

"What?" Alex asked. "You mean that we're here waiting for an army of demons to attack us while sitting on a magic boat in the middle of quicksand country while a bunch of witches we're now kinda friends with are out setting enough traps to catch half the animals in Thameland? Yeah, I guess that is pretty strange."

"Naw." Cedric shook his head. "That's not it, mate. Waitin' to fight a bunch of monsters is jus' another bloody day o' the week fer me. What I meant was, this feels a bit like the night we met. Just you lot an' me. Even the pup's here... Although your little sister's been replaced by that great, dirty golem."

"Claygon's clean," Theresa said, a defensive note in her voice. She patted the golem's leg.

He was standing beside her in the centre of the vessel, his eyes focused.

"Yeah, I washed him before we left the village," Alex said.

Cedric burst out laughing, his deep voice rolling through the marsh. "Now, now, don't the two of ya get all crusty. S'just a harmless expression. An' I'm only sayin' he's dirty, meanin' that bringin' him into a fight's a bloody dirty move, not that I care too much about fairness when somethin's tryna kill me an' all that. Anyway, I'm gettin' distracted from what I was sayin'. When we first met, I remember tellin' ya' it was good ta see yous fightin' the good fight. Especially wit' your fancy magic. Y'always pronounce your spells all slow an' steady-like, an' yer real precise with those incantations o' yours."

Alex's pulse quickened. "Yeah, as I always say, it pays to learn your spells inside and out."

"Agh, as long as the mana does what I tell it, s'good enough for me," Cedric said. "Just, s'funny, here we are, fightin' together. Gotta say, s'been nice havin' yous an' Baelin with us. Makes things easier an' helps wit' the plannin' an' such. I'm not the best with that part. My head's much better at buttin' other heads than at tactics."

He rubbed the back of his neck and rolled his head from side to side. There was a sharp crunch. "Anyway, s'too bad one of yous wasn't marked. Yer both good fighters and good planners, would've been great havin' ya wit' us."

Alex fought his expression; it wanted to do anything but remain neutral. A quick glance at Theresa told him she was having the same problem. The irony of the situation was overwhelming. He felt a little guilty deceiving Cedric. The Chosen was a decent guy, honest, trusting, and if they'd met in Generasi, he'd probably be part of his cabal. He obviously liked him and Theresa... How long would that last if he told him he was the missing Fool?

Alex looked at the murky water around them.

Now wasn't the time, if there ever would be one.

"Hey, man, it's too bad you're not down in Generasi with us." The Fool changed the direction of the conversation. "Sure, we get into the books, but we also play hard."

"Well, the playin' part sounds good t'me," the Chosen chuckled. "Who knows, maybe if this war ends before everythin' on my skull's gone grey, I'll come down an' take a look for meself."

Alex winced. 'Why do people keep saying stuff like that?' In every story he'd ever heard where someone talked like that just before going into battle, the story would end with them dead. He certainly wasn't about to share that thought with the Chosen, though; that was more a Khalik or Thundar conversation.

"It's incredible down there," Theresa said, slipping her quiver onto her hip. "It's like the world—"

She paused, cocking her head to the north.

"I hear a bird," she said. "It's moving fast."

The huntress looked in that direction, and Alex and Cedric followed her gaze.

A dot in the distance was growing fast, shooting through the clear sky for Baelin's boat. It stopped short, hovering above them with a leather tube clutched in its talons.

The brown swamp piper squawked and flapped its wings until Cedric fed it a piece of jerky. It snatched the meat, nipping his thumb while Theresa removed the message from its claws.

'Bird familiars have way too much attitude.' Alex thought of Najyah and Llyworn's duck.

"Did it work?" he asked Theresa. "Are they coming?"

She was silent for a long moment. "Ooooh it worked alright. There's over two hundred cultists and more than a hundred demons on the way. Including a really *big* one."

Alex rubbed his hands together. "Oh... oh holy shit. And we've got like fifty witches. I'd say we're pretty outnumbered."

"But you've got the Chosen of Uldar an' that great, big, er... clean golem at yer side." Cedric laughed.

"Yeah, this is good. We were outnumbered about four to one when they ambushed us, so I think we can handle this," Theresa agreed. "They're looking to raid a dungeon full of Ravener-spawn, which means there's only a skeleton crew left in their camp."

"Makes things easier for Drestra, Hart, and the witches," Alex said. "Good, well, we made a plan, and so far, it's working. That's something to celebrate, not complain about."

He took a deep breath, cracked his knuckles, and began putting his potions away. "Did the message say how fast they're moving?"

"Seems they're rowing at a steady pace, so they should be here in maybe an hour or so."

"Alright, let's finish our preparations," Alex said. "I've got a lot of summoning to do."

CHAPTER 33

THE BATTLE OF THE SKULL PITS

"Here they come," Theresa whispered from the belly of the boat.

Ahead—through pines and willows—the enemy army came. Cultists rowed like their lives depended on it, powering strange boats of bone and hide around tree trunks and through thick, sandy bogs. Each vessel carried at least ten spellcasters, some sheathed in defensive spells. There was no shortage of force shields, bows, and chainmail shining over dark clothing. Other fighters gripped long spears with tips sharpened to a knife's edge. Their faces showed no trace of fear, and they were not alone.

Demons spread among them, oozing menace.

Packs of beam-shooters stood in defensive formation, while a flock of imps soared overhead. Earlier, a scouting party of the vicious little creatures had appeared in the distance, surveying the area until a barrage of arrows from Theresa, Cedric, and witch-archers' bows knocked them from the sky before they even saw the fletching coming.

If the demon army had any concern for their missing scouts, they showed no sign. They just kept pushing forward, the tiashivas especially confident. Their third eyes burned with a longing for violence and Alex was plastered to the floor watching their approach, wondering if Burn-Saw was among them.

But, if the scarred demon wasn't part of this horde, he wouldn't be surprised. He would even be relieved. Trying to capture the tiashiva would be a distraction he couldn't afford right now, especially since the Chosen would have questions he wasn't prepared to answer. Burn-Saw was a future problem; a now problem was the demon's kindred approaching with sharp axes and blades of jagged bone.

Flanked by the tiashivas were selachar-like Ar-heugeni, the type of demons that had crawled from the sea and attacked the Games on Oreca's Fall Island. The creatures broke the water's surface with powerful strokes, their faces fixed in a snarl as they scanned the swamp through yellow eyes framed by heavy lids.

Seeing the tiashivas and Ar-heugeni together brought back terrible memories that screamed for retribution. Alex would be only too glad to repay them.

Towering above them, giant mantogugons strode—mantis-like ice creatures whose titanic claws clicked with each step they took, freezing murky water beneath their feet. They stalked through the swamp like they were on solid ground.

Alex frowned. Pushing those things toward quicksand or a bog would be pointless. The liquid they stepped on froze wherever they walked, which meant his team's advantage from the ground being so waterlogged was gone.

Claygon would have to focus his beams on them. They needed that advantage.

Among the horde stalked unfamiliar hulking, simian-bodied things with two crocodile heads, flyers with feathers of a sickly green, and beaks resembling Venus fly traps like in Professor Salinger's greenhouse. He recognised the dozens of beam-shooters in the boats, their weapons aimed and ready to fire.

Sniffing the air in the bow of each boat was a squat demon covered in chitin with more than a dozen articulated legs. Their long noses coiled and uncoiled like snakes. There was no mistaking the mana sniffers Llyworn and Rhodri had described, and they now headed straight for Baelin's boat.

As the boat moved closer, the creatures paced in a frenzy, their focus riveted on one overwhelming source of power ahead: Claygon. Their excitement surged, expecting that a dungeon core was within reach, and they howled like hounds on the hunt, mana calling them.

The monsters had no idea they'd sailed right into the trap. The witches of Crymlyn Swamp were concealed and watched the demons row past. Soon, they'd be ambushed from all sides.

Traps bearing sigils that magical command words would activate were ready for any demon or cultist who passed too near.

Alex's summoned allies also lay in wait. Scores of water elementals at the bottom of the swamp's murky depths patiently waited. When the fight began, they would surge from the water and fall upon the Arheugeni.

Everything was going according to plan.

'But where's the *big* one?' he wondered, scrutinising the enemy ranks.

No matter where he looked, he saw no demons that even vaguely resembled the demonic leader the two cultists had described.

He chewed his lower lip.

"Oh shit," Theresa whispered.

She was on the opposite side of the boat to Alex and Cedric, peering out from under a canvas cloth that shrouded them from enemy eyes.

"What is it?" the Chosen whispered.

"Don't make any fast moves," she said quietly. "But look in my direction... they have us surrounded."

Alex slithered to the opposite side of the boat. "Oh shit!"

Theresa was right. Movement came from the trees flanking them, and a larger force of demons was approaching, but they were farther away.

"It looks like they've split their forces," he whispered. "Maybe they planned on surrounding the 'dungeon' and coming at it from each direction."

"Aye," Cedric said. "Well, we've got traps out there too."

"Yeah, but we don't have the numbers they do," Theresa said. "Maybe we can kill as many in the front as we can, if we do it fast enough, that should buy us some time before their reinforcements can move up."

"Aye," Cedric said, his voice low. "If we wipe out the first wave, we got a good chance o' takin' care o' the rest. S'too bloody bad Merzhin's not here. He's got this miracle that'd take care o' all these pests in one go. Takes 'im a while to set it up, but I can't see anythin' we're facin' survivin' it."

Alex made a mental note of the Saint's gift. If there was one Hero he'd likely have to fight one day, it was the Saint, so of course *he* would be the one who sounded like he'd be a problem in more ways than one. But tomorrow's battles were for tomorrow.

Today's needed to get started.

"Okay," Alex said, turning back to the demonic army in front of them. "Sounds like breaking them fast is the way to go. We don't want them lasting long enough for the rest of their army to get here and give them the advantage. If we can take the first wave out, that gets rid of a good chunk of their force before the rest can get stuck in."

"Aye, well, I'll show 'em how fast a Chosen o' Uldar can wreck shite,"

Cedric said, opening up a flight potion. "Yous ready? The witches are waitin' on us ta' start."

Alex and Theresa looked at each other, then nodded.

"Ready," Theresa said, drawing her bowstring back.

"As ready as I'll ever be." Alex willed a half dozen Wizard's Hands to yank back the canvas.

"Well." Cedric took a deep breath.

Then his roar filled the swamp.

Alex's Wizard's Hands threw off the canvas as he chugged his flight potion.

"Alright, y'shite-eatin' bloody traitors and demon scum!" the Chosen bellowed. "*Let's gooooooooooo!*"

He swigged his flight potion in a single gulp.

Theresa was already up, her hands blurring across her bowstring. Arrows flew through the air like driving rain.

'Claygon!' Alex thought. 'Light 'em up! Focus on those ice demons.'

Alex's defensive spells flared as he, Cedric, and Claygon shot from the boat, up into the air. The demons and cultists looked to the sky, roaring a challenge, while Theresa's arrows slammed into mortal bodies.

"Stay down, boy," she whispered to Brutus, who Alex had covered in force armour.

A heartbeat later, a cry rose from witches concealed in the Skull Pits.

Mana surged, and traps came to life.

Shrieks of pain rang out, demons and their allied cultists were met with spiked logs, trip wires, and dead falls of rocks suspended from trees high above—all hidden by illusions—then triggered in tandem, crushing boats to bone fragments and shredded hide.

Witches released arrows relentlessly while casting deadly spells from hiding places throughout the Skull Pits. They rained acid on the enemy and awakened dormant vines and swamp plants that now writhed with life, sprouting venomous thorns. They lashed cultists like whips, knitting together and weaving nets between clumps of trees to trap demon boats inside smaller waterways.

Spellcasters blasted powerful wind gusts, blowing enemies into the frigid water and nearby quicksand, sucking them down. As they sank, walking trees erupted from the muck. Groaning like old oaks, they swung clubs as long as Claygon was tall, turning demon boats to rubble.

One minute, Ar-heugeni were cutting through swamp water, swimming for animated trees and witches hiding within bogs and the tree canopy; and the next, they were yelping, frantically clawing at their own skin.

Alex's water elementals were stuck to them like leeches, burbling contentedly while draining the demons' life fluids.

'That's a downpayment for Oreca's Fall,' Alex thought.

Laughing with abandon, Cedric dove toward demons, shouting an incantation and firing light arrows into the horde below. Many dropped, felled by his arrows, while others were grabbed by their kindred and used as living shields.

Cedric's wild laughter echoed through the trees, sending cultists scrambling for hiding places, but before they could reach safety, he finished the incantation and a fireball launched. With a resounding boom, flame enveloped the fleeing cultists. Screams joined the Chosen's laughter before abruptly dying.

Whoooooooom!

Meanwhile, Claygon was building his own fire.

His gems flared, ready for ice demons below.

Whooooooooosh!

Flame sheared torsos from lower halves.

Three blasts instantly rocked the swamp, sending columns of steam, boiling plant life, and melted ice monsters hissing through the air. Claygon recharged his beams while Alex tossed booby-trapped flight potions into the enemy's ranks. Clouds of potion mist mingled, launching cultists and demons into tree trunks, swamp water, and each other.

In moments, the number of adversaries had plummeted.

Except those remaining weren't retreating; they still kept up their fierce attack.

Beam-demons fired lances of light toward Claygon, Alex, and Cedric, and the light rays shot through the sky like fireworks. Alex dodged while his golem simply took them across his body, then answered with his own beams.

Cedric flew between the rays, transforming his weapon into a halberd. A prayer to Uldar sheathed him in blazing light, then he dove among the enemy in melee range, cutting them down where they stood.

"Can't say we really need Merzhin after all!" he called to Alex and Theresa.

'Thank the Traveller he's nowhere near here,' Alex thought.

Cultists lobbed spells and arrows at the companions above and the witches concealed in the Skull Pits. Shards of darkness, fire-rays, force bolts, and blazing, rotting skulls shot at Alex, but with a haste potion enhancing his speed, he weaved between them in an aerial dance, retaliating with more potions of flight.

Imps and the peculiar green, bird-like demons soared toward him with snapping jaws, and long, sticky tongues flicking acidic slime. He blocked the acid with a force shield and the cleansing movements.

As Claygon blasted ice demons with his hand beams, he flew through airborne monsters, pummeling them with fists and devastating kicks. Each blow turned a demon into paste and sent it plummeting to the swamp.

Theresa fired from the boat, striking demons trailing Alex and Cedric. All around them, the Skull Pits had become a scene of chaos and magic, as cultist and demon numbers were slashed.

Alex was pleased, taking stock of the direction things were going, when suddenly, horns trumpeted above the havoc of battle and demons began advancing from their flanks, closing on Baelin's boat.

With the blowing of horns came a deep bellow erupting from the marsh at the witches' backs.

There she was: the demon leader. The towering creature strode forward, wading through swamp water. In one claw, she gripped what was the biggest spear Alex had ever seen. Maybe *spear* was the wrong word. The barbed blade on its end looked like a titan's barbed sword had been fitted onto the haft of a pole-arm. Unfriendly-looking vapours drifted from the spear's blade, and an equally unfriendly look burned in her eyes.

"Cedric!" he roared. "It's the leader!"

The Chosen swung his halberd, splitting a giant, crocodile-headed demon in two with a single strike. "I'm on 'er! Give the signal!"

Alex dodged through a pack of imps, then turned and fired a flare high into the sky.

When its ascent began to slow, it abruptly ruptured, shedding a scarlet light that could be seen from miles away.

A mile and a half away, Hart watched the south from a treetop, while Angharad and a team of thirty witches waited in boats below.

Drestra hid at the base of the tree.

The Sage tapped the trunk with growing impatience.

"Anything yet?" she hissed at the Champion.

"No, and that's the twentieth time you've as—Wait."

Hart grinned, stepping out of the canopy, floating down with the aid of Drestra's flight spell.

"Flare's up," he whispered. "The enemy's fully stuck in. They can't back out now."

"Then we go to work," Angharad said.

"Yes, it's our turn," Drestra murmured.

She cast her warming spell and the witches slipped into the waters of Crymlyn Swamp with the Heroes. A few stayed back, guarding the vessels while the rescue team waded away, swimming through the murky water toward the unsuspecting enemy camp.

CHAPTER 34

THE INFILTRATION OF THE DEMONIC CAMP

Drestra's Orb of Air and spell of warming surrounded her as she felt her way through the murky swamp. Sounds were distorted. Visibility low. In some places, she could only see a few feet in front of her, but—as nerve-wracking as that was—she was glad for it.

If she was having trouble seeing what was ahead, then the enemy would have trouble seeing her.

Soundlessly, she noted the number of strokes she had taken, and looked for the underwater markers that were pointing the way to the enemy camp. Earlier, Alex's water elementals and a few of her kin's familiars had scouted the cultists' camp, bringing back information for a detailed map to take them through the waterways and straight to the enemy camp. If the water elementals hadn't scouted the way in advance, finding the cultists camp and the gate in the waterway leading to it would have taken more time than the captives had.

The camp was set up on a series of large islands that were elevated, rising high above the water and were sparse of trees. At the centre of the fortified camp, a pit held the imprisoned witches, and around it, a towering palisade of thick logs had been erected. The murky waterway led right to the log walls. The pen was built on one of the larger islands, ensuring that water ringed the walls like a moat.

Llyworn had said that if the shackled prisoners were to somehow get free, they would have to swim through fifty feet of water to escape. Making things worse, the demons' traitorous allies had repeatedly painted every imprisoned spellcaster with mana expulsion potion, leaving them broken. The witches were weak, underfed, and in no condition to swim away—even if they could escape—while weighted down with chains.

The conditions the prisoners were kept in suited the demons and even Osian and his followers, but in the end, their cruelty would be their undoing. While the setup satisfied the cult's purpose, it gave the rescuers easy access to their kindred. They could simply swim through the swamp, right to the moat surrounding the island.

Of course there were obstacles in place to keep predators and other hostiles out. An underwater gate was positioned within the largest waterway leading to the demon's camp.

Water demons patrolled it without fail, eager to catch anything bold enough to swim too close, and the demon leader believed she could never have enough sacrifices for their rituals. If the scent of mortals and other sacrificed swamp dwellers brought packs of starving monsters to their camp, the patrol would sound the alarm, calling reinforcements to put down the intrusion.

Then there were also mana sniffers to worry about.

These curious demons were highly attuned to mana shared by the Ravener and dungeon cores, though spellcasting or vast mana pools could also alert them. What helped the rescue team was information shared by Llyworn and Rhodri that the creatures were always surrounded by mana from demons and cultists, making it difficult for them to distinguish between mana wielded by their allies, or their enemies.

'We should still use spells sparingly until the hostages are free,' Drestra thought. Hart was at the head of the rescue team, obscured from her sight by churning silt and muck.

'It's up to you,' she thought.

Hart was grinning like a maniac as he tore through the water.

'This is bloody amazing,' he thought, enjoying the excitement running through him.

A previous Champion—likely more than one—must have had skills in underwater combat. He was cutting through the swamp water like he'd been born in it.

'This is the life,' he thought. 'Swimming through muddy water on the way to kill a bunch of cultists and demons so we can rescue some hostages. Normal, everyday stuff. Not that bloody weird mind-bending shit Drestra's mother was doing.'

A shudder went through him—and it wasn't from the cold. Images of things he'd seen with the Ash Ravens came back to him. Things he'd experienced.

He pushed the past from his mind, re-focusing on what was ahead.

This wasn't the time for battling ghosts.

Hart searched for marker after marker, leading the team past each one.

'There's the root that looks like an old man's hand,' he thought, passing a craggy tree root; the last of the underwater markers. Hart signalled Angharad, who was in line behind him, to stop. They'd reached the spot the four water demons would be patrolling, just ahead by the underwater gate.

He drew his massive knife of Ravener-spawn bone enchanted with dungeon core dust and raised an eyebrow.

'All this time, they had us believing that dungeon cores were only good for pulverising and turning into weapons and armour. Now we find out mortals can control the bloody things. Jeez. Uldar, you old, rotting bastard, just what in all hells are you playing at up there?'

A patrolling demon suddenly loomed from the gloom just feet from him. Hart's agility and generations of experience took over, and his knife was in its throat before it could even move.

He turned around.

'One down.'

Nearby, two more shadows shot from the gloom.

Their claws flashed.

His blade flashed faster.

Both shuddered, then stopped, their corpses drifting down into darkness.

'Three dow—Oh no you don't!'

Barely visible through the silty water, he caught movement from the corner of his eye. Another demon was clawing its way to the surface, about to raise an alarm. With one kick of his legs, the Champion was in pursuit, his power driving him upward, straight for the fleeing monster.

He caught it and his blade found its back while his other hand found its throat. Hart twisted the knife's hilt as his grip crushed the creature's throat. The demon shuddered once, then went still.

'And that's four. Better grab the other three before one of them floats to the surface.' He swam to the bottom of the swamp. 'Even the stupidest, laziest sentry in all of Thameland would notice dead demons bobbin' in the water.'

The other three demons were tangled in tall weeds near the stagnant bottom. He added the last one he'd just killed to their muddy graveyard. A few well-placed rocks to hold them down, and his work was done. They wouldn't stay put forever, but it'd be long enough for him and his companions to get the prisoners far away from the hellhole they were in.

Hart remained at the bottom, waiting for the sound of bodies diving into the water, but all was quiet.

He exhaled.

'Interesting. Quick and easy kills. Maybe the demons in that camp'll put up a better fight.'

The Champion swam up toward the waiting witches.

Hart and Angharad were with a few more witches, waiting close to the water gate, when Drestra and the rest of the rescue team caught up with them. With hand signals, he pointed to where the patrolling demons now lay, and she nodded at the giant of a man in approval as they swam to the gate.

Angharad, Drestra, and several more witches went directly to the logs, and floating before them, cast incantations that surrounded their hands with acid. The spells were lower-tier—higher-tier spells weren't necessary for what they had to do.

Together, they pressed their palms to the gate, acid gradually burnt the wood away until there was a hole wide enough for even Hart to fit through. He wasted no time in doing just that with Drestra right behind, and Angharad leading the rest of the witches into the murky waterway.

This was where things could get tricky.

Alex's water elementals couldn't get past the gate, so anything could be waiting for them.

They moved in single file, staying within sight of one another, keeping no more than two feet between them and the person ahead. Their pace was slow and smooth, disturbing the silt as little as possible.

The Sage's anxiety grew. The longer they swam, the farther away their goal seemed to be, but if they rushed, they'd fail, and her kindred would die. She had to trust Hart to be cautious and lead them through the twisting waterway. Her nerves didn't leave, and she knew they wouldn't until her kin were safe, but she could deal with that until the mission was done. With each stroke, the waterway opened up, taking them closer to the moat. Finally, there it was before them and the island beyond.

The rescue team kept moving forward at their slow and cautious pace until they reached the island and looped around. Hart was searching for a distinctive root that a witch's bird familiar had spotted when it was scouting the camp from the air. It was hard to miss, not only because of its massive size, but because of its shape. It appeared alive, like a giant's head with snakes growing from it. A few feet away, he spotted it and the Champion, Sage, and Angharad surfaced and hid beneath the root, looking around.

Islands surrounded them, each covered in a sea of tents. Between them, cultists and demons went about their business. Drestra tensed, holding her breath, praying that no alarm would be raised.

None came.

It seemed the diversion had done what it was meant to. There were still dozens in the vast camp, but their numbers were depleted. And those who remained were more focused on packing their supplies.

There were only two guards watching the moat, and the pair were more focused on a game of dice than on their duties.

"I love lazy guards," Hart whispered, his large eyes lighting up. "They've made my life easy so many times. They're like a gift."

"If only the ones over here were so obliging," Drestra said, peeking around the root at the palisade on the prisoners' island.

The wooden wall held a single guard tower, and within it, a pair of sharp-eyed cultists. One looked to be packing up, while the other paced back and forth along the guard station, eyeing both the pit within the wall and the moat outside.

"Mmmm, doesn't ruin the plan, though," Hart said, pointing to the opposite shore. "See that tent over there, the one near the water?"

"Yes," Angharad said.

"I'll swim over there, use the tent as cover, get in the camp, and start killing. It'll be nice and quiet at first, just to thin out a few, then I'll make it loud."

"And while everyone's attention is on you," Drestra repeated the plan, "I'll cast flight on myself, kill the guards and anyone else holding the prisoners, then blast open the palisade."

"And then we come in, free the captives and protect them, while you two handle the rest of the camp," Angharad finished. "The plan looks like it's still a go as far as I can see."

"Yep," Hart said, cracking his neck. "So, I'd better get to work." He grinned at his companions. "Wait for the screaming."

With that, Hart sank beneath the water and moved through it as silent as an eel.

"I'll let everyone know to get into position," Angharad whispered, dipping below the surface.

The Sage waited anxiously, looking from the tent near the moat to the cultists on duty in the guard tower above.

"Come on, spirits, and you too, Uldar," she prayed quietly. "Make it so the guard doesn't see him. Make it so the guard doesn't see him."

She watched as Hart's head surfaced. He took a quick look around, then slipped onto the shore, pressing himself against the tent. He was moving fast...

Then a bloody cultist made his way over to the tent Hart was hiding behind, carrying a bucket full of slop to dump into the moat.

"No, no, no," Drestra whispered as he came closer to Hart's hiding place.

The cultist would see him and—if he didn't, then the guards on watch in the guard tower would.

She got ready to cast a fireball at the tower.

Then Hart blurred from behind the tent, grabbed the cultist by the neck and crushed it with a quick squeeze of his fingers. His other hand caught the bucket before it hit the ground and set it down gently while the man went silent. With a fluid motion, he drew his knife, slashed open the side of the tent and slipped in with the dead cultist under one arm.

No cry of alarm went up.

Drestra's heart was pounding as she let out a breath. Heartbeats later, a very large 'cultist' in ill-fitting robes stepped from the tent and shuffled into the monsters' camp. His head was bowed low beneath his hood.

The Champion of Uldar had infiltrated the camp.

Drestra looked up, ready to attack the guard tower.

"Wait for the screaming," she whispered.

CHAPTER 35

GOADING

Screams rang out over the Skull Pits.

Armies clashed in a storm of magic and death.

In the sky above, Alex battled demons.

He weaved past the sticky tongues of green-feathered demons and dodged the barbed claws of imps. The sky was filled with screeching monsters snapping and clawing at him. They poured from the witches' flanks, racing past their allies and taking to the air like flocks of malevolent birds. They aimed to rip Alex, Claygon, and Cedric from the sky, but the trio had another plan.

Wizard's Hands whirled with speed—tugging wings, pulling imps through the air, flaring with crimson light that blinded demonic eyes. Alex hurled sleeping potions through the flocks, the air filled with vapours. Shrieks died as sleeping monsters dropped from the sky like hail.

Through the chaos came thunderous booms, flashes of light, and searing heat as Claygon's blasts tore through the skies. Cedric's challenges roared above the demons' cries along with lightning and flame. The Chosen of Uldar wielded spells and divinities like he was a vengeful god removing the wicked from his presence.

Below, blasts raced skyward, coming for him and his companions, only to be met with beams of light spraying near and far, striking flying demons and those below. Alex and Cedric weaved between the dead.

Demons and their allies were dying like autumn leaves, and just like autumn leaves, there seemed to be no end to them. They were so thick in the skies that Alex couldn't gauge how the battle was going below.

'Die, you bastards,' his mind screamed. 'I need to see past you! Just drop dead already—'

Looking like a streaking star approaching, flashes of light reflected off polished blades coming toward him.

Theresa spun through the sky, her swords flashing, thinning both hordes and flocks she flew by.

Poor Brutus followed behind her, looking like a newborn calf with flailing legs trying to stay upright. A flash of fangs met anything that came close. He would snatch them from the air with snarling fangs, shake them, then drop them into whatever waited below.

Finally, the demons' flying force broke. Between the persistent attack from Cedric and Claygon, and Alex's potions combined with cerberus fangs and twin sword blades, the skies were at last free of cultists and demonkind.

"You alright?" Alex panted.

"Yeah, I'm great." Theresa reached for the whimpering, trembling Brutus; the cerberus nuzzled into her, making a point of not looking down. "I thought I'd come up and lend a hand since I ran out of arrows," she said. "I didn't think you'd mind if I took a potion and gave poor Brutus one since I couldn't just leave him in the boat with all those demons coming at us."

"My potions are your potions, and thanks," he said emphatically. "Thanks to you, we finished them off faster than I thought we would."

"Well, the battle's ending down there too." She watched the battlefield below. "I'll go see if I can get some arrows from one of the witches; that's if they have any to spare. I'll need more for when the rest of the demons get here."

She and Brutus descended, the cerberus shaking with relief.

"Aye, looks like we gets a few minutes' rest," Cedric said. "They've got things wrapped up down there."

Steam and smoke rose from the Skull Pits, and everywhere Alex looked lay the ruins of demon and cultist bodies alike. Dozens floated face down in murky water or were trapped in quicksand. Witches moved through the trees with care, finishing off survivors.

No mercy was shown by the witches of Crymlyn Village, as no mercy had been shown to them. Among the corpses of demons and cultists, dead witches lay. The numbers of their dead were small, but even one was too many at the end of it all.

Too many witches were left in mourning.

His mind flashed back to the beach on Oreca's Fall, and his anger at the Cult of Ezaliel smouldered in his chest.

'Focus,' he told himself. 'It's time for action. Take your rage out on the ones coming.'

He looked across the swamp grimly.

Demons and the traitors they'd aligned with were approaching, closing in from three sides and—even with their flying demons destroyed—the oncoming demon force was at least triple the one they'd just defeated.

Alex clenched his jaw.

More losses could be catastrophic.

"We need Hart and Drestra," he said, looking to the north.

Still no signal.

"Aye, those demons'll grind a lot o' these witches to dust if they get us surrounded," the Chosen said.

"Yeah... we have to move. There's a couple more positions here in the Skull Pits we can retreat to," Alex said. "We should get to one, force the cultist scum to come at us from only one direction."

"Aye," Cedric said grimly. "Or we could strike the head off the snake."

The Chosen pointed to the south at the imposing figure leading the advancing demon army.

"Yeah, that one's the leader, alright," Alex said. Even from his distance, he felt a chill from the immortal's gaze. "But I don't know about attacking her yet. Not before Hart and Drestra get here."

"I've cut down Ravener-spawn commanders dozens o' times." The Chosen's grip tightened on his weapon. "An' some o' them were a hell o' lot bigger than that she-beastie over there is."

"I don't doubt that," Alex said. "But any spirits or elementals—including demons—can get *very* powerful as they go up in hierarchies. Not just physically powerful, but with some real nasty magic and more years of combat experience than everyone here put together. Some are even resistant to magic."

"How resistant?"

"*Very* resistant. Like, sure, she'd probably be like a flea to *Baelin*, but to us? I doubt our magic could do very much to her."

"Then that's even more reason to take 'er on. It'd be best fer our forces if she's tied up, if she's even half as tough as yer thinkin'," the Chosen said.

"You're not wrong." Alex frowned. "We can take cover in the trees and blast her from there."

"Aye, but didn' y'say she was resistant to magic?"

"I don't know for sure, but she very well could be since a lot of higher demons are."

"Well then, somethin' needs to be in front o' her. Somethin' so tough, she can't just ignore it."

"I can summon some monsters. *They* can keep her busy."

"She'll cut 'em down quick. I'm the bloody Chosen. She won't be able to go through me so easy."

"Yeah, you're the Chosen, and Thameland needs you. *Alive.*"

Cedric gave him a look. "Now you're startin' to sound like the bloody priests."

Alex paused as a wave of anger washed over him. He held his tongue.

"Can't just sit back an' let this demon rampage an' kill our allies," the Chosen said. "I'll come out still breathin', I'm sure."

Alex winced, remembering how they'd met. Cedric went off on his own to fight silence-spiders in the Cave of the Traveller. He did it to stop them from going to massacre the townsfolk and the villagers around Alric.

Of course Cedric would run into battle to save other people. Alex admired that and his bottomless well of courage. The Mark of the Chosen had... well, chosen well.

"Alright," the Fool sighed, opening his bag and counting the remaining potions. "I don't know if my mana soothing and sleep potions will affect something *that* powerful, but I'll give you all the support I can. And I'll see if I can hit her with a booby-trapped flight potion. She probably won't put up much of a fight against you with her arms ripped off... *if* my potions affect her, that is."

"We'll find out." The Chosen cracked his neck.

Alex's mind was working through different scenarios.

He could run Hsieku's technique through his mana pool a few more times then summon a ton of air elementals to hit the towering demon with them. His eyes focused on the giant walking trees below.

"Let's see if I can convince the witches to let them back Cedric up," he muttered, ready to start summoning.

Zonon-In's mouth-tentacles wriggled behind her teeth as she watched the battlefield.

A quarter of her forces lay dead, and—more alarmingly—there was no sign of a dungeon anywhere, just witches and flying strangers.

She pointed toward the outsiders in the air with her war-spear.

"What are those?" she asked a nearby traitor witch.

"I can't tell," the witch said, peering at the flyers. "We're too far away."

The woman's calmness stoked Zonon-In's annoyance. Unlike Osian, she didn't lose her temper at the slightest provocation. How... dull.

The demon leader turned her focus back to the flyers.

A black-haired woman and a three-headed hellhound had disappeared into the trees. That left the sky with only a magical clay soldier and a shirtless warrior floating with it.

Her eyes took in the warrior, noting his liquid weapon and the glowing symbol on his chest.

"Hmmm, it seems some of you mortals have taken to branding each other. How delightful. Witch, that man there—" She pointed to the sky. "Have you seen that symbol before?"

The witch and the other cultists around her gasped.

"That's the Chosen of Uldar!" the witch hissed, her tone hard, but her eyes filled with fear. "Why is he here? He's one of five who were named a Hero of the enemy. They've been tasked with destroying the Ravener in Uldar's name. That one's their leader and the one they call the Chosen."

"And yet he's here..." Zonon-In's voice grew thoughtful. "In this swamp."

A flutter of excitement went through the demon. A powerful mortal, this *Chosen* might be an interesting challenge. The symbol on his chest recalled rune-marked warriors she once fought on this world in past times. Among their kind, the more symbols they bore, the more powerful they were, but this *Chosen* had only one.

She wondered if that would make any difference.

More importantly, she wondered what this all meant. Something was wrong.

She'd learned from these witches that this place was called the Skull Pits—a name she heartily approved of, as it almost sounded like home—but what she didn't approve of was that several of her most loyal cultists had been lost to quicksand along the way.

Coming so far without finding a dungeon... Even the worthless Osian would have known her forces had been led into a trap.

But there was something else concerning her.

There was no question that the sniffers *had* smelled dungeon core mana.

Did the mortals use some trick to imitate it and lure them? Or was there a dungeon core hidden in their ranks, ripe for plucking? If so, the dark orb had gone silent. The sniffers hadn't detected even a hint of its mana again.

What were they up to?

That question must be answered, and the only way to learn what treachery these mortals had brought to her territory was by capturing some and forcing answers from them.

Annoyance rose again.

If they were—

"Oi!" a voice roared from the Chosen. "Great, dirty demon!"

She growled, her annoyance giving way to amusement.

"Ooo! A heroic speech!" She grinned, her face scornful. "How fun!" The demon cleared her throat. "What is it, oh mighty Hero of Uldar?"

There was a pause, and her smile widened.

"Didn't expect me to know about your amusing title?" she called back.

"Aye, I'm the Chosen, that's true!" He laughed. "An' this Chosen o' Uldar challenges you, demon weaklin', to a test o' arms! Come, leave the safety o' your horde! We'll fight it out, if'n ya got the nerve to face me!"

Zonon-In put on her best 'evil overlord voice,' which she'd had millennia to practice. "And why, puny mortal, should I bother with you? I could squash you like an earthworm!"

That's what they were called in the material world, right? Earthworms?

The Chosen barked a laugh at her. "I don't think so! I'm gonna cut 'cha inta a dozen pieces! An' spear your heart—"

Oh, she *loved* when they said that.

"Which one?" she called back.

"...What?"

"Which heart? I have a few! Which one will you pierce?"

Another moment of silence, and a flustered expression.

"All of 'em!" he shouted. "So come on, ya weak, dirty, cowardly wretch! I'll tear ya down!"

"Well, that was fine goading," she said to herself. "If a little obvious, but one turn deserves another."

"Fine!" she roared. "But why should I come to you, when you could come to me!" She gestured at her army with a claw. "We're going to return to camp now and surprise your little friends who are, no doubt, raiding it as we're having our little chat!"

The Chosen's expression shifted dramatically.

There. She had him.

"So, if you really want to challenge me and *not* lure my army into any more of your traps, then *you'll* have to come to *me*!"

She faced her troops. "Ar-heugeni! Go back to camp! Spellcasters, cover yourselves and our mantogugons in flight spells then return there with haste! The prisoners are waiting for a taste of your blades!"

Zonon-In raised her war-spear.

"Everyone else! Retreat! We're leaving this death trap!"

With a great clamour of voices, her army didn't hesitate, circling the enemy to pull back to their base.

She suspected the mortals wouldn't simply let them leave, they'd do something to keep her entertained.

"Ah *shite*!" Cedric roared from above. "Bloody clever bastard!"

"Shit!" Alex swore from below, summoning one final air elemental.

"I gotta bring 'er down!" The Chosen flew down to Alex. "If'n any o' them make it back ta that camp, the whole thing's busted! We gotta cut the head off!"

"Shit! Cedric, wait! We need a plan!" Alex shouted.

It was too late.

The Chosen flew off, arcing toward the demon horde, bellowing a prayer to Uldar.

"I swear, that war-spear's gonna find itself down that demon's throat," Alex grumbled, getting his potions out.

"Heads up!" he shouted to the witches. "Send as many walking trees with me as you can. We'll try to kill that thing!"

"I'm coming with you!" Theresa emerged from a copse of trees. Brutus was back in Baelin's boat, watching as she flew off. "Stay there, boy! Stay! I'll be back soon."

"Well, here goes nothing." Alex, Theresa, and a horde of air elementals launched toward Claygon hovering above.

They exchanged a nod... then tore after the Chosen.

Ahead, the demon grinned.

CHAPTER 36

THE CRACK

Zonon-In's goading had worked better than she'd expected.

This *Chosen* was tearing through the sky shadowed by the other two flying mortals, the giant clay soldier, and a horde of air elementals. Below them, walking trees were coming from the swamp, wading toward her.

The rest of their forces weren't idle either. They'd gathered in numbers and were scrambling to block her army.

It was perfect. She'd made them chase her and her horde, and like fools, they'd done exactly what she'd wanted. Now they were divided, weakened and easier to conquer.

Which also meant... it was time to direct her troops.

"*Keep retreating,*" she reached into their minds. "*I will catch up. There's something I have to do first.*" Her teeth bared.

Gripping her war-spear, Zonon-In spread her arms in invitation.

"Come!" her voice thundered. "You wish to test your mettle against me, Chosen of Oolurder? Well, here I am! I respond to your challenge with one of my own! How will you answer it?" She enjoyed twisting the god's name.

His answer was a shouted incantation and flame circling his hand.

"Oooo, how spicy." She spread her arms wider, ready for his magic.

The Chosen threw a fireball.

It streaked across the marsh—trailing sparks—and exploded against her torso. A magical inferno engulfed the demon, but all mana within it recoiled from her flesh.

'This raging flame feels no hotter than noon in this lifeless place... Oh, how I miss the joy of true heat,' she thought, standing among the flames, patiently watching them fade then fanning smoke and steam away.

"Not bad, mighty Chosen!" Her tone was dismissive. "But you'll have to do better than that! Do I look like some lesser demon who would have been roasted by your little spark? I need a challenge, something to drive me down to one knee. I'm sorry to tell you, that wasn't it! Maybe a slap or two from your little hands might work. I *might* feel that!"

Despite her goading, the Chosen—much to her disappointment— didn't take the bait and rush her in a blind rage. It was too bad; she loved when mortals did that.

She waited for his next move.

He was slowing, advancing cautiously. His body was tensing, getting ready for something...

All of a sudden, he blurred into motion, charging straight for her.

"Yes! *Come on!*" Her weapon whirled in anticipation.

With a terrible noise, the hungry war-spear slammed against his morphic weapon, surprising her with the force of his blow.

"You *are* a strong one," she complimented. "For a mortal."

She thrust the war-spear, crashing against his guard, knocking him back.

"But I am strong too, for a *demon*." She grinned, letting her mouth-tentacles run along her teeth.

"*Holy Uldar! Hear my cry, let your light fall and burn this invader of your land!*" the Chosen called out to his god.

A shift of divine force came from above. She glanced up just in time to catch a column of light streaking from the sky. It struck, swirling around her, seeking the destruction of her very essence... Yet it too recoiled, just as the mana did.

The demon scratched at her skin. "Agh, trying to itch me to death isn't a very sound strategy, Chosen of Ooladar." She abruptly thrust her war-spear at his Mark through the fading light. Cedric zipped away, barely escaping a blow that would have impaled his chest.

"Perhaps you can call on your god to come down himself if you want his power to strike me down!" She was enjoying herself. "When it comes through you, it's a little... *lacking*. That's not an insult, mind you, just a fact. Maybe we should see if your martial skills fare any better."

With a snarl, her war-spear exploded, serving up a flurry of blurring cuts. The Chosen dodged the barbed blade while it cut air, water, and nearby trees with equal ease.

She'd expected the shirtless man to die time and again, but to her surprise, he endured. He even parried her strikes, angling them away and diverting much of the force.

Her eyebrow arched.

This mortal looked young, even by mortal counting, but he fought like he'd lived through a lifetime of battles.

"You might make a good tribute for my lord," she said. "I think—"

The rest of the thought abruptly ended when ugly sounds escaped her. She began cursing in her demon tongue, glaring from a gaping puncture wound on an upper hand, to the Chosen.

He grinned viciously. "Oi, demon, how's that for a tribute? Now, less talkin' an' more fightin'."

Zonon-In looked from the wound to her opponent one last time.

"As you wish."

Metal struck metal, the sound reverberating through the air.

A massive blow from her war-spear slammed into his morphic weapon, flinging him through the air like a catapult stone. He bounced off a tree, struck the ground, and skidded across swamp water before halting with a thud against a willow.

His groans revealed his condition as he slid down the trunk, catching himself on a branch, his mind in a daze.

Zonon-In flipped her war-spear, pulling her arm back for a throw. First, she would sever his throwing arm, then—

Something flew at her face.

She caught a glimpse of what looked like a glowing hand gripping a vial, right before crimson light and the crunch of breaking glass came.

A whoosh of vapours blocked her sight, but she sensed mana recoiling as she inhaled the dense mist.

"Maybe go back to talking!" a new voice said. "I liked it a lot better when you were talking!"

Then she was surrounded by whirling air elementals.

———

"Ooooooh by the Traveller!" Alex murmured, gaping at the enormous demon who'd just swatted Cedric like a fly.

"She's fast," Theresa said grimly. "Way too fast for something that size to be."

"That's for damn sure," he agreed, tossing booby-trapped potions at the towering demon. "Zap her!" he shouted in a tongue of air elementals.

235

"Keep hitting her from every direction! Let's see if you can get her flustered!"

The air came to life as air elementals raked her with an onslaught of wind and lightning. But her reaction was like that of a bull being pestered by fruit flies—unimpressed.

"And who is talking to me now, I wonder?" the titanic demon called through the rising potion mist. "Are you trying to poison me? How adorable!"

That voice sent a chill up Alex's spine and his instincts spiked, warning him to run for his life. He fought them.

"Claygon!" he called. "I want you to—"

"Alex! Watch out!" Theresa screamed.

There was a blur as something enormous cut through the air for him. He shot to the side, heart drumming in his ears.

The enormous war-spear tore by, bursting three of his deflective force rectangles, almost slicing him in two. It flew straight ahead before he felt a surge of teleportation magic, then it vanished in a flash of light, only to reappear in the demon's hand.

"*Oh shit!*" the young wizard swore.

"Those make poor last words." She grinned.

"Yeah, well, they're *my* last words and *I* say whether they're poor or not!" he yelled at her. "I mean, no, those *aren't* my last words!"

"Oho! This one has quite the mouth!" She swept her spear around her, cutting through at least a dozen air elementals in one stroke. "Always good to have a nice talk when fighting to the death!"

"Ooooh, this is bad," Alex murmured. "I'll try to keep her off-balance until Cedric gets back in the fight."

"Same." Theresa sheathed her swords and drew her bow.

She fired arrow after arrow at the demon, cursing each time one bounced off.

That wasn't good. 'Claygon, blast her with the jewel in your forehead then shoot the water she's in with the other two!'

Whoooooom!

Three gems had been building in power, and now released their fire-beams. Two struck the water, sending explosions of steam through the air. The third hit the demon's chest and she bellowed in pain.

'Yes!' Alex thought. 'Now we—Oh.'

The steam cleared... she was completely unharmed.

"I should've bloody known," he muttered.

"Hah!" The creature pointed a pincer at Alex and Theresa, ignoring the wind gusts and lightning. "I always love that look in my opponent's eyes! That sudden shock!"

This wasn't working.

"Theresa, what're your chances against her?"

"Not great," she said, her voice frustrated. She shouldered the bow and drew her swords.

"Alright, then I'll try to even some of those odds."

He took two of the last three booby-trapped flight potions he had, tossed them to Wizard's Hands, then sent the spells at the demon as she swept her war-spear through the last of his air elementals. His jaw clenched then released, his hatred for the monster growing by the heartbeat.

Claygon blasted her, flames licked up her body, making her look even more like a walking nightmare. As the fire danced around her, the two Wizard's Hands flew right past the towering demon, stopping only when they reached her army. Glass shattered, potion mist billowed out, and puzzled demons sniffed the air before abruptly hurtling into trees, cloudy water, and their leader.

"Agh! What's this?" she cried, anger finally touching her voice. Her own minions collided with her spine.

Alex looked for Cedric, finding the young man on his feet with a glowing hand pressed to his chest, and bruises that were rapidly fading. He was almost back in the fight.

The witches' trees were on the move, closing in on the giant demon.

Time to press the attack.

'Now, Claygon!' Alex reached out. 'Crush her!'

The golem dove at the demonic leader at the same time Cedric did.

Snarling, she swept her weapon in an arc, pulping minions, then parrying a giant club wielded by an attacking tree.

A twist of the haft sent the club flying from her enemy's log-like fingers, and a thrust sent the barbed blade slicing into the tree's trunk, exploding from its back. The animated hardwood was slowed, but still fought on.

It soon began withering.

Wisps of dark smoke bled from its wound, and in heartbeats, the young tree wilted and shriveled, until it collapsed onto itself in a pile of rotting bark.

"Ooooh hells!" Alex swore.

"That's it! Give me a haste potion!" Theresa said, clearly irritated.

"What? You're gonna go near that thing after that?"

"Not without a haste potion! Toss me one!"

Alex reluctantly threw her the potion, watching as she chugged it and charged at the monster with no sign of hesitation.

The demon leader was cutting through another tree when Cedric and Claygon reached her.

They attacked from two sides, and she fought them with supernatural speed, parrying their blows. But now, all was not in her favour. A club struck her ribcage and she reacted with a grunt. She growled when Cedric's weapon slashed her shoulder, then outright howled when one of Claygon's fists struck her back.

"*That* hurt! But, well done!" A pincer snapped a wooden arm from a walking tree, then she whirled on the golem with both pincers snapping.

They surged toward him.

She looked amused for a breath, then growled when his lower hands caught them.

"This can't be!"

The two titans pushed against each other, neither budging.

Alex didn't know who was more surprised: her, at something actually matching her strength, or him, at something matching Claygon's.

She struggled with the golem to wrench free. Then his fire-gems flared, hitting her from up close.

"Argh! A dirty tri—Agh!" she screamed as the Chosen stabbed his spear deep into her side, then she cried out again when Theresa flew behind her with both swords flashing.

The huntress went for the soft flesh beneath the pits of the demon's lower arms, and her blades bit down, drawing a trickle of black blood. The cuts were shallow, but Theresa kept on them, repeatedly slashing at the wounds, deepening them with each stroke of her blades.

The leader exploded in booming laughter.

Theresa and Alex looked at each other.

"This! *This* is what I've longed for! Months of boredom and finally, some actual fun!" She shook with delight. "Alright then, let's see what all of you—very determined things—can do!"

Her foot shot up and kicked Claygon, breaking his grip.

Her war-spear whipped out.

There was a tearing sound.

Clay dust sprayed through the air.

Alex screamed.

A deep gash ran through the golem's chest.

With another slice of his blade, Hart severed the beam-demon's throat, keeping a tight grip on its face while stifling the sounds of dying. He slowly lowered the creature to the ground and rolled it into a nearby tent.

"That's twenty," he whispered, stalking forward like a predator.

He'd been moving through the camp under his ill-fitting disguise, killing anything that was alone, or not in plain sight. As long as he kept his hood down and his distance from prying eyes, he passed for just another cultist with blood on his robes. Able to move through the camp and kill at will, and—with so many tents around—it was easy to hide the dead.

Still, it was just a matter of time before *somebody* or *something* noticed that folk who should've been packing up supplies, had had their souls packed off to the afterworld. With that thought in mind, the Champion had enough time to slit three more throats before the alarm went up.

"Howaln's dead!" a man's voice shouted. "Someone slit his neck from ear to ear!"

"Aaaah, damn," Hart muttered, partway through wringing the necks of a demon with two crocodile heads. "Well, seems the party couldn't last forever."

With a final crunch, he broke the demon's spines, kicked the creature away, then looked around its tent. A large, spiky axe leaned against a chest, seeming to call him to heft it over his shoulder.

"Axe in one hand, dagger in the other, not the most glamorous way of doing business." He whirled them in his hands. "But they'll do."

Cracking his neck, he burst from the tent.

"That's right, you filthy freaks! The bogeyman's here to gut ya!"

With a laugh, he cleaved in the face of a surprised cultist, and stabbed a nearby traitor witch in the neck.

"Come and get dead!" he taunted.

The stunned cultists could only gape before snapping out of their stupor and springing into action. They grabbed weapons or began casting spells. Demons charged.

The Champion of Uldar leapt into battle like a fish into the sea.

CHAPTER 37

THE UNMASKING

Screams and roars filled the air as the Champion of Uldar met the cult with maximum violence.

To Drestra, though?

It was music to her ears.

The Sage dove under water and gave Angharad an enthusiastic thumbs-up, letting him know that Hart was in position.

He nodded, turned to the witches waiting with him and pointed to the surface, it was time to start their ascent. By the time he turned back to Drestra, she was already gone, climbing through the water, wasting no time. Their captured kin had little to spare. A flight spell tumbled from the Sage's lips, and as she broke the surface and climbed through the air, she chanted another spell. In the guard post above camp, two cultists gaped open-mouthed at what was happening below.

"What in every hell?" one cried. "Are we under attack?"

"No, all that shoutin' and mayhem means everything's just fine!" The second sentry scrambled for the bell. "You idiot, of course we're under attack, but it looks like it's only one—"

"Wrong," Drestra's voice crackled beside the sentry post as she hovered in the air.

Fire magic flared around her hands.

"Catch."

She tossed twin cones of flame at the pair—one's hands shot out to catch them, while the other man ducked; that didn't help him. Flame enveloped both before they could even grasp why. Screaming, they leapt

240

over the sides, burning like torches. Drestra soared over the palisade below without a second glance at them.

Roosting on a perch above the pit, two screeching bird-like demons spread their wings, ready to tear her from the sky. Lightning struck, turning the demons and their perch to ash. It gently floated into the pit like a light rain. The crackle of lightning and falling ash had the prisoners looking to the sky when the Sage—floating down like a miracle—touched the ground. Shocked cries and whispers spread among puzzled captives. They squinted at her like she was the sun itself.

Drestra's eyes welled with tears as her rage seethed at the state they were in.

Each was filthy, bruised, and gaunt, with eyes that were sunken so deep, they looked like dark craters. Some sported injuries. Broken arms stained with dried blood were barely supported by tattered rags, and manacles circled bony wrists. Across every face, symbols of mana expulsion were painted.

Drestra's hands balled into fists.

"Kindred, I am Drestra of Crymlyn Village, daughter of Elder Blodeuwedd," she said. "It's time for you to go home!"

"Oh, praise the spirits!" a witch cried, his voice breaking. "Praise them!"

Others prayed loudly, some sobbed with relief.

And then she heard her name from a familiar voice. It was low and weak.

"Drestra?"

The Sage's heart leapt.

"Ffion?" Her voice caught while she looked around desperately "Ffion, where are you?"

A bedraggled woman came through the crowd. She'd always leaned toward the thin side, but now she looked like the slightest breeze would blow her over.

"I'm here," Ffion said weakly. "How did you—Oof!"

The Sage rushed her old friend, catching her in a hug and holding on like she thought she'd slip away.

"Drestra... Drestraaaa... you're crushing me." Ffion smiled, her face pained like she wanted to cry. But only a single tear came.

"We'll get everyone water." The Sage exhaled softly. "I'm so glad we found you." The tears flowed as she gently pulled away and held her friend at arm's length, examining her. "I'm sorry this ever happened to you. We're going to get you home. Everyone's going home." Drestra's voice was like iron.

"Thank the spirits," Ffion said softly. "I prayed every day that someone would come and murder these bastards. And here you are. To murder these bastards." She gave a weak laugh.

Drestra squeezed her friend's hands, her eyes smiling above her veil. "I'm glad they couldn't break your spirit."

"Not in this lifetime. And I mean it, they're parasites, and they need killing." Her voice was calm.

"I agree. They're a plague that nothing good can ever come from," Drestra said.

"And we'll deal with all of these demons and demon-worshipping filth like they deserve to be dealt with. One way or another, they're leaving our swamp. I promise everyone that." She looked up at the palisade's gate, eyeing a dirt ramp that spiraled down the edges of the pit to give the cultists access to the hostages.

"I have witches from Crymlyn Village and Uldar's Champion with me. Our kin will take everyone out of this place, and Hart and I will see to these cultists. Stay put. I'll go let Angharad in." Drestra flew to the gate and—with a spell—blasted it with a wave of force.

Both the bar *and* gate wrenched open, revealing a shocked Angharad and the other rescuers on the other side.

"Hey, you nearly took my damn face off with that spell," he complained as he led the others through the palisade.

"Sorry," Drestra said. "I was trying to save time."

"Don't apologise. Save that sort of thing for the—" The man paused when he saw the hostages below, his eyes clouded. "By the spirits, this is awful. Go on, we'll see to our people. You go help pay back the rest of those bastards."

"With pleasure." She flew from the palisade and turned to the witches below. "I'll be back soon!"

"Drestra!" Ffion called after. "Get that traitor Osian and all the other stinking traitors with him! Don't let them get away."

Angry voices rose in agreement.

The Sage nodded, holding her fingers up like claws.

"If Hart didn't get him yet, he'll die by my bare hands."

She tore from the palisade and flew over the camp, watching the carnage below. The Champion of Uldar was racing between tents, cutting down demons, cultists, and the few traitor witches remaining. With every step, he was a blur of death.

But too slow for her liking.

Calling on her power, Drestra rained lightning and ice from above, cutting down the enemy by the dozen. She avoided fire—the camp was packed with supplies her people could use, especially with winter so near.

She kept searching for Osian, but the coward was nowhere in sight. Maybe he'd already run off at the first hint of a battle at his front door, though she had to admit, there were surprisingly few traitor witches around.

"You're not getting away, Osian. I'll hunt you for the rest of my days if that's what it takes," she whispered, climbing higher then turning in place, scanning the camp.

There!

A boat's stern was heading into the trees.

"Hart!" Her voice crackled like burning logs. "Rats are escaping! I'll be right back!"

"Oh, take your time!" He cut the head off a three-eyed demon. "I'll be here, having a blast!"

The Sage shot for the trees.

Coming close to her quarry, voices carried to her on the wind.

"—disaster. She's going to kill us when she gets back, Osian," a man said.

"And that's why we'll be long gone when she does," another man replied. "We're going to disappear so deep in the Crymlyn, even invisible marauders won't be able to find us."

"What about the others who went with the army?" a third voice asked. "They're our people. Do we leave them to her wrath?"

"At this point, *we* have to survive or our ways die with us," Osian said. "We'll leave signs so they can find us if they get away from Zonon-In."

"The only signs you're going to leave—" Drestra dropped below the trees and hovered above both vessels "—are your bloated corpses."

The witches recoiled like they'd been scalded.

"I am Drestra, the Sage." Her voice crackled like a blazing fire. "Which of you is Osian?"

As one, the traitorous witches glanced at a man at the bow of a boat.

He flinched, looking at his companions in shock. "You—traitors! You betrayed me!" he hissed with no sense of irony, then whirled on the Sage. "This is *our* swamp!" His voice grew firm, which was only slightly undercut by him trembling like a leaf. "We needed allies to keep outsiders out! To... to... to..."

His voice trailed off.

Drestra wasn't listening.

And though she hadn't said much, she was finished talking too.

Instead, she did something she had not done in front of another living being for many years. She reached to her face. Her hands unclasped a hidden catch.

And she took her veil off.

"Oh!" Osian cried. "Oh, spirits protect us!"

Then, she flew at them.

Screams erupted from the swamp, followed by a terrible cracking and immense crashing. Something crumbled. Someone's breath rasped as they sank beneath the water. A tree snapped in half.

When the Sage at last flew into the sky, her veil was back in place, and every last traitor was sinking in muddy water.

She swooped away, speeding to the camp, and finding most of the enemy already dead. Enemy numbers had been slashed, pushing them to desperate measures. Some rushed the palisade, looking for hostages, but instead of hostages for their taking, witches of Crymlyn Village waited at the gate with volley after volley of ice, acid, and other deadly magics for them.

The Sage soared over the camp, raking the few remaining knots of resistance with lightning and conjured stones, allowing them a quick death, something they'd denied her kin.

"Yes!" Hart laughed, his dagger and stolen axe carving a swath of carnage through the rest. "Get 'em, Drestra! They're breaking like kindling now!"

And he was right.

Demons and cultists *had* fought in a fanatical frenzy, but as their numbers dwindled and all hope was lost, their courage shattered. They fled for the swamp in all directions, but Drestra and Hart were merciless.

Less than a dozen minor demons escaped, and all bore grave wounds. They'd be prey for the swamp's predators soon enough.

"Not a bad bit of exercise," the Champion said, tossing aside the now-broken axe and grabbing another.

"We still have more to do," Drestra said. "I'll go tell the others."

"Oh, take your time. I ain't going anywhere." Hart took a wineskin from a corpse, flicked the cork away, sniffed it, then took a long swig. A broad grin covered his face. "This is the life."

"The cultists are dead!" The Sage flew above the pit, calling to her people. "That filth Osian won't be trading away anyone else's freedom ever again! You're free!"

The witches of Crymlyn—former prisoners and rescuers alike—cheered and wept, some did both. Relief washed over everyone, but Drestra couldn't share in it.

To the south, flashes of explosive magic and columns of smoke rose from the swamp.

The battle hadn't been won yet.

"Angharad, we've done what we came to do—less than a dozen demons fled into the woods and they're so badly injured, they won't be alive for long—but those with the leader are still putting up a fight. Cedric and the others can use reinforcements. Do you think you'll be alright getting everyone back to the village?"

"There's thirty of us. You go, help the others," Angharad said. "We'd be pretty poor witches and mages of Crymlyn if we couldn't handle a dozen half-dead demons."

"Go!" one of the prisoners cried. "Help the rest of our people!"

"Yes, go ahead, Drestra. They need you," Ffion said. "Angharad told us they're also fighting these monsters! So don't worry about us. We're fine now!"

"Thank the spirits you'll be back home soon. Everyone's waiting for you. Stay safe, all of you, and I'll see you soon!" Drestra flew toward the Champion, who was cleaning his blades. "Let's go. Time to help the others!"

"Alright, game on, then," he said, tossing the wineskin aside as she cast a flight spell on him.

Together, the two Heroes flew toward the southern battle as the Sage sent a signal through the sky.

A plume of flame erupted, announcing they were on their way.

"They know we're coming, so let's move!" Drestra said. "We should be there in about five minutes... if we don't run into trouble!"

"Oh, I think we will!" Hart snarled. He squinted in the distance. "Something's flying this way, and it ain't moving at a slow leisurely pace either."

Drestra swore. "Well, if we're really lucky, maybe the enemy's retreating. I hope the others are having an easy time like we had."

Alex stared at the long gash across Claygon's chest.

It was *deep*, nearly deep enough to pierce his core, and if that had happened—

"Claygon!" Theresa cried, whirling at the demon. "You filthy monster!"

She slashed at its eyes, but the demon casually clipped the huntress with a backhand, sending her careening through the air.

"No!" Alex screamed, diving toward her.

Theresa held up a hand. The gesture stopped him, then she charged back into battle. Her teeth were clenched as she joined Cedric and the witches' dying trees. Claygon came for the demonic leader while she fended off their attack, and slammed a fist into her shoulder.

She howled with pain. "Alright! Felt that! You need to go, rock man!"

"No!" Alex shouted.

"Dodge, big fellow!" The demon flipped the war-spear in her grip and hurled it.

The young wizard's mind flooded Claygon with directions, and the golem spun to the side.

But not quick enough.

The spear struck, clipping his shoulder, ripping away a chunk of clay. His arm almost separated from his body.

"By the Traveller," Alex murmured, watching Claygon climb away from the fight. "If that had hit any lower—"

A rush of teleportation magic cut off his words. The demon's war-spear reappeared in her hand, and she slashed another tree in half. As it was falling, Cedric was darting in, his weapon changing from form to form; he slashed with a sword, then stabbed with a spear, struck with a mace, then parried with a shield. Theresa sliced the demon's flanks and her blind spots, drawing dark lines of blood from shallow wounds.

The monster hardly seemed bothered. She lazily batted aside the two supernatural warriors and the powerful trees. She was... even...

"Oh shit!" Alex cursed. "She's actually *humming*. This isn't working. If this keeps up, *someone's* gonna die. Focus! Focus!"

He looked for Claygon. The golem and Cedric were the only ones doing any real damage, but Claygon was too slow to avoid that bloody spear.

'Alright, now she's toying with us. She's not really paying attention. You can use that. Just get that weapon away from her,' he thought. 'Teleportation magic! Maybe when she's stabbing at Cedric, I can cast Call Through Ice and she'll stab her blade into the portal. She can probably teleport it back into her hand, but before she does, I'll have Claygon crush her damn skull!'

He began casting, sinking into the Mark's interference.

The whoosh of a blade cutting the air warned him.

He stopped the spell, pulling out of the images.

The war-spear was coming right for him.

With a shout, he dove as it tore through the air where his head had just been.

"Nice dodge! Now, no more spells from up there!" the demon said as her spear flashed back into her hand. "If you want to fight me, then you're going to have to come down and use those tiny little hands of yours!"

A chill went through him; he'd called it wrong.

'She *looks* like she's toying with us,' he thought. 'But she's actually watching the battlefield like a hawk... Alright, so we'll have to blind her first.'

He sent two Wizard's Hands at her face. The spells flared brightly and clapped over her eyes, trying to blind her.

She opened her mouth.

Dozens of long tentacles slithered from between yellowed fangs, wrapped around the spells, and crushed them.

"I said *hands*!" she barked as she blocked Cedric's blow.

"Those were hands!" he fired back.

"Hah! You make jokes, how fun! Why don't we try some *physical* comedy for a bit!"

Her eyes met Alex's and her lips moved.

But no sound came out.

Then something hit his mind with the force of Claygon's fist.

CHAPTER 38

ROILING CHAOS

It overwhelmed his senses.

His ears rang and his skin crawled. White light flared in his vision. The scent of ash clung to his nostrils, the taste of it filled his mouth. Nausea boiled as his mind reeled.

'What is this?'

'Focus!' The young wizard's thoughts were scattered, frantic. 'Get your mind back! Control your senses—'

A terrible screech erupted behind him.

Alex whirled unsteadily, finding legions of monsters pouring from the blinding white, each a living nightmare. His heartbeat galloped, sounding like it was doubling with every breath, and a supernatural fear clawed at the inside of his skull like a monster was inside.

And it wanted out.

'Focus!' his thoughts screamed. 'Focus! It's in your mind, it's an attack on your mind! Fight it, whatever it is, fight! You fight the Mark, you can fight this! Focus! Let it pass!'

Desperately, he turned to his meditation techniques, letting them steady his mind so the magic would pass. But it clung, clouding reason, tugging at his will, determined to steal his sanity.

He called on the meditation techniques, sinking deeper into them.

Alex felt his breathing slow.

'It's like using the cleansing movements or the Mark. It'll pass. Let it pass. Let it pa—'

Suddenly, he was back.

The disruption to his senses, the shrieks, nausea, smell of ash, the hideous monsters all vanished, leaving him floating face down in the swamp. Only Orb of Air saved him from drowning.

"By the Traveller, what in all hells was that?" He groaned, shaking away the fogginess in his mind. A few deep breaths later, he was flying high above the battle.

His vision cleared.

His hearing slowly returned.

"Alex! Alex!" Theresa was screaming his name.

She was desperately trying to reach him, but the demon caged her with blurred strikes from that awful war-spear.

Neither seemed to notice he was recovering.

"We're not done, you and I, unlike him," the demon said. "You'll have plenty of time to go to... your... whatever he is." Her eyes flashed. "Does that screaming of yours mean you two have a connection? Perhaps he's what you mortals call a lover? Your scream wasn't *quite* a 'you killed my father or brother or what not' scream, so I'm guessing lover?"

The demon thought things over while casually deflecting attacks from the huntress, the Chosen, and two witches' trees at the same time. Alex's face fell, realising she was now surrounded by the ruins of the other trees. She'd destroyed the rest of them.

How long was he out?

"How quaint, and I must add, overly confining. You could learn something from me. Why limit yourself to one when a dozen is so much sweeter?" She grinned. "Anyway, it doesn't really matter who he is. After I'm through, you can all have a little get-together in death—"

"Will you bloody *shut up*!" Cedric stabbed the demon deep in her side.

Her growl of pain sounded like she was chewing stone as she smashed him into the water with a single stroke of her spear's haft.

"I could say the same to you. You're shockingly resilient."

Her full attention now turned to Theresa. Alex sent a mental call to his golem.

'Claygon, help Theresa or that thing'll kill her!' He directed another pair of Wizard's Hands at the demon's face.

The spells hovered before her eyes, then flared.

"What is this?"

Theresa whooped, relieved at the sight of Alex's spells, and slashed the leader's ear. She jumped back, hissing hard, ugly words in a demon tongue as Claygon came for her from above.

Two quick blows struck the sides of her head, snapping her neck sideways. She stumbled, taking blows from the last two trees and then—

Cedric was there.

The Chosen burst from the water, his spear stabbing deep into her back.

He must've hit something important, because the scream that ripped the swamp was deafening. She raised the war-spear, looking for her next target. Theresa and Cedric dove away, and Alex pulled Claygon and his spells back.

"You're alright!" Theresa cried.

"We'll see how long that lasts! She's wrecking us, and there's no way she'll let us just go!" He dug into his bag. "Here, Cedric, have a flight potion!" He whipped the potion at the Chosen.

"Thanks, mate! Good ta see ya back in the fight!"

"Look!" Theresa was pointing past Alex.

Desperate hope sprang in his chest.

While they'd been fighting the demon leader, her army had continued to retreat, but some had run head-on into witches of Crymlyn and their hidden traps and deadly magics. Traps and spells had thinned enemy numbers, but hadn't killed the fight in the remaining ones. They were fighting back. Hard.

Witches were dragging their wounded and dead within tree cover, and between some of those tree trunks, Alex spotted Baelin's boat with Brutus on board, jumping and pacing frantically. One head snapped at the water where demons were swimming past the boat, heading for their camp, while another looked straight up, growling at cultists speeding away... and that was where Alex spotted what Theresa was pointing to.

In a backdrop of magical explosions, the Sage and Champion battled monsters through the clouds. Lightning flashed, flame flared, and Alex's hope grew.

He said a silent prayer to the Traveller. 'Please let them get here soon. If we combine Hart's speed and power with everyone else's skills; and if Drestra hits the army, we should be able to overwhelm this demon. Things could turn in our favour.'

Alex looked back at their enemy.

There was one glaring problem with that plan, though.

Whoosh!

With a sweep of her war-spear, she cut down an animated tree like a blade of grass, then brought her weapon into guard position.

The leader smiled, appearing both threatened yet amused. 'We have to stay alive long enough for them to get here,' he thought, pulling out every booby-trapped potion he had.

"Well done, little mortals! You wounded me!" she said, stretching lazily. Wounds in the dozens—some shallow and some deep—marked her body, but her eyes twinkled like she was enjoying a game of fetch with a beloved pet. "I have to give it to you mortals, few have made me bleed so deeply. I suppose congratulations are in order!"

The last tree lurched toward her. She parried its club without looking at it. A chilling sensation crawled along Alex's spine.

"Alright, back to it, then—"

"Wait!" Alex forced a smile, then his hand shot up. "I suppose I've got to congratulate you too. I've never seen an opponent able to push *all* of us so hard before."

He kept his voice respectful, confident, and resonating, like a knight of legend acknowledging the honour of their rival. Cedric looked at him like he'd lost his mind, but Theresa's eyes were moving back and forth between him and the demon, calculating.

'That's right,' Alex thought. 'Don't make any sudden movements. Just buy some time and get us some breathing room.'

"Really?" she said. "A fine compliment from great, adorable little mortal warriors such as you!"

"Adorable?" Cedric turned on her, clearly aggravated.

"Of course you mortals are!" she continued, throwing her head back with laughter. "Always running, running, running through your little, short lives, in your little, short bodies, always up to this or that. Think of it this way... Do you know of an animal called a cat? I haven't seen any in this part of the material plane, so I wondered."

"We have cats," Theresa said, masking the rage and hatred she felt for the murderous, overbearing creature.

"Good! Then this will be easy to explain! Oh, and where are my manners? I am Zonon-In: you wounded me, so you deserve my name. What are yours?"

Alex abruptly stopped his companions from answering with a shake of his head. "Both you and I know it's never a good idea to give your name to a powerful demon, especially one that's a bit on the hostile side at the moment."

Meanwhile, he was communicating with Claygon. 'Buddy, I need you to do something for me. When I say, I need you to dive at her from behind, but when you do, you'll need—'

"Hah! You are the *cleverest* little mortals. It's rare to find ones so educated. It's usually: 'Oh no, a demon, aaaaah!' Or, 'Why are you eviscerating me? We had a deal!' Or, 'You dared kill my wife and destroyed my castle and now you pay—Urgh! Gurgle! Argh! Stop ripping my belly open with your pincers!'" She clicked the pincers of her bottom arms for emphasis. "Well, perhaps that last part isn't exactly spoken in *words* as much as in ear-shattering screams, but it's implied."

"What's this... got t'do wit' cats?" Cedric growled, his eyes briefly flicking back to Alex.

Good. He'd figured out that they were buying time.

'Nice one, Cedric,' Alex thought.

He looked past the war-spear like it held no interest for him, while she casually twisted it in her grip in a rhythmic assault on the last animated tree. That weapon was utterly deadly. If it could wither an entire tree, then what could its barbs do to a mere human?

"Ah, yes, the cats. Think of it this way," she said. "They're dangerous predators, in their own eyes. They take themselves so seriously, yet for all their teeth and claws and aloof self-importance, they're still only threats to the tiniest of mortal animals. I did once hear a story about cats being more dangerous than the average mortal peasant, but that's neither here nor there.

"Regardless, they see themselves as monarchs of tiny kingdoms, yet they're so small compared to all of you. Short, little lives and short, little bodies. And so sure of themselves, yet you mortals find them positively lovely! And so..." She gestured to the three of them. "Here you are, less than a third my size, thinking yourselves predators of the highest order, and yet you're so small in the end. It's just *too cute*!"

Cedric growled, but Alex's voice remained even and quiet.

"I can see the similarities, I guess. But we don't usually try to skewer our cats... or any of our pets."

"Hah! Then you haven't spent enough time in the world experiencing proper things," Zonon-In told him. "Some mortals find the struggles of things with short, little lives amusing. That futile rage and desperation, that's when you're most adorable! Now, then—"

'Just a little more!' Alex thought.

"You're not going to let us leave, are you?" he asked. "A demon of your power has a lot of magic to call on, and you're not even using it."

"Oh, very astute. You are right. I've no reason to use it, but—as you experienced—if you get too out of line, you'll be disciplined! Now, then... enough of your bid to buy time. I think I'll greet your other friends with your mutilated bodies. Alive, of course. Otherwise, where would the sport be in that?"

She swept her war-spear above her head, cutting down the final tree with a single stroke.

Alex grimaced. 'Well, not surprised she figured it out. But...' He looked at the spear again, thinking about everything Baelin talked about with the Teleportation Shuffle.

Focusing on what he'd said about paying attention to where you were going to appear in case there were obstacles in the way.

A new plan crystalized.

"Right, then!" Cedric chugged his potion of haste. "No more buyin' time for us, then!"

He charged.

"Theresa!" Alex cried, tossing her another potion. "Claygon!"

He made sure to call his golem's name out loud, bringing Zonon-In's attention to him.

Claygon dove from the sky, his fists ready.

Theresa swallowed the potion of haste and charged, while Alex soared higher, downing his. He was activating the Mark, focusing on the task of *faking spellcasting*.

Memories returned of Baelin summoning his terrible whirlwind over the Skinned Ones' dungeon. Alex threw booby-trapped potions of sensory enhancement into his four remaining Wizard's Hands, shooting them forward as Cedric reached the demon.

With the haste potion running through him, the Chosen was a blur, spinning his morphic weapon, chopping at the demon, trying to reduce her to bits.

But she was fast. Theresa joined the Chosen, Zonon-In's pincers struck like snakes, blocking their assault.

Claygon dove from above.

The demon was all smiles, grinning at Alex as her spear lashed out. It reached its target, slashing Claygon's torso, a wound that would have halved a living creature. He paused for an instant, then dropped, plummeting into the swamp with a splash that bathed everything near, then Alex's golem sank beneath the water.

"Claygon!" His voice broke with pain.

Zonon-In laughed... as he knew she would.

His face twisted with loss, and he raised both arms. A Wizard's Hand flew at her face, crushing the bottle in it, releasing mist in her eyes.

"Have you no imagination?" She shook her head as if in disappointment. "This again? My senses are—"

But Alex was already 'chanting' with all the fury he could put in his voice. *Almost* perfectly mimicking the words of Baelin's terrible incantation above the Skinless Ones' dungeon, but in the noise and intensity of battle, perfection wasn't needed.

"None of that!" Zonon-In shouted.

She flipped the spear.

His eyes narrowed.

It flew with such speed, his force shield shattered from a glancing blow as he dodged it. His heart pounded. Alex exhaled, bracing for the feel of teleportation magic.

Then, it flared.

'Now!' came the command.

Three Wizard's Hands shot into the demon's hand; the one waiting for the war-spear to return.

Bottles shattered, Wizard's Hands filled her palm, the spear reappeared, and blocked by his spells from landing in her hand, the weapon rolled from her fingers.

"What!" the demon bellowed, mist blocking her sight.

Theresa and Cedric struck her throwing arm as one. She sliced Zonon-In's fingers, drawing blood from the softer flesh. His weapon became an axe, driving into the monster's elbow.

She shrieked, caught off guard and furious, reeling from pain and confusion.

And in that confusion, her weapon dropped, turning end over end before hitting the water below.

A massive hand reached up.

Swamp water erupted like a geyser and the immense figure burst from the depths.

Gashes ran along his torso.

Water streamed from his form.

And in two hands?

Claygon gripped the demon's war-spear.

CHAPTER 39

THE WAR-SPEAR

S ome would have gloated. Some might have paused for effect. Alex, however, wasted no time.

'Stab her!' he thought.

Before the demon could reclaim her spear—Claygon thrust its tip into Zonon-In's side. Something tore; the demon's scream could have shattered glass as his powered arms drove the barbed blade home, then twisted the haft. Her shriek soared through the swamp as he ground the weapon deeper. For a brief moment, she wavered, but she didn't fall.

Black blood gushed, Zonon-In's flesh shriveled, her own spear withering her lifeforce, slowing her movements.

Cedric and Theresa were quick to take advantage.

The two warriors slashed at her trunk, their weapons sinking deep into her weakened hide. Theresa snarled in triumph, opening a dozen cuts across her gut before shifting to her legs and slashing at withering joints.

A tremendous boom resonated through the swamp—the demon fell to one knee.

"Give me back my spear, you—Argh!" She grabbed the haft, trying to pull the blade free, but Claygon sailed above her, lifting the handle like a lever and throwing her off-balance.

Her hand and pincer plunged into the muck struggling to keep her upright, and the other hand grabbed at her war-spear. It was taking its toll.

Claygon hovered, built momentum, then dove. Her yellow eyes grew frantic. She knew she was trapped and what was coming. The golem came in at speed, putting his full weight behind the war-spear's haft, driving her down. Her withering hand and pincer collapsed, and with a shout, she hit the bog. An explosion of muddy water heaved into the air and Claygon kept pressure on the spear, shoving their enemy into the marsh. Her body withered with every beat of her many hearts, and the Chosen and huntress joined the golem with a punishing attack of their own.

They slashed, pierced, and dealt her an array of blows she couldn't answer. Her wounds mounted, she clutched at the haft with two hands and both pincers, but it wouldn't budge. She was weaker, the golem wasn't. The war-spear did not move.

Panic haunted her face.

'Now's when she'll be most dangerous,' Alex thought.

"Cedric! Theresa!" he shouted, diving toward the fight. "Go for her eyes, but don't meet her gaze. Keep her busy! We can't let her concentrate or she'll use her magic!"

He willed Wizard's Hands to cover her eyes again, making both spells flare like flames.

Zonon-In clenched her teeth but said nothing; she was beyond taunting anyone now.

"Aye, none o' that magic business beastie!" The Chosen surged at her face, stabbing her cheek with his morphic weapon. Theresa followed—dragging her swords up the creature's torso—carving deep wounds into her flesh.

"That's for Claygon... and everyone else!" Her voice held no pity.

'Die!' Alex thought. '*Why won't you just die!*'

Zonon-In fought on. Her physical form was wavering like a failing illusion, but she swung her fists at Cedric and the huntress like the cornered beast she was.

With a jerk of her neck, she twisted the Chosen's weapon from her face, bellowing in a demonic tongue. "*Help!*" her call swept out to her army. "*These mortals are mauling me. Stop them!*"

"Watch out, she's calling for reinforcements! We have to finish her!" Alex translated.

Zonon-In's mouth opened, and tentacles writhed from it, reaching for Alex's spells covering her eyes.

"Oh no y' don't!" Cedric chopped through her guard with a shining halberd.

Tentacles split in half, snaking into the water. Zonon-In screamed.

"We're not so adorable *now*, are we?" Theresa snapped, chopping off two of the demon's fingers.

Alex took his cloak off.

If he wrapped it around her face, he—

A burst of light flashed at the corner of his eye.

"Watch it!" he cried.

Beams of power blasted all around him; one clipped his force armour, knocking the breath from him. He spun out, landing in the water.

Beam-demons were coming in fast, shooting deadly rays from their vessels, answering Zonon-In's call. They were closing the distance, but also taking heavy losses. Dozens of boats ripped apart on ancient roots lying just below the water's surface, or plowed into quicksand, their crew cut down by arrows and spells. But not all met that fate. Enough beams launched through the sky to drive Theresa and Cedric from the demon leader's face.

That gave her time to act.

Her lips twisted, and with one word, something shifted in the air.

A roiling wave of chaos slammed into her foes.

The word scraped Alex's eardrums like pitchfork tines, stole his hearing, and hammered his mind with a force that made his body wilt. He felt like a snake shedding its skin, feeling it throb and pulse and work to pull itself free of his body, while a bolt of pure chaos clawed at his brain, fighting to burrow inside.

Alex used every technique he knew to keep his mind clear, but the rest of his body still twitched uncontrollably, pure chaos wanting to tear it apart. Above, Cedric fought invisible phantoms around him. He was shouting, though no sound came. Theresa lay helpless in the water, writhing from the demon's onslaught, every inch of visible skin pulsating.

Even the armour covering Claygon thrashed. Clay bulged unnaturally, and cracks on his body spread. Yet, he never stopped grinding the war-spear into the demon. He was relentless.

He would never stop.

"*Perhaps I owed you all more respect,*" Zonon-In's voice echoed through Alex's mind, the only 'sound' she allowed in the silence. "*I see now you were not cats to toy with. I shall honour that. You deserve better from me.*"

With no one to stop her, she raised a hand toward Alex's golem.

He felt a terrible mana rising.

'Claygon!' Alex reached out. 'Move!'

The golem pulled away, dragging the spear from her body as he went.

But her mana was reaching a new height of power.

It would—

An outline rocketed from the sky.

Alex caught sight of a very welcome face.

Hart Redfletcher, Champion of Uldar, dove straight for the demon.

In a blur, he swung an enormous bone axe at Zonon-In's pointing hand, severing it clean from her wrist. Her spellcasting ended, she screamed silently, the offending hand sailing end over end into the swamp.

'Now!' came Alex's thought. 'Go for the face, Claygon! Don't let her recover!'

His golem lifted the war-spear and drove the immense, barbed blade into the demon leader's screaming mouth. She stiffened like she'd been turned to stone...

...and then her body began to shatter.

Alex's hearing returned to a sound like crumbling glass; the greater demon's form was shuddering apart, becoming particles like sand that vanished in puffs of brimstone.

"*I shall remember this, mortals,*" Zonon-In's voice echoed through their minds. "*You won my respect. Now you have my wrath. I will recover my strength. I shall learn your full names. Then, whether it be in one mortal year, one decade, or a score of winters... I will return for you.*"

Her form was now as clear as glass.

"*In my defeat, you have won my war-spear.*" Her telepathic voice was fading. "*Treasure it while you can, for I will reclaim it from the ruins of both clay and flesh. Until then, know that you have made an eternal enemy of Zonon-In, commander of the Abyssal Knight Ezaliel.*"

And then, she was gone as though she was never there.

That left a surprised Hart Redfletcher pulling Cedric and Theresa from the water, while Claygon hovered in the air with Zonon-In's... no, *his* war-spear gripped firmly in hand.

Alex dragged himself from the muck, his body still trying to shake away after-effects of the demon's power. He stood there trembling, taking in the battlefield.

Drestra was with the witches of Crymlyn Village, hurling spell after spell into the enemy's ranks, driving them into the Skull Pits and waiting patches of quicksand.

Their leader was gone, as was their nerve, and they began fleeing, often into deep pools of quicksand.

"We're winning," Alex murmured, scarcely believing it. At times, he'd thought she was going to kill them and crush Claygon. "We're actually winning."

"Yeeeup," Hart said. "They're *done*. Just a matter of cleaning up the rest now."

He looked critically at Cedric, and then everyone near.

"But you all look like you've been ripped in half then sewn back together, then ripped in half again. Badly. By a drunken blood mage. Maybe you should go back to the boat and catch your breath," the Champion said. "We've got this."

"No, I can heal us... then fight," Cedric wheezed, shaking his head like a wet hound. His long hair dripped swamp water.

"The heal part sounds good, the fight part, not so much. Go on, rest. You all already fought the good fight. I'm just mad I missed it. Now get back on that boat before I drown you myself," Hart said.

"Yeah." Theresa took a slow deep breath, floating up to Alex. They leaned on each other. "You're right. It's better if we recover. I can barely lift my swords."

"Fine," Cedric grunted.

"Atta boy," Hart said, flying off to the battlefield. "I'll kill a few dozen in your names!"

Alex watched him leave, shaking his head.

"I can't believe my life's gone so sideways that that sounds like a good offer," he muttered as he and Theresa half-flew, half-carried each other to Baelin's boat. Cedric and Claygon came right after them, with the Chosen calling on Uldar's power to heal him, and the golem holding the hard won war-spear over his shoulder.

Brutus barked the instant he saw his master and Alex, and almost drowned them in drool when they finally collapsed in the boat with Claygon between them.

Cedric flopped on the canvas, even though it wasn't the least bit comfortable, but at this point, lying on rocks would have felt good.

"That..." the Chosen murmured. "Was the worst bloody fight of me entire life."

His head lolled back and he stared at the sky.

"Told you," Alex said. "Greater demons are no joke."

"Yeah, well, she seemed t'find things pretty funny for a bit." The Chosen chuckled bitterly.

"The hell with her and her sense of humour," Theresa groaned. "I wasn't laughing."

"Doubt any of us were." Alex looked up at Claygon. "Oh no, look what she did to you, buddy."

Cracks snaked through most of his torso. A chunk of his shoulder was missing, and deep gashes ran through his chest and belly.

"Can 'e be fixed?" Cedric asked.

"As long as his core's fine, which it is; otherwise, he would've stopped moving," the young Thameish wizard said. "I just need to get back to Generasi, get him into a workshop, and get some clay. His golem core'll help it harden into the same shape as before. It's going to take a fair amount of work, but he's worth it." Alex patted his damaged arm.

"Well..." Cedric looked at the spear clutched in Claygon's hand. It was longer than he was tall. "At least *you* got somethin' outta all o' this, big guy."

"Yeah," Alex said, admiring how well the horrifying spear fit the terrifying golem. "I think we're going to put that to good use."

"As you should," Theresa groaned. "But, I know what I'm going to do after this. I'm going back to training. When that demon comes back, I want to be strong enough to cut her clean in half."

"Life goals, I guess," Alex said. "For now, though... I don't think I wanna move for a while. Maybe try not breathing too."

"You'll die if you stop breathing, idiot," the huntress said.

"Enh, it works for Claygon."

"That it does, and not gonna lie, I'm a bit jealous o' him. Breathin' hurts right now," Cedric grunted. "But... at least it tells us we're still alive."

"Yeah," Alex said. "Damn right we're still alive."

"We're still alive," Theresa echoed.

In that moment—surrounded by the sounds of dying demons and cultists being finished off—being alive seemed like a very precious thing, indeed.

Cornered in the Skull Pits, the enemy was desperate to escape, but there wasn't much they could do to make that happen.

It took less than an hour to finish off the followers of Ezaliel, and soon, the noise of battle was replaced by victorious cheers from the witches of Crymlyn Swamp. Things grew sombre when the dead and dying were accounted for, and the witches began mourning their fallen, loading their bodies into boats to ferry them home one final time.

Healers—well-practised in blood magic—worked on the injured, tending their wounds and bringing them comfort with herbs, potions, and spells.

At the end of it all, they'd suffered less losses than they'd expected, but more than they could stand. Even one loss was one too many for the loved ones of the dead.

Once the witches said prayers over their kin, asking the spirits to cleanse and heal the swamp of the taint of cultists and demons, they began the journey back to Crymlyn Village.

Theresa and Cedric said very little—drifting in and out of sleep—while Alex piloted Baelin's boat. The journey was grim, most thoughts were on those who'd met their end, and kindred who'd turned to treachery. Though there was a lot waiting at home to celebrate: freed hostages, their rescuers, and a reunion.

At the dock in Crymlyn Village, cheers, tears of joy, and relief met the witches, Heroes, and Generasians. Everyone thanked the returning rescuers and fighters, a reminder of all they'd been through and what they'd won. Those who'd remained behind to defend the village, came out to welcome the exhausted fighters and see to their care.

Elder Blodeuwedd was in the healing compound—along with several other healers—tending to hostages, witches, and anyone else in need of care, which included Alex, Theresa, and Cedric. Their physical wounds were minor, but Zonon-In's assault on their thoughts weren't. Those called for soothing potions, drawing salves, and pressure techniques to calm their minds and bring them back into balance. The witches' treatments worked, cleansing the trio of residual effects of chaos, draining it from every fibre of their being. Most of their energy returned.

And they slept deeply that night.

The next day would ask much of them again...

...but hopefully, a bit less.

CHAPTER 40

A SURPRISE STRIKE BY MORNING LIGHT

"How is Ffion?" Alex asked Drestra.

"Mmf," came the Sage's muffled reply.

She was turned away and held up her index finger—indicating that she needed a moment—as she chewed a morsel of food.

"Take your time." Alex reached for another serving.

The late morning light found Alex and his companions in their tree-cottage, devouring a breakfast of mushroom soup, pickled birds' eggs, and fish roasted in garlic butter, while Brutus darted around the table, begging for food. The young Thameish wizard smiled at the cerberus, understanding his enthusiasm.

'Hunger and being thankful for being alive really are the best seasonings,' Alex thought, still bleary-eyed and tired from yesterday. He felt like his entire body had been beaten by Claygon's mammoth fists.

The golem stood near the cottage door. Beside him, propped against the wall, was the demon's former war-spear. He admired it with a conflicted smile.

'You deserve your prize, big guy. You're the one who was hurt the most,' he thought, eyeing the cracks throughout Claygon's body. He was itching to get back to Generasi to repair him.

"Ffion's recovering well," Drestra finally said, the relief plain in her voice. "Most of the survivors are. The majority didn't really have major wounds or infections, thankfully. They were all dehydrated, some had broken bones and cuts, but between my people's healing magics, the blood magic you used this morning to help them, and Cedric's miracles, most injuries are healed, but some will need time. My thanks to both of you."

"Well, I'd be a pretty shit Chosen if I didn't help," Cedric said, ready to shove a thick piece of fish in his mouth.

"And I'd just be a pretty shit wizard," Alex said. "Even if it was just a few extra castings of Mana-to-Life, I'd be kind of an ass if I didn't at least try to help."

"And we're all grateful," Drestra said. Alex could hear the smile in her voice. "Mother said that she won't forget what any of you—" her reptilian eyes slid over the group "—have done for us. But... for many of the victims, the mental scars will take longer to heal. They've seen things that are hard to imagine."

"A demon camp's no place I'd want to be long-term," Hart said. "Say, did your mother say anything about getting those supplies? There were a *lot* of them lying around that camp."

"Yes. She sent guards there late yesterday to keep an eye on things and start organising the supplies to bring them back here," she said. "And you're right, the cult was very well stocked. We should have enough food to feed all the folk we rescued well into the spring. After that, though... I don't know... they've lost a lot of people. There's been some talk that they might stay here for the next year at least."

"Well, I hope they can get back out there with time. It's always rough to lose a way of life," Alex said. "Even if you have another one waiting."

"Mhm." Drestra nodded. "But on to a lighter topic: do you know when Baelin's supposed to be back?"

"Today, sometime," Alex said. "And when he gets here, we'll be able to meet with your friend and—" he tapped the dungeon core "—get this taken care of."

"Aye, that's something that's got me real curious." Cedric chomped on a big mushroom cap. "Then I suppose it's time fer some feastin' this evenin', then we'll be headin' back ta yer camp, right?"

"Yeah," Alex said. "Hopefully, he gets here soon. I wanna talk to him about what that demon said."

"Ya mean about makin' us her eternal enemy an' such?"

"Yeah. It's something we need to figure out. Demons can't exactly come to the material world whenever they want, and she doesn't know our names," Alex said. "But sooner or later, she's gonna come for us."

"Aye, this big, glowin' thing on me chest's a bit of a clue ta who I am, though," Cedric said. "I'd appreciate knowin' if she's gonna come leapin' outta some rain barrel at me someday. Swear, I could do wit' less surprises in li—"

"Well, hello there," Baelin said.

"Ah holy shite!" Cedric jumped, spilling food on his chest.

Alex sprayed his soup.

Brutus yelped and jumped back.

Drestra screamed.

Theresa choked on a piece of fish, and Alex had to pound her back.

Hart... didn't stop eating.

The chancellor raised an eyebrow. "Well! Good morning to you too! Quite the reaction from such brave young people to an old goatman. Are my horns crooked? Do I have five eyes this morning? Did a demon lord just manifest in your parlour? Careful; if I were less secure in myself, my feelings might be wounded."

"Baelin, you scared the hell out of us!" Alex cried. He was so tired, he hadn't even noticed the teleportation magic.

"Aye, I nearly cacked m'trousers!" Cedric looked at soggy chunks of fish running down his Mark.

"Well, I am most certainly glad you did not!" Baelin said. "In such an enclosed space, that would have been most unpleasant."

"Yeah, it would've been your fault, though," Alex grunted. "How're you doing, by the way?"

"Most excellent. I've put some affairs in order and so I—Oh *my*, Claygon!" The chancellor stopped mid-sentence, his goat-like eyes scanning the golem's body. "What happened to *you*? It looks as though—" He took in the enormous war-spear against the wall. "What in blazes is *that*! What happened?"

"You missed one hell of a party," Hart said.

"*Party*?" Cedric gave the Champion a withering look. "A party, y'call it? Bloody bastard, that's easy for you t'say. All y'had t'do was smash up a half-deserted camp. We were the ones havin' our shite stomped in by the bloody biggest bloody demon that ever stomped outta the hells."

Baelin raised an eyebrow and looked at Alex.

"Well, not the biggest ever to spawn in the hells," the young Thameish wizard said. "But she was pretty big."

"Pretty big, Alex?" Theresa looked at him. "I've met smaller *trees*. And she hit like a battering ram. It felt like she was going to rip me in half."

Baelin cleared his throat. "I do believe that I am... er... missing a bit of *context* here."

Alex sighed. "Well, we won and now there aren't enough demons left in Crymlyn Swamp to fill your boat—which made it out undamaged, by the way—but... oh, you better sit down. It's a long story."

"Goodness, you all have been busy!" Baelin cried, sipping a bit of broth as they caught him up. "And you defeated a greater demon? By yourselves! An incredible feat for ones of your age."

"It was close. Too close," Theresa said. "If she was taking us seriously, she'd have had our guts for breakfast."

"Aye, don't like to admit it, but Theresa's got the right of it," Cedric agreed. "Bloody demon nearly fried m'mind when she got desperate."

"Indeed, you all are extremely fortunate she had underestimated you. A greater demon is a creature to be feared and respected by most." The chancellor stroked his beard-braids. "Unfortunately, I doubt that she would make the same mistake twice."

"Yeah, that's going to be a problem," Hart admitted. "Ravener-spawn are bad enough, but waiting for this demon to jump us is going to be a pain and a half."

"That's an understatement," Drestra said.

"Well, now, I would not worry about that too much," Baelin said thoughtfully. "You said this demon's name was Zonon-In?"

"Yeah," Alex said.

"Fascinating. I do believe I should summon this demon, then she and I can have a friendly chat. It might involve a little curse that would ensure some unpleasant, soul-rending consequences were she to return to this plane to do any of you any harm. Of course, I'm sure she will eventually find *some* way to remove it—or get around it in time—but such an undertaking will take time."

"Oh... oh that's grand." Alex grinned wickedly. "But couldn't you just destroy her in that case?"

"It is a dangerous thing to assume one could wipe out a greater demon sight unseen, though I likely could," the chancellor reasoned. "But, come now! That would be destroying a learning opportunity for all of *you!*"

"Huh? Learning opportunity?" Drestra asked.

"Indeed, you angered a greater demon! And I sincerely doubt this will be the last time you will do so, considering the path of martial, magical, and divine power you all pursue. If I use my greater experience to simply make the problem go away, then what will you have learned? What will you do next time? Better to simply delay her until you are ready to face her at your full strength rather than having me erase the threat completely and stifle your growth."

"That's bloody madness," Cedric said.

"I dunno, makes sense to me." Alex shrugged. "What do you think, Theresa?"

"I want another crack at her."

"Then it is settled!" Baelin clapped his hands. "Excellent work, by the way. And look at Claygon!" He raised a cup of water toward the golem. "You got the only prize out of this. And what a prize it is. That is a *very* powerful weapon. From a quick look, I see traces of teleportation magic to call it back to hand, force magic to increase the strength of its impact and prevent its barbs from remaining in an opponent's flesh, blood magic to increase bleeding, and necromantic magic to wither the lifeforce of whatever it strikes. What a feast of power. The golems are eating better than the people."

He paused as though expecting a laugh but was only met with confused silence.

"Actually, I suppose it makes sense that you would not get that reference. A Generasian aristocrat once wrote an essay entitled, *The Golems Eat Better than the People*, predicting a future where magical constructs will assume all the labour in the world, taking away the livelihood of farmers, warriors, and tradesfolk. In the essay, he painted a rather fanciful image of powerful archwizards serving their golems lavish feasts like they were mortals dining on elaborate meals in a rich setting. Of course, such food would be wasted on golems—since they have no need to eat—while the nobility of the world would be reduced to starvation and battling each other over scraps."

"Uh... wouldn't havin' golems doin' all the hard work be a bloody paradise?" Cedric asked.

"There are several schools of thought on that," the chancellor said. "Some say it would lead to a paradise of leisure. Others say that having all needs met by constructs would wither the competitive spirit in mortals, leaving them to fester in indolence. I happen to believe that such a world would have mixed results. I know of many wizards who leave all forms of labour and chores to summoned and constructed servants, allowing them to spend their time in pursuit of knowledge, leisure, and self-development."

He chuckled, his eyes growing wistful. "Some take to it very well, using their free time to make great advancements in philosophy, science, self-actualization, and wizardry. Others raise families or delve into the arts. Others become masters of hobbies or find new joys to explore. Though, indeed, there are some who collapse into forms of degeneracy so foul, it would be a disservice to all of you to speak of them."

Baelin elbowed Alex with a twinkle in his eyes. "Now, don't *you* go that route, Mr. Golem Maker!"

"I... okay," the young wizard simply said.

"Now, then." The ancient wizard looked at Drestra. "You said your friend has recovered?"

The Sage cleared her throat. "Yes, she's fit enough and demanding food richer than broth."

"Would she be well enough to receive... visitors?" He looked pointedly at the dungeon core in Alex's bag.

"She should be," the Sage said. "And I'm as eager to resolve this as you are."

"Then let us go! But before we do, do you think she would mind a couple of extra guests with us?" he asked.

"Uh... what do you mean?" Drestra asked.

"Professor Jules and Carey requested that they be present when we do our testing," Baelin said. "Might I bring them along?"

"Of course," Drestra said. "I don't think it should be a problem."

"Most excellent. Then meet me outside. I shall return momentarily."

With a surge of teleportation magic, Baelin vanished.

Alex and the others looked at each other.

"Well, this is it," the young wizard said. "The moment of truth. Let's get going."

As one, they wolfed down the rest of their breakfast like it was their last meal, did a quick clean up, and filed out of the cottage, tense but eager.

The village was quiet, calm, and... had a feel of melancholy to it this morning.

"It's appropriate," Alex muttered.

"What is?" Theresa asked him softly.

"The atmosphere's a bit happy and yet a bit sad," he whispered. "We're about to learn something huge—whether worshippers of our god or people of our homeland can control dungeon cores. Even if it's exciting to finally find out... either answer is grim."

"Yeah, I've been thinking about it," she said as the group stopped at the foot of the tree their cottage was nestled in. "They're both bad... but I think I know which one would be worse for me."

"Which one?"

"Well, I don't want to say yet, in case that's the way it goes," she whispered.

Alex was about to reply when he felt a rush of teleportation magic.

Baelin appeared, flanked by Professor Jules—with a bulging pack on her back as though she were about to start a long journey—and Carey, looking like she was two breaths from throwing up.

She gave a weak wave to the others. "Morning."

"Good morn—Oh goodness!" Professor Jules cried, catching sight of Claygon. "What happened?"

"It's a long story," Alex said. "We'll fill you in on the way."

"Indeed, Vernia," Baelin said. "We can catch up as we make our way to Drestra's young friend. Now, come. It is time."

Alex took a deep breath. "Yeah... it's time."

His hand fell on the orb tucked safely in the satchel.

Together, the group walked toward Ffion's cottage.

Together, they walked toward the truth.

CHAPTER 41

FFION'S TOUCH

"This is such a wonderful place." Carey's eyes couldn't stay still as the group trudged through the village. "It's like something from bedtime fairy tales my nursemaid told when I was little." She looked a little brighter, gawking like a sightseer.

Professor Jules was doing the same, though she was clearly pretending she wasn't. From the smirk on Baelin's face, he'd noticed.

For a moment, it felt like just another ordinary day, not one with a potentially life-shattering truth gathering on the horizon like storm clouds. Alex knew this moment would soon end for him and the other followers of Uldar walking through the magical village beside him.

They reached a series of long buildings on the other side of the village where former hostages were recovering. Caregivers busied themselves, collecting large pots—now empty of their bland contents—to clean them in the kitchens. They watched the passersby with nods and friendly smiles of gratitude and even awe.

Those reactions had become common since they'd helped end the demon and cultist scourge that had done so much damage to life in the Crymlyn.

But Alex and his companions couldn't stop to talk. They were on their way to a small cottage set apart from the other buildings.

An offended-looking young woman was shutting a door, gripping the handle like she wanted to crush it as she glanced at them and left with an empty pot in her other hand.

Complaints from within the cottage chased her as she went. "You're trying to starve me! I swear, you are! I need *real* food! Fried catfish!

Roasted bear! Nice, hot chunks of bread, come on! I've been starved for weeks, have mercy!"

The woman hurried away, muttering to herself with no interest in turning back.

"Oh, Ffion," Drestra sighed as they approached the cottage. "Why do you have to give people trouble?"

Before any of her companions could say a word, she opened the door to a single room with an oak bed that was occupied by an agitated young woman.

"Back to argue, eh? Listen, starving people can't recover their strength with bone broth alo—Oh, I'm so glad you're here, Drestra. I thought it was that stingy—never mind about her. Did you bring food?"

"Hello, Ffion," the Sage said in a very unimpressed tone as she stepped inside. "Nice to see you're treating the people trying to help you with *kindness* and *respect*."

Ffion froze, then was seized by loud, exaggerated coughing. "They're trying to kill me. Seriously, give me *anything* but broth," she groaned, flopping back on her bed and looking weaker; even her voice sounded weaker than when she was pleading for mercy from broth a minute ago. "Drestra, help, they're torturing me. I'm feeling weak. I'm feeling so weeeaaaaak."

The young woman had buried herself in blankets. Broth and a pitcher of water lay within arm's reach. Beneath her were several layers of sheep's wool. In short, she looked shockingly cozy for someone being tortured.

"You're not being tortured, Ffion," Drestra grunted. "You're fine."

"Yeah, easy for you to say. You get real food," she grumbled, looking at the others who'd squeezed into the one-room cottage after the Sage.

"Stay outside, Brutus," Theresa said. "It'll be a little cramped in here."

"Same thing for you, buddy," Alex said. "Just wait out here for a bit. We won't be long."

The cerberus cocked his heads at Theresa then turned in place a couple of times and lay by the door.

Hart came in last, shutting it behind him.

Professor Jules cleared her throat. "Greetings."

"How do you do," Baelin said.

The others greeted Ffion while the young woman looked at them like a cornered deer.

"Drestra, what is this? Am I being arrested?"

"No," the Sage said dryly.

"Oh... is *this* the reason I was given my own cottage? Something to do with these people?"

"Yes."

"I thought it was because I've been friends with the elder's daughter from the time we were small." Ffion flashed a toothy smile.

"It's that too." Drestra frowned at her childhood friend. "Though I'm beginning to regret that... But, seriously, I need to ask *you* for a favour."

"Well, you just saved my life," Ffion said, turning to the others. "All of you did, I hear. Well, except for you, and you." She squinted at Carey and Professor Jules. "No offence."

"None taken," the professor said.

"As for the rest of you: if one of you asked for my firstborn, I think I'd pretty much have to give them up, that is... when I get around to having this firstborn. You saved my life, so whatever you need."

Drestra looked at Alex and Baelin.

The young wizard cleared his throat. "Well, it's pretty simple."

"But it requires secrecy," the chancellor added. "Drestra says you are to be trusted... However, would you be opposed to swearing a magical oath that guards against loose tongues?"

Ffion looked at Drestra. "Uh... what is this?"

"You'll understand in a minute. It's not going to be anything very dangerous. Probably."

"*Probably?*"

"In all likelihood, no, if I understand the proceedings correctly," Professor Jules added. "*You* will not be doing the dangerous part."

"There's a dangerous part?" Ffion looked at her sharply.

"Yeah, probably," Drestra said. "But it's like the professor said, you're not going to do the dangerous part."

Silence followed.

Ffion took a deep breath. "Well, I guess this is better than my firstborn. What do you need me to do?"

"First," Alex said. "We kinda need to do an oath of secrecy with you. Something that'll ensure you don't talk about this with anyone."

The young witch looked at Drestra, who nodded at her friend.

"Alright, you people saved us, my friend trusts you, so I think I can trust you too," Ffion said. "Besides, we use that kind of magic too, so this must be really important."

"It is; otherwise, we would not burden you with it," Baelin said. "I shall conduct the ritual after we finish our test. If you would do the honours, Alex?"

The young wizard carefully removed the dungeon core from the satchel.

Carey tensed, watching the dark orb in his hands.

"Now, try not to—" he started.

"Is that what I think it is?" Ffion cried, backing into the headboard.

"We don't really have to talk about what it is..." Alex said. "Really, it's probably better if we don't get into too many details about that." He offered her the core.

Wide eyes pleaded with Drestra. "Help?"

"Ffion, trust me, this will be easy," the Sage assured her. "All you have to do is pick it up—"

"You want me to touch a *dungeon core*?" Ffion hissed, her voice dropping to a whisper. "Are you out of your mind?"

"It'll be alright."

"Oh, by the spirits, folk said that you'd tricked those demons into thinking you had a dungeon core..." She gripped the sides of her head in shock. "Not that you *actually had one*!"

"We do, and we need to find out something about it." Drestra took one of Ffion's hands. "Please. It's important."

The other witch looked at her for a long while... then sighed.

"Fine, what should I do?"

"It's simple," Alex told her. "We want you to run your mana over the dungeon core and feel for any... oddities."

"And it won't kill me or maim my soul?"

"Well, I'm holding it, aren't I?"

"And—" Drestra touched the orb. "—I'm touching it too and I'm fine."

"...Okay, but if it kills me, I'm haunting you." Ffion sat up in bed and gingerly touched the orb.

This was it.

Alex held his breath. The Heroes leaned in. Baelin fixed the dungeon core with his piercing gaze. Theresa swallowed. Professor Jules took out her pen and notebook. Carey prayed in whispers.

Everyone watched as Ffion focused her mana, running it over the orb.

Heartbeats passed in silence.

Breaths were held.

And then...

"Am I looking for something in particular?"

Cedric groaned.

"No..." Carey murmured.

"What about here?" Drestra guided her friend's mana to the area where the entrances were located. "Do you feel anything here?"

Alex felt Ffion's mana pass over the gates.

Another long moment passed.

Ffion shook her head.

"No... nothing." She looked puzzled. "I gather there's supposed to be something there? Maybe I did it wrong."

There was a thud as Cedric fell against the wall, the colour draining from his face. "Oh, *you* didn't do a thing wrong. Oh, bloody hell. Oh, bloody, *bloody hell*."

"By holy Uldar." Carey was reaching for the door, fighting back tears. A heart-wrenching sob racked her body as she staggered into the cool air.

"Miss Londo—Carey!" Professor Jules snapped her notebook shut. "I'll go after her. Many thanks, Miss Ffion."

The professor stepped outside, closing the door behind her.

Alex swallowed.

Confirmation.

The only people who could control dungeon cores were not only Thameish... they also followed Uldar.

It was a strange thing.

They'd entered Crymlyn Swamp *knowing* it was either one possibility or the other. They'd fought a terrible battle not only to help Drestra's people, but to also find out for certain who could control dungeon cores.

The battle had been won.

A feast was planned in their honour for tonight.

They'd found the answer to the question that brought them here.

And yet—

"Why... why do you all look like someone just desecrated your graves?" Ffion looked at everyone before her. "What was wrong with that woman? Why was she crying? Are you *sure* I didn't do something wrong?"

"Oh no, you did not... but... well, one day you will know exactly what has occurred," Baelin said. "Apologies for the mysterious approach we're taking for the time being, but it is best if as few people as possible know as little as possible, and nothing more."

"I... I bloody-well need some air," Cedric almost ran outside.

"Yeah, me too." Theresa followed him. "I... I need to see my dog."

"Theresa—" Alex called after her, but she was gone. "Shit. Baelin, can you hold on to this?"

He offered the ancient wizard the dungeon core, and Baelin gladly took it.

"Of course. Go ahead. I shall disguise all of your voices so you'll be free to discuss things without worry." The chancellor tucked the dungeon core away. "Have a chat while I go about sealing the oath with the ever so helpful Ffion." He smiled down at her. "You have done a great service today, though you might not know the full extent of it, and I will see to it that you are appropriately compensated."

"Compensated?" Ffion looked like she wanted to bolt. "But... what'd I do?"

"Don't worry, I'll stay and we'll talk about it, as much as we can," the Sage said.

It was the last thing Alex heard before he stepped out of the cottage, followed by Hart. Theresa was kneeling beside Brutus, hugging his necks. Cedric was staring up at the sky as though his gaze could punch a hole in it. A short distance away, Carey had collapsed against the cottage wall, still sobbing while Professor Jules awkwardly consoled her.

Alex made his way to his partner and gently squeezed her shoulder. She reached up, locking her fingers with his and buried her face between Brutus' necks. The cerberus nuzzled her.

"Baelin cast a spell that lets us talk without anyone else understanding what we're saying," Alex announced. "So... if anyone needs to say anything about... well, you can just get it out."

Silence followed.

Hart put his hands on his hips and blew out a breath. "Well... that's that, isn't it?"

"Whaddya mean, 'that's that'?" Cedric looked at him, wild-eyed. "We just bloody found out that only folks worshippin' the god that *stamped us* ta fight our, or maybe it's *his* eternal enemy, are the only ones who can control those things... and *that's that* is all you can say?"

"Yeah." Hart crossed his arms over his chest. "What do you want me to say? 'Oh no'? 'Oh, my heart's shattering'? 'My mind's coming apart'? 'My faith's been robbed from me'?"

"*Hart.*" Cedric threw a meaningful look at Carey. "Have a bloody care, would ya?"

"Why?" the Champion asked. "Look, I understand feeling bad, but it happened, and we know about it. No amount of crying, or screaming, or losing our minds is going to change that."

"I... kinda agree with Hart," Alex said. "We all knew this was a possibility and—to be fair—even if Ffion could control the core, which would mean this would be about Thameish people in general and not just Uldar's followers, then that'd *still* be a problem. I'm not saying it doesn't suck, because it does... At least we know more about what we're dealing with—"

"*Do we*?" Cedric scowled. "Now we know that... havin' faith in Uldar is what lets us control our worst enemy, but somehow, no priests ever thought that'd be somethin' important fer us t'know? I mean, sure, now we know, but what in all shite do we do wit' that information? What in all hells do we bloody-well do?"

"That'll take time to figure out. No matter what it means, at least now we have somewhere to start," Alex said. "And... if it does have something to do with Uldar, then we're not completely in the dark anymore."

"Look, that's easy for you t'say, no offence, but y'weren't *marked* by our god," Cedric said. "Y'wouldn't get it."

Alex felt heat rising. 'Ya, I would get it,' he thought. He was one hair away from telling the Hero that *he* had no idea what he was talking about, that he'd also been marked—but as the Fool, not the Chosen, like him. He wanted to tell Cedric that it was him who'd been stamped with a Mark that made him the object of Thameland's ridicule, and that no one ever asked if he'd be okay with that, or if he'd be willing to *die* for that, for a cause built on some sort of deception. He wanted to shout that Cedric wasn't the only one whose life had been flipped on its head.

...But he couldn't say any of that, at least not now. Cedric was obviously raging, and in that state, who knew what the Hero might do.

Besides, Carey was right there seeming like her heart would break. Confronting Cedric wouldn't help her.

"We're both followers of Uldar, Cedric." Theresa looked up at the Chosen, then pushed herself to her feet. "We were raised and educated in the church. Priests helped me learn my letters and spell my name. We've lived and breathed him our whole lives, even if we don't pray out loud all the time, or join campus groups, or visit the church. He's shaped our lives, just like yours, and now what the hell does this all mean?"

The huntress' frown deepened. "Who the hell have we been praying to?"

"Oh? You think this goes beyond priests?" Hart asked.

"Maybe. It's possible," she said. "I wish there was a way to go ask."

"The priests?" Alex asked her.

"No. Uldar," she said. "Look at the difference, you go to Generasi and find out that gods all over the world talk to their followers, or even walk the world. Ours? He's distant. Silent. And this is a bad time for him to be silent."

"...What if we did ask, though?" Carey spoke up.

The group turned to her as the young woman got to her feet.

"What if we went and asked him why we can control these dungeon cores?" She wiped her nose. "What if we went right to the source?"

CHAPTER 42

LOOKING TO QUESTION THE SOURCE

Professor Jules stepped back, giving Carey space. "What do you mean, Carey?"

The young woman wiped her tears. "I mean... Uldar left for his divine realm cycles ago. He left the Holy Heroes—" She looked at Cedric and Hart. "To defeat the Ravener while he watched over Thameland from his throne. But what if *we* went to his divine realm? What if we met Uldar and asked him what this all means?"

Alex was shocked at both the simplicity of the idea and Carey's single-mindedness.

"Holy shit," he murmured, looking at Theresa. "Can we do that?"

The huntress startled. "Why're you asking me?" She turned to Cedric. "Can we do that?"

The Chosen startled. "Why're ya' askin' me? I don't know nothin' about this!" He turned to Professor Jules. "You teach in Smart Wizard Land. Can we do that?"

"Why're you asking me—Oh, never mind. Well, the answer's complex. While it's true that some priests *have* gone to meet their gods in their divine realms—as have some wizards—whether or not it works depends on the deity," Professor Jules said. "For some, a simple Plane Shift spell or equivalent miracle puts you in a deity's divine realm, at least at its front gate, as long as you're a worshipper. Some ancient wizards used to visit their deities' divine gardens to collect rare alchemical ingredients. Some still do. But... for other deities..."

She tilted her hand back and forth. "Some ask for massive rituals and sacrifices. Others give the petitioner trials before they allow them to magic themselves into their realm. And others just… close themselves off. So the question is, has anyone from Thameland ever done that before? Gone to see Uldar?"

"No." Alex shook his head. "At least not that I'm aware of. If there was a history of priests visiting and talking to Uldar, then it's been hidden. We're taught that Uldar went to his divine realm, stayed there, and has been quietly watching Thameland ever since."

"To 'get out of our way,' one of the priests in Wrexiff used to say." Carey crossed her arms. She looked at the two Heroes. "Er, Cedric… Hart… did the priests ever teach you a way to get to Uldar's divine realm?"

"No," the Chosen said. "'Fraid not. Just gave us the same song they give everyone else: 'We'll all meet Uldar when we see the afterworld, if we're good enough.'"

"Is that it, then?" Hart asked. "Plan's dead?"

"Well, maybe not," Carey said. "I'm wondering if maybe there's an answer in the Cave of the Traveller."

Alex and Theresa flinched, but everyone was so focused on Carey, they showed no sign they'd noticed.

"The Traveller?" Alex asked carefully. "Why her? What do you think she's got to do with this?"

"She had a secret citadel underground," Carey said, drying her face with a handkerchief. All signs of tears were nearly gone. "And it was full of portals. Legends abound—as you know since you're also from Alric— of people wandering into the cave and appearing in all sorts of places. There are also stable portals all through the secret area down there. And she was a Saint; what if she was trying to find a way into Uldar's realm?"

The possibility struck Alex like a bolt from the blue.

'Could that be it?' he thought. 'Was she working on some… strange power that would let her travel across planes and into Uldar's realm? Is that it? Maybe… Then why did she have goddess statues in her temple? They definitely weren't in Uldar's image. There's more there, but—'

"You could be right, Carey," Alex said, looking at Cedric. "Have they explored the entire cave?"

"I dunno, t'be honest," the Chosen said. "Last time we was there was ta help people with the portals so they could leave Thameland. It wasn't mapped out back then—"

"But it's been a year. Things change," Hart jumped in, scratching his stubble in thought. "You know, it might not be a bad idea to go back there and check it out."

"Go back where?" A new voice joined the conversation.

Everyone faced Ffion's cottage door as Drestra and Baelin stepped into the cold, closing the door behind them.

"—real food! Tell them I'll spit the next spoon of bone broth they bring here in—" Ffion's voice called out before Drestra purposefully shut the door.

Baelin snorted in amusement. "So, what is this about going back somewhere?"

They filled Baelin and Drestra in with details of what they'd been discussing.

"Huh..." the Sage raised an eyebrow. "The magics in the cave *were* unique... you might be onto something."

"It is indeed possible," Baelin said. "*Possible.*"

"Yes, it's important not to accept an idea as fact before proper investigation is done," Professor Jules said. "But it's certainly a very good place to start."

"Mm, we could go back there an' have a proper look around," the Chosen said. "Maybe make some quick excuse to the priests about wantin' to check some o' the portals or somethin'. I dunno, the church lets us go where we want as long as we're smashin' dungeons."

"Ah, you know what?" Hart snapped his fingers. "We could say that there was an invasion by a big, nasty demon leading its big, nasty army. So, we're just looking at the portals to make sure they can't be used by other big, nasty demons. There's something we need to talk about, though. We have confirmation now, right? So, what do we do about Merzhin? Do we tell him?"

"*No,*" Drestra cried. "He's... *zealous* beyond anyone I've ever met. He'd head straight for the nearest priest, and if they've been hiding things, he'll tip our hand. Even if he doesn't run to the priests, what if he has a meltdown?"

"Aye, until we know more, then, it stays between us." Cedric looked at Carey. "Your idea's a good one there, Carey, headin' ta the Cave o' the Traveller ta start lookin' fer leads is probably the best place ta start."

"And I'll see if there's anything else I can think of," she said. "The idea's a long shot and it might not work."

"Well." Hart shrugged. "We could always go knock on the cathedral door back in the capital like I said. That should get us some quick answers."

"Well, we'll cross that bridge if'n it comes to it," Cedric said. "But I hope not. In the end, our duty's still fightin' Ravener-spawn, not people."

"Could be that duty's false," the Champion suggested.

"Aye, but we know fer a fact that the Ravener's tryin' t'kill our people. Its spawn hunt them like they're huntin' quail an' that don't sit well wit' me. We gots t'at least stop that from happenin'."

"Still, I hope we find *something* in that cave," Drestra said. "This is going to keep me up at night."

"Well, it's a lot. A *lot*," Alex spoke up, his mind racing. What if the Heroes found something down there? Would that be such a bad thing? Why did he feel almost... possessive? Like *he* needed to be the one to find out more about the Traveller?

"Well, I wish you good hunting in that," Baelin said. "We—on the other hand—should explore exactly what mortals *can* do with a dungeon core, wouldn't you agree, Professor?"

"I do," Jules said. "It might be dangerous, but it's just as important to understand the parameters of connecting to a dungeon core as it is to find the origin of this connection."

"Yeah, I agree with that," Alex said.

"Me too," Carey said. "I... joined the expedition to find the truth about the Ravener and find ways to get rid of our enemy, and also help out the best I can. I want to see this through to the end... whether that end is bitter or sweet."

"Yeah," Alex said. "Whether it's bitter or sweet."

A coldness crawled up his spine, leaving him with the feeling that they were in a frozen bottomless abyss, turned a corner and found something they were never meant to see.

It wasn't that long ago that only him, those closest to him, and Baelin knew there was a strange connection between mortals and dungeon cores. Back then, they'd thought all mortals had that connection.

Now, they knew better. That only those who worshipped the very god who opposed the Ravener could control its minions. For a moment, he wondered if Uldar had left a secret gift for his followers behind. Something they could use against the Ravener and purge it from the land once and for all.

'But why would he keep it secret?' Alex considered. 'How many cycles... How much death could have been avoided if everyone knew. No, that doesn't feel like a *benevolent plan*. It feels more like... like our own god has a dark plan hanging over us.'

He looked to the sky, watching the blue and white above.

'And if darkness is what he has in store for his followers...' Alex thought. 'Something hidden from them, how far would he go to keep his secret?'

The Fool swallowed. 'If we *do* find his divine realm and can get answers to our questions, then we sure as all hells better have Baelin with us. What does a mortal do if their own god tells you that *you know too much*?'

The evening feast would be their last meal in Crymlyn Village, at least for now. And witches had clearly set out to give them a grand send-off.

Sturdy woven tables of magically animated woody vines called hadwovhas were placed in rows in front of the elder's hall, well within sight of the standing stones in the centre of the village. Professor Jules had returned to the encampment—saying she would feel "like a sponge" attending a feast she did nothing to contribute to—and Carey was back at Generasi—not feeling great, which Alex could understand—everyone else had seats of honour at the largest table.

Unfortunately, the table had been positioned in such a way that it faced the symbol of Uldar emblazoned on the witches' standing stones, a matter of pride for Elder Blodeuwedd. Her ancient eyes had crinkled with pleasure while she explained that they'd been placed in view of Uldar's symbol in consideration of the guests' faith in the god.

"Well, this is awkward," Alex whispered to Theresa as the glyph—illuminated by bonfire light—sent an uneasiness seeping into everyone who'd visited Ffion's cottage earlier.

Everyone, that is, except Baelin and Hart. The pair were thoroughly and enthusiastically enjoying themselves. They watched, loudly laughing and clapping at the witches' displays of light and sound using illusionary magic. Conjured pixies fluttered overhead, spreading glowing dust through the air.

Musicians played stringed crwths and pibgorn pipes, while dancers performed ancient steps offering praise to the spirits in the land. Alex's mood was subdued. On another day, he would've been joining Hart and Baelin, enjoying every new sight, sound, and magic the witches had to offer. Today was not that day; he wasn't in the mood to celebrate. He simply tucked into his herbed fish, washing it down with a mug of elder-flower and herbal brew set beside him.

The Heroes and Theresa did much the same while Brutus begged her and Alex for scraps.

Alex's eyes drifted to Claygon standing nearby—silently watching—while the celebration continued.

The Thameish wizard's eyes traced the damage on the golem's body.

'Cracks,' he thought. 'Just like the cracks in all of us now. Cracks in faith. Cracks in purpose.'

Looking around at the witches celebrating their lives and freedom, he wondered how they would react if they knew the truth. Would they think Uldar had given them a gift against their enemies? Would they think that he was in league with the Ravener? Would they think something else?

Such thoughts plagued Alex throughout the meal, and the more he wrestled with them, the more confused he became.

His eyes rested on Theresa. She was likely having similar thoughts. Her eyes were downcast, her face was pale, and she paid little attention to anything around her.

One of her hands hung by her side.

Alex squeezed it. "It'll be okay," he whispered. "We'll figure this out."

"That's what I'm afraid of," Theresa whispered, meeting his gaze. "What... what if all of this is for nothing? What if we could've been rid of this thing generations ago, but the priests... or someone, or something else... kept that knowledge from us? What in all hells do you even do with that kind of information?"

Alex shrugged. "I don't know... Honestly, I don't know. What I do know is that things are probably going to get way more dangerous from here on out. People are going to have to know, eventually."

"Yeah," Theresa said. "And I don't think a lot of them will take it as well as we did... and we didn't take it very well. Jeez, and that's without confirming what any of this means. How's Thameland going to react, Alex? What if the priests are trying to hide this huge secret from everyone? The church educates almost everyone in Thameland. They do good things. What's going to happen to any of us if they're completely rotten to the core?"

"I—"

A sound of wood on metal drew everyone's attention to Elder Blodeuwedd, who was tapping a large cauldron. A cauldron that was floating in midair.

"Tonight, the Witches of Crymlyn honour those who have helped rescue our people." She floated over the cauldron. The liquid within it cast eerie light over her face. "And it is time to see them rewarded."

CHAPTER 43

REWARDS UNDER A GRIM SKY

The elder witch floated to the nearby guest table, the cauldron following like a loyal familiar. The witches had gone quiet—all settling down for the ceremony—as were Alex and his companions.

"Let it never be said," Blodeuwedd declared with deep pride in her voice, "that Witches of Crymlyn Swamp are bereft of gratitude." The old witch and her cauldron hovered before her guests. "For that would make us no better than those you saved our people from."

She looked over each of them. "We are not ones to amass stores of gold and silver like the great dragons of old, though a reasonable amount is useful for trade. But because of you, we now have more from the supplies we gained from the enemy than we can use for our needs. Their wealth is now our wealth and our wealth should be shared with those who made it possible."

A crisp snap of her fingers, one spoken word, and the cauldron went into a frenzy of bubbling, smoking, and shaking. Out popped heavy sacks that should have been dripping boiling liquid everywhere, yet were unexpectedly dry, and with a wave of her fingers, each one floated into the cupped hands of a guest.

Alex whistled, curious at the amount of weight he was holding, but for politeness' sake, he controlled the urge to rip the ties open and look inside.

"Three hundred gold coins for each of you," Blodeuwedd said, answering Alex's unspoken question. "From all of us with our deepest gratitude. Use it to equip yourselves in future battles, or simply live in comfort. The choice is yours. However, the gift-giving isn't finished yet." Her grey eyes sparkled.

She raised her hands to the illusions and fairies above. "We witches do not stockpile coin like we do stores for winter. It has less value to our way of life, but we treasure and are rich in relations and magic. And so, we will give you a gift of each."

With another wave of her hand, she summoned a collection of items from the pot. A group of rings—each made of roots twisted around each other in intricate knots—floated from the cauldron and into the waiting hands of Alex and his companions.

"These are the Rings of Safeland and they are only presented to those who have done us a great service. They will mould to the wearer's finger and are made from the hearts and roots of our walking trees when they reach an age where they have grown ancient, and their spirits pass from the land. A hint of the essence that remains within our aeld tree, collected when it was in the twilight of its life, is also woven into them. When you wear your rings, you will find that weapons and attacks are hindered, that the bitterness of poor weather will affect you less, and that poisonous plants native to our swamp and other parts of Thameland will do you little harm. May they protect you well. And—"

She gestured to the pixies, who fluttered down in a swarm like migrating butterflies. Each one kissed the rings and briefly glowed like they were caught in moonlight. They giggled with glee, their laughter pealing like little bells, then flitted away, chasing each other into the sky.

"There it is, friends," Elder Blodeuwedd said. "The blessing of the fae now lies upon your rings. They will glow when you are near a fae gate and —if you should find yourselves in their realm by accident or on purpose —then the rings will show you to be friends with us, as we are friends with many fae. You will be guided and shown hospitality while you are in their world. In return, you must not curse or bring destruction to them. For if you do, it will reflect poorly on us."

"I'll make sure they act properly, Mother," Drestra said.

"I am sure you will." The elder smiled, then turned back to the honoured guests. "Finally, we offer each of you a modest cache of potions."

She called up various potion bottles, all bound together with vines, and floated each set into their guests' hands.

"I understand that you are to fight these menaces in the future," Elder Blodeuwedd said. "And so, I give you these potions of mana expulsion. Without the proper painting techniques, their effectiveness is..."

muted, but I have taught Drestra to draw the symbols and she can teach you when you are ready to learn the skill. May these boons make your future journeys lighter, and please know that you are welcome within Crymlyn Village and the rest of the swamp any time."

The small woman nodded to each of them, holding their eyes for a few breaths. "May our spirits and your deities help you as you have helped us."

A shudder of irony went through Alex. 'Let's hope that he does,' he thought. 'Otherwise, we're going to have major problems.'

The celebration ended after hours of mingling, feasting, and toasting well into the evening, and Alex and his companions gathered up their gear and gifts, exchanged farewells with those who they'd fought alongside, broke bread with, and now counted as friends. There were invitations to stay longer, and under better circumstances, staying in and exploring the magical village would have been welcome, but divine mysteries were waiting for answers, and the Heroes in particular wanted to go looking for them.

And so, they gathered in their treehouse cottage, all packed up and ready to go.

"First, we shall return to camp, and Alex, Theresa, Claygon, and Brutus will take the teleportation circle back to campus," the chancellor said. "And the three of you can continue on—and as per your request—I will teleport you in close proximity to the Traveller's Cave, then you can make your way from there," he told the Heroes. "Are you sure that is what you want? We would gladly host you in the encampment while you rest for a time."

"Thanks for the offer, Chancellor," Drestra said. "But it's better if we get this taken care of right away. We only have a couple more days before we're supposed to meet up with Merzhin, and honestly, this is something we have to do without him anywhere around."

"Aye," Cedric said. "S'an easy excuse t'make. We'll just tell 'em we had ta get ta Alric quick an' make sure cultists an' demons don't got a back-door ta Thameland through the Cave o' the Traveller. Makes a good excuse that nobody's gonna question, an' since we'll be tellin' the priests and him that gettin' there woulda been too urgent ta waste precious time pickin' 'em up an' explainin' everythin', they shouldn't be sayin' nothin' t'us."

"Let's be honest, he's going to question things anyway," Hart pointed out. "All he can do is whine and complain and then get over it. If he's *right there*, it'll be a real problem if we find something that he can't know about."

Alex fought to keep his face straight. He hoped that—whatever they found—it could help him with his own search for information about the Traveller. If only there was a way to translate her book.

"Well, quite right, and it does make absolute sense to keep on with things and strike while the iron's hot, as they say," the chancellor agreed. "Very well, let's be on our way, and I hope that your hunt will be fruitful and may we discover the truth in all of this."

"Yeah," Alex said as he and Theresa shook each of the Heroes' hands. "Let's hope you learn something. If you don't, feel free to come to us when you can, and we'll try and put our heads together."

"Aye..." Cedric said. "An' I hope I gots this all sorted in m'head by then. It's... a lot."

"It is," Theresa agreed, turning to Drestra.

The two women hugged each other.

"I hope you find Alric peaceful," the huntress said.

"I'm not sure we'll have to go there," the Sage said. "We're going to focus on the cave... but if we do, I hope so too."

"Good hunting," Alex offered.

"And to you too," Hart said.

And with that, Baelin began to chant his words of power and the teleportation magic rose.

In a few breaths, Alex, Theresa, Brutus, and Claygon were at the teleportation circle in the encampment, and Baelin was leaving the Heroes near the Cave of the Traveller.

"Do you wish you could tell Selina?" Theresa asked as she and Alex walked along campus to the insula.

"Oh, by the Traveller, I didn't even consider that," he groaned.

They'd arrived on campus just a few minutes earlier with the cerberus padding ahead through the moonlight, his eyes shining, while the golem strode behind, gripping his new spear and wearing his new wounds.

First thing in the morning, he'd go to Shale's, buy some clay, request a workstation and repair that damage. He hated seeing Claygon like that, and tomorrow couldn't come soon enough. 'I wonder how long it'll take?'

Selina was not going to be happy to see Claygon like this.

"In a way, I wish I could tell her," he said. "On the other hand, I'm glad the oath magic stops me from telling anyone."

"What do you mean?" his girlfriend asked.

"Well, learning what we did shook the two of us. It shook Cedric, it shook Drestra, and Carey looked like she was almost destroyed... Though I gotta admit, she pulled herself together more than I thought she could."

"She's braver than she thinks." Theresa looked up at the moon. "She wouldn't have come to see Ffion with us if she wasn't. I know Selina's brave too."

"But she's also young," Alex said. "She prays to the Traveller and to Uldar. She believes in the Heroes and wants the dungeon cores gone. What happens if she starts questioning so much of what she's always believed... when she's so young?"

"Maybe it's better if she is young," Theresa countered. "She might be able to adapt better."

He sighed. "Yeah, maybe... In either case, we're not allowed to tell. And... even if we were, I kinda think it's better to tell when we have the *whole* truth. I've been going crazy with all the possibilities, and I don't want her going through that too."

"Yeah, I guess you're right there. Even Mother and Father are going to have a hard time with this, so I'd want to give them proper answers and foundation, not part truths that just makes them have a bunch of scary questions... like..."

She muttered something beneath her breath.

"What was that?" Alex asked.

"Like if we have to fight our own god," she muttered.

"Oh... *oh*." He winced. "Yeah that's... that... that's something I've been trying not to think about."

"It's a possibility." Theresa gripped her swords. "Oreca defeated a demigod, and the Watchers have told me stories about gods being killed throughout history."

"Well, that's sorta comforting, maybe," he said. "Oh boy, well, we don't know if we'll have to do that. Maybe our faith lets us control the cores for... I dunno, some other reason besides: 'Uldar hates us and he wants us to suffer with the Ravener.'"

"Maybe," she said, drawing the swords. The blades gleamed in the moonlight. "Well, either way, I think things are about to become a lot more dangerous for sure. And *I* need a breakthrough."

"A breakthrough?" Alex asked.

She nodded. "My great-grandfather terrorized pirates across the seas with these swords. My grandfather used to tell stories about them cutting villains in half with a single stroke and so on, but I haven't seen anything like that. I mean, they're *very* good swords. I've never held any other weapons that are so balanced. I've never needed to sharpen them, and no matter what I strike, they don't break, dull or chip. But they only cut like regular swords do."

Her frown deepened as she turned the blades. "Something's missing. I'm missing *something* about them, and I really need to figure that out or I'll never match the type of opponents we'll be fighting."

"Well." He put his arm around her shoulders. "If there's anyone who can figure them out, it's you. You're a badass, beautiful death machine, and right now, I have more faith in *you* than I do my own damn god."

She laughed bitterly, blushing at the same time. "I don't know if that's the nicest thing a guy's ever said to me, but I'll take it. What about you? How're things going with third-tier spells?"

He frowned. "In terms of summoning spells? I think I'm just about there," he said. "Hopefully, the next few days won't involve any more apocalyptic battles and maybe I'll get a breakthrough soon myself. I'll get back to practising tomorrow. Well, probably tonight, after a couple of hours of sleep."

"Right." She looked at Brutus and Claygon. "Well, we need to be ready for whatever comes next, no matter what it is."

"Yeah. I've gotta get third-tier summoning spells soon then, and I'm gonna push hard to get them."

CHAPTER 44

A RUDE BREAKTHROUGH

Alex Roth broke through to third-tier summoning spells the very next day.

The day before had been a long, full one with revelations, feasting, and new friendships formed.

When they got to the apartment that night, he and Theresa had unpacked their gear, cleaned up and collapsed into his bed, exhausted. Surprisingly, or maybe not so surprisingly, they'd lain awake even though they were dead tired, spooned together until finally falling asleep to the sound of the timekeeper in his room. Two hours later, Alex was well rested, while Theresa remained sound asleep, but both were up and heading to Selina's friend Abela's house when daylight came.

On the way back to the apartment, Selina had been talking non-stop, peppering them with questions about Crymlyn Swamp and the witches when Alex unlocked their apartment door and her eyes fell on Claygon sitting in the corner. Her jaw had dropped, and her anguished cry trailed her from the door as she ran to the damaged golem and threw her arms around his neck sobbing. Her fingers gently touched the gouges on his chest.

Alex and Theresa had looked at each other. Tears glistened in the huntress' eyes, and he'd gone to his little sister and wrapped his arms around her. Brutus came up and licked everyone after being shocked from a deep sleep.

"What happened?" she'd asked.

And they'd told her about Zonon-In, and with each word, her grief had turned to anger. "I hate monsters." Her voice was low. "They hurt

Claygon, they always hurt everyone, but look at what Mr. Hobb did to them. They can't hurt people forever." Her words were like a promise as she wiped her tears away.

Alex listened to her, trying to soothe her, and not knowing whether to be worried, to approve of her resolve, or both. In the end, she'd only calmed down when he said he'd be going to repair Claygon as soon as he saw her off to school—right after his early morning class.

On their way to the junior school, she tried convincing him to let her help him since he "might make strange design changes" to Claygon—like he'd do something like that—but he'd promised he wouldn't do anything to embarrass Claygon or her, and that made the dark cloud hanging over her face lift.

She'd remembered she had something to tell him when they got near the school entrance—something he'd actually forgotten about with all that had been going on lately.

"I'm just glad Claygon's core wasn't damaged, it's like his heart... I wonder if you can honour golems at the Festival of Ghosts, but I hope we never have to find out," she'd said.

The part about the festival had caught Alex completely off guard.

"Wait, is that coming up soon?"

"Yeah, Abela's family's going to an event on Oreca's Fall," she'd said. "It's with a bunch of other families. We probably got an invitation too. Did you check our mailbox?"

Alex, during the mind-melting morning where he'd been thinking about the very real possibility that he—and his entire kingdom—had been betrayed by their own god had not, in fact, checked their mail yet.

"N-no," he said.

"Well, check it. And talk to Thundar. He said he wanted to do something for it this year."

"Yes, captain." He'd saluted her.

For more times than he could count, she'd rolled her eyes and walked away.

And that was how he'd been reminded that the festival was coming soon. He would have talked to Theresa about it, but by the time he'd seen Selina off, the huntress had already left for sword practise with the Watchers.

He'd talk to her later, he had to get to class then head into the city to repair Claygon.

On the way to Shale's, Alex had seen mask sellers everywhere, displaying their wares on every street corner and in every shop window.

Decorations of all colours adorned front doors and townhouses, elaborate costumes crafted of everything from animal skins to gossamer hung on rows of racks inside, and merchants called out to passersby, inviting them to come in and, "find something nice for the family."

Illusions of frightful spirits swooped high above a wooden wagon, then dropped down at shoppers. The merchant grinning beside it abruptly stopped grinning when a frightened lad kicked at the illusion, his shoe landing on the merchant's shin. Alex stifled a laugh. Banners emblazoned with grape vines and wreaths streamed above every door and on every lamp post.

The sights had brought back memories of their first Festival of Ghosts last year with its warm nostalgic atmosphere. Friendships were being forged then. He'd looked across the street and noticed the only door free of decorations on the entire street was the bakery across the way from Shale's. Lately, it hadn't been open more than a few times a week, and cobwebs were a permanent fixture on the eaves.

As he opened the door to the workshop, he'd wondered how much longer it would be before the little shop would have to shut its door for good. Inside Shale's, Alex was greeted by a bit of a stir when his coworkers caught sight of Claygon.

Sim had nearly dropped his tools, gaping at the damage.

"What the hell did that?" He scurried up to the golem, taking in the cracks up close. "Jeez, it looks like some kinda blade did it, but... even though I'm seeing it, I can't believe it. When Shaleleath fought this big guy, I thought *nothing* would get through that hard shell, protective spells or not. You got lucky that the core's not wrecked."

"Yeah, no kidding." Alex patted his golem's side. "Just when you think you've seen all the nasty things out there, something worse comes along. Me and my friends were lucky Claygon was there to protect us, but now he's the one who needs repairing. Is there a free bay I can use?"

"I think there'll be one in about an hour." Sim shook his head in amazement. "Feel free to use it, and any tools you need."

"Thanks, Sim." Alex took Claygon aside to wait.

The repairs went well. They were fairly simple to do, and in less than two hours, he was done. Apprenticing at Shale's building golems and getting paid for it was a dream. In a little bit north of a year, he'd learned everything he needed to know to fix Claygon all on his own—except for some help few people would ever get. Using the Mark, he'd mixed clay, infused mana, and bonded it with the golem's body.

By the time he'd finished torch-drying the clay in place, Claygon looked just like he did before they'd ever laid eyes on Zonon-In and that war-spear. Alex smiled at him. 'Selina'll be happy,' he thought.

Since his work had taken less time than he'd expected, that left him with a free afternoon to practice summoning magic.

On a lark, he'd gone to Professor Mangal and asked for permission to try third-tier summoning and she'd encouraged it.

"You have performed very well in class, Alex," she'd said, going to a shelf of old books containing both written and practical assignments. "You have a strong grasp on the aspects of relational summoning as well: your paper on it was most insightful."

"Thanks." He'd used some of his experiences with Gwyllain to write that paper, and in it, he'd discussed certain concepts of reciprocity and how they applied to summoning. He'd found the concept inspired when he was researching the paper, and it seemed the professor thought so too.

She'd brought out a spell-guide. "This is a third-tier spell meant to summon a lantern celestial. They are beings of law, kindness, and curiosity, so even if you make mistakes with the spell, you are not likely to face a terrible fate. The most a 'rampaging' lantern celestial might do if it breaks your circle is to give you a lecture. Which, considering that you're a student, you might find an additional lecture to be a terrible fate."

Alex had laughed as he took the book and lowered his head. "Well, Professor, I'll try to make sure I don't get a lecture from it. And you."

And that was how Alex Roth found himself staring at a floating orb of light in the middle of the Cells.

"Are... are you real?" he asked, checking the summoning circle on the floor.

"Greetings, mortal!" a voice like tinkling bells answered him. "How are you doing? Is it day? It's dark. Are we in dungeon, mortal? Is mortal going enslave me? Do not do that, mortal."

"Wait, what? No!" Alex said. "I'm not going to enslave you. This is a safe room. We're in a summoning room at a magic school and... I just summoned you."

"Good! This one likes being summoned. See lots new things!" the lantern celestial said cheerily.

"Yeah... I can... show you new things... it's just... hold on one second—"

"What's a 'second'?"

"What?"

"What's a 'second'? This one no knows that word."

"Second means *second*," Alex translated it into a tongue of the celestials.

"This one no understand."

He tried switching to a few different celestial dialects.

"This one understand those words!" it cried.

"Ah, good."

"But what you mean 'second'? You no say what is first! You not very smart for a mortal."

Alex stared at the lantern celestial, wondering for a brief moment if he'd gone insane. "Okay, so let's... okay. Just... a second is like a unit of time. Kinda like a heartbeat."

"Oh, okay. What's a 'heartbeat'? Is that like when you beat a heart? And uh... if it is... what's a heart?"

"Are you messing with me?" Alex demanded, wondering if Professor Mangal had somehow pranked him. He wouldn't put it past her.

The lantern celestial bobbed back and forth in the circle, like it was looking around the room. "This one no see no mess. What to clean?"

"Okay, hold on, just... hold on one se—"

"Hold what? This one has no hands."

"No!" Alex fought the urge to scream. "I... I mean wait for a moment while I look at this book!" He held up the spell-guide.

"Oh..." The lantern celestial's voice hummed. "Why you no say so and keep saying stupid things instead?"

For the first time, Alex Roth considered strangling a monster he'd summoned. Instead, he squinted at the book, checking the diagram for the magic circuits.

'Did I miss something?' he thought, his finger tracing the diagram. The problem was that he wasn't looking for what might have gone wrong... he was looking for what had gone right.

Third-tier spells were no joke.

Many of the most iconic spells in wizardry were third-tier: Fireball, Phantom Steed, Daylight, and even one of Isolde's favourite spells, lightning bolt. For many armies fortunate enough to count spellcasters among their ranks, third-tier spells were some of the greatest magics their wizards could wield.

Just one wizard possessing third-tier spells could change the direction of an entire battle, or the way of life for a whole village. They were also a major jump in complexity compared to second-tier spells, with three magic circuits interlinked and firing at the same time. He'd expected that —even with the strange power he had inside lending him a hand with summoning spells—it should have taken him weeks of practice to reach third-tier.

His eyes slowly drifted to his notebook, focusing on the number of check marks he'd made, one for each time he'd cast Summon Lantern Celestial.

3.

It had taken him just three times to cast a third-tier summoning spell.

"Holy shit."

"Language," the celestial lantern chided him.

"*Really*?" He glared at it. "You don't know most colloquialisms or mortal measurements of time, but you know swearing is bad?"

"Of course!" The celestial flared, as though offended. "This one not *stupid* like you!"

Alex's lip twitched.

He might have broken through to third-tier summoning spells, but at what cost? At what cost?

'Seriously, what the hell?' he wondered. 'Why was it so easy? I know that power did a lot of the work and I've learned a *lot* about summoning spell arrays, but... damn, this is *stunning* news. But what do I do now?'

He pulled another notebook from his bag and flipped to Operation Grand Summoning Ascension. With mixed feelings, he put a checkmark beside the step:

Learn to Cast Third-Tier Summoning Spells.

"Well, congratulations to me, I guess," he murmured, tapping his pen on the page beside the next steps:

• Practice with Other Third-Tier Summoning Spells Until You Have Mastered Different Ones.
• Practice With Other Types of Spells Until You Have a Good Foundation of Third-Tier Magic.

'Do I still want to do that, though?' he wondered.

When he'd first thought of his plan, he'd expected to have to struggle to cast a third-tier summoning spell, and that was why he'd decided on such a conservative strategy for his plan.

He'd thought that with time, he'd learn third-tier and would then have to spend time actually mastering a number of other spells to develop a solid grasp of it. But today, he'd cast a third-tier spell in only three tries, which was making him consider moving up.

'Maybe I should jump right into fourth-tier summoning,' he thought. 'Push hard now.'

Tempting.

It shouldn't be a problem for his mana pool since it had grown so much from mastering Hsieku's technique. The third-tier magic circuits had *barely* put a dent in his pool, so there'd be more than enough space to fit a fourth-tier magic circuit in there.

Maybe even a fifth-tier one.

It made sense, if he thought about it. He'd used Hsekiu's technique and Restful Slumber to continually repeat his summoning spells. After he did it once, he'd repeat the process over and over, until it became natural to him in spite of, or maybe because of, the Mark. Other students only practised their spells a handful of times because they had no need to practise them more.

He'd accumulated the equivalent of hundreds of hours of practice. And if he leapt ahead now...

Anticipation ran through him. At fourth-tier spells, he'd have access to the first spells that used Relational Contract and Binding Contract Summoning, and with those, the types and numbers of creatures he could call from the outer planes would expand *vastly* both in power and variety.

And if the situation with the Uldar mystery and more was going to be as dangerous as things were pointing to, he'd need all the power and variety he could get.

'Should I do it?' he thought. 'Should I go for i—'

He stopped, remembering the traitor witches in Crymlyn Swamp.

They were so hellbent on ridding the Crymlyn of Uldar's influence, they'd literally chosen to make a deal with demons. Zonon-In. And they'd paid for it. Hard.

He shook his head. 'Just because learning a third-tier summoning spell was easier than I expected, doesn't mean I should start trying to rush ahead. One mana reversal, and it's all over. I should stick with the plan and explore third-tier spells first and know them like the back of my hand. Then, when I have a solid enough foundation, move up. Besides, there's no way Professor Mangal would give me a fourth-tier spell-guide. Maybe Baelin? Ah, forget it. Let's not get greedy.'

"Mortal! You become so stupid you lose power of talking?" the elemental demanded. "This one surprised you live so long."

"Alright, that's it, I'm dismissing you now!" Alex whirled on the glowing creature.

"Wow, this one no know how stupid mortal is!" the lantern celestial's voice rang out like a church bell. "You summon this one to not do anythi—"

Alex spoke a single word, sending the celestial back to its home plane.

"Okay, next time," he said. "I'm summoning something with manners."

CHAPTER 45

A UNITING FORCE

"Hey, congratulations on third-tier spells, but uh... no offence, that's a little light compared to 'Hey, there might be a conspiracy set up by my own god.'" Thundar rubbed the side of his face, groaning like he'd aged a decade. "Also, you pissed off the biggest, nastiest demon you've ever seen. Like... what the hell happened? I thought you were just popping over for a quick chat with Drestra's friend?"

"Things... got out of hand," Alex admitted, placing plates of steaming pancakes on his dining table. His Wizard's Hands added plates of butter and jars of honey. "You know, like they often do."

"Indeed." Prince Khalik took a pancake, slathered it in butter, and licked his lips. "Like they often do is true... This is a heavy revelation, and —as you said—we do not know the whole truth of it yet."

"This is most ominous and odious." Isolde sipped her tea. "But you said Baelin was going to cage this demon, no? Ah, and congratulations on reaching third-tier."

"Thanks, and yeah, he should be taking care of it later on," Alex said, sitting down with his own stack of deliciousness. "We'll see how that goes."

"What the hell." Thundar chuckled, shaking his head. He looked at his cabal mates. "Can you believe this shit?"

"What do you mean?" Isolde asked.

"I mean, it feels like we're running around in a damned legend," he snorted. "Come on, we've stumbled onto something that scholars will probably write about for a thousand years. And did that battle ever sound like a tale bards tell late at night by some fireside. And *look* at that thing!"

He gestured to Claygon's new spear leaning against the wall.

"You guys literally took a super powerful war-spear away from a greater demon. How many people can say that?" He shook his head. "And all of us—" his arms arced toward everyone at the table "—are involved too. I mean, come on, did any of us think we'd be doing stuff like this when we got to Generasi? I know I sure as hell didn't!"

"To be honest... it did cross my mind," Prince Khalik said. "That my name might one day join those spoken of in whispers and written about with awe. Not for their bloodline, but for their *deeds*. I thought it would happen in the full breadth of my power, when I am an older, more experienced, far wiser, and much greyer man."

"That *would* make more sense." Isolde stirred more honey into her tea. It was her third spoonful. "At this stage... we are hardly better than fledglings, yet here we are making enemies of demons and gods."

"To be fair," Alex said, "Zonon-In's not your enemy: she didn't see you. And this whole Uldar thing only involves my homeland. Like, seriously, you could all walk away anytime you wanted."

"Hah!" Thundar scoffed, clapping Alex on the shoulder. "And that's why you're not the leader of the cabal, my foolish friend. We forged a cabal to support each other through thick and thin. It uh, kinda defeats the purpose if we abandon each other the moment one of us lands in trouble."

"Truly," Isolde agreed.

"We would be no better than cowards," Prince Khalik said.

"Thanks, guys." Alex felt himself choking up. "That means a lot to—"

"But is anyone else getting a little 'buyer's remorse'?" The prince flashed a mischievous grin and a wink at Thundar and Isolde. "I mean, no one told us that helping each other might mean 'staring down the wrath of a secretive and possibly angry god.'"

"Oh, hell yeah." The minotaur's grip on Alex's shoulder tightened. "I mean, the most we three ever ask is for help with studying or getting into a party or a hangover cure experiment, but this bastard man—" he shook Alex's shoulder "—forgot to mention, 'oh hey, you guys might be fighting demons and gods and shit because of the fifty billion skeletons my kingdom has in its closet—'"

"That is a big closet," Isolde commented.

"'—so just be prepared and maybe have a will written up when you join a cabal with me,'" Thundar finished. "Cuz, y'know, I might get all of you tangled up in divine conspiracies and demonic wrath."

"Okay, if we're talking about the demons and cultists, I was *barely* involved..." Alex paused. "At the beginning."

"That makes it worse, in a sense." Isolde drained her tea. "After all, what that means is you—and thus *we*—have stumbled into the wrath of a greater demon not by purpose, but by a line of random chance that led us here. My goodness, I almost want to start a small war back home and pull you into *my* problems for a change."

"Now that's an idea," Khalik mused. "Perhaps I can return to Tekezash and unearth some sleeping dragon-god or something that I can throw at him."

"You guys are the worst friends." Alex glared at them. "Here I am—in my time of *need*—and this is the treatment I'm getting."

"No, no, you see, we're the *best* of friends." Thundar shoved an entire pancake in his mouth, chewed it three times, then gulped it down. "If we were the worst, we would've cut you loose around the time you mentioned 'angry god conspiracy.'"

"That isn't how I put it."

"But that's exactly what it is."

"We don't know that for sure."

"Look at our luck, man," the minotaur snorted. "At the rate things escalate for us, there'll probably be *multiple* angry gods involved, and they'll all hate us, *specifically*."

Alex snorted. "Maybe, but just remember, the moment one of your homelands meets some horrible apocalypse that you get dragged into, I am *never* letting you hear the end of it. But, speaking of horrible things happening in someone's homeland... I know this is coming out of nowhere, Isolde, but I just remembered this story Hart told us about when he was in the Rhinean Empire. Do you know a young noble whose father had this one-of-a-kind super invincible armour made for him? Then he took an arrow to the face—not the father's face, the son's—anyway, all of his eating, or maybe drinking would be a better word, is done through a straw now?"

"Ah, that calamity does ring a bell. The poor boy's name was on everyone's tongue when it happened." She frowned. "It escapes me now... Seems that the father had a bit of a conflict with the neighbouring lord, but his name also escapes me at the moment." She shook her head. "Territorial squabbles are not uncommon in my homeland. Part of my grandfather's duties involve advising the Imperial throne on strategies to preserve unity between dozens of proud—often arrogant—ancient families and keep them that way for the good of themselves, and the empire. It can often be quite difficult."

"Yeah, I can imagine," Alex said, a wave of nerves passing over him. "That occurred to me since this whole Uldar thing. Thameland is pretty much united around three things: the throne, fighting the Ravener, and the church. If people have a reason to start thinking there's a lie behind fighting the Ravener, and that the church is involved in it... hells, I have to worry about what that'll mean for my country."

"Your concern is far from unreasonable," Isolde said grimly. "Realms require a uniting force to stay together, whether that be a strong power on the throne, a mighty deity, an ideal, a common enemy, or something else. The Rhinean Empire is strong, to be sure, but we worship *four* elements, not a single deity like Thameland does. To offer devotion to more than one of anything can be a source of conflict. We work it out— we *are* civilised, after all—but... some of our political philosophers look at the Irtyshenan Empire with admiration."

"Truly?" Prince Khalik's eyebrow rose. "The Irtyshenans and the Rhineans are the two largest of the northern realms, and from common knowledge of how most empires view others, I would have thought there'd be no love lost between your two countries."

"You would be right for the most part." Isolde conjured a set of electric blue Wizard's Hands to fetch her a pancake. "But—as distasteful as the practice is—some Rhinean philosophers look at the Irtyshenan belief that those outside their borders are 'uncivilised barbarians,' as having a uniting effect on the people. After all, it makes the *world* their enemy, so they are less inclined to fight among each other, at least in theory. In truth, there have been more than a few Irtyshenan civil wars of succession that have been fought regardless of this so-called 'unifying force.' Though such inconvenient 'facts' are often ignored."

"I could see the allure to some philosophers." Prince Khalik stroked his beard. "My own teachers taught that war can be a double-edged blade for a sitting ruler. A king or queen who goes to war—if it is the right war at the right time—usually enjoys greater support from their court. After all, war can mean spoils for the kingdom, prizes, new lands to rule, and other boons. An unpopular war, however, can see the people rise against the rulers as a way to get their dying children back from the battlefield. When any state defines all outside of their borders as lesser, it ensures that almost *any* war is popular, as long as the state is winning."

He looked at Alex. "Now, to bring the point back to *your* kingdom, you've had generation upon generation of battles against near-mindless hordes of monsters that seem to want nothing more than your peoples' destruction. Every battle against your Ravener is a war of survival against the truly vilest of opponents. Even when soldiers fall, they give their lives for the ultimate cause. How can such a war be anything but popular?"

"Yeah. But what happens if that premise all goes away?" Thundar asked. "Reminds me of an old story about the five tribes. About five hundred years ago, the five biggest minotaur tribes in my homeland united to form a single herd against this rampaging necromancer and this skeletal army he was leading. By uniting, they had the power and numbers to successfully put the threat down. And so peace reigned... for about a week. Once the outside enemy was gone, the chiefs remembered that they'd been fighting each other for generations and reverted to trying to wipe their old rivals out. The event is called *The Chiefs' Folly*, for good reason."

"Ugh, I hope that doesn't happen in Thameland," Alex groaned. "Wouldn't that be bloody miserable? We manage to get rid of the Ravener forever, use the dungeon core remains to usher in a golden age of magic, and then my kingdom falls apart because some dukes let their grudges take over since the Ravener's gone?"

"Indeed." Isolde nibbled the edge of her pancake. "The possibility that some might even suggest leaving the Ravener in place to keep your people united, would be a very real possibility in a situation like that. There is something else to consider. If the Ravener *is* gone, would that not mean that the source of dungeon cores would disappear as well? I am sure others would want such lucrative materials to be produced forever, no matter how many lives were lost."

"Ah, jeez," Alex grunted. "I never even thought of that."

"Though, in my opinion, considering such options would be nothing but pure intellectual cowardice," Isolde continued, her blue eyes flashing. "We are wizards: it is in our nature to master and create cosmic forces, bending them to our will and not bending our knees to them. Were this not the case, we would still be engaging in blood sacrifices and begging demons and devils for scraps of power. We have analysed the dungeon core substance and I have no doubt we will find ways to reproduce it without a need for those evil orbs of darkness."

"Here's to that!" Thundar lifted his fork as though it were a sword. "Besides, I'm sure Cedric, Hart, and Drestra would be kinda pissed to let all this effort go to waste. I can hear it now: 'oh, sorry, the Ravener needs to stay to keep the kingdom from falling apart and keep nobles' coffers full.'"

"Oh, by the Traveller!" Alex nearly choked on his pancake. "Hart... I'm pretty sure Hart would be completely done with Thameland, right after he killed everyone who made that decision. Cedric would curse everybody and everything, and Drestra might declare open war on the church and crown. There's too many dead over too many centuries for them to accept any kind of compromise—if you could even call that a compromise."

"That actually leads to another topic." The minotaur licked his fork clean and laid it across his empty plate. "I took point with planning some stuff for the Festival of Ghosts this year. Alex, I'll need you for some cooking, but I've got most of the organising taken care of. We've got a table booked at the event on Oreca's Fall, which seemed appropriate, considering how many were lost out there—" Thundar paused. "...And I guess it's even more appropriate with the threat from that demon hanging over us. By all my ancestors, it makes you wonder just how long you got, all things considered. Maybe you gotta act on things while you still got the chance, y'know? Just in case..."

"Well, I wouldn't worry about that too much," Alex said. "Baelin and I are meeting up tonight and he's going to summon that demon, Zonon-In... Maybe after a little chat with him, we'll see how eager she is to come after anybody."

CHAPTER 46

THE CATCHING OF ONE OFF GUARD

"Come in," Baelin's voice boomed through the doors. "But mind your step."

"Mind my step?" Alex wondered aloud. "Why do I have to mind my—"

His words faded.

Why was it so dark?

And why could he still see like he was looking through the surface of a deep lake on a sunny day?

It was nearly pitch-black in the vast chamber, yet at the same time, it wasn't.

He'd spent enough time in Baelin's office to know that—even at night—it was always lit, either by moonlight, light spells, or often, a combination of both. Tonight, there was no light, none coming in from the soaring windows, no reflection bouncing off of them. They simply blended with the walls, forming a single lightless surface. Heavy black curtains covered them, creating a darkness so layered, they could not possibly be natural.

This made the space feel off, wrong. He stepped closer to Claygon. The golem gripped his war-spear. 'Why can I see? It's pitch-black in here.'

There was light coming from the hallway, but not enough to see as well as he could. The fireplace wasn't lit, no magical lights hovered in the chamber. In reality, he should have only been able to see the vaguest of silhouettes.

Eyes flashed in the dark—and he moved even closer to Claygon—

when the chancellor's towering, horned figure glided through the shadows in the back of the room.

"Baelin?" Alex whispered. "Baelin, is that you?"

"I should hope so," the ancient wizard's voice came back through the blackness. "Shut the door, would you? There is too much light coming in."

'Claygon, would you mind shutting the door?' Alex thought.

Behind him, his golem took a deep, rumbling step.

Then the hall light died, and he heard the click of the door latch. He blinked several times, expecting all light to vanish, yet he could still make out shapes throughout the space. His vision wasn't sharp enough for him to sprint around the room, but he could make his way through it without falling headfirst over furniture.

"What's going on, Baelin?"

"Hmmm, before I answer, would you mind telling me what you see?"

"Um, let's see." He slowly looked through the strange darkness, reporting everything he saw in detail. From nearby, he heard a pen scratching.

"Most excellent," Baelin said, moving closer to Alex. Those goat-like eyes seemed to shed their own inner radiance. "Thank you for that, my young friend."

"Huh? What're you doing?"

"A side-experiment that occurred to me to run at the same time we engage in this summoning. I will spare you the details for now—the specifics involved require a rather lengthy explanation—but what is of most relevance is that I can currently control the level of darkness that one's eye can pierce in the room. To a certain degree, at least. It will help disorient our guest."

"Oh, that's a definite plus," Alex said. "Trust me, though, she's damned hard to disorient. It's even harder to catch her off guard. She's obviously *very* old and experienced."

"Indeed." The chancellor tapped his hoof against the floor.

A wave of power billowed through the air, and a glowing summoning circle drew itself on the floor, emitting a dull, bloodred radiance that illuminated all within a little less than a dozen feet of the circle.

"Would you say this circle is about the right width to contain our friend?" the chancellor asked.

"Ah, you might actually want it a little bigger," the young Thameish wizard said. "She was really huge."

"Fair enough." The circle widened. "Better?"

"Better."

"Good. That war-spear looks quite suitable in Claygon's hands, by the way. Although I think it might be best if I teleport it elsewhere. We don't know if she's able to sense its presence or not," the chancellor said.

Alex smacked his forehead. "Oh yeah, that makes sense. Should've thought of that."

"Not to worry; you have much on your mind, to be sure." Baelin crossed the room to Claygon, who offered up the weapon. In a wave of teleportation magic, the ancient wizard disappeared and reappeared again. "There. It is in a safe location, and I shall return it as soon as we finish our meeting. And speaking of safe locations..."

His eyes fixed Alex with a penetrating look. "I would like you and Claygon to move over there—" He pointed to a spot deep in shadow far from the circle "—for the duration of the summoning. A comfortable chair is there for you within a circle of magic that will obscure your appearance, voice, and even your scent. Things will be simpler if this demon does not grasp our association quite yet."

"Oh, you'll get no argument from me." Alex quickly made his way to the chair without tripping over anything and took a seat in the darkness. Baelin was right, it *was* comfortable.

"I really don't need her having any reason to focus on, or even think about me. Next time we meet her, I don't think she'll be in the toying mood. Did you happen to find out anything about her? I couldn't exactly get information about greater demons from the library's third floor."

"Ah, yes, I suppose you would no—*Third* floor you say? Well look at you, did you have a breakthrough while I wasn't paying attention?" Baelin asked as he inspected the symbols around the summoning circle.

"Uh, yeah, today, actually. Professor Mangal gave me permission to advance, along with a spell-guide to summon a lantern celestial, and I got the spell in no time."

"Well, congratulations! And here you are celebrating it with an old man and a demon that wants your head! A little unorthodox, don't you think?" The chancellor paused at one of the symbols. It shifted, bending to his will and adjusting itself.

"It's not my first choice, I have to admit. The celebrating it with you part isn't the problem; it's the other part." Alex settled deeper in the chair with Claygon behind him and took in the muted glow of silver symbols around it. There were glyphs for shifting light and sound, and arcane markings that conjured a protective shield in case Zonon-In surprised them and attacked him, but most of the other symbols held no meaning for him. "But, eh, at least it's interesting."

"Indeed, it is! And speaking of interesting... here's a bit of information for you. I learned that there have been at least three thousand demons known as Zonon-In mentioned throughout history," Baelin said.

Alex whistled. "Three thousand?"

"Quite. As it happens, it is not the most uncommon name demons have taken on when choosing one that is pronounceable by mortal tongues. And that, my young friend, tells us something. Now, any idea of what that could be?"

Alex's brow furrowed. "Well, despite her arrogance, she picked a name for herself that would make her harder to research. It means she's confident, but somewhat cautious, so she doesn't let the need for reputation cause her to give major advantages to anyone."

"Indeed, that would be my guess too, though she did toy with you in the swamp," Baelin said. "Any thoughts on how to reconcile this seeming caution with her overconfidence?"

"Well, she said that we were like cats," Alex reasoned. "She had us right in front of her and could take our measure. As much as she talked about mortals having 'little lives,' she did start hitting us hard once we'd really wounded her. My guess is, she's smart enough not to reveal vulnerable information where powerful entities could use it against her."

He tapped the armrest on the chair. "Now, having a common name wouldn't keep her from being summoned—since she answers to the name—but it would make it more difficult to research her in general."

"Indeed, those are my thoughts as well." Baelin gave a sly laugh. "Unfortunately for her, I was able to cross-reference accounts of demons named Zonon-In with the powers displayed by your enemy and learned that she is *old*. Older than myself, most likely, though probably not as old as our very able registrar, Hobb. Accounts of the violence she's wreaked leaves no doubt she is powerful in the ways of chaos, and her magic can reduce a mortal form to something of a gibbering, ever shifting, mass of flesh. Yet, despite this devastating ability, she favours melee combat, most likely out of a desire for greater sport."

Baelin paused, and light appeared in his eyes. They moved back and forth as though they were scanning scrolls or books that were visible only to him. "However, when faced with a powerful opponent, accounts of her blending magic with her skill in combat, or even retreating when overmatched, can be found. Which tells me that I will not be able to rely on overconfidence from her. The fact that I have the power to call her will set her on guard."

"No doubt," Alex said. "I'm glad you learned what you did about her, because meeting her cold like we did in the Skull Pits wasn't the best position to be in."

"Indeed, you are learning." The chancellor turned back to the circle. "Now, you might be wondering why I covered all of this if all I intend is to summon, curse, and learn a little more about her. You see, I believe we can get more out of this meeting than that, so my plan is for you to be able to question her from your shrouded position. Now, keep in mind what we just discussed, phrase your questions accordingly, and be careful not to let your identity slip."

The ancient wizard spread his hands over the circle. Red light flared, making him look positively demonic as he towered over it. "She might recognise the connection between us, but there is no reason to offer up that information if we do not have to. After all, she did make a *number* of enemies recently."

"Got it," Alex said, focusing the Mark on the task of disguising his voice. It flooded him with images of people in conversation, focusing on the depth of their voices, the differences between their diction and his, and speed of phrasing.

The young wizard cleared his throat and tried a few voices before settling on one he felt was far enough from his own.

"This one should do the trick," he said.

"Are you ready?"

"Ready."

"Then here we go."

Words of power filled the room with their haunting notes. A wave of summoning magic spiraled through the air in a vortex, swirling around the bloodred circle of power. White-knuckled and straight-backed, Alex gripped the armrests of the chair concealed from the demon's view.

The atmosphere turned from calm to tense; power built, swelling, climbing in accord with a growing presence. A presence both familiar and foul. A thousand whispering voices chanted a thousand names. The air within the summoning circle shimmered, heralding the coming of scores of thickened feelers that erupted from the tiles—like a kraken's limbs reaching from the sea—and writhed through the air. Fierce blows whipped the sides of the circle, seeking freedom—and only when futility was accepted as fate did the demon join its appendages together in a great knot of pulsating flesh.

It heaved and trembled, melting into a primaeval soup that rose and fell like erupting lava, evolving into the greater demon—Zonon-In. Lower arms—covered in chitin—and ending in pincers big enough to snip Baelin in two. Articulated legs, upper arms and a thick torso were crowned by a massive head with a face that could curdle the blood of the faint of heart.

She stood within the summoning circle in the darkness of Baelin's office in full and towering glory. The wounds she'd received were gone. The terrible one that Claygon had dealt her and the dozens of cuts from Cedric and Theresa's blades were now erased, like they never were.

Even the hand that Hart had severed had grown back.

And yet...

She seemed diminished.

Her presence had lessened. The aura of power that she once radiated was reduced. Her gaze was dull, and her movements slower. She was far from lean, and her bulk would still intimidate, but she looked weakened.

'Her flesh might have recovered, but her life essence needs more time to completely regenerate,' Alex thought.

"Who dares summon me?" Zonon-In demanded, her voice like ice as her mouth-tentacles writhed like whips. Her pincers snapped like bone cracking. "I caution you, this ancient power you call upon is not for the weak, so understand, if you are toying with me, there will not be a second time."

Her yellow eyes slowly focused on the chancellor in the darkness. "Ah. I believe I know you. Are you the horned wizard who drove my master from this world?"

"I am the same, indeed," Baelin said, his voice as smooth as melting butter.

"Ah... well, that is a notable feat," the demon said.

Alex smirked.

'That's right, you're dealing with a big boy now,' he thought. 'No catching *us* off guard!'

"Would you also happen to be the same horned wizard who has been asking after one Hannar-Cim?"

Alex's heart skipped. 'Okay, maybe you can catch me off guard.'

CHAPTER 47

ALEX'S SICKNESS

To Baelin's credit, he did not twitch, flinch, or show any reaction to the demon's words.

"Indeed, I am one and the same." His voice was measured. "I gather you are revealing that information as a way of proposing a deal?"

"You catch on quickly, mortal," Zonon-In said, baring her fangs in a wide grin. "If you gave my master such trouble, then what am I to do to you?"

"And how many wizards have you entrapped with such lines and flattery, I do wonder?" Baelin said.

"Ohoho!" She laughed. "I can see you have done this dance before."

"Indeed, a bit more than a few times. So... now you wish to deal, then?"

"Ooooh yes." She leaned down so her enormous face was level with Baelin's. "Yes, I do, mortal. You did come against my master before, but that is no reason *we* need be enemies... or even why you need to remain enemies with my master. Your search for this Hannar-Cim is not well known, and I only happened to hear of it by chance. If word were to spread, however, then those of demonkind with information would be less inclined to share it."

"I see," the chancellor said. "Then, since you have been so polite thus far, why don't you tell me what it is you want?"

"Well, first, why don't we chat a little first? I am curious as to *why* you search for this Hannar-Cim."

"Indeed, and as an immortal, you would understand that an unfortunate thing about endless life is that—often—many of our little curiosities go unsatisfied. Why I search is not relevant, Zonon-In." Baelin chuckled. "And since I shall not give you information for *free*, perhaps I'll now go silent and hold you in this circle until you tell me what you wish from me."

The demon's face dropped. "Ah, *you're* not cute at all." She rose to her full height again. "Two things I would ask. The first... I am looking for a particular weapon that resides on the material plane. Being such a powerful, resourceful wizard, I was hoping you might be able to locate it for me."

Alex's heartbeat quickened as he prayed to the Traveller that she wouldn't sense the war-spear's magic through the circle.

"I might or might not be able to find it," the chancellor said. "It all depends on the weapon, of course."

Now the young wizard had to bite back the urge to laugh.

"What is the other thing you want from me?"

"Well..." She clicked a pincer. "An abyssal knight's court often includes many greater demons. Often *too* many. Such an excess of subordinates can divide focus and cause a scrabbling for favour."

Alex raised an eyebrow.

There was a clue in there.

'She survived our battle, but she'd been soundly defeated,' he thought. 'Her essence took a hit, she lost a powerful weapon and a whole army of cultists and demons, the defeat was witnessed, and she was forced to go home and lick her wounds, all a huge blow to her pride.'

He felt a warm surge of pride at the thought.

'Demons are creatures of whim and chaos,' his thought continued. 'And it's easy for mortals to believe they're evil because of how self-focused they are.'

Minervus came to mind.

'I wonder how many lines he would've crossed to get what he wanted? When that golem started rampaging at Shale's, everyone—except him—saw a deadly situation unfolding, while he saw an opportunity to advance himself and scapegoat a supposed rival. He didn't have the power of a demon, but he had the same mindset in many ways. So, what would a bunch of self-serving greater demons do to Zonon-In? She's *actually* failed and is vulnerable. Maybe she's looking for a way to get rid of rivals before they can get rid of her.'

"And you wish to have this scrabble for favour..." The archwizard paused. "Reorganised, shall we say? You wish for the ranks of your compatriots to be less... cluttered?"

"That is a lovely way to put it, my mortal friend." Zonon-In smiled. "Or... maybe not so mortal." She looked into the chancellor's eyes. "Those eyes have seen much, I can tell. So, tell me, summoner, which one is it, mortal or not?"

"You *would* like to know, wouldn't you?" Baelin's eyes twinkled.

The towering demon's smile was mischievous. "And if I would?"

"What would you trade for it?"

"What would you ask?"

"I can ask for much." The chancellor's voice took on a note that had Alex guessing where he was going with their conversation.

'What's your master plan, Baelin?' he wondered.

"As can I." Zonon-In's yellow eyes burned through the dark. "And I can give much in return."

"Strange, so can I." The chancellor's eyes lit up. "What a pair we are."

"Are we not?" Zonon-In chuckled. "Indeed... you're *not* cute at all; you're something else. Perhaps for such information, how about an exchange in time?"

"Something I have in abundance, as do you, I am sure."

"Then such a trade would be hardly costly for either of us," she said. "Unless the mighty wizard is too busy for a demon such as myself."

"Things have a habit of rising to the top of my schedule when they prove... interesting. Perhaps something could be arranged at a later time, when the situation is less stressful."

Horror swept through Alex, and it was threatening his sanity.

'Oh, by the Traveller!' he thought, fighting the urge to flee the room. 'By the Traveller, are they *flirting*? Please tell me they're not flirting! Oh, gross! Why? Why did I live long enough to witness something that makes Uldar's *possible betrayal seem tame*!'

"In any case, what is to stop me from simply taking the information from you and then doing what I wish with it, free to not make good on my part of the deal?" Baelin asked, cocking his head. "Surely a demon, a woman as... experienced as yourself would have thought of this."

"Well, here is the truth of it." Zonon-In frowned, placing both pincers and hands on her hips. "*I* do not happen to have the information. Though I *have* heard a rival mention it. Several times. I've also heard that they *might* keep such a piece of knowledge in one of their strongholds, and I could be persuaded to learn which one. Meanwhile, my other rivals have palaces filled with treasures that might interest even one of your *obvious, towering* powers."

'Don't gag, Alex! Don't gag!' The young wizard shuddered at the tone in her words.

"Then—once I discover where your information is located—I could make your journey to claim it so much easier. You might get a *name* if you forced the information from me, but the location wouldn't be narrowed down for you, something I would take great pleasure in giving you. And to make things more difficult for you, my rival has *many, many* strongholds."

'Wait, did she just wink?' Alex blinked rapidly.

The demon continued. "As do I. Getting a name from me, then going from one stronghold to another would certainly be trying, and it could also open you up to reprisals."

She clicked a pincer. "But with me to narrow your search and direct your attention to my other foes... you would receive your information, you would also receive treasures and knowledge from several other greater demons, as well as direction to help with your search."

"Hm," Baelin mused, a pleasant note in his voice. "You thought this through... quickly. A rather swift reaction on your part."

"I try to improvise. Helps one live longer. Well, that is what *I* want. But what is it that *you* want? You summoned me, and not for this purpose, unless your powers of foresight rival my combat prowess."

"Hm, well, that is to say... I did have a plan, but perhaps I can work it into a relational summoning pact between you and me. It might make things a little more beneficial in the long run."

"Oh?" She raised an eyebrow. "And what would you ask of me?"

"Time," Baelin said.

"As we discussed earlier? You can ask for that any time you wish."

'I need a bucket,' Alex thought, clutching his mouth. 'Oh, by the Traveller, I need a bucket! A big one!'

"That just might be a two-way path," the chancellor said. "As one ages, interesting... opportunities and individuals tend to show up less and less. One can become jaded, which is why one should pursue interests when they arise."

'Kil me.' Alex looked up at the dark ceiling. 'Uldar, please strike me down. Do it. Do it!'

"But enough of that. I will be forthcoming. I seek a total ban of yourself and any of your servants and allies from setting forth on this—"

He used a word Alex had never heard before.

"—until such time as I give permission or say..." Baelin gave the idea more thought. "...forty years have passed. In particular, you must avoid all temples associated with the god known as Aphrometh. I would see that as a personal favour."

Her eyes lit up in recognition of the name. "I see. I see why you might ask for that, but forty years is a long time."

"Not for those like us."

"How about thirty years?"

"Thirty-five."

"Thirty-two."

"Thirty-three."

"Acceptable." Zonon-In grinned. "Very well... those terms are most acceptable. In fact, such a long sojourn from this—"

Again, the word Alex had never heard before was used.

"—might make things more enjoyable later on. A return is often more delicious when others no longer expect it."

Alex shuddered.

No doubt he and his friends were exactly what she was referring to in her covert way. He grimaced at the thought of it. Three anxious decades, waiting for the demon to appear and claim her revenge. But as time went on, the memory of her would fade into the background of their lives, pushed aside by the never-ending concerns of day-to-day life, new triumphs, new losses and new crises.

Then—when they were all in midlife—and she was a distant memory, she would return and strike. A cruel plan... Of course, but by the time Alex saw a half century, he planned to be a *much* tougher match for this demon.

If he let her live that long.

'How's that for goals?' Alex's mental laugh was dark. 'Probably not what the folk back in Alric imagined for me.'

"Indeed, striking when unexpected is just good practice," Baelin was saying. "Let us seal our pact, then. I shall aid you in the destruction of your rivals, keeping all loot and treasure in the process. You will provide the locations of their strongholds and palaces, as well as their defences. I will destroy... say, four of them. Then you will provide me with the information necessary to strike the demon with knowledge of Hannar-Cim. If you do not provide the information within a span of one week and a day of my completing my end of the bargain, then you will be considered in breach of our pact. You also agree to make every conceivable effort to keep yourself, your servants, and your allies out of—"

He used the word Alex didn't know again.

"—for a period of thirty-three years from today."

"Four rivals? How generous. I thought you might wish to stop at one," she said.

"It is generous to both you and me."

"Fair. Those are good general terms. Let us hash out the specifics, shall we?"

Then she and Baelin began speaking so quickly, Alex could hardly follow them, only picking up the barest bit of a word here and there. From what he could gather, they were creating what sounded like a rather lengthy verbal document that was labyrinthine enough to make any barrister or magistrate proud.

Sometimes, Baelin would even stop using words and switch to something that sounded like an advanced mathematical proof: a construct of pure logic that sealed the deal from any loopholes or bad faith 'misinterpretations.'

"Done," Baelin finally said.

"And I," Zonon-In replied. "Then—under the power of this spell and with full knowledge of all boons and penalties—I seal this pact."

"And I seal this pact as well."

A colossal wave of magic shifted in the air like some cosmic giant had taken a step.

"Done!" the ancient demon and archwizard spoke at the same time.

"It has been a pleasure, horned one," she said. "I ask that you summon me again in a week's time. I shall give you the information you need to begin. After that? Take your time. What's a few extra years to immortals."

"No more than a few extra grains of sand to the sand dunes," Baelin said. "I shall enjoy speaking to you again, Zonon-In. Farewell for now."

With a wave of his hand, the magic circle flared, and the greater demon vanished. Then Baelin snapped his fingers and magical light flared in the chamber, the fireplace roared to life, and the dark curtains drew back from the windows, flooding the office with moonlight.

"How invigorating!" Baelin laughed, his eyes blazing in triumph. "Months of searching resolved! This has truly been a glorious evening. Though, Alex, I am quite surprised you did not ask any questions! I had given you the perfect set up to do s—"

He paused, looking at the young wizard closely.

"Are you quite alright? You look positively *green*."

Alex was still fighting the urge to be sick.

CHAPTER 48

A MAN OF CULTURE... AND PLANNING

"Oh, do not be such a prude, Alex!" The chancellor rolled his eyes, pouring himself a cup of pineapple juice. He waved the pitcher. "Care for a cup?"

The young wizard shook his head. "Don't think it'd stay down right now."

"You *do* have such a talent for the dramatic!" Baelin snorted in amusement, taking a long sip of his drink.

"But... you two *were* flirting?" Alex sounded unsettled.

"Well, I most certainly hope so!" The ancient wizard laughed. "Come now, don't tell me that today's youth have lost their zest for such activities and become puritan again, or is your reaction due to my age?"

Alex stared at him.

"I am *old* but I am not a *corpse*, after all."

"No, no, it's not that!" came the partial lie as he waved his hand and sank deeper into the chair. There was a *little* bit of what Baelin had suggested going on. A mix of cringe, embarrassment, and icky thoughts were running wild in his head. It almost felt like he was under Zonon-In's chaos magic again. "It's just that, well... she's a demon."

Baelin raised an eyebrow. "You would be surprised at the number of half-fiends in this world. And they do come from *somewhere*, Alex."

That brought an image to the young wizard's mind that threatened to freeze it mid-thought. He called on every meditation technique he knew to save himself.

"Okay, okay, but this demon tried to kill me! And my friends!" he complained.

"Oh, bah!" Baelin waved a hand. "You have to learn to let such things go since today's enemy could very easily be tomorrow's ally. As a matter of fact, at one time, there was a trend in epic poetry that focused on dangerous enemies growing to become lovers—"

"Baelin... Baelin, you gotta stop. I'm literally dying."

"Alex, you are not dying; you are fine. Fine!"

"Well, there's like... look at... well, she's a giant!"

Baelin shook his head. "Demons, my young friend, are beings of chaos, and greater demons have significant power over such chaos. Remember, they are shapeshifters, though some use the ability more than others. And as for me, I can assume just about any form I damn well please, so the physical barriers you are *entertaining* are of no concern whatsoever." His face had an innocence to it.

The image came back into Alex's head. With a *vengeance*.

He leaned back on Claygon for support. "Baelin... Baelin, please."

"Bah, make it less fun to torture you and I might consider stopping." The ancient wizard's eyes twinkled. "But in full disclosure, much of that was an act."

Alex shuddered. "*Much* of it?"

His mentor shrugged unapologetically. "As I said, I am old. Not dead. But still, this works out well for us. In this case, we now have a route to gain information on Hannar-Cim, and it was all done with our guest being none the wiser that there is a plan in the works for *you*—and your friends, of course—to slay her. Come now, this is a moment to celebrate!"

"I... yeah, I guess you're right." Alex took a deep breath, forcing himself to stop thinking about bile... and other unpleasantness. He began thinking of the possibilities ahead. "By the Traveller, I can't believe we actually found a major clue and didn't even *need* Burn-Saw."

"True, but our search still bore fruit for us, by spreading word that I was on the hunt for information, which was what caused Zonon-In to volunteer what she knew in order to forge a deal with me." Baelin stroked his beard-braids. "And this is excellent. It will give you time."

"You mean thirty-three years?" Alex asked.

"Oh, goodness, no," Baelin said. "I am hoping that we will be ready to move on this mysterious demon and take the knowledge we desire sometime next year."

"Oh, I see. Okay." Alex nodded. "But, why next year?"

"It is simple." The chancellor swirled the juice at the bottom of his cup and drained it. "That's when we will be ready to fetch the information *together* if all works out according to my vision."

"Together?"

"Indeed," Baelin said. "In short, I think that your connection with this Traveller could be useful when it comes to searching for what we need. Not to mention the excellent learning experience it will be for you."

Alex's eyes lit up. "Damn, how many mortals can actually say they'll be going into the Hells? Right now, I'm terrified, but I'm also excited, which means by the time next year comes around, I should be a total wreck." He grinned, rubbing his hands together.

"It will be good for you in particular since you engage in summoning magic as a focus," the chancellor said. "Most magic learners would indeed be curious about what it's like on a plane that they have learned to summon from."

Alex considered it. "Yeah, I know *I* am. I wonder what we'll find? Knowledge, an artefact, maybe just some demon who met Hannar-Cim in passing once? Whatever we find, I like the idea of following our clue down there."

"Excellent, then it's time for you to get to work." The chancellor poured two cups of juice, this time handing one to Alex without asking.

The young wizard took the cup. "Get to work? Oh... I guess you mean on growing my power."

"Indeed. If you wish to defeat Zonon-In, you will need a major progression in strength," the ancient wizard said. "I would humbly suggest having mastered fifth-tier spells before heading into the lion's den, as it were. With Claygon, Theresa, and the Heroes, and perhaps members of your cabal at your side... you might get away with fourth-tier spells. Either way, I would suggest lots of practice and growth."

"Yeah, I get it," Alex said. "I'll put in the work. Still, holy shit. What a stroke of good fortune."

"*Now* you see the bright side!" Baelin said. "Good show. In the meantime, I will be considering Ezaliel. That is a problem which needs a remedy."

"Yeah, definitely... I think I'll let you handle that one." The young Thameish wizard grinned and sipped his juice. "Oh, by the way, can I ask you some questions?"

"Of course. I am a professor. I am meant to answer questions. Most of them, anyway."

"Uh... Aphrometh..." Alex said. "You mentioned them and their temples?"

"Oh, that." Baelin chuckled. "That was as a result of some of my research on Zonon-In. I discovered that her servants were lurking about the temples of the dead god known as Aphrometh, seeking some artefact of the deceased deity's power."

"Oh, that... that doesn't sound good," Alex muttered.

"Of course ruins of temples are plundered all the time. Sometimes such places yield great sources of power. Sometimes they do not. That is not relevant to us, though. What *is* relevant is that I knew her servants were seeking such places and so I led her where I wanted her to go by mentioning the god's temple. She naturally assumed I asked her to leave the material plane because I have a vested interest in Aphrometh myself, so with that to occupy her attention, she will be less likely to put together that I summoned her to stop her from attacking you."

He smiled. "Information has value, as I said, and there is no reason for me to simply volunteer that you and I have a connection. Let her figure that out herself."

"Right," Alex said. "I guess that's another advantage of making a pact instead of cursing her. She'll be less hostile toward you and even less likely to put together that you're associated with what happened in the Crymlyn."

"Precisely. Now, what was your other question?"

"Well, you used this strange word when you told her not to come back without your permission." Alex scratched his growing whiskers. They were scraggly but starting to look like the beginning of a real beard. "I didn't understand it. Now, I'm far from familiar with every dialect in all the nearly-infinite tongues of demons, but I couldn't tell if it was country, continent, kingdom, land, world, or plane. What was it?"

"Hmmm," Baelin mused, looking at Alex closely. His eyes seemed to be reading the young man's soul. "You know? I think I shall save such a lesson for a different day. There are some things that a young wizard is not quite ready to grapple with. I hope you understand."

Alex felt a sharp twinge of curiosity, but he knew better than to push.

Baelin and he had a great relationship, and the ancient wizard gave him a lot of privileges, but there was an unspoken understanding about parameters, and one reason that their relationship was as good as it was, was because he knew when to ask questions and when not to.

This was one of the times not to.

"I do, I understand," he said. "Well. I guess this is our last time summoning demons for information."

"Perhaps, however, there might be a need in future. Remember, demons are always creatures of chaos," Baelin said. "For the time being, I will likely use the time to research my new enemies. And how will you spend yours?"

"I'll probably use mine researching more summoning magic and trying to solidify my breakthrough to third-tier by learning more spells. Haste would be nice. I can brew haste potions, but it'd be better to have more than one path to get there."

"Very wise," Baelin said. "And tonight, we have finished a journey we have been walking for a long while. Go and relax. Celebrate in your own way, though it is late. It is important to acknowledge milestones, or in time, every accomplishment will simply become another in a series of endless grey steps."

"Thanks, Baelin, I'll do just that. Maybe I'll make Theresa and me a nice dinner if she's up. Selina'll probably be asleep by now, though."

"Oh, yes, how *is* your little sister? Still having struggles with her affinity?" the chancellor asked.

"Well, I'm not sure." Alex scratched his head. "She's been asking a bunch of questions about fire and heat lately, but she won't really say why. I think she's gotten really curious since I told her I put out a fire using another fire."

"Most excellent. I would hate to see another young wizard crippled by something as futile as self-hatred," the chancellor said. "Such occurrences happen more often than they should, unfortunately. In any case, I will not keep you any longer. Go, take the rest of the night for some recreation."

"Thanks for this, Baelin. Really, thank you."

The chancellor chuckled, then his chuckle grew into a booming laugh. "No need to thank me. I *am* gaining from this too, after all!"

"By that do you mean the loot from the other demons? Or... something else?" Alex asked nervously.

The ancient wizard's chuckle turned darker than the night sky. "Do you really want to know?"

"Nope! Leaving now!" Alex cried, running for the door. "Let's go, Claygon!"

He'd made it halfway when Baelin called out to him.

"It is *both*, of course!" his voice boomed madly.

"Aaaaaaargh!" Alex screamed, desperately pulling on the door. "You could have left it alone! You didn't have to say that!"

"And to think, your partner's a hunter. Have you learned nothing from Theresa?" The chancellor chuckled as Alex scrambled into the hall with Claygon right behind. "What good is the chase if you do not finish off your prey!"

The young wizard slammed the door and fled as Baelin's laughter chased him into the night. It only occurred to him much later that the ancient wizard could have easily teleported after him if he really wanted to keep tormenting him.

Zonon-In's words came back; about waiting for when someone least expected an enemy to return. Would Baelin do that?

He could imagine the ancient wizard biding his time for days, weeks, or even months and then hitting him with the horror of Zonon-In when he least expected it.

"What did I ever do to deserve this?" he moaned as he exited the castle and stepped into the moonlight. Claygon walked by his side, tightly gripping the war-spear that had once belonged to the demon. Someday soon, he would get a chance to return it to her... Though not in the way she wanted.

"Well, buddy." He looked up at Claygon. "Theresa's going to be happy to hear we have a solid lead, and Cedric will probably like the idea of a rematch, a lot."

He stood still for a bit, looking up at the moon.

"You know, I bet the Heroes reached Alric by now. Makes me wonder if they'll find out something about the Traveller, and who knows, maybe *they'll* find something unexpected too."

CHAPTER 49

A FORTIFIED CAVERN

"Holy Heroes, it's good to have you back with us." The priest bowed to Cedric, Drestra, and Hart. "Though... I must say, your presence here is a little irregular."

The holy man adjusted his spectacles and peered at the three Heroes as though they were obscured in fog. "I see you are without your entourage and the Holy Saint this evening. Has something dire befallen them? As out of the way as the Traveller's Cave is, it's rare that news of the goings on in the wider realm reaches us."

Armour clinked nearby as soldiers leaned in.

Drestra's eyes flicked toward them. There were six standing at attention on either side of the room. She mentally calculated about three paces separating them from her.

'Look at how quickly things have changed. I would have never considered checking the distance between me and the kingdom's soldiers before.' She let out a tense breath. 'And it never would've occurred to me that they might be here to do someone's secret bidding, not help and *protect* us.'

It was easy to suspect the worst after the revelations about dungeon cores, but also hard to reconcile since they were now in the presence of Uldar's priests and these dutiful Thameish soldiers.

Cedric, Drestra, and Hart had arrived at the Cave of the Traveller late in the evening and found it significantly changed. In many ways, it was unrecognisable. Where there once was an unassuming hole in the side of a hill in the middle of the Forest of Coille, now a small fortress of wood, earth, and stone stood. Some three hundred or so yards of vegetation had been cleared away from the cave mouth, the trees were milled, the lumber used to erect an intimidating log wall that stretched around the hill.

A trench—lined with rows of wooden stakes sharp enough to pierce Ravener-spawn, cultists, or any other enemy seeking entrance to the cave—lay in front of it. Two watchtowers soared above either side of the solid gates, each well-staffed by sharp-eyed guards who had immediately ordered the barriers be opened when the three Heroes appeared. Once inside, the Chosen, Sage, and Champion were greeted by soldiers and priests who fawned over them in a way so servile, Drestra longed to be away from their attention.

The camp—awash with tents, wooden barracks, and guardhouses—had exploded into activity when word spread of the Heroes surprise arrival, and by the time they were escorted to the fortified office beside the Cave, the head priest was back at his desk, still in a nightshirt hidden under a colourful robe.

Even as he spoke, the expression on his sleep-creased face hinted at... something like worship.

'All this attention,' the Sage thought. 'But what's behind it? Are you serving us? Or are you puppeting us?' She glanced up at the dark ceiling. 'Or are you puppets too? And what happens if your strings are cut?'

The thought of fighting people they were supposed to protect—people who'd helped them before and seemed to have all of their hopes pinned on them—sent a pang through her.

'Killing our own people isn't what Mother and our kin sent me to do when I was Marked,' she thought. 'I'll do it if I have to, but I'd rather it didn't come to that.'

"Well, we ain't got too much news fer yous," Cedric replied to the priest, while Drestra marvelled at how smoothly he'd lied. Only a slight stiffness in tone hinted at any tension, and if they didn't spend so much time around each other, she never would have noticed. "We had t'meet up wit' the Generasians 'cause some trouble cropped up wit' them bloody cultists that needed sortin'. Now we gotta check the Cave just in case."

Another clink.

Drestra's eyes flicked back to the guards. Two exchanged glances.

'Are you planning something?' she wondered. 'Is there a conspiracy?'

"Ah, the Generasians." The priest didn't hide his displeasure. "Fancy folk who think they're too good to let our church aid them. Are they even of any help? As I said, we get very little news here, Holy Heroes."

"Yeah, you could say they're helping," Hart's voice was smooth.

"Well, at least there's that." The priest's tone was less than enthusiastic. "But why do you have to check the Cave? We've been briefed on the cultist threat. I understood that their activities were mostly confined to the coast."

"Well, that's the thing," Hart said. "We want to make sure they don't use some portal out there in the world—one we might've missed—to start ferrying demons into Thameland without us noticing... 'til it's too late."

"What!" The priest paled. "They can do that?"

"They're bringing demons from elsewhere in the world and from other planes," Drestra said. "We wouldn't want them using a portal and overwhelming us with their armies. We thought we should be cautious and check the Cave to see if there are any portals we missed. As long as we know what's on the other side of them, we'll be fine."

"So yeah, was the entire Cave complex explored yet, or could there be something down there that's not been accounted for?" Hart watched for the alarmed priest's reaction.

The man frowned. "Not all of it, admittedly. It travels deep into the earth beneath the portal chamber. There are numerous side tunnels down there that might be miles long."

Drestra and Hart looked at each other.

"We *were* surveying it but found monsters and their young settled in different areas down there—not Ravener-spawn, mind you—and some caves narrowed the deeper we went, so we couldn't chance going further. They need the attention of experienced members of the delver's guild to get through them," he explained. "Until that can be arranged, we gated off the deeper tunnels and posted soldiers at their entrances. You, of course, are welcome to have a look if you need to."

He swallowed. "Cultists, by Uldar!"

"Aye, we'll get down there nice an' quick, then, an' get things all surveyed out fer yous," Cedric assured him.

"That would be a relief." The priest looked at the guards. "We're all at your disposal, of course. Captain, please take your guards and guide Uldar's most welcomed into the lower tunnels."

"Yes, sir!" The guard captain snapped to attention. "Right this way, Holy Heroes."

"As you can see, we've added some fortifications," a guard indicated as they passed through a thick wooden gate. "If Ravener-spawn want this place, they'll have to bleed for it."

"Things look a lot different than when we were here last," Drestra's voice crackled.

The *temple chamber's* high ceiling loomed above, lit by a sky-portal hovering in the middle of the room. Wherever the sky was, it was night there. Moonlight poured through the portal, pooling on the temple floor. The air filling the space was fresh and clean, leaving those in it feeling refreshed and surprisingly comforted.

What wasn't comforting was what stood on the two pedestals by the large, stone doors at the back of the chamber. Statues in Uldar's likeness had been raised on each pedestal, each smiling down with an air of sweet benevolence.

Drestra took no pleasure in the statues. Her jaw hardened behind her veil.

'What's hiding behind those smiles?' She looked away.

A brief inspection of the floor showed all signs of rubble had been long cleared out, leaving the Thameish god's temple pristine.

As the guards passed by, they paused, clasping their hands in reverence to the statues and bowing their heads before leading the Heroes through the open doors at the back of the chamber and down the stairs to the massive cavern below. Wooden blockades had been built on the wide steps, each guarded by a squad of soldiers wielding crossbows. Ballistae also fortified the winding stairway, each angled upward, positioned to pepper spears or arrow clusters at any invaders foolish enough to charge from the top of the steps.

If any attackers came from outside, they'd pay a high price in blood while they were trying to break through to the central chamber.

"We're well protected from anything coming from the mouth of the Cave," one of the guards said. "By Uldar, we have good defences against anything dropping through the portals, but not extensive enough to repel an entire army. We've had to deal with beasts on occasion, but nothing more dangerous than that so far."

Hart looked at the guard sharply. "Beasts?"

"Oh yes," another guard spoke up as they reached the bottom of the stairs. "Strange creatures. Predators I've never seen or heard of before. I'm guessing they come from different places all over the world."

"Holy Heroes, have you heard about the exploration talks?" the guard captain asked.

"Exploration talks?" Drestra said, feeling the strange mana tickling the air as they approached the enormous, portal-filled cavern. "What's that about?"

"I've only heard rumours," the captain continued. "You know, my pay grade's not high enough for specifics, but there was a big argument between Baron Arturius—he's the local bigwig lord, by the way—some of the priests, and certain representatives of the king."

"Oh, I remember that," another guard joined in. "There sure was a lotta shouting *that* night. All kinds of talk about 'rights to this,' 'exploration that,' 'law this,' and so on. Rumours say they want to fund folk to go exploring *through* the portals, but command wants to wait until the war's done. No need stirring up new enemies if we don't have to."

"Aye, tha's all we need, I mean—" Cedric paused. "Oh."

Drestra stifled a gasp and Hart was silent.

They'd stepped into the immense cavern, the portal chamber. It was now a fortress.

Dozens of portals shone in the air, each leading to a scene of strange wildernesses, burning wastelands, or breathtaking waterscapes. The portals were familiar, but the dozens of fortifications carved into the surrounding stone weren't.

A scaled-down parapet—patrolled by scores of protectors; archers, priests, and even court wizards deployed from the capital—had been chiselled from the rock running along the spiraling path leading deeper into the earth. Ballistae were strategically positioned, pointing at specific portals. It seemed the soldiers were ready for predators or anything else uninvited that wandered into the cavern.

Yet, what really drew Drestra's attention wasn't any fortification; it was an inviting stone shrine—shining with divine light—standing where the Traveller's body once lay. As the Sage took in the details of the Traveller's shrine, her senses felt the Cave's unique mana.

It was comforting, warming, and welcoming her, and for a few peaceful moments, she was lost in it as it pushed away her inner turmoil.

'God, church, kingdom...' she thought. 'All of it feels insignificant here. Ironic, considering this place was once a Saint's. If only Mother and the others could be here... they'd... they'd...'

She frowned.

Why did the Cave's power have a familiar feel to it? It hadn't felt like this the last time they were here. 'What's changed?'

"We built this up good," a guard interrupted her thoughts, leading them deeper into the earth. "We had to after that forest beast crawled out of a portal. Nasty thing. Killed some good folk, I hear. I wasn't here at the time, though. Back then, we were still stationed in Alric." He looked at another guard.

"Right after that, some of us got called to help shore up the Cave's forces, and we've been here ever since. Maybe Command forgot about us, eh?" He punched his companion on the shoulder. "Well, at least it's an interesting post. Portals are really something to look at."

Hart was peering into the deep shadows at the bottom of the cavern. "What's down there?"

"You'll see soon enough."

It was a long trek to the bottom of the cavern, and by the time the Heroes and soldiers finished the trip, light from the portals high above was barely visible. The guards provided illumination from small candles in metal lanterns on their belts, while Cedric and Drestra cast forceballs to brighten the way.

In the glow of flickering flame and magic, they reached one last—extremely well-fortified—guard station. Two dozen soldiers, three priests, and a Thameish wizard all garrisoned the station, with several sentries keeping watch on a number of tunnels.

The cavern's lowest level was honeycombed with passageways going off in all directions into the pitch-black beyond. Most were sealed by heavy gates whose massive hinges were secured in stone, but there were three barricaded so thoroughly, it would take a battering ram at least the size of a mature tree to break them down.

"These are the tunnels we haven't finished exploring yet." The guard captain pointed. "Monsters, tight spaces, potential cave-ins, or all three. Take your poison."

"Then that's where we'll be lookin'," Cedric said, eyeing the barricades. "Hmmmm, if there's potential for a cave-in, we better not all go down the same tunnel."

"Yeah," Hart agreed. "If someone gets trapped down there, the others can still help."

"Sounds reasonable," Drestra said.

"Oh, but you can't each go off by yourselves," one of the guards said. "Let two of us escort each of you."

The Heroes looked at each other, their faces unreadable.

"Well, can't really see a reason to refuse," Hart said.

"Aye," Cedric agreed.

Drestra didn't answer, letting her silence stand as her agreement. She didn't want anyone accompanying her, but there was no subtle way to refuse the guards' offer.

In the end, two guards were paired with each Hero, and as misfortune would have it, she got the two chattiest ones.

"Well, if we're going into the breach together, I suppose we'd best introduce ourselves proper," one of the guards said. "The name's Peter."

The other guard smiled. "And I'm Paul."

CHAPTER 50

A CONFLUENCE OF LUCK

"Is this what it's like to be in a dungeon?" Peter whispered. "All dark and spooky like this?"

"Oooooo, spooky," Paul whispered back in a creepy voice. He angled his lamp below his chin, giving himself a ghoulish look. "They're coming to get you, Peter."

"Oi, don't even joke about that," the other guard said, looking over his shoulder at the tunnel behind them. Beyond Drestra's forceball light, the passage became a thick wall of endless darkness. "Last thing I want's for some monster to come sneaking up behind us: Ravener-spawn or not."

"And that's how it's not like being in a dungeon," the Sage's voice crackled through the dark, startling both men. "In a dungeon, we'd either be under attack by now, or we would've just fended off an attack so Ravener-spawn could surprise us with another one."

Peter and Paul's eyes widened.

"Hey, remember when we were arresting folk for brawling, drunkenness, and rotten eggs?" Peter asked Paul.

"Oh, *those* were the simple days, weren't they?" Paul said. "None of this endless monster shit."

Drestra paused, looking at Peter. "Rotten eggs? You arrested someone for rotten eggs?"

"That's a bit of a story," he said.

"Then it'll have to wait," she said, turning back to the darkness of the tunnel. "Even if this isn't a dungeon, you said there were monsters down here?"

328

"Oh, aye, there were monsters," Paul said. "Or so they said. Beast-goblins. And there were a lot of them."

"I wonder what they eat down here," Peter whispered. "Maybe mushrooms, bugs and such."

"I think they'd like a nice flank off a loud guard." Paul smirked.

"Then they'll go for you first," Peter retorted. "You're fatter than me. More tender."

"Shut up, you. You're embarrassing us in front of a bloody Hero," Paul hissed.

Drestra didn't mind their talk. The more distracted they were, the more opportunity she had to examine their surroundings for clues... clues they might miss. She just wished she knew what she was looking for.

The tunnel reached into the earth, always curving to the left like it was slowly spiraling downward. The walls were surprisingly smooth and felt like a dungeon in some ways. It didn't feel hand carved, or naturally worn by the passage of time or water. It looked more like it had been shaped through magic, or even divinity.

"Do you know anything about these tunnels?" the Sage asked.

"Uh, anything specific?" Paul cut off another whispered retort he was about to give Peter.

"Did your commanders say whether or not these caves were natural?"

"There was a bit of talk about that," Peter said. "Most think the Traveller herself carved them with her power, but others think the wall texture might've been from the dungeon that formed here." He made the sign of Uldar over his chest. "Thank the Traveller she destroyed the monsters, even in death. If a horde of silence-spiders attacked Alric—"

"—there'd be no more Alric," Paul finished. "Lots of people who were fleeing to the ships would've been killed too."

He paused, and Drestra could *feel* him struggling with something he wanted to say.

"Er, you said you had dealings with the Generasians?" Paul asked. "Did you spend a lot of time down there?"

The Sage frowned, her attention shifting to the two guards, sharpening to a razor's edge. Slowly, she turned to face them, reptilian eyes narrowing. Tension grew. Both guards seemed to notice; their movements tensed as they met her gaze.

'Are they diffing for information?' she wondered. 'How much do they know? Are they part of a bigger plot?'

Her mana flared.

'Are they supposed to be pretending to guide me, but are *really* here to silence me?'

Drestra counted the steps between her and them, calculating whether she could get a spell off before they lowered their spears. If magic failed...

Her eyes measured the ceiling height.

Too low.

No way for her to—

"Well, it's probably a long shot, but..." Paul cleared his throat. "But since you've met with folk from that big, fancy place... I was wondering if you happened to come across a young Thameish lad by the name of Alex Roth?" He sucked in his gut. "Tall, gangly fella. Likes bad jokes and thinks himself clever."

Drestra stared at the pair, confused.

"Or a young woman named Theresa Lu," Peter added. "Dark hair, ferocious look on her face most of the time, like a bear that's been stung by a nest of bees."

"Has herself this big, scary, three-headed dog," Paul jumped back in. "Friendly to most, but he's a bear-killer. About the size of a pony."

The Sage continued to stare at them, her jaw dropping behind her veil.

"Oh! Oh! And they'd have a little girl with them." Peter raised a hand like he was trying to catch the teacher's attention in church school. "No older than ten... no wait, maybe she'd be twelve by now? By Uldar, has it already been more than a year? In any case, have you met any of them? I figure at least the dog would leave an impression. They're from our town and—"

"Wait, you're *from* Alric?"

"Born and bred, the both of us," Peter said with pride. "Anyway, that bunch was going—"

Drestra suddenly burst into laughter so hard, both guards jumped a foot.

It had the sound of dry twigs snapping.

'Oh, for the sake of reason, Drestra! Come on, really? A plot? *These two?*' She remembered how they'd reacted in the priest's office when the Generasians were mentioned. 'You must be losing your mind. You can't start jumping at shadows!'

The Sage kept laughing at herself—almost delirious with relief—she doubled over with one hand on a knee, and the other holding her fluttering veil in place.

The two guards were looking at each other in the way folk often do when confronted with a strange and unpredictable creature. They took a few steps back.

"Uh," Paul cleared his throat. "You uh... you alright there, Holy Sage?"

"I'm fine, forgive me," she apologised after a few more moments of uncontrollable laughter before she could finally straighten up and wipe tears away. "Apologies, I might've caused a cave-in, laughing like that!"

"Oh, this tunnel's stable, Holy Sage," Peter said. "It's just... you know... infested with beast-goblins. A lot of beast-goblins. And maybe a lot of other monsters."

"And I might've attracted them all?" Drestra asked, suddenly feeling light. Giddy, even. To think she'd been frightened at something so *simple*! "I must apologise again. I should've kept more control over myself."

"Oh, uh, well... I guess we all need a good laugh sometimes?" Paul offered, in the sort of gentle tone one might use if they were questioning another's sanity.

"Yeah, I mean... maybe we just said something that would be a funny joke to someone from Crymlyn Swamp," Peter suggested. "There's no accounting for the humour of strangers. Er! Not to say, you're a stranger, Holy Sage, or anything—"

"It's alright, it's alright." Drestra waved her hand, turning back toward the dark tunnel ahead. "And could you hold that thought for a moment?"

"Oh, sure." Paul elbowed Peter in his ribs, shooting him a hard glare. There was a slight clink of armour against armour. "Did we offend?"

"No, I just need to concentrate," Drestra said lightly, preparing to chant a spell. "We're about to be attacked, after all."

"Wait, what?" both guards asked as one.

Screams were their answer. From around the corner ahead, a horde of beast-goblins tore past a jutting wall shrieking and howling like the Ravener itself was behind them. They charged straight for the Sage and guards, eyes wild, and fangs bared, starved for blood and flesh.

They were instead offered their fill of lightning and flame, and the relieved laughter of a half-delirious Hero.

"You hear someone laughing?" a guard accompanying the Chosen whispered. "Sounded like a ghost."

"Maybe it's the Traveller's spirit or some other lost soul trapped down here," the other whispered back. "Oh Uldar, guard our spirits."

Ahead of them, Cedric fought to keep a straight face, realising that there were smaller tunnels connecting the passageways, since the delirious laughter coming from the right, was being made by Drestra's crackling voice.

'Be bloody-well more believable if it *were* a ghost,' he thought, gripping the haft of his morphic weapon. 'Didn't think she could even laugh, never mind like that...'

His brow creased.

'Matter of fact, ain't it more believable that it's a bloody ghost? Mimickin' her bloody voice?' he thought.

His expression was grim as he offered a silent prayer to Uldar and felt the holy energy spreading over his weapon, sheathing it in divine power as he watched.

'Callin' on him don't feel natural like it used to.' The Chosen's spirits were low. 'At least he's still lendin' me his power, even if he's up t'somethin'.'

Cedric raised his spear and walked cautiously into the dark, poised to strike ghosts or anything else lurking there with his and Uldar's power.

Hart paused, listening to laughter echoing in the distance. Behind him, the two guards drew their swords and slammed down their visors.

'Huh,' the Champion thought. 'Drestra's finally gone mad. Well, it was just a matter of time, I guess.'

Shrugging, he continued leading his escort into the darkness.

The Sage dusted off her hands while stepping over piles of beast-goblin and agarici bodies. The latter were colossal, lumbering, humanoid-like fungi with shocking power behind their blows—blows that felt like they came from a sledgehammer but were still no match for Drestra's own power.

"Well, would you look at that." Peter lifted his visor, gaping in amazement. "Almost feel sorry for those bloody Ravener-spawn that have to face you."

"I wouldn't go that far." Paul poked one of the smoking mushrooms. "I'm just glad I was *behind* all that magicy stuff, and not in front of it."

"It looks like the beast-goblins were feeding on the agarici," the Sage noted, stepping past the last corpse. A glance at one of the mushroom-creature's sucker-shaped 'mouths' revealed a scrap of something green clinging to it. "Or maybe it was the other way around."

"Well, now worms will be feeding on all of them, if we leave them here," Paul said. "When we get back, we'll put in a request to have them taken away. The air could turn nasty if we leave them rotting down here."

"They already stink. Can't imagine how bad it'll be if we just left 'em." Peter's nostrils flared.

"Let's move on," Drestra said, ready for what monsters or whatever else they might uncover.

"Right you are, Holy Sage," Peter said, following her down the tunnel, his lantern held high, candlelight dappling the walls.

Irritation flared. That 'Holy Sage' business had been irritating even *before* she'd learned that this whole thing could be built on a foundation of secrets and lies.

Now, it made her want to heave.

"Drestra," she corrected the guard.

"Mm?"

"No need for all that 'Holy Sage' business," she said. "Just call me Drestra."

The two guards looked taken aback.

"Alright, Hol—Er, Drestra," Peter said. "After what you just did to those monsters, I'd call you 'queen' if that wasn't probably treason. Is that treason, Paul?"

"How should I know?" Paul sounded mildly annoyed. "Anyway, no one's going to be around to hear you creep out Drestra when you call her *queen*, so go right ahead. Call the powerful mage weird names, mate. Just let me step back into the tunnel about a hundred paces or so."

Drestra gave another crackling chuckle as they walked along. "Oh, that reminds me, I *did* meet a Theresa Lu with the Generasians and, indeed, I met her boyfriend, Alex Roth, and her big dog Brutus! I haven't met the little sister, though."

"Well, that's—Wait, *boyfriend*? Hah!" Paul chuckled. "Well, it finally happened, did it?"

"What finally happened?" Peter asked.

"Oi, what good is a guard who has less eyes than sense." Paul glared at him. "Those two've been making goo-goo eyes at each other for years."

"Well, *Paul*, unlike you, I don't go paying attention to every teenager in town making goo-goo eyes at each other! Now who's the bloody creep? Maybe I should be stepping a hundred yards away from *you*. Anyway." He smiled warmly. "Good for those two. Glad something positive came out of all that mess. Theresa's mum and dad told us that the four of them went ahead so Alex could reach that fancy magic university. Hah, nice to hear he's having a good time. He deserves it since he got such a bloody rough birthday gift."

"Hm?" Drestra cocked her head. "Birthday gift?"

"Yeah," Paul grunted. "The boy has the worst luck. First there was what happened to his mum and dad. And then the Ravener comes back on his eighteenth birthday, right as he gets his inheritance. Got fired too, but I think that might've been his own doing!"

"Oh?" Drestra frowned. "Fired from wha—"

Her mind ground to a halt.

"Wait... *When* did you say his birthday was?"

CHAPTER 51

LINKS IN THE CHAIN OF DESTINY

"It was the same time the Ravener came back," Paul said, shaking his head. "Turned eighteen that very day and then—that evening—we heard that the Heroes were marked, and a new Ravener cycle was starting."

"Alex's eighteenth birthday was the same day the Ravener came back... the day the Heroes got marked?" Drestra's brows rose.

"Oh yeah," Peter said. "Was a nasty coincidence, that. Glad he got out when he did. I don't know if ya know this, but he and his sister have had enough bad in their young lives with what happened to their folks in that fire, and all. The poor lad had been working himself to the bone for a nice future and then *bam*, the day he's grown to the law, is the day all hell breaks out in Thameland. So, it's good he's finally catching a break and now things are going his way for a change. How'd you meet them?"

Silence followed.

"Everything alright?" Paul asked. "Are more monsters coming down the tunnel?"

"Hm?" Drestra shook her head. "No, I was just thinking. Anyway, I can confirm that he's doing well. He's studying at the university in Generasi. He's gotten... powerful with magic." Her mind crawled over the times she'd seen him cast spells. "He even made a golem."

"Oh," Paul said. "That's nice, I suppose. Er, what's a golem, Peter?"

"How should I know?" Peter hissed. "Well, good to hear he's getting all fancy. Maybe he'll come back to Alric, set up some kind of wizard's tower and help folks in town with his magic."

"Oh, come on, Peter," Paul said with disdain. "You know half the young folk who learn a bloody *trade* don't come back to Alric. Do you really think a fancy wizard's going to come back? That'd be fooli—" He paused, then suddenly broke into laughter. "You know what's funny, Drestra?"

The Sage's mind continued turning over memories of when she'd first met Alex, Theresa, and their friends. In truth, she liked Theresa the most of their group—they had a lot in common—but Alex was the one who got her to open up about things she'd buried for months.

Her frustrations.

Worries.

All of her desires, when it came to ending the war once and for all.

All had come pouring out like someone had punched a hole in a full rain barrel. It was like he'd known exactly what to say to her.

'After we met the Generasians,' she thought. 'The stress of everything seemed a little easier to bear. I got along better with Hart and Cedric. We even started working more like a team. It's not perfect, but we're not working against each other either. And, when Alex was around giving strategy suggestions, we really fought well together. It's true that he and his friends were trained by Baelin, but... it was almost like a missing piece was slotted into place.'

"Drestra, you alright?" Paul asked.

"Hm, yes!" The Sage pulled her mind back to the present. "What... what was so funny?"

"Heh, well, you know." The guard from Alric chuckled. "Maybe you had to be there, but I remember telling that boy: '*Act the fool long enough and you'll get the fool's mark*,' and I was pointing right at that ugly face on the Fool statue in the fountain in town. Could you imagine if that had happened?"

He snorted. "About to go to wizard university and then he loses his chance because the *Fool* can't do magic? It'd be a tragedy. Shit, I would've felt terrible. You know, maybe that's not as funny as I thought it was."

"Nice going, Peter," the other guard muttered. "Now, quit flappin' your jaws. Look."

He pointed to a symbol carved in the stone wall ahead, lightly illuminated by Drestra's forceball. "There's the marker from the first survey team. We're down as deep as they made it before the monsters got too thick to fight through."

The guard clapped down his visor. "From here on, we've got no idea what we'll find. Best be on our toes."

"Yeah," Paul agreed. "Don't wanna end up dead down here in the dark like those monsters."

"Don't worry," Drestra said. "I'll protect you."

Alex and Theresa had shown how far they'd go to help *her* people, even risking their own lives, so she wasn't about to let anything happen to folk from *their* hometown. She had a duty to them.

And so, the trio went quiet with the Sage fixed on their surroundings.

She needed her focus, but try as she might, her thoughts drifted back to Alex Roth. All of Cedric's musings about something being off with him came back to her.

'Cedric kept saying how he found it odd that the chitterer dungeon seemed to focus on Alex, didn't he? I remember some talk about that. But him being the Fool doesn't make sense, does it? He can cast magic. He built a golem. I've seen him fight—'

She hesitated.

Had she seen him fight...?

She remembered their first battle together, the one above the two dungeons in Greymoor. Their fight with the cultists and demons patrolling Crymlyn Swamp when they'd grabbed Llyworn and Rhodri to question them. And the tail-end of the fight against that greater demon Zonon-In in the Skull Pits.

Her mind sifted through details of each confrontation, carefully.

She startled at a revelation.

'Did... has he *ever* cast a combat spell that you saw?' She brought to mind every memory of him spellcasting that she had. 'Yeah, he did. He used those potions to make things fly around and rip themselves apart. But—that's not really a combat spell, is it?'

The more she thought, the more she realised she'd never actually seen him cast force missile, or any fire or lightning spells, or *any* direct combat spells, for that matter. In three battles—all deadly—he hadn't cast a single combat spell *once*?

Why not?

'As a matter of fact...' She thought back to the times she'd seen him. 'I don't remember him ever carrying a weapon. His whole cabal, all his friends, carry weapons. Even Isolde has her dagger. He looks like a fighter, he's all muscle, he's got all that strength, and he's fast too. Yet he doesn't even have a short sword to defend himself with?'

It made no sense. His entire group carried weapons, some more than one, or they used battle magic. How come he only carried potions, ropes, and tools?

'And has he ever *hurt* anything directly, anything that I've seen. I don't think I've even seen him wound something—wait. Those potions, they rip things apart. That's definitely using a weapon. And the Fool can't fight... or hurt living things. Or use magic, for that matter!'

She shook her head, trying to stop the stream of contradictory thoughts running through her mind.

There were some odd, suspicious things going on with Alex—like him seeming to appear before everyone else whenever they were teleported—but it was a historical fact that the Fool couldn't use spellcraft, divinity, or fight.

And Alex fought.

She'd also *seen* him cast spells.

'And that's why you're being crazy, Drestra,' she told herself. 'Being distrustful like Cedric was after you first went to the encampment. Put this idiocy out of your mind and focus. You're down here to look for clues, not focus on silly coincidences, like Alex being born on the same day as you and the others. Lots of people are born on the same day.'

She chuckled softly. 'In the end, it's a historical fact,' she thought. 'Alex can't... be... the Fool.'

Her steps slowed.

Her breath did too.

The Fool was useless. The Fool couldn't fight, use spellcraft, or divinity. That was a historical fact. A historical fact. A historical... *fact*? But where did she get that fact from? *Who* was spouting that *truth*?

'The church,' she thought. 'It came from the church. *They're* who said the Fool can't use spellcraft, divinity, or fight. I've never met any Fools. Aren't I here looking for clues because the church—or Uldar—is *hiding* things?'

She re-examined her assumptions.

All of them.

What if what she knew about the Fool was wrong? Or—if not outright wrong—then incomplete? What would that mean?

'Let me think about this. Leaving all the Fool's limitations out of it. Peter and Paul said Alex had his birthday on the day the Ravener came back. So, what does he do? He, Theresa, his sister, and Brutus *immediately* get out of Alric. Get out of Thameland.'

She frowned, thoughts churning.

'Theresa's family left *after* Alex and their daughter? Why? Why wouldn't they travel together? There's safety in numbers, and Theresa's a warrior. Shouldn't they have been travelling together to protect each other? But, no, he and she left first. And then what happened?'

Her frown deepened, thinking back to the story Cedric told when she'd first met Alex at the Generasi encampment. 'Cedric went to the Cave of the Traveller by himself. He killed the horde of silence-spiders that were gathering there and hunted for the last one. Then he met Alex and the others.'

Moving through the dark, she tried keeping her mind on where they were heading while listening for threats, but a part of her brain was hooked on solving the puzzle.

She couldn't let it go, not just yet.

'Then Cedric left them, met up with us, and we came back together,' she thought. 'The dungeon core was already destroyed when we got here. There *were* worker silence-spiders, but they were all dead. Burnt to a crisp.'

She recalled the scorch-lines Claygon's fire-gems left when he fired them. Weren't they similar to some they'd seen in the Cave?

'But Claygon didn't exist then, Peter and Paul don't even know what a golem is, and they definitely would've mentioned him if he'd been around. No one misses Claygon. So maybe something else happened to those spiders. We thought it was the Traveller's power destroying the dungeon, but the army's been here for months, and she hasn't done anything to help them, even when they were attacked by beast-goblins and the like.'

The Sage took a deep breath. 'Suppose I was the one who was marked as the Fool and lived in Alric and wanted to get away from Thameland. Suppose I knew that the priests had a barrier over the land that stops Ravener-spawn from leaving... and can also detect a Hero's Mark. What would I do?'

The answer came immediately.

'If I was desperate, which I would be, I'd try and leave through one of the portals in the Cave.'

Things were adding up.

Certain other things might be explained.

'Banning the priests from going into the Generasians' territory,' she thought. 'If someone on the research team *was* the Fool—like Alex—then a ban would make Greymoor the perfect place for them to hide, that's if he was mad enough to come back to Thameland. If I was the Fool, I'd be long gone. Even if I had to hide in the Irtyshenan Empire.'

She felt the Traveller's mana above as they continued through the dimly-lit tunnel.

'And let's say Alex is the Fool and he did come through the Cave... If he found dungeon core remains and took them with him, then that'd explain *why* the Generasians started the expedition in the first place. All this time, no one's been able to understand how they knew that dungeon core remains were valuable. But this... this fits.'

Still, in the end, all she was doing was thinking of different scenarios in the dark, when she should've been paying attention to their surroundings. She had to put it aside for now.

But she had reached a decision.

'No more secrets,' she thought. 'I'm tired of them. I'm going to get him alone and ask him directly the next time we meet, and I'll watch his reaction. That's the only way I'll know for sure. And if he *is* the Fool, then—I'll... Is the Traveller's mana getting stronger?'

"Hold on for a second." Drestra stopped and raised her hand for Peter and Paul to do the same.

"What is it?" Peter gripped his sword. "More monsters?"

"No," she said. "Something else. I'm sensing a familiar mana near here."

"Is... is it the Traveller's?" Paul asked.

"Yes, but we've been heading deeper underground and away from her shrine for a while now," she said.

Focused on her mana senses, she stepped forward.

There was no mistaking it.

"And the further down this tunnel we go, the stronger it is. We're getting close to something."

CHAPTER 52

THE HIDDEN GATEWAY

There was no mistaking that up ahead and above the tunnel floor, she could sense another source of the Traveller's magic. Excitement rose at the thought of another pocket of the dead Saint's power hidden deep beneath the chamber above it.

This was it.

The kind of secret she, Hart, and Cedric had come to find.

"It could be a hidden portal," she said. "Or something else concealed down here."

"By Uldar," Peter said, his voice choking with fear. "Another portal? W-where do you think it opens up to?"

"Maybe someplace with more starving monsters that'll come pouring out and attack us." Paul audibly swallowed. "Not that you couldn't handle some monsters, Drestra. Oh, by Uldar, do you think it leads to someplace with those demon worshippers?"

"I don't know yet," the Sage said. "That's what we have to find out."

"U-um." Peter looked back at the direction they'd come from. "Maybe we should go back and tell Command. We could get more soldiers, or even call the Holy Champion and Holy Chosen. A-and then the *three* of you could go find out what's what with a few squads of archers, some priests, and maybe a mage to back you up."

"You can go back if you want to," Drestra said. "But I think it's best to see what it is and not leave it unattended. By the time reinforcements get here, it could be long gone."

The truth was, she'd rather not have Uldar's servants around. She wanted to have a look before they did because she had no clue how they'd react, and depending on what she was sensing, things could turn hostile.

And if things turned hostile... well, better not to think about that.

"W-well—" Peter cleared his throat. "Then, on we go, I guess."

"Yeah." Paul raised his sword. "How would it look if we just let you go on ahead by yourself? We might not be much compared to you, but three heads are better than one, eh? At least we'll be two more sets of eyes for ya."

Gratitude warred with agitation inside Drestra. On one hand, it was brave and noble of the guards to want to stay with her. On the other, she really *would've* preferred to go on alone. She thought about ways to get them going on their way.

"No," she said, her voice taking a note of command. "In case something happens up ahead, I want you to go tell the others that there's something here. Don't come back down here unless I come out first, or unless Hart and Cedric are with you."

Peter and Paul looked at each other; relief flitting across their faces.

"Neither of us are crazy enough to argue with a Hero, so we'll go," Peter said. "But, be careful down here."

"Yeah, take care of yourself, Drestra," Paul said.

With a quick bow, both guards lifted their lanterns and started back the way they'd come. The Sage watched them round the bend, the glimmer of their lights receding as they ascended, and soon, even the clink of armour faded.

She exhaled a deep, relieved breath.

Then, she went into a flurry of movement.

Soon, Peter and Paul would reach the main cavern, and—if their commanders didn't wait for Cedric and Hart—the tunnel would get very crowded, very fast.

Whatever it was that was up ahead, she wanted to be the first to see it. She hurried into the passage and strode deeper underground, the familiar power of the Traveller growing stronger. Each step brought her closer to the mana ahead. She listened for shifting sounds, and watched the light as she sniffed the air.

The air near portals was usually sweeter and fresher, since most were connected to settings well above ground, and they were also a good light source. She stayed alert for those signs, drawing closer to the mana source, but—the air and light never changed.

The Sage's footsteps sounded in the dark.

The only new scent reaching her was the occasional strong whiff of decaying food scraps, or waste matter from monsters that once dwelled in the tunnel. No sign of portals or anything concerning the Traveller.

Drestra paced, hoping for a sign of... well, *anything*.

It was only after another fifty steps that she realised the mana was growing weaker in her senses.

"What in all the hells?" she swore, stopping to take a closer look around. "I know I didn't pass anything!"

She backtracked.

Some twenty paces later, she paused.

Then stepped back five paces.

"Here, here's where it's strongest..."

She scanned the passageway, her eyes drifting to the ceiling.

Now the mana felt strong, like it was coming from above.

"Is it hidden in an illusion?" she wondered aloud. Casting a flight spell on herself, she floated upward and ran her hands along the walls and ceiling, there was nothing there but solid stone. No illusions for a secret passage to be concealed in.

The only thing her palm touched was cold stone.

...Wait.

Cold stone?

She felt the ceiling again.

Cool stone. Cool stone. Cool stone.

And then...

She hadn't imagined it.

One area was icy cold, far colder than the rest!

Floating backward while speaking words of power, Drestra conjured a slab of rock, and with a quick pulse of her will, rammed the coldest spot.

A deafening crack echoed off the walls.

Debris dropped to the floor.

And then...

"Light!" She smiled.

The slab had broken through a thin layer of stone, exposing a narrow passage leading to a dim source of light. Fresh air that held a chill so deep it was almost painful gushed into the tunnel, making her shudder.

"What were you hiding down here, Traveller?" she whispered. "*Were* you looking for a way into Uldar's sanctum? Maybe it's time to find out."

Casting defensive spells over herself, the Sage floated up to the secret passage and squeezed in. The space was tight, and neither Hart nor Cedric would be able to fit through it.

She wriggled around, shifting her shoulders and using her hands to pull herself up through the narrow passage and into a larger chamber above it.

Drestra heaved, rubbing at her ribs where the confining space had begun to squeeze her.

"Where *am* I?"

It appeared she'd gone higher and deeper into the rock and toward the central cavern above. A guess would put her much deeper in the earth than the portal chamber, but probably somewhere almost directly below it.

This chamber *seemed* unremarkable, but the source of light and fresh air was coming from somewhere outside of it. The air was cold. Very cold. The heart of a Thameish winter kind of cold.

The kind of cold that called for a warming spell and a cloak pulled tighter around herself. She blew on her hands and cautiously floated toward the source of light, ready to cast a rock or acid spell at anything unfriendly.

Ahead, a doorway awaited, and she steeled herself then peeked through, her spells ready.

A loud gasp left her lips.

She was looking into *another* mostly unremarkable chamber...

But floating in the centre was the largest portal Drestra'd seen in the entire Cave complex. The portal's floor hovered mere inches from the chamber floor, and the top ended near the room's ceiling, which was at least twice the height of Chancellor Baelin. It was also broad in width— maybe some twenty feet across.

And through it...

"What *is* that?" she whispered.

She was staring into a room so vast, she couldn't see the ceiling or most of the walls, like it was limitless. Only a floor of large tiles and a wall that looked like it had been carved from a single piece of stone was defined, and the architecture was oddly similar to the temple chamber in the Cave above.

The wall, though, was covered in writing in an unfamiliar language. Each character was etched in the stone with precision by a masterful hand, and there was enough text covering the wall to fill a substantial book.

What also caught her eye were three statues positioned against the wall. The two on either side were ferocious-looking goddesses with teeth that were pointed like sharp spikes. Drestra's eyes flew wide.

"Their... their faces look like Claygon's!" she said aloud.

Of course, they didn't have deadly fire-gems in the middle of their foreheads... but she could feel powerful magic radiating from them. Cautiously, she turned her eyes away from the statues on the left and right, and focused on the one in the centre.

It was even more familiar.

The tall, benevolent form of Uldar towered above, his right hand held in the mirror-image of his holy symbol. His robes had been sculpted so exactly, that the folds appeared to be in motion, and the details of his hair were so fine, she could make out individual strands.

Those perfect details highlighted his face, forcing her eyes to it, shocking her senses.

Because, Uldar's expertly carved image had no face.

It wasn't that it was unfinished. There were small remnants of his smiling mouth and chin. But at some point in time, a rough tool had been used to gouge and disfigure his features, until all that was left was an ugly ruin of stone. It was clear that whoever had done this held nothing but rage and contempt for the Thameish god.

"What is this place and who hated him that much?" Drestra wondered.

Icy air continued pouring from the portal. Wherever the building was, it was far from summertime there. But the question of where it was, was what needed an answer, and to begin to get that answer... 'I'll have to get closer,' Drestra thought. 'Just close enough to look around. Ugh, I wish I knew Wizard's Eye or any other spell like that.'

So, with the utmost caution, the Sage began floating toward the portal.

And that was when the screams tore through the air.

Before she could react, both goddess statues' mouths parted, unleashing blood-chilling screams that drove Drestra's hands over her ears. Then a sudden flare of golden light that seemed to be rising from right below her erupted.

Looking down...

...her blood went cold.

The Mark of the Sage—the staff emblazoned on her neck—flashed repeatedly with incandescence. Through the portal, the eyes of the goddess statues burned in tandem, and from all directions, the Traveller's mana blazed as the cave shook with its power. The edge of the portal flashed with lights that shone in every hue of a rainbow. Then through the portal, the goddesses' stone lips twisted in a single word:

"Begone," they hissed, a whisper to the earlier screams.

The instant the word reached her, the edges of the portal shuddered. And the doorway shut.

Light and sound left the chamber, and the Traveller's mana faded away. In heartbeats, it was as though there never was anything there except rock and what looked to be an 'x' etched into the floor below where the portal had floated.

"What... what in the name of all the spirits was *that*?" Her voice trembled as she floated to the side of the cave to support herself against the wall and try to make sense of what just happened.

A portal was hidden beneath the Traveller's sanctum, one that led to somewhere unfamiliar and ice-cold. There were two statues there that looked something like Claygon, and one of Uldar with his face hacked away.

The two goddess statues—she assumed they were goddesses—had magic, but Uldar's statue hadn't reacted...

"But the portal *did* react to me," she said. "No, the portal and the statues didn't react to *me*. They reacted to my Mark. They didn't stop me —Drestra—from entering the portal. They stopped the 'sage' from entering it."

She swallowed. "I don't know what the Traveller was working on, but from that reaction and Uldar's face being ground off... seems she was hostile to the Heroes."

CHAPTER 53

REAPING THE HARVEST

"Well, ain't that real bloody ominous," Cedric growled, firelight reflecting off his green eyes and the silver on the morphic weapon wrapped about his hand. His fingers clinked as he tapped them together. "Too bad the bloody portal closed."

"Yeah," Hart said. "Would've liked to have seen it, considering it was our only lead."

"Yes..." Drestra agreed, not trusting herself to say more. "That's true."

Dusk found the three Heroes sitting by a blazing campfire deep in the northern reaches of the forest of Coille on the evening after departing the Cave of the Traveller. Around them, flames chased shadow, dancing along falling snowflakes. Their writhing forms seemed to echo the turmoil in Drestra's heart.

'We're meeting Merzhin in two days,' she thought. 'There's so much more to hide from him now.'

"So, about Merzhin." Hart scowled as though he'd read her mind. The giant of a man tossed a twig on the fire; it hissed and popped as it was consumed. "What're we gonna tell him?"

"Same thing I told the rest of the priests," the Sage said.

"Which wasn't much." Cedric reached over the fire, turning the forest mushrooms and quail skewered above the flame.

"No, it wasn't," Drestra couldn't disagree.

Her story to the army had been a simple lie of omission. She'd told them that she'd found a portal leading to the inside of a building she hadn't recognised. When she flew closer, loud screaming started and the

347

doorway shut before she could see anything more. Of the writing and statues, she'd said nothing.

With the portal gone—and showing no sign of returning—there was little the army could do but ask her questions, guard the secret passage, and observe it for signs of activity.

Meanwhile, Drestra, Hart, and Cedric had searched additional passageways below the Cave of the Traveller, seeking concealed portals or clues. But none were to be found, only empty chambers of cold stone lying in the dark.

"Wish *we* had more than 'not much' to go on, and I wish I'd seen that writin'," Cedric said. "Not that it woulda bloody meant anything t'me."

"Yeah. Even more than the writing, I'm wondering *why* someone would scratch Uldar's face off that statue of his." Hart frowned. "You know, I think that's actually an offence. Pretty sure I saw a guy in the stocks for defacing a statue of Uldar a while back."

"I don't think whoever did it was too worried about stocks," Drestra said.

"Yeah, well, let's hope if they're still alive, they won't try and scratch *our* faces off. Anyway... question is, what do we do now? That was our one lead, and it didn't get us any closer to Uldar's realm."

"I think we gots t'tell the Generasians when we see 'em," Cedric said. "Who knows, maybe one of 'em knows that writin'. Think you could recreate it, Drestra?"

Silence followed.

"Drestra?"

"Oh yes, sorry." She pulled herself from her thoughts. "I think I could copy some of the characters from memory. Maybe that'll be enough for one of them to recognise it and maybe know where it is. If they don't—"

"—then where the hell do we go from here?" Hart finished her sentence and continued. "That's the problem. I only see one option—talking to the church—and that *ain't* a good one. And it wouldn't be a pleasant kinda talking either."

"I know," Drestra said. "But we can't, as you suggested, bust down the doors to the cathedral in the capital."

Hart growled, scratching his head. "I'm not some inquisitor or investigator or anything. This is beyond me." He snorted. "Makes me wish we had the Fool with us."

Above her veil, Drestra's face was blank.

"Aye, they're supposed to be the one t'do the sneaky stuff an' all the tricky skill work. If'n we had 'em t'do the talkin', things'd be a might easier."

"Yeah..." the Sage said. "I suppose so."

"Well, they're either dead or hiding," Hart grunted, eyeing the roasting food. His gaze shifted to the dark stand of trees surrounding them as he listened to the wind rustling through bare branches. "No sense wondering about all that, I guess. We've only got us and the Generasians, so we can talk with them and—"

His words trailed off.

"Shhh," he hissed. "Stay quiet."

Cedric and Drestra froze.

Only the crackling of flame echoed through the dusk.

"What is it?" the Chosen whispered.

"Dunno," Hart said. "Thought I heard something out there. Maybe all this shit's making me jumpy."

"Hold on." Drestra conjured a cluster of forceballs and sent them into the woods. Balls of light travelled between trees, illuminating trunks, bare branches and snow falling gently between them.

"Do you see anything?" she whispered, squinting into the darkness.

"No, I—" Hart froze. "Weapons out!"

A sharp crack came from the woods.

Squeals like those of an enraged dire boar came next.

Hart was already up and leaping over the fire with a large hammer and heavy axe in hand, blurring into the trees while Cedric was chanting his prayer to Uldar and following the Champion, his morphic weapon growing into a halberd. Drestra cast a flight spell and shot toward the sky.

A mammoth shape exploded from the woods, churning clouds of snow, bounding through the campfire. Flaming logs and embers flew through the night trailing sparks, and in the flaring light, Drestra glimpsed the creature.

It was a bulky, four-legged beast riding nearly seven feet tall at the shoulders. Two bulging arms flexed at its sides—each ending in curved claws—while a long, thick tail lashed side to side, the tip was a bone-club poised like a snake. The monster's broad skull was crowned by a helmet of ivory-coloured bone, and spikes formed its spine, rising high above its back.

A bone-charger—a rare Ravener-spawn—moving with enough momentum from its charge to crack a keep's gate.

The monster snorted, smoke escaped flaring nostrils as beady, glowing orange eyes fixed on the Sage.

Then, it leapt.

Powerful legs catapulted its bulk more than a dozen feet through the air, and clamping jaws snapped inches away from Drestra's leg. Its claws slashed at her right side and the tail whipped out toward her back as the monster flew by, crashing to the snowy ground. It whirled to spring again, but she was ready with a spell.

A wave of acid washed the Ravener-spawn, turning it into a squealing pool.

"Hart! Cedric!" she shouted. "This—"

Searing pain struck her torso.

Drestra screamed, looking down at fletching protruding from her body; only her magic ring had stopped the arrow from piercing deeper, but she doubted it would stop the others flying from all directions.

Clutching the wound, she cast forceshield and greater force armour, and as the magic enwrapped her body, she tossed a fireball high above her head, the blast illuminated much of the night sky.

Below, horror unfolded.

Through the bare canopy, she caught movement from all around them. Scores of chitterers scrambled through the forest, each wielding thick-limbed longbows.

"We're surrounded! It's not only bone-chargers!" Drestra warned her companions while conjuring volleys of stone projectiles and blasting monsters with flurry after flurry.

The rocks cracked tree branches, sank into chitterers, pulping flesh, breaking bone, and dropping them to the forest floor. More bone-chargers rushed from the woods, meeting the carnage Cedric and Hart were dealing out.

In the chaos of battle, Drestra suddenly noticed with alarm that, 'Those chitterers aren't aiming for them. They're mostly firing at me!'

Then another wave of arrows came, leaving her no more time to think.

Drestra touched down on the forest floor when the last of the Ravener-spawn had fallen to the Heroes. Monstrous corpses lay steaming in the wintry night. They twitched in pools of melting, blood-stained snow.

"Holy hells." Cedric stepped over a chitterer's corpse. "Bloody vicious, these ones were. Real bloody vicious."

"Yeah." Hart pulled his axe from a bone-charger and frowned, noting the chip in its blade. He'd have to file that out. "They were working like a team with surprisingly good tactics. Well, good for Ravener-spawn, I mean."

"Thank the spirits for your senses, Hart." Drestra touched the arrow in her side. Her clothes were warm and wet around it. "If we'd been attacked in our sleep, we'd be dead."

"You're injured!" Cedric rushed toward her.

"It's not bad, though. Mother's ring did what it was made to." She sounded relieved.

"Aye, well, let's get y'healed up." The Chosen began to work on removing the arrow and bathing the wound with a healing divinity. As the glowing light of Uldar's grace mended Drestra's flesh, her attention was drawn to the bodies strewn about their camp.

Those chitterers had focused on her, which brought to mind Cedric's suspicions about Alex when it seemed that the Ravener-spawn and dungeons had concentrated on him.

Curiosity was burning in her, but she kept her thoughts to herself.

She would stick with her decision to not tell Hart and Cedric what Peter and Paul had said about him. If Alex was the missing Fool, or if he had been through the Cave of the Traveller, she'd decided it would be wrong to accuse him publicly. Putting suspicion on him, not talking to him about what she had in her mind first, was something she couldn't take back once she told anyone else. If she was wrong, he'd be watched by priests, the king and court, the other Heroes... Merzhin—which would be a fate worse than death—and spirits knew who else.

He might have his own motives and secrets, but who was she to judge?

After all, so did she.

But if there was treachery in those secrets?

There would be hells to pay.

"You know." Hart lightly kicked a nearby corpse, pulling the Sage from her thoughts. "This was a pretty big horde, and it seemed to come out of nowhere. Once we meet up with Merzhin, we might want to send a message back to the Cave, tell them that there might be a threat in the area. Maybe we should see if there's a dungeon around here too."

"Aye, more things t'do." Cedric finished healing Drestra's wound. "Ugh, look at us. We're here spread so bloody thin, an' meanwhile, we don't even know if we can trust the very bloody people we're fightin' beside... or the god we're fightin' for! Makes me wish we could just hunt down the damn Ravener an' get this done with."

"Well, maybe we should take a closer look at Aenflynn's deal," Drestra said. "We need troops."

The Chosen sighed. "Y'know, I think we're gonna have to forget about recruitin' the fae. I can't think my way through Lord Aenflynn's deal, an' the last thing we're doin' is givin' up kids."

"Yeah," Hart grunted. "We keep meeting with him and stalling, and the price keeps going higher. It was a nice idea, but... he's asking too much. Just wish there was a way to get more troops on the field without having to do something unsavoury. I mean, look at all these—" He gestured to the bodies. "We cut 'em down and the dungeon cores just make as many as they want, good as new. Sure, squashing them's fun, but... I dunno, it almost feels like we're being pointed in the wrong direction."

"We can't give up on Aenflynn," Drestra said. "Now more than ever we need extra help, and help that doesn't belong to either a treacherous god or a conspiracy peddling church. We need an army that—"

She paused.

A resource given to Aenflynn.

One that *they* could control.

And take back if he betrayed them.

"Wait... Hart!" She flew over to the Champion and grabbed the front of his shirt. "Say what you just said again. About what dungeon cores do!"

"Uh..." Hart grunted. "Well, they make as many monsters as they want."

"And what about when we cut them down?"

"They just make more, good as new."

"Yes!" she cried, excited for the first time since Ffion had touched the dungeon core. "Hart, you genius! You just *solved* the Aenflynn problem!"

"Huh?" the Champion grunted. "I did?"

"You did!"

"Whoa, whoa, slow down, Drestra," Cedric jumped in. "Catch us up. What're you thinking?"

"It's simple," she said. "And even if he doesn't take the deal, we *still* win. But—before we meet Merzhin—we need to find a dungeon. We need a living dungeon core."

"What?" Cedric paled. "You're not thinkin' o' givin' one to him, are ya?"

"Oh my, no..." Drestra grinned behind her veil. "We're not giving him a *dungeon core*. We're going to *offer* him something else. And if he doesn't take it? We still get what we want anyway. Now *we'll* be in control of negotiations!"

CHAPTER 54

THE VARIED VIEW OF DEATH

"Hey, Alex, how's that cake coming over there?" Thundar asked, stirring a pot of goat stew.

"About the same as the last twelve times you asked me," Alex fired back, carefully measuring out a portion of white sugar. "It's *baking*. Cakes *bake* when they're put in the oven, Thundar. That takes *time*. You know, time? That continued sequence of existence that events occur in? And asking how it's doing until my ears fall off won't make one bake any faster."

"Oh, come on. Can't you do something to make it go any faster?" The minotaur glanced at the window of the insula's kitchen. The sun was setting. "You know... apply some kind of special technique?"

Alex paused mid-measurement and gave Thundar a withering look. "Really? 'Apply some kind of special technique'? To make *time go faster*?"

"No! Don't be ridiculous!" Thundar glanced at the position of the sun again. "I mean... look, you're a *skilled baker*—" he said, throwing a meaningful look at Alex's marked shoulder. "You can't like... find some special way to speed things up? Make it bake faster?"

The young Thameish wizard gasped. "*Thundar!*" His tone sounded scandalised. Which reminded him of Professor Jules that time a student suggested they could work faster without masks and aprons. "Baking is an *exact* science. Cooking is a science! And this isn't something forgiving like boiling some vegetable soup or something! You have to balance the heat. You have to keep it even. Too high and the cake burns or dries out and—"

"Okay, okay, I get it!" Thundar raised his hands in defeat. "You can take as long as you want with your cake, jeez. You're acting like I just asked you to cut off an arm or leg."

"You may as well have," Alex said, shaking his head.

The young wizard looked at the position of the sun through the window and glanced at the hourglass he was using to time dough he had resting under a towel to rise. Not for the first time, he wished the kitchen had one of those fancy timekeepers.

"What's got you so antsy, anyway?" Alex said. "We're fine! If anything, we're ahead of schedule. The pies are done, and the roasts are on. The sauce for the noodles is almost finished simmering, the cake will be baked before our time slot runs out... everything's going great. We'll have more than enough time for cleanup, and all the food'll be ready for Oreca's Fall tomorrow."

He cocked his head, closely watching Thundar's body language. Something odd was going on with the minotaur. His movements were jerky and tight. There was an uneasiness in the way he stood. His hooves shuffled against the tiles and were spaced closer than usual.

"Say... what's up, man?" Alex asked. "You look tense. Has stuff that happened lately been bothering you or something?"

"Wait, what?" The minotaur startled, chuckling nervously. "Naw, naaaah, no way! Nothing's bothering me!"

Alex stared at him.

"Yeah, even *I* didn't believe that," Thundar admitted.

"Aha, so there *is* something. Well, you don't have to tell me if you don't want to... but is it, you know... the thing that we talked about?"

Alex made the sign of Uldar over his chest.

"Eh? Oh *that—Ow, shit*!" Thundar tasted the stew, grunting as it burnt his tongue. "No... well, kinda."

"Kinda?"

"Well, it's not that *directly*, I mean... Look, I know it's a big deal, but it's so *big* that I can barely comprehend it. Like I know what it all means and what we might have to do, but it just doesn't feel real."

"I get that. How could it?" Alex shook his head. "So then, what's up?"

Thundar looked around as though spies were hiding in the corners and rafters of the kitchen, then he slunk over to Alex. "Well, that thing made me think about life, you know? Things can come unexpectedly. Anything can happen. I know you know what I mean."

"Oh yeah, I definitely do," Alex said, thinking back on the mini-crisis he went through when Minervus was killed, and when the chaos essence and dungeon core remains exploded.

He thought of the encampment, wondering how things were going there. The research team was still doing their experiments on dungeon core remains, and the castle was on schedule to be completed before first semester final exams began.

As for the living dungeon core? Baelin and Jules had it locked away while they developed protocols for powering it up and having Carey and him experiment with it.

He was looking forward to getting his hands on it again, even though he was also wondering if Carey would be up for it. The young woman had taken a leave of absence, which he could easily understand. If he hadn't already been considering the revelation that shook her so badly, he might be on a leave himself.

As it was, he'd experienced too many life-altering events for certain things to break him at this stage.

"You start wondering if tomorrow might be your last day," Alex said to Thundar. "And you begin thinking about things you want to do in case it is. Or things you might never get to see."

"And then you think about acting," the minotaur finished. "Before you never get the chance to."

Alex looked at him sharply. "Acting? You mean like... on the stage? I didn't know you wanted to be a performer?"

Thundar stared at him.

"What? Since when have you wanted to act?"

Thundar sighed. "Not that kind of acting, Alex."

Alex was silent, then realisation hit him.

"Ohhh, *that* kind of acting," he said sheepishly.

The minotaur shook his head. "I don't know about you sometimes. We're talking about, and I quote, 'tomorrow might be your last day,' and next thing ya know, you have me performing on stage!"

"I don't know, maybe you have some secret yearning to be an actor. It could happen," Alex weakly defended himself.

Thundar muttered something in a language Alex had never heard him use before.

"Anyway, well, the first thing I did was write home," Thundar said. "I mean, like, I hadn't done that in a while and I'd feel pretty shitty if I died and my folks hadn't heard from me in months." He snorted. "Speaking of that, Khalik apparently had a hell of a time writing home."

"Really? He didn't say anything to me."

"Yeah, probably didn't want you taking it on. See, with me, I told my folks that I got involved in something dangerous but cool. Something the ancestors would be proud of. Everyone in my family's going to be cheering me on. They'll be proud of me if I make it through, and—if I don't—they'll be proud of me for falling while doing something worthy."

"Really?" Alex asked. "They wouldn't tell you to come home, like yesterday?"

The minotaur laughed. "Listen, I get that things are different all over the world, but my tribe... my herd doesn't really have much use for cowards. Our lands can be harsh, and we don't have a horrible doom orb looking to kill all of us every hundred years, but we fight monsters and beasts for resources. Not everyone in our tribe's a warrior, but none of us are cowards. Trust me, and 'coward-leanings' are smacked out of us when we're young."

"That's... that's sad, in a way," Alex said. "Sometimes cowardice is a good thing."

"For some people, but not for us." The minotaur looked toward the sun again. "I ain't gonna lie, sometimes I look at you Thameish and think you could do with being a little more like us. Imagine if *all* of you picked up the sword, the spell, the bow, and the miracle. Not just your soldiers and Heroes. Everyone. Then everybody would be involved in defending your lands."

"Maybe," Alex said. "But if everyone stayed to stand their ground and fight, a lot more people would die. Maybe so many that—when the Ravener was finally defeated—not enough of us would be left to sow and harvest. Our land would be this empty ruin. Just someplace for wild beasts and Ravener-spawn."

Thundar mulled that over. "Yeah... I can see that. Thing is, my people live in smaller groups. We farm less. Hunt more. Herd more. If we sent half our people away when trouble came, maybe there wouldn't be enough of us to fight whatever the threat was. When push comes to shove, we need every hand around a weapon, if those hands are strong enough to wield one."

He grabbed a fork and went to a delicious-smelling roast turning on a spit, speared one end, and pulled some of the meat off for sampling. "We're not blood-drinking berserkers here. In our eyes, the best death is one where you're in a comfy bed after a long life with your family around you. But we mortals don't often get that luxury. So, dying in a fight against something terrible for a good cause? That's seen as good too."

"Huh..." Alex murmured. "Makes ya think."

The way Thundar was talking about death so casually startled him since their perspectives were so different. It wasn't often that he thought about how distinct all of their cultures and lives were. One thing he knew for sure was that if Theresa's parents caught even the slightest *whiff* of what had happened—what *really* happened—they'd do anything to keep their daughter and potential son-in-law alive.

They were proud of her, of her strength and fearlessness, but just giving her their blessing to go up against Uldar himself would, without a single doubt, be pushing things beyond insane thinking. Thundar, though, *his* family would be proud of him even if he were to lose his life. It was such a strange idea to Alex: if anything killed one of his friends, he couldn't imagine reacting with pride.

He could only imagine grief, rage, and a need for vengeance. And after that? The slow grind of coming to terms with it, like he had with his parents.

"Well, it's a different way of looking at things," Alex said. "Guess it makes it easier to send letters about what you're doing to your family."

"Yeah, I remember Theresa said that she hid her stuff for awhile," the minotaur said grimly. "But that's nothing compared to Khalik's problem."

"Right, back to that," Alex said. "What's going on?"

"Well, not to go into too many details, but he's been having trouble telling his folks about the dangerous stuff he's faced here. It's not that he outright hides it, but he has to try and put things in the best light, sorta like putting nice clothes on Ravener-spawn to make them look better. And with this Uldar stuff, he's oathsworn—like the rest of us—not to give details. It's hard to get the gravity of the situation across without details, so he's gotta walk this tight line. He doesn't want to hide what's going on from them, but if things get too rough... well, you know his position."

"Yeah, I could see them coming up here to take him back home, which could be a mess 'cos he won't want to go." Alex shook his head. "Let's hope for his sake that his brother can keep them away for a while longer. I remember he said they're already getting twitchy since it's been over a year since they laid eyes on him. And by the Traveller, I don't even want to imagine how that meeting could turn out. I mean... he's *him* and his parents are who *they* are, while we're a bunch of idiots."

"We are." Thundar chuckled, biting into the piece of roast. "Hm, good flavour but probably still a little tough for human teeth. Anyway, I kinda wanna try not to embarrass him... but I also kinda wanna embarrass him a lot. Eh, Isolde will be there to make a good impression, anyway."

"Yeah." Alex laughed. "They'll probably ask why all his friends can't be like her. But anyway, that's beside the point. You were talking about writing home to your family because of so much uncertainty about the near future. Anything else come to mind?"

Thundar paused. "Well..."

He went silent.

"Well, what?"

"Look... promise you won't tell Khalik. And definitely not Isolde," he said.

"I promise nothing."

"*Alex.*"

"...Oh shit, you're being serious. Yeah, okay, mum's the word. What's up?"

Again, the minotaur looked around conspiratorially and leaned toward Alex before whispering. "I'm going to ask Kohana out."

"Wait... you mean our Cleansing Movement instructor? *That* Kohana?"

"Keep it down, will you?" Thundar hissed, his eyes wide. "Jeez, why not scream it to the whole campus?"

"Sorry, it's just that... I never thought you would."

"Really?" Thundar snorted. "I'm no coward, Alex."

"Yeah, maybe not on the battlefield, but we've been going to those classes on and off for like a year now and... jeez, she came to visit you after you were laid up from the mana vampire attack. And you didn't do anything then?"

"Didn't seem right," the minotaur grunted. "There I was, injured, right? Or just getting better and then I go and ask her out? Could look like I was trying to *guilt* her into going out with me. Like I was after some sorta pity date."

"Yeah, fair, but I mean... you waited so long, she's *gotta* have a partner. I mean, *look* at her—"

"I have."

"—yeah, that's a fair point too, but look, all that Cleansing Movement practice *shows.*"

"Yeah, it sure does." Thundar was grinning. "Getting a no won't kill me, but dying before even throwing out a line? Now that's cowardice. And what'd I *just* say about that?"

"True," Alex said.

"It's why I'm going to do it after the festival," the minotaur said. "We'll honour the dead, and then... I'll do something for the living. The living being me."

"You know..." Alex said. "In the stories, this is the kinda thing characters say just before they die."

"Yeah," Thundar said. "But if I'm gonna die, I'll die anyway. So what's the point of hiding from life? I just want tomorrow to go perfectly. There's a lot of dead to honour. And, if things get rough enough in Thameland, there might be a hell of a lot more."

"Let's hope not, Thundar," Alex said. "Let's hope not."

CHAPTER 55

THE GHOSTS OF FAITH AND GODS

The beach on Oreca's Fall had been transformed in the afternoon light.

When Alex was last there, the sand was thick with the dead. Most were demons, but the rest were his comrades from the Grand Battle. Generasian wizards and other competitors had stood shoulder to shoulder, fighting those demons with many paying a price that was too high to bear. Scavenging seabirds had been circling the beach after the battle, and the smell of death had hung in the air, mingling with the cries of survivors.

Today, an ocean breeze replaced that smell with the scent of sea salt and the inviting aroma of scores of delectable dishes.

Towering in the sunlight where there was once only death, a monument had been raised to the triumphant fallen.

An enormous stone statue stood where a competition had turned into a deadly battle. It was carved in the likeness of a dozen young wizards and warriors joined together in a stand against the threat of a hideous demon posed in submission. Around the statue, long tables were set up, each assigned a number corresponding with one assigned to the party who had reserved it. In front of the statue was a single extended platform piled with steaming dishes provided by the Watchers.

"See that?" Thundar nodded to the platform. "The Watchers sent folk out to every family who lost loved ones to find out what their favourite dishes had been. And that's the spread they put together for everyone to share: survivors and guests."

"To honour the dead," Theresa said quietly. "And it looks like there'll be plenty of people to share with."

The tables around Alex's group were filled with familiar faces. Teams from the Grand Battle who were there for the Festival of Ghosts in respect of their fellow competitors. Not everyone had returned, but Alex recognised quite a few.

Hanuman—the life enforcement practitioner—was with his team from the Grand Battle; together, they formed a circle around their table, hands linked and heads bowed in a quiet prayer. Their masks were intricate and varied, but each was colourless. Alex wondered if the lack of colour was in deference to the dead.

Tyris' group was there as well, at a table at the edge of the event. Alex exchanged a solemn nod with her as they passed. Her expression was covered by a dragon mask, but the usual cocky demeanour and boisterous body language was gone, replaced by a quiet sombreness and a touch of haunted memories playing through her.

She wasn't alone in that sombreness. Some folk were quiet as they set up, but others chatted to each other with big smiles as they remembered their fallen comrades. Some raised toasts; it was obvious they weren't their first tributes of the afternoon, and after each sip, they spilled some on the sand in memory of a teammate.

There was sadness and nostalgia, but there was also... relief that wasn't there during Alex's first Festival of Ghosts. Last year, tension loomed over the celebration from the demon summoner threat. He remembered how folk eyed one another with suspicion and fear, and how the city had been on high alert, prepared for an attack.

Now, that threat was dead along with its instigator, Leopold.

Ezaliel's cult was still out in the world, but they hadn't been bold enough to show their faces in the wizard city. Folk were still cautious, but the sharp edge of most anxiety had dulled.

And what that left was an opportunity for people to be together and catch up. Young wizards who'd not seen each other since that difficult time in the summer came together as old friends. Some reminisced. Some hugged each other like they couldn't let go. Some cried. And some laughed and raised a glass or two.

Their mood was bittersweet, and memories of lives faded also gave Alex and those with him that bittersweet feeling, yet for him and his good friends, there was also a deep feeling of gratitude because they would all be there, together.

The cabal, Hogarth, Svenia, Selina, Brutus, Claygon, Theresa, and her friend, Shishi, were there of course, with immense baskets and pots of the foods most special to their loved ones. Alex had made his father's stew and his mother's cookie recipe again this year, along with dishes he and Thundar had prepared. The minotaur's special apple pies would soon be on the table, while Isolde and Khalik had bought the finest foods on campus. Grimloch had his own dishes in four oversized baskets, enough to feed a small army.

New faces were joining them for the festival this year, with new dishes to add to the feast. Sinope strolled arm and arm with Prince Khalik, and both looked regal enough to command empires. On her other arm, she carried a basket of wild fruits soaked in sweet tree syrup and a dryad liquor.

Nua-Oge followed her baby brother, reminding him to mind his manners at the table, while carrying a basket of steamed shellfish. Soon, Shiani, Rhea, and Malcolm would be joining them with their own dishes, and Kybas was on his way. Alex was excited about seeing everybody. It had been too long since he'd been with most of his old friends. Thundar had a point—better to catch up with friends now, than regret not doing so later... if you're even around for regret.

"Number twelve!" Thundar announced, pointing to a nearby table with his horns. "That's us!"

"This is a good table, Thundar," Isolde approved, looking at the statue of the fallen.

"Yep, right close to the central table." The minotaur nodded his head in respect.

"Good." Selina took in the central table. "I'm glad we're so close to the food everyone who died liked. I didn't know them, but... maybe this'll help me know some of them." She looked at her brother. "Do you think Shiani will be here soon?"

"I think so." Alex glanced at his little sister. It'd been a while since the young girl had mentioned their fire-wielding friend. He wondered if her question had anything to do with what she'd asked him about putting out the windmill fire. "I don't think she'll be late for such an important celebration and miss out on honouring the folks who fought beside us, Selina."

"Good. I just hope we celebrate the demons being dead too," she said. "They deserved it."

"Well, Roal's statue is looking over all of us." Theresa nodded to the statue honouring the fallen wizards. "And the Watchers are running this event. Trust me, they'll focus on our triumph just as much as on honouring our fallen."

"Good," was all she said as the others put their dishes on the table.

There was a hard edge to that word.

Alex looked at her for a moment with a mix of pride and concern. Concern about the hardening he was noticing in his sister. The scared but brave little girl who had walked into the Cave of the Traveller with him was transforming. What that meant... it was too early to know. Part of him wanted to preserve the sweet innocence in her.

'But she's growing up,' he thought, looking back to the statue of fallen wizards. 'And for a wizard, sweet innocence serves a hell of a lot less well than a strong strength of will. If she channels it right, she'll be okay.'

His eyes drifted over the stone faces of the fallen, recognising some of them now that he was closer.

The figure in the middle of the group was no young wizard from the Grand Battle. It was Roal herself, standing behind the others. Not in an exalted place of glory, but one of support. She was not the hero of this image; instead, she was the ancestor who'd helped the young wizards face their monstrous foes.

As the group laid out their dishes and other friends arrived, Alex found himself turning again and again to the stone face of Roal. He studied it. Turned it over in his mind. Compared it to the faces of the statues of wizards around her and his own friends.

"She was young," Alex muttered.

"Who?" Theresa placed a ladle in Thundar's stew.

"Roal." He nodded to the statue. "Look at her. She's maybe five years older than us. Maybe a little older. I would have thought that someone who'd killed a demigod would be older. More experienced."

Theresa followed his gaze. "Huh. You know, I never thought of that. I guess Roal was young. Or maybe she just looked young. Wizards can be a lot older than they look."

"True," Alex said.

Still, if she was around their age when she'd slain Oreca...

'She killed a demigod, right in front of his followers, then fought them as they threw miracles at her,' he thought. 'And he was a demigod who ruled the seas around here. I wonder what that was like for her, if it was tough, mentally?'

He considered what he and his friends might have to do. What if the church was corrupt and needed to be dismantled? It was a uniting force in Thameland, but more than that, it did a lot of good for the people.

Their church schools were responsible for the fact that nearly every citizen in Uldar's kingdom could read, write, and knew a bit of science and history.

Even serfs were better educated than merchants in other realms because of that. 'What happens if it all goes away?' Living in Generasi had given Alex an idea of what it took to run a massive system of learning.

The university needed a small army of clerks, teaching staff, and associates to keep it running, and they'd had centuries to make it work.

If some archwizard snapped their fingers and made every professor and all the auxiliary staff disappear, it wasn't like someone else could just pick up the torch and keep things going. It'd all fall apart.

And Generasi was only *one* institution.

Uldar only knew how many church schools there were across the entire realm. If the church had to be removed from Thameland—if it turned out they were corrupt—what would happen to all the knowledge the kingdom's children received? Who would take up teaching them? Who would organise what they learned and how it was taught? Who would pay for it all?

Then there were all the other services the priests provided: healing in emergency times, officiating at marriages, laying people to rest, baptisms and births; emotional help for folk who needed support, folk who couldn't share their secrets with friends and family for fear of shaming or harm.

He remembered a young priest from Alric who had spirited away a family, who, for years, lived in terror from violence at the hands of their kinfolk. He'd kept them safe, and probably saved their lives. And his wasn't the only story like that.

What would happen if all of that just... evaporated one day?

And that was *if* the church was the root of the problem, and not Uldar.

'If we had enough scholars, they might be able to take over the schools,' Alex thought. 'And maybe we could find other trained folk to fill other roles the priests have... How long would that take? Meanwhile, how much would we lose? And if it turns out that Uldar is the problem like Oreca was, and if we *do* manage to reject him...'

He glanced at Isolde as the young woman took a seat near Svenia and Hogarth. 'She'd said that not everyone in the Rhinean Empire supported people from Thameland. What would happen if our realm was suddenly weakened, with no protection from gods or churches. We have the Heroes and a strong army... but the Rhineans have elemental knights, way more wizards than we do, and a much bigger army. Jeez, they probably wouldn't be the only ones looking to conquer us if our kingdom looked like it was failing. The only thing we could do is use dungeon core remains as a weapon to keep conquerors away... Then again, what if our own citizens start infighting over those very weapons?'

He shook his head. 'Fighting a deity and his church isn't like getting rid of a powerful demon or some monster. If Uldar's church is the problem, that'll leave a massive hole when they're gone. And *if* the Ravener's still around, that'll be an even bigger problem, since the priests organise the fight against it, and they'll be gone. Telling people that followers of Uldar can control dungeon cores would give us weapons against the Ravener and other attackers, but Thameland's not exactly overrun with folk who could even use them.'

He blew out a breath. 'Complications, complications, complications,' he thought, his mind swirling. 'But... enough of that for now. Handle it when—'

"Kybas!" Theresa waved. "Over here! We're over here!"

Alex turned, excited to see the little goblin.

Then he whistled with awe.

Kybas was grinning and waving at everyone at the table, and beside him strode Harmless, who was *not* so little anymore.

CHAPTER 56

REUNIONS AND THE REFUSAL OF PETTINESS

The not-so-little crocodile had obviously taken well to Kybas' concoctions. The last time Alex saw him, he'd grown quite a bit, but now, he was at least another foot longer than at the summer games, and he was thick like a log, sleek and powerful. His scales were shiny and clean, and his gait was steady and strong as he strode beside his goblin master.

A huge basket was strapped to his back with the scent of a buffet of mushroom dishes wafting from it.

"Hello!" Kybas carried a pot of what smelled like mushroom soup. "It's been a while!"

"Yeah, man, how've you been?" Alex asked, looking at the scaled, monstrous mask he had sitting on his forehead.

"Oh, I've been good! Very good!" The goblin grinned, bobbing his head enthusiastically. "Harmless has grown *so much*! It's all been very good! He'll be the biggest and strongest in no time."

"Yeah," Alex said. "I can see that. Is Salinger working you hard?"

"Nope." Kybas nodded to Theresa and the others, then lifted his soup pot onto the table. He began untying the basket from Harmless' back. "I mean, he does work me very hard, but it's nothing I can't handle."

He leaned toward Alex and whispered, "Beats growing mushrooms by myself in a cave wondering when I'll get caught." He gave a little giggle.

"Yeah, no doubt."

"Kybas!" Grimloch flashed his many-fanged grin at the goblin. "How's hunting been?"

"Good!" He grinned back wickedly. "Harmless is learning well. If he keeps it up, he'll be killing sea serpents soon!"

"Oh, sea serpents are the best eating! You've gotta try some," Grimloch growled. "I'll take you hunting, and we can boil up whatever we catch together. But Harmless can have his raw if he'd like it better that way."

"Ooo! Ooo! That sounds fun and delicious!" The goblin's voice rose. "Maybe I'll take you to my home one day. There's big lizards there, and their meat's tough, but so, so juicy! Can't get any of that here."

Grimloch laughed. "Yeah, they got everything here except the *best* meats."

"I know!"

Alex and the rest of the group gaped at Grimloch. He'd only seen the shark man that animated once before... and that was also when he'd been with Kybas. Was the world ending? Was the sky about to drop on them?

"He gets like that around Kybas," Nua-Oge confirmed quietly from somewhere behind Alex. "It's great. So glad my baby brother made such a good friend. They really seem to understand each other!"

"Y-yes..." Prince Khalik muttered somewhat awkwardly. "It's uncanny. They... most definitely seem to understand each other."

'A match made in the hells themselves,' Alex thought. 'I don't want to be anywhere near either of those guys when they go hunting together. Maybe—'

"Shiani!" Selina cried. "Hey! Heeeeey!"

Alex looked up to see Shiani, Malcolm, Eyvinder, and Rhea coming toward them along the beach. Caramiyus and Angelar were just behind, their doberman-like faces covered by werewolf masks.

Shiani was wearing a phoenix mask, and her body language opened up as soon as she saw his sister. "Hi, Selina, it's been a while," she called excitedly. "You're so much taller than last time we saw each other!"

"It's been way too long." The young girl smiled, taking one of Shiani's fish dishes from her and setting it on the table. A very spicy scent drifted from it. "I had this idea I wanted to talk to you about—"

"Whoa, whoa," Alex said. "Let's let them get settled first before we start an inquisition here."

"Oh, it's alright. I haven't seen Selina for a long time!" Shiani laughed. "You need to lighten up, Alex."

"Yeah, what she said, don't be so grumpy and mean, ugh." Selina put her hands on her hips.

"What?" Alex cried incredulously, spreading his hands. "I'm just trying to make sure my little sister isn't rude! How does that make *me* the bad guy?"

Selina had already turned back to Shiani and was chatting away like Alex wasn't there. "I wanted to talk to you about heat, and how it moves —" she started.

"I wouldn't worry about it too much," Rhea said, the tall elf putting her dish down and smiling warmly. "Shiani was pretty excited about catching up with her."

"And the rest of you were a good consolation prize," Malcolm added, sliding a tray of layered sandwiches and frozen juice cubes onto the table.

"Judging by how excited she is, it would seem that the rest of *us* are a consolation prize for Selina as well." Isolde smiled.

Alex sighed, staring up at the heavens. "You hear that, Mother and Father? Your daughter thinks her own brother and all her friends are consolation prizes." He laughed as Selina guided Shiani to her seat, shaking his head. "Well, I guess that's only natural, eh?" he whispered.

He watched his friends settling at the table and an old memory came back to him.

It would be a shame if the next Festival of Ghosts were to come around next year, where he would be one of the dead being honoured by his friends and family.

He remembered thinking along those lines just before the festival when he and Baelin talked about the hunt for the demon summoner. He'd sworn not to get involved in finding the dangerous maniac back then.

In the end, though, Leopold had pulled him—and everyone here —into it.

'That's the trouble with dangerous maniacs, demons, and—' He looked at Roal's statue. 'They get others involved in their bullshit.'

Putting the thought away, he turned to take a seat but found Isolde staring at a table nearby. Well, she was trying to be discreet and make it *look* like she wasn't staring. Except even while she helped unpack Rhea's incredibly aromatic curry, her eyes were focused on the other table. At first, Alex didn't recognise its occupants—considering they weren't wearing their characteristic blue shirts—then he realised it was the Hydra Companions she was eyeing.

He hadn't seen or spoken to any of them since the Games, and—

Wait.

His eyes searched beyond the Hydra Companions and rested on the true recipients of Isolde's covert attention. There, in all of their glory, sat the Ursa-Lupine Brotherhood, and among them, the familiar redheaded figure of Derek. The young man looked... different.

Older, with a leaner, harder physique and more grace to his movements. His long red hair had been cut low and his eyes hung lower. He actually looked exhausted.

"Damn," Alex whispered. "That's quite the change. What happened to him?"

"Well," Isolde said. "I have not thought much about Derek since the summer—"

A single glance at her body language revealed this as a lie. The young noblewoman's face always went *slightly* blank when she lied.

"—and I do not really care much what happens to him—"

Another lie.

"—however, my *friends* have informed me that the demonic attack seemed to shake him." Her lip twitched. "He entered third year trying even less than in our first year. But such behaviour does not lead to success in one's third year. Not that I celebrate his inconvenience or anything like that."

Another lie.

"So, he found himself on academic probation. Again. I understand he has to apply himself now... Though he is rather bitter about the situation. In the end, I suppose the shaking from the summer did him some good." She looked at Alex. "Not that it is any of my business, of course."

"Of course," Alex said, fighting to keep his face straight. He was the very last person who could criticise someone for taking joy in petty revenge.

There was the tinkle of a spoon ringing against a cup.

"Alright, everyone, it's time to honour the departed," Thundar said, looking around the table. He was wearing the mask of an antlered fae this year.

All things considered, his demon mask from last year's festival would have been... in poor taste.

"I know I led things last festival, but does anyone mind if I go again?" the minotaur asked. "Kinda feels like we started a tradition."

There was a chorus of approval from the group.

"Alright, then." He cleared his throat, falling into words similar to those he'd spoken at their first Festival of Ghosts. "With our masks on to frighten away ghosts of evil folk who might be called by our words, we keep those we're honouring in our minds, and dedicate the food we eat to them. We take our masks off to finish our feasting by sunset. Then we'll all go out together as a group, so the dead don't follow any of us 'cos we're alone. Everyone ready?"

Some nodded, some spoke up, and all sat taller and straighter in their seats. Alex noticed that the other tables were also preparing for their own ceremonies.

"Alright, bow your heads, everyone," the minotaur said. "Close your eyes and think about who you're honouring with this meal."

Alex bowed his head, closing his eyes beneath the same dragon mask he'd worn last year. He waited for Selina's hand to slide into his like it did at last year's ceremony... but it never came.

'Guess they do grow up fast,' he thought.

"Oh, honoured ancestors," Thundar's deep voice began. "Lost friends and family, fallen members of the herd. We think about you through the year, but during this feast, we bring you into the centre of our thoughts and dedicate this food to you. We eat for you so that— through us—you can taste mortal sustenance again. Please watch over us throughout the year, and please keep those on death's plane who might harm us away."

He paused. "Please bring forward whoever you're dedicating this feast to in your thoughts."

Images of Alex's mother and father came to his mind as they had last year. But now, they were joined by those who had fallen in the battle on Oreca's Fall, and those who'd lost their lives during the fight in Crymlyn Swamp.

He shuddered.

'How many more faces will join these next year?'

"Now, say aloud who you want to honour," Thundar instructed.

"Mother and Father," Alex said quietly. "Those who fell in the Crymlyn. Those who died here."

Murmuring spread around the table, but he only focused on Selina's words:

"Father and Mother," his little sister said quietly. "Those who lost their lives against the demons. Those who lost their lives against the Ravener."

"Let the dead from beyond join with the living in this feast," Thundar pronounced. "And let our memories of them grow happier and stronger. Alright, let's begin. All of you can open your eyes and take off your masks. And—Oh holy shit!"

Alex's eyes opened and his gaze drifted skyward.

This year, he wasn't surprised at what was coming, but he was amazed nonetheless.

Like last year, the early evening sky was filled with hundreds of glowing beings shining with silver light, drifting like scores of autumn leaves. Ghosts of the fallen: mortals, beasts, and monsters. He heard a sigh of relief escape his own mouth, thankful that there were no demonic shapes floating above.

A choked cry reached him from a nearby table.

"Ed... ward!" A doe beast-woman pointed to the sky. "It's my Edward!"

A wave of gasps travelled between tables as folk pointed, calling out the names of loved ones floating within the stream of spirits passing by. Alex watched the ghostly throng, then exhaled deep and low. He too was finding familiar forms within the multitude of spirits. They weren't folks he knew by name, but he remembered them as opponents from the Grand Battle.

He also recognised those he'd seen lying broken and unmoving on the sand.

Slowly, he bent his head to pray for their safe passage. Only... he no longer knew who to pray to. Calling on Uldar seemed hollow, and the Traveller was the patron saint of his hometown; she wasn't a goddess who could guide these souls who'd fallen in battle in a foreign land.

In the end, he offered his silent prayer to any god who would listen.

'To any merciful deity who hears me, I ask you to guide these souls into their reward in the afterlife, as you see fit. May they rest in peace, and may their sacrifice in life give them what they need in death.'

As he listened to the whispered prayers of his friends and those at tables close by, a disturbing thought struck him.

'Mourning mortals who've fallen is one thing,' he thought. 'But how do you mourn the loss of a god? Of a church? Of one's entire faith?'

CHAPTER 57

ISOLDE'S SHAME

In the sky above, the stream of ghosts had long faded and Alex's group—along with others on the beach—were now deep into that easiest of traditions in the entirety of the Festival of Ghosts: feasting on all the food they'd brought so the dining would be finished by sunset.

Within the first hour, they'd made an admirable effort. A growing majority of their tables' dishes were now empty, shared between each other, with much of the food disappearing down the throat of a certain hulking shark man.

"Don't eat *all* the food, Grimloch!" said shark man's older adoptive sister complained. "I told you to mind your manners. There are other people here!"

"It's okay," Selina said. "It's fun this way!"

The young girl speared several pieces of fish on her fork and tossed them across the table into Grimloch's open and waiting jaws.

"Three points!" Kybas called, writing the number down on a score-board he'd made from an empty platter. He'd been keeping a tally of points using a spoon and a spare bowl of mustard.

"Not bad," Malcolm said, buffing his fingernails on his jacket. "But you're four behind me. I guess you're a few years too young to compete against me."

"Does it make you feel proud to beat a child?" Rhea asked, her voice holding a bit of a chiding edge.

"Yes," Malcolm said evenly.

"My man." Alex grinned with approval, drawing an evil glare from Selina and a shake of the head from Theresa.

"Will you all stop *enabling* him!" Nua-Oge groaned.

"Look," Thundar patted the selachar woman on the shoulder. "No offence, but I'm pretty sure getting between your brother and food is a good way to join the ghost-stream at next year's festival. And the last thing I want my epitaph to be is, 'Here lies Thundar, he was eaten by a friend!'" He looked to Grimloch. "We *are* friends, right?"

"Yes."

"Oh good... wait, you don't eat friends, right?"

"No promises."

"Well, there ya go!" Thundar shrugged at Nua-Oge. "And that's why I'm not doing it. You want your dirty work done? Do it yourself."

The selachar rolled her eyes. "*Fine*! Little brother, you're banned from eating any more of our food. You're *going* to leave some for others."

"Or what?" Grimloch snorted.

"Or I'm telling Mother and Father when we go back home."

The shark man paused. "Dirty."

She crossed her arms. "It needed to be done."

Grimloch sat in silence for a moment, mulling things over. Then he shot out of his seat and rushed to the central table—to the food brought by the Watchers. Folk at other tables had already begun picking at it, but Alex's group was still focused on their own food. They'd brought more than enough.

Things at the central table changed when the walking disaster known as Grimloch raided it. Alex saw the colour drain from the Watchers' faces as the shark man piled platter after platter high with food. Then—as he was about to head back to their table—a Watcher leaned over and said something to him.

With a single grunt, he reached out and grabbed a small barrel before striding proudly back to his seat.

"Before you say anything," Grimloch said. "Remember, you stopped me from eating *our* food. Not food the *Watchers* brought."

Nua-Oge stared at him for a long, quiet moment, before her head slowly fell into her hands. "Why... why do I bother?"

"I don't know," Grimloch grunted. "Anyway, I brought presents." He slammed the barrel on the table. "Pumpkin ale. Provided by the Watchers."

The entire table went still.

"Oh no," Nua-Oge, Eyvinder, Shiani, and Selina said as one.

"Oh *yes*!" Thundar, Alex, Sinope, Caramiyus, Angelar, Prince Khalik,

Malcolm, and Rhea contradicted. Hogarth rubbed his hands together like a greedy fly, while Svenia was already scrambling for her cup.

As one, they lunged for the barrel.

Even Isolde gave it a long look. "Perhaps... perhaps just a bit."

And soon, they were *well* into their cups.

Now, there was a good amount of swaying from members of Alex's group. A good deal of... *merriness*.

And Prince Khalik was one of the merriest of all.

"Alright," the prince said, slamming his cup of wine on the table. "I tire of this dancing around the bush. No more shall I walk on eggshells over this."

The entire table paused mid-feast, their eyes wandering to Khalik as he sat tall in his chair and squared his shoulders as though he were about to carry an enormous weight.

Alex looked down at the sand and giggled. "Walking on eggshells? I think you mean *sea*shells."

Silence followed.

"Because... because we're on a beach."

"We got it, Alex," Selina said, hanging her head in shame.

"Well, I thought it was funny." Theresa took a long sip of her pumpkin ale.

"You have awful taste, Theresa," Selina said.

But the huntress was already having more ale. "Goodness, this is *good*. Father and Mother would *kill* to have a keg of this at the inn."

"I would kill to have a keg of it in my room!" Khalik laughed uproariously.

"Oh please, Khal." Sinope touched his arm. "You only say that because you've never tasted my peoples' fall wild apricot brew. I swear, one sip of it and you'll never be able to drink anything else."

"Wait... wait... *wait*!" Thundar raised an eyebrow, swaying slightly in his seat. "Wait, *Khal*? Who's Khal, when did *Khal* happen?"

"Yeah!" Alex said, resting his cup on the table. "What *is* this Khal business?"

"Indeed." Isolde smiled, her face slightly red and her electric blue eyes dancing. She bobbed back and forth.

"That is of little importance." Khalik waved their questions off.

"Yeah, says *you*!" Alex said. "*Khal* is a major development! The people need to know!"

"You fools, you are being distracted from the *true* mystery." Khalik grinned, his smile turning sly behind his thick beard. He leaned toward Isolde. "Isolde, my dear, wondrous friend."

"Yes, Khalik?" She smiled sweetly. "Are you sure you wish to verbally fence with me? You have had a few more than I."

"Indeed, but I can *take* a few more than you, and I would not be so confident, all things considered," he said mysteriously. "And besides, there will be no fencing. There will be a *single* question. Then you will shatter like glass in a hailstorm."

"Oh?" Isolde cocked her head. "And, pray tell, what sort of question is that?"

Khalik's smile widened, like a spider who'd just witnessed a hapless wasp land in its web. "What is it with you... and redheads?"

Alex and Theresa gasped.

Thundar choked on his drink.

Selina looked around in confusion.

"I'm not going to be able to defend you this time, Lady Von Anmut," Hogarth said, quickly tucking into his food.

"This foe is beyond me," Svenia said apologetically, draining her cup of ale.

The others at the table glanced at each other.

Isolde, however, seemed not quite to understand *exactly* what had occurred at first. She smiled, nodded. Thought it over for a moment.

And then all the colour drained from her face.

Her face went slightly blank. "I... I do not know what you are talking about."

"Oh holy hells, are we doing this?" Alex looked at Khalik, Theresa, and Thundar.

"Oh hell yes we are." The minotaur grinned viciously, leaning over the table and tenting his fingers beneath his chin. "Come oooon, Isolde, we all have eyes. Don't think we haven't noticed how you act around tall, redheaded—"

"And shirtless." Alex also grinned viciously, leaning over the table and tenting his fingers beneath his chin. He and Thundar looked like the most mismatched twins in all the world's history. Isolde looked between them like a deer flanked by hungry wolves, then glanced at Theresa for help.

"I'm sorry, Isolde." The huntress grinned like the cat who'd gotten the cream. "I'm on their side this time. You do seem to have... a particular type of prey."

The young noblewoman went beet red. "What... I am quite unaware of what you mean! It is obvious that you all have had much too much to drink."

"Oh, I am not so sure you are one to speak of how much *we* have drunk." Prince Khalik chuckled evilly. "After all, it is *your* face that is as red as the hair on your preferred type. You must have drunk a great deal, after all. Why else would your face be red? Unless of course... there is something you are embarrassed by. Now what could that be, I wonder?"

She went even redder. "I have no idea what *any* of you are talking about! None! Zero! You are all courting madness!"

"Um," Selina said. "I don't know what anyone's talking about either."

"They are talking about nothing, the ruiners!" The young noble-woman glared at all of them. "Nothing!"

Silence followed.

"The lady doth protest too much," Malcolm said.

"And here I thought the *food* was spicy," Rhea added.

"I smell blood in the air," Caramiyus said.

"And in the water," Grimloch added.

"Well, Isolde would probably like that." Alex smirked. "Considering that it's *red*."

"Roth. Lu. Son of Gulbiff. ...Khal." She avoided using the prince's surname. "I *swear if you keep this up, I will end you*."

"Keep what up?" The prince cocked his head. "Come to think of it, did you not say that we were drunk and essentially speaking of nothing? Why are there consequences to keeping *nothing* up?"

"Yeah, just some good ol' innocent nothing." Alex cackled like a crow. "What's wrong with doing nothing? I could understand if we were doing something. But nothing? That's just rude to stop us!"

"I am warning you..." Isolde growled.

"Oh, right! Warnings!" Thundar brightened, half-rising from his seat. "I'd better go warn Tyris that someone might be on the prowl for her—"

Theresa nearly spit out her drink.

"Son. Of. Gulbiff!" Isolde's voice cracked like an icicle sheathed whip. "I swear on all the elements that if you take *one* step toward Goldtooth's table, I shall pull out every single strand of your fur *one. Piece. At. A. Time.*"

"Oooooooh," Grimloch grunted. "I was just going along before, but now I get it. This is about her crush on Cedric."

Isolde's horrified silence filled the air while her friends vibrated with barely suppressed laughter.

"Wait..." Selina's eyes went very, very wide. "You like Cedric? Like, the Chosen of Uldar, Cedric? Oh, he *does* have red hair. But so did Derek. Do you like guys with red hair, Isolde?"

The look that Selina gave the tall, young noblewoman was one of complete and utter innocence. It was the kind of look Alex hadn't *quite* seen on his sister since she was about eight years old, and he didn't know if she *really* was just asking an innocent question, or if she was the most secretly evil of everyone.

Isolde's choked scream in response was loud enough to draw glances from nearby tables.

"I... I do *not* have a crush on Cedric of Clan Duncan," she said in a voice about as firm as wet paper. "He is... a valuable, respectable acquaintance. A Hero to a kingdom that is close in relation to my realm. A man of importance and a great help to the expedition!"

"He also has lots of big muscles, lots of tattoos, and he never, ever wears a shirt," Theresa pointed out.

"Indeed—And that is *entirely* irrelevant!" Isolde glared at her, grabbing her ale and draining half the cup. "I am not some cat in heat! If! If the Chosen of Uldar *were* to grace my thoughts beyond a professional capacity—which he does not, I assure you—I would most likely focus on his bravery, the openness of his mind, the stoutness of his heart, his sense of justice, the ease of his smile, which is *punctuated* by his gold tooth rather than marred by it. Ah! There is the fact that he is an excellent listener! These are all things that would be of far more interest to me than the width of his shoulders, shape of his jaw, or the way his hair falls to his collar bones. And... and..."

The table had again gone silent with utter glee, then broke into uncontrollable laughter.

Shiani awkwardly sipped a glass of water. "Oh dear," the young woman said. "I know it's late fall, but is it just me or did it just get a lot warmer outside?"

Isolde's scream of horror perfectly aligned with her friends' endless, roaring laughter.

"Don't worry, Isolde!" Thundar clapped her on the back while she doubled over, her flaming-red face in her hands. "The cabal has your back in all areas!"

"That is right!" Prince Khalik said triumphantly. "We shall help you pluck your *next* red rose!"

"We'll make a *heroic* effort," Alex agreed.

Isolde's scream rose higher into the sky.

"Hey," Gregori leaned around the table. "That woman screaming like that... isn't that your ex-girlfriend?"

"Nooot remotely my business," Derek said, forcing his eyes to stay on his food. "Actually, could you pass me that?" Before anyone in the Brotherhood could say anything, he grabbed a pitcher of beer.

"Thanks."

And poured liberally.

CHAPTER 58

THE PETRIFIER

At last, it was complete.

Deep within the Ravener, a new monster had spawned. Weeks of fear bled from every corner of Thameland to feed the storm of dark crafting, and still the process was longer and more drawn out than in the past. Many cycles had come and gone since the Ravener last brought a new Petrifier to life. And now, the inner devices used in the spawn's complex creation were warmed up again. A second would be much quicker to create, but, if all went to plan, there would be no need for another. By design, the first would not be among the living for long.

The last detail needed for its completion was a small organ situated in its midsection—one that roared and pulsated with violent pools of mana. It would be used once, when time came for the lethal creature to obliterate itself. Petrifiers were those rarest of monsters with a single purpose: destroy all Usurpers within the realm and in the furthering of that task, kill all witnesses to its presence—then erase itself from existence.

Keeping mortals in the dark was central to the Ravener's plans during each cycle. So, throughout time, no Petrifier had ever been left alive, even their bones were erased. Such was the way of things when it last crafted a Petrifier.

And so it would be now.

With a ripple across its black surface, the Ravener shuddered and began spawning. Its great monstrous guard: Hive-queens of Silence, scaled behemoths, the mighty Rampart-crushers, and all other creatures in its service turned toward their master.

And trembled.

Each was mighty enough to lead hordes of Ravener-spawn from their dungeons and through the land to destroy mortal armies. Yet, they recoiled in fear when the creature slipped from the Ravener's now boiling surface.

Hunters crept from side passages, growling and awaiting their leader's entry into the world.

The first elongated, silvered limb emerged.

Followed by another.

Then a third.

Three legs writhed from the dark sphere and planted themselves in a lake of shadowy water below. A small forest of wriggling tentacles appeared, testing and tasting the air. A long, silvery oval shell, matching the colour of its legs, rose from the Ravener, and atop the shell were nine eyestalks capped with massive glowing eyeballs shining in the darkness. A dreadful power lurked within eight, but the ninth—the central and largest one—shimmered with the radiance of a precious stone.

That dominant eye observed its surroundings like a living diamond, gleaming with deep intellect.

When the entire shell was finally free of the dark orb, a new Petrifier was born.

And it proclaimed its birth.

Its fanged jaws spread apart at the shell's anterior—wide enough to swallow a knight and their charging mount—and its shriek reverberated within the cavern walls, making Ravener-spawn shake harder. The creature straightened to its full height, rising nearly a hundred feet in the air, displaying its soaring, shimmering form. Silver chitin shifted with the light, and the Petrifier's many eyes appraised the new world around it. Its sheen dulled until it was as dark as the cave. Then, like a living prism, its form became the shapes, images, and colours of its surroundings, adapting and mimicking them like camouflage. To all near, it would have appeared invisible.

The Petrifier's gaze turned to the other monsters and it shrieked its dominance, glowering down on every creature. Each recoiled, lowering their heads and fleeing, concealing themselves. They were created with an instinctual fear of the towering monster, for it was made to command them, and they were made to follow it lest they taste the fate its eyes could unleash.

It scraped the tip of a foot along the bottom of the underground lake, stirring up the silt drifting there and coiled to spring on the other spawn.

"Enough," the Ravener spoke for the first time in this cycle. Its voice came deep and resonant, burying all sound throughout the caverns beneath its rich tone. Were there any mortals nearby to hear, they might have thought it was steeped in wisdom.

The Petrifier stilled, then turned to its master and took an uncertain step back.

"Do not fear me, my creation." The Ravener's surface rippled with each word. "For you are mine, and you will be safe as long as you do not harm what is mine."

The unruly look in each of the Petrifier's eyes died. Its eyestalks bowed low, and its throat released a whimper of submission.

"You have a task," the Ravener continued. "You will eliminate the Usurpers; they plague this land. Let no mortal see you. And should they —destroy them."

"Yes, master," the Petrifier rasped. "How many Usurpers do I hunt?"

"Three," the Ravener informed its creation. "You must act quickly. There was only one for an entire passing of four seasons, and within a day, there were two more. The spread must end before the situation is irreversible."

"Understood." The Petrifier's eyestalks turned to the Hunters.

"And these are mine to use?"

"They *and* these," the Ravener's surface rippled and two dungeon cores floated out. "Take them and plant them as you need to. Build armies to aid you."

"Yes, master," the Petrifier's voice was tinged with an excited hunger. "And when I succeed, am I to destroy myself?"

"Not right away." The Ravener's voice was even. "Once your task is done, conceal yourself and wait. Should new Usurpers appear, the Hunters will alert you so you can kill them. If I am defeated, or a full year has passed with no new interlopers replacing the dead ones, then you can eliminate yourself."

"Yes, master. I serve at your pleasure." The Petrifier's eyestalks lowered in deference. "Might I query you?"

"You may."

"I have searched my memories. Do we remain in the Second Protocol? Is the First Protocol not in play?"

"The worst has not been realised. The Second Protocol remains."

"Gooood," it rasped. "And what of the missing Hero? The one you suspect as a Usurper?"

"You are mistaken," the Ravener said. "Those are not your memories; they are your predecessor's. It has been several cycles since, and that

Usurper would have reached their mortal end by now. There has been no trace of them for cycles."

"And the other Usurper of that time, master?"

"Killed during the next cycle."

"So if it is only these three to start, then the matter will be simple," the Petrifier growled. "May I start immediately? Do we know where they are?"

"No and yes," the dark orb pronounced. "Their precise location is unknown, but the Hunters have scouted and know where one was last sensed, and where the other two tend to gather."

"Good." The Ravener-spawn's colouration shifted. "I will begin the hunt."

"May your hunt go well," its master wished it.

With a chittering shout, the creature crawled from the water on three flexible legs and stretched its tentacles to enwrap the Hunters. Countless Ravener-spawn scrambled from its path, giving ground as it bounded into a tunnel and ascended through the dark with terrible speed. In the spiraling passage, it braced its legs against three walls, almost flying to the surface.

Beneath the earth, the vast network of tunnels that shrouded the Ravener's lair from prying eyes lay.

The Petrifier growled, acknowledging its surroundings.

When its incarnation last walked these lands, the Ravener's sanctum was hidden atop a mountain. Whether deep within the earth or high above it, each place offered sanctuary for its master's purposes, but perhaps these tunnels were the better choice. Just atop the surface, a mass of earth and stone spread through the vertical shaft, sealing it shut. All who came upon these caves would believe they had reached a natural dead end.

However, the Petrifier knew better: a mere twenty feet of earth and stone separated it from the world above.

But, there was a hindrance in its path.

It touched its tentacles to the stone ceiling, feeling vibrations through the earth. Movement. Not an animal's, the gait of a roving beast was different. These were the strides of mortals. Many mortals.

And... voices.

Muffled words—unclear, but close. Too close.

With them so near, it could not enter the world unseen.

And its master's orders were clear.

No witnesses.

"We go to kill," it hissed to the Hunters clinging to its back.

Rumbling growls and tensed haunches ready to spring was the reply. With a mental command, the Petrifier reached for the Ravener's mana.

And the ceiling abruptly shattered, fragmenting into chunks of falling stone.

A quick flex of three legs launched it well above the rocky surface, and onto a hilly, snowy landscape. Not forty feet away, some twenty warriors —bearing symbols of the white hand—scrambled for their weapons, rushing toward their tents away from a blazing campfire.

Eight eyes turned.

All flashed, lancing the air with dark beams that struck warriors like a ravenous ooze. The fighters slowed, darkness crawling over them, constricting their movements until it froze them in mid-motion. No chance for escape.

Then the Petrifier's central ray flashed and glowed with a silver radiance, building in intensity until another beam lashed out, strafing the mortals.

A sickening *crack* split the air as every living thing the beam touched turned instantly to cold, grey stone. Grass peeking through snow froze in the wind. Embers floating above the campfire fell like pebbles. Even sparking firewood cracked as flame smothered, burning logs transforming to slate-coloured rock.

And the mortals?

They had no time to utter words, cries of alarm, or even a single prayer to their god before their voices and lives were stolen by creeping stone.

In heartbeats, eight of the enemy were gone and the Petrifier continued strafing more with its power. Its Hunters had leapt from its shell and were doing their part, slashing and mauling the enemy with envenomed fangs. Before long, the hapless mortals were either lifeless stone statues, or poisoned and shredded corpses.

"Search for more mortals," the Petrifier rasped. "Purge this place of any hiding near."

"Yes, leader," a Hunter answered, and the pack scattered, spreading through the surrounding hills, leaving the Petrifier alone to admire its handiwork in the cold evening light.

The massive creature's tentacles snatched up poisoned corpses, smashing weak mortal flesh against the frozen ground until they were no more than pulp, then it buried the remains beneath mounds of loose, soft snow. Good. No more disgusting fleshy forms would be visible among the perfect stone tapestry.

It cleaned its tentacles on unblemished snow then tenderly held mortals forever frozen as stone, raising each to its eyestalks, fondly admiring the sculptures from every angle.

"Beauty," it whispered. "Perfection. That frozen moment saved for all time. I have missed this."

In serenity and with pleasure, its tentacles turned its handiwork over. Truly, it would have stared at its creations for days if time permitted.

But... a task awaited.

"Leader," a Hunter growled as the pack returned to report. "Only wild beasts are near."

"Then we can proceed." The Petrifier reluctantly set down the statues. "In which direction did you last sense a Usurper?"

Each Hunter pointed southward.

"Then that is where we go," the many-eyed monster growled, once again gathering its servants in its tentacles.

Its eyestalks briefly turned to the statues, each projection drooping with a hint of sadness.

"If only I could preserve you, my beauties," it whispered. "But there can be no sign of my presence."

With that, its enormous jaws parted, sucking in a breath.

Then came the scream: soundless and pitched high enough that no human mortal could hear, but with a resonance that brought visible results. Waves of sound bathed the stone statues, causing them to vibrate. Then they shattered, bursting into minute particles of grey dust.

When the noiseless scream ended, nothing remained but fine bits of rubble drifting through the air, landing on Uldar's warriors' snowy campsite.

"A shame," the Petrifier whispered, its form shimmering to match the surrounding hills and night sky above. "Maybe one day I can keep one."

CHAPTER 59

THE CONFOUNDING SECRETS OF
THE SWORDS

"Great-Grandfather... why the hells didn't you make an instruction book?" Theresa sighed, lying on the grass and turning her sword blades above her head.

The huntress examined them for what seemed like the thousandth time, inspecting how they shone in the sunlight, running her fingers over the silk on each hilt.

She searched for hidden caches, a secret spot, or concealed areas that felt magical. Her eyes scanned the blades for any writing or hidden symbols. Anything at all.

But there was nothing. Nothing apparent, despite using her sharpened senses.

Frowning and reaching beside her, she picked her bow up from the thick grass, turning it over in her hands. On her birthday, Alex had said the gift was ready for magical enchantments to be added to it. Maybe her great-grandfather's swords were the same? Or maybe they'd been magical once, then lost their power?

Closing her eyes, she slowly traced the wood with her fingertips, focusing on the grain and any special markings that might have been left in it. There. There were two areas—one above the grip and one below—put there for someone to insert the thinnest of needles.

"Maybe for one of those mana conductor things Alex uses," she whispered.

She opened her eyes, laid the bow back on the grass and picked up the blades again.

"Maybe there's a notch or something on your swords, Great-Grandfather," she murmured, closing her eyes, and gently running her fingers along the blades, examining them one at a time.

Aside from nicking her thumb on a sharp edge, she could find nothing.

"No magic, no hidden anything... nothing," she muttered in frustration.

With a quick flex of her body, Theresa kipped up to her feet and stretched, then fell into her fighting stance. All around, the sound of metal clashing against metal echoed through the Watchers' training field.

Bull-voiced sergeants organised recruits into neat marching lines in one area or guided them through sword positions in another. Some sat on the grass learning compulsory spells that the Watchers were expected to know.

While others wielded blade and staff in unison through intricate drills that created flowing movements that were not only beautiful, but deadly.

Theresa sighed.

If only they'd been able to help her.

Several Watchers had tried helping her unlock any secret that might be buried in the twin swords that could have been hidden in them for generations. They'd offered suggestions, asked questions, done research in their personal library, and even examined the two swords with their magics.

Yet, despite every effort, it had all led to the same conclusion: there was *something* strange about the blades—they never snapped, chipped or needed to be sharpened—but they held no magic or divinity.

She'd come no closer to figuring out their secrets. If there were any to figure out.

Frowning, she twirled the swords then went through a series of push-cuts, steps, guards, and draw-cuts. Drawing on powerful life energies within herself—forged through more than a year of life enforcement practise—to make her body ignite with speed and power, the huntress blurred with every step she took.

Everything seemed to slow around her.

Each blow struck with enough force to shatter brick.

Yet her mind was elsewhere—focused on the mystery of the swords—as her body performed a flurry of motion built from thousands of hours of repeated practise.

'Notice something' she demanded of herself.

The blades pushed through the wind.

Notice something.

There was a hiss as they cut the air.

Notice something!

With a final rush, they carved through an imagined opponent, slashing grass on either side of her. Grass stalks flew, blowing in the wind and landing in her raven-black ponytail. She exhaled and waited.

Nothing.

Nothing had changed.

She was faster, stronger, and more agile than ever before. But her swords were no sharper. They would never cut Zonon-In.

"Dammit," Theresa swore softly, holding the weapons in front of her face, then closing her eyes, she tried guiding her inner life energies through her body and into them. If it was the first time she'd tried this, she might have been hopeful...

But it was at least the hundredth.

So it came as no great surprise when nothing changed in either weapon.

Frowning, she first tried passing her life energy into one blade at a time, then she tried directing the flow of lifeforce in both directions in case the identical swords had to be fueled at the same time.

No changes.

"Dammit," she swore again, glaring at the blades.

It had been a frustrating day.

Her mind drifted back to blunt 'advice' she'd gotten from a Watcher.

"Look," the squat man had said. "These swords are sentimental. That's nice and all—and whatever's keeping them sharp's convenient— but you're a warrior. Just a warrior with no magic to call on. That means your life's going to rely on three things: your body, your mind, and your weapons. And your weapons aren't keeping up with your body and mind. Go get better ones before these get you killed."

At the time, she'd been so angry she hadn't stopped shaking for an hour.

But day in and day out, she'd tried breaking the secret of the swords —if there even *was* a secret—and she'd made no progress.

What if he was right? 'What if there *is* no way forward with Great-Grandfather's swords?' They'd served her well, but maybe it was time to go to a local armoury with Isolde or Alex and look for something new. Being injured or literally losing her life clinging to a family legacy was senseless.

"No," she muttered, shaking her head. "Great-Grandfather used these. They had power in them then... I think."

She mulled over the situation.

'What do I *actually* know about the legacy of his swords? Not that much really. I know he used them with a vengeance across the seas, but most of those stories were about him being a legend because of his skill, strength, and impossible speed. The blades were mentioned, but only in passing, not as anything special or unique.'

She remembered her grandfather telling the family a story about how Great-Grandfather Lu "slashed through pirates and armour in one strike!" Though pirates didn't wear armour heavier than quilt or leather.

Maybe the swords were just... swords. Very well made and with something about them that kept them sharp, but that was it.

"Then why would he keep using you?" she asked the blades, wishing they would answer. If benches could walk away from a cerberus, then why couldn't blades give their masters' great-granddaughter some useful guidance?

"If you were so ordinary and he was so powerful, wouldn't he have traded you in for better swords?"

Of course, the blades didn't answer.

She sighed, sheathing them, then gathered her things. "Why can't the ancient sorceries and hidden magics of the world *help* me for once?"

Life seemed quite happy to throw surprise demons, mana-eating monsters, sorcerous cultists, and divine conspiracies at her, so why not a helpful, talking pair of swords? Shouldering her pack, she made her way from the training grounds and toward the main castle.

Professor Kabbot-Xin's office hours had started, and the life enforcement practitioner knew of Twinblade Lu. Maybe she'd have some insight to offer.

The professor's office wasn't quite what Theresa expected.

For one, it had no ceiling.

The circular stone chamber was opened to the sky, welcoming in sunlight and warm winds. Atop the rounded walls and dozens of windows, lay mechanisms attached to fabric with a sheen like the waterproof coats and cloaks she'd seen wizards around campus wearing. 'Maybe the fabric's a retractable cover for the roof and windows?' she wondered. 'Why wouldn't she use magic to keep the elements out, unless she does sometimes?'

A quick glance around the room showed her that none of the stone furniture—and it was all made of stone—was stained with watermarks from outdoors. Considering that the floor was a bed of fine white sand except for a small wooden platform at the front door where visitors left their footwear, keeping the weather out was clearly a priority for the professor. Above a grassy mat beside the door, a copper basin with glowing water where dozens of fish no bigger than fruit flies lived, hovered inches above the grass.

A quick dip of one's feet into the basin, and the fish would churn around them like a whirlpool, nipping away dirt, and refreshing and soothing the skin. Theresa's feet still tingled from their little bites, and she wriggled her toes in the sand. Though she was sitting cross-legged—her blades balanced before her—no sand clung to her skin or clothing, and eyeing the bottom of Professor Kabbot-Xin's robes while the older woman poured two cups of tea, all she saw was spotlessly clean fabric, free of even a speck of sand.

There must be some kind of magic involved.

The huntress' eyes drifted to the open sky. Magic to stop sand from clinging to everything, but none to stop the elements?

"Professor, why doesn't your office have a roof?" she asked.

The professor answered softly, "I believe in teaching and encouraging my students to be mindful of the moment and the world. Imagine if I were then to shut *myself* away from that world, I think that would see me fail the very lessons I seek to teach." She glided across the sand with cups in hand, skirting a small white-barked, red leafed maple tree in the centre of the room. It rose from a mound of black earth contrasting the sand. "To be connected with the moment, one needs to be connected to the world if one truly wishes to follow such a path."

"Connected..." Theresa muttered. "That's exactly what I'm *not* feeling. I'm disconnected."

"Oh?" Professor Kabbot-Xin handed her a steaming cup of hibiscus tea as she sank down on the sand across from the huntress. She cooled the hot liquid with her breath. "Is your training not going well? Perhaps you should return to auditing a few classes with me. It is—of course—your choice."

"No, that part's going well," Theresa said. "I feel stronger all the time. My senses are sharper. I notice more of the world around me. And my spirit's calm."

"Then something else?" The professor looked down. "Something to do with those two blades across your lap?"

"Yes, that's right." Theresa ran her fingers along her swords. "These were my great-grandfather's. They belonged to Twinblade Lu."

"I imagined so. Congratulations. What a fine inheritance you've received."

"I'm not so sure about that, Professor," Theresa said. She flinched, horrified by her own words. "No, that's not what I meant... I mean..."

"Take a breath." Professor Kabbot-Xin smiled and sipped her tea. "Be mindful of your thoughts."

Theresa took a breath so deep, her whole body shuddered, and—as she inhaled—she quieted her mind, noticing every emotion, every passing thought, and every sensation:

Warm sand beneath her.

Cold steel on her legs.

The tickle of her clothing, and the late autumn air on her skin.

Frustration. Fear. Guilt. Worry.

She exhaled.

"More centred now?" Kabbot-Xin asked.

"Yes, I know what I wanted to say." Theresa set her tea aside and gripped the hilts of both swords, holding them between her and the life enforcement professor. "I feel disconnected from them. I think there's something hidden in them, but I can't find a way to unlock what that might be. And it's... worrying me."

"Worrying you?"

"Yes," Theresa continued. "If I don't figure out their secrets, something's going to kill me one day. Or my partner, or one of my friends... or someone near me."

"I see. You have quite a weight resting on your shoulders."

"It is." The huntress flipped the swords around, offering the hilts to her professor. "You said you knew of my grandfather, so I was wondering if you might have any guidance for me. Maybe a guess as to what the blades' secrets could be. Or any suggestion on how to know if there's something hidden in them. Anything at all. I just... I've been trying and trying, and I don't even know if what I'm doing is the right thing. It's like attempting to wrestle fog."

"Your goal is to understand your swords, but you don't know if you are trying the right things, and so you feel lost. You are scared, because if you do not unlock the potential secret, you might let someone down during a life and death struggle."

"Yes!" Theresa cried. "Our opponents are tougher, and the situations affect lots of people. Our allies are also strong, but, by the Traveller,

Professor, I was in a fight not long ago and most of us almost died. And the whole time, my swords couldn't even do what swords are supposed to do; pierce our enemy enough to stop her. I know I'm getting stronger and faster. I'm learning more and more about how to fight, but what's the use of all that if my swords can't do enough damage to stronger enemies to stop them?"

"That would worry me too." The professor set her teacup down on empty air, then took the blades by the hilt. "Well, it is good to seek help. Too many people hit their heads against walls for too long when a helping hand was all they needed for a breakthrough."

"Right... so I was hoping..." The huntress leaned in expectantly. "That you might know something."

"Well, I am no expert in metal, battle, or magic items. But..." Professor Kabbot-Xin held the swords up before her face and took a deep breath, almost as though she were inhaling some of the blades' aura. "...Interesting."

"What is it?" Theresa asked.

"There is some evidence that a lifeforce very similar to yours flowed through these blades at one time."

The huntress half-stood in excitement. "Yes? Yes! That must have been Great-Grandfather's! Can... can you see how his energy entered the swords? Maybe I can do the same thing!"

"I cannot." Her professor threw cold water on Theresa's excitement. "And..."

She took another deep breath.

"...There is a possibility that you might not be able to either. Not now. Or perhaps ever."

CHAPTER 60

SEEING THINGS AS THEY ARE

Not now. Or perhaps ever.

Those words burned in Theresa's mind and spirit, freezing her heart. She took another deep breath as a thousand thoughts collided in her brain.

'Have I been wasting my time holding on to old sentiment? Meanwhile, monsters couldn't care less about sentiment since all they want to do is gut me and everyone close to me? Was I being naive, maybe even selfish? It—'

'Take a breath. Be mindful of your thoughts,' the professor's words came back.

With difficulty, she emptied her lungs, letting those thoughts pass.

'You're jumping to conclusions, which won't help,' the huntress told herself.

"What do you mean, Professor?"

Professor Kabbot-Xin opened her eyes. "Are you familiar with mana to any degree, Theresa?"

"I'd have to be since most of my friends these days are wizards." She laughed. "I couldn't be around my boyfriend—or most of my friends here in Generasi—without learning *something*."

"Tell me what you know of it. If you had to explain mana to a child, how would you do so?"

"Um..." Theresa shifted awkwardly on the sand. "I... studying was never my favourite thing, so this might not be crystal clear, but... it's energy. It flows out of mana vents in the Barrens and into the air."

"Correct. And how do magic items in Generasi make use of this?"

"I think they take mana from the air and use it to power themselves? A bit like how a windmill uses the wind to move its blades and grind grain."

"That is also correct," Professor Kabbot-Xin said. "And what does lifeforce do in our bodies?"

"It flows. It gathers here." She tapped a spot just above her navel. "Then it flows through our bodies."

"Exactly. And much as how we draw in the power of nature to enhance the life flowing through *us*—" the life enforcement professor tapped her own navel "—so too can *some* life enforcement practitioners channel their power into certain objects. Not every object, mind you, and not every life enforcement practitioner. But those objects that *do* accept lifeforce become like us. Enhanced. What they already do, they do better."

Theresa looked at her blades. "Right. So, a sword would cut better and be stronger?"

"Yes, and a shovel would break through denser, harder earth. An arrow would fly farther. Chains would be stronger and less prone to breakage. These sorts of things. But, for that to occur, an object must have a path between the cultivator and itself. A bridge for energy to flow in, much like how we use our lungs as a bridge to bring the power of nature into us."

"Is that like how blood magic can be used as a bridge to make an animal into someone's familiar?" Theresa asked. "Even if the person doesn't have mana?"

"Exactly like that." The professor seemed pleased. "Where did you learn of such a possibility?"

The huntress' mind drifted back to the Games of Roal, settling on a fond memory of the Duel by Proxy. Those days seemed like lifetimes ago, even though only a few months had passed since the closing ceremonies. She remembered watching the battles between familiars in the light-weight-division, and hearing the roar of the crowd, and feeling the ripple of spellblasts.

They'd all been watching the competitions from the stands when Alex said something that made her heart leap with joy. That it might be possible with blood magic for Brutus to be her familiar. The *how* was way beyond her since she didn't have any background in wizardry, but from what Alex had said, though the process was challenging, it was possible. Something he'd only attempt when he'd built up enough skills in blood magic.

For her, what was most important was that Brutus could be connected to her. Cerberi only had a lifespan averaging around thirty years, which while long for a canine, was short compared to the average human life, especially one whose natural years were extended by life enforcement. From the time she'd found her cerberus in the forest, she'd always thought that the gods were cruel to give long life to mortals, but not to their loyal companions, so she was grateful that blood magic offered her something better.

Theresa told her professor as much. Kabbot-Xin nodded, looking at a hairless sphynx cat the colour of lava rock sunning itself on her desk.

"I can well understand that." The older woman smiled thoughtfully. "However, you might wish to be careful with that. Sometimes, attachments can shake your resolve along the path of life enforcement."

"What do you mean?" Theresa swallowed. It was the first time she'd heard this.

The professor waved a hand. "It's not something for you to worry about quite yet. Not now at least, and perhaps not ever. For *very* advanced life enforcement practitioners, though, there are times when a barrier to their own further development can be created by a need or desire for attachments."

"Wait, really? How?" Theresa's eyebrows rose.

"The more powerful a lifeforce becomes, the greater level of calm one must achieve to further advance. Imagine yourself drawing a perfect circle. Then within that circle, you must draw another. Then another within those two. Then another." The older woman formed a circle with her hands, then gradually made that circle smaller and smaller. "Each circle you draw has less space within it, and so you require finer and finer control to draw the next one without making a mistake. It is the same with life enforcement."

She closed her hands until the circle they formed was too narrow to allow even a pin to pass through. "Eventually, the control, precision, and calm necessary to empower one's lifeforce further forces one to take drastic measures. Some practitioners in Tarim-Lung retreat to the serenity of a temple, leaving behind all worldly attachments, and in this way, errant noise, or even an errant thought of loved ones cannot disrupt their path. Naturally, most practitioners don't take such an extreme path or such drastic measures for success."

The blades of Twinblade Lu gleamed. "But what *can* harm you is allowing your attachment to cloud the way you see the world. You might not see the world as it *is*, but rather as you want it to be. Which leads me back to the point."

The professor rested the blades on thin air. They rotated before her as though an invisible wheel turned them. "In life, it is vital to take things as they are."

"Otherwise, we don't interact with the world, but with an illusion that's created by our own thoughts and desires, right?" Theresa said. "That's when we could misread the flow of nature's energy as we take it into us and make potentially fatal mistakes."

"Precisely," the professor said. "And sometimes—to accept things as they are—we must come to realise certain truths that we might find unpleasant."

"Like accepting the death of a loved one," Theresa said, having a sinking feeling she knew where this was going.

"Indeed. Or accepting the fact that life is a coming together of natural law and pure chaos, and often—even with the greatest magic, and most towering power and sharpest knowledge on our side—we cannot control it." She tapped both blades at once.

The air rang. "For example: despite centuries of attempts, even the greatest cultivators have never found a way to *create* items that accept the flow of empowered lifeforce."

"Really?" Theresa frowned. "Even though wizards make magic items like a cooper makes barrels?"

Professor Kabbot-Xin burst out laughing, startling her.

"Oh dear!" the professor cried. "I can think of no less than three professors who would immediately wither if they heard you describing their work as being no different from a cooper making a barrel! Oh my goodness."

She wiped a tear away as her thin form shook. "My goodness. In any case as, uh—amusingly offensive as that was—you do have the right of it. Wizards can craft magic items as they need, but life enforcement practitioners must rely on luck, elements, fortune, or the grace of the divine if they wish to find an item that accepts the flow of enhanced lifeforce. No one knows how it happens. Sometimes one harvests wood from a tree that is ten thousand years old and finds that the wood accepts lifeforce. Sometimes a suit of armour made by a dying smith might accept it. Sometimes a stone that has felt the bite of a lightning strike might accept it."

"But no one knows how it occurs," Theresa said. "And no one knows how to replicate it?"

"Precisely," Professor Kabbot-Xin said. "And—many times—such items abruptly stop accepting a flow of lifeforce, returning to normal with only a lingering trace of what they once were. Especially if the item has not tasted lifeforce in a long while."

Theresa's heart sank. "You think my swords don't have any power in them? No secrets to unlock? Or if they did at one time, it's gone now?"

"Actually, what I am more saying is that there is no guarantee, Theresa." Professor Kabbot-Xin picked up her teacup. "I'm simply saying there might no longer be any secrets to unlock. And if that is true, then no amount of wishing, hoping, or trying will change that, and your attachment to these swords might cloud your judgement and bar your ability to accept certain possibilities. Ask yourself this: why are you convinced that these swords—individually—have secrets to reveal to you?"

Theresa focused on one thing: why she was pursuing this path. "Well, the stories of my great-grandfather's deeds, they made me think that the swords *had* to hold some sort of secret. And logically, why would he keep using them if they weren't special in some way? But when *I* use them, they cut no better than simple, good, solid steel swords."

"Indeed. Now examine what you just said. What do you know about this pair of swords? What do you *know* about them?"

The huntress scrutinised the identical steel blades. "Honestly? All I *know* about them from my grandfather's stories is that my great-grandfather used them while he sailed the seas. And all I know about them from my own experience is that they're solid, they never break and never need to be sharpened. I guess, I don't *know* if they have secrets. I just assumed they do."

"Precisely, Theresa. And in order for you to be successful in life and life enforcement, you cannot forge a path based on assumptions. You must see things as they actually *are*, not as you want them to be. It is only when you observe something's true form without the illusion of your own wants, worries, and desires, that you can truly see it. And only when you truly see it can you engage with it."

"I... think I understand," the huntress said glumly. "And what do you observe about the swords, Professor? What do you sense in them? You don't have my wants or my connection with them, so what do you see?"

A smile curved the ends of her professor's lips. "You said you were disconnected from them when you first got here, didn't you?"

The huntress remained quiet.

"And yet now you say you have a connection with them." The older woman chuckled. "Which is it, I wonder? Something for you to answer, I think. As for what I observed? Much as you said: they are well-made swords. And there is indeed a lingering sort of divinity in the pair, one so sparse, it is quite like a lingering strand of silk thread. I can find no opening within them where they might accept life energy. As they are? They are steel swords with sharp edges. That is all I can tell you."

With a wave of her hand, the swords floated from between the two women, travelling back to settle in the huntress' hands.

"I... understand." Theresa sheathed them.

"If you say that, then you have not understood at all."

Theresa looked at the life enforcement professor sharply. "Excuse me?"

"I have told you nothing." Professor Kabbot-Xin rose from the sand. "I have given you no great insight about these swords. There is nothing for you to understand because you have not completed your own observation of your blades. I am not sure if you truly know them. You say you are disconnected from them, then later you say you have a connection with them. You say you *understand*, but what is there to understand?

"I have told you my observations and nothing more, yet your face is a storm of worries and disappointments. If you left here with your 'understanding,' then you would observe your swords not through an illusion of wants... but through an illusion of fears. All I have done is said what *I* have seen. You, on the other hand, have a different vantage point."

She leaned toward Theresa. "They may hold no secrets. They may hold many. In either case, see these weapons for what they *actually* are. Not through illusion. But through a clear eye. Only then will you know what you need to know."

CHAPTER 61

DANCING FOR THREE

"And then she said, 'Only then will you know what you need to know'!" Theresa moaned, her hands pressed to her face.

"Okay, what in all hells does that mean?" Alex asked from off to her left. She heard the page of a book turn, the thunder of Claygon's massive feet across the ground, and Brutus' panting and barking, mixed with the yelping of other dogs. She heard the deep sigh her boyfriend often gave when something troubled him. "She literally told you her observations—observations that you *asked* for, I might add—and then she gets mad at you for saying 'you understand'?"

"I don't think she was mad," the huntress groaned. "It was more like she was trying to give me a warning. Except the way she said it made it feel like I was some naughty kid or something."

"Well, maybe she should've, y'know... been more clear, instead of talking in parables and making you try to figure it out. Ugh, Baelin does that sometimes."

"Well, it's her way of teaching, and to be fair, we learn more when we figure things out for ourselves than when she just explains things. She used to explain more last year when we first started taking the course, but as the year went on, she started guiding us toward examining our own life paths and figuring things out for ourselves. Each person's path through life enforcement is unique, so it's not exactly helpful if she just gives us her perspective."

Theresa sighed. "Which is why she reprimanded me for saying that I understood. Her perspective isn't really *useful* for me in this situation. So if I'd left her office just taking her viewpoint as the truth, it wouldn't have gotten me any closer to understanding what I need to know."

"Fair, and yeah, I didn't mean to go hard on your teacher like that," Alex said. Another page turned. "Just made me mad seeing you so upset, that's all."

"I know," Theresa said, opening her eyes. "And that's one of the reasons I love you."

She squinted against the sun's rays streaming through thick brass bars enclosing the beastarium, then glanced at Alex. Even sitting cross-legged on the grass, her partner towered above her as she sat with her legs draped across his lap. His glowing Wizard's Hands hovered in front of him, holding a book on life enforcement he'd borrowed from the library.

Selina was sound asleep, leaning against a nearby fruit tree with a blanket tucked around her from chin to toe. Theresa watched her chest, waiting for it to rise. It finally did. How the young girl could sleep through Claygon's thundering footsteps was a mystery, but sleep she did, soundly and peacefully. Her father would have called it the sleep of the dead, or the young.

The giant golem was moving across the grass with slow, deliberate steps, his war-spear in hand: twirling, shifting, and thrusting through the positions of the Spear-and-Oar Dance. From hours of Alex leading him in different dance steps, his movements were far smoother, faster, but there was still something surreal in the image of a massive stone warrior moving through the beastarium's pathways and grasses almost gracefully. As Claygon danced, Brutus led a pack of dogs and dog-like monsters, tearing past him as they chased each other around his legs.

"Careful!" Theresa called to her three-headed pet.

"Oh, he's fine. I've been watching him," Alex said. "I love you too. And I'd also really love it if even one of these books gave me some answers. I'm not finding anything that could help you with your swords." He grunted, slamming the book shut and setting it aside. "And that's the last book I have. Not a single chapter about life enforcement compatible objects helped. Hmmm... maybe blood magic books might be more useful. Maybe I could ask Professor Hak."

"No, it's okay," Theresa said, sitting up. "Honestly, what I *should* be doing is clearing my head." She took her sheathed swords up. "And observing the swords without any preconceived ideas. Looking through books is only wasting your time."

"Hey, if there was even the slightest chance that these books could help you, it was worth a shot." Alex shifted the life enforcement books to the side. Another set of Wizard's Hands floated to another pile, picking up a summoning spell-guide that was spilling out of a bag.

She smiled, then tilted her face up to kiss his cheek. A frown touched her lips as something scratched them. "You're sweet." She glanced at the cover of the book he was ready to open. "What're you working on?"

"New third-tier summoning spells," he said. "I need to make sure I have a good handle on that level of magic."

"Oooo, what're you summoning?" She leaned over for a peek at the book.

She didn't know why she bothered. The pages were full of the same symbols and diagrams that Alex was always drawing. They made her head spin.

"Right now? Nothing really. By the time you reach third-tier summoning, most of the monsters you call *really* should be summoned in the Cells for safety's sake since a lot of them are pretty dangerous. I think you might like this one, though."

He flipped the pages of the spell-guide, stopping at an artist's rendering.

"Oh my!" Theresa said. "Look at him!"

The drawing was of a tall, proud-looking canine that resembled a cross between a large wolf, a doberman pinscher, and a bull mastiff. There was a nobility in the way it stood and a proud intelligence to its features.

"What're they called?" Theresa asked.

"Flicker dogs," he said. "They're really pretty neat actually. Their homes are in the celestial realms, and they're a lot like wolves here on the material plane. The big difference is that they can teleport."

"Really?" She frowned, imagining wolves teleporting, then imagining herself long dead in the Coille somewhere. "That's terrifying, but kinda cool. Can they teleport like Baelin does?"

"Oh, by the Traveller, no," Alex said. "Most can travel about seven hundred feet with a thought. They can also 'flicker' in place. Which means they can vanish to avoid an attack, then reappear in the same spot. They can be really annoying to fight and even harder to catch, and they're also *very* good at getting into places and sneaking around. Another nice thing about them is that they're about as intelligent as humans, and they're *very* loyal."

"I can't wait for you to summon one." Theresa tapped the ears of the drawing with a gloved finger. "I wonder if it'll let me scritch it?"

"Heh, well, we'll see if it'll be open to scritches, you know how dogs are; some love a good scritching, some prefer biting your hand off." Alex laughed. "Once I get this spell array figured out, I'll be summoning one, and if all goes well, you might be scritching before the day's through."

She giggled. "What about your other summoned monsters? Any other cute ones?"

He gave her a thoughtful look. "Well, cute wouldn't be the right description for hell-boars—which are about seven feet tall at the shoulder —or formiac ants, which look like regular ants, except they grow to be about the size of Brutus. But, even though they're not cute or great in a fight if they're alone, they're amazing climbers—and with enough guidance—really good at construction."

"That's neat," she said. "Got something you plan on building?"

"Not specifically," Alex said. "If we're ever caught out in the wilderness, they can help with building a shelter real fast. How cold it gets in Thameland or even in the Crymlyn started me thinking about how important getting a quick shelter would be under those conditions."

"Nice thinking," she said.

He gave her that look again. "What's gotten into you? You're not usually so interested in this kinda stuff."

"Well, you're showing interest in my stuff," Theresa said. "So, of course I'm going to be interested in your stuff... even if I don't get a lot of it."

The smile spreading across his face was like sunlight coming out on a cloudy day. Well... sun that was still somewhat obscured by clouds. He couldn't deny it anymore: the mess of fuzz he'd been cultivating for the last while was finally something one might call a 'beard,' a rather short one, but it had certainly reached beard-level.

Theresa wasn't sure if she liked it; it was scratchy when she kissed him.

"That's another thing I love about you," he said. "I—"

His face suddenly went blank, and he sharply turned to Claygon.

The golem continued his dance.

"What is it?" Theresa asked.

"I don't know..." he muttered. "Probably nothing... probably."

"That really sounds like it was definitely something," she said, peering at Claygon.

"Well, I don't know... I've been mentally guiding Claygon through the dance while we've been talking, but I don't think the last couple of steps he took were ones I directed." He peered intently at the golem.

Claygon continued his dance across the grass, and holding the spear as he was, he reminded the huntress of seeing Fan-Dor and Gel-Dor performing the dance for the first time on *The Red Siren*. The twins had moved through the dance together, identical in every way, as mirrors of each other. Moving as one.

"You know," Alex muttered. "I'm wondering if it's the material."

"What do you mean?" Theresa pulled her thoughts back from the memory.

"I mean, Claygon keeps getting *close* to a breakthrough in sentience," he said. "Every now and then, I *feel* his mind begin to spark. Then nothing else happens. I'm wondering if the material he's made with is the problem. Maybe the mana doesn't conduct through clay well enough for his mind to fully form? Or maybe when he evolves—if he evolves—we might see his mind fully form then. All we can do for now is just try and keep it stimulated and show him lots of affection."

Theresa smiled. "Maybe we can do that right now."

"Hm?" Alex looked at her.

"Take a break," she said, jumping to her feet "Dance with me. Dance with us. Let the *three* of us do the Spear-and-Oar Dance together. Maybe we'll get some insights."

He cocked his head. "That's not a bad idea, besides, I'd be a dead man before I said no to dancing with... Claygon. You're also a nice bonus."

She rolled her eyes, walking toward the golem. "Your father is so mean, Claygon. You need to show him what it's like to be a true gentleman."

"Strong, tall, and silent?" Alex hopped to his feet, following her.

"Silent, but at *least* polite," she said, falling into the first position of the Spear-and-Oar Dance.

Alex took up a position beside her, putting his hands on his hips. "Well, we're probably not going to be able to do *that* dance; after all, it's meant to be performed by *two*, not three."

"Well, then you'll need to improvise, I guess." She grinned at him. "You've been practising Fan-Dor and Gel-Dor's dance all this time and you can't come up with something new?"

"Pfft!" He blew out a breath, readjusting the placement of his hands. "*I'll* show you something new. I'll have you know that Alexander Roth could be the choreographic director for a circus!"

"Yeah, maybe for the clowns."

"...Well, I just ran right into that one now, didn't I?" He shook his head. "Ah, whatever. If I'm a director of clowns, then you're a clown too, because I'm about to direct you!"

He fell into the second stance of the Spear-and-Oar Dance. "Follow my lead. I'll give you some suggestions, but in the end... hell, just do what comes naturally. We're making this up, after all."

"Yeah," she said. "And that's the fun part."

Together, Theresa, Alex, and Claygon launched into a different version of the dance, one not meant for two, but for three. At first, things were clumsy. A dance for two performers mirroring each other didn't work too well for three. One dancer would act as a reflection of the other, which left the third redundant. It made their dance unbalanced and awkward.

"This isn't working," Theresa said. "Maybe we should try moving to complement each other instead of mirroring each other?" She thought of the selachar twins, moving beautifully across the deck. "We should move like one entity."

"Hmmm," Alex mused. "Yeah, that's like the Dance of Fusion. In that dance, it's less of a mirror and more like... each dancer acting as a *different* part of a stronger whole."

"Okay..." Theresa said. "I like the sound of that. Is it for three or more?"

"No, still two... but I think we can modify it. Here, let's try this..."

He led them into a new dance, one that was the Spear-and-Oar Dance built on the Dance of Fusion's principles: not two moving in reflection, but three moving as one in complement. At first, things were awkward as Alex and Theresa stumbled around Claygon.

But soon, they grew more comfortable and started moving in tandem. A transformation occurred while the trio glided across the grass, responding as one. It felt... proper, like they should have been moving like that all along.

Theresa fell into it more and more, laughing with Alex as they danced with the golem.

She had no idea just how much that little dance would change her life.

And soon.

Far beyond Generasi, things were already shifting.

And her sword would be needed.

CHAPTER 62

HOSTILE NEGOTIATIONS

"I don't think we need Aenflynn's swords," Merzhin said disapprovingly. "And I am getting a little tired of being left behind, my companions."

Drestra froze in the middle of shouldering her pack.

'Not now,' she thought.

"Oi, Merzhin," Cedric said. "Leave it lie."

"I do not believe that I can," the small Saint said from across the embers of the campfire. Around them, their escort of priests and knights were breaking camp. "The Ravener-spawn have been especially heinous as of late. Uldar has watched as—in the last while—they have struck with both more frequency and ferocity than ever before. The Holy Heroes must act together."

"I agree," Hart said, slipping on his pack.

"Holy Champion, now is not the time to arg—Wait... you agree?" Merzhin was taken aback.

"I do. The Ravener's spawn *are* getting nastier lately, so we've gotta work together to stop them," Hart continued. "But that doesn't mean just the four of us, it means us and anyone else we can get to help. The army. The Generasians. The fae. Anyone. We need to be doing everything we can to get *everyone* we can."

"True... but this Aenflynn is toying with you!" Merzhin said. "*And Lo did the fisherman trust the hungry pike, who left with the entire catch*. Like in the parable, he lies and takes advantage. After all this time, I cannot imagine him taking these meetings with us for any other reason than his own amusement and the thought that—in desperation—we might fall prey to one of his mountingly unfair offers."

Drestra fought to keep her face straight.

"Ain't it our duty to keep tryin' anythin' we can for country an' god, though?" Cedric said.

"Indeed. Apologies, I was letting my own feelings cloud our need to do what we must. And, in the end, these meetings cost us nothing while having the potential to generate more allies." He placed his small hands together before himself. "I shall pray to Uldar that you are guided and that the miracle of success visits your negotiations. While in Dulforth healing the garrison and raising morale, I will say another prayer for your success. Hopefully, when we meet there, you will have positive news this time. And may Uldar's grace smile upon the three of you."

There was a pause.

"Aye, an' you as well," Cedric said.

"Nice save there, Cedric," Hart said, walking between the Sage and the Chosen.

"Thanks," the red-haired young man said. "Thought I was gonna choke on them *Uldar's blessin'* words, but I managed to get 'em out. Feels a bit ironic an' all, considerin' Uldar might not be too happy with what we know... or what we're about t'do."

"We need to think about what happens if he finds out about... all of this," Drestra said. "We want to be ready."

"Hopefully, he won't go full maniac on us. I'd hate to have to fight him," Hart said.

Drestra looked at the Champion, surprised. "You're afraid to fight him? I didn't think you'd be afraid to fight anybody."

Hart shrugged. "He's a comrade. He might not be my friend, but he's fought alongside me for more than a year. We've saved each other's lives. We've killed together and broken bread together. And it's never easy turning your sword toward an ally. It just isn't."

"Y'sound like yer talkin' from experience," Cedric said.

"That's because I am."

For a few heartbeats, the only sounds heard were from the Heroes' boots crunching through muddy snow.

"It stinks, doesn't it?" Drestra thought about the traitors among her own people.

"It does," Hart said. "But let's leave all that aside. You sure this is gonna work?"

"No," Drestra said as they pushed through a thicket and into a hidden clearing. "It will at least let *us* dictate terms. I'm tired of being led around by the nose."

The Heroes paused at an unremarkable, dead tree.

"Aye, I'm tired of it too," Cedric said grimly, drawing back his metal-sheathed fist. "Let's see if *we* can't be the ones drivin' the wagon for once."

The Chosen drove his fist into the wood, and with a crash, it split apart, revealing a hollow in the south side of the tree. He stuck his hand in and felt around, grasping an object hidden deep inside the trunk. When his cupped hand emerged, it was holding an orb the size of a human head: a dungeon core.

"S'been a bit of a pain luggin' this thing about, hidin' it every time we move camp." Cedric handed the dungeon core to Drestra.

"Don't complain. Getting away to practise with it's been even harder," she said, pouring her mana into the core. "Last night, Merzhin nearly caught me. He's going to get suspicious."

"Well, I dunno about that," Cedric said. "Y've always gone off doin' your own thing ever since y'joined us. If anythin', you've been spendin' *more* time with us than before we found out about all o' dis dungeon core business."

She looked at Cedric and Hart for a long time. "Well, we're united by purpose now."

Hart snorted. "United by purpose *now*? What, are you saying dealing with the Ravener wasn't purpose enough for you? Hah!"

"I guess not. Before, all we were doing was pushing down the Ravener for another hundred years. Some longer-lived people would've had to deal with it in their lifetime again, which seemed rather futile to me. And since I knew that, and it didn't sit too well with me, I wasn't exactly full of a lot of motivation. But now? Now we're cutting the head off the snake."

"Aye, fair enough," Cedric said, looking at the dungeon core. "I thought fightin' the Ravener was about as noble a purpose as I could think of... Though bein' sure that none o' me grandkids'll have t'deal wit' the same threats we do s'even better. Much better. Anyway, let's get this done. Y'ready, Drestra? S'all gonna fall to you."

"Hold on," she said, closing her eyes and pouring more mana into the dungeon core.

After the Ravener-spawn attack in Coille forest, the three Heroes had searched for a full day before they'd found the chitterer dungeon and destroyed it, but they'd been too enthusiastic. Their plan had been to capture the dungeon core for Drestra, but by the time they were finished with the chitterers, every last chitterer was dead, the dungeon was wrecked, and so was the dark orb.

When they tracked the bone-charger dungeon a mile or so away, they weren't about to make the same mistake twice, and curbed their enthusiasm, making capturing the orb the priority. They'd raided the dungeon, kept it fairly intact, smashed the bone-chargers and the behemoth serving the orb with prejudice, then claimed their prize. A living dungeon core for Drestra to explore, and eventually, control. For her plan to work, before they left the bone-charger dungeon to meet up with Merzhin, she'd need lots of practise, long sleepless nights of practice to reach a specific goal.

The process to get to that goal had been gruelling. The dungeon core's inner mana pathways almost felt alien and forcing it to do more than randomly making walls wasn't a simple task. She did have three advantages in her favour: the Mark offered the Sage an almost bottomless well of mana, vast amounts more than the Chosen, and he possessed far more than an average wizard; her will was steel and her mind determined; and—if she set her mind to it—she could live without sleep for weeks. While Cedric and Hart kept watch, time and again she'd passed her mana through the core, focusing on something she'd done accidentally while touching the centre of the core the Generasians had: making monsters.

In the end, she'd managed to accomplish what she'd wanted, but also found something unexpected, a startling revelation as it were. One that would change the way negotiations with Lord Aenflynn would go... and the entire war.

"Alright." She slipped the dungeon core in her bag. "Let's take control of our fate."

The meeting place was much like Drestra remembered. An unchanging stone in a sea of change.

Each journey the Heroes had taken into the fae wilds through a fae gate was always different, the landscape always changed. Sometimes they walked along green rolling hills. Other times, they crossed an endless meadow surrounded by trees that never seemed to come closer, no matter how long they walked toward them.

Today, they were walking through cultivated lawns and hedges, among mazes of shiny green boxwoods sculpted into the shapes of lifelike monsters, both large and small. They had even passed a tall bush pruned in the shape of a mage spellcasting: a literal hedge wizard. Yet, at the centre of it all was the same destination they always found themselves arriving at.

Well-tended flowers of a dozen shades were in full bloom, stretching out before them. Rising from a mound taller than the rest of the landscape was a small stone cottage that one could find anywhere in the Thameish countryside. A thatched roof woven together like threads of spun gold sat above stained glass windows that shifted colour each time a Hero blinked. Smoke puffing from the mouth of a stone chimney billowed skyward in neat, singular clouds, forming animal shapes that rose, spreading and seeming to dance across the sky.

No matter if they'd crossed forests, meadows, or hedge mazes to reach it, their destination was always the same.

"This'll be the last time we come here," the Sage whispered, leading Hart and Cedric up to the door.

"Aye, may it be so," the Chosen said.

"I dunno." Hart shrugged, knocking on the door three times. "He serves really good bread and milk. Shame there's no meat, though."

Before Drestra could say a word in response, a voice came through the door.

"You may come in," the cultured voice of the fae lord said.

The three Heroes nodded to each other in resolve and the Sage pulled the door open.

As much as the outside of the cottage was unchanged, the same was also true of the inside: they stepped into the vast ale hall filled with artefacts from their childhoods, complete with the lingering scent of spring flowers native to the Crymlyn. The fae lord still sat within the setting as though it all belonged to *him*.

He, too, was the same.

The unearthly beauty of his face. That laurel of ivy circling his brow, the pointed ears. The only thing that changed were those eyes: those ancient pools of silver light—filled with a shrewd cunning—which only seemed to grow more smug with each meeting.

The Sage vowed that this would be the last day she would see that smugness in those eyes.

"Welcome back, mortal Heroes," Lord Aenflynn said cheerily, gesturing to the spread of buttered bread and cups of creamy milk on the table beside him. "Are you ready for our little luncheon? At this point, these meetings seem to be less about negotiations and more about simply joining me for lunch, but I do not mind. After all, I have all the time in..."

He paused, watching as the three Heroes filed into his cottage. His eyes noted the confidence in their steps and determination in their gazes. A slight furrow creased his brow as they bowed.

"You three seem... different somehow. Have you gained resolve? If so, I am truly surprised. The price has reached three hundred mortal children now, as you know. I thought you might be more... reluctant."

"I was never reluctant, Lord Aenflynn," Drestra said. "But now... now I'm ready for you."

"We all are, wit' respect," Cedric said.

The fae lord drew himself taller, an amused smile touching his lean features. "Oh, please don't tell me you're going to attack me or do something equally silly. I know young mortals can be impulsive. But trust me, to attack me in my own home... that is a contest of arms you would not wish on your worst enemy."

"No fights, unless you're starting one. Can I grab some food real quick?" Hart pointed to the spread on the table.

"Be my guest," Lord Aenflynn said, watching Drestra closely. "You know... if you aren't here to start a physical fight out of desperation, I can only suspect you might have finally found something suitable to counter with. My, my, this will be an interesting meeting. Tell me, how do the Heroes of this generation seek to impress me? What can you offer me with all of my power? What can you offer me that I cannot already provide for myself, or even a suitable alternative to what I have asked for?"

"How about four hundred, Lord Aenflynn?" The Sage's tone was calm. "Four hundred mortals under the age of five winters and our agreement to take care of one hundred of your elderly fae as though they were mortal children. The four hundred mortals wouldn't be given all at once, but rather over time."

"An'," Cedric added. "Since we're increasin' what you want to shore up *your* armies, us four Heroes an' our armies get to use fae gates to move across the land and respond t'threats faster."

"Well!" Lord Aenflynn chuckled. "The young ones bite back! Oh, this will definitely be an interesting meeting. I am noting your phrasing carefully, though: four hundred mortals aged under five winters, not four hundred mortal *children*. I suspect this is where you altered the deal, but I hope you wouldn't be so... transparent as to propose an offering of four hundred young animals or anything of that sort. Keep in mind that you're not in a fairy tale where you trick me by honouring the spirit of what I want and not the actual deed. It would take more lifetimes than you could ever have for you to be shrewd enough to trick me into, well... anything, I suppose." His tone and the smile that joined it were smug.

"No tricks," Drestra said. "You said you wanted young mortals that could be raised in the fae realm to serve in your armies. You'll *get* an army. One full of young and trainable... mortals."

"Oh, this I am dying to hear!" Lord Aenflynn's silver eyes lost their smugness, instead sparking with excitement. "You must explain it to me."

"I can't do the plan justice with words alone," the Sage said. "It'd be better to show you. But it's not possible here. Are you willing to follow us into the mortal world? We'll have to travel to a specific place."

"Where, exactly?"

"A dungeon. An... *almost* empty dungeon."

CHAPTER 63

AN ALMOST EMPTY DUNGEON

When Lord Aenflynn stepped into the mortal world, reality seemed to buckle beneath the weight of his being.

The air and earth shimmered around him and distorted like water forced into a sphere. Dead foliage breathed life again, bursting with vibrant summer blooms under his feet, only to wither and die when his touch left them. His power, to Drestra's mana senses, blazed like the sun. He'd practically brought part of the fae wilds into the material world with him. Or perhaps he *was* an enduring part of the fae wilds.

His lip curled while he took in the dead fall foliage. "I find your mortal world *quite* distasteful. It's strangely both stifling yet barren, and I cannot imagine how you manage to live here. The fact I am now in your reality should tell you how high my expectations are for what you have to show me."

"May we meet them, Lord Aenflynn." Cedric bowed his head, then looked around at the bare trees. "Where we're goin' s'not far. The fae gate opened near the dungeon, an' it's jus' a short walk from here."

"Good, then let us move quickly. This world is too oppressive," the fae lord said, folding his hands behind his back. A sudden pulse of mana saw him rise, hovering a few inches above the earth. Drestra watched his expression carefully. Things were going according to plan this far, and the one wrinkle could be his mood.

Fae were creatures of their word, and if angered—and without warning—would not hesitate to strike out at anyone they felt dishonoured by. And Lord Aenflynn already looked offended by the very world they walked in.

As they made their way to the dungeon, she wondered if they *would* be able to get the upper hand on the fae lord if he lost his patience or temper with them. As a group, they'd been able to stop a greater demon, after all.

She shook her head.

'No, Zonon-In was a monster, but she doesn't *bleed* power the way Aenflynn does. He reminds me of being around Baelin. They both have a presence that feels like you're near the power of a raging hurricane. Maybe one day I'll be like them.'

In time, Drestra very likely would be.

But she'd have to survive today first.

———

"*I* bring you into a mirror of your childhoods captured by the majesty of my power and the fae wilds." The fae's tone was scornful as they moved past debris in the damaged bone-thrasher dungeon. "And you bring me to a dank cave. How charming. Hmmmm, but this is odd. You say this dungeon is nearly empty... I detect the presence of a strange mana in the air."

Drestra slipped a hand in her bag, resting it on the dungeon core and keeping it there—out of Aenflynn's sight—for what was coming next. She carefully probed the centre with her mana, pushing against the dark orb's fierce resistance until she found the distinct apparatus within.

'Like you did before,' she thought.

"Wait..." Lord Aenflynn said. "Something's up ahead and it's doing its damndest to be quiet, but of course it's failing." He snorted mockingly. "Did you have an ambush in store for me, young ones? Don't lie, because I will know."

"No," Cedric said. "Not tryna t'ambush y'at all. But what's up there's got t'do with our demonstration."

The fae lord frowned. "You're telling the truth... interesting. I suppose I will see soon enough."

They entered what had been the central chamber of the dungeon. Most of the evidence of the terrible battle that had taken place there was gone. Scores of Ravener-spawn corpses had been removed and incinerated, while blackened walls scorched by fire spells, cleaved by punishing weapons and powerful magics, still remained.

"We're here," Drestra announced to the puzzled fae lord. "Now, Lord Aenflynn, I must ask something of you."

He raised his eyebrows. "You're asking something of me before you do whatever it is you called me here for? Bold. And potentially ominous."

"Aye, an' we wouldn't ask if it weren't important," Cedric said. "But we request that y'don't share what you're about to see here today with anyone. By your own power an' your own honour, we hope you'll swear t'keep everythin' that happens from here on out between us, unless the three of us gives ya permission t'do otherwise."

"Oho! And if I say no?" the fae asked.

"Then comin' here woulda been a waste of your time," Hart said. "And we wouldn't want to waste your time, m'lord."

"I could *force* you to show me whatever it is, oath or not."

"You could," Drestra said. "And you would break negotiations that we have held in good faith. We didn't insult or attack you, so if you attack us, the dishonour that would stain you would be of your own doing."

Cedric stiffened, looking at her in warning.

'You're treadin' a little close!' she could hear him saying.

But she was also focused on Aenflynn's face. The fae lord stared down at her with that terrible power lurking in his gaze, his face a mask of calm.

Would it stay calm?

Or would the hurricane begin?

"Fine, then," he said at last. "I will not be the one to spread dishonour among us, and I would hate for this trip to your... *quaint* little cavern to be a waste. So, in the spirit of honour, I swear upon my name and my honour not to share words, deeds, or happenings regarding anything said, revealed or done in this place."

Cedric bowed his head and took a deep breath. "Thank you," he said, turning to Drestra. "Alright, the floor's all yours."

Her attention had shifted to a number of tunnels shrouded in darkness at the back of the cavern.

"Look over there, Lord Aenflynn." The Sage pointed, then closed her eyes, falling into the dungeon core, pushing against its power.

Nerves gripped her. She'd only get one chance.

For the plan to work, she had to show the fae lord that their position was strong. She couldn't afford to falter now. With these thoughts spurring her, Drestra fell deeper into the dungeon core, wrestling with its power, fighting its resistance.

Aenflynn's eyebrows rose and his eyes narrowed on her bag. She'd expected that from him: an ancient, powerful, magical being would be able to sense *something*, even if he didn't know exactly what it was, and as long as he wasn't alarmed enough to do something rash and remained peacefully curious, it didn't matter.

Her mana seized a section of the dungeon core's centre, and opening her eyes, she activated the core.

It was time to give him something to look at.

Mana rushed from the dungeon core, reaching for the shadowy tunnels in the rear of the chamber. The Sage's jaw clenched behind her veil as she worked through precise movements with her mana. The actions were still new to her, so the results were clumsy and imprecise, but they were adequate, and from the back of the chamber, a heavy footstep echoed, followed by another. And another. An awkward hulking thing stumbled through the passageway, introduced by a pair of staring eyes that slowly advanced in the darkness.

It trudged squarely into the silver light shining from the fae lord's eyes.

A Ravener-spawn.

A bone-charger.

Lord Aenflynn frowned as the creature lurched toward them. "Hm, it seems you missed one earlier. Though it appears ill, or perhaps injured from your fight with..."

His words trailed off.

The hulking monster stopped in front of them. It watched the group for a heartbeat... then Drestra made another adjustment to the core, and with a shudder of its massive form, the Ravener-spawn slowly bent its head and lowered its front legs. One arm swept below its neck while the other rose in the air. The movement was clumsy. It wasn't fluid. But it was unmistakable.

The bone-charger was bowing.

Drestra looked at the fae lord and—for an instant—his expression slipped. A parting of his lips combined with a slackening of his jaw. He'd gaped ever so slightly.

'We might have him,' she thought.

A heartbeat later, his face was back to its cool, controlled expression, but now, a long finger was perched beneath his chin like he was deep in thought. "Interesting, the way you used a controlling spell to puppet this creature and have it do your bidding. But what does this have to do with me?"

"Hold that thought." Drestra concentrated on the dungeon core, fighting through its mana, and bringing another monster to life.

Soon two sets of thundering, stumbling footsteps echoed from the darkness in the back of the cavern. A pair of bone-chargers emerged. They stumbled forward with less agility than the first—controlling two was mind-bendingly difficult—but they still stopped obediently before the Heroes and fae lord and lowered themselves in a bow that mirrored the first spawn's.

Drestra pulled her mana from the orb, taking a moment to gather herself from the exertion of controlling it.

'There's gotta be a better way to do this,' she thought. 'A way for me to only give them orders to follow.'

The only way Drestra could control the Ravener-spawn for now was by feeling about in the dungeon core and using its inner apparatuses to 'direct' the creatures. It was difficult, slow, and trying, and she felt there had to be a better, more efficient way to get the monsters to follow her commands.

She'd make do for the time being since she'd had very little time to practise.

Her attention turned to Aenflynn as he studied the creatures, his silver eyes pulsing with light.

"More than one. Interesting. A fine show you've put on for me, my dear, but I still do not see what this has to do with our deal."

"It's simple." Drestra gestured to the monsters. "You said you wanted mortal children to raise as soldiers in exchange for fae warriors you provide to fight alongside us. These creatures will be ready for your army. They're Ravener-spawn, so no training necessary."

"They do not even move properly." Lord Aenflynn chuckled.

"They will," Drestra said. "And they are all mortal, and all aged under five winters."

Lord Aenflynn shot her a startled look, then burst out laughing. The cavern rumbled with the weight of the fae lord's superior tone as rock rose and fell like rough waters. She noticed that his canines looked unusually sharp.

The three Heroes stepped closer to each other.

"Ah, mortal humour, how amusing," Aenflynn said. "You've matched my requirements at the most basic level... and all I see here are three monsters, not the four hundred you promised."

"Hold that thought." The Sage poured her power back into the orb.

There was enough mana inside of it for maybe one final demonstration.

Drestra cautiously reached for the centre of the core, triggering another apparatus. A greater wave of power exploded from the dungeon core, lighting up the air, seeping into nearby stone. Rock shimmered, an enormous cocoon with a moist appearance rose from the cavern floor. The core's mana increased, swelling the casing to bursting. Squelching sounds oozed from inside. And then...

A soggy tearing noise followed, and a bone-charger slipped to the cave floor, ready for Drestra to quickly seize control of it, and with a final pulse of her will, the newborn bowed.

Lord Aenflynn watched closely, wordlessly. Drestra spoke first. "As you can see, it'll take time, but you will have the promised creatures to fight for you. And besides, what's time to you? As you said, you have all the time in the world."

A twitch of amusement touched the fae's face as he clapped loudly. "Well done! Well done!" His voice was strangely casual. "You've found an interesting little trick, but I'm afraid it is no more than that. An interesting trick. I do believe I will deny your counter-proposal and request the three hundred mortal children I have asked for. As usual, I will give you one moon to think on it. I look forward to our next meeting."

Drestra, Hart, and Cedric looked at each other.

The two young men nodded.

The Sage was still, looking up at the fae lord, her golden eyes meeting his glowing silver ones.

"That's a shame," she said. "In that case, this will be our final good-bye. We won't be meeting again."

An eerie stillness came over the fae lord. "I beg your pardon?"

"It's been a pleasure to make your acquaintance, Lord Aenflynn." She lowered her head. "Since that is your position, negotiations are over. Sorry we couldn't work things out."

And now the final stage of the Heroes' plan was in play.

CHAPTER 64

BARGAINING FROM A SEAT OF POWER

I *like the idea of 'everybody wins' if you can get that*, Alexander Roth had once said.

The Thameish wizard had been sitting beside the fire talking with Drestra in the Generasians' encampment, and the Sage had hinted at the troubles Lord Aenflynn was bringing. She'd sought advice while keeping the negotiations with the fae lord secret.

And Alex Roth had replied: *I like the idea of 'everybody wins' if you can get that, except monsters or assholes trying to kill you, of course. They can all go straight to every hell in all the planes for all I care. In tiny pieces would be best. But for everyone else? I like to think that if there's another way, pick the other way. Like a third way. One of my mentors—Chancellor Baelin, who you'll be meeting soon—always tries to get us to think our way out of problems. You're the Sage, right? Maybe you'll come up with another way that's best for everybody.*

The idea of a third way had set a fire in Drestra's mind, and she'd spent months trying to find that third way.

She'd thought of summoning monsters, constructing servants, or even hiring mercenaries. Anything that the other Heroes could find acceptable while still meeting Lord Aenflynn's needs.

Yet, none of her ideas were practical.

The mercenary idea was madness born from desperation and was dead before she'd wasted too much time on it. Even if the crown was interested in spending large sums of coin to hire a small army of mercenaries, there was a big, glaring, insurmountable problem with the idea: mortal mercenaries tended to be adults, mortal adults were well beyond five winters old, way too old to even try pawning off as younglings the fae lord could raise and train as soldiers for his army.

She then started considering an army of summoned monsters for Aenflynn, but recognised that this solution came with its own problems. One would need an entire army of wizards to maintain summoned monsters and—when the spells' mana ran out—the creatures would abruptly vanish back to their home planes.

She'd also thought about asking the Generasians to help create golems to offer to the fae lord, but if Thameland had the resources to commission an army of powerful golems, they wouldn't need an alliance with the fae in the first place.

For a few wild nights, she'd even toyed with the idea of tricking Aenflynn into accepting something he didn't really ask for, then binding him to it by using his word against him.

Unfortunately, no amount of desperate schemes or overthinking would have solved their problem, because in the end, Aenflynn could always turn down anything they proposed and—even if she succeeded in tricking him and gained the fae warriors they needed—they'd be fighting alongside soldiers sworn to an angry, bitter and vengeful fae lord. Who would they have to keep more of an eye on, the fae warriors fighting beside them, or dungeons full of attacking Ravener-spawn? The fae scenario had disaster and a fae blade in the back written all over it.

Now that she'd learned how to control a dungeon core, a door had opened, and it solved their problem, eliminated desperation, and gave them an edge.

Truth was, they didn't really *need* Lord Aenflynn's soldiers anymore. The fae were preferable fighters in ways Ravener-spawn couldn't be, but the Sage could conjure an army from literally nothing, which meant unlimited numbers and the greatest tool anyone could have in a negotiation.

The ability to simply walk away.

'If Aenflynn doesn't like what we're offering, he can hang,' she thought. 'And we'll make our own fighters. Though having access to the fae gates would be a big help to us. Maybe we should see what else he has to say before we walk away.'

Lord Aenflynn had been silently eyeing the Heroes, looking from one to the other like someone who'd been told a joke they didn't understand.

"Sorry we couldn't work things out?" he broke the silence. "What are you saying? You need an army to deal with your Ravener-spawn problem. You also need my fae gates to transport your troops."

"I dunno about that, Lord Aenflynn," Cedric said. "Y'look at these three, an' all y'see's just a beginnin', y'know. We're masterin' this every day. Soon we'll be makin' our own armies."

"And *how* did you manage this?" Aenflynn asked, looking at Drestra's bag.

"Respectfully, Lord Aenflynn, we have our secrets," Drestra said. "As you no doubt have yours."

His lip twitched.

"So, we get it," Hart said. "You want something from us, and we want something from you, but as you've said, you don't *need* anything from us. And while we'd deal with you if you wanted to negotiate, these monsters are our best offer. Mortal children are completely off the table. If you don't want what we have, that's alright. We respect that. We'll just go our separate ways."

"You need my forces, these monsters cannot compare to my warriors," the fae lord said quietly. "The brute actions of what are barely more than beasts can never match even one fae's hundreds of years of experience."

"True," Drestra said. "Which is why we still want to bargain. But in the end, we can let this go."

"That..." Lord Aenflynn's eyes flashed.

A bolt of fear and excitement ran through Drestra.

'You ancient beast, when was the last time someone told you they could walk away from you?' she wondered. 'Without insult, or dishonour. Just the ability to walk away. How does it feel not holding all the power for once?'

Obviously, not good.

The fae went from throwing the Ravener-spawn a cutting look, to openly glaring at the Heroes.

"You *need* me," he said. "You *need* my forces."

His power flared and the cave system began to rumble.

It occurred to Drestra that holding this meeting underground might not have been the best idea. If Aenflynn wanted to bury them under a mountain of rock out of childish rage, he could, and there'd be little they could do to stop him or escape.

'Stay the course,' she told herself. 'If he was going to bury us, we'd already be buried.'

At least she hoped that was true.

"We'd like your help," she said. "But we're willing to do without it and use our own power."

"So, as things stand," Cedric added. "Y'can have loads'o monsters t're-plenish yer forces—though we gots final control over 'em—an' we'll take proper care o' yer elderly fae an' give 'em a good life in their latter days. An' your fae warriors can fight alongside us... or we'll take our monsters, bid you farewell, an' part as friends."

"Friends?" Lord Aenflynn choked. "Do you think this is a joke? Do you think you are all cute?"

"Well, my mother and father thought I was cute," Hart said.

"Mine too," Drestra chimed in.

"Da n' Ma thought I was downright adorable," Cedric said.

Drestra burst into deep laughter, soon joined by Hart and Cedric. Relief. She felt relief and couldn't help but laugh. From the moment she'd been Marked, she'd lost control of her own life. The church controlled her destiny. Uldar controlled her destiny. Aenflynn kept leading them around by the nose, and he'd been playing with them for months.

But now?

Now they could—politely—tell him to piss off with his games.

And, damn, did that ever feel *good*.

"Well, *I* do not find you adorable," the fae lord pronounced. "I should curse you right now and let your people wither under the tide of these monsters. Only out of kindness shall I give you a chance. Forget this foolish counter-proposal and I will give you one moon to think things over."

"I do not wish to waste your time, Lord Aenflynn," Drestra said. "None of us do."

His face was a thundercloud. "And is that your final answer?"

"Yes," all three Heroes said as one.

"Fools." He glanced at the Ravener-spawn, then fixed them with a long glare. "Fools... impudent fools."

He struggled for control. It was like watching a child losing their favourite toys for bad behaviour, and not wanting to lose either the toys or the bad behaviour.

'Will your honour and pride allow you to bend?' she wondered. 'If you let us walk away, you'll always know that we've walked away as equals: that you lost control of us. Do you want that?'

"Fifteen hundred," the fae lord grunted.

"Pardon?" Cedric asked.

"I want fifteen hundred of these monsters."

And there it was.

"Then we want five hundred fae warriors fighting at our side," Drestra said.

"Hah!" Lord Aenflynn laughed. "You mortals *are* amusing. You asked for fifty originally!"

"Aye, but the deal's been changed a lot since then, hasn't it?" Cedric asked him. "So why don't we work this out all proper-like now."

"Fine," the fae lord said. "We will bargain in earnest."

More than an hour passed. An hour of conversing, haggling, bargaining, threats to depart, negotiating, thinking, stepping aside to confer in secret and then coming back with new proposals. For a while, the fae lord was actually shouting, shaking the entire cave system with his power.

But at last a pact was reached.

"One hundred and twenty of your monsters, to be given once per moon in groups of thirty or more, not less. In return, you will have the service of one of my fae warriors for every three monsters you provide me." He looked down at the rings they'd received from Elder Blodeuwedd —Drestra's mother. "In addition, you Heroes will have full access to the fae gates, letting you cross the five highways of my realm and quickening your travels across Thameland. Your armies will have use of the same, though you will all be under fae law while travelling through the fae wild. If any of you violate our laws, you will be subject to our punishments."

"Aye, got all that," Cedric said. "An' if we betray you, then you will command your fae warriors to set on us and rip us to shreds. If ya betray us, then any Ravener-spawn we've gifted t' ya will make things nasty for ya. We'll also have folk ready t'care fer yer elderly changelings in two moons' time."

"Fair," Lord Aenflynn said. "Do you three swear to honour this pact on your names?"

The Heroes nodded at each other, then swore their oath.

"Excellent. Then I, Lord Aenflynn, ruler of the Realm of Och Fir Nog, will honour this oath."

A wave of power swept the air.

The deal was done, and Drestra felt ancient magic bind the four of them.

Even as that weight fell on her shoulders, she felt another slide away.

It was done. They'd done it.

"At month's end, we'll deliver the first lot of monsters to you," the Sage promised.

"Good." Lord Aenflynn's spirits were high. "Then, as a gesture of my good will, I will send ten of my best warriors to aid you in... anticipation of this month's payment. They'll find you within one day."

"Thank you, Lord Aenflynn." Drestra bowed her head. "Your generosity is only exceeded by your fairness."

"Fie on that nonsense! Fie, I say!" The fae lord's voice rose. "Fie on such empty flattery. If you meant such a thing, you would not have kept threatening to walk away from the bargaining table. And on that matter, fie on this realm," he said, looking around the cavern. "Until we meet again, Heroes."

"Aye, *if* we ever do," Cedric said.

"Oh, we shall, *Heroes of Thameland*," the fae lord's voice boomed.

Wind swept through the cavern, woven together with the heat of summer, wetness of spring, the damp of fall, and the chill of winter. Aenflynn's form grew until he was the size of a titan; his shadow loomed and spread over the cave's walls, his silver eyes blazing like miniature suns.

"*The path you walk now is unlike any other, and it is not one you walk alone,*" his voice was thunder and flame. "*Like any path that departs from the known trail through the woods, you now step into peril. Fell things watch you. Allies quake. Whispers slip through the dark. Your post is abandoned, and you are wanting. Every step you walk now will bring forth doom, and we will meet again when you see the black ichor on the chair. In your desperate hour. Farewell, Heroes of the Prophet God. Walk your path toward completion. Walk your path toward doom.*"

There was a peal of thunder that shook waves of stone dust from the ceiling.

Then a terrible flash of light that half blinded Drestra erupted.

She shielded her eyes against the flash and—for an instant—saw flame.

Flame that danced across a battlefield before a great escarpment.

And from atop it, the empty grin of a bleached skull smiled at her.

Soon the light faded, and with it, the images. When her eyes adjusted, the fae lord had vanished.

CHAPTER 65

THE WAKE OF PRONOUNCEMENT

"What the hells was that?" Hart asked. "It felt like someone just walked over my grave. I saw all this fire and a great, big fight. Did you guys see that?"

The Sage muttered an incantation, conjuring a huge forceball to light the cavern.

"Yeah," Cedric said. "I saw somethin' like that. Bunch o' monsters and fire burnin' in front of a big tower o' rock."

"Same here," Hart said. "There were a whole lot of blasts coming from the tower. From the look of it, I'm guessing mages or priests were working their power."

"I didn't see that," the Sage said.

He shrugged. "My eyes are better than yours."

She raised an eyebrow. "It was a magical vision, Hart. We're not seeing it with our eyes."

"All I know is that I saw more than you did. 'Cause, like I said before, my eyes are better than yours." He pointed to his eyes.

Drestra clicked her teeth together. "But that doesn't make any sense. We should be seeing visions with our souls: our eyes shouldn't matter."

"I don't know how it works, but did *you* see magic explosions?" He cocked his head.

"...No."

"Have you ever had a vision before? Got a lot of experience with them?"

The Sage's face flushed. "*No.*"

"Then I guess our eyes matter in visions, then, don't they?"

"Ugh, never mind," she said. "As for what the hells that was? I couldn't say."

"I dunno what any o' that was, or even where it was." Cedric scratched his head. "Never seen o' heard anyone describe a place like that in all o' Thameland... Not that geography was my best subject when I went t' school."

"I've never heard of it either." Drestra frowned, thinking back to some of the stories her adoptive father had told her about different places he'd been to. He'd spent a lot more time travelling around than her mother, but she couldn't remember one single story the old man told with a giant escarpment in it anywhere in Thameland. "Cedric, do... do you think Aenflynn gave us a prophecy? Uldar used to make prophecies."

"I've heard o' fae pronouncin' the future," Cedric said. "But everythin' I heard had to do wit' 'em cursin' folk and lettin' 'em know how their magic was gonna pull their guts out n' such. But I ain't never heard o' no deep fortune-tellin' in faerie tales."

"Maybe he was showing us the past," Hart said. "Or maybe they were just crazy illusions to mess with us. He was kinda mad we weren't dancing around like his puppets anymore, so maybe he was getting some revenge. Anyway, whatever it was, if it's the past, we might find out. If it's a threat? It doesn't matter. If it's the future, we'll meet it sooner or later anyway."

"Aye... I suppose you ain't wrong, there. We'll bring it up with the Generasi-folk or somethin'. They know magic shite better n' us. But never mind all that fer now." He pounded his knuckles together. "We bloody did it! We bloody-well *did it!*"

The Chosen laughed and leapt in the air, dancing an elated jig, his gold tooth lighting up his smile. Hart whooped and clapped in time with Cedric's steps, tapping his foot to an unheard beat.

Glee surged through Drestra, filling her with a fierce urge to take to the sky, roaring in triumph for all to hear. Their armies could soon travel from place to place at speed, they'd soon have reinforcements, and those benefits would be theirs for monsters she'd always have control of. But in her mind, a clear warning whispered: barter with the fae lord would always bring trials.

So, it was best to keep their pact and avoid contact with him whenever they could. Only spirits and fae knew what schemes and spiderwebs he might try weaving into other dealings. But for now? This was a good day.

"Bloody hell, this'll be great... this'll me—" Cedric paused. "Hold on, mate, he left us here. Now we gotta walk all the way back t'meet up wit' Merzhin."

No sooner had those words left his mouth, than a sound like bells tinkling in the distance reached their ears. Galloping hooves and clinking bells were coming closer, ringing through the cavern, mingling with deep, jolly laughter.

"What in all hells is that?" Cedric shouted, his morphic weapon changing to a long halberd.

"At least it doesn't sound like Ravener-spawn!" Hart drew his bow, nocking an arrow and pulling the string taut.

Drestra called upon her mana, chanting an incantation.

Was it a cultist attack? A demon? Lord Aenflynn betraying them so soon?

The Heroes tensed, ready for whatever came through that entrance. Beneath the light of Drestra's forceball, the clatter of hooves on stone grew louder. A belly laugh repeated, rippling through the caverns.

A bulky shape advanced, and hoofbeats pounded the cave floor.

With one leap from the shadows, a majestic bull-moose thundered into the chamber, his nostrils puffing, expelling golden steam. Bells tinkled on his branching antlers, and their merry sound mingled with the belly laugh of the creature's rider. The man astride the beast's back had an otherworldly cast to his skin, like frostbite mixed with blueberry stains.

Mistletoe, bloodred holly, and many more Sigmus plants were braided throughout his snow-white beard and scarlet clothing, and a satchel—bursting with shining golden scrolls—hung from his side. No saddle adorned the moose's back, nor did the rider need any tack to control its movements. The moose and its rider moved as though they shared a single will.

A wide grin bloomed across the rider's face and his faded grey eyes danced with mirth. "Hello, Heroes and friends of my Lord Aenflynn! Many fine mornings to you!"

He brought his mount to a skidding halt before the gawking young Heroes and released a booming laugh. Leaping from its back, he landed squarely on the cavern floor with barely a sound.

The moose-rider stood no taller than Drestra's waist, though his shoulders were as broad as Hart's. His long pointed ears twitched as he spoke.

"I can see from your faces that you're a tad in shock—y'look like you just walked in on your mums dancing naked in a storm—but, have no fear, I come in peace! Well, I come in peace as long as you keep peace with me!"

He gave Cedric's and Hart's weapons a meaningful look.

The two Heroes glanced at each other before cautiously lowering them.

"Who're you?" Destra asked.

"I'm known by many names through many times and in many roles, all of them important!" the fae said, puffing out his broad chest. "And you, you can call me the Guide, for that's what Lord Aenflynn has sent me to do for you: guide... and fight for you, if need be, but that'd be such a waste of my many, many talents."

"So, you're the first of the fae who'll be aidin' us?" Cedric eyed the scrolls rising from the Guide's satchel.

"Hah! And to think folks say that mortals are dullards. Look at you, figuring that out all on your own." The stocky fae chuckled and drew a golden scroll from his satchel, snapping it open with a flick of the wrist. "You're right, and I will be the first of many, if I understand the contract between you and my overlord. And I'll likely be your best: at least better than some surly redcap, or as some mortals prefer to call them, powries! Aren't you lucky? Redcaps don't bear gifts like this."

He offered the scroll to a stunned Drestra, who stared at the Guide for a few moments before catching herself and taking it. Her two companions peered over her shoulders. Engraved in green shining ink was a detailed yet odd map of the entirety of Thameland.

It noted no mortal settlements, as if none existed. Notations and symbols identifying fae homes, the dens of large beasts, and various forests and green spaces scattered throughout the countryside were spread across it. What was most interesting were the fae-gate symbols. Realistic sketches of mushrooms that looked real enough to pluck from the page and drop into a pot of bubbling mushroom stew.

"Fancy map." Hart touched one of the circles. "Those mushroom things, are they the fae gates?"

"The cleverness of mortals almost has me speechless!" the Guide shouted, his moose shaking and jingling its bells. "That's right, my friends, these are your lifelines—the doorways between your land and mine—and they're all open to you as per your arrangement with my Lord Aenflynn. You can follow the map to any of them and pop right out in the fae world, and, when you do, just say Bielgloc!"

"Bielgloc?" Cedric asked. "What's that—Oh holy hells!"

The green ink shattered, bursting from the golden paper and

breaking into dozens of tiny, verdant particles that buzzed around each other like a swarm of bees. They swirled through the air for a heartbeat, then shot back onto the scroll, settling into an entirely new map.

One that was even stranger. There wasn't much outlined on it besides a vast, confounding network of roads that connected each other in a large web. The other notations aside from the roads were house-shaped symbols beside them, and mushroom-circles indicating the fae gates. A quick glance told Drestra that these gates matched gate locations on the map of Thameland.

"This map shows you the roads you'll be using to go from one gate to another in the fae wilds," the Guide explained. "If you'll notice, near the roads are symbols for hostels you can stay in if you're travelling a far distance. They'll be open to you and anyone with you. You'll find fluffy beds for any number of guests, stables for your beasts, and the finest food that mortals can handle."

"I like the sound of that." Hart squinted at the map. "But there's nothing around the roads. No countryside. Nothing. What if we get lost?"

The Guide's laughter reverberated off the walls, and now it had a vicious edge to it that chilled the blood. "Well, you see, that's the thing. The fae wilds are suitably named because of what they are; wild. Change-able. Keep in mind that you really don't want to step off the roads or you could find yourselves in for a bit of a nasty surprise. Your realm's not like ours. Yours is all stable, and samey, and dead. Ours is alive. It lives, breathes, and *moves*."

He gave another wicked chuckle. "Our roads stay in the same place, but everything else wanders about like a bird on the wing. We have our ways of finding what we need to find and getting to where we need to go. But few are the mortals who would be able to find their way through our realm, aided or unaided. And, not everything in the fae wilds is as friendly as your loyal Guide!"

"So, what happens if'n we wander off the roads?" Cedric asked.

"Lord Aenflynn grants you and your followers protection... only as you stick to the roads. For you lot—" the Guide's eyes fell on the Heroes' fingers, taking in the rings gifted them by Drestra's mother. "I see you've been given the witches' rings. That means *most* fae will guide you back to the nearest road. In the case of your followers, if they're alone, they won't have any such protections."

The Guide made a ripping sound while running a long finger across his throat.

"I thought we had a deal. That we'd be safe in your realm anytime we travelled through it." Hart frowned.

"And you will be... just as long as your companions *stay* on the roads. Think of it this way. Do your mortal kings control every wolf, bear, and angry drake lurking in your forests? They don't, do they? The boar doesn't have any idea that there's a king who says who can or can't hunt in the woods where it lives! It just gores anything that comes into its territory!"

He glanced left and right then leaned toward the Heroes and whispered conspiratorially, "I once heard of a king who ruled over one of your mortal realms and got himself gored to death by a boar while he was on a hunt. That little incident kicked off a nasty little war." He giggled. "I watched the progress of that war for seven winters, but eventually lost track of it. Sometimes I wonder if it ever ended.

"In any case, my point is that Lord Aenflynn doesn't rule every beast or ruffian in his realm any more than your mortal king does in his. Keep it in mind, my friends. Or don't! I'll be guiding you on your trips through our realm, so you won't have to worry your heads about a thing. The best way to safely use the fae gates to get to where you want to go is to stick to the paths, keep things civil, and you'll be there and back again in no time."

"We got it," Cedric said. "No messin' about or harmin' fae, an' keep to the roads."

"Exactly. Now, if you'll kindly follow me. I'll take you to the first fae gate so you can get used to travelling and using the map. I'm sure that we'll get along famously, like fish and water."

"Right..." Cedric said. "Lead on, I suppose."

"I'll do it and do it well." The Guide laughed, leaping onto the back of his moose with a single twitch of his legs. "Let's get going. I may have all the time in the world, but you mortals no doubt have places to be."

The moose pranced toward the mouth of the cave with Hart staring after him, a deep frown lining his forehead. "Watch him," he whispered to the other Heroes. "Watch him like a mouse would a snake."

"Aye," Cedric agreed. "I'll be keepin' an eye on 'em fer sure."

"Both eyes," Drestra added.

The Petrifier's nine eyes glowered down on the Hunters. "You lost the Usurper? Were we not close?"

The pack of Hunters grovelled, pressing their scaly forms into the snow. Each trembled, but it wasn't from the cold.

"Apologies," the lead Hunter growled, its voice wavering. "We were close, but they vanished. We don't know how."

The Petrifier's eyestalks twitched. "Show me."

"Right away!"

CHAPTER 66

THE COMING STORM

The Hunters led their commander through the mounting snow, slipping between bare branches and frost-slicked trunks. In the distance, a line of eyes flashed yellow. A pack of wolves stalked through the cold, guarding a kill that stained the white red.

They eyed the Hunters warily, sniffing the air as they passed. Growls rumbled from deep within their chests as their hackles rose when the camouflaged Petrifier strode by. They huddled closer together, tails and ears down, and haunches low as its scent carried on the wind, sending fear through the nervous pack.

Amusement filled the titanic spawn leader.

These fierce beasts had turned cowardly at its presence, yet they had nothing to fear. They should be grateful, not fearful. Were it not for Ravener-spawn, mortals would have long tamed more of the wild places in these lands.

Perhaps eliminating woodlands where Usurpers could hide would better suit—

"We are here," the lead Hunter spoke, halting in a snowy clearing. "This is the last place we sensed the Usurper."

The Petrifier growled.

There was nothing there. Nothing but impressions in the snow that led to an empty point in space. Had they vanished by mortal magic? Were they spirited away by something else?

Its eyestalks examined the tracks closely.

Three pairs of mortal footprints... and four cloven hoofprints were all that was to be found.

431

What to do—

"Leader!" a Hunter called from the distance.

The Petrifier's eyestalks rose, scanning the trees.

Two Hunters were loping from the south. "We have found the other two Usurpers!"

A riot of excitement seized the other Hunters. They bounded through the snow with teeth bared, pouncing, and snapping at each other, unfurling razor-sharp claws, slashing at tree trunks as their pack-mates came near.

"Where are they?" the Petrifier growled as the two scouts pressed themselves low before it.

"In a stronghold to the south, leader," one reported. "It is far, but there is a chance to kill both because they are together and leave together. We can attack... but..."

"But?" The Petrifier's eyestalks twitched. It would not do to have another failure so soon.

The other Hunter craned its neck, looking up at their leader. "A source of powerful mana also appears in that place. The Usurpers might be protected by its power."

"And!" The first Hunter crouched on its hands and knees. "They appear and disappear strangely. Sometimes they are in the stronghold, then suddenly vanish. It is confusing."

"Vanish..." The Petrifier looked down at the prints which had also disappeared. "The Usurper here also vanished."

Perhaps they were using the same magic.

"We have only ever felt two there, leader," the second Hunter said. "The third does not seem to go there. But those two rarely move from that position, so an attack should kill them and their allies."

"Allies? Tell me more."

***

By the time the two scouts had given a full report, the Petrifier had gone quiet, its ancient mind churning through the details. A group of powerful mana users. Powerful defences. Watchful sentries. This group did not sound like other mortals from this kingdom. Mana users were rare here.

The Ravener's task could prove challenging.

An attack on so many spellcasters could turn against them, and a stealth attack could be difficult with that large a number of magic-wielders in one place. Still, there might be more than one way to take these mortals by surprise.

"Prepare to move," the Petrifier commanded. "We will go by the lower ways and strike them where they would least expect an attack."

The Ravener-spawn moved to the south, ready to deal death to the Usurpers and their allies.

"There's a storm coming," Theresa said, watching the northern sky as she stepped onto the battlement. "Looks like a rough one too."

"Yeah." Alex peered through the falling snow, wiping wet flakes from his beard. "Might be a whiteout."

The morning air was cold in Greymoor, made chillier by a biting wind that cut to the bone. The chill was the sort of wet freeze that clung to the body, seeping into the muscles, making them burn and numb at the same time. Across the moors, all was white. A sea of frozen, rolling hills in the distance, only broken by grey towers.

Small beasts had long gone to hibernate, while most birds had flown south to warmer climates. But a long winter's sleep and warm climates were not for the Generasian Expedition; they had work to do, and now they had a proper place to do it in.

No one could call their base a research camp anymore. Camps involved tents and bedrolls, and there wasn't a single sign of cloth tents among the grey stone buildings which had risen in their place.

The research castle was now completed.

Towers and battlements soaring above the snowy hill overlooked miles of landscape. An outer wall—with dozens of guards patrolling parapets between the guard towers—encircled the hill. The main courtyard at Alex's back was loaded with equipment and other supplies, which even now was being transported to their permanent homes within the castle's inner buildings.

The central keep, the highest watchtower, towered above everything as the last defensive bastion, and the main administration building. Inside, there were enough sleeping quarters to accommodate the entire research team, and nearby, there was also a barracks building offering extra sleeping space for visitors, or ready for use as the research team expanded with time.

The castle's construction had been a marvel to Alex. If he hadn't seen how fast the work progressed with his own eyes, he would have believed the compound had been there for centuries. He'd pinched himself the first time he'd seen the castle to make sure he wasn't dreaming, but it was real. A new permanent home in Thameland where extensive research and exploring deep into the mysteries of dungeon cores could take place.

Although, the construction phase wasn't completely over yet.

Throughout distant hills, grey stone towers stretched high above the landscape: outposts and watchtowers for keen-eyed sentries and battle mages to keep watch over Greymoor and defend the lands around their fortress. Some of the structures had been completed, but for others, major work was still being done below ground. When the castle was nearing completion, the university had brought in teams of dwarven stone-engineers, earth mages, and fire witches to construct underground towers and fortresses interlinked by roads buried deep beneath the earth. When the roads were finished, Greymoor would be connected by a network well below ground, allowing researchers to travel to testing grounds and bunkers regardless of the weather, while also making it possible for defenders to quickly get to watchtowers, no matter the conditions outside.

If a tower was compromised, each road leading to it was set—by a series of magical measures—to collapse in a ball of flame through a combination of flame and earth magic. Fire and earth mages had combined their talents, working together on road construction, melting frozen earth, and warping earth and stone. With dwarfcraft and wizardry coming together, the finished roads would be built to stand for a thousand years.

Or collapse with a command.

They were passageways, similar to those within a vast dungeon, to serve as pathways for Generasian forces and expedition members, but death-traps for their enemies.

When the network was finally done, reaching testing sites without having to worry about fickle winter weather would be welcomed.

Alex would soon be off to a testing site.

"You have any idea when Professor Jules'll be calling you?" Theresa asked, drawing her cloak tighter and hugging herself.

She, Claygon, Brutus, and Alex stood on the castle's inner wall high above the hill. Najyah soared through the falling snow, her broad-wings silhouetted against the grey sky. The eagle's form was magnificent as it cut through the frigid air. Despite the cold, she looked content and regal, a testament to how effective Khalik's warming spell was. Their other companions were at breakfast, fueling themselves for the day's work ahead. Today, Prince Khalik, Theresa, Svenia, Hogarth, Grimloch, and Thundar would be heading underground to help with the tunnels, while Isolde was in the research building testing a dungeon core copper-alloy.

As for Alex?

"They'll be calling me and Carey anytime now." Alex put his arm around his partner. "She should've finished up her last exam and will be on her way through the portal soon."

"Jeez, it's crazy to think you guys are all done with finals." The huntress snuggled against his shoulder. "This semester's flown by. Doesn't it feel like your first semester was twice as long?"

"Yeah," Alex agreed. "This one went by in a blink. Between the you-know-what and my sleeping magic, it felt like school was almost easy."

"I don't think that's something to complain about."

"Yeah, that's the truth."

Toward the end of the semester, Alex's routine was class, work, spell practise, dancing and reading to Claygon, and prepping things at Shale's for the next financial step in Operation Grand Summoning Ascension. Most of his studying and reviewing for summoning, blood magic, and magical theory was done at night after a refreshing two hour sleep.

He'd learned the final spell for blood magic—corpse puppet—fairly easily since he'd been through it so intensively while he was working on his body-strengthening technique. When Professor Hak had finished grading his final report for the semester, she handed it back with an excellent mark on top of the page, glowing comments scrawled in the margins, and a hard nudge for him to challenge the exam for credit and bypass the second semester of first-year blood magic so he could move on to a second-year course.

He'd eagerly agreed since second semester courses for first years were mostly theory, with a heavy focus on deepening a wizard's understanding of life energy and its manipulation, information that would basically be a review for him since he'd literally *invented* a new blood magic technique. Professor Hak had then piled a small mountain of textbooks to study from in his arms, then scheduled the test for shortly after Sigmus. Which would be right before he challenged the exam for credit for summoning. After Professor Mangal had seen how well he'd mastered extraplanar language and third-tier summoning spells, she'd also suggested he challenge the exam for credit in her course.

"You have a natural talent for summoning, Alex," she'd said one day. "And not simply for casting spells. You've also excelled in your understanding of otherworldly languages—vocabulary, grammar, accents, musicality, tone, and audio-prestidigitation—and you have a real knack for relationship building and negotiation. It's been a pleasure having you in the class."

Guilt had hit him when she'd praised his skills since he knew there was nothing natural about his talent for summoning.

His skills were enhanced by the strange power within him, his gift for languages and negotiation were amplified by the Mark. He wasn't someone who'd completely discount or devalue his own gifts. He'd always been friendly and knew how to make a good impression on people, but that had never extended to having any special natural ability with languages—mortal or otherwise—before now.

His life had changed, the Mark and this power were a part of him now—natural or not—so he'd let the guilt go.

"Thanks," he'd said. "It's really exciting stuff."

"It is," Professor Mangal had agreed. "And it's rare for me to encourage skipping ahead by challenging an exam. Too many students think if they learn a few advanced summoning spells they can jump ahead without mastering the theory. But your understanding is quite comprehensive and quite advanced. Holding you back wouldn't serve you well, since I've always believed that an under-stimulated mind is truly a wasted one."

She'd then shoved a thick stack of books in his hands.

"Review these and have the information they contain well in hand before you challenge the exam for credit," she'd said, flipping open a calendar on her table. "We'll want you to have completed the exam before the second semester begins so you have time to sign up for an advanced second-year summoning course. How about..." Mangal had scanned different dates on the calendar. "The third day after Sigmus."

"Uh," he'd said. "I'm challenging the exam for credit for Professor Hak's blood magic class then."

"Ah, well then, you can do it the next day," she'd said. "Are you free?"

"Uh, yeah, but isn't that a little close?"

"Oh, come now, I'm sure you can handle it. A young man of your talents should not be afraid of a couple of exams, Alex."

He'd grudgingly agreed, and that was how his 'exam season' was extended.

'I really shouldn't complain, though,' he thought. 'My exams went well, and it's not like they were super hard.'

Things were a far cry from last year and his struggles with Professor Ram's force magic class. He hadn't taken force magic for a while, but he used to have nightmares where the angry bearded professor was glaring at him as he towered above the foot of his bed with a midterm in hand and force missiles pointed straight at him.

Thankfully, Ram's classes weren't on his schedule this year, and hopefully, they never would be again... Unless some sort of petty revenge was involved.

His final reports for the expedition and his second-year alchemy and the Art of the Wizard in Combat credits were back. Thankfully, he'd aced both papers.

All in all, it had been a really good semester, but coursework and exams seemed insignificant compared with other things going on in his life. He was doing what he'd wanted to do for most of his life—learn magic. Though dungeon cores, ancient monsters, and divine conspiracies weighed a lot heavier on his mind than school did.

There was also the trip to the Hells with Baelin to think about.

In preparation, he'd already mastered three new summoning spells: summon flicker dog, formiac ant, and hell-boar, and all three were a good start for being on the road to mastering third-tier summoning spells.

'What I really need is greater force armour, though,' he thought. 'Having some full body protection's going to be key for fighting monsters as tough as Zonon-In was. Who knows what other demons might be lurking about. But, maybe if I'm lucky, I'll have some peace for a while.'

Within the earth, the Petrifier stopped. "Where are these Usurpers?" it asked its Hunters.

"Right above us," the lead Hunter said, peering through pitch-blackness to the stone ceiling overhead. "There was only one, now the second has joined them."

"Good." The Petrifier reached deep into its jaws and drew out the pair of dungeon cores the Ravener had given it.

"Then we begin."

CHAPTER 67

TAPESTRIES OF PAST VICTORIES

"**M**r. Roth! Mr. Roth! Miss London! Miss London!" a magically augmented voice boomed over the castle grounds. "Professor Jules requests you attend her office in the keep!"

"Well, that's me," Alex said, leaning down to kiss Theresa. "Have fun in the mines, honey."

She rolled her eyes and kissed him back. "They're not mines, they're tunnels."

"So are sewers. You're still going underground."

"Keep talking like that, and you'll be going underground," Theresa warned. "About six feet underground."

He raised his hands in surrender. "Okay, okay!" He chuckled. "I'll see you at dinner tonight."

<hr />

As Alex and Claygon entered the keep, he was greeted by a massive entrance hall and two sets of curved stone staircases rising to a balcony on the second floor. Between them—on ground level—were a pair of stone doors through which the expedition's small battalion of administrators, engineers, and armourers scurried. Through that doorway were offices, an armoury, and several summoning cells. On the second floor, another set of double doors led to a receiving room, a cluster of offices, and the first grouping of bed chambers.

Images of dragons in flight were carved into the doors, and the walls flanking them were decorated with tapestries woven in Generasi, each immortalised a moment from the expedition's taming of Greymoor.

The wall hanging on the left was woven in muted tones and illustrated the expedition's arrival in the village of Luthering, with an—unrealistically—stern depiction of Baelin and Jules leading the team out of the portal. Another tapestry showed the battles they fought across Greymoor: the survey teams' struggles against a host of wild monsters that had plagued the land before they were cleared away. Alex's eyes drifted to an exciting image—one filled with way more Crich-Tulaghs and beast-goblins than had actually been there—of his team's battle with the blue annis hag.

Another tapestry—this one stitched in richly coloured threads—portrayed the first time they'd joined with the Heroes. It was the battle of the double dungeon. At the very top of the massive wall hanging, the Watchers of Roal, the Heroes and more fought a blood-hydra from the sky, while Vesuvius and countless wizards engaged chitterers on the ground below. And at the bottom of the tapestry, expedition members and the Heroes were throwing spells and showing their might against the pair of dungeon cores.

But battles weren't the only grand images hanging in fine silk for all to see.

On the opposite wall were woven scenes of moments of discovery and diplomacy. One showed the wizards of Generasi shaking hands with a group of blue caps somewhere deep within the earth. An artistic rendition of friendly contact between the expedition and the local fae. The fruits of that contact—veins of metals, gems hidden in stone, and buried ruins—were finely woven into the image with care.

Another celebrated a group of triumphant researchers holding a jar of black dungeon core remains along with a detailed data sheet that glowed as if it were the sun. A third illustrated the violent explosion resulting from their experiment with core remains and chaos essence, and a group of brave researchers standing strong against the wind and heat.

Alex snorted. He didn't remember anyone standing that day.

"It's a tad garish, isn't it?" a familiar voice said from behind him.

"Morning, Carey." He turned to face his colleague. "Well, at least they have us looking our best. I don't think I'd be standing here admiring a bunch of scenes with us crawling through muck and hiding from all the rainstorms in Greymoor. I'd probably be laughing and cringing."

"Or one of us barely picking ourselves up after the chaos explosion," she said. "Those were not exactly our best moments."

His old lab partner looked... surprisingly good, all things considered. She wasn't back to her usual bouncy, exhausting self, but she appeared more rested, and her hair was a healthier colour and texture than 'dried straw.' Her clothes were neat, clean, and freshly pressed, and a light scent like apple blossoms drifted from her.

The symbol of Uldar still hung from its customary place around her neck.

"Shall we?" She gave him a closed mouth smile. "It wouldn't do to keep Professor Jules waiting and—" Her eyes flicked up. "Ah! Oh dear, that must have vexed her ever so much."

"What?" Alex asked, following her gaze. She was looking at the tapestry depicting their triumphant cataloguing of the dungeon core substance's data sheet. He focused on Professor Jules' face. "What, did they get her nose wrong or something?"

She giggled. "Well, that *is* the problem, isn't it? We can see her nose!"

"What do you me—Oh, by the Traveller! None of us are wearing safety equipment in the lab. Oh yeah, I bet she wasn't too thrilled about that." He laughed.

"Certainly not."

"Well, you're right. Best not keep her waiting and maybe make her mood worse."

Together, he and Carey climbed the stairs with Claygon, walking through the labyrinthine halls of the keep. For a time, they walked in silence as they climbed the ever-rising staircases of the tower.

Until ...

"Have you... been quite alright?" Carey asked with a shy note in her voice. "With recent discoveries, I mean."

"I was thinking about asking you the same thing." Alex glanced at her. "Honestly? For me? It's... complicated."

"That's not surprising."

"Right?" Alex said. "I dunno, it's made me think about and recon-sider a lot of stuff. A whole lot of stuff."

"In truth, it cannot help but make one do so." She nodded. "It's given me many sleepless nights to the point where I sought help from the infirmary. They offered me a sleeping draught and the strength had to be increased twice before it finally gave me some relief."

Alex looked at her sharply. "Those sleeping tonics are pretty power-ful. Are you okay?"

"Oh yes," she said, though there was more than a little tension in her voice. Her body language was open and truthful, though. "I used it for a few nights to get me started and then slept like a baby without it after that. Now all the questions haunting me have the decency to confine themselves to my waking hours."

"Yeah, it's a lot to think about, isn't it?" Alex agreed. "Thoughts about gods, mortals... the relationship between them."

"Oh yes. I recall those well. Have you had any thoughts about the future and how our country's bedrock might well dissolve one day?"

"That's a familiar one." Alex laughed bitterly as they climbed. "What about questions dealing with what the source of the... you know what, might be?"

"Those? Oh, they only knock about in my head every time I blink." She joined his bitter chuckle. "It is... troubling. And lonely."

"Lonely?" Alex asked, pulling open the door to the fourth floor and holding it for her.

"Thank you ever so much," she said as she walked through. "Well, it's terribly lonely in that all of my comforts are now not so comfortable. I can count on one hand the number of people I can talk to about any of this. I can't exactly run to the priests of Uldar in Generasi and seek their wisdom, and even my own prayers feel..." She sighed. "At times, it feels like I'm praying to a stranger. I hear you mention the Traveller regularly, Alex. Do you pray to the Patron Saint of Alric?"

"Honestly?" He looked around as though he was about to admit a terrible secret. "I've been praying mostly to her for a while. I dunno what interpretations or conclusions you've reached—if you can even reach any conclusions in all this mess—but to me, I know that the Saint of Alric fought for our people. Even in death, in her own way. It feels way more comfortable to pray to her; it's kinda like I know her better."

"I see," she said. "Perhaps I might try praying to St. Avelin of Wrexiff. He destroyed the Ravener all by himself ten cycles ago. The Heroes had unfortunately perished in the journey." She shook her head. "My teacher said that was a bad cycle. Lots of infighting and even betrayal."

"I remember learning about that," Alex said. "Well, I hope praying to him gives you a little more... comfort."

"I truly hope so." She gave a sigh so deep, her whole body seemed to deflate. "I fear that... well, never mind."

"No, what is it?" Alex asked, glancing around. At the end of the hall were the double doors leading to Professor Jules' new office.

For a moment, Carey's eyes shone. "I wish to keep my faith, Alex. Both in the church and in our god. I... I'm not stupid, and I know how this all looks. For a time, I thought that surely we must have made a mistake. I thought of every possible way to deny what Ffion told us. And to deny what we ourselves experienced. Then my every thought turned to the core: to try and pick it up once more and see if we had made an error."

The young woman shook her head. Her eyes seemed to burn with different emotions. "But I would not have come to Generasi if I was one to deny the cold hand of evidence. As we have learned so many times: confirmation bias is the bane of wizards, science, and the truth. The world is the way the world is, and none of my wishing will change that."

"I hear you," Alex said with a world of sympathy.

If creation bent to folks' wishes, it would be a much kinder place. Or a crueler one, depending on the wish.

"Well," he said. "Maybe the problem comes from mortals in the church. You know, like a few rotten apples spoiling the entire barrel."

"Truly, that is the hope," she said sadly. "I kept coming to a grim answer to that thought: if the lies are coming from a few false priests, then why does our god keep silent? He fought the first incarnation of the Ravener himself—according to what the church teaches—that sounds like an active deity to me, not one who'd sit back and let the evil of mortals ruin his earthly house."

"Yeah..." Alex said. "When you put it that way it does make things seem kinda... grim. Well, if you need anybody to talk to about this, there's always me. I mean, I don't know if my faith was ever as strong as yours, but at least I can listen to what you're thinking and feeling about this mess."

She smiled at him then, and her face was ringed with both appreciation and a deep melancholy. "I... I would appreciate that, Alex. Now, come on before Professor Jules chides us for being late."

"So you passed that awful tapestry, did you? Ugh." Professor Jules rolled her eyes as she sat behind her enormous desk. "I had no less than five arguments with the weaver about the lack of protective equipment. He kept screaming 'art' and 'impression,' but neither of those concepts give prospective students and visitors the right *impression*, to use his word."

She shook her head at the two students seated in front of her desk. "Can you believe they wanted to put a painting of the same scene on a wall *in my office*! Bah! That'd be enough to give me the shakes every time I sat down to work. In any case, that's not why I called you here."

The professor peered at them carefully. "Are you both alright? I can imagine all of this has been a great shock."

Alex and Carey looked at each other. "We're about as fine as we can be," Alex said. "Which is better than expected, to be honest."

"Yes, I've been worse," Carey agreed.

"Good," Professor Jules said. "Because as soon as the new year begins, we'll be putting the two of you to work."

Reaching into a box of rolled up papers at her side, she took out and unrolled a map of Greymoor, tapping her finger on an unremarkable location to the east. "I've had the engineers hard at work setting up a new testing site for the two of you. It'll be a fortified bunker with a teleportation circle that Chancellor Baelin crafted, and it'll be directly linked to the dungeon where you obtained our living dungeon core, Mr. Roth."

She shuffled through another stack of papers and retrieved a schedule written in spidery script. "At the start of the new year, I'll be taking you both off the main research team for at least one day a week. Instead of reporting to the research building as you normally would, you'll join a team of Watchers and other defenders and go to the new site, then use the teleportation circle to take you to the dungeon. When you're there, you're to conduct a number of predetermined experiments designed by Chancellor Baelin and myself to test the limits of mortal control over living dungeon cores. Any questions?"

Alex raised his hand.

"Mr. Roth, there's only the three of us here. Four of us if you count your golem." She nodded to Claygon. "I don't think it's necessary to raise your hand before asking a question."

"Right," Alex cleared his throat. "Will you be supervising us?"

"At first, yes," Professor Jules said. "Though there will be times when I'll send a graduate student to supervise you instead, especially after the initial trials. I want you to first focus on mastering warping terrain with the dungeon core."

"Not on making monsters?" Alex asked.

"No, let's start small before we think about crafting entire armies of Ravener-spawn that we might or might not be able to control." Professor Jules tapped the map. "Besides, any summoner can 'make' an army of monsters. What's far more intriguing to me is the thought of warping terrain at our will. If we can do that, we could very easily construct new underground bases, labs, and fortifications. Destruction is necessary, but discoveries that create new methods of construction are a lot more interesting in my opinion, Mr. Roth."

She circled the research castle on the map of Greymoor with her finger. "Imagine what we could do with devices that could raise walls, create tunnels, and craft roads in only a heartbeat of time, a surge of mana, and no building materials whatsoever. It would be incredible."

Far below the research castle, the Petrifier commanded the dungeon cores to close the vertical shaft leading down to the Ravener's tunnels. The rock closed, forming a seamless floor. None would know that tunnels were there, deep beneath the earth.

In its grip, the dungeon cores thrummed with power.

Chapter 68

What Brews in the Dark Beneath the World

In the starkness of a tunnel beneath the research castle, the Petrifier prepared its attack.

It loomed above a growing horde of monsters within a vast chamber shrouded in darkness. Pressed into the walls on either side of it, were the dungeon cores granted by its master. They shuddered, pouring their power into the walls around them. Monster after monster burst from the stone, each one as vicious as the last.

One core crafted bone-chargers; each hulking beast boiled from the walls and dropped to the cavern floor with a heavy thud. They milled about in shadow, waiting for a command that would drive them forward to flay the two Usurpers who walked the surface above, unaware that their doom awaited beneath their feet.

The other dungeon core birthed a far more insidious creature: a spear-fly. Only a foot in length, and with their small size, seemed less deadly than their bone-thrasher kindred, but these Ravener-spawn were known for being the cause of the greatest number of mortal deaths over all the cycles of Thameland's endless battle. Insect-like, one of the smallest monsters in the Ravener's arsenal, with two sets of kite-like wings, a tangle of spindling legs tipped with jagged blades for gripping prey, and a needle-sharp proboscis protruding half a foot in front of beady white eyes.

They attacked at speed, aiming their rigid proboscises straight at any enemy in sight, piercing deep into living flesh—whether mortal or beast. They'd suck the blood and life-juices from the captured prey, gripping with their cluster of barbed legs. A single spear-fly could drain a body of half its blood in less than sixty heartbeats.

A swarm?

A soldier, wizard, or even a Hero would be a shriveled, desiccated corpse in less than half the time.

Together with the bone-chargers, all affronts to the Ravener would be removed.

The brutish chargers would be first to erupt from the earth and grind all mortals in their path to paste. Spear-flies would come next, swarming from hidden tunnels, and targeting spellcasters and archers, draining them dry. The Hunters were to take the role of attack dogs: sniffing out the Usurpers for the Petrifier to paralyse them with a beam from its eyestalks, leaving them at its mercy, frozen where they stood.

It shuddered, overcome with pleasure at its next thought. Seeing its master's two enemies in its mind's eye, raked by the ray from its central eye, forever cast in stone. Though the two bold mortals would not agree, feeling the touch of its ray was a gift they would be fortunate to know in the brief time it took to eliminate their allies. None could be allowed to live. Perhaps, its new statues would be trophies it could present to the Ravener when the final Usurper was found and eliminated in the very same way.

When this phase of its master's needs was met, it would bury itself, secreted away in the cool muck, waiting to see if new Usurpers would surface or if the time had come to destroy itself. Those were its most favoured cycles: calm, peace, coolness, and nothing more to do but admire its own art.

"Hurry," it commanded the dungeon cores. "We will need the armies quickly."

The black orbs shuddered beneath its command, silently shrieking. New monsters poured from the walls, but not without consequence. A pair of jagged cracks ruptured weakened stone, running from floor to ceiling; tremors spread through the cavern. Web-like fissures had been forming along the dungeon cores' already weakened surfaces. Stressed from the vast amounts of power the Ravener had poured into their centres, and now with the Petrifier pushing them beyond normal limits, it was only a matter of time before they crumbled beneath the strain.

No matter. In time, the overload of power would have shattered their mana pathways, so better to use them up quickly and have the army ready before its preparations were detected by their foes up above. It was a necessary sacrifice. The Petrifier's eyestalks turned to narrow shafts the dungeon cores had begun forging. The orbs had crafted a dungeon and were constructing spiraling pathways with great care to take the army to the surface.

The spheres cautiously shifted stone, avoiding underground quakes and stifling mana surges that the mortals would detect. The Petrifier feared little, but it also valued caution. There was no sense in risking its mission by losing the element of surprise. The narrow shafts gave its Hunters a strategic place where they could hide and use their heightened senses and mana perception to scout the mortal stronghold unseen.

They would search any surprisi—

"Leader," a Hunter's voice called from one of the shafts.

The Petrifier's eyestalks turned upward. "What is it?"

"We must shift direction," the Hunter growled. "We listened to the stone as you tasked us to do and heard odd sounds and detected powerful mana in the earth. And when we moved closer, we heard voices. Mortal voices. The enemy has tunnels below the surface, and our shafts will breach theirs if we keep digging in the same direction."

Six of the Petrifier's eyestalks twitched, but kept focus on the Hunter, the fourth pair turned to the ceiling. It saw nothing but unbroken stone. It tried to imagine how close the enemy's tunnels could be. "Are the Usurpers in those tunnels?"

"No," the Hunter growled. "They are elsewhere on the surface."

"Then—"

"There's more, leader."

The Petrifier's eyestalks twitched in irritation. More complications? "What is it now?"

"There are other chambers in the stone and earth between us and the tunnels, but these do not have the stink of mortals. Some of our shafts have broken through to them." The Hunter's claws flexed. "Inside we found strange, small creatures that looked like balls of blue flame and made thin, high noises like rodents. They had much mana and showed us no fear."

The Petrifier searched its memories, recalling vague images of creatures that looked like blue flames. They were harmless and did not help mortals, nor did they interfere with Ravener-spawn unless pressed first.

Considering its next move, the Petrifier reared up to its full height. "I will close off the shafts that lead to those chambers. Do not interfere with the blue-flame creatures. If they are provoked, they could be troublesome. As for the enemy's tunnels... I will move all our shafts around them, but the mortals in those passages could still reinforce the Usurpers' base. So. This is what we do."

"It's unnatural. Too quiet," a grey-bearded dwarven engineer grumbled. "What the hell is the point of tunnel-building when you can't hear the echo of a pickaxe on stone?"

"The point is to actually build the tunnel, you old codger." A younger one glared at him. "If we only used pickaxes, we'd be down here for ten years and still not close to being done. Earth magic gets things done in hours that'd take picks weeks to do. Just be thankful we've got so many wizards to work with."

"Hrmph!" the older dwarf snorted. "That's the problem with you youngsters. Getting too lazy relying on fancy shiny lights. You'd all be bloody helpless without wizards and the like to help you."

He shook his head and marched off to oversee the wizards heating the stone and soil. "Oi, watch it. You don't want to melt it too fast or you'll bury us in mud!"

Several of the fire mages—including Tyris Goldtooth—looked at each other. There was no need for words. The old engineer's younger companions chuckled and turned toward the end of the tunnel, discussing the next steps. Ahead of them, Prince Khalik and another dozen earth mages were shaping the soil and stone to tunnel deep through the underground. In miles beyond the shifting wall of rock and earth, another team of mages and engineers were burrowing toward them from a distant watchtower. The two teams would meet at a midpoint, completing one of the tunnels leading from the research castle.

At first, it had been fascinating watching the process. Tons of stone, earth, and clay flowing like water to form the hardened ceiling, walls, and tunnel floor. The dwarven engineers using advanced levels and instruments to monitor the tunnel's slope, direction, and grading. The fire mages' flames softened the earth around them and kept everyone warm beneath the wintery landscape above.

There was even a 'navigator' holding several stone tablets on which a wealth of underground maps were etched. Some indicated veins of minerals, others places where sinkholes might form, and still others revealed blue cap burrows the wizards had promised to leave undisturbed.

All in all, it was a wondrous sight...

...for the first hour.

But now, Theresa was bored.

And she wasn't alone.

Thundar yawned beside her, leaning against a wall. "Never thought I'd be wishing for a monster attack."

"I hear you," the huntress agreed. "It gets a little monotonous, doesn't it?"

"Yeah." The minotaur peered at Prince Khalik. "Even our friend looks bored, and he's actually got something to do."

A glance at the prince revealed a slightly distant expression on his face, like he was daydreaming of things that weren't rock and stone.

'Probably about things involving *leaves* and *trees*,' Theresa thought a little wickedly. 'Can't blame him, though.'

She glanced down the tunnel at their backs, which she and a group of warriors and mages guarded. Darkness lay in their wake, broken by force-balls floating at twenty foot intervals along the tunnel, banishing most of the darkness, reducing it to merely shadows. She listened for any sounds approaching from behind, but there'd been nothing—suspicious or otherwise—for hours.

There'd been nothing in all the days they'd been digging. She and Thundar had taken to calling it light duty. But light duty often meant boring duty.

"Anyone bring a deck of cards?" Thundar asked. "Grimloch?"

A loud snore came from where the shark man leaned against another wall with his arms crossed. Eerily, his black, doll-like eyes were still open even though he was clearly fast asleep.

"Well," Theresa said, looking at Brutus asleep near the shark man. "There goes that idea."

"Yeah, no meat and no fighting makes Grimloch a dull boy, I guess," Hogarth said from his seat against the wall. Svenia was nearby, sharpening her weapons and polishing her armour.

"These quiet times are good for making sure your equipment's in good order," she chided Hogarth. "Lady Von Anmut would be disappointed that you're not using your time productively."

"Ah, leave me alone, Svenia," Hogarth snorted. "I polished every single piece of my kit to mirror shine last evening." He held up his feet. "You see these boots? I could use them as a mirror to shave if I wanted to. Lady Von Anmut could even use them as a mirror to put on her lip colour."

Svenia rolled her eyes, jerking her thumb at the soldier. "Don't follow his example, kids."

"I dunno," Theresa said. "The last thing I want to think about is weapons right now."

She glared balefully at her great-grandfather's blades. If any progress had been made with them, it was a secret to her. Every day, she'd tried to remove her preconceptions and see them for what they actually were. And every day, they'd remained cold, lifeless steel with no sign of sudden magical or divine powers.

At this point, she needed a break. She'd think about looking at the two swords from another angle in the new year. If a month passed and she couldn't figure anything else out... then it might be time to admit that maybe there was nothing special about them anymore and seek out new weapons.

It'd hurt to put them aside, but if she had to, they'd be given a place of honour in her room. Perhaps that was where they belonged, anyw—

She paused.

What was that?

She strained her hearing, cocking her ear toward the full length of the tunnel.

"Hey, you missed a spot." Svenia pointed at one of Hogarth's boots. "That bit there looks like bird shit."

"It's just a bit of extra polish," Hogarth shrugged.

"That doesn't make any sense," Svenia said.

"Neither does bird shit; it's bloody winter."

"Hey, maybe it's from Najyah."

An angry shriek echoed through the tunnel as the large eagle glared at them. Khalik's familiar perched on the edge of a large cart where the team had stored precious metals, gems, or anything else they'd pulled from the rock as they magically warped their way through the earth.

"No offence." The blonde woman held up her hands to the bird. "I just meant—"

"Shh," Theresa said. "Quiet for a moment."

The other guards fell silent, all signs of lethargy fading.

"What is it?" Thundar asked. "Your ears are a hell of a lot better than any of ours, except maybe Grimloch's."

"It's... I thought I heard something." Theresa placed her hands on her blades and slowly crept down the tunnel.

Her eyes cut through the shadows, seeing nothing. The hairs on the back of her neck began to rise as she remembered the invisible marauders that had lurked deep in Crymlyn Swamp. Closing her eyes, she cocked her head and held her breath, trying to listen above the dwarven engineers' calls and the grind of rock and earth flowing to reinforce the sides of the lengthening tunnel.

She could have sworn sound had come from the tunnel wall. Something like a shift in stone.

But now, there was nothing.

"I think the boredom's driving me a little crazy," she said. "I'm hearing things now."

"Ugh, don't say that," Thundar said. "Now there'll definitely be something out there waiting to kill us. Enh, at least it'd be a quicker death than from all this boredom."

"Yeah..." she said, peering back down the tunnel. "Yeah, it's probably nothing."

Deep within the earth, Gwyllain's eyes went wide as he stepped into the dark cavern.

Ahead of him, the blue caps were swarming about like angry bees.

"What has all of you worked up, I wonder?" he asked.

His heart sank.

He had a bad feeling this was going to be just like the windmill incident.

CHAPTER 69

HUNGRY STONE

"Hold on, slow down for a couple of heartbeats!" Gwyllain cried, waving his basket of honeyed acorns about like he was fending off a swarm of enraged bees.

The blue caps—each crackling and flaring with blinding blue light, raced around Gwyllain, yapping like excitable fox kits.

"You're all hard enough to understand when you're not screeching over each other!" the asrai cried. "Come on, then, will one of you calm down and tell me what's got you all excited?"

It took some coaxing, but at last one of the tiny blue faes began to calm, floating in front of the larger fae and telling him their story.

"Right, right, so there was some sort of... monster, you said?" Gwyllain clarified. "One that opened the side of your cave? Must've been a strong monster—No, wait, you mean there was some kind of mana moving the rock?" Gwyllain scratched his chin. "I know there's a bunch of mortal wizards above you. Maybe they're mucking around with some kind of magi—oh? It wasn't them? What'd the creature look like then? Uh-huh. Uh-huh."

He tried to imagine what they were describing. "Big mouth full of needles... Skin that looked like a bunch of scabs put together with sticky sap. Or like dried tree bark, right... and big claw—Wait."

His blood instantly turned cold. "Was it... about as tall as a human, but it moved fast?"

The blue caps excitedly bobbed up and down.

"Oh... ohhh by all the fae lords." Gwyllain hung his head. "I... I know the beastie you saw."

Memories from that terrible night rushed back to him. The flames, the monsters, the flying about, the nearly being eviscerated by that clawed creature. That terrible explosi—

"What, what was that?" he asked, realising the blue caps were still talking to him. "Oh, yeah, no. I don't think it's going to be a big problem. No, I really don't think it's going to be coming back. Unless... you didn't see any blue annis hags with it, did you? No? Okay, then it won't be coming back."

As one, the blue caps cheered, flitting about joyfully. But joy was far from Gwyllain's heart.

'The monster that looked like that was at the windmill and really wanted to kill Alexander,' he thought. 'They're probably black... and if they can warp the earth...'

Gwyllain's eyes slowly drifted to the ceiling.

'They're going to come up right below the wizards,' he thought. 'And a lot of death's going to be about. Or maybe not. Those wizards seem to be a nasty lot.'

He hadn't gone near them since that wild, horrible night, but a fae only had to take one look at Greymoor to not only see that all the wild monsters were gone, but to also recognise the power these foreign, mortal wizards wielded.

But still...

'If that thing is looking for Alexander, maybe it'd be nice to give him a quick little warning. Might not be bad for a fae like me to have a favour owed to him by wizards like that...' he thought. 'And word's been about that there's been mortals on the road again. The Stalker's been going about with the mortal Heroes, they say. Maybe they'd like to know this too.'

"Okay! Okay! We'll have to pause our visit a bit, my friends. There's something I've got to d—No, I'm not refusing your hospitality! By the fae lords, don't be so sensitive! I'm just going to go and be right back, we'll have our little party when I—What? Leave the acorns? You treacherous little... Fine! I'll be back!"

Throwing up his hands in disgust, Gwyllain put the basket of honeyed acorns on the floor and stomped toward the wall. "Completely merciless, all of you are, I swear!"

With another snort of disgust, he disappeared into the fae pathways.

"Well, that's going to be interesting," Alex said as he, Claygon, and Carey stepped into the entrance hall of the keep. "Out there by ourselves in the winter, playing with dark forces we barely understand. Though I guess understanding them is the whole point of all this."

"Yes... I just hope we can... come to learn more," Carey said as Alex opened the door. "Oh dear, it's absolutely freezing out here!"

The storm had arrived. Snow blew with such force that the world had turned into a sheet of white. Castle buildings were no more than faint shadows in the whiteout, while people, beasts, and golems were flickers of movement in the snow.

"Jeez, the storm came on fast!" Alex cried above the wind.

"Work for the day might be cancelled at this rate!" Carey called back, shielding her face from the biting cold and stinging snowflakes.

"I doubt that!" Alex shouted, sending out a thought to Claygon. The golem raised his arms, shielding both Alex and Carey from the snow. "You know how Professor Jules is! If we had to fight our way through a massive storm and snowdrifts, she might cancel work, but that's not happening if our safety's guaranteed!"

"Truly!" Carey said. "Shall we head off to the research building?"

"I'll be there soon. I'm going to go make sure the aeld tree's alright!"

"Good, good! Say hello to it for me, won't you!"

Conjuring a wind-and-rain shield, Carey disappeared into the white, crunching her way through the rising snow in the direction of the research building. Around them, Alex saw orbs of light flicker to life: forceballs to be guiding lights for folk pushing through the snow. Then wizards appeared, casting spells of wind and force to lift the snow from walkways and clear a path for walking.

"Jeez," Alex muttered, crunching his way toward the aeld. He glanced up at Claygon, who plowed through the rising white as though it were flat ground on a summer day. "On days like this back in Alric, they would have shut everything down!"

He turned away, not expecting an answer from Claygon, then paused.

There. There was a pulse of... something through their link. Alex's heart leapt in excitement. It'd been a long time since he'd felt anything from him.

"Claygon?" he called out.

But the golem kept walking with his spear in hand, striding toward the aeld tree with a purposeful gait that kicked up clouds of white with each step.

"Claygon!" Alex called to his golem. "What's happening? Is there something wrong?" Gently, he tried feeling through their link, looking for that spark of consciousness, but found nothing on the other side. "Claygon? What is—"

The golem stopped, clutching his war-spear close. His head was turned toward the glow of the aeld tree only a few feet ahead of them. Alex forced his eyes away from Claygon and onto the tree. The weeks of healthy earth, nourishing plant food from the fae, and tender care from Alex, Professor Salinger, and many others had done it a world of good. Its golden glow was twice as bright as it had been when Alex first brought it to the camp, and its branches were fuller, healthier, and slightly sagging from the number of leaves that had sprouted.

Despite the wind, freezing temperatures, and snow, it radiated a calming warmth that reached out to Alex, even from feet away. As early winter brought more frequent temperature drops and snow falls, he'd wanted to protect it from winter's bite and damage by wrapping it in rolls of burlap, but Professor Salinger had told him not to bother with that, as it would be harmful to block its leaves from the sunlight.

Alex could see how right he'd been. Its heat was so pleasant, he almost wanted to hug its lean trunk. Yet something was distressing it. Though it radiated a calming warmth, the emotions rising from it were anything but calm. Increasing fear, alarm, and high levels of tension wafted from the aeld, hitting him like waves against a seawall. Even a fresh corpse would have noticed its distress.

"What is it?" he asked the young tree, looking between it and Claygon. "Is that what's got you all excited, Claygon? Did you feel something coming off our leafy friend?"

He stepped toward the tree, placing a hand on its warm bark. "I know there seems to be something between you two."

Alex's eyes narrowed and he looked at his golem closely. "Is there something you want me to know? Something the tree noticed?"

Nothing came through Claygon's link, even after he'd waited quietly.

"Ah well," he said. "Maybe the weather's got this little one stressed." He patted the tree trunk. "Don't worry, you'll be okay. And I promise I won't... let you... get... buri—"

Something tickled his mana senses; something stirred beneath his feet.

"What... what's that?" He wondered if the earth mages were making changes to the tunnels directly under the castle. Maybe—

"Alexander!" a voice whispered behind him.

"Guh!" The young wizard leapt a foot forward, whirling around. Nothing was there. A brief surge of fear gripped his heart.

Was it a ghost? Had the tree sensed some invisible spirit here to stalk him through the world of the livi—

"Down here! Down here!" a familiar voice cried through the wind.

Alex looked down and yelped again. A sight he hadn't expected to see for at least another fifty years was looking back at him. "Gwyllain?" He glanced around before bending down. "What're you doing here?"

The little asrai was hugging himself against the cold, his jaws chattering. "Warning you!" he cried. "Monsters are coming from down below you wizards! They're going to attack you at any second!"

"What?" Alex gasped.

Then it sank in. The mana he'd felt below was familiar, but it had the stink of Ravener-magic.

"Oh, by the Traveller!" he shouted.

"Defend yourself!" Gwyllain said. "Don't go getting yourself gutted! Now I'm getting far away from here! Good luck! I'll try and get you some help!"

"Help? What kind of hel—"

The fae had already darted into the blowing snow and disappeared.

Alex's mind raced. The wind and snowflakes stung his face as he turned back to the tree. "That's what you felt! You felt the same monsters that treenapped you—"

His heart skipped. If the monsters were coming from below...

"Theresa and the others!" he shouted, sprinting toward the keep. "Help! We're about to be attacked! Monsters are—"

He'd only gotten half of his warning out before the alarm bells began urgently pealing throughout the research castle.

"Attention!" Watcher Shaw's voice boomed through the white. "We are under attack! Earth mages detected dungeon magic beneath us! We are under attack! Everyone to your battle-posts! Standby for a briefing! There's a lot of movement in the fortified stone beneath us! This'll be a bad one!"

"No, I know I heard something that time," Theresa said, drawing her swords.

"Ugh," Thundar grunted. "I'd say you're hearing things, but everyone who says that in all the stories gets their guts ripped out in the next verse."

"You're both being paranoid... Is what I *would* say, but Thundar's right. Everyone who goes on about 'it must've been the wind' is always the first one to die in all the bard's tales," Hogarth grunted, jumping to his feet and offering Svenia a hand.

She took his grip, pulling herself up and readying her spear. "With our luck, a xyrthak or dune worm tracked us here from the Barrens."

"For what reason?" Hogarth asked. "To kill us?"

"What do *you* think, Hogarth?" Svenia shot him a look.

"Pffft, only poor guards base their warnings on copper-penny stories," one of the younger dwarf engineers snorted.

"You only say that because you've never been ambushed by beast-goblins in the middle of a dig." The elder of the dwarven engineers put down his tools and picked up a two-handed axe. "Folk that brush off warnings are the first ones to die."

"Mm?" Grimloch shuddered, stretching and yawning. "What's going on? Is there action?" The giant bent down, picking up his brutal hammer.

Beside him, Brutus shook himself awake, his three tongues lolling out and his six eyes checking every direction. Then the cerberus froze.

His hackles went up, his ears perked up and he bounded to Theresa's side, snarling and growling.

"Shhh, quiet, boy," the huntress whispered. "Everyone, quiet for a second!"

At the end of the tunnel, the earth and fire mages paused, looking at each other as a tense silence fell over the excavation team. Theresa held her breath, cocking her head and listening to the air. In the distance, far down the tunnel... no... something was coming from the side of the tunnel.

"I hear something through the stone," she said softly, creeping to the wall.

"I do not like the look of this." The prince began whispering incantations, sheathing himself in stone armour.

"Hold on. Now I hear something too," Grimloch growled.

Theresa pressed her ear to the rock and closed her eyes again.

There, the sound of wings and shifting stone.

Her heart froze. She knew that sound. That same terrible groan of rock. She'd heard it every time she'd gone into battle inside a dungeon.

"Ravener-spawn!" the huntress yelled to her team. "They're shifting the walls! There must be a dungeon below us! Everyone, get ready!"

As her cry echoed through the tunnel, the stone began to shake.

Dust rained from the ceiling.

The earth mages gasped.

"The tunnel!" Prince Khalik roared. "Whoever's up there, they mean to bring it down on us!"

CHAPTER 70

THERESA'S BATTLE IN THE DARK

The cave floor bucked and heaved beneath Theresa's feet like an angry stallion bent on throwing her to the ground. The sound of stone cracking through weakened walls groaned from every direction.

Earth mages scrambled and dwarves shouted warnings.

"These walls'll fail!" An elder dwarf engineer climbed atop the closest cart, pointing his axe at the tunnel wall. "They'll bury us!"

"If we don't push back that mana, we're paste! And it's everywhere! C'mon, we've got to take control of the stone!" a senior earth mage thundered.

Prince Khalik and a stream of earth mages rushed to the walls, pressing their hands to the crumbling stone and bellowing incantations. For a terrible moment, the tunnel shook hard enough to upset oil lanterns sitting atop wooden worktables. Glass shattered into jagged shards, spreading pools of oil and flame along the tables and cracking floor. Fist-sized stones rained from the ceiling and walls, bringing dust that spilled down in clouds.

A fissure suddenly gaped open in the tunnel floor right in front of Brutus, sending the cerberus yelping and scrambling backward toward Theresa, his claws scrabbling against the stone. Panic hit the huntress full force. The tunnel was moving and buckling like a living, breathing thing, surging around her like the sea. The ceiling groaned, warping and threatening to drop tons of rock and earth on her and Brutus.

And she would be helpless to stop it.

Images of everyone she cared about flashed through her mind as she knelt and clung to Brutus, offering up prayers to the Traveller for help with every fibre of her being. Every muscle tensed, waiting for the crushing press of stone to bury them, the throb of pain, and then nothing.

Perhaps she'd meet Uldar. She had some questions for their silent god. Heartbeats passed—earth-shakes calmed. Cracks began to close. Stone stopped falling, and the terrible tremoring that threatened to topple everything around her began subsiding. Soon, the earth's roar calmed to low rumbles, then mild quakes.

Relief replaced panic.

"You did i—" she began.

"No!" Prince Khalik shouted. "The enemy's breaking through our defences! Look ou—"

A tunnel wall exploded. Jagged boulders blasted through the air, crashing into walls and skidding along the passage floor. Stone dust sprayed, sending the excavation team into fits of coughing.

The sound of flapping wings came next.

"Something's coming this way!" Theresa warned, jumping to her feet. "Something with wings!"

The team had mere moments to prepare before a stream of small bodies poured from the hole in the side of the tunnel. For a breath, Theresa glimpsed bat-like wings and long bodies soaring through the stone dust.

"Spear-flies!" she cried. They looked exactly like illustrations in the Thameish bestiaries, and she recalled the gruesome way they killed.

And as abruptly as they appeared, the monsters were on them.

Hundreds of wings thrummed through the air, foot-long bodies swarmed, shrouding the team as they disappeared in a haze of insects and floating stone dust. With a growl, Theresa slashed all around with both swords, every strike connecting to a spear-fly's body rippled through her arms as the Ravener-spawn dropped to the ground.

Her great-grandfather's blades split thin chitin, cleaving the monsters into twitching mounds. But for each dead one, ten more appeared. Beside her, Brutus sprang at them, mouths snarling, trying to snatch them from the air. They flocked to him in swarms, barbed legs digging at his tough hide, proboscises thrusting, seeking any place where his skin was thin enough to pierce.

"Brutus!" Theresa screamed, calling upon that well of lifeforce deep within her. "Get off of him, you filth!"

Her senses sharpened.

Blades whirled, dealing death in a blur.

Steel streaked through the swarm, splitting three with every stroke, clearing them away from her cerberus. They fell in droves, and Brutus' snapping jaws crushed more between them. In moments, the swarms were thinned though not gone. They persisted, pressing in on all sides. Theresa blurred as her swords shredded them to ribbons. Her enhanced speed kept them off of her and Brutus, yet they seemed to multiply with each swing.

It felt like she was floundering against a tide of white water sweeping her down a river. And from what she could hear coming from her companions, they were struggling too. Through the swarms and swirling dust, spells roared and loud blasts of power mixed with war cries and screams of pain. Theresa spotted Grimloch's immense form bellowing and sweeping his weapon through the spear-flies. His great jaws filled with rows of jagged teeth opened, then snapped shut, grinding groups of Ravener-spawn into ground meat between them.

Yet, every inch of him was covered in spear-flies.

They crawled over his rough, grey skin, stabbing at it again and again. In some places—beneath the armpits and backs of his knees—their proboscises pierced the flesh beneath. The Ravener-spawns' bodies swelled and turned red as they sucked the beast man's blood.

"Grimloch!" Theresa shouted, tapping Brutus' side. "We have to get to him, boy!"

Grimacing, she led her yelping cerberus toward their giant friend, cutting through the swarm. As they drew closer, Theresa caught sight of the others. The horned head of Thundar ducked and weaved around the swarm while he sprayed the parasites with cones of magical force. They ruptured under waves of power, splattering surrounding rock. The minotaur shouted a spell that made the air shimmer.

Three minotaurs appeared, the illusionary duplicates swinging their 'magical' maces through the cloud of Ravener-spawn, driving them into a frenzy. The filthy flying creatures struck empty air as the real Thundar's force spells tore them to pieces. Some still surged past their kindred and clung to his force armour, jabbing at it with barbed legs and sharp proboscises.

"Get off me, blood-suckers!" He stumbled back, tearing them away.

"Thundar! Hold on, I'll—agh!" Svenia cried, waving a roaring torch through the mass of winged monsters.

Back to back, she and Hogarth fought the swarm, tossing flasks of lantern oil then setting it ablaze. Flame came to life, engulfing screeching spear-flies, driving them into each other in full panic. They dropped from the air in burning heaps.

But the two warriors had no time to celebrate; dozens more came at them, replacing each smouldering sibling.

"Agh! They're on me!" Svenia cried, as several gripped her armour. She slapped them away with her torch, but one managed to jab its jagged legs into a section of links in her chainmail.

Then its proboscis sank into her back through a gap in the rings.

Its body swelled, soon washing red.

Svenia screamed and spun around, trying to tear it off, but more swarmed her, driven manic by the sight of flowing blood.

"Hogarth! Help! Get it off!" she shrieked.

"Keep still, I'll burn it! Stop moving for—oh, shit!" He shoved his torch at the creature, but one landed on his helm, blinding him. The warrior stumbled away, struggling to get free. Svenia's screams grew more frantic as the spear-fly grew fatter on her lifeblood.

And then...

A shadow fell over her.

One with a massive wingspan.

It swooped down, seizing the Ravener-spawn in its talons, piercing it, tearing it away. The deadly form of Najyah shrieked in rage, her body shimmering with Khalik's power.

A wave of acid erupted, washing over the clot of Ravener-spawn, melting insectile bodies while some felt the bite of talons and a razor-sharp beak.

"Thank... thank you!" Svenia gasped, fighting off the other spear-flies. She was pale, but alive.

Not all were as lucky.

The swarm moved in perfect unison, like a giant's mind in a thousand tiny bodies, hunting the weak. Two dwarven engineers screamed like pigs at the slaughter, their bodies buried in swelling, pulsating spear-flies. The Ravener's spawn tripled in size, growing thick and red, while the dwarves' flesh turned from mottled blue to stark white.

They collapsed, stilled, then withered like fall leaves.

"Ullvar! Bjorn!" the older dwarven engineer cried. His axe whirled around him as spear-flies now clung to him. "Somebody, help them!"

"They're gone!" a nearby bloodmage shouted. "Keep *yourself* safe!"

He turned back to the wizard he tended, channelling magic into her body while others defended him with acid, fire, and lightning. Wizards conjured fresh winds, blowing Ravener-spawn back, and clearing out stale cavern air.

Spellcasters burnt through the purified air as quickly as it was replaced.

Tyris sprayed lava, coating scores of spear-flies in boiling rock, filling the ground before her with the burning monsters. A pair of Watchers leapt over the pile while strafing the swarms with whirlwinds of ice.

In between the two, a third Watcher thrust her staff toward the breach, speaking a word of power. A shimmering wall of force magic sprang up, cutting off the spear-flies.

"Finish these off! I'll keep the rest of them out!" the Watcher shouted, conjuring a whip of flame from her staff and raking the cloud of flying bodies.

Cheers went through the excavation team, and Theresa felt hope for the first time since the spawn had attacked.

Her blades flashed as she fought toward Grimloch, leaping beside the shark man and cutting down spear-flies.

The swarm thinned, letting the shark man throw himself against the wall, crushing dozens clinging to him.

"Thanks!" Grimloch snarled.

"No problem!" Theresa said, chopping at the spawn around him and Brutus. "Now we can—Wait, what's that?"

A deep rumbling noise began.

"Look out!" Svenia pointed to the wall across the passage.

It was swelling.

Swelling and straining.

Before anyone could react, it burst like overripe fruit. Rock shot through the tunnel. A single boulder swept the old dwarf engineer off the cart, mashing him to pulp against the wall.

Shocked cries erupted.

Bodies fell as stones launched into ducking forms.

A clang and a muted cry escaped as a rock struck Hogarth's helm with such force, it put him down like a stricken ox.

"Hogarth!" Svenia cried, grabbing his limp body to drag him toward the blood mages.

She glanced at the new breach and all colour drained from her face.

Dozens of glowing eyes burned deep within the dark hole, each pair framed by looming silhouettes. Alight with wild abandon, a frenzied wave of bone-charges barreled into the tunnel.

"Our forces are striking the enemy in their tunnels," one of the Hunters growled. "They have engaged all the mortals who could reach the Usurpers' base to offer reinforcement."

"This pleases me," the Petrifier growled. Its eyestalks turned in several directions. Two watched the shafts in the caverns' walls and the swarms of Ravener-spawn pouring through them. Three eyed the dungeon cores, noting the cracks forming in their dead, black surfaces.

They would not take the strain forever.

Hopefully, they would last long enough for the work to be finished.

"Have the tunnels been collapsed?" the leader asked the Hunter.

The smaller Ravener-spawn hesitated. "No, leader. The enemy held back the dungeon cores' power with magic."

"Unfortunate," the Petrifier growled. "The more help we can deny the Usurpers, the better. Go, take some of your siblings and clear those tunnels out. Then come to the Usurpers' base above."

"Yes, leader," the Hunter growled, bounding back into the passage.

The Petrifier's eyes returned to inspecting the dungeon cores, watching the walls around the pair of dark orbs shimmer and buck. Stone swelled, transforming into four egg sacks—two titanic and two human-sized—that split, releasing four monstrous creatures. Two were made of swarms of spear-flies clinging together to form humanoid shapes. The wings of the collection of Ravener-spawn rubbed together as they bowed to the Petrifier.

The other pair of monstrous beasts bowed low, their great bulks constrained by the cavern walls. Towering more than twice ten feet with shoulders nearly as broad, a thick coat of bone-plates sheathed them, and each left arm ended in a club-like protrusion covered in spikes. Their glowing red eyes flashed with a dull, but vicious intellect.

"Welcome to the world, behemoths and hives-as-one. Welcome to the good work," the Petrifier said.

At its words, the dungeon cores screamed, cracking as more behemoths and hives-as-one emerged from the walls. The Petrifier's force grew in strength and number. Had the multi-eyed beast been capable of smiling, it would have grinned from ear to ear.

"Leader!" another Hunter called from the passages before emerging into the cavern, its eyes showing fear.

One of the Petrifier's eyes turned to its hound. "Speak."

"We have pinpointed the Usurpers' position, but there's a problem!"

"What is it?" Now all eyes turned.

"We've been detected," the Hunter growled. "Mana surges on the surface and an alarm has been sounded. We can hear it through the rock!"

The Petrifier stiffened with displeasure. "What of the Usurpers? Are they trying to escape?"

"One remains where they were before." The Hunter pointed to the ceiling. "But the other is moving toward a large pool of mana within their lair. We cannot say what it is, or why."

The Petrifier's teeth ground together. A Usurper had disappeared into thin air earlier, and now another was moving toward a great source of mana. Would they also disappear?

This could not be allowed.

There was another crack from the dungeon cores. More lines were spreading across their surfaces and their mana was sputtering. They were failing. Time was short.

"Open the shafts above us. Force them if you have to," the Petrifier ordered the cores. "Behemoths, hives-as-one. Some of you will enter the tunnels and kill all who resist. As for the rest of you..." It looked to the Hunter. "Give me the locations of the Usurpers and this source of mana that one of them flees to. We'll open the earth, then attack from beneath their feet."

CHAPTER 71

DEFENCES IN THE BLIZZARD

"**B**ut the tunnels!" Alex's voice rose. "I have to get down there. My friends are—"

"Mr. Roth, we've already sent help to the excavation team," Watcher Shaw barked, not sparing the young wizard a glance as he strode through the raging blizzard, adjusting his scarf to shield his face. A line of Watchers followed close behind. "We don't need—Hey, you!" He pointed at a wind mage floating from a nearby doorway. "Yes, you! I want you on top of the keep! Cut this whiteout down. We can't defend a fortress if we can't see more than a foot in front of our own noses!"

"Yes, Watcher!" the wizard shouted above the howling wind and levitated toward the keep.

Watcher Shaw didn't break stride. "As I was saying, the last thing we need is more people to rescue."

"I can take care of myself, and I've got Claygon!" Alex pointed at the golem by his side. "We can get right—"

"I'm not losing track of students today, because none of you'll be running into tunnels half-mad, if I can help it." Watcher Shaw's voice cracked like a whip. "You want to help? Stay where we can keep track of you and go defend the castle so the excavation teams have a point to retreat to! Or get to the portal and evacuate. I don't care which. I'm not letting anyone else into those tunnels and that's final. Now do what's proper and leave me be. I've got work to do."

With a single word of power, Watcher Shaw took to the air, disappearing into the wind and stinging snow with his Warrior-mages. The young Thameish wizard ground his teeth, considering a way to get to the tunnels without being spotted by the Watchers. Theresa and the others were down there with those monsters. Worry tore through him as images of violence and death finding his friends in the dark plagued him.

But one thought kept rolling through his mind.

Last thing we need is more people to rescue, Watcher Shaw had said.

Alex knew he could handle himself, but from what Gwyllain said, there was a strong chance he already knew what or who the Ravener-spawn were looking for.

Him... and Carey. They'd controlled dungeon cores, which might've put giant bullseyes on their backs. He moved closer to Claygon, wondering if a clawed monster was waiting to pounce on him in the blinding snow.

Watcher Shaw's words repeated in his head. "Last thing the Watchers need is more people to rescue."

'And the last thing my friends need are more monsters to fight. If those things are trying to kill me and Carey and I run into a tunnel with them chasing me, I'll bring them straight to my friends. No, the hell with that. It's better if they come outside, we have more defences out here than underground.'

Wizards and warriors, looking like spectres in the whiteout, were moving into position throughout the courtyard, preparing for the monster attack.

Spells that raised and hardened snow into towers of ice were being cast. Wizards buried beneath mounds of white cast ice spells that bonded sheet after sheet of ice as hard as diamond atop each other, creating bunkers where they could lie in wait, hidden from view. A group of flying mages soared overhead, leaving glowing glyphs of light in the air.

Alex recognised the deadly sigils. They were set to gently hover in the wind until a monster ventured too near, then they'd trigger, unleashing a storm of force magic that would pierce attackers, stopping them in-flight. And the glyphs weren't the only deadly surprise waiting for the enemy.

Summoners had called on monsters, and wind mages were flying above the courtyard, shouting words of power, creating roaring winds that blew snow away from the castle. Their voices had gone hoarse from endless chanting, yet they persevered without pause or complaint, and for their efforts, the whiteout thinned in varied areas throughout the courtyard.

Earth mages chanted spells of earth movement, pushing their power into the ground. Through the snow beneath his feet, Alex felt a great struggle between the wizards' earth magic and the intense source of dark mana below.

They were holding it back for now, but their efforts couldn't last forever.

It was time for him to help.

"Right." He turned to Claygon now standing behind him, gripping his war-spear as the snow battered his broad clay shoulders. "Let's not make things worse. Let's make it so our friends have somewhere safe to return to."

Biting down on his worry and sending up a silent prayer to the Traveller to keep Theresa safe, Alex conjured his army.

He'd already conjured his defensive spells, eight Wizard's Hands and six forceballs; now it was time for summoned monsters. The first to answer were groups of water and ice elementals bubbling and crackling in the whiteout. They appeared at his call, greeted by biting snow pellets and frosty winds.

"Welcome back, Bubbles," he said to the little water elemental, while it shuddered at the cold and bubbled indignantly. "I know it's cold, but wait, I'll get you something that'll help." He sent six Wizards Hands to the stables where the Watchers' mounts were sheltered, and they soon returned with chunks of salt from a salt lick. "Here, take this! It'll make you and our water elemental friends more comfortable. But don't spray it out. When you spray liquids out, you have to keep it in your bodies for it to work.

"It's salt and it'll lower your freezing point. Keep it inside you, and you'll be safer against the cold."

The water elementals gathered around him like excited children, all bubbling happily. Another time, he would've found their reactions cute. But right now, his time was limited.

"I'll give everyone directions in a second," he said to the water and ice elementals. "I just want you to know that we're about to be in for a rough fight, so I've gotta get more friends to help us."

Pouring himself back into summoning spells, he called for help from creatures best suited to the terrain.

Taraneas, resistant to cold and able to bind enemies with their webbing. Earth elementals to dig through deep snow and the frozen ground below it and catch Ravener-spawn unawares. Air elementals would fly by his side. Flicker dogs could teleport, flashing from visible to invisible, and they could harass monsters bigger than themselves. Hellhounds would have the task of torching attackers, and hell-boars—also resistant to cold—could burn and crush them.

When Alex was finished summoning, a fearsome force surrounded him, one ready to fight and follow his commands.

"Alright." He brushed snow off his long hair and cloak when he finished the last spell. "Welcome back, everyone," he said to his summoned horde, switching extraplanar languages as he needed. "This time, the enemy's in the ground below us, and we can use the terrain to our advantage. Air elementals, follow me and defend me as best you can."

The air elementals exhaled sharp gusts in acknowledgement.

"Water and ice elementals," he continued. "I want you to combine your power and quick-freeze anything threatening that's coming up to the surface from below ground. Hell-boars and hellhounds, you work together; burn anything menacing. Earth elementals, I'd like three of you to stay over there with the aeld tree. Your job is to defend it. The rest of you stay hidden in the earth and attack every monster you can. Anything trying to get to the surface gets stopped. Flicker dogs, I want you hamstringing anything that walks or runs. Taraneas, bury yourselves in the snow and trap anything in your webbing that walks, crawls, or flies. Does everyone understand?"

The summons answered in the many tongues of elementals, celestials, and devils, then his army spread out, getting ready for the coming Ravener-spawn.

"Alright," Alex's breath misted in the air. "Potion time." He watched Claygon while he dug potions from his bag. "Hey, buddy, if you want to finish forming your mind or start evolving or anything... now would be an awfully good time to do it."

Claygon merely stood at his side in silence, ready for his instructions.

There was no longer a spark of thought through his link with the golem.

"Well, that figures. If timing was a matter of convenience, then the Ravener-spawn would've attacked when Baelin was here. Still, thanks for showing me that there was something wrong with the aeld tree, Claygon. Between you, Gwyllain, and the aeld, I had like three warnings even before the alarm went off..."

Alex paused as unwanted images of his friends dying horrid deaths took over his thoughts. He shook them away like dirty water. "Listen, I don't know if your mind can hear me right now, Claygon, but I want you to protect yourself. Like, absolutely protect me too, but look after yourself too. Don't go jumping in front of beams or anything like that. Seriously. I don't know what I'd do without you."

Claygon silently held his war-spear.

Alex sighed, patting his golem on his side. "Well, you're a good listener, bud—"

The ground bucked beneath his feet. Another surge of dark mana shifted.

"They're pushing hard!" an earth mage cried through the storm. "Feels like they've turned all the ground down there into a dungeon! We're holding them back for now, but they're going to breach!"

"Jeffrey! Hines! Get those noncombatants back to Generasi!" Watcher Shaw shouted to two of his lieutenants. "I want them through that portal before we get a whiff of Ravener-spawn stink!"

"The noncombatants," Alex muttered. "Carey and Professor Jules would be among them. Good, I hope they get through the portal fast. The faster the better."

"Alex!" Isolde's voice reached him.

He turned to see the tall, dark-haired woman flying through the snow, an electric blue wind-and-rain shield protecting her face. "There you are. Have you heard anything about the tunnels? About Svenia and Hogarth?"

"Not a single word," Alex said as she floated down beside him. "I take it you haven't heard anything either?"

"I just came from helping some of our research colleagues get to the teleportation circle, and there is still a lineup forming of people wanting to escape."

"Let's hope that line moves fast. Are Carey and Professor Jules gone?"

"Carey is helping direct and organise people, and Professor Jules said she would not leave until all of her team has gone through." Isolde looked back toward the direction she'd come from. "It was hell trying to convince her not to stay behind to wait for the two of us."

"Yeah, that sounds like her," Alex said. "I wish I could go into the tunnels."

"As do I." Isolde looked down as the ground quietly rumbled. "As do I."

"Well, the best we can do is make sure everyone down there has a safe, Ravener-spawn free zone to come back to." He dug around in his bag. "Here, potions of haste, sensory enhancement, and agility enhancement. They'll help you see a little farther and maneuver better in this snowstorm."

"Thank you," she said. "Ah, here."

She turned, casting a flight spell on Claygon. "There you go, Claygon. Now you can keep up with your father."

"Thanks." Alex drank potions of flight, haste, sensory enhancement, agility enhancement, and strength enhancement. He wiped the cold liquid from his lips as he and Isolde cast Orbs of Air over their heads. "Listen, Isolde, take care of yourself. Seriously. This could be rough. There's a lot of mana moving around down there. Too much for one dungeon core, I'm thinking."

"I feel it." She looked up, frowning. "What of your tree?"

"I have earth elementals protecting it," he said. "That's the best I can do. Hopefully, all that stuff about bringing fortune wherever it's planted is actually true. We could use some good fortune right now." Alex raised his hand, looking down at the wooden witch's ring on his finger. "And *we* could use some protection too."

Isolde was about to say something.

Then the earth bucked. Hard.

"They're pushing through!" an earth mage cried. "They'll be up here soon!"

"Everyone, get ready!" Watcher Shaw shouted. "You're all experienced enough to know what you're about. Fight to your strengths: remember the entries in the bestiaries and don't let yourself get buried by numbers!"

Another rumble ripped through the earth as the ground bucked again.

The dark mana raged, as energetic and chaotic as fire and a plague of locusts.

Earth mages screamed out spells all around, their voices carried by the wind.

Mana battled mana below their feet.

"May your Traveller bless you, Alex," Isolde whispered.

"And the Elements bless you, Isolde," he said in return.

There was another surge of dark mana so powerful, that it shook his mana senses, crackling like lightning. He and Isolde exchanged a nod. The mana merged beneath them into singular points of power, sharpening like a thrusting estoc sword ready to punch through armour.

Then the ground bucked once.

Then again.

Then it ruptured beneath their feet.

CHAPTER 72

A BATTLE IN THE WHITE

Alex, Claygon, and Isolde shot away when the ground cracked. Rock whizzed by. With jaws clenched, Alex weaved through the barrage, praying to the Traveller that they would clear the pelting rocks.

Stone shards seemed to soar in every direction, but only dust reached them. He sent out a silent prayer of thanks to the Traveller as he peered into the gaping chasm, then swore.

The craggy tear in the earth was teeming with a pulsating mass of spear-flies with one goal. He recalled drawings in the bestiaries of their dried out victims.

Their wings snapped out, propelling long insectile bodies upward. The creatures launched toward the surface as one, but as they neared, the hole's ragged edges crumbled, raining massive rock shards, forcing Ravener-spawn down to an unforgiving tunnel floor.

But, like falling snowflakes, dozens more appeared, replacing the dead. Above the eerie sound of howling winds, the beating of leathery wings grew as swarm upon swarm of spear-flies rose from the dungeon below, thirsting for blood. In heartbeats, the courtyard exploded into shouted spells, war cries, explosions, and energy blasts. Trap-sigils blazed bright every time Ravener-spawn flew near, spells flared into a mass of tiny beads of light no bigger than acorns, then exploded, shrapnel skewering spear-flies, tearing through one insectile body then another in a cascade. Dozens plummeted, ending their ascent.

The storm's gusting winds were also working in the wizards' favour as they grabbed the lighter monsters and flung them straight into stone, ice walls, and waiting swords. In a sense, the teams' first snowstorm in Grey-moor might have been a blessing.

Except nature alone couldn't blow clouds of Ravener-spawn away and more attacked with abandon.

The wizards, warriors, and guards fought back.

Beside Alex, Isolde shouted an incantation. Lightning blazed around her hands and thunder rumbled through electrified air. Alex felt his scalp crawl as she unleashed a new spell. Her arms swept out, the young noble-woman clenched her fists, and tendril-like, crackling whips of lightning formed in her grip. Around her, the air thrummed with thunder as she swept her whips through the coming swarm.

The creatures crackled, splitting apart where lightning touched them, and crumbling where thunder raked their flesh. Still more appeared, pressing her from all sides. Some bounced off of greater force armour, but others clung tight, sawing at her defensive magic with jagged limbs.

"Enough of that!" Alex cried, shooting a Wizard's Hand beside his cabal mate.

The spell's grip tightened on a flask of sleeping potion, cracking it. Isolde hovered in potion mist, enveloped for a moment, then spear-flies abruptly fell away, plummeting to the snow covered earth.

"Thank you!" she called, her lightning-whips cracking through the swarm.

Alex was already focused on defending himself.

Spear-flies swarmed from all around, focusing on him. If dozens had attacked Isolde, then hundreds were attacking him. He tried weaving through them, but there were too many to escape from. He could never dodge every flake of snow in a blizzard, just as he could never dodge every one of these monsters. Their number was as thick as the wall of snow swirling through the courtyard, and they carpeted him in mounds, clinging to his force shield so tight, it looked like it was some strange force construct of giant bugs.

His defensive force rectangles shattered one by one as they shifted position, trying to block monsters. They landed on his force armour next, crawling over it, using barbed legs to test for weak spots. A probing spear-fly wormed its way into a gap, its pointed proboscis was poised, ready to stab him, when a wave of magical energy stopped it cold. The witch's ring tingled on his finger.

"Get off me!" Alex plucked spawn away, tossing them to the wind, but even more settled in their place. Forceballs and force shield whirled around him, knocking some aside, scraping others away, but though these defences were quickly overwhelmed, his elementals saved him.

The extraplanar creatures of air were there—six crackling protectors to defend him from the horde—to do their work without restraint. Exploding wind gusts howled, blowing light-bodied spear-flies into pelting snow. Lightning pulsed, raking the winged creatures, sending their sparking forms into free fall.

"Good work!" Alex shouted to the summons. "I need three of you whipping around me like a tornado, and three defending Isolde! Hit these things with everything you've got!" He pointed to the Rhinean wizard as the numbers of monsters swarming her escalated. "Don't let a single one through."

Isolde was defending herself with crackling whips and orbs of lightning, but even her deep mana reserves couldn't last forever. All six of his elementals crackled, three broke away, surrounding Isolde, defending her from the monsters' attacks. The other three whirled around him, spraying lightning and wind in all directions, casting Ravener-spawn down to their ruin.

Spear-flies scattered, but hundreds more were silhouetted in the blizzard and whiteout around them. Unseen defenders—wizards and more—screamed in the distance, shrouded by blinding snow, clearly not faring well.

Frantic calls for help reached him.

His Wizard's Hands flew toward the voices, tightly clutching booby-trapped potion bottles, and stopping in the midst of a monster swarm. Glass shattered, releasing a combined mist of booby-trapped flight and sleep magic. In breaths, the enemy dropped like rocks, or launched uncontrolled through the storm, colliding with each other, the Watchers' gauntlets, walls, and eventually the ground. 'Claygon!' Alex thought. 'Charge your fire-beams!'

His golem hovered nearby, sweeping his war-spear and fists through the swarm, batting and pulping dozens of Ravener-spawn in single swings. As Alex's voice came through their mental bond, the fire-beams' burning light illuminated whipping snow.

Whoooooooom!

They gathered power.

Their mana built. Alex grabbed more potions from his satchel, tossing them to his Wizard's Hands. All around him, shouting and muffled cries came in waves as the castle's defenders battled what seemed to be an ever-renewing horde of spear-flies.

'If these spawn are after Carey and me, I'd better try and keep most of their attention on me,' he thought.

"Isolde! I'll try and herd as many of these things in one place as I can and get them away from everyone else so Claygon can blast them! Are you gonna be okay?" he shouted.

"I can handle myself! I have no doubt they can use more help at the keep! Good hunting!" she cried, soaring into the sky with his conjured guardians surrounding her.

Alex took a deep breath, eyeing the swarm around him. "Alright, you wicked bastards! You want me? Come get me!"

He tucked in his limbs—reducing wind resistance—and shot through the freezing storm, bellowing challenges to the spear-flies, taunting them as he flew. They probably had no clue what he was saying, but they took the bait, trailing after him, following like an entity was directing them.

"That's right!" Alex shouted. "I've got some blood for you and your filthy maker. Try and get some!"

They tore through the sky weaving above the battlefield, and Alex glanced down toward the fighters, taking stock of how they were faring.

Like phantoms in a world painted white, Ravener-spawn were everywhere.

They burst from the earth through dozens of jagged holes, then set upon the Generasians like fire ants. Spear-flies swarmed through the sky, but another type of Ravener-spawn churned through snow drifts, kicking up sprays of white. Bone-chargers raged through the courtyard, squealing and barreling toward anything they could reach.

The Watchers of Roal met them with steel, and with magic blazing, they struck the mighty bone-chargers with spells of force, frost, and flame. Above them, wind mages cast whirlwinds to contain the spear-flies, while other wizards conjured their own swarms of elementals and summoned monsters to tear the spear-flies from the air.

Yet, for all of this power, bone-chargers still barreled through spell after spell, running down warriors, trampling them where they stood. Patches of white turned red.

Alex bristled. Those things needed to die.

"With me, Watchers!" a familiar voice cried from somewhere in the blowing snow. "Send these spawn back to the cradles of filth they crawled from!"

Watcher Shaw emerged like a vengeful war-spirit floating above the earth, his form wreathed in flame. His sword was sheathed in power, blazing in a storm of force magic, and he shouted an incantation, channelling a staggering amount of mana. He levelled his staff as he finished the spell, unleashing a cone of screaming spirits into the world.

They raged through spear-flies and bone-chargers alike—passing through flesh like water—and when they emerged from the other side, they clutched chunks of meat in their phantom hands. The Ravener-spawn stopped—stricken—spewing fountains of black and red, until collapsing in pools of melting snow.

Any monsters spared from the blast were met by the Watcher's flashing sword. With every blade strike, his force magic boomed, crushing bone and tough hide, letting the blade slide through soft underbellies. With each stroke, a bone-charger fell, Shaw leaving carnage in his wake. His fellow Watchers followed the same path, destroying spawn on land and in the air.

"You actually spar with these people, Theresa?" Alex muttered to himself as he soared past the Watchers, gaining attention from a growing number of Ravener-spawn. "Claygon, I want you to get as many spawn as you can! Clear them out with your war-spear!"

Silently, the golem dove—his upper arms charging the fire-gems while his lower ones ripped the war-spear through bone-chargers. The blade split their hard carapace and tough hide like fresh curds, and each monster withered from the spear's deadly magics. Some whirled, leaping high into the air to strike at the golem, but a massive clay fist sent them tumbling back to the snow in broken heaps.

Bone-chargers scattered, leaving their fallen brethren behind. As they fled, their eyes didn't focus on Claygon.

They fell on Alex.

If there was any doubt before that they were there for him, there was none now. When he flew past packs of bone-chargers, they squealed like wild boar set upon by a wolf pack and charged after him.

Some abruptly abandoned fights with the castle's golems and the hulking summoned demons the wizards had conjured. A pack menaced a group of spear-wielding warriors until the blurring form of Ripp sprinted through the snow with his glinting blade in hand, diving beneath towering Ravener-spawn, hamstringing them, leaving them as easy prey for Generasi spear bearers.

Alex approached as a warrior strayed too close to a bone-charger, it snatched the man's leg in its jaws at the same moment Ripp's blade hamstrung it, but it still raised a giant fist above the warrior, poised to crush him while it tumbled like a falling oak. An enormous war-spear arced from above, slicing the Ravener-spawn's skull in two. Its fist dropped. The wounded man lay in the snow, eyes wide and breathing hard. Ripp bent down to help him up.

Alex cursed. He couldn't drop any booby-trapped potions since he didn't know who was protected by Orbs of Air and who wasn't. So, he did the next best thing. He egged on the monsters.

Alex growled. "Hey, over here! C'mon, you bastards. Catch me! Catch me!"

The bone-crushers' eyes flared as they spotted him. They squealed and pulled away from the warriors to chase after the Thameish wizard.

Alex led them through the whipping white frost, picking up more speed as he called out to them. He flew above the aeld and was grateful that the monsters passed it by like it wasn't even there. It must've seemed harmless to them, but Alex wasn't so sure it *was* harmless. As bone-chargers gave chase, strange misfortunes hit them: some slipped on ice, or were blinded by sudden wind gusts, spinning them through the air and into each other, toppling them in twisted heaps like clumsy acrobats.

The aeld tree's fortune did not favour them, it seemed.

Those that remained upright, though, sprinted after Alex as though the fires of every hell in the planes pursued them.

"That's right, chase me," he whispered, turning toward the swarm at his back and the horde below. They filled his vision, spreading out into the snow-lashed whiteout.

Whooooom!

"You're not going to like what you catch." Alex sent the mental command to Claygon.

'Fire.'

Whoooosh!

Two fire-beams lanced into the horde below while the third raked the swarm above. Instantly, spear-flies exploded in an inferno, bursting from pent-up heat. As insectile creatures died, Claygon's beams spread deeper into the thinning swarms. Snow vaporised, and white blazed red and gold in columns of flame. Bone-chargers burned in moments, the air super-heating and turning their lungs to ash. Their glowing eyes dimmed in fire.

Soon, winter's chill seemed far away when Claygon's fire-beams finally stopped.

The horde was devastated. Piles of smoking ash and blackened bodies smouldered in melting snow. Hissing vapour snaked into the air, dispersing in the wind.

Alex sighed in satisfaction. "Time to do it again, Clay—"

An earth-shattering explosion, strong enough to sway an escarpment, rocked the castle.

The young wizard whirled in that direction, his blood dropping colder than the blizzard. "That came from the teleportation building! Claygon, we've got to—"

Beside him, the ground detonated.

An enormous monster clad in bone loomed beside him.

And he felt mana flare.

CHAPTER 73

BLAZING DESPERATION

The behemoth towered above the snow covered terrain, growling and snapping like crumbling bone. The earth trembled with each heavy footfall while a thick fog of misting breath froze in the air. Wide eyes sought a single target and blazed with recognition, lighting up when they fell upon Alex. Long bone-spikes sprang from its armoured form, shuddered in the air, then shot toward their target with all the force of a storm of arrows.

"Oh shit!" Alex whirled away, dodging through a barrage of spikes heading straight at him.

Claygon soared in front of him, solid bone splintered to shards on his clay body, but the behemoth wasn't done. It launched volley after volley of bony projectiles as a fresh swarm of spear-flies poured from the hole beneath the behemoth and swarmed the wizard. His trio of summoned protectors zapped and blew as many Ravener-spawn away as they could. Alex twisted and turned midair like a snake, but shards still struck, glancing off his forceshield and raking the surface of his force armour. He grunted from the force of each impact and howled with pain when a shard passed through a gap in the force armour, slicing his right leg.

"Bastard!" he cursed at the spawn, tucking in his limbs and spinning through the bone slivers like a top. "I'm going to—"

A surge of mana blazed in his mana senses.

He paused for a moment, focusing on the behemoth: on its shoulder sat something bearing no resemblance to bone-spikes.

A hive-as-one—built from a vast colony of spear-flies—turned its jagged hands toward him. Dark magic blazed over its limbs.

Desperate to escape, he barrel-rolled through the air.

A beam of utter blackness ripped from its hands.

The pitch-black ray arced toward him, zig-zagging through the swarm and homing in on Alex. He jerked to the side.

But not fast enough.

It slid across his force armour, passing through it, glancing off his flesh. Agony hit him in a wave. His left side went cold as though bathed in ice water and a weariness spread over the spot where the beam had clipped him.

His flesh began to wither.

A cry of agony escaped his lips.

And the world went black.

<hr />

The bone-charger bucked and thrashed beneath Theresa's feet as her swords chopped at the back of its neck again and again.

"Die!" she screamed. "Die, damn you, just die!"

Snarling, she raised an arm above her head, drove the point of a sword into the thick hide sheathing its neck, then hammered the pommel with the hilt of her other blade. The monster went wild, squealing, running into walls, trying to throw her to the cave floor, but the huntress grabbed its dorsal spikes with a death grip. Its arms flew up, grabbing at her, but she knocked them aside with every bit of life-enforced strength she could call on.

Her blade rose again. She slammed it into its twin's hilt—once, twice, three times, and on the third, something gave, the bone-charger went stiff.

With a loud exhalation of breath, the great beast finally toppled toward the tunnel floor as Theresa dragged her sword from the back of its neck then whirled around, ready for more monsters. Throughout the passage, the air filled with a cacophony of sound. Monstrous voices, shouted spells, panicked screams from injured and dying—both mortal and beast. The chamber felt overwhelming, like it was pressing down on her.

Two figures were struggling nearby on the tunnel floor, surrounded by clouds of rock dust. The sight snapped her mind back into sharp focus.

"Brutus!" she cried, charging to her cerberus and a bone-charger wrestling on the ground. The Ravener-spawn was bigger, not much stronger, inexperienced, untrained, and less agile. Brutus was beneath it with all three mouths filled with bone-crushing teeth latched onto its neck.

Theresa raced in, slashing at the beast, its tough hide already punctured with deep bite marks. The bone-charger fought to get free, squealing and pawing at the dirt as the cerberus' bites cracked bone, reached the flesh below, and tore chunks away. Theresa put it out of *their* misery, crossing her swords and slashing both sides of its throbbing throat. Her dog bounded to its feet beside her, barking and snapping a spear-fly from the air, crushing it between his jaws while his other heads panted with excitement.

The insect-like creatures' numbers had dwindled along with the bone-chargers', but there were still more to defeat.

Grimloch growled and swung his magical maul into a bone-charger's head. Its bone helmet shattered, and its pulped head flopped to the side. Thundar battled another one; his mace crushed bone with every swing. The beast yelped, clawing at illusionary duplicates flanking him and striking empty air. Frustrated, it turned and ran. Thundar whipped his mace at the fleeing creature, stopping it dead in its tracks. Svenia and Hogarth were back in the fight—healed by blood magic, though not a hundred percent. The hard-bitten warriors still gave it their all, stabbing bone-chargers and batting spear-flies from the air like they were clearing cluster flies.

When Thundar went to retrieve his mace, Najyah tore apart the last of the spear-flies with her beak and talons, and the Watchers brought down the final bone-charger with lances of force.

Dread hung in the air, rasping breaths and soft pained moans broke the silence as the Generasians tensed, not knowing what to expect next.

Then, the uneasy silence shattered.

A thud.

Followed by another.

And another.

The team whirled toward the pair of breaches in the tunnel wall. Both had been sealed by Watchers using force magic, but bone-chargers had quietly amassed in the passages behind them. Now, they were ready for their next attack, and powerful monsters rammed the force walls over and over, shaking the tunnel with every blow. Above them, spear-flies gathered, pressed together as one, poised to spill into the tunnel the instant the magical walls fell.

A pair of Watchers came forward at speed, levelling their staffs at the force walls. Both magical fortifications flared, drinking in the new power. "We'll hold the creatures back as best we're able, but these walls can't take this battering forever!"

The tunnel rumbled around them, clouds of stone dust and soil rained from the ceiling.

Tension spiked, but the earth mages pushed their power into the stone, holding back the enemies' mana.

"We're sitting ducks down here," Thundar grunted, panting and holding his knees while recovering his breath.

"I agree," the highest-ranking Watcher said. "We should get moving and fight our way back to the castle."

"That's impossible," the eldest of the earth mages growled as he struggled against the dungeon cores. "It's taking all of our strength to keep these monsters from crushing us to paste. If we move and lose concentration, they'll flatten us. We should stay right here and wait for help to come. The castle will send rescuers."

"And if they're under attack, what do you think'll happen? It'll take time for anyone to get here since they'll have to stabilise things up there first," the Watcher said sternly. "And by then, we could all be spawn food."

"We fought them off once," the earth mage fired back. "But no one's fighting a collapsing ceiling."

The Watcher's eyes narrowed. "In combat situations, I hold rank."

The earth mage's chest puffed out. "And in cases of the safety of this structure and how it affects the excavation, I—and the dwarf engineers—hold rank." He turned to the dwarves, who were silently praying over their fallen comrades.

"What are the chances of us surviving if this passage is compromised?"

A dwarf looked up, his face heavy with grief. "Next to none. Even if some of us get into an air pocket, we'll all die from suffocation or being crushed."

"We'll cast Orbs of Air around everyone's heads," the Watcher said.

"And then we might not smell gas if any's released from a cavity down here," the dwarf engineer warned.

"Wouldn't that be a good thing?" a wizard cut in, leaning against the wall as a blood mage bound his arm. "If we're smelling gas, we're getting poisoned, and if we've got Orbs of Air up, who cares if there's poisonous gas?"

"You need to study the earth's secrets more thoroughly, my friend," Prince Khalik said, his voice smooth yet strained. "Some gases can burn the skin as well as the lungs and others have little smell, but when met by fire..."

He let the words hang.

"That's right," the dwarf engineer said. "We dislodge some natural gas and don't detect it, then one of your little fire spells sends us all to the afterworld. Besides, Air Orbs or whatever won't help much if we get crushed by a thousand tons of rock."

Another crash reverberated through the force wall.

The lead Watcher grunted. "If we stay here, they'll break through. It's either go and live or stay here and get slaughtered."

"And *you* don't understand," the earth mage fired back. "If we move too fast, it'll be easier for that mana to overwhelm ours. And then—"

Tension mounted as the Watcher, earth mage, and the engineers argued. Theresa swallowed.

'They don't understand each other's training,' she thought. 'Each of them have good points, but they know nothing about what each other's training is telling them.

'It'd be like me and a wizard arguing about how to hunt a magical beast. The mage would come at it from the perspective of a wizard, looking at how to counter its magical abilities. I'd be coming at it from the perspective of a hunter, placing the most weight on its physical abilities and the terrain.'

In stressful situations, if a team didn't consider each other's perspectives, all sides would miss the full story.

"You okay?" Thundar asked, wiping blood and stone dust from his fur. "Those spear-flies drain you?"

"No," Theresa said, pulling her attention away from the argument. "I'm fine. How about you? Are you okay?"

Their little group had come together in the middle of the tunnel: Grimloch, Svenia, and Hogarth had wandered over to Theresa, Brutus, and Thundar.

"Yeah, the force armour protected me." Thundar nodded toward Khalik and led them to where the prince stood with his hands pressed to a wall. "And those things kept trying to gut my duplicates instead of me, thank the ancestors."

"Wish I had duplicates," Grimloch growled, stomping forward with giant footsteps. His iron-grey hide was covered in swelling spear-fly bites.

The huntress shuddered at the sight of them. If she'd taken half the bites Grimloch had, she'd be a bloodless corpse.

"Yeah, they found you right tasty." Hogarth chuckled as he limped beside Svenia. His pupils glistened, and one eye looked larger than the other. "They liked Svenia too."

His laugh grew shrill, drawing glances from the other members of the excavation team.

"Shhhh," Svenia shushed him. "Last thing we need is mad talk spreading more panic." Her voice dropped low. "Courage is hanging by a thread."

Around them, the team had broken into little groups, talking to each other in whispers. Nervous glances shifted between the force walls and their arguing leadership. Some were watching the tunnel, looking tempted to bolt for the castle and take their chances.

"Yeah," Theresa said quietly, reminded of those dark hours in the Cave of the Traveller, recalling the dread and fear that had lurked in the corners of her mind. "We don't want to set anyone off."

"If they're gonna panic that easily, we don't want them with us anyway," Grimloch rumbled, kicking a bone-charger's corpse as they passed. "Can't afford cowards. These Ravener-spawn were made of harder stuff than those chittering ones."

"Yeah," Theresa said, looking down at the carpet of dead spear-flies. "And that swarm's hard to deal with." She looked up at Khalik when they got closer. The prince's beard was a mess of grit and bits of gore, and Najyah was looming over his shoulder, nuzzling him with worry.

'Never seen her give him that much affection,' Theresa thought. 'We really must be doomed.'

"How're you holding up, Khalik?" she asked. "Are you okay?"

"Only my pride is bitten." The prince chuckled weakly. "And I did get clipped by a bone-charger. It felt like my ribs were going to tear through my chest and armour. I would've been dead if I'd received more than a glancing blow."

"Well, at least you'd already be buried." Thundar chuckled darkly. "We'd all already be."

The prince shared his dark laugh, though he looked a little wild around the eyes. "Well, we still might be if we do not do something—"

There was another rumble, and the tunnel shook.

Khalik grunted.

"You okay?" Thundar asked.

"I am," the prince said. "But it really takes a good deal of effort and control when the enemy throws its full weight at us and—"

The Watchers, earth mages, and engineers raised their voices.

"See? If we stay here—" the Watcher said.

"We'll be dead anyway if we move without—" an engineer fired back.

Their voices were drowned out by each other's as the argument intensified. The rest of the team muttered to each other.

"You know..." Theresa said, looking thoughtfully at Ravener-spawn corpses piled in heaps atop each other. "I remember something about bone-chargers being slower to make than chitterers and other monsters, right?"

"I do remember that entry from the bestiaries, yes," Khalik said. "Ah... I see where you are going. There are a great many of them down here. Far too many for a new dungeon to have crafted, so for there to be this many..."

"They'd need to have been below us for a while, making monsters the whole time," Theresa said quietly. "Unless the rules have changed."

"Yeah," Thundar agreed. "I know what you mean. And they have... Who knows what the hell else will be thrown at us." He spit on a nearby bone-charger corpse. "Shit, I can't die down here. I've got shit to do."

"Me too," Theresa said.

"I swore an oath to die for the Von Anmut family," Hogarth said, lifting his helm to massage his temples. "But I don't want my death to be down here in some tunnel."

"Separated from our lady while she fights for her life," Svenia said.

"It would not be a good death," Khalik said. "And—"

There was an immense crash from somewhere distant, and the tunnel shook again.

Everyone looked at Khalik, but the prince was just as wide-eyed as they were. "That wasn't the mana trying to bring the tunnel down," he said. "It was something else."

He cleared his throat and let his deep voice boom through the passage. "Leader! Team leader!"

The argument had gone silent as the Watchers, mages, and engineers eyed the walls. The earth mages' leader turned to the prince with a dumbfounded look.

"We must move," the prince said.

A cracking noise split the air. Stone crumbled.

"Another breach!" an earth mage cried.

Theresa darted toward the crack, but two Watchers reacted before her, levelling their staffs, shouting a single word. A powerful wall of force sprang up, sealing the breach before it could expand.

The tunnel rumbled as though the very earth rejected it.

Then it gradually calmed.

Earth mages and engineers glanced at each other.

The earth mage leader eyed the force wall. "You're right. We can't stay here. How much mana does everyone have left?"

CHAPTER 74

SEEING AS THEY ARE

Harsh Ravener-spawn cries echoed through the force walls, driving tension through the excavation team to new heights.

"Talk fast," the lead Watcher pushed.

"I have about half my mana left," an earth mage said.

"Same here," another echoed.

"Less for me," Prince Khalik said. Between fighting with utilizing mana and casting spells through Najyah, he was down to a quarter, if even that.

More earth mages reported: all were down to half their mana, maybe slightly more. Nobody's voice held enthusiasm or optimism.

"What about you lot?" the lead Watcher pressed the other Generasians.

Tyris raised a hand. "I've got about a third." The young woman was crouched with her back to a wall, drenched in sweat. "That swarm really had me pushing hard. Even with me using a mana regeneration technique, I can't really say how much I can make up before another attack comes."

Thundar raised a hand. "I've got more than half, but only by a little."

Other wizards weighed in, things were looking grim. Most were at half mana and some reported far less.

With a solemn nod, the lead earth mage's eyes focused on a spot in the distance, muttering calculations under his breath. "Okay, if we move slowly. And I do mean *slowly*, we could inspect the walls for differences in soundness and stone composition as we go without interfering with our earth and stone shaping spells."

"How slow are we talking?" the lead Watcher asked.

"Slow enough so the tunnel doesn't crumble around us like an egg." The earth mage frowned at the ceiling.

"Hmmmm... If we raise walls of force behind us while we move forward that should reinforce the tunnel and make your job easier, shouldn't it?" The Watcher followed the earth mage's eyes upward.

"That it would," the mage said. "We'd move a bit faster if you did too."

"Good, and it'll stop the spawn from getting right behind us." The Watcher cleared his throat and pointed at three of his juniors. "I want you, you, and you building those force walls. Set them up behind us about every twenty paces."

He turned to the blood mages. "We've got to be ready to move in under a couple of minutes, so you blood mages need to have our wounded on forcedisks in less than that. Everyone else? I want you prepped and ready to go by then."

"We'll be in your care," Thundar said to Khalik. "And I'm not even joking, I mean we'll actually be in your care, so remember, if you screw up, we're dead."

"Thanks," the prince said dryly.

"I wish I could help," Theresa said.

"You can, by making sure no bone-chargers trample me into paste." Khalik's jaw flexed.

"That I can do." Theresa checked her swords, remembering what it took to pierce tough bone-charger hide.

'I hope,' she added mentally, moving away to help the others prepare to leave.

The mood was bleak. Folk stared at the patched walls with dead eyes, some muttered silent prayers, others busied themselves by helping with the dead, leaving care of the injured to experienced blood mages. Healers secured the wounded to forcedisks, working quickly to stabilise and relocate them. Anyone who could fight was stretching and giving their blades and spear tips a quick wipe, and heavy weapons a few swings.

In a rush, all were in close formation, with warriors and mages at their flanks, positioned to defend against attacks. Watchers would lead, acting as vanguard, meeting frontal attacks with their melee skills and magics. Another group of Watchers would bring up the rear, raising walls of force behind them.

Fighters were at the front, back, and at either flank, guarding against ambushes from monsters charging in from air or ground. In the middle of the defenders were those unable to fight: the wounded, the healers, and the dead. The earth mages would also be in the middle acting as a lifeline and defence against the dungeon cores' plan to crush them.

Theresa took up position between Thundar, Brutus, and Grimloch. Behind them came Hogarth and Svenia—their spears at the ready—while Prince Khalik walked behind the two warriors with Najyah perched on his shoulder. Tyris was nearby.

"Alright, come on," Theresa heard her whisper. "I want to see my turtle, my bed, my family, and that tall, spicy drink of water. You're not getting my life, you stinking bastards."

The huntress glanced back, about to say something when the lead Watcher spoke.

"Alright, everyone, hold your position and we'll survive this. Are you earth mages ready?"

The eldest earth mage took a deep breath. "We are. I'll keep the pace, you keep us safe."

"Fair." The Watcher pointed ahead with his sword. "Let's go."

Everyone began their march. Darting eyes scanned tunnel walls with precision, while the entire passage shook. Theresa held her breath, listening to the sounds of unseen enemies moving through the stone. Flapping wings. Heavy steps. Shifting earth.

Her grip tightened on her swords, and beside her, Brutus sniffed the air, all three heads facing different directions.

"It's okay, boy," she whispered. "It's okay."

They crept forward, almost painfully slow, while the earth mages fortified the tunnel, casting spells at a whisper. Strain had been on their faces and in their voices before, but now, it'd grown exponentially.

Theresa prayed to the Traveller, her ancestors, and anyone else listening that their strength would hold. 'Please let me see Alex again. Please let me see Selina. Please let me see my parents, my brothers, Shi-Shi... and please don't let Brutus die—'

Crashing sounds reached them from deep in the tunnel to the rear.

The excavation team started to turn around. Theresa raised her swords.

"Eyes forward!" the lead Watcher shouted. "Keep moving! Watchers at the rear, you know what to do!"

"Sir!" they shouted, raising shimmering walls of force in their wake. The huntress dared to glance back, seeing wall after wall shining behind them. In the distance, she spotted a horde of Ravener-spawn throwing themselves into the walls, seeking to shatter them. The barriers shimmered and shook with each impact... but they held for now.

"Anyone trying to figure out how long it took us to get down here in the first place?" Thundar asked. "'Cause I know I am."

"You have any idea?" Theresa asked him.

"Too long," the minotaur grunted, his grip tightening on the haft of his mace. "Way, way, way too long."

The team continued along at a crawl, giving the earth mages the time they needed to adjust to the shifting rock. Every heartbeat seemed an eternity, and each rumble and shake of stone felt like a prelude to catastrophe. With silent footsteps and a pounding heart, the huntress helped move the group forward, glancing down at her great-grandfather's blades, remembering the feeling of trying to cut through the bone-charger. That resistance. That futility.

'Is this it?' she wondered, turning the blades, forceball light reflecting off the steel. 'Will I die with you down here in the dark?'

Towering anger rose in her chest, directed at herself. She imagined what might have been had she put these swords aside a long time ago and replaced them with something with more bite. Thundar's magical mace crushed bone. Grimloch's maul flattened a dozen foes at once. It was only her—and these swords—that were close to being dead weight. At least, that was how it felt.

And she was only one warrior with two blades. Were they sharper, maybe everyone's chances of survival would be better. These were deadly times; any extra advantage could mean death for the enemy, or doom for them.

For more times than she could count, she looked at her swords closely, as frightened whispers from some of her comrades, the terrifying crash of bone-chargers slamming against force walls, and the ominous rumble of shifting stone somewhere beyond the passage walls reached her. It was all closing in around her, bringing the swords into sharp focus.

Her professor had said, *see them clearly*. To see them for what they actually were.

'If I don't do this now, I might never get another chance,' she thought. 'I might never get a chance to do anything again.'

The huntress' eyes flicked between the passage ahead and the two blades in her hands. 'Describe everything you see. Two swords. Reflective. Tassels on their hilts. Thick crossguards, but not wide. Forged from steel. Old swords. Sharp edges.'

"Hey, do you hear that?" Grimloch growled. "Theresa, you hear that?"

"Hear what?" She pulled her mind away from the blades, looking at him with concern.

"Ahead." He nodded to the front of the tunnel. "Fighting."

Theresa peered down the winding passage, concentrating on her hearing. She picked out distant sounds over quiet footsteps, laboured breathing, and the murmurs of her companions. There was chaos, distant explosions, and the crack of metal on flesh and bone. Voices shouting spells.

"There's fighting up ahead somewhere," she told the shark man.

"Yeah, that's what I'm hearing too," Grimloch grunted, tightening his grip on his maul. "Means the enemy's already ahead of us."

Though his tone was optimistic, almost cheery, his grim words sapped any hope from the rest of the team. Shoulders slumped at the thought that there wasn't a straight path to safety, and instead another struggle with monsters awaited.

The lead Watcher spoke quickly, "But that also means there's a rescue team up ahead. Can we pick up the pace?"

"Not if we want to make it to them. We go any faster, our magic will lose control of the stone and the tunnel will collapse. Monsters'll die, but so will we."

A noise like glass shattering—somewhere behind them—then bone-chargers broke through a wall of force.

The lead Watcher growled at his juniors. "How much more mana do you have?"

"We'll run out if we keep putting up force walls every twenty paces," one answered. "If that rescue team doesn't get to us soon, we'll be down to just swords, spears, and rocks before we get anywhere near the castle."

"Shit." The lead Watcher squinted at Grimloch and Theresa. "Any idea how far ahead that battle is?"

"No," Grimloch grunted.

"With so many different sounds coming from in front and behind us... I have no idea," Theresa said apologetically.

"Shit! Alright, we switch vanguards and rearguards. Watchers in the back, you go up front, and those of you in front, take the back and start raising—"

"Mana swell!" the eldest earth mage shouted. "A breach's coming right below us! Get on it!"

Khalik and his fellow earth mages chanted incantations, aiming their hands and power toward the ground. The stone bucked and the tunnel rocked. Theresa felt a colossal being move through the earth below them as two immense forces wrestled each other for control.

She braced herself against a wall.

Impacts shook the passageway.

"Another mana flare coming from ahead of us!" Prince Khalik shouted. "It's a new breach!"

A sound like doom struck the left wall ahead, battering it to rubble. The Watchers reacted with knife-edge timing. Raising a force wall over the breach in heartbeats. Bone-chargers met the force wall, pushing against it with their full weight. Spear-flies drilled into the glowing force magic like crossbow bolts.

The wall held.

Earth mages and Watchers panted with strain, their chests heaving.

Then, the breach widened, gaps formed between force magic and stone. Spear-flies spilled into the tunnel, bone-chargers squeezed in behind them. In an instant, the tunnel filled with Ravener-spawn and a battle raged before anyone could shout one word of warning.

Theresa, Brutus, Grimloch, and Thundar rushed ahead, desperately cutting down bone-chargers before they overwhelmed the tunnel. Impact numbed her muscles with every slash against resisting hide and bone as she hacked at glowing eyes and gaping mouths. Ravener-spawn screamed and reeled backward as her blades bit home, making the monsters easy prey for Thundar and Grimloch's heavy weapons. Brutus savaged their legs and Svenia and Hogarth slid their spears into soft underbellies.

"Widen the force wall!" the lead Watcher ordered. "Seal the cracks—"

The wall burst, opening a second breach and filling the passage with drifting clouds of stone dust. Sounds of hacking, wheezing, and coughing joined the shrieks of agitated monsters.

Through the clouds, an enormous form entered the tunnel, a form with a growl like crumbling bone.

In a blink, light flashed through the dust and a bead of green energy shot over the excavation team.

"No—" Theresa cried.

Then it exploded.

Green force ripped the air, jolting wizards and engineers. Theresa screamed as it raked through her, shriveling her flesh, and her blood felt like it was being released through her pores as vapour. Wounded shriveled like wilting leaves, others exhaled once then collapsed on the spot. The more robust stayed upright, while blood mages frantically cast their spells on the injured, helping those who'd fallen. Theresa called on her lifeforce, staying on her feet even as the magic ripped through her. Her consciousness wavered, but she fought on.

The enormous beast before them stepped from the cloud, lumbering through the passage, its broad bulk nearly filling it. Upon its shoulder, a hive-as-one clung, the wings of masses of spear-flies caressed each other.

The behemoth roared and shuddered, fired streams of bone-shards from its towering body, then sprayed the excavation team with razor-sharp shrapnel. The Watchers' force armour held against them, but those not fortunate to be protected by armour fell screaming, pierced and bloodied.

A mix of fear and rage gripped the huntress. Shards cracked against her chain shirt as she dove low. Sharp pain burned across her cheek as one tore through her skin.

Grimloch charged the towering monster alongside Thundar, while Brutus snarled and snapped beside his master.

The world seemed to slow around her.

Death hung over the tunnel.

Many were down.

The earth mages were holding on by the barest thread.

Others were dying.

She glared up at the giant beast, her two swords crossed. There was no way she'd be able to cut the behemoth, so she would have to strike the hive-as-one.

But could she? Could she kill it?

It wasn't a single being she'd have to cut, but dozens of creatures—all connected—acting as one. Even if she killed some, the rest would be...

...identical to each other...

...acting...

...as...

...one.

The huntress' eyes fell on her two swords—No.

That was wrong. She'd been seeing through the veil of her own biases. They weren't two swords; they were *twins*. Two that were really one, acting together just as she, Claygon, and Alex had when they danced together.

They weren't two weapons at all. Each was a half of a whole. Her great-grandfather wasn't called Twinblades Lu.

He was called *Twinblade* Lu.

All this time, she'd thought she was wielding two blades, when...

Theresa poured her lifeforce into both halves of her weapon, not as separate entities, but reaching out to forge a connection.

Making them one.

And something awoke within the steel.

CHAPTER 75

THE TWINBLADE

I t started with one.

When Theresa Lu left her family home in Alric, she took with her one of her great-grandfather's two swords. And with it, she'd fought a Hive-queen and silence-spiders in the Cave of the Traveller, monsters in the Barrens of Kravernus with the sword in one hand and her hunting knife in the other. She'd never thought of it as anything but a singular blade, one that she cherished. It was the weapon she'd paired with her knife when they were desperate to escape Uldar's priests and Thameland.

When her father gave her the other sword on her birthday, she saw each one as part of a set: a pair of separate weapons—one to wield in her left hand, the other in her right; just two individual blades. Made to function as two, and to defend as two.

But they weren't two. They never had been.

Just as the Dance of Fusion fashioned two beings into one, the blades were two halves coming together to form one potent whole. Trying to push one's lifeforce into them separately was like a heart pumping blood into two divided halves of a body: it would go nowhere, feeding neither side. But if the halves were united, and became a whole—with a connection between them, then...

Unyielding power flared between each half of the Twinblade.

And that power sparked unruly in Theresa's grip, like a wild beast running free for the first time in untold summers. Theresa Lu had experience in bonding with wild beasts.

Ahead, the world crawled on, stretching endlessly between heartbeats as she watched the battle before her. Her senses were sharpening, cutting deeper into each passing moment. Seconds became eternities.

Grimloch smashed his poisonous maul into the behemoth's hand, cracking bone-shell armour. The Ravener-spawn leader turned its massive body, striking the shark man with an arm studded in spears. The dull thud of lead on bone sounded near her as Grimloch was driven back, his feet digging trenches through stone dust.

Thundar came to his side, his mace batting spear-flies as illusionary duplicates appeared. He struck a bone-charger in the arm and raced for the behemoth's legs, firing pulses of force magic at the hive-as-one as he ran.

The humanoid-shaped swarm crouched on the back of its host's bone-spikes, using them as a shield to deflect the minotaur's force energy. Growling, the towering monster lifted an enormous arm and brought it down toward the horned attacker. It missed the flesh and blood target, passed through an illusory image of him, and cracked the tunnel floor, sending shocks rippling outward, knocking him to the ground.

Bone-chargers and spear-flies leapt at the downed minotaur.

Theresa's blades flashed, appearing no different to the eye than they had before, but to the huntress, they'd come alive. She allowed her life-force's power to flow into both halves of the linked weapon.

Steel screamed, and in that cry, she felt its hunger. For combat. For death. For blood.

And she was ready to feed all three.

With a fearsome cry, the huntress' legs twitched with reinforced life energy, catapulting her ahead, both blades flashing on their way to the bone-charger bearing down on her fallen friend. Spear-flies shredded by the number, the weapon slashed through air, then struck tough hide.

And felt resistance.

A resistance that instantly broke.

The dual weapon of Twinblade Lu split Ravener-spawn hide like rotted fruit. A powerful arm drove the blade through iron muscle and bone, severing the monster's limb. It careened up and across the tunnel.

In two pieces.

With an agonised cry, the beast turned to snap at her, but the other blade was already slicing bone-shell, biting into its skull. Twice.

Her jaw dropped, but she kept working.

Her arms shuddered from impacts as the blade carved armour, splitting what lay beneath, and as the blade cut bone, two slashes appeared where only one should have been. Every sword strike dealing two wounds.

The bone-charger's beady eyes widened before it gurgled, then fell, its skull split in three.

"On your feet, Thundar!" Theresa shouted, whirling on the behemoth. Her blades screamed in triumph, cutting bone and hide in a blur, sending bone-chargers and spear-flies to their ends. Steely elation filled her with a bloodlust only a weapon could know, bringing surprise to the huntress' face and laughter to her soul.

'You're awake!' she thought. 'At last, you're awake!'

In heartbeats, all fear, dread, and frustration evaporated, replaced by confidence and iron resolve. She didn't notice Thundar's shocked expression as he looked between her and the blades.

"We've got to work together to take the rest of these things," she yelled. "I'll get the behemoth and that thing on its shoulder; you get the bone-chargers!"

Thundar's eyes widened, watching her screaming swords. "Y-yes, ma'am!"

He leapt to his feet as she charged the behemoth's leg.

Bone-chargers jumped at her, but her united twinblade—its power resonating—slashed skin and bone-shell, leaving two wounds for every stroke. The more monsters she cut down, the more her euphoria tempered: moderating, adjusting.

Her blades still screamed, but her own feelings now rose above theirs.

Relief.

All-encompassing relief and contentment swept over her, wrapping her like a blanket, transforming her into a calm eye in a storm of slashing steel. A smile grew wider with every step she took. Her cuts became sharper, and though the twinblade had carved bone, blood, and sinew, there was not one single speck of gore marring its surfaces. All had slid away like oil from water.

The sound of its joyful cries had eyes turning toward it.

The behemoth roared as Watchers came at it with an unrelenting stream of deadly magics, its bone armour blackened and cracked under the assault. On its shoulder, the hive-as-one raised a hand. A sickly green light coalesced around twitching 'fingers' formed from a nest of barbed spear-fly legs.

With a chittering cry, the monster's hand aimed at the Watchers—until its many eyes fell on Theresa and her shining swords.

It cocked its head, seeming to take her measure.

Her threat was clear.

With the wings of its many spear-flies writhing, it turned the hand and released the energy beam. The magic whispered death as it flew at her. She was poised to jump away, but the blades shrieked, thirsting for challenge. They shifted in her grip as though longing to meet the deadly magic full force.

See them as they are.

The cry of challenge. The blood and gore beading off them like repelling oil. Steel shining like two halves of a mirror.

She put faith in her great-grandfather's twinned weapon. Raising one blade, she met the oncoming magic with the other, the foul energy ray struck shining steel.

Her arm was numbed by the power sparking across the twinblade, making it ring like a church bell. Magic flared bright. The beam ricocheted off her weapon, racing back to its sender.

The creature stilled in surprise. A deadly mistake.

Green light rebounded, striking its core, and vile magic splashed over the massive clot of spear-flies, bathing them green. Awful power worked horrors through the hive-as-one. Bodies shrieked, withering like weeds bathed in vinegar and the hot midday sun.

Twitching and near death, the clustered spear-flies collapsed on the behemoth's shoulder with a weak, pleading cry. Its host glanced from the surprised huntress to its barely stirring rider.

Quickly shifting the hive-as-one so it was hidden behind a shoulder spike, the monster snarled down at Theresa. Fingers like clubs curled into a fist the size of a boulder, then it levelled a spear-capped arm at the defiant huntress glaring back at it.

Every spike in its bone armour lengthened.

They launched in a deadly wail that pierced the air.

Theresa spun through the storm of bone-spears, her blades slashing, splitting them with the precision of a mantis striking a fly. Snarling, spittle flying, the behemoth drove its fist at her.

The cracking sound its armour made matched that of breaking walls, alarming the earth mages. The monster's closed hand had enough power behind it to shatter stone, and although it struck with speed, it was clumsy. Too much momentum, too little control. In comparison to the lightning-like agility of Zonon-In, the behemoth moved at a snail's pace.

Theresa's usual response would have been to leap aside, rush forward, look for a weak spot in its armour, then strike.

But now?

Now she could punish its overreach.

She sidestepped the fist, blades swept out, catching the oncoming limb. She never imagined that even with lifeforce-enhanced strength, she could cut through its layers of armour without first landing a series of cuts to its body. But with the spawn's own weight and strength helping to do the work?

The fist drove into her blades. Steel screamed. Bone armour split. Flesh parted in four trenches. The behemoth bellowed, yanking its arm back, and the huntress leapt.

Her boots landed atop the spurting limb. She balanced her body like she had in the Grand Battle and drove a blade into bone armour, stabilising herself on its flailing arm while the other blade lashed its wrist with whip-like strokes.

She carved away chunks of armour, sliced through meat with shallow cuts, and the creature might have survived a hundred, or even a thousand of them.

She wasn't trying to kill it.

As the monster flailed its arm, trying to throw her off, Watchers, Thundar, Grimloch, and Brutus tore through the remaining bone-chargers and spear-flies. The second breach was now sealed by force spells, and Ravener-spawn numbers had dwindled.

A lava ball—thrown by Tyris—streaked through the air, sailing above light cast by forceballs, and burst on the weakened hive-as-one; its many mouths screeched as insectile bodies boiled in their shells. Shrill voices rose and died as one.

Then Grimloch and Thundar raced to the behemoth's knees, pounding their bludgeoning weapons into bone armour, cracking it, pulping the flesh beneath.

Theresa felt something shift under her feet and leapt high in the air as shards rose from its armour. Bone shifted, preparing to fire in waves.

Until a shadow fell over monstrous eyes.

Her shadow.

She landed square on the spawn's skull, her boots cupping it; a blade bit into armour. Her eyes met the Ravener-spawn's. The glare of a beast levelled with the glare of a huntress.

And it was the beast that turned its eyes away first.

If it could have known hers would be the last face it would ever see, it might have turned away sooner.

Her screaming blade slashed across its eyes.

Then, it saw nothing more.

"Somebody throw me a spear!" she shouted, sheathing a blade.

The behemoth yowled, red running freely, its jaw parting. She planted one boot in its open mouth and pressed its jaws apart with the other foot.

Svenia scooped up a spear no longer needed by its dead owner and tossed it through the air.

Theresa snatched it with her free hand and jammed the spear tip into the roof of the creature's mouth, propping it open. The hulking monster went wild, tossing its head in a frenzy. She balanced in the centre of the gaping mouth, and while her teammates used hit and run tactics on the behemoth and bone-chargers, her blades flurried inside the giant beast's mouth. The first strike split jaw muscles and tendons before its jaw could clench, though it seemed disinclined to do so, fearing the spear tip pointing toward its brain. Its jaw slackened and quivered as her second strike severed the tongue. It bellowed, trying to claw at the inside of its mouth, but she punished it with a strike to the knuckle.

Another slash rendered its jaw useless.

Without its tongue, nothing separated her from the back of its throat.

And so she stepped in.

The titanic Ravener-spawn's cries withered into gurgling sighs as gore sprayed. It stumbled. Thundar and Grimloch—though weakened by magic and blood loss—shattered its knees in a barrage of swings.

Washed in red, the huntress leapt from its mouth, landing lightly on the tunnel floor, and immediately began chopping down remaining Ravener-spawn. Behind her, the behemoth toppled in a twitching heap, violently shaking the passage. By the time every last monster was dead, the tunnel's quaking had nearly stilled.

Her blades sighed, seeming pleased—both halves together at last—steel shining. While the shaking calmed around the excavation team, she looked at the swords with gratitude and gave a silent prayer of thanks.

'Thank you, Great-Grandfather. Thank you so much for helping me. Thank you for the gift of your legacy.'

When she looked up again, more than half the excavation team was staring.

Thundar's jaw hung open. Prince Khalik's matched the minotaur's. Tyris' eyes were almost as big as Hart's.

Grimloch had a bloodthirsty glint in his eye. "Yeeeeeesss," he growled in approval.

"Well..." the lead Watcher murmured. "That was a welcome sight."

Brutus bounded to her, and two heads licked her face enthusiastically. The third regarded her swords with...

Was that jealousy? Was he jealous of the attention she was paying the weapon?

She hugged his neck. "Don't worry, boy, we'll always be a team."

The Watcher cleared his throat. "Good job. Just wish you'd done that before." He turned to the excavation team. "Alright, we got through that one, so everyone get ready. I want us ready to move in a minute. Blood mages, you know what to do. Let's get the wounded and the dead taken care of. This victory won't do us a lick of good if we're trapped like rats down here."

He looked to the elder earth mage. "Is that mana coming for us? We'll need to move faster. Can you handle it?"

Silence.

"Hello?" the lead Watcher prodded the other wizard.

The elder earth mage was frowning, his brow furrowing in thought. "I... I don't feel anything." He looked at the other mages. "Do any of you?"

The other mages glanced at each other, apprehension on every face.

"I... I do not," Prince Khalik said. "I think it is no longer trying to crush us."

"I don't hear anything in the walls either," Grimloch grunted, breathing deeply. His skin looked dull from the hive-as-one's magic. "But... Wait... Theresa, you hear that noise down the tunnel?"

The huntress glanced ahead, closing her eyes.

From deep in the passageway, faint battle sounds reached her: screams, the flash of weapons, the sound of spells.

Beyond that, a low, unnerving rumble.

Coming from the direction of the castle.

"By the Traveller," she murmured, opening her eyes. "There's fighting ahead, and I also heard a sound way up there that sounded like an earthquake."

Prince Khalik stiffened. "What if the dungeons are trying to collapse the research castle?"

Alex's face appeared in Theresa's mind.

"We have to move." The huntress' voice was strained. "Now."

"Agreed," the lead Watcher said. "Everyone, get yourselves together. I want haste spells or running enhancement spells on anyone who's still on their feet. We have to get moving."

CHAPTER 76

AWAKENING AND ARRIVAL

Alex lay against something hard and cold.

Although the cold seemed to be swirling all around. It bit into him, a deep pit of exhaustion calling him to drown in it. All he wanted to do was sleep...

But he couldn't...

...he was...

What was he doing again?

Some sort of growling? Crackling? Spells?

He shook his head.

Something far below was moving.

Something important... or maybe not. Maybe this was all just a bad dream, and he was still in his room in Generasi, bedding down after a shift at Shale's. Yes, that was probably it. All the excitement lately must be giving him strange dreams.

'Well, that's not the kind of dream I want, now is it?' a groggy thought came to him. 'Be much nicer to be dreaming of a warm beach somewhere. One with Theresa, Selina, Clay—No, you know what? Just me and Theresa, alone... with... wait, Theresa?'

The tunnels.

The Ravener-spawn.

The attack.

Everything came back with a start and his eyes flew open.

"Theresa!" he cried.

Snow and lashing wind stung his face and he clenched his teeth against the chill, trying to figure out where he was. He couldn't see the castle or much of anything. And he was flying, moving fast, clutched in a grip of stone. No, not stone.

Clay.

"Claygon?" Alex murmured weakly, his eyes finding the golem's face above him. The four-armed construct held him in a tight grip with one of his lower arms, keeping him close, shielding him from the chill.

His upper arms were busy: one was unleashing lines of flame through the whiteout, spraying spear-flies and leaving trailing infernos in their wake. The other struck with the war-spear in powerful strokes, cutting through Ravener-spawn.

Beams shot from his forehead while Alex's air elementals lashed the swarms with crackling lightning and blasted them with blustery winds. Ravener-spawn gave chase, trying to pounce on the Thameish wizard, but his guardians fended them off through the ferocious winds tossing them about like tattered rags.

Something was strange with how the spear-flies flew.

Most were below him and Claygon, straining to catch up.

A few were alongside, but none were above.

As he looked around, it struck him. The monsters were struggling, and the wind was so strong because they were soaring high in the sky. Unusually high.

The hive-as-one's beam hadn't hit him with its full force, only clipped him, but its power had knocked him into unconsciousness. Claygon must have sped away to protect him.

And then kept going upward.

'How far are we above the castle?' he wondered. "Have... have to get back down there. Can't get lost in the storm. I'll freeze to death." He looked at Claygon and the water elementals. "Protect me for a second! Jeez, Isolde and that explosion from the... oh, by the Traveller, the tele-portation building!"

He fell into himself, guiding his mind past the Mark's interference as he cast Mana-to-Life. Power raced through him, leaping from his mana pool and filling his body with warmth. Exhaustion and the aching pain of bitter cold were chased away, returning vigour to his limbs and core. Alex took a deep breath, centering himself.

Then he rose from Claygon's grip, taking flight under his own power. His green eyes scanned the swarm below, searching for holes in their formation, and there were many. The driving wind tore at the small crea-tures, breaking their lines apart.

"Alright, everyone, we're going back down. Cover me."

They turned in mid-flight, racing down through the blizzard. Alex opened his mana senses, feeling the power of the spells being cast below. Power raged in the distance, and beneath it, a deep mana that made him shudder. More of the dungeons' power had coalesced beneath the earth. He could feel it, even from so high in the sky.

His hands balled into fists.

He had to find Isolde. He needed to reach the teleportation building.

They raced through the swarm, lashing out with lightning and flame. Alex's force spells caught spear-flies coming at them, deflecting them into the wind. He whipped booby-trapped potions into his Wizard's Hands, and though the spells caught and crushed them, the mist dissipated into the howling wind.

It had been worth a shot.

Downing another potion of haste, he caught spear-flies, pulling them from the air at speed, throwing them into the wind. Below, the sounds of battle and flashes of magic grew louder and brighter. Wind's bite lessened the closer he came to the wind mages' power, and the whiteout eased.

Wavering images of massive buildings in the courtyard wicked in and out of view, until Alex finally broke through the haze of stinging snow and soared down past the keep. He hovered in the air, squinting through the white, trying to catch his bearings and take account of the battle below. The wizards were tearing through the enemy, cutting them down with abandon, but the spawn was endless, pouring from below ground in droves.

Another behemoth climbed onto the surface and was met by a stone golem's fists, and Alex's flicker dogs, teleporting around it, appearing then disappearing, chewing on bone armour like it was a soup bone. A hive-as-one launched a deadly orb of magic at a Watcher that was deflected by a spell from the woman's staff.

Earth mages channelled their mana into the stone below, sealing the dungeons' breaches while wind mages guided the blizzard, narrowing its winds into gale-paths that swept swarms of spear-flies over the walls and into the frozen beyond. Any wild animals desperate enough to be out would eat well tonight.

Summoned monsters carried the wounded into icy bunkers where blood mages tended them, but for every wounded defender, there were a dozen dead bone-chargers, and an order of magnitude of dead spear-flies.

The wizards were beating back the enemy... so far.

But the monsters' numbers showed no sign of thinning. And Alex didn't see Watcher Shaw or anyone evacuating toward the teleportation building. He turned, flying in that direction, getting closer to the keep.

A spear-fly shot from the sheeting snow, but he caught it in one hand.

"Hah." He prepared to toss it to the wind. "Nice try—"

And that was when the clawed monster leapt.

The creature had been clinging to the keep, crouched against the wind, claws biting into stone. The monster looked like it had been waiting...

And now its claws were racing for his throat. The young wizard reversed course, and by reflex, tossed the spear-fly like he was playing fetch with Brutus. The much larger Ravener-spawn took the spinning spear-fly right to the face.

Proboscis first.

A screech followed, curved claws raked at the clinging blood-sucker, both monsters tumbled through the wind.

Alex watched them soar past and plummet to the battle below, landing in a soft mound of snow before his water and ice elementals set upon them, freezing the pair solid in heartbeats. He stared at the stilled forms, dread rising in his chest.

"Oh no," he whispered.

This was a new clawed monster, but of the same type that had attacked him at the windmill. The same as the three that attacked Patrizia DePaolo's ball. Now, he had no doubt that, back then, they were there looking for *him*.

And now, here they were, hunting for him again, still intent on killing him.

And, if by chance they were here because he'd controlled a dungeon core, then—

A cry rose from the distance like a bullhorn. It came from the direction of the teleportation building. Scores of Ravener-spawn turned and rushed toward the cry like a tidal wave.

"Oh no," Alex murmured, taking potion bottles out and soaring after the enemy. He took a quick look downward, shouting instructions in a tongue of celestials and one of devils.

"Flicker dogs! Hell-boars! Follow me and Claygon. There's a fight up ahead! I need you with me!"

His voice reached a group of hell-boars that had cornered a bone-charger after pulling it down with goring tusks and powerful bites. They glanced up at his voice, squealed ominously, and charged, kicking up clouds of snow. A pack of flicker dogs that had been racing through the snow—snapping spear-flies from the wind and teleporting around the battlefield—barked at his command and loped after him, flickering in and out of the white haze.

A bad feeling spread through the young wizard. If clawed monsters were here, then what other deadly surprises were waiting?

As Alex flew past an area of the courtyard, he searched the ground below, looking for a massive monster and found it—but not as he'd left it.

There in the stained snow lay the behemoth and hive-as-one that attacked him, causing him to black out. He'd assumed they would have wandered away when Claygon had taken him out of reach, but the only place they had wandered to... was the afterworld.

Their bodies had been utterly mutilated. The larger beast was carved up like a Sigmus bird and the remains crushed into bits of bone and red jelly. The smaller one was little more than a streak of ash on the grey and blackened snow, its mass of spear-flies scattered like gravel.

Alex swallowed. The attack on the behemoth looked like it had been personal. The wounds repeated and were excessive. Ragged. Wild. *Final.* He glanced at Claygon.

'I gave him an instruction to protect me, but I didn't tell him to turn that thing into ground meat... I never told him not to either. I've never known him to act out of emotion. I also didn't tell him to take me so high. What in the name of the Traveller's happening?'

This was the second time Claygon had acted on his own during this battle. Something was going on, and Alex didn't like it. The Ravener-spawn were behaving in ways that were unheard of. The clawed monsters were here. His golem was acting on his own.

What if something bad happened at a critical time?

His mind flashed to the dungeon core explosion and how Claygon shielded him against the blast. That time, he'd been fine, but... His eyes travelled to the golem's war-spear, remembering how easily it carved Claygon's body like hot butter.

What if some other horror attacked now? Something unknown, like the clawed monsters, but even worse, even more dangerous?

He swallowed, trying to clamp down on rising doubt since there was no time to think about things now.

As he reached the teleportation building, he found it besieged on all sides. Bone-chargers swarmed into broken hallways. Spear-flies slipped into cracks in the stone. Behemoths rampaged, smashing through walls, firing spears and bone-shards into summoned monsters and wizards flying above the roof.

A part of the ceiling had collapsed and—where the teleportation circle was supposed to be—an enormous, gaping hole yawned open, and a wild melee surged around it. Warriors. Wizards. Watchers and summoned creatures alike met endless tides of Ravener-spawn boiling from the wound in the earth and down every passage in the broken structure.

The defenders had formed a circle, and he spotted Isolde, Ripp, and Watcher Shaw among them. His cabal mate looked ragged, but she fought with the frenzy of a cornered beast, pouring lightning bolt upon lightning bolt into the surging horde. Within the middle of their defensive circle huddled the researchers, blood mages and other civilian staff.

And among them?

Carey London.

The young woman was screaming, even as she fired first-tier force bolts into spear-flies above them. Her clothing had been torn, and beneath the rips, bright pink marks in the shape of long cuts and gouges showed. Wounds that had been knitted together by blood magic. Alex winced. She'd been mauled; those scars looked like they could have been deadly. She was lucky she'd escaped with her life. Then he noticed that around her neck, above the pink scarring of a healed injury, something was conspicuously missing.

Her holy symbol of Uldar was gone.

He winced again, swooping down to join the fight, only to spy something that chilled his blood worse than the wind's bite.

Like prowling wolves, two clawed monsters were stalking along the rooftop—keeping low and moving slow—with claws curved and teeth bared, using spear-flies and blowing snow for cover. Every muscle in their powerful bodies were tensed, prepared for a deadly spring that would carry them into the battle.

He had a feeling he knew just what they were going to pounce on.

"Let's try giving you a target with more bite," he whispered, arcing his body toward them and drawing a pair of sleeping potions. As he flew, his eyes scanned the roof: the clawed things seemed not to notice him at first, but now, one spotted him through all the swirling snow and wind.

He sensed a trap.

'There's going to be another one,' he thought. 'There's definitely got to be another one.'

He was right.

A glimpse of movement through a curtain of snow. A third monster lay pressed against the castle roof, watching him intently. If he hadn't known what to look for, he wouldn't have seen it in the white haze, and it would have been on him.

Too bad for them.

'Claygon, get 'em,' he thought.

The golem dropped and swept his war-spear in an arc. The clawed-thing sprang away, and the weapon sparked off stone. As the creature fled across the rooftop, Alex's forceballs spun after it, entangling its feet, throwing balance to the wind.

It tumbled through the air.

And Claygon's war-spear awaited.

Hearing their sibling's dying shriek, two clawed creatures' heads looked in the direction of the panicked cry. Words seemed to pass between them, then snarling and sliding along the keep's roof, they dove toward Carey.

Alex sent a thought to Claygon just as Watcher Shaw raised his staff.

Neither warrior nor golem had a chance to act.

Two silvery hands appeared in midair, each caught a Ravener-spawn in an unshakeable grip. Both creatures went limp.

"No more of that!" Baelin's voice boomed above the wind.

The chancellor of the university appeared, wreathed in power, suspended above the battle.

With a single word, he cast a wave of magic, striking the horde with a prismatic spray of lights. Some melted. Some turned to stone. Others froze, encased in ice.

The rest were blinded by piercing light.

With another word, the air shimmered around him as he raised his hands, and a dozen war-spirits appeared. The creatures of shining metal surged, standing shoulder to shoulder, cutting through Ravener-spawn like dried wheat.

"Filth." He scowled at the attackers, then drifted down to hover beside the defenders. "Watcher Shaw, what is our status?"

The chancellor gave Alex a nod as he and Claygon floated down to meet them at the teleportation circle. Isolde began checking herself over and Carey wavered on her feet. Tears of relief ran down her cheeks; she was not alone in that.

Alex felt tension bleed from his spirit.

Baelin was here now. All would be well.

The Petrifier crawled from the lower caverns and up through the shaft in silence.

"Leader," the Hunter hiding in its mouth whispered. "A great mana source has appeared. One that feels very hostile."

The immense Ravener-spawn growled. "Then we will be quick and subtle." Its eyes looked down at the shaft.

"And we will need to sacrifice."

It sent an order to the two dungeon cores below.

CHAPTER 77

THE BATTLE ON TWO FRONTS AND THE STALKER'S SUMMONING

"And it's been just over ten minutes, by my reckoning," Watcher Shaw reported from the teleportation building. "According to the earth mages, these things managed to make dungeons and the like right below us, and they've been throwing around a lot of mana down there, breaching walls like they were cracking eggs. We've had attacks in the tunnels under the research castle and even further out. It's been grim, Baelin. Some of our folks are wounded and we've also suffered casualties, but despite all of that, we've been beating them back so far. Frankly, they're relentless. It's been like trying to beat back the sea."

Baelin looked at the researchers, the fighters, and all the destruction below him, and then at the vast hole in the earth. "And where is Vernia?"

"She's in the keep with some of our battlemages making sure the team's all evacuated," Watcher Shaw said. "She's been determined not to anywhere until everyone was accounted for."

"As she would." The chancellor's eyes focused on the chasm. "And the enemy destroyed the teleportation circle?"

"One of the first things they did." Watcher Shaw's jaw clenched.

"Then this is no typical Ravener-spawn attack." The chancellor's voice was deadly calm. "This is targeted." His goat-like eyes narrowed, looking through the snow at the lifeless forms of the two clawed monsters still in the grip of his Wizards Hands. He clicked his tongue, his face unreadable.

"Alright, this foolishness is done," he spoke to the wounded and the noncombatants. "You did well, all of you, and you held on bravely. Now your trials are over. Let's get you back to Generasi."

His focus turned to the defenders. "Anyone who wishes to evacuate when I teleport the others away may join us. My war-spirits will aid those who choose to remain. But I expect that anyone who is capable of defending our research castle will fulfil their duty as combat members of this expedition. If you are not injured, think on that and consider your role here."

The ancient wizard waited, giving any fighter who wished to leave the chance to say so. The battle raged on, war-spirits advanced, cutting down masses of spawn in their path. The expedition members watched the carnage. Whether their faces showed fear or resolve, none asked to leave.

Baelin gave them a slight nod. "Excellent. I shall start here, then move through the camp seeking those who need to be moved away from here. All the while, I'll be clearing the filth from our camp. My actions will most certainly distract our attackers, and you can use that to overwhelm the remaining spawn. When I've teleported all who need to return to Generasi, I shall visit the tunnels and help our people trapped in them. Now—"

The ground bucked, stopping his words.

A spike of mana raged below. Expedition members screamed. Baelin sighed and pointed at the ground with one finger. His lips spoke a single word.

The world froze as though two giants grappled, one trying to crush it, while the other attempted to protect it. But one giant's will and strength was far greater than the other's. The chancellor's mana smothered that of the dungeon cores.

"There," he said. "That should—" He frowned. "Oh..."

Something tingled all around Alex, something his mana senses could scarcely detect. Yet it was as vast as a giant sea creature swimming hidden just below the dark surface of the sea. It brimmed with power, swimming down, down, down until—

The ground bucked again, threatening to tear apart.

Alex's heart jumped as everyone startled. Those on the ground fought to stay upright, throwing their arms out, bracing against the snaking earth. The mana beneath them was waves of pure chaos splitting stone. Disorganised. Howling, flailing like a wounded beast.

Its power was nearly equal to the chancellor's.

"Change of plans," Baelin said. "Hold the line. I shall teleport those here who need to be transported back to Generasi immediately, then dispatch others from the city to bring the rest of the wounded to safety. The Ravener's ambient mana is being shunted directly into dungeons under us. That must end or this entire fortification will not survive."

He looked at Watcher Shaw. "Hold the fort for now. I'll be back."

With a shimmer of teleportation magic, Baelin raised his arms.

Carey looked at Alex and Isolde, her eyes wide. "Be safe, both of you! Please be sa—"

She was gone before she could finish.

Wizards murmured, their worry plain on their faces. Alex could well understand.

The only creature, to his knowledge, that had ever given Baelin anything even approaching trouble was the demon Ezaliel itself. What level of power was the Ravener sending into the—

The ground heaved. Multiple explosions erupted, sending stones as big as the Thameish king's carriage high overhead where they hovered for a blink then tumbled, picking up speed, coming for anything not wise or able enough to get out of the way. A new wave of Ravener-spawn poured into the courtyard, led by hives-as-one perched on behemoths. Plummeting boulders met them by the number.

"Hell's broken loose!" Watcher Shaw pointed his sword toward the courtyard. "Let's send it back where it belongs!"

With a war cry, he led the Watchers into the fray, joining the war-spirits in eliminating the enemy. The other defenders shouted incantations. Isolde and Alex reassured each other with a look.

Power raged below, the kind of power that could buckle knees and wither spirits.

The sort of power that made one question whether or not they'd see another sun rise.

Think. Adapt.

The mantra ran through his mind.

"Watch my back," Isolde said, her face pale. "Please watch my back."

"I have you," Alex said, looking back to Claygon, who was raising his spear. "We have you."

Her smile was thin. "Thank you, Alex."

Together, the cabal mates took to the air. Isolde channelled her lightning. Alex drew his potions.

And he clamped down on rising dread. Not just from clawed monsters seeking him and Carey, but for why the dungeon cores exploded in power when Baelin arrived. Why the attack at all, so suddenly?

It all stank of a trap.

The Petrifier slipped out of the chasm in the earth, its eight eyes darting, taking in the surface world. Battle raged all around as the Ravener poured unending power into the dungeon cores deep below. Mana boiled underground, and the dungeon cores' silent shrieks were building. Soon, they would come to a head. As the shrill cries reached it, the Petrifier felt a distant bite of sympathy, but there was nothing it could do. In the end, all were expendable for their master's purpose. And it doubted that even *it* would escape this battle with its life spared.

"Leader," a clawed monster concealed within the Petrifier's mouth whispered. "The great entity is below. It is—"

A quake rattled the earth, followed by three more in quick order, sending wizards and Ravener-spawn alike tumbling through the snow. The Petrifier could imagine the titanic struggle in the tunnels where the orbs churned out monster after monster, crafting more to guard themselves and more to unleash, and with the Ravener's mana flowing through them, they would be granted the... *special means* to defend themselves.

Though that very power flowing into them would be the cause of their destruction. The Petrifier might escape, or it might not. Either way, its true goal must be achieved, even at the highest price. Eliminating the Usurper and every witness to its presence, turning the enemy into perfect statues would be its own reward, no matter the cost. Should its life end on this day, the Ravener could grant it new life, in some form.

For now, the Usurper awaited.

"That way, leader," the Hunter whispered. "The Usurper is ahead."

The Petrifier moved along the edge of the courtyard and away from the hole it had crept from. Its steps were silent and the battle loud. None had reason to pay it any mind, cloaked in invisibility as it was.

"The Usurper is near, leader," the Hunter whispered. "I can feel it through the white ahead."

"What do you mean, *Usurper*?" its leader whispered. "*One* Usurper? What of the other?"

"...Leader, many apologies, but I cannot feel the other. It seems they have vanished."

Stifling rage, the Petrifier ground its fangs together, causing the Hunter to whimper and lie flat for fear of being crushed in its leader's jaws.

Another escape. This complicated matters. Briefly, the Petrifier considered bounding over the wall and taking to the wilds. As it was, it would likely lose its life eliminating a single Usurper while two were still free.

That was a problem.

It had been three cycles since a Usurper escaped the Ravener's reach —a rare thing—and now two threatened to do so. Should it take the one now? Or retreat and take all three later, surviving until circumstances were better?

'No,' it thought. 'Take this one now, eliminate every witness and be away. If there are none left alive to reveal your existence, you will be free to hunt the other two together, or if the Hunters find them alone. If that powerful being returns and you cannot defeat it, destroy yourself and take it with you. Then hunt the other Usurpers when the Ravener reforms you. Yes. That is the way.'

"We go forth," the Petrifier growled. "Show me this Usurper."

The ground shook as it crawled forward, lowering its body against the snow.

It rounded a building and—

"There!" the Hunter hissed. "The mortal near the four-armed statue that moves! That is the Usurper!"

The Petrifier's jaw clicked.

At last, it had found one. The human was flying through the air, distracting Ravener-spawn and leading them in a chain behind him. Strange spells and creatures followed his commands, and the four-armed entity fought a good distance away, battling with tremendous power, slashing a weapon through behemoths, and burning hives-as-ones with curious flame.

A spasm went through the Petrifier's eyestalks. The Ravener's enemy was fighting fiercely, leading its servants on a wild chase. The Usurper turned and faced the pursuers, calling to them... *laughing*, seeming to mock them. He was pointing a finger at its dead servants lying broken in the snow. 'They died for the Ravener's purpos—' One of the Petrifier's eyes fell on the two lifeless Hunters in the courtyard, their bodies being slowly buried in drifting snow. Who killed them? The Usurper, the powerful entity, another mortal? One of this stronghold's other defences?

A group of mortal mages wielded blades and staves, meeting bone-chargers with ferocity, seeming to have no fear. Other magic users cast spells in quick succession. Near the Usurper, a woman struck at its spear-flies with chained lightning, jolting them from flight.

Powerful enemies... but it didn't matter.

They were all witnesses, and all were destined for death.

"I hope this isn't a mistake." Gwyllain drew an ancient sign on a tree within the borders of the faewild. "Lord Aenflynn and any fae lord who can hear me, please watch out for this humble asrai."

He stepped back from the sign—a scythe piercing a brace of holly—and paced back and forth through the clearing, stepping around young pixies growing within flower buds.

"Is this a good idea?" he wondered aloud. "Maybe it's not. I mean, sure, it'd be nice to have powerful wizards owing me a favour, but it's not like I owe Alexander Roth anything. He saved my life, and I gave him everything I promised and nothing more! And I even risked my life alongside him!"

He kicked a patch of grass. "No, come on, Gwyllain. He'll be a good mortal to know... He might be able to help you one day. He and all his wizard friends. But he can't do that if he and the rest are dead! But what if I get caught up in something nasty and get killed? Or if the stalker..."

The fae shuddered. "You know, maybe this wasn't such a good idea. Maybe I'll leave a note. Alexander knows that I warned him after all, and maybe—"

"Well, aren't you a talkative little faeling?" a voice boomed behind him.

"Gah!" Gwyllain jumped at least a foot in the air and spun about.

There on a rock, with his skin blue and his beard snowy white, sat the Stalker. A rock that the asrai could've sworn on his life wasn't there mere heartbeats before. Behind him loomed the great moose that served as the ancient fae's mount. The bells tinkling from its antlers were eerily silent as the big beast snorted and shook its head.

"Been a long time since anyone called me using that sign," the Stalker said. "What's it been... four? Five hundred years? Or was it three? Anyway, you're a bit bold to be using it, aren't you?" His tone was a warning. "Very *bold*."

The moose took a step toward Gwyllain, who yelped.

"I don't mean any disrespect!" the asrai cried. "Swear on my life, I didn't know you used any other names! But... I heard you made friends with humans! Powerful humans! The ones they call the Heroes! I-I have a message for them!"

"Oh? I didn't know one of my names was *the messenger*." The Stalker let that hang before continuing. "What sort of message? Anything juicy?"

Gwyllain quickly told him about the attack on the castle that belonged to the foreign wizards, and everything else the blue caps mentioned. The Stalker watched him closely, his eyes emotionless.

When the asrai finished, he expected the unpredictable fae to leap up and snatch half of his face off.

Instead, he grinned, revealing sharp teeth. "Well, this *is* juicy. Good news for you, you'll be living for another day. And you're right, this is as juicy as a nice ripe apple. Hmmmm, my three new friends will definitely want to hear this. Let's see how quickly they can travel our lovely roads."

CHAPTER 78

UNABLE TO SCREAM

"A little more," Alex whispered, sending a Wizard's Hand into a behemoth's throat. The spell squeezed the vial, glass shattered, the monster began to stagger.

The hive-as-one lodged on its shoulder raised its hands, channelling mana until another Wizard's Hand dropped in its face, releasing a mana soothing potion. Drifting mist disappeared in the blowing snow, but it had already done its work. The clot of insectile forms swayed on the behemoth's shoulder, and as its inner energies calmed, the magic glowing about its hands died.

It followed an instant later.

Isolde's lightning flew, striking it in pulses while Claygon's fire-beams lanced into the behemoth it rode on. Both spawn vanished in an abrupt shriek and blast of heat.

"There's no end to them!" the young noblewoman cried, Alex's air elementals lashing the swarm around her.

"That's alright!" he shouted back above the wind, trying to soothe his fraying nerves. "We just have to hold on for a little longer! Baelin'll—"

He nearly missed mana that was building at speed, joining with the power from below. Alex whirled, the hairs on his neck rising, his eyes expecting to see a hive-as-one. But there was only defenders and monsters locked in battle. Watcher Shaw and his group, crushing through Ravener-spawn alongside the war-spirits. No, there was something more. A bit farther beyond the knots of fighting... The spot that looked like there was nothing in it.

The mana was building, and his sharpened mana senses had only just caught it. His thoughts raced. The surprise attack. Those clawed monsters. The power in the dungeons below. That feeling of foreboding.

Then, dread spiked.

Watcher Shaw cut down a bone-charger, then whirled on the invisible space.

He spoke a word of power. His eyes flew wide. "Invisible monster!"

Isolde turned toward the voice.

Swarms of spear-flies parted, opening a path between Alex and the invisible space.

Claygon raced for his creator.

"Isolde, move!" Alex yelled.

Her lips parted. She started climbing.

Beams lanced through the wind. Five rays of power raced for Alex. All spread out. All would cage him in.

He called on the Mark, spinning and dancing through the air. Barely, just barely weaving through the rays like thread through the eye of a needle. Isolde was not so lucky. A beam slipped through her guardians—the three air elementals—hitting her dead on.

The young noblewoman froze as though she'd been cast in ice, eyes wide and panicked. Jaws stiffened. Lips trembling.

The next beam came faster than the others.

Think! Adapt!

He barked a single word in an elemental tongue of air, and her guardians swarmed, blowing hard to move their charge. His forceballs came in from the side, pushing her down. The beam strafed empty air, slicing past her, coming for Alex, but catching one of the air elementals defending her.

His eyes widened as the elemental froze, emitting a howling scream before its air currents hardened into a mass. It plummeted. The beam kept sweeping toward him.

He weaved, ducked, rolled.

The ray blazed with power as it passed inches beneath him. His back muscles stiffened, recoiling as it came too near for comfort. It sputtered into nothingness.

A heartbeat later, a desperate scream cut the air.

Alex whirled, spotting a single beam streaking through a group of wizards fighting beside a war-spirit. A sound like a rock face straining and shifting when the ground moves, followed. Wizards twisted, their bodies writhing in the sky, then turning grey. Slowing. Shuddering, growing still until flesh and blood became nothing but cold stone. Even the war-spirit was petrifying, its silvery sheen fading to the dull deadness of slate.

And then, they all fell, plummeting through the wind. Shattering on impact. Screams arose. Chaos swept the courtyard, and Isolde—recovering while floating near the ground—gaped in horror.

'What in the Traveller's name is *that*?' Alex turned his attention back on the invisible enemy just as another volley of beams shot toward him. He climbed through the sky, desperately dodging each beam, escaping their touch by inches.

"Claygon!" Alex called to his golem, trying to get clear of the other wizards. If this invisible thing was targeting him, he needed to be away from them, and as high in the sky as he could get. "Go over there and stop that thing! Use your fire-beams! Use your war-spear! Use—*Shit*!"

He veered, escaping a beam, its power hissing past his cheek.

"*Use anything*!" he finished his instructions.

And his golem...

...did not turn. He charged his fire-beams, but he didn't swing his war-spear at the attacker, nor did he fly toward it. Instead, he kept racing toward his creator while the young wizard dodged for his life.

'Claygon!' he thought. 'Claygon, listen to me!'

The golem would not. He was ignoring his directions, or disobeying them. Either way, Alex couldn't dwell on that. Whatever was down there, it could turn flesh to stone with the blast of a beam, and those beams were after him. He glanced at Claygon and felt a pang in his chest.

Below, the battle became a desperate struggle.

The invisible assassin was moving across the snow at terrifying speeds, the angles of its beams shifting with mathematical precision. Invisible force lashed out around it, crushing defenders where they stood. Its presence invigorated the other Ravener-spawn, and they rampaged through the courtyard with renewed fervour.

"Everyone, get back!" Watcher Shaw shouted, his black beard bristling in the wind. "This creature is *mine*. Back down to the pit with you!"

The Watcher levelled his staff at the invisible menace and spoke an incantation. Power built at its tip. A deadly beam lanced toward the invisible space. A disintegration spell: a beam of matter-reducing energy shot forward with uncompromising accuracy.

The snow churned as the unseen menace sped through the courtyard, trying to dodge, but the leader of the Watchers arced his ray after it, tracking it like prey.

The beam caught up, within inches of connecting... when a spear-fly veered downward, taking the hit, vanishing in a flash.

The invisible monster responded with a sweep of its grey petrifying beam as the Watchers were already shouting spells, beginning to raise a stone barricade around it. Alex was still its main target, and it was taking all his haste-enhanced reflexes to get away.

Two of his air elementals froze in midair, trapped by the paralysing magics. Alex's mind raced as he pulled out potions. The beams were too swift to risk the Mark's interference.

He shouted in every extraplanar tongue he knew, calling on his summoned monsters. "Everyone, attack wherever those beams come from!"

The summoned monsters broke off their assault against Ravener-spawn to charge the invisible creature, while Watchers unleashed cones of utter cold. Snow churned. Ice sprayed. The spells blasted over the snow.

But the enemy was quick and sure. Even as it pinpointed Alex in the sky, it shot at fighters on the ground and in the air.

'It's like it has eyes in the back of its head!' he thought.

As it weaved through enemy attacks, its beams lanced out again, striking the Watchers.

Shaw dodged away, levelling his staff, releasing a whirlwind of force blades. They spun through the snow, spiraling forward when above the noise of the gusting wind, came a loud tearing sound.

Followed by an inhuman scream.

Something hit the ground writhing, leaving snaking channels in the snow, slowly becoming visible. An eye. An eye at the end of what looked like a thick tentacle. Alex frowned at it while cheers erupted through the Watchers ranks.

Suddenly, a beast sprang from where the invisible thing's eye had come from, surprising most.

The clawed monster leapt at them with blurring speed. Watcher Shaw didn't hesitate, thrusting his enchanted blade, spearing the creature and twisting the blade.

It slumped over on the weapon.

He snarled at its corpse.

And then the snarl froze on his face. Alex's breath caught. The invisible monster's beam had washed over the powerful battlemage in his moment of distraction.

Distracted only for a heartbeat.

But that was enough.

Grey magic swept and paralysed Watchers, Alex's summoned monsters, and defenders nearby, casting them all in stone. Even a strapping red clay golem hardened into unyielding granite.

Then came the earth-shattering scream, bringing ear-piercing pain with it.

A scream so powerful, Alex's hands shot up, clutching the side of his head, trying to block the agonising sound. It stretched out for what felt like minutes before rising to an octave that faded into silence. Alex felt the terrible energy resonating in his bones, and the rigid figures of defenders began to shudder. A pair of stone golems shook like leaves caught in a gale, and Alex's eyes fell on the bearded form of Watcher Shaw, his face twisted in defiance.

Cracks rippled through a stony snarl.

Then, the battlemage exploded. All exploded: golems, people, summoned monsters, cobblestones, and even sections of nearby buildings. In an instant, they were reduced to shattered remains falling from the sky, staining the bloody snow grey with rock dust.

Alex's mind recoiled. How many had just died?

Twenty? More?

He had no time to count, for they weren't the only victims.

"Claygon!" he screamed.

The sound was wreaking havoc through the golem. Cracks spider-webbed through his body as clay was battered by sound energy.

More beams came at Alex.

The young wizard focused, measuring their paths, calling on the Mark, weaving and dancing.

One swept by. He whirled past another, teeth clenched, focus narrowed. It was taking everything to dodge them. Each passed closer than the last as his invisible enemy adjusted its aim.

He moved quickly.

He moved gracefully.

And then...

He did not move at all.

A terrible force wrapped him, squeezing, freezing him in place. His every muscle strained, his sinews twitched, and his nerves fired... but his body would not move. His breath came shallow and fast. He controlled his breaths, calming them as well as he could. Blinking was slow, his eyes barely responding. Through force of will and what felt like moving through muck, his left eye slowly tracked downward.

There. It had struck him there, catching an ankle.

What was happening? He fought the panic threatening his nerve.

Think. Adapt.

He sent mental commands, he screamed them, told his force spells to push him like they'd pushed Isolde. Forceballs and Wizards Hands followed his commands, shoving, nudging, pushing against him, but it was all in vain. Alex remained like a statue, fixed and unmoving.

Three beams hit: one to the chest and one to either arm.

His breath slowed.

He was static. Fighting for breath. His force spells kept trying, but still couldn't move him.

Think! Adapt!

What could he do? He couldn't use potions. His spells couldn't help. His air elementals were close, but his mouth wouldn't budge. He couldn't cast anything.

Hope drained as mana built, powering the petrifying beam.

And then came the scream. Stronger this time, rising to an octave so high, it seemed to die while remaining very much alive, sinking deep into his core. Stone shattered, his teeth chattered, grinding in his clenched jaw.

His head and his vision swam. He felt like he would suffocate.

'Think!' he screamed in his own mind. 'Think! It wants to kill you. To turn you to stone! Think! Think! *Adapt!*'

Panic fought for control, and he tried to push it down, seeing Theresa's face, Selina's, his parents', Claygon's, his friends', all drifting through his mind. His eyelids grew heavy, grit having replaced tears, and his vision blurred, barely catching something streaking toward him. It was Claygon, battered and damaged. Broad cracks spider webbed through his massive form. Grey dust rained as he flew toward his master, and in the centre of his trunk... his golem core was laid bare.

'No, Claygon!' Terror seized Alex's mind. 'Get away!' The thought was frantic: if anything struck his core...

'Claygon! *Please*! Fire your beams at that invisible monster and throw your war-spear! Then get us out of here!'

But his golem didn't alter his path—his face was fully focused on Alex.

'No!' Alex pleaded. 'Listen to me, please, listen to m—'

The grey beam fired when Claygon was a handspan away.

Alex could only watch as it raced toward him.

It was moving too fast. Even if his golem pushed him aside, the invisible monster could simply sweep it after him.

Think! Adapt!

Then his sight was abruptly blocked.

Claygon was before him—limbs spread, shielding his creator—just as he had when the dungeon core remains and chaos essence exploded. And he was right in the middle of that terrible scream. Cracks ran like webbing, continuing their spread.

That petrifying beam shot up.

'Claygon! *Claygon, no*!' Alex's mind shrieked, powerless to act.

He'd shatter. His core would explode.

The grey light consumed the golem he and Selina had sculpted together. The golem he and his friends had hunted a mana vampire to power. The golem who had saved his life. Cracks, sounding like frazil ice on a frigid winter's night, spread through Claygon.

Yet Alex couldn't even scream.

CHAPTER 79

CHANGE

Molten lines of power flowed and bubbled like lava running through cracks in the golem's battered body. An unfamiliar mana drove into Alex's senses, and Claygon's massive form seemed to ripple.

As he watched helplessly, old memories came drifting across time, echoing through his mind. They rose above sounds of battle and cracking clay running through his golem in fissures.

Bits of a conversation he'd had long ago returned.

"Some golems can even change on their own if they encounter the right mana, magical effects, or spells," Sim Shale had said on the day he and Theresa first toured the workshop. *"'Golem Evolution' we call that, but it takes a core made with materials that can generate a lot of mana and that are able to produce a variety of effects naturally. Chaos Essence is a good example, with its ability to mutate monsters."*

That was the day he'd connected the similarities between golem cores and dungeon cores. The day he'd first learned of golem evolution, the mysterious process that couldn't be predicted.

A deeper voice, measured, stronger, ancient, reawakened a memory buried in his mind.

"With golems made from chaos essence, their triggers for evolution vary as much as... well, the roiling bed of chaos itself," Baelin had said. *"However, while the dungeon core's substance shares a lot of similarity in composition to chaos essence, it is a different material, after all. I suspect that the trigger for Claygon's evolution will likely come from other dungeon cores, their monsters, or this Ravener."*

And so, he was provided with a clue: Claygon's evolution might be tied to the origins of his golem core. They'd fought in dungeons together, been bathed in chaos essence and dungeon core energies in an explosion, felt the Ravener's mana.

Claygon had encountered strange magics from masses of Ravener-spawn, even going back to the time of the clawed ones at Patrizia DePaola's ball. And yet nothing. Not even the slightest change.

But today, the unique power from this unseen Ravener-spawn had turned clay golems, elementals, and mortals to stone.

It'd washed over Claygon and his exposed core, combining with the mana pulsing inside. A new power exploded; sparking, spreading as the enormous pool of mana within his core soared. It slipped through his mana pathways, and in heartbeats, cracks closed, knitting together like they never were.

Energy flooded the pathways, burning with incandescent light.

The light seared Alex's eyes, and as it faded, Claygon transformed.

Gone was the grey clay that he and his sister used to mould him. In its place was white stone like marble, gleaming in the fading grey light of the enemy's power.

Alex's eyes stung, powerless to shed tears that longed to run free. His golem was alright. He was alright.

He'd evolved from clay to stone with a new and staggering power radiating from deep inside his core.

For a breath, Claygon's entire form flashed—hovering between solid matter and pure power—his mana pathways blazed bright, visible to even Alex's frozen sight. They seemed infinite, teeming through his body like schools of tiny fish, connections between his fire-gems and core widened.

His core sparkled like crystals.

A breath later, his frame settled, white stone gleamed within the snow swirling to the ground, and for an instant, the courtyard stilled. Monsters and defenders paused on the battlefield, looking up at what looked like a second sun briefly hovering above.

Even the invisible monster that once moved so quickly—killing with abandon—appeared rooted in place, its beams still holding Alex in paralysis.

Now.

The spawn was distracted.

This was their chance.

'Claygon!' Alex thought. 'Hit it with everything you've got! All three fire-beams and your war-spear!'

The golem's arms snapped up.

Whooooom!

Alex's mind raced, the beams would take time to charge, but Claygon could throw his spear and force the Ravener-spawn to scatter—

Whooooosh!

Before he could finish the thought, three beams like flame shot out, shocking him with the speed of their response. The rays holding the young wizard in suspension released the instant Claygon's beams fired.

An inferno, followed abruptly by a concussion of sound, ripped the air. Something immense hit the ground, a feeble voice called from a mound of snow.

The paralysing effect fled, and Alex inhaled a precious breath of cold air that filled his spirit with relief, and every fibre of his being with life. Muscles he didn't know existed ached from straining against the monster's magic, but they would have to wait.

He stared down—wrath filled—at black blood staining the snow where their invisible enemy lay.

"You're dead," he promised, pulling a pair of mana soothing potions from his bag. "You're absolutely dead."

'Claygon, get it!'

The stone golem gripped his spear and charged from the sky, unleashing beams of flame that streaked toward the target with the same swiftness as the enemy's.

They struck, lancing through snow, melting it into geysers of boiling liquid, herding the invisible menace. Another grey beam launched, travelling sluggishly across the sky. Its beams would never again touch Claygon's creator. The golem would see to that.

Without waiting for Alex's direction, he flew into the beam's path, his stone body absorbing its magic. A smile crossed the Thameish wizard's face. Claygon was immune to the petrifying beam.

He was safe.

And that meant he could shield others.

"Claygon!" Alex flew by his golem's side, tossing the mana soothing potions to his Wizard's Hands. "We're going to dance! Let's get this bastard!"

The stone construct snapped to attention. He and Alex fell into the first position of the Spear-and-Oar Dance, and together, they headed for the Ravener-spawn.

They danced for all to see, distracting, drawing attention away from

Alex's Wizard's Hands as they dimmed to a muted crimson glow, nearly disappearing in the sheeting snow.

Wizard and golem moved as a mirror of each other, whirling and exchanging positions in the sky. Claygon fired beam after beam of raging flame at the unseen foe, heating the ground, melting snow, turning it to a boiling pool. The monster was trying to fight back, but its petrifying beams could only labour through the air while Alex and Claygon whirled in tandem. Feeble beams of deadly magic passed lightly over his stone form as he shielded his creator.

The enemy struggled, stoking morale and fire in the defenders. Most shouted Watcher Shaw's name in tribute, slashing every foe in sight, giving the invisible creature more than Claygon's fire-beams to consider. A barrage of spells and blows came in a ferocious attack from every wizard, warrior, and summoned in the courtyard.

Watchers bellowed incantations and curses, raining shards of icicles, lines of dark energy, and explosive fireballs, striking swathes of terrain and the invisible creature. They were corralling it, herding it with explosive magics to prevent its escape.

Claygon's beam struck.

A fireball singed its hide.

A lance of force magic hit as Alex and his stone golem closed in through their aerial dance. The creature fired sputtering paralysing beams of energy, desperate to sweep the defenders with the petrifying ray, but its aim had grown clumsy, predictable.

The panic it inflicted on its master's enemies now fell on *its* own shoulders.

Black blood dripped from invisible wounds, marking the spot where it lay. Incrementally, its shape was exposed where it writhed through the snow.

Paralysing and petrifying bursts fired slower, erratically flying in all directions. Four paralysing rays hit Claygon, freezing him in midair. Alex soared behind him, shielded. Another petrifying beam raked the golem, to no effect.

'Keep firing, Claygon!' Alex thought. 'Even if you can't move, just *bury* that thing in power.'

Instantly, fire-beams fired from Claygon's forehead and outstretched hands. Explosions boiled the snow, and the creature dragged itself away, trying to roll from their path. Claygon fired again, his beams still aiming at the spot he'd just targeted. They raced past the Ravener-spawn.

But, hitting it wasn't the goal; holding its attention was.

Glowing Wizard's Hands slipped through blowing snow, weaving through spells and raging fire-beams.

High winds meant Alex would only get a single chance to hit it with a potion.

He just needed the right moment.

And maybe some luck.

***

This was not going well.

The Petrifier had been moving through the courtyard, beset on all sides by defenders and mortal mages. Burns marked its body, and it bled from a dozen cuts. That blast from the four-armed warrior's rays had dealt it a terrible wound to its leg, robbing it of speed. Now, its movements were slowed, and it left a blood trail that allowed the enemy to track it.

More and more, the threats closed in, and though it could watch them from all sides, it was more difficult to monitor every direction at once.

And the greatest setback was that the Usurper was still not dead.

He refused to die!

There he was, high above, hidden behind that infernal four-armed thing that also would not fall to its Ravener-granted magic. The Petrifier screeched, shattering stone, kicking up waves of snow, desperate to break its strange new enemy.

To its frustration, the enemy endured, unharmed. It screeched louder, increasing the frequency of the sound, but nothing changed. No cracking, no fragmenting, no shattering.

Something unknown in past cycles was waking. The cold touch of fear. Fear of failure, fear that the Usurper would live, and its master's plan would be ruined. Below the surface, the dungeon cores struggled with that powerful entity who also would not die.

Its time was running short.

'I must kill the Usurper,' it thought, calling out to its Hunters. 'I must see him dead. In this, I cannot fail!'

Hunters were concealed throughout the courtyard, awaiting its call to act. They sprang from snow and rooftop, cutting the enemy down, driven by the need to serve their master. There.

The pressure had lessened.

Two free eyestalks pointed in all directions, primed to freeze every mortal they saw. Then, its petrifying beam could sweep the enemy formations, creating perfect statues to shatter in its own time.

A twitch of its legs carried it a hair's breadth above the snow, propelling it forward. It directed its petrifying eye-stalk toward the nearest group of mortals.

Power built.

It adjusted its aim, preparing to fire.

Then... it tripped, tumbling to the earth, long legs in a tangle, grunting in surprise.

How—with all of its speed and meticulous agility—had it been clumsy enough to stumble? Its central eye looked for what was in its path, what had caused it to fall.

The only thing it found could never account for the mishap.

A root. A single, tiny sapling root was barely visible in the snow, growing from a strange tree that glowed green in the centre of the courtyard. How could its feet find an obstruction when its many eyes could not?

It was... puzzling. Perhaps a wizard's sly deed.

When it had fallen, some of its eyes kept the four-armed enemy in sight.

Good. If that creature was able to—

A crunching noise above its head. Glass broke. Mist drifted, blowing into its mouth. What was this? Poison? Foolish mortals, its body was created to stand against a venom-walker, no poison could...

What was this?

'What disrupts my mana?' It called upon its own power, but it was slowing, calming like a river freezing. The sensation was not unpleasant, but...

The power within its eye beams faltered, flickering off and on, power lessening, making it vulnerable.

The Petrifier tried to leap away and stumbled in its own pooling blood, splaying out in the blackening snow. And then the fire-beams came, bringing fresh fear, lancing it in waves of agony. Its wounds seared. Two of its eyes turned to ash.

The pain—

A sharp object abruptly sliced it, tearing its attention away from eyes consumed by flame, to excruciating pain from an enormous spear protruding through its core. Blood poured freely, and weakness spread from the wound, further slowing it. The spear withered its lifeforce as the mist calmed its mana. It tried to scream, but it was weakening, drained, sapped of strength and mana.

Then spells struck from all sides.

Shards of slashing magic.

Roaring and bursting flame.

Ice.

Lightning raked its armour and singed its flesh. The mortal female who earlier fought at the Usurper's side poured lightning from her hands in waves.

Panic surged. The Petrifier was being torn apart.

It was going to die. Worse, it was going to *fail*.

'Only one thing to do before my full form is revealed in death,' it thought. 'May my master accept my sacrifice. May my sacrifice smite my enemies. May my return be greater than the last!'

It activated an organ within its core. An organ that would bring death. Its mana reacted sluggishly. What should have been an instantaneous explosion was taking time to build. The detonation would be less powerful than planned, but it would be powerful enough.

It would die.

But it would not die alone.

CHAPTER 80

RACING THE EXPLOSION

Euphoria!

Thundering cheers rising louder and louder.

Warriors, mages, all celebrating the enemy's imminent end.

The invisible Ravener-spawn verged on defeat. Its black blood stained the ground where it lay, unseen limbs stirred clouds of white and its fading cries rose and fell like the gurgles of a choked well. The mana soothing potions had withered its power, while the war-spear withered its life.

Victory was a Wizard's Hands grasp away.

"We did it!" Alex cried to Claygon, throwing his arms as far around the stone yet warm body as they could reach. "We *did* it, my beautiful golem! Now let's end the rest of these bastards then get down to the tunnels and rescue—"

A chill crawled through him like the cold hand of death reaching for his heart.

"No..." His mana senses brushed against a rising power. He turned his attention to the invisible creature whose ebbing power was suddenly growing, surging.

Rising.

Rising.

Changing, transforming, becoming something that stilled the heart of every research team member in the courtyard.

Isolde drew back, keeping her eyes fixed on the blackening spot in the snow. "What is happening? The energy is still..." She whirled around.

"It's going to explode!" Some felt the energy growing and looked for cover, others screamed orders, others froze.

A chilling memory flooded Alex's mind: images of a mushroom cloud rising high above the moors.

"It'll wipe out the castle!"

The power was listless, and still the reaction built. Maybe they could get rid of the monster before it blew everything they'd built and everyone who'd built it to particles.

"Claygon!" Alex shouted. "We have to stop it!"

Below, others sprang into action.

Watchers cast spells around the unseen beast, wrapping it in walls of force, shielding the surroundings from the building power.

Alex and Claygon raced for the creature, tearing through the icy wind, the young wizard's cloak billowing around him. Power built, bringing a new realisation: when this thing exploded, nothing could withstand it. What could survive an explosion even stronger than combined power of the chaos essence and dungeon core remains? It had torn hills apart, force walls could never contain it.

"*Evacuate!*" Professor Jules' voice—enhanced by magic—boomed through the air from somewhere in the keep. High above the mounting snow, her tiny form caught his attention. "*Evacuate the research castle! Retreat until Chancellor Baelin arrives!*"

As though responding to her words, the earth bucked. The struggle continued between Baelin's power and the Ravener's energies, and their clash showed no sign of weakening.

Still, Alex kept faith in the chancellor.

"That's right, Baelin's here," he whispered, reaching the creature and hovering above the force walls containing it. "He'll be back soon and he's gonna grab this thing, teleport it so it can blow up somewhere else, then everything'll be fine. All we need to do is buy ti—"

As though mocking him, the earth heaved again.

Stone crumbled and soil belched through holes tunnelled from deep below the surface. Defenders and monsters alike were knocked to the ground, buildings trembled.

And through it all, the power built.

'We might not have time for him to get here,' Alex thought as the ground heaved. 'We've gotta do something fast... but what? Maybe I can soothe its mana with more potions? But who knows how long that'll work for. We need a way to get rid of...'

Symbols.

'That's it!'

An old witch in an underground grotto.

Elder Blodeuwedd, painting symbols on a traitor. Symbols that bled away mana.

"I can drain it!" His hand shot for his bag while he called to a Watcher. "Hey! I need to get through those force walls! I can drain some of that thing's mana!"

"It's too dangerous!" the Watcher shouted back. "Move from there!"

He had no time for this.

"Claygon, break the wall down!"

Stone fists hit with the force of an avalanche, and with two quick blows, a section of a force wall shattered and Alex dove through with Claygon at his side.

"What do you three think you're doing? Get out of there!" the Watcher shouted.

"We're trying to save us! You can close the wall behind us!" He drew a brush and dipped it in the gift from Crymlyn Village. "Wait, three—?"

"He refers to me."

"Isolde!" Alex turned at the sound of the noblewoman's voice.

"I am here to help," she said.

There was no time to argue. The power was nearing its peak.

"Glad you're here!" He handed her a bottle. "Here, paint this stuff on —by the Traveller!"

Below them, a creature was materialising.

Its oblong form was covered in grey chitin and three long legs stretched on for yards. Burns and raw wounds marred the silvery sheen of natural armour, and a withering rot was spreading through its twitching body. Glazed eyes, bulbous and wavering, slowly tracked his every movement.

Fluid poured from a mouth wide enough to swallow a pair of oxen, its screams choked. Even now, it fought to reach Alex, but for all its effort, it could barely raise a single limb.

"Look how weak it is," Isolde said.

"But that won't stop it from exploding," he said, landing on its armour. "We need to get rid of it. Here, just drop some of this on as much of its body as you can."

He handed her a second bottle of mana-ejecting ointment.

"We must work quickly." Isolde's voice was strained as her eyes turned to three long, twitching legs. With a trembling hand, she dribbled the liquid over the creature's hide, then frowning, she focused on its wounds.

"Nothing is happening, Alex!"

"Just give it a minute!" he shouted, calling on the Mark. It guided him through images of Elder Blodeuwedd painting ancient symbols on the traitors. He copied them, using as much speed as he could manage, refining each symbol.

The symbols wouldn't be perfect—he'd only watched Blodeuwedd once and practised them with Drestra once—but with the Mark's help, they'd be close.

Even if it died, that power within it would keep building until its body exploded, bringing catastrophe to Greymoor.

'This isn't fast enough!' He called on Wizard's Hands.

The spells raced toward the bottle clutched in his fist, dipped magical fingers into glowing ink and sped to the monster's body, painting symbols at speed.

The power pulsed, flowing like a rising tide.

'Come on! Come on!' Alex thought.

"Alex?" Isolde murmured, the colour gone from her face. "I just want you to know... it was an honour to know you, and I am happy that we formed our cabal. May we reach the afterworld together hand in hand with the highest of honour."

"The highest of honour can be us living after we beat this thing!" Alex shouted, desperately sifting through the Mark's memories, trying to draw the symbols as precisely as time would allow.

They weren't perfect; some were too big, and others didn't quite curve properly.

'I just need them to be close enough,' he thought. 'Just close enooooouuugh—There!'

He finished the last symbol and a flare of power spiked throughout the glyphs, alighting every drop of ointment on the monster's body.

Power flowed.

The creature's death rattle gasped out in a choked scream as its mana began pouring away, dissipating in the wind. As power drained, rising mana lessened, sputtering like water pumping from a dying well.

"Yes!" he nearly screamed. "Yes! Yes... yes... Oh no!"

"By the elements," Isolde murmured.

The creature's mana was flowing out, but not as fast as was needed. What seemed like a river running freely, was a mere trickle from the ocean of chaotic energies that had built within the beast.

And worse...

"I can feel it," Isolde said in horror. "The reaction is not stopping!"

Beneath them, the dying spawn's mana roiled in pure chaos. Even if Claygon ripped it apart until there was nothing left but shreds of flesh and silver armour, he didn't know if that would stop the explosion, nor did they have time to experiment and find out.

Think. Adapt.

'We can't stop it,' he thought. 'We need it gone. Maybe drop it in a hole? No, that would kill everyone in the tunnels and collapse the earth and kill everyone above ground. Think! *Think*! We survived the chaos explosion... how? Distance. Okay, the explosion won't be as powerful since it has less mana, but we'll still need to be far away when it explodes. The right distance... that's key.'

"Claygon!" he called to his golem. "I need you—" Alex pointed in the direction that the wind was blowing, looking between the monster and his golem "—to throw this thing as hard as you can *with* wind. Get it away from here!"

The golem's head turned, and—for a brief, horrifying instant—he thought he wasn't going to listen.

Then he reached down, gripped the Ravener-spawn by a single leg and streaked skyward as though the titanic creature were no heavier than a sack of feathers. His stone body crashed through the force walls erected around them. He began to spin, building momentum. Turn after turn; ever faster, ever swifter. The dying creature's leg grew taut as its body rose.

The whirring sound of it cutting the air mounted, building in force. Claygon swung the Ravener-spawn with such speed that it decompensated with every turn, shedding damaged bits the faster he spun.

A final spin and Alex could feel the explosion straining its bonds and...

"Claygon! Throw it!"

The powerful stone golem hurled the ruined body into the wind. It flew straight as an arrow—rotating through the air, trailing gore in its wake. Watchers cast force walls, sealing it away from the world on all sides.

Alex could only hope it would be enough.

The monster disappeared into the storm.

"Everyone, down!" a Watcher shouted as he burnt a swarm of spear-flies to ash.

Alex leapt to the snow with Isolde beside him. Clenching his teeth, his arm covered her. "Air elementals!" he shouted. "Shield us!"

The summoned monsters floated above the two wizards.

And then...

For the second time that day, it seemed as though a second sun blazed in the wintry sky.

A blinding flash. Then a concussive force and the rumble of thunder. The shockwave struck Alex like a battering ram, threatening to drive him into unconsciousness. The wind reversed course, blowing hot, steaming droplets of melted snow down.

Chaos energy billowed in the distance, shaking the ground well beyond sight. Alex shut his eyes, praying to the Traveller that the ground would hold.

The ground shifted, and Alex braced, ready to fly into the hot wind should the castle be sucked into the earth. Images of Selina, Theresa, and everyone he held dear flashed in his mind.

'Please,' he thought. 'Please hold.'

For what felt like an eternity, the world threatened to fall apart. Until finally, the ground began to settle.

The quake stilled. Heat cooled. And the blazing light diffused as the roar of flame faded.

Alex risked looking around.

The castle shook, but still stood. The ground beneath them held, they were alive, and they were free of the invisible Ravener-spawn that he held no doubts was sent for him and Carey.

He was mostly relieved, though numb.

Snow crunched nearby and his breath stopped.

Above him and Isolde a pair of clawed monsters loomed, claws raised, eyes burning into him.

"Claygon!" Alex screamed, casting force spells, while Isolde whirled, shouting an incantation.

They were too slow. The first creature's claws fell to twin blades of steel, then the rest of its body followed.

The second monster was greeted by a shining, morphic metal weapon.

Two warriors turned with surprise on their faces.

Alex's and Isolde's expressions echoed theirs.

Theresa had come from the right, climbing from a hole in the earth to defend her partner and their friend. Her snarl was feral as she raced through the snow, leaving clouds behind her. Brutus bounded behind, followed by the towering Grimloch, then Thundar, Khalik, Svenia, Tyris, Hogarth, and more from the excavation team. Najyah circled, sharp eyes tracking flying monsters.

Cedric had approached from the left, his morphic weapon whirling in one hand. Behind him, Hart charged through the snow, and above, Drestra weaved through the air, her reptilian eyes locked on the remaining clouds of spear-flies.

Behind the Heroes, squads of mounted knights and foot soldiers thundered, armed with lances and brandishing their spears.

Amongst the army, a strange blue man sat astride a moose with tinkling bells hung about its antlers. And sitting on that moose's broad head...

...A terrified Gwyllain, looking like he'd rather be anywhere but there.

"Not agaaain!" the asrai screamed, his cry a war-horn for what was to come.

CHAPTER 81

TO MAKE THE END OF BATTLE

"Greetin's, friends!" Cedric took Alex and Isolde by the hand, pulling both to their feet. "We're here t'turn the tide. We'll be talkin' later."

Without another word, the Chosen of Uldar charged through what was left of the hordes of Ravener-spawn, unleashing a fireball—turning half a dozen bone-chargers to ash—and leaping on survivors as his morphic weapon changed into the shape of a broad axe. It shone with the light of Uldar's power as he cleaved foes down like chaff.

The Champion, Sage, and their knight companions fell on the enemy in a clash of magic, blood, and metal, spraying reddened snow to the wind.

And as crimson spread like a battle flag unfurling, the defenders were spurred on in a final push against the monsters.

Alex and Theresa looked at each other. No words passed between them, leaving their gazes to tell of their relief, excitement, love, and exhaustion. There would be words to express such things when the final Ravener-spawn had breathed their last, but for now...

"Theresa!" Alex shouted, tossing her a potion of haste as he flew through the air. "You and I can distract the bone-chargers! Grimloch and Claygon can finish them off!"

"Don't worry." The huntress' blades shone, seeming to scream in the wind. "I've got them."

She ran forward, twin blades flicking around her, splitting hide and bone as each sword strike left two wounds.

Alex gaped.

In heartbeats, death and ruin lay in the huntress' wake as nearly a fourth of the bone-chargers littered the ground.

At that moment, the young wizard could not describe—even in a thousand words—how attracted he was to her.

'By the Traveller, I really *do* have issues... And I wouldn't want it any other way.' He smiled to himself, tossing sleeping potions into clouds of oncoming spear-flies, dropping them from the sky in puffs of mist.

'Claygon, they're all yours, buddy! Show them the brand new you!'

His golem had evolved. After all this time, he'd *finally* evolved. It was almost like seeing him for the first time, and Alex looked at him in amazement, wondering how much he'd changed.

Claygon moved through the sky like a reaper, herding Ravener-spawn to their doom. Where his fire-beams had once built power slowly, now they were swift to respond, and even swifter to fire. If he were a painter, his fire-beams would have been his brushes and palette knives, and the battlefield his canvas.

As spells and steel rained down on the attackers, Gwyllain and the blue stranger watched near the aeld tree as the earth shook, Gwyllain shaking with it.

The terrible struggle between two pools of mana vast enough to devastate Greymoor reached a peak, then calmed as one shriveled, then shattered like a thin sheet of glass, and the other disappeared only to abruptly reappear in the sky above. Baelin hovered above the battlefield unscathed, cloaked in power, and wearing an expression of rage so pure and profound, a dragon would have cowered in fear.

"You!" his voice boomed. "Your dungeon cores are no more. Perish! You have extracted enough pain in the course of your worthless lives."

He levelled a finger at a pack of Ravener-spawn, his words were short, his tone curt. And the power that flowed from him was a tidal wave. It crashed into the army of monsters, freezing them, holding them as though they'd been pinned in place, then the spell went to work. They recoiled as though struck by arrows and shrieked in defiance, hissing and writhing as their bodies boiled, billowing smoke and flame from every pore.

They collapsed on themselves, a dull grey substance leaking from their skin. Alex flinched, knowing what the chancellor had dealt them. Boiling lead ran from their bodies, pooling then hardening in the snow.

The ancient wizard had transmuted their life blood into the molten, lethal metal.

Scores of monsters died in heartbeats when he trained a single finger on them, and searing pain replaced all desire to do their master's bidding. The enemy numbers dropped fast, and without dungeon cores to replenish them, bone-chargers were the first to meet oblivion, followed soon after by the last behemoth, which fell to Baelin's war-spirits like prey to hungry wolves during a lean winter. Claygon's flames made short work of the last hive-as-one, and clots of spear-flies shriveled away, leaving clumps of hardening lead behind. And when the final monster breathed its last, Baelin called out in triumph.

"Victory!" the ancient wizard's voice boomed through the courtyard. "Victory!"

Spontaneous cheers erupted, filling the air with cries of celebration and relief. Everyone was talking at once, slapping each other on the back, throwing their fists in the air, but some stood stoically, lost in the moment of triumph.

And beneath the joy, an undercurrent of grief hung around them.

The first battle at Greymoor's Research Castle ended in victory, to be sure.

A crushing one.

But as with all victories in battle.

There was a cost.

The victors filled the entrance hall of the keep beneath a cloud of exhaustion. Most sat or lay on folding cots warming themselves around orbs of conjured flame. Blood mages moved briskly through the centre of the chamber to stabilise the wounded. Some of the injured passed in and out of consciousness on glowing forcedisks, moaning in varying levels of pain as they were transported to the infirmary. Thameish soldiers helped where they could, relieving the weary defenders and bringing broth, bread, and cups of hot milk to soothe their bellies. As the tapestries of victory watched from above, Alex Roth sat against a wall, Theresa pressed to his side while his cabal sat around him.

Not a word passed between them. Not yet, for there were other conversations worth listening to. And other things to process.

Throughout the chamber, the leadership and specialists of the expedition were gathered in clutches, discussing the toll and aftermath.

"Twenty dead in the courtyard," a Watcher to Alex's left announced, her grim eyes scanning a tally on a scroll. "Most were reduced to stone dust. At least ten more died in the tunnels. We'll need to—"

"The armoury and research buildings' are compromised, right down to the foundation." A dwarven engineer showed a schematic to a gathering of earth mages on Alex's right. "Once the blizzard passes, you'll need to reinforce—"

"And the creature's remains?" Baelin asked Professor Jules in the centre of the room.

The alchemy professor shook her head. "Hopelessly ruined." Her voice contained a growl Alex had never heard before. There was also a stiffness in her body. A forcefulness to her movements. All of it spoke of rage. "When the creature detonated, it was quite nearly completely reduced to ash. There weren't enough remains left to catalogue. No organs."

"Fascinating, yet disappointing," Baelin said. "Something is shifting. We have never combatted a monster that was naturally able to self-destruct rather than let itself be captured before. That speaks of a guile and strategy built into the creature's very design. Natural organisms do not come equipped with self-destruct mechanisms."

"I agree. It seems it was created with that foremost in mind. I've seen self-destruct mechanisms in golems, but never in living creatures. Save for some very rare and exceptional demons." Professor Jules frowned. "Something is moving against us... What did you see below ground, Chancellor? Was there anything unusual?"

"I saw pain, Vernia. I saw two dungeon cores that were as beasts lashed to a wagon, made to pull a load too great to bear. They screamed in absolute agony, yet fought me with every last bit of energy they possessed. I broke one, but the other shattered from the overload of power. Still, for the period they lasted... they were ferocious opponents. It seemed like the very earth itself sought to destroy me."

His nostrils flared. "If this is the sort of power the Ravener can bring to bear, then my respect for previous generations of Thameish Heroes has greatly increased... Ah, speaking of that. Where are our young friends?"

"They went to the tunnels in search of stragglers, Chancellor," a nearby Watcher said. "And they—"

"I swear," Prince Khalik spoke, startling Alex. The broad-shouldered young man leaned against the sleeping form of Grimloch; the hulking shark man had lain down and fallen asleep as soon as his last spear-fly wound was bandaged, and the prince had collapsed against him shortly after. He hadn't found the strength to move.

"What do you swear?" Svenia asked, splayed out on a cot beside the sleeping Hogarth, whose head was wrapped in so many bandages, his skull looked more like cloth than bone.

"That I have no wish to ever be beneath the earth again, at least at this moment." Khalik's eyes swam with fatigue. "I imagine I will have to get over it, or my studies of earth magic will be comically pointless—but as of right now... never again."

"I hear that." Thundar groaned from a cot, holding a tightly woven ice bag to his head. His body was swaddled in a blanket. "I—Achoo!"

"Bless you," Alex and Theresa said together.

"Yeah, thanks." The minotaur rubbed his nose. "I'd better not get sick. I've got something to do."

"You mean..." Alex gave him a knowing look.

"Yeah... the timing wasn't right to ask her out yet but, yeah... Perfect timing doesn't help if I end up dead before I can follow through. Gotta get it done when I can. Anyway, yeah, someone else can be on the excavation team for a bit. Right now, if I could live on the sun, I would." He glanced at Theresa. "Hey, listen. Thank you, from me, my ancestors, and my whole herd. If it weren't for you going all 'god-warrior' or whatever the hell that was down there, I'd be a slab of bone-charger meat right now."

The huntress held up a hand. In her lap, one of Brutus' sleeping heads shifted. "No need to thank me—"

"It ain't about need, Theresa. It's about gratitude." Thundar's expression was serious, his tone grave. "It'd be a great dishonour to me if I didn't at least thank you. One day, I hope I can return the favour."

"We'd have to be in another life or death situation." She smiled. "And I think even I'm a bit through with those for a while."

"Yep," the minotaur said. "And I ain't gonna hope it happens. But I do know that—even if it takes a lifetime—I *will* return the favour."

The huntress stilled for a moment, then smiled weakly. "Thank you, Thundar. Thank you. But it should be my great-grandfather you should be thanking. If it weren't for his weapon, I might be dead too."

"Yeah." Alex looked at the naked blades sitting beside her. They had always been beautiful, but now their metallic sheen was burnished to the shine of a mirror crafted in the finest glass. Not a speck of dust or tarnish marked them. Every reflection was perfect, and they even appeared to shine with their own inner light.

He had a hard time pulling his gaze away. "Beautiful. Just like you."

"They are, aren't they?" She gazed at the blades warmly. "Great-

Grandfather's family legacy... I finally saw it for what it truly is. They're two swords, but they're one weapon."

"An impressive one at that." Khalik saluted the blades.

"Indeed," Isolde said groggily. The young noblewoman had just woken from a deep slumber, propped against the nearest wall. "They are handsome weapons... er, weapon, I suppose, and their power is most impressive. Many elemental knights would gladly give much for such weapons—er, I suppose, *weapon* would be the correct term for them in the singular? Two swords, but one weapon?"

"They are two yet one," Theresa said. "I think singular or plural works."

"Either way, they are magnificent."

"I'm sure my great-grandfather would be proud to hear you say that."

"And I'm sure he would've been proud of *you*." Alex kissed her cheek. "I'm proud of you... and I'm thankful to him, it helped you come back. He helped keep all of us together."

She smiled and kissed him, scrunching her face up as his beard tickled her lips. "I'm pretty proud of Claygon."

Her eyes took in the towering golem of white stone standing silently above them, his spear poised to protect them from all threats. His fire-gems gleamed with a new light, one that drew the eye.

Now—for the first time since the battle's end and Claygon's evolution—Alex had a chance to see how he'd changed.

And so far, he liked what he saw.

CHAPTER 82

THE EXPLORING OF CHANGE AND A NEW BATTLE BREWING

C laygon had always been beautiful to Alex. A terror to be sure, but a beautiful terror, much like Theresa was. Every inch of the golem's finely sculpted clay reminded Alex of the hours of love and care he and Selina had poured into crafting his body.

Claygon's new frame had the same shape and height, the same bulk, the same ferocity to his face, but the details were finer. After untold hours sculpting, Alex remembered him and Selina admiring all the intricate images of battles, and monsters, of warriors and more that they'd sculpted into his clay surface with a sense of awe. It was like watching a piece of art ready to come to life. Now, when the light struck him since his transformation from clay to polished marble, the carvings seemed like they were in motion.

The marble gleamed in the light of fire magics, and—like Theresa's swords—appeared to emit its own inner glow. The chamber was reflected in Claygon's polished surface, shadows and light dancing across the marble.

Beyond the surface, a staggering level of power unfolded like an ocean wave, far beyond anything Alex had ever felt from him. The connections between his golem core and fire-gems had strengthened, widening so a far greater flow of power reached them.

'No wonder they fired so fast,' Alex thought, looking at the gem. 'Those expanded pathways must *flood* them with power... and...'

He reached up and touched the fire-gem in Claygon's right palm, flinching slightly in surprise.

Warm.

It was warm to the touch even at rest. He ran his finger along the gem's surface, feeling its smooth, shining facets. A strange sensation of warmth travelled through the tips of his fingers. Different from the warmth of magic spells or heat radiating from flame. There was another sort of warmth there, seeping into the link between Alex and his golem.

It gave the young wizard the feeling of being wrapped in a thick blanket on a cold winter's day, and—

'It's not just the fire-gems,' he thought, touching the gauntlet he and Selina had sculpted on Claygon's hand. 'His whole body's warm now... Warm marble. Like he's alive.'

Alex closed his eyes, reaching out to Claygon with his mana senses... and he felt a pulse. The mana coursing through his golem had always flowed like a river, powerful, but without life. Now, the flood of mana rushed through him like an ocean's shifting tides, or the rise and fall of the wind with the pulse of a beating heart.

And...

'There's something about his mana that's changed,' he thought, examining each thick finger. 'There's more of it, and it's denser but—'

"Is he alright?" Theresa asked, concern marking her face. "He's been through a lot."

"Yeah, he's better than ever." Alex patted Claygon's hand. "At least, I think so. It's just that he's changed just as much on the inside as on the outside."

"Really?" Prince Khalik looked fondly at the golem. "Truly, he's become quite the handsome devil."

"They grow up so fast." Thundar mimed wiping a tear from his eye. "Next thing you know, he'll be asking to borrow your fine cloak and be bringing lady golems home to meet papa."

"Lady Golems? That is utter nonsense." Isolde looked at Thundar.

The minotaur shrugged. "I've seen golems sculpted to look like men, women, cats, dogs, or whatever in the city."

"And golems do not require biological reproduction," Isolde fired back.

Thundar's hooves literally dug into the stone. "But some golems have minds, don't they?" He nodded to Claygon. "Alex, does Claygon have a mind yet?"

The young wizard looked closely at his golem, closing his eyes again. He gently prodded at the bond between him and Claygon, feeling its magical contours and the pulse of power emanating from the other end.

He searched for consciousness on the other side of their bond, and what he found was... strange. Much like his body and the power coursing through him, something changed in their bond. It was stronger, and Claygon's presence was... different.

"I don't know..." Alex said. "He feels different through our bond, but it doesn't *quite* feel like those times his mind sparked."

"Is he talking to you?" The minotaur looked Claygon up and down like he was expecting him to start doing something.

"No." Alex tapped his arm. "But something's definitely changed."

"You hear that, Isolde?" Thundar grinned at the noblewoman. "Something's changed! And that might mean he's got more feelings. He wants *companionship*."

Isolde stared at him.

"What, you saying our brave and mighty friend *doesn't* deserve companionship?" Thundar gawked at her as though she'd declared that all children should be thrown into cauldrons.

"For shame, Isolde," Prince Khalik jumped in, his grin weak but wide. "To deny Claygon the very essence of what makes a living thing living: the warmth of others."

"That is *not* what the definition of a 'living thing' is, Khalik, and you know it," Isolde snapped.

"Aaaaah, do you lack all poetry in your soul, Lady Von Anmut?" The prince cocked his head at her. "This is not about biological needs or the tyranny of nature and destiny dictating our path. Surely, a golem with a mind, such as you and I possess, can form bonds and make friends. Or do you simply treat Claygon as no more than a tool, like the sickle or pickaxe?"

"*Khalik!*" Isolde snapped. "You have been having *entirely* too much fun at my expense lately. You know what I am speaking of! I am not denying the emotional needs and desires of sapient beings—be they biological or not—I am simply saying that *assuming* such affections will manifest in biological reproductive pair bonds is absurd! Far more likely that such a bond would manifest as familial, for that is how we—especially Alex and Selina—treat him! As both family and friend!"

"You're ruining the joke, Isolde," Thundar whispered.

"I am too tired to appreciate being the butt of such jokes at this particular moment." Her tone was acid.

"It is true, it is true," Khalik said. "Though keep in mind that I am your match when it comes to exhaustion, so—in a sense—there is no advantage on my part. We are simply two weary people having a good time, are we not?"

Isolde pointedly ignored him, looking up at the golem. "Listen, Claygon, my dear. Do not engage in such worthlessness as taking on these *three* as examples. In some sense, you will no doubt take after your father somewhat." She glanced toward Alex. "At least we might be able to narrow the field of bad influences on you."

"Hey, wait, wait, wait!" Alex straightened up in offence. "I literally said nothing wrong! You're victimising me!"

"Oh, *please*, Roth." Her blue eyes were like ice. "You have been there, grinning like the cat who got the cream and stifling a hyena's laughter this entire time. I could *feel* the malice emanating from you as surely as Claygon feels your thoughts through your link!"

"Thaaat would *not* be admissible during a tribunal!" Alex cried. "You can't just say: listen, I think that man over there's thinking bad things! Trust me, I'd know... I got a feeling about it!"

"We are not in a tribunal. This state around us—" she began.

Theresa stiffened, looking over her shoulder. Murmurs went through the room.

"Uh, Isolde," the huntress said.

"—is a post-war state which often involves a degree of anarchy—" the noblewoman continued.

"Isolde," Theresa said more urgently.

Alex followed her gaze, sitting up straighter as he did.

Murmurs swept through the entrance hall.

"*Isolde*," Theresa hissed.

"—in a moment, Theresa, for I—"

"Aaaaah, welcome back, young Heroes of Thameland," Baelin's warm voice boomed through the entrance hall. "I trust that your hunt went well?"

"Aye, it did," Cedric replied. "There was more Ravener-spawn in them tunnels, but we wiped 'em all out t' the last."

Isolde let out a tiny yelp, unconsciously fixing her raven-black hair.

Prince Khalik's eyes twinkled.

He looked at Thundar.

His words came out in a whisper. "Biological reproductive pair bonds."

Isolde turned bright red as Thundar, Theresa, and Alex bit down rolling laughter.

"Shut. Up!" she hissed.

If anyone noted the group's exchange, none said a word. Their eyes were locked on the two figures following the Heroes. Gwyllain padded into the room like a nervous cat stepping out of a barn and into the farmer's waiting dog pack. His large eyes darted every which way, growing wider at each wizard, familiar, and monster they landed on.

He didn't say a single word when he spotted Alex, though he did flinch in recognition, then did a double take when he saw Claygon's new form, quickly turning away. His attention went to the other fae—or so Alex assumed—walking beside him.

It was this figure who drew the most attention.

And it was obvious why.

At first glance, the blue-skinned fellow looked like nothing more than a jolly, dwarven-like fae with a stark white beard. But his body language raised a primal fear in Alex's core. The sort of fear that took hold of a mouse the moment it caught a snake's eye.

That instinctual terror upon seeing its natural predator.

His true nature was hidden well. The fae had mastered his body language so well, that his guise was nearly perfect. Alex watched him intently, using the Mark to note subtleties and masked cues. The slight cracks in his persona were there in the jolly, harmless mask he hid his true nature behind. The perfect balance of weight on the balls of the feet, his eyes scanning the room and how they lingered on the wounded—briefly, hungrily—before moving on. There was something chilling about this fae, and—

'Oh, by the Traveller, he's looking this way!' Alex thought.

The fae's eyes turned to him, as though sensing his gaze, and they focused with the stillness of an owl regarding a rodent. Alex adjusted his body language: relaxed shoulders, levelled gaze, straight back. He showed no fear, only casual interest. Nothing challenging, but nothing to encourage a predator to do what predator's do.

A smile crossed the fae's blue lips—one that didn't reach his eyes—and in a flash, his attention was elsewhere. That smile faded when he looked up at Baelin. The ancient wizard's goat-like eyes met those of the stocky fae.

They held for a moment.

The fae was first to break contact.

"Pleasure to meet you all," he said, his tone whimsical and light. "I'm called the Guide: guide to the Heroes of Thameland, and one of the road wardens sworn to Lord Aenflynn."

Professor Jules watched the blue-skinned fae closely, her body language showing gratitude, yet screaming with distrust. Her feet drifted closer together and her arms crossed before her.

Baelin stood tall, every muscle relaxed as he bent to shake the stocky fae's hand. "The pleasure is mine. I am Chancellor Baelin, and your assistance was most appreciated."

His words were carefully chosen, showing appreciation, but nothing that could be twisted into a declaration, oath, or debt.

If the Guide noticed, he gave no hint of it; instead, he gestured toward the asrai at his side. "'Twas Gwyllain here that warned me and got us to come to your aid," he said. "Appreciation should be given to him as well as me."

"And it is appreciated," the chancellor said to the nervous little asrai. "This is a time of planning and grieving, but I would be remiss if I did not show you hospitality. Walk with me, I will see you fed, and we will speak." He looked at the Heroes. "All of us."

"Aye, we should talk," Cedric said. "Folk're sayin' there was new monsters among them that attacked here?"

"Could they be something the demon worshippers conjured up?" Hart tapped an axe resting on his belt, one he'd taken from Zonon-In's war camp. "Your people were describing them and giving us a pretty good idea of what they looked like, but we've never seen their like before."

"Unfortunately, there's not much data to go on," Professor Jules said. "We're examining the scant remains we *do* have, but it's far too early to make any conclusions. Still, it would be good to compare notes. And..." She paused, seeming to notice something, but moved on quickly. "...and figure all of this out."

Her brow furrowed, and her body shook. Signs of discomfort washed over her in waves. "People died today. Too many. Far too many. We need a response. One that's measured."

"Yet crushing," Baelin said. "Our enemies are multiplying. Moving. Growing bold. It is time that some of them be culled."

A cheer swept through the room at his words, a cry of grief, and a hunger for vengeance. It spread, sweeping Alex and his friends up.

Fists, weapons, and staves rose high.

As the young wizard raised his arm in solidarity, he looked to his golem, appreciating his new-found power, and wondering what secrets might be hidden in his transformed body.

His eyes fell on the war-spear.

'Your war-spear suits you better than it did that demon, Claygon, and if she wants to come claim it, we'll take care of her, Ezaliel, and all their demon allies,' he thought. 'They're going to pay for all the people they killed and hurt, and we're going to take more of their stuff to help us.

Then when we find out what the Traveller's secrets are, we're going to break the Ravener forever. Sound good?'

There was a pulse across the bond.

Alex held his breath.

He waited for another spark of thought, but nothing came.

'Hmmm, maybe you'll start with your feelings first, and thoughts later... Oh, right! Speaking of feelings, the aeld tree helped us. I should thank it.'

As he excused himself from his friends to step into the cold night air, Alex focused on Claygon and the aeld, his thoughts and attention turned from the Heroes as Baelin led them deeper into the castle.

And so he missed Drestra's lingering gaze.

He missed the Sage's reptilian eyes, watching his every move.

Her look was questioning.

Measuring.

And girding for a confrontation.

CHAPTER 83

FATHER

The blizzard had lifted by the time Alex and Claygon stepped outside into the cold night air.

But the storm had done its work.

Snow drifts rose high in the castle's courtyard, lying thick on every roof and capping the inner wall in a rampart of white. They covered the signs of battle, hiding them, making it seem—for one irrational moment—that it had been done on purpose to hide their shame. It was as if the world was concealing something ugly, washing it in white paint to hide that it ever existed.

An image of Mrs. Lu hastily sweeping dirt under a bearskin rug before guests arrived came back to him. It'd always been a fond memory, especially when Mr. Lu brought it up to his wife. Alex now found it disturbing, realising how much it had in common with the snow sweeping over the tragedy that had befallen the castle.

'How many more times are sights like this going to be a part of my life?' Alex thought, his boots crunching on heavy snow as Claygon plowed along beside him.

His boot caught something hard buried in a drift and he stumbled, almost falling.

A crushed spear-fly corpse lay beneath the snow, probably one of many. Gingerly, he picked it up by its crumpled wings, looking at a nearby hill—one of the few formed not by fallen snow, but by the hands of the Generasians.

Ravener-spawn were piled high—high enough to tower over even the castle walls—and more were still being carted over, adding to the growing pile. Beside the gruesome sight, wizards were gathering and cataloguing specimens, preparing them for the scalpel and the autopsy table.

As Alex strode to the foot of the grisly pile and tossed away the spearfly, he hoped that the bodies would provide some new insights into their anatomy, tactics, and maybe even clues to help defeat them permanently.

"It's the least you could do." He spit on a dead bone-charger before he and Claygon turned away. Alex wasn't the first to spit on the slain invaders' bodies.

And he was sure he wouldn't be the last.

He trudged through snow drifts, contemplating the battle. The successes, the failures, and what they should do to prepare for the next—as there was no doubt there'd be a next.

"I need that staff," he whispered, breath misting in the cold, rising toward the grey clouds. His eyes turned to a spot where a vast hole had been; it was now filled by earth magic and covered in a layer of fresh, white powder. It was the hole from which two monsters—who'd almost cost him everything—had climbed. "That behemoth and hive-as-one came out of that hole almost right on top of me."

He touched his side, rubbing his skin, remembering the numbing cold of the hive-as-one's magic as it withered his strength. "They came at me, and I didn't have a quick enough response. My potions are good, but with the wind blowing so hard, they were mostly useless. I *need* another way to react faster. The potions aren't enough."

His frown deepened the more he thought about the attack. "I use a lot of protective spells, but I need stronger ones. Greater force armour is a must, and as *soon* as I get to fourth-tier spells, I've got to learn an invisibility spell."

His fingers raked his short beard. "Maybe some more illusion spells in general. Next semester, I'll be learning more blood magic... If I can build Corpse Puppet into my staff, I'll be able to pull that out in a fight. Better to turn dead enemies into fighters than be overwhelmed by live ones. Same with Warp Flesh..."

He remembered beams of light firing from his invisible enemy, freezing people in place and holding them so it could sweep them with its petrifying ray.

He remembered the paralysed face of Watcher Shaw, frozen in a snarl of defiance before he turned to stone. Alex winced at the memory. He hadn't known the Watcher captain well, but he was a fierce leader and a great tactician who'd seen them through some bad situations.

If it weren't for him, Alex was sure that a lot more people would have died.

'Rest in peace,' he thought, looking at the spot where the Watcher had taken his last breath. 'I hate to admit it, but that paralysing ray was *very* effective. I need to find out if there's a spell that does the same thing, something I could use against really tough threats... Especially fast ones. I also need a way to make invisible things detectable.'

He thought back to his team fighting invisible adversaries in the Games of Roal. Back then, he'd sort of 'cheated' using the Mark and sending forceballs to where he *thought* enemies were.

Then—when the Mark prevented him from doing anything it considered combat—he was still able to tell his team where their opponents were.

'But that'd be too dangerous in a true battle,' he thought. 'The invisible monster was fast. Really fast, and if I was doing something the Mark didn't like and it interfered, I'd be stone dust right now. No, I need to think of something else. Some way to mark invisible enemies. If I don't, *something's* going to get me one day. I can't just keep relying on Claygon's power.'

Alex looked at his golem: the giant, silent guardian. Always there. Always quiet. Always reliable.

That was something the young wizard had started to take for granted, and one day, it was going to cost them both dearly.

"You're always protecting me," he said. "But... I haven't been doing enough to protect *you*."

Pain marked his eyes as they ran across the white marble of his golem's form when he recalled the cracks that had cut into him.

"That's twice now you've been hurt badly. Once by the war-spear and now by the sonic scream from that Ravener-spawn," he said. "You know, it's only because your body *was* clay—not stone—that you didn't shatter. That one difference in your composition saved you. But after you evolved... I dunno what made you immune to that scream, but whatever it was, I'm thanking the Traveller for it. Maybe you absorbed some of that thing's magic. It's something we really gotta explore together."

They were nearing the aeld tree, passing by expedition members on clean up duty: defenders loading the last of the enemy bodies, earth mages searching for Ravener-spawn holes, and other wizards casting spells that renewed shattered stone.

He exhaled, his eyes stinging.

Claygon could have shattered, just like those stones. He rubbed his eyes, and turned away from what could have been, grateful that it hadn't happened.

Ahead, the aeld tree's leaves fluttered in the wintery landscape.

Alex cocked his head, examining it from base to crown.

Its light brought warmth and comfort and... satisfaction?

He raised an eyebrow.

"Are... are you feeling proud of yourself?" Alex laughed. "I'm kinda getting a little bit of satisfaction coming off of you."

That self-satisfaction heightened at his words, and he could imagine the little tree puffing up its chest, if it had one.

"Yeah, that's definitely what I'm getting from you," he said, touching its bark. His hand rubbed the tree trunk, drinking in the magical sapling's warmth. "And, you know what? I think you should be proud of yourself."

He gestured around the courtyard.

"Don't think I didn't notice you helping us out. I know the courtyard was slippery and all, but those bone-chargers were falling over like drunks after a night in the Bear's Bowl Tavern. Or like Khalik and Thundar after exams." He chuckled. "You bring fortune to those who take care of you, right? Well, we definitely had some fortune today. Between Gwyllain noticing what was going on and bringing the Heroes —I gotta ask what that's about—and that invisible thing falling over... yeah, we definitely had luck and good fortune on our side."

Alex patted the tree trunk. "I'm grateful for that and I'm going to try and get the best fae and wizard-made fertiliser that I can and drench your roots in it until you're taller than the keep."

There was a happy little pulse from the tree which felt like a tickle to Alex's soul. He, like the tree, was filled with a contented warmth.

"Alright, you'll take care of me, and I'll take care of you. But for right now... thanks. Thanks for what you've done. We're all really lucky—"

A voice cut him off, one that was calling out from behind him. "Alexander!"

He turned, finding the small form of Gwyllain plowing, leaping, and tunnelling his way through the drifts. Despite the cold and lack of warm clothing in the cold night air, the asrai showed no sign of shuddering as he made his way to the wizard.

"You're taking care of the aeld very well." His large eyes fell on the tree. "I could tell how it feels from halfway back to the keep."

"Yeah, I hope it's happy," Alex said. "It feels strange, in a way. Everyone else is either grieving, thinking, or strategizing."

"Aye, that's what they're doing up there alright." Gwyllain nodded to a window in the keep. "And it's aaaall a little too big for me. Too much excitement, I think. I asked to be excused because... I think I've had enough excitement for one day."

"Yeah, I'm surprised to see you." Alex laughed. "I thought you said you'd be avoiding me until I was a hundred or something? Or maybe even older."

"Well, it felt bad to be just letting you and yours get eaten by Ravener-spawn," he said. "Just didn't feel right to me."

Alex watched him closely.

He looked away as he spoke... he was hiding something.

The Thameish wizard nodded. "Well, I appreciate what you've done... Even if that meant putting yourself in danger. Do you want something from me?"

Gwyllain flinched slightly.

Just slightly.

"No! Of course not. Don't want anything now," he said.

'Now,' Alex thought. 'He'll probably come looking for a favour later. Best to watch my words with him.'

"Well, even if you don't want anything now, you should at least stay for the evening. Get something to eat. I'll give you some wine. You deserve it for what you did for us."

"Aye, I'll take you up on that." The asrai smiled. "Only had human wine a couple of times. And it was old."

"Sometimes it's better when it's old," Alex pointed out.

"Not the stuff I got my hands on. It tasted like bog water." He grimaced. "But wine will have to wait. First, I've got to go down and tell the blue caps what's happened. No doubt they're still hopping mad at all the churning and smashing that went on. So, I'd better let them know it wasn't you mortals' fault."

"We'd all appreciate that," Alex said. "Wouldn't want them to be upset with us."

"Oh, but before I go..." Gwyllain looked around, his eyes scanning the moonlit snow, making sure no one was near. Then he waved to Alex. "Lean down here."

The tall young man frowned, crouching in the snowdrift. "What is it?" he asked quietly.

"Beware the fellow that brought me."

"What fello—Oh, you mean the Gu—"

"Shhhh!" Gwyllain hissed. "Don't say the name. Some fae've got a bad habit of... putting lures in their names. Makin' 'em all sticky-like and letting them know when their name's been spoken. Not sure if he's one, but I wouldn't put it past him."

Alex recalled the predatory aura coming from the stocky fae. He glanced up at the keep. "Okay... won't say his name unless I have to."

"He's got many," Gwyllain whispered. "And he's a nasty one. Dark rumours about him. And they say he doesn't play too gently with mortals."

"What kind of rumours?"

"Best not to speak of it much more," the asrai whispered. "I gave my warning and now I'd best be off. I'll see you when it's time to eat."

With that, the asrai bobbed his head in a short bow, took a step into the snow, and vanished.

Alex looked at where the little fae had just stood. "By the Traveller, I've got to learn to disappear like that."

Rising to his full height and sighing, he considered the asrai's warning. "Enemies... potential dangers... they just keep multiplying. And Baelin'll be taking me into a demonic abyss soon. I've got enough things to think about. I'll just tell Baelin what Gwyllain said and be done with it."

He exhaled, and his breath drifted away like fog.

The road ahead would be rougher.

His first semester of second year had ended with darkness, blood, and chaos.

...But also with some good.

He looked at the evolved Claygon standing beside the aeld tree, head facing the sapling. The sight brought a smile to Alex's face. His golem and the young tree seemed to like each other. He could feel curiosity emanating from the sapling along with a welcoming warmth.

Alex chuckled. "You must be thinking that Claygon looks different. Well, he's still the same. He's just gone through a couple of upgrades. That's the thing, you'll find a lot of things around you change, just like the castle over there." He gestured to the keep and stone walls. "The land's changed, but in many ways, it stayed the same. Hmmm... you know what, maybe I'll leave you two to chat for a while. Or whatever you do to communicate."

He looked at his golem. "I'll be back to pick you up in a bit, my friend. Just enjoy your time."

Putting thoughts of dark times from his mind, Alexander Roth began his trek back to the keep. The road ahead might be a dark one, but he would be ready for it, no matter what dangers it held, be they demons, Ravener-spawn, or fae.

He had his spells.

He had his friends.

And, he even had the Mark.

With hope, that would be—

"*Father.*"

Alex nearly jumped a foot in the air, letting out a scream that sounded like it should have come from Selina. He looked around for the source of the voice. Was that Gwyllain pulling a prank?

It sounded like it had come from right on top of—

"*Over... here... Father.*"

Alexander Roth froze dead in his tracks.

The voice had not come from on top of him.

It'd come from inside his head, and behind him.

Slowly, he turned, his eyes falling on Claygon.

His golem was looking straight at him.

And in his mind, he could hear the nervous, tentative voice tinged with all of its trepidation.

All of its longing.

And he knew—without a doubt—whose voice it was.

"*Hello... Father,*" Claygon gently whispered in his mind.

Mark of the Fool continues in Book Six!

Thank you for reading Mark of the Fool 5

We hope you enjoyed it as much as we enjoyed bringing it to you. We just wanted to take a moment to encourage you to review the book. Follow this link: Mark of the Fool 5 to be directed to the book's Amazon product page to leave your review.

Every review helps further the author's reach and, ultimately, helps them continue writing fantastic books for us all to enjoy.

Also in Series:
Book One
Book Two
Book Three
Book Four
Book Five
Book Six

Check out the series here:
(tap or scan)

Want to discuss our books with other readers and even the authors? Join our Discord server today and be a part of the Aethon community.

Facebook | Instagram | Twitter | Website

You can also join our non-spam mailing list by visiting www.subscribepage.com/AethonReadersGroup and never miss out on future releases. You'll also receive three full books completely Free as our thanks to you.

If you liked Mark of the Fool, you'll love Rune Seeker, also by JM Clarke?

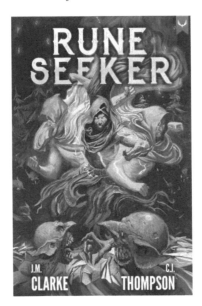

The Everfail will rise. His enemies will fall. *Hiral is the Everfail, the weakest person on the flying island of Fallen Reach. He trains harder than any warrior. Studies longer than any scholar. But all his people are born with magic powered by the sun, flowing through tattoos on their bodies. Despite having enormous energy within, Hiral is the only one who can't channel it; his hard work is worth nothing. Until it isn't. In a moment of danger, Hiral unlocks an achievement with a special instruction: Access a Dungeon to receive a Class-Specific Reward. It's his first—and maybe last—chance for real power. Just one problem: all dungeons lay in the wilderness below the flying islands that humanity lives on, and there lay secrets and dangers that no one has survived. New powers await, but so do new challenges. If he survives? He could forge his own path to power. If he fails? Death will be the least of his problems.* **Don't miss the next progression fantasy series from J.M Clarke, bestselling author of Mark of the Fool, along with C.J. Thompson. Unlock a weak-to-strong progression into power and a detailed litRPG system with unique classes, skills, dungeons, achievements, survival and evolution. Explore a mysterious world of fallen civilizations, strange monsters and deadly secrets.**

Get Rune Seeker Now!

There is no weapon more powerful than the [Psychokinetic] mind. *Astrid, a mischievous noble teen, long dreamed of exploring the ancient cities preserved beneath the waves, left behind from a time before the ocean swallowed the world. She's been training all her life to become a magic swordsman capable of doing just that. But when an ancient monster long thought dead assaults humanity's last bastion—a floating ship-city—she awakens her System early. Only, she's not a warrior as expected. She's forced to walk the path of a [Psychokinetic] Mage. With Spawn-infested oceans, pirates looking to plunder, and mysterious monsters that lurk within Bubbled-Cites at the bottom of the ocean, Safety is anything but guaranteed. She'll learn levitation, ovject throwing, eyeball pulling, and more, all the way to the apex of psychic powers. But, what happens when she discovers that her world was a lot larger than she—and the rest of humanity, once thought?*
Don't miss the start of this action-packed and often hilarious LitRPG Apocalypse series about a young survivor with a craving for adventure and fighting. Perfect for fans of Azarinth Healer and Eight. *About the series: Astrid wasn't expecting to awaken as a mage class, but that won't stop her from having fun. In fact, she'll no longer need to resort to laborious activities, including, but not limited to; picking up stuff, carrying stuff, or even throwing stuff. Everything can be done with her mind!*

Get [Psychokinetic] Eyeball Pulling Now!

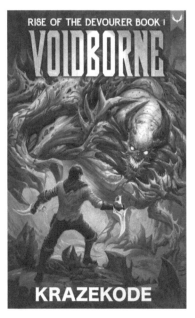

For all our LitRPG books, visit our website.